INTERNATIONAL

BOOKS BY

Carlos Fuentes

Where the Air Is Clear
The Good Conscience
Aura
The Death of Artemio Cruz
A Change of Skin
Terra Nostra
The Hydra Head
Burnt Water
Distant Relations
The Old Gringo
Myself with Others
Christopher Unborn

Christopher Unborn

Carlos Fuentes

TRANSLATED FROM THE SPANISH

BY ALFRED MAC ADAM

AND THE AUTHOR

VINTAGE INTERNATIONAL · VINTAGE BOOKS

A DIVISION OF RANDOM HOUSE, INC. · NEW YORK

FIRST VINTAGE INTERNATIONAL EDITION, OCTOBER 1990

English translation copyright © 1989 by Farrar, Straus and Giroux

Library of Congress Cataloging-in-Publication Data
Fuentes, Carlos.
    [Cristóbal Nonato. English]
    Christopher unborn / Carlos Fuentes ; translated from the Spanish
by Alfred MacAdam and the author.—1st Vintage international ed.
        p.   cm.—(Vintage international)
    Translation of: Cristóbal Nonato.
    ISBN 0-679-73222-5
    I. Title.
    [PQ7297.F793C713   1990]
    863—dc20   90-50296
CIP

Manufactured in the United States of America
10 9 8 7 6 5 4 3 2

The author is grateful
for the help—both creative
and critical—of his friends
JUAN GOYTISOLO
and
PROFESSOR ROALD HOFFMAN

Naturally,
to my mother
and my children

Contents

Prologue

I Am Created

The body is the part of our
representation that is continuously
being born.

Henri Bergson

"Mexico is a country of sad men and happy children," said my father, Angel (twenty-four years old), at the instant of my creation.

Before that, my mother, Angeles (under thirty), had sighed: "Ocean, origin of the gods."

"But soon there shall be no time for happiness, and we shall all be sad, old and young alike," my father went on, taking off his glasses—tinted violet, gold-framed, utterly John Lennonish.

"Why do you want a child, then?" my mother said, sighing again.

"Because soon there will be no time for happiness."

"Was there ever such a time?"

"What did you say? Things turn out badly in Mexico."

"Don't be redundant. Mexico was *made* so things could turn out badly."

So she insisted: "Why do you want a child, then?"

"Because *I* am happy," my father bellowed. "*I am happy!*" he shouted even louder, turning to face the Pacific Ocean. "I am possessed of the most intimate, reactionary happiness!"

Ocean, origin of the gods! And she took her copy of Plato's *Dia-*

logues, the edition published in the twenties by Don José Vasconcelos, when he was rector of the University of Mexico, and put it over her face. The green covers bearing the black seal of the university and its motto, THROUGH MY RACE SHALL SPEAK THE SPIRIT, were stained with Coppertonic sweat.

But my father said he wanted to sire a son (me, zero years), right here while they were vacationing in Acapulco, "in front of the ocean, origin of the gods?" quoth Homerica Vespussy. So my naked father crawled across the beach, feeling the hot sand drifting between his legs but saying that sex is not between the legs but inside the coconut grove, around the svelte, naked, innocent body of my mother, crawling toward my mother with the volume of Plato draped over her face, Mom and Dad naked under the blazing and drunken sun of Acapulque on the day they invented me. Gracias, gracias, Mom and Dad.

"What shall we name the boy?"

My mother does not answer; she merely removes the tome from her face and looks at my father ironically, reprovingly, even disdainfully—not to say compassionately—although she doesn't dare call him a disgusting male chauvinist pig. What if it's a girl? Nevertheless, she prefers to overlook the matter; he knows that something's wrong and can't allow things to stay like that at this point in time and circumstance and so he solves the problem by nibbling at her nipples as if they were cherry-flavored gumdrops, cumdrops—postprandial but prepriapic jelly beans, puns my dad, in whose prostatic sack I still lie in waiting, innocent and philadelphic, with my sleepy chromosomatic and spermatic little brothers (and sisters).

"What shall we name the boy?"

"Things exist without anyone's having to name them," she says, trying not to reactivate their old argument about the sex of the angels.

"Of course, but right now I'd like a taste of that pear in heavy syrup of yours."

"You and I don't need names to exist, right?"

"All I need right now is that sweet thing of yours."

"Just what I mean. Sometimes you call it the Hydra and other things."

"An' figs, sometimes."

"And figs, sometimes"—my mother laughs—"as your Uncle Homero would say."

"*Our* Uncle Homero," my father jokingly corrects her. "Ay!" Even he didn't know if he was complaining about that undesired family tie or roaring because of the precipitate pleasure he did not want to see lost in the sterile sand, even if he knows, stretched out on his belly, that both good and evil are merely violent pleasures, and thus they resemble and cancel each other out in their infrequent eruption. As for the rest: kill time and kick ass.

"Yeah, yeah, go ahead and howl, or laugh at the old guy," said Angeles, my mother, "but here we are on vacation in Kafkapulco, in front of the ocean origin of the gods, guests in his home."

"His home, bull," blurts out my father, Angel. "It belongs by rights to the peasants from the communal lands he stripped it away from, damn the old moneybags and damn his granny, too."

"Who happens also to be your granny," my mother says, "because you and I say 'sea' to refer to the 'sea,' but who knows what its real name is, the name the gods utter when they want to stir it up and say to themselves 'Thalassa. Thalassa. We come from the sea.' "

Blessèd mother of mine: thank you for your multitrack mind—on one track you explain Plato; on another you fondle my father, while on a third you wonder why the baby must necessarily be a boy, why not a girl? And you say Thalassa, thalassa, well named was Astyanax, the son of Hector, well named (Angeles my mother, Angeles my wife looks toward the wrathful sea); well named was Agamemnon, whose name means admirable in his resistance (and what about my resistance, moans Angel my father, if you could only see how my Faulknerian chili pepper resists, it not only survives, it endures, it perdures, it's durable stuff). Well named are all the heroes, my mother murmurs, reading at her vasconcelosite tome with its elegant Art Deco typography, to postpone with her first mental track the unrepeatable pleasure playing on the second: heroes who share the root of their identity with Eros: Eros, heroes. What shall we name the baby? What are we going to do today, January 6, 1992, Epiphany, and the anniversary of the very day of the First Agrarian Law of the Revolution, so that he's conceived on ancient lands belonging to the community improperly appropriated by our uncle and lawyer Don Homero Fagoaga, and so that he will win the Discovery of America Contest on October 12 next? In which of my mama's multitrack mind's circuits and systems am I going to be onomastically inserted? I shudder to think. The paternal genes send horrible messages: Sóstenes Rocha,

Genovevo de la O., Caraciollo Parra Pérez, Guadalupe Victoria, Pánfilo Natera, Natalicio González, Marmaduke Grove, Assis de Chateaubriand, Archibald Leach, Montgomery Ward Swopes, Mark Funderbuck, and my mother repeats the question:

"Then why do you want a son?"

"Because I am happy," bawls my dad. She throws away the green volume published in 1921 by the rector of the University of Mexico, Don José Vasconcelos, with its thick Platonic pages that survived, look now your mercies, the murders at La Bombilla and Huitzilac, the massacre of the students in Tlateloco Plaza in 1968, the principal cadavers and the subordinate cadavers, the dead with mausoleums and the dead in potter's fields, those dead on marble legs and those dead without a leg to stand on: what shall we name the child? Why the fuck does it have to be a boy? Because the contest rules state:

TO WHOM IT MAY CONCERN: The male child born precisely at the stroke of midnight on October 12, and whose family name, not including his first name (it goes without saying the boy will be named Christopher), most resembles that of the Illustrious Navigator, shall be proclaimed PRODIGAL SON OF THE NATION. His education shall be provided by the Republic and on his eighteenth birthday he will receive the KEYS TO THE REPUBLIC, prelude to his assuming the position, at age twenty-one, of REGENT OF THE NATION, with practically unlimited powers of election, succession, and selection. Therefore, CITIZENS, if your family name happens to be Colonia, Colombia, Columbario, Colombo, Colombiano, or Columbus, not to say Colón, Colomba, or Palomo, Palomares, Palomar, or Santospirito, even—why not?—Genovese (who knows? perhaps none of the aforementioned will win, and in that case THE PRIZE IS YOURS), pay close attention: MEXICAN MACHOS, IMPREGNATE YOUR WIVES—RIGHT AWAY!

> TOMORROW MAY BE TOO LATE
> WHEN THE FROST IS ON THE PUNKIN
> THAT'S THE TIME FOR DICKIE DUNKIN
> THE MOMENT IS AT HAND
> THESE NINE MONTHS WILL NEVER COME BACK AGAIN

So, ladies and gentlemen, let's get procreating! Your pleasure is your duty and your duty is your freedom! In Mexico we are all

free and anyone who does not want to be free should be punished!
You can count on your judges, after all: have we ever let you
down?

And she, at least on the track given over to her consciousness, no
longer puts up any resistance, no longer says: What if it's a girl? What
shall we name the girl, huh? She only said it's beautiful making love
like this at noon on the beach my love, ever since you said don't
take care of yourself anymore, Angeles, I want to give you a child
right next to the sea, I started getting hot, for the first time in a year
I shaved my armpits and also the hair that peeks through the slots in
my chair asada in this Acapulcoesque incandescence, the sun, not
the sun, no my love, but your cherry jubilee in my hungry mouth,
your scherezada from Tampique with its chilis and little beans which
I'm digging up with my long finger, your cunt, your raccunto, your
ass chérie, your cherry ass, Chère Sade, flagellated by my furious
whip here on the beach of Kafkapulco, but a private beach my love,
sometimes private property does have its virtues, right Prudhon?
Pardon?

Shhh, my love, let me imagine your chers rassés, your ché arra-
sado, let me live, Chère Sade, in the feverish calendar of your opec-
and-one nights, let me swim in the colors you sweat, your
chromohydrosis, I yearn for your yen, if only for only thirty seconds
over Tokyo, I pokey-you now your ass which is all the asses that bore
you my love, the waves carry grass to your ass, my Arabian mare,
my divine Angeles, I drink the wine of your nalglass, I hear the toll
of your knelglass, I bury my nose in your knolgrass, Oh your Mexican
ass my Angeles mía, the color of sweet quince, the smell of rotten
mango and fresh red snapper, your historical ass, Angeles, febrile
and Phoenician, dancing the Roman rumba, Spanish and spunning,
Turkissable, Castilian and Moorish, tinged with Aztec, nahuátl nal-
gas, Cordobuzzable buttocks, Arab pillow of the almohades, ass on
horseback and ass on camelback, second face-double cheeks—what
is your name? What shall we name the baby? What says the Plutonic
part of your Platonic book? Have you run out of words, darling?

My father dared to look at her. She had an illuminated halo over
her head, which is to say (she was saying) more illuminated than
ever when she said what she had to feel or felt what she had to say
or listened to what she had to hear, but her halo dimmed, saddened,

when the idiots, the jerks, the dimwits, the flatfeet wore it down: my
mother, her halo very brilliant on this brilliant afternoon, was complaining about it, with her elbows jammed into the sand, exiling her
questions:

"And what if it's a girl, contest or not?"

"And what if it's twins?"

My father stares at my mother's elbows and desires them almost
more than her snatch: nubile, sensual, exciting elbows, buried in the
sand. The dry smell of the palm-leaf roof: a dry coolness. Coconut
and mango and scallops with Tabasco sauce. The sea is the Pacific.
The farther out you look, the more the water seems to burn. Thalassa.
Thalassa.

And my father once more sucks her nipples as if they were Sucrets,
with the very rhythm of respiration: Air, Hera, Air, Eros, Air, Heroes,
Angeles, Scheherazade, Certified Pubic Accounter, First Novelist,
drown yourself in the waters of time, wet your syllables my love, ass
of my angelic amour (my mother is loved, in case you missed it, by
my father on the beach and I am about to be created) in Acapulco.
I am happy at noon and I want to have a son in a country of happy
children and sad men before the time for happiness ceases to exist,
and even if Mexico exists so things turn out badly for us, in front of
the ocean origin of the gods.

"Isabella," if it's a girl we'll name her Isabella, whimpered my
mother, hanging on to the mainmast of my father's caravel, suddenly
shifted into her unconscious track, it may be a girl. My queen. What
shall we name the girl? Well! Does it have to be a boy? Well! We'll
call her Isabella, Isabella the Catholic, Isabella the Chaotic.

My Queen: give me America, give a little America to your little
Angel. Let me come near your Guahananí, Angeles, caress your Gulf
of Mexico, tickle the delta of your Mississippi, excite your Cuba, get
engulfed in your Gulf of Darien.

Give me America, Angel: come on, my Martín Fierro, here is
your pampa mía, give me your Veragua, come close with your Mar-
acaibo, take my Honduras, snuggle up with your Tabasco, kiss my
Key West, Vene, Vene, Venezuela, anchor in my Puerto, Rico, just
leave your Grand Cayman right there, let me feel in the Hispaniola,
ay Santiago, ay Jardines la Reyna ayayay! Nombre de Dios:

May God Give You Your Name, my son, Name him, name him,
he's coming, he's out! The only one among millions, silvery and
quick, the gay bandolero, the swashbuckler, the matador, escaping

from the myriad company of the chromosomatic legions. Name him, he's out, nothing can stop him now, with all his genes on his back, bearing, oh my God, bearing all that we are.

"Hey! Genes are to blame for everything, is what Uncle Fernando Benítez said."

"Certainly: Hegels are to blame for everything, is what Uncle Homero Fagoaga answers."

"That's a fact," confirmed Uncle Fernando:

Angel, Angeles, bearing all that we are from our very origins, everything is inscribed in him, ay, my dearest DNA, he's going to find your egg, Angeles, your sperm, Angel, bearing, my God, name of God, nombre de Dios, Hispaniola, my Queen, by God, bearing, Christ, Christ, Christ . . .

CHRISTOPHER

Now they've found one another, he's swashed and buckled his way through the forest of blood and sweat and throbbing mucosities an' impatience (and impatience, son, Uncle Homero corrects, with Don Andrés Bello's grammar book in hand). Now I've come out pained and paining, separated forever from the only company I've ever known: my packages of cells, my belovèd generations armed with precursory cells, patiently stored in my father's pouch, regenerating themselves constantly but hopelessly, my true grandfathers and great-grandfathers, my transitory though authentic parents, my internal genealogy, adiós! Ay dios! Out I come, running, crying, borne by the hot blood and inflamed nerves of my new father, leaving behind what up until now I knew and loved, amé, ahimé, oh me, oh my . . . I lounged God knows how long in my father's pruny cave, and now my father is tearing me out of my internal genealogy, far from my secret family tree of inside fathers and grandfathers and great-greats and great-great-greats I belonged to up until this moment when *this* man decided to do what he is doing: throw me off balance, tear me up by the roots, nip me in the bud and ejaculate me, expel me from the peninsula, me ejaculated, she fornicated, dismissed, beginning my voyage in the middle of my true life. No one knows me, they're having a ball out there and they don't know that

HERE I COME!

accompanied by the invincible haha armada of my one billion brothers and sisters, little Christophers an' Isabellas (and Isabellas, shouts

Uncle Homero, furious) crackling like whips, in close formation, rolling out of my father's barrel of fun, then abandoned all to the accidents of the black tunnel, fighting upstream in my mama's Delaware, her salty mine and truffle war, the swift, lubricious infantries inside my mommy's Thermópelos, Vulvar boatmen, little heads and long tails. We are legion, said Lucy, whipping and snapping, jumping hurdles, over the walls of the inhospitable mucous cavity that will end up being the walls of my homeland, the steaming baths of acid secretions that dry up our salty juices, Salaam Salamis, lost in the deserts of the wrong cylic exits, Luther's Turnpike, no exit on this expressway, the Labyrinth of Solitude, ay! I see them die like flies because they're out of gas, because they have two heads and twelve toes, because la cucaracha cannot walk without grass, they die by millions on the roadside, all around me, my soul brothers and sisters, Fred Waring and his Pennsylvanians, Guy Lombardo and his Royal Canadians, the Andrews Sisters, and the Hermanitos Brothers, les misérables who did not make it to the goal victorious. *Victor who?* Go! The millions of sperm fallen into Niagara, oh watery Waterloo of my decimated fraternity, thermopiled, forever separated from our young precursory grandfathers and from all the memories the sexy couple on the beach know nothing of: battles and songs, names and tastes, goodbye forever, you never escaped from the prison pouch of he who is about to become my Lord and Father, and the rest of you have perished in the battle against the juices and the blood and the perverse tunnels of her about to name herself *Mamma Mia*, we are being beaten up in the dark alleys of the cervical mucosity, no left turn through the unblocked cervix, a river of glass drowns me, I'm slipping and sliding spermatically, only a few of us remain now, whipping and snapping, exhausted, nature is not kind, nature is implacable, nature doesn't weep for us, my poor agonizing brothers and I, I?

ALONE AT LAST, AT LAST ALONE

. . . . Terror . . . . Pain . . . . and I, alone once more: I the only one who made it to Treasure Island: my mother's egg awaits me in its hiding place. She on her throne of blood, Queen of the Angels—Isabella, Angeles, opens her arms to me, the Champ, victorious over the millions of soldier boys and girls dead in the useless race to get to where I am, warm and cozy, avid and sad, asking for a room of my own. A sperm for an egg. Mother, there is only one. Now p'tit Christophe is all tangled up in his roots, now no one can save him from his fate, now il piccolo Cristoforo has met his destiny, let him now speak listen *know*: there he is. He had no time to jump on his horse.

You'll see, Angel, my mom told my dad when they separated and rolled on the hot sand and then embraced once more and then he licked her elbows while I lodged myself singular and triumphant in the uterus of Isabella of the Angels, who told my father once more: "You'll see, he'll be born when you want, I swear to you my love, I'll have him for you on time, sure I will, God I love you, ever since I met you, I couldn't sleep all night long I was so damn happy, what does it matter, I swear I'll give you a son because that's what the rules say, that's it, I'm no longer demanding the kid be a girl, no Isabella, only Christopher, just as long as you go on whispering into my ear what you've always said to me, honey:

"In Mexico, the whole problem is one of attitude—toward men with power and toward women without power."

"Come back."

"I never went anywhere."

"Come here."

"I was waiting for you."

The two of them here lying on the burning sand in the Acapedro calderoon where life is a dream, happy, a land of sad men but happy children, but before time runs out for happiness *but* in Mexico where everything turns out badly for us but now only you and I holding hands, naked, exhausted, on our backs, with our eyes closed against the sun but with my halo spilled all over the sand like liquid stars. And from the heavens it rains, the sun is just a tiny bit clouded over, the wings of the big bad bumblebee cover us and from up above it rains on us, butterflies? petals? plumes? tropical clouds? You bet.

"Look," said my dad, "it's coming from up there."

"Smell," said my mommy. "It's shit."

Over their heads flew a pair of buttocks like the trembling wings of an uncertain bat, white and bland, drained of blood by the vampires of the sun: a man was flying across the wide Mexican sky, hanging from a blue-and-orange-striped parachute, tugged over Acapulco Bay by a roaring motorboat, kept aloft by hanging on to a tightrope in the thick air was our Uncle Homero (sixty years old), clad in a yellow guayabera, without his pants on, dripping the skyborne revenge of Montezuma, fleeing from the guerrillas in Guerrero, fearful and trembling, fleeing diarrheic with terror, followed by a sign written by a skywriter:

WELCOME TO SUNNY ACAPULCO

Homer, oh mère, oh mer, oh madre, oh merde origin of the gods: Thalassa, Thalassa.

"Now what are you going to do?"

"Tomorrow's another day."

"When? When will it be that kind of day?"

"The boy has to be born, understand?"

"But he's so all alone. Nine months alone. With whom will he talk?"

"With your mercies benz."

"Who?"

"The reader, just the reader."

WELCOME TO LIFE, CHRISTOPHER PALOMAR

1

The Sweet Fatherland

The fatherland is impeccable and adamantine . . .

Ramón López Velarde
The Sweet Fatherland

1

El Niño comes running up from Easter Island, tepid and sickly, the offspring of death by water, beating against the Peruvian coast, suffocating the anchovies and algae in its hot embrace, kidnapping the vital equatorial nitrates and phosphates, breaking the vast food chain as well as the procreation of the great sea fish: heavy and sweating El Niño swims, hurling dead fish against the walls of the continent, stupefying and putrefying it all, water sinking water, the ocean asphyxiated in its own dead tide, the cold ocean drowned by the hot ocean, the winds driven mad and pushed off-course. Destructive and criminal, El Niño flattens the coasts of California, dries out the plains of Australia, floods the Ecuadoran lowlands with mud. My uncle, Fernando Benítez (eighty years of age), is flying toward the Usumacinta River, weeping for his lost fatherland, at the very moment that my Uncle Homero Fagoaga flies over Acapulco, in diarrheic fear, fleeing from the guerrillas. And so my father recapitulates, while I make frantic efforts to hang on to solid ground in the uterine oviduct as I head for the cavity of this woman who is preparing to be my cave for who knows how long, the space which she and I are supposed to share for who knows how

long a time (I hope they—it's the least they can do—inform me about
the meaning of this word "time," which I'm starting to think is of
capital importance if I am to understand what the fuck is happening
to me, how I am to live with and without them, inside and outside
of myself and of them), and they should get busy and tell me when
I was conceived, how much "time" I have to spend here inside, if
I'm going to get out someday or not and where, if the answer is
affirmative, I'm going, what all this means, "place," "space," "earth,"
my new home now that I've left (or was thrown out of) my old house
of skin and sperm between my father's legs (he threw me out, the
miserable bastard, just for a fleeting moment of pleasure, right? oh!
how ever to forget that deed, how ever to forgive him?) where I was
so comfortable with my secret genealogies, one big happy family now
scattered, scattered to the four winds, and all these questions I have
(time? what is it? how much is there? when do I begin to count the
days of my life? inside my father's testicles? inside my mother's egg?
inside of outside? now that I've passed into my mother's possession
just because of my father's pleasure? I ask in despair: for how much
"time"?), all my previous security and serenity completely destroyed
by the lusts of Mr. Angel Palomar y Fagoaga, Esq. (twenty-four years
of age—but we already said that), about five feet ten inches tall
(descriptive news for your Mercies Bends), with yellow, panther-like
but shortsighted eyes (this we knew) and olive, gypsy-like complexion
(this we did not know), who before the entire world will attempt and
presume to be my father; okay, I have to tell you I love you, Dad,
that despite everything I adore you and that from now on I will live
in imaginary complicity with you and that I depend on you to tell
me where I am, where I come from. Once you've told me my name
and given me my time—they say this is my time, tell me what country
this is, where are we? where do you want me to be born? Is it true
what my genetic code is telling me?: that there is no other land like
this one? and that it's either a blessing or a curse that there is no
other land like this one? that it's true that *someone* (He, She) never
did to any nation what he or she did here, that now our problem is
to administer our wealth? that we're not really ready yet for democracy? that the Tlaxcaltecas are to blame for everything? that you've
got to admit the Indian is right, even if he isn't? that we should go
out and lynch some lousy Spaniards? that you are foolish men, foolish
men, you who accuse women unjustly? that we have not come to

live but to dream? that there is a Ford in your Future? that in a crisis we rise to meet the challenge? that God denied us talent for journalism and movies but made us geniuses at survival? that: why doesn't my father want me to be a girl? just on account of that fucking contest? because of the little Christophers?

He said he wanted to have a son (me, zero years) with her because if I were conceived on Twelfth Night, with a bit of luck I'd come into the world on Columbus Day. My mother sat up as if she were on springs, covering her breasts with the university classic. A boy conceived on the beach January 6 might show up on time on October 12?

"And what if he's born in September?"

"He'd win the Independence Day Contest, but it isn't the same."

"Of course not. Hey, where were we on the 15th of September last year?"

"Facing the palace balcony in the Zócalo, watching the first apparition of the apparition."

"And October 12 last, where were we—bet you can't remember."

"Standing in front of the monument to Columbus on Reforma."

"She was carried in a sedan chair through the streets to the Columbus monument in order to proclaim . . ."

"She never speaks. She only cries once a year."

"You're right."

"And don't talk about her in that tone of abject admiration. Instead, answer these three little questions right off the top of your head."

"Shoot."

"Here goes. First: what are we going to name the baby?"

"What is the matter with you, you stoned? Christopher!"

"And if it's a girl?"

"Okay, okay. Isabella. The Chaotic."

"Second question: what language will the baby speak?"

"Spanish, of course."

"And all those new slangs, what about them? Spanglish and Anglañol, and the Anglatl invented by our buddies the Four Fuckups and . . ."

"And the language of our Chilean girlfriend Concha Toro, and the frog-speak of the French chanteuse Ada Ching. Adored Angeles: please realize that we live in an arena where all languages fight it out."

"Don't change the subject."

"Shoot."

"And third: in what country will our son be born?"

"Easy: in the Sweet Fatherland. You go on reading Plato, Angeles. I read Ramón López Velarde."

"Ramón who?"

"López Velarde, Ramón. Born June 15, 1888, in Jerez de Zacatecas. Dead at the age of thirty-three for having strayed from the old park of his provincial heart and wandered into the noisy concourse of the sunken-eyed and made-up metropolis in order to die. These days a shot of penicillin would have saved him from his minor but in those days fatal infection. On a June morning in 1921, the poet Ramón died with his pockets full of papers without adjectives."

"Who did he look like?"

"It seems he looked like me. Just a bit, so they tell me. Olive skin, almond-shaped eyes. But he wore a mustache and had pouting lips."

"What did he write?"

"The fatherland is impeccable and adamantine," said my father.

"Impeccable and . . ." My mother stopped, clearly disconcerted. "Is this where our son will be born?"

2. *Fatherland, Your Mutilated Territories*

On the day of my conception, Don Fernando Benítez is flying toward the forest of the Lacandons along the border bound by the Usumacinta River. At a given moment, his eyes cloud over, he feels a premonition of darkness, and tries to imagine the nearness of a volcano, a village, a river. He wants to give them names so he can say them to himself and to tell to the young helicopter pilot flying him to the Frontera Corazos airport:

"Young man, show me from up here the territories of the fatherland. Tell me, what remains of Mexico?"

He is asking the pilot to help him see from the air the totality of the newly mutilated Sweet Fatherland. He could almost see, beyond the Lacandonan forest, the territory of the Yucatán, ceded exclusively to the Club Méditerranée in order to create the Peninsular Tourism Trust (PENITT), free of any meddling by the federal government, in order to pay the interest on the external (eternal) debt, which this year would reach, according to calculations, $1,492 billion—a pretty sum to celebrate the five centuries since Columbus's arrival and our division and conquest. And right now they are flying by special permission over the CHITACAM TRUSTEESHIP (Chiapas–Tabasco–Campeche), ceded to the U.S. oil consortium called the Five Sisters until the principal of that external debt is paid. Of course the debt only grows, assuring the foreign companies a possession in perpetuity. And he didn't want to see, beyond that cloud bank, the besieged half-moon of Veracruz, along the coast from Tampico to Cotzacoalcos, and inland from Veracruz to the foothills of the Malinche, lands ceded to an incomprehensible war, an agrarian revolution according to some, a U.S. invasion according to others: it all depends, gentlemen, on which television channel you watch in the evening. The fact is that no one can communicate with Veracruz, so what's so strange about the fact that suddenly no one can communicate with Acapulco? It's impossible to fathom those mysteries. What are you saying, Don Fernando? You can't hear over the noise of the motor. I said that Veracruz has become materially impenetrable because a line of soldiers, shoulder to shoulder, helicopters, right, this is a helicopter, Don Fernando, no, you don't get what I'm saying, and antiaircraft guns have closed to invaders the whole strip along the Perote Ridge to the Lakes Tamiahua and Catemaco. And Don Fernando has no desire to turn his eyes toward that atrocious nation on the northern border: Mexamerica, independent of Mexico and the United States, in-bond factories, smuggling, contraband, Spanglish, refuge for political fugitives, and free entry for those without papers from the Pacific Coast to the Gulf Coast, one hundred kilometers to the north and one hundred to the south from the old frontier, from Sandy Ego and Auntyjane to Coffeeville and Killmoors: independent without the need of any declaration, the fact is that there no one pays the slightest attention to the government in Mexico City or Washington. And Don Fernando would also have wanted to look toward the Pacific and understand just exactly what had happened to the entire coast to the north of Ixtapa–Zihuatanejo, the whole thing, including the coastal zones of Michoacán, Colima, Jalisco, and Nayarit, Sinaloa, Sonora, and Baja California: why didn't anyone ever talk about those lands, to whom did they belong, why were there no explanations, why was the Republic of Mexico only a kind of ghost of its ancient cornucopia-shaped self?

He saw a narrow, skeletal, and decapitated nation, its chest in the deserts of the north, its infarcted heart in the exit point of the Gulf at Tampico, its belly in Mexico City, its suppurating, venereal anus in Acapulco, its cut-off knees in Guerrero and Oaxaca . . . That's what was left. That was what the federal government, its PANist president, its PRIist apparatus, its financial bourgeoisie now totally addicted to the public sector (or was it the other way around? It was all the same now), its police imposed on an army that had disbanded out of discontent and demoralization, its new symbols of legitimization, its August Founding Mothers and its National Contests, and its thousands of unreadable newspapers . . .

Don Fernando Benítez was on the point of vomiting out the helicopter window when he hesitated, secretly fearing the horror of symmetry: how to vomit on vomit?

"Do you believe in the Virgin of Guadalupe?" he asked the pilot.

"The what?" the pilot said (the noise, his earphones).

"I'm saying that only a miracle like the reappearance of the Virgin can save Mexico . . ."

"No, we're not going to Mexico City," shouted the pilot. "We're going to Frontera . . ."

Fernando Benítez closed his eyes and squeezed the young pilot's shoulder. "Only a miracle."

Although for him that miracle, behind his clouded vision, consisted in being able to remember a mountain, a village, a river, and to repeat under his breath now, the noise of the motor of no importance: Nevado de Colima, Tepoztlán, Usumacinta . . .

Sweet Fatherland, impeccable and adamantine: the forest of silk-cotton trees, the silvered velocity of the river, the crocodile and the ocelot, the monkeys and the toucans under the vegetable vault. And a column of smoke that rose from the heart of the jungle: the forests cut down, the new highways, the drilling of the Five Sisters, the changed course of the river, the traces of the past wiped away forever by mud slides and oil spills: Yaxchilán, Planchón de las Figuras, the forest of the Lacandons . . . The Invisible Sweet Fatherland.

3

Take a break, You Mercedesful Readers, and listen to the story my father is telling my mother on Epiphany as they clean off the shit that rained down from heaven, and the two of them (I think) prepare to fill me in on everything that led to *this instant*, my most immediate postcuntly, but which doubtless I shall only remember at the moment in which my little head begins to function within my mother but outside of her, if I can put it that way, independent of her. At what moment am I worthy of respect and consideration? At what moment am I more important than she is, with as much right to life as she has, at what point? I ask. They are not wondering about any of this; they are on the beach where they have just conceived me without being certain of the success of their labors, remembering what happened days before, then years before, adding layer upon layer to the where and the when that I got right away. They are and will always be something like the simultaneous captivity and freedom of my "person."

"Where are we?"

"In Acapulco."

"What's going on?"

"Well, you and I are going for a swim so we can wash off Uncle Homero Fagoaga's shit."

"No, I'm not asking you about us but the circumstances outside ourselves."

The President of the Republic will address the nation with his message for the New Year 1992, year of the five hundredth anniversary of the disco . . .

What are the people of Acapulco doing?

They are gathered in the cement town square (decorated with sculptural hummocks) in order to hear by way of loudspeakers the words of the President of the Repu . . .

But it's impossible to understand what's coming out of the loud-speakers, so the townspeople did not hear the core of the presidential message of Don Jesús María y José Paredes, in which he ruffled the feathers of the nation's political deadwood by solemnly announcing that the most important obligation of a president of Mexico in the nineties was to choose his successor and then die. "There should be no former presidents; there should only be candidates," he said cryptically, thus opening the door to every speculation: Is our national Chuchema going to die when he leaves office? Is he going to commit suicide? Will he be a candidate for something????? These were questions that kept the nation busy for the entire First Month of the Quincentennial by adding their complicated symbology to the other new items in the country after the election that followed the events of the year '90. Item: the first victory by a candidate from the clerical, right-wing PAN (National Action Party) over the monolithic power of PRI (Revolutionary Institutional Party), deforcer of all the governments and all the Senates since 1929 and author of directed democracy, national unity, industrialization, agrarian reform, the rise of the bourgeoisie, the Mexican miracle, the opening, the reform, the bonanza, the collapse, the austerity, the moral renovation, the eternal debt, the earthquake of the Fifth Sun, the revenge of the oligarchy, and, finally, the bust of the year '90, was in the last analysis a Pyrrhic victory (says Uncle Don Homero Fagoaga, looking down on the corrupt Bay of Acapulco) since the first PAN president found himself obliged to govern with the cadres, organizations, and structures of the PRI, with the Confederation of Workers of Mexico, with the National Peasant Confederation, with the National Confederation of the People's Organizations, with the bureaucracy, with the technocracy, administrators, and officers of PRI. It turns out there were no others, said Colonel Nemesio Inclán (an undefinable number of years old), chief of the Mexico City police force, as the green slime dripped off his chin, while he tossed back a shot of root liquor on the deck of the floating discotheque, Divan the Terrible, anchored in front of Califurnace Beach in Aca, forever hugging the pillow on which his mommy had died. We must create new civic powers, a real civil society, the young and fiery secretary of SEPAVRE (Secretariat of Patrimony and Vehiculation of Resources), Federico Robles Chacón (thirty-nine years old), said to himself, from the balcony of the palace in the center of the Mexican capital, but first we've got to blow up all the terrible symbols of Mexico as if they were last year's fireworks. *Plus ça change*, murmured his rival Don Ulises López (sixty-four years old), the head of SEPAFU (Secretariat of Patriotism and Foreign Undertakings), observing the full length and breadth of his Guerrero fiefdom from the heights of his ranch in the Los Breezes subdivision. Named Permanent Minister so he would never give up either his position at the apex of the political bureaucracy or his well-earned seat as captain of (private) industry, Don Ulises contemplates the emblematic phrase that all of you can see on all the bare ridges of the country and which he has ordered installed in neon lights on top of the Roqueta Lighthouse:

CITIZENS OF MEXICO: INDUSTRIALIZE
YOU WON'T LIVE LONGER BUT YOU WILL LIVE BETTER

And then there is the no less lapidary, embroidered motto that adorns the headboard of his bed: CRIME DOES PAY.

The child has to know what country this is and who governs it, right, Angeles?

"Right, Angeles," she said in a mocking imitation of my father even as she gave in to his arguments: self-evident, as the South Americans who sent us El Niño say, this wind that tumbles me, barely conceived, around in my mother's womb.

The net result is that I'm obliged to admit, from the egg on, that I am Christopher plus my Circumstance.

My mother asks three questions:

In which country will the child be born?

What will the child's name be?

What language will the child speak?

But I have my own questions, selective Readers.

Will I be that child?

How can I know it unless I know three things:

What is my time? What is my space? And last but not least, what is my circumstance that they tell about as if they were heeding my prayers without listening to a noise coming from deep down, so persistent that it was a brother to silence, similar to the purring of a pack of cats, who recall in their every movement, in their every noise, their savage origin, but disguise it with their silent gliding about the house, which is itself a fearful memory of the movement of a panther about to spring: that's how the faint noise of the trailer trucks sounded as they headed in and out of Acapulco, loaded with the products that the sterile resort needed but didn't produce: from New York cut steaks to toilet paper, from cases of Taittinger to hairpins; paper, pens, and pickles; mustard, muscadet, and melons; bikes, bricks, and billy clubs:

everything had to be brought from far away and the noise of the trucks that brought it all was the most pervasive noise of all; who would ever turn to stare at an eighteen-wheel truck, its refrigerated trailer, its smoking jaws, its vulcanized extremities, its poisonous exhaust pipes, its inevitable dashboard Virgins?

No one. Except today.

Leading the truck armada, the albino boy wearing a black leather jacket stopped, jumped out of the truck, raised his rose-colored hand, looked from behind his wraparound sunglasses toward the port from the heights of the seized communal lands of Santa Cruz and said: "We're not going in today; today we stop right here. Something's going on today. Let's not get involved, okay, guys? Today we stay out of Aca."

He looked with disgust and surprise at the discolored hand he'd raised and instantly concealed it. He desperately looked for his black glove. He saw it on the seat in the truck cab, climbed up, grabbed it, sat down on the driver's throne, and as he put it on he glanced at the icons on his dashboard: votive lamps, the Virgin of Guadalupe, Mrs. Margaret Thatcher, his swarthy little mother, and a photo of the Lady, the Mother and Doctor of all Mexicans. The union bosses ordered him to add that picture to those of the Virgin, his Mother, and the PM. First Bubble Gómez balked at the idea and was on the point of spitting out his eternal chewing gum: at least his holy little shrine was his, just his and not the property of the PRI or the union! But he'd grown fond of the photo of the Lady, word of honor, it even went well with the other three, and the proof of his fondness is that every so often, to pass the long hours he spent on the highway, the driver blew bubbles with his chewing gum until they burst; this was his maximum tribute to life: Bubble Gómez, bringing to the sterile resort indispensable provisions, transporting from one place to another the wealth produced elsewhere, totally unaware of the irony of Hispanic wealth, imported, unproductive Road to Santiago, gold of the Indies, treasures of the Hapsburgs, electric gadgets from Texas, treasures that escape like water through our fingers, only the symbols remain, only the continuity of the symbols is ours.

Now SHE IS THE SYMBOL.

I saw her—he told the huge man with the bushy mustache sitting next to him with a tiny thirteen-year-old girl dressed as a Carmelite nun sitting on his lap—like, well, one of us, a woman of the people, despite the jewels and feathers, like a real pal. Didn't he think so, too?

The mustachioed man stepped down from the truck. "Come on, Colasa. The truck isn't going in. We'll go on foot."

He slammed the door shut and said to the albino: "Don't let her fool you, man. That bitch is the whore of Babylon. This is the Ayatollah Matamoros giving you the true facts."

He raised two fingers in benediction, rested his other hand on the tea-colored girl, and told the driver he could quote him if he liked.

Bubble Gómez started his truck and popped a bubble right in front of the Lady's photograph.

4. *Mother and Doctor of All Mexicans*

 She was seated before the mirror: she looked at herself, surrounded by powerful, pore-perforating spotlights. She had no time to remember herself. She hadn't been allowed to look at herself in a mirror for more than a year.

The squad of makeup artists and hairdressers fell on her. First they erased her face, the one she was wearing, the one she had when she'd walked into the makeup room. She did her best to see and remember that face, but they didn't give her the time. To remember her earlier face, the real one, the original—that was certainly impossible. She had even come to doubt she ever had an original face.

She shut her eyes while they marcelled her hair and refused to accept what she'd just thought. She wrinkled her brow to cling to the shred of memory and the makeup girl said, señora, please don't frown like that.

She decided that this morning, before they put her on exhibit again, she would remember herself; soon there would be no time. She would be taken away from the mirror. A year after her enthronement, they allowed her to look into the mirror when they made her up. But she preferred to try the impossible: to remember herself as she was before all this. And she couldn't. The present was too strong, it washed away her memory and left her abandoned on the isle of the present moment, as if her present could be her salvation and not, as her soul warned her, her prison. She even came to think that memory was her worst enemy, the shark in a blind and opulent wave that kept her on its crest but without ever moving her, fixed forever in the terror of the past.

For that reason it was such a valiant act on her part to yawn in front of the mirror and decide, against, despite the fact that this morning, before they put her on exhibit, she would remember the girl who worked for two years in the secretarial pool of the Secretariat of Patrimony and Vehiculation of Resources (SEPARVE) on Avenida de los Insurgentes.

What was she like?

That was the problem: the last two years seemed an age to her and how was she going to recognize herself in a thin, tall shorthand-typist, well stacked, or so they said, with chestnut-mousy lank hair, pale makeup that was a bit too much for her because she had very pretty cinnamon skin, and wearing a pants suit bought in the Iron Palace with the savings from her previous job, one she indeed did not remember.

Her job at SEPARVE she certainly did remember, it's when she was the girlfriend of Leoncito, the mortician from San Luis Potosí Street, not very far from the Secretariat. They would meet in the Vienna Café in Parque Hipódromo, because that garden was the only oasis in these neighborhoods, where the diesel buses and dump trucks raced with their exhausts wide open (in Mexico, Nader is Nadir; this is where the Nothing with Nader Society was founded, Nader Enemy of National Development), vomiting clouds of poison onto the dead trees: they would drink cappuccino and eat chocolate pastries with German names and he offered her, so she could dress up a bit, so she would not appear so simple, well, so that he could feel proud of her, some ribbons, which were always left over after the national holidays in September, tricolor ribbons, green, white, and red, with the mortician's favorite letters printed right on the knot: RIP.

"Even when we celebrate the Day of the Cry of Dolores, people die, you know," he told her in pedagogical tones.

Of course someone laughed at her for turning up at the office decked out that way, but so long as she pleased her boyfriend Leoncito, their sneers rolled right off her back; actually, she rather liked the fact that they took more notice of her, even if it was just to take their minds off the flood of national disasters and all the other secretaries. Before, all they did was fool around or gossip about romance, movies, and soap operas, but now, suddenly, they gossiped about foreign debt and devaluation and seizing savings, my God, and she had nothing, nothing, nothing except her coquettish ribbons, the tricolor flag and the RIP, and a few wilted flowers left over from old wakes that Leoncito gave her.

Not that she was blind and deaf, no way. When she went in to take dictation (from the old-fashioned functionaries who still didn't use dictaphones or who were afraid to have their voices on tape or leave any evidence that might be directly attributed to them) or went from office to office with letters to sign (there were no executive secretaries higher up than she was to give her the *listen here don't you think that you or anyone else around here is going over my head to get to the boss*), she would pick up a word here, a word there. Of course, she understood nothing. And when she walked out of conference rooms where a pool of secretaries labored to immortalize each parenthesis, each comma, each subordinate clause created by the teams of economists who replaced each other at roller-coaster speed even though their verbal chorus was always the same (the economists, unlike the politicians, aspired to have all their words immortalized), she wondered if someone somewhere could really understand the prose of the ten thousandth National Development Plan.

But then two things happened, one after the other. Dr. Federico Robles Chacón came to the ministry cursing right and left about the language of economists, saying, to think that in the eighteenth century Montesquieu called economics the science of human happiness, thank you, Carlyle, for correcting him and calling it an abysmal science, a grim science. And the day she became the handmaiden of the interministerial committee, tricolor ribbons, dictation notebook, and all, Robles Chacón happened to say: "Mae West doesn't wear feathers and beads and she doesn't put on her diamonds just to take a walk through Central Park at midnight."

Then (an event that changed the course of Mexican history forever) Robles Chacón, doubtless because he happened to be talking about a woman, intuitively looked for a woman in the interministerial meeting room. He looked at her and his words died right in his mouth.

This . . . is . . . what we did . . . with . . . our . . .
oil
　　p
　　　o
　　　　l
　　　　　i
　　　　　　c
　　　　　　　y

He stared at her intensely, stared at her wilted flowers, her tricolor
ribbons, and their funerary letters; he snapped his fingers as if he
were about to start dancing flamenco, and out of a nearby closet
came a tiny little man, who sprang to attention like a soldier, wearing
a tuxedo and patent-leather pumps with black bows on them.

"Okay," said Robles Chacón, "give me the gross national product
figures per capita . . ."

"Well now," the man replied in a faint voice, "if we observe the
parameters of the increase in the GNP in global terms of 300 billion
pesos, in relation to consumables imported at the rate of 75 percent
of exports, but without overlooking the increase in salaries at the rate
of 49 percent and prices adjusted according to the indices of real
inflation, which occurred at the rate of 150.7 percent, and if . . ."

"Okay," interrupted the minister, "now describe the same situation
in Guinea-Bissau . . ."

". . . at the rate of 296.8 percent, we come to the conclusion,"
said the man from the closet without stopping, "that the foreseeable
increase in the demand for work will be on the order of approximately
two million new jobs, while their incidence in the demand for goods
and services will fluctuate sharply, as long as it does not necessarily
coincide with the need of infrastructures valued according to classic
parameters with a public expenditure deficit on the order of . . ."

Robles Chacón slammed his fist down on the table with such force
that his thick aviator glasses almost fell off. "This proves, gentlemen,
that there's a liar hiding behind each one of these statistics. The only
truth unspoken in all of what you've just heard is that the vast majority
of the people in Mexico and Guinea-Bissau are *screwed*."

The statistician, like a sleepwalker, went back to his closet, but
Minister-for-Life Ulises López, head of the Secretariat for Patriotism
and Foreign Undertakings (SEPAFU), stood up in a rage and said
that Dr. Robles Chacón's zeal to disparage the science of economics

in favor of old-fashioned gunslinger politics was all too well known.

"The obvious truth about Mexico," Robles Chacón responded without looking at him, "is that one system is falling apart on us, but we have no other system to put in its place."

"Yes, we do," said López, his entire being pomaded, bald, brushed, and gray, "we have a system of economic and scientific competence that will never fall apart, because, after all, economics is an exact science."

Robles Chacón, who was, after all, Professor Horacio Flores de la Peña's favorite disciple, took no notice. "The cemeteries are full of statistics. But since you can't eradicate discontent with statistics, we'll have to do it with action. But since action is hard to take and since, moreover, actually doing something can lead to chaos, I suggest we utilize neither action nor statistics and use imagination and symbols instead."

Ulises López said aloud that he would come back to the inter-ministerial meetings when dreamers and people who didn't have their feet planted firmly on the ground, poets, what have you, were kept out of them. He furiously tossed a mint Life Saver in his mouth and walked out of the meeting room pounding his heels into the floor like an angry flamenco dancer.

But Robles Chacón didn't even blink. He looked at her again. He perched his glasses on the tip of his nose. He pointed a finger at her, which made her tremble with fear as she had never trembled before, except when she saw the titanic courage of Superminister Ulises López, with his experience and his years facing down the insolence of the young upstart Dr. Robles, so she dropped her pad and pencil out of pure fright when the minister exclaimed: "Look at that girl. Do you see her? What do you see? A miserable secretary. Well, I see the same thing Bishop Juan de Zumárraga saw four centuries ago. I see a little Mexican virgin."

She blushed. "Oh dear, sir, I'm afraid you don't know what you're saying."

But he was already on his feet, dark and tense, nervous and thin, a kind of bureaucratic Danton: at age thirty-nine, the youngest minister in the regime of President Jesús María y José Paredes (fifty-five years old), haranguing the cabinet with a conviction that demolished his own personal ideas in favor of the system that, devoid of ideas, served the collectivity. He had predicted all the catastrophes: loan after loan to pay the interest on a debt that grew and grew because of the new loans which never put a dent in the principal; devaluation after devaluation, export agriculture to pay off a bit of some other debts in a declining world market; lack of hard currency to import food for a growing population; a money printing machine with inflation at Brazilian, Argentine, at Blue Angel levels; pressures, dismemberments, and finally—he collapsed in his chair, exhausted— the need to save something, whatever could be saved.

"Are we going to be a Weimar without democracy or a utopia with symbols?"

Robles Chacón maintained a religious silence for an instant. She said she believed she actually crossed herself and covered her eyes. But the minister broke the silence with a roar, again pointing to her, my God a thousand times over, at her, at her, so modest in her pants suit from the Iron Palace, with her ribbons in her hair, the ones her boyfriend from the funeral par . . .

"I say it again: look at her. Look at that girl."

"At me? At me, sir? Why look at me?"

"What do you see, fellow ministers? Don't bother telling me. A secretary from the pool. I know. But take a good look at her braids, her tricolor ribbons. What do you see written on them? I know. Don't bother telling me. You blind men see RIP. But I, maligned though I may be, I see PRI."

He breathed deeply. "For starters, we're going to make her queen of the office. We've got to do all this without haste but without pause. But remember one thing. The only thing this country is interested in is the symbolic legitimization of power."

They never left her alone from that moment on. In the office they changed her funerary ribbons for those of the party, they brought her by Mercedes to a new house surrounded by walls in the Pedregal district, a house for forgetting, she told herself, because she recognized nothing there, wanted nothing there, and everything she touched she forgot: white walls, built-in furniture, white just like the walls, as if they'd put her inside an egg, a house made for white forgetting, yes, they sent Leoncito off to sell coffins in Empalme Escobedo, she never saw him again, they disappeared her into this white shell in El Pedregal, they never let her see anyone, talk to anyone, only hear boleros all day long through a loudspeaker system reaching all over the house, even the bathroom, even her pillow, listening to boleros so she would know she was dominating and not dominated by the world of the machos, only in the bolero were women triumphant, punishing, inflicting pain, dominating, and beating down the whimpering macho who passed from his little mommy to his little Virgin, to his little whore, it's all in a bolero, if you know how to make it fit, so that she would be told, subliminally, through the loudspeakers, day and night, sending the message directly to her subconscious as if to compensate for her being locked up, a man singing to her from the invisible heights of the romantic heaven of celebrity and love and security where it's the women who have power and the men who are impotent:

> You *are to blame*
> *For* all *my anguish*
> *And* all *my grief* . . .

and after this solitary cure for one year and three months, without knowing what was going on outside, came the army of hairdressers, makeup artists, seamstresses, dressmakers, and hat makers who invaded everything, dressed the house with models and stoles, clouds of crepe and chests filled with sequins, platinum wigs, and snakeskin bustles.

One day they all left her alone. Then Robles Chacón returned with all his people. They stared at her in astonishment. But she was more astonished still. What were they looking at?

They hadn't let her see herself. The minister said that she needed no mirrors just now, she would have to get used to them later on, little by little: mirrors not allowed in the mansion of blindness in El Pedregal, just boleros. She could only see herself in the others' astonishment, above and beyond the always energetic words of Robles Chacón.

"Gentlemen: the deeper the national crisis gets, the more obvious it becomes that we cannot be satisfied with quick-fix solutions. Mexico has always managed to save herself because she has known how to turn everything into an institution—even her vices, alas. Poor Argentina can't even manage that; even its vices are chaotic and insignificant. Not here. Now we see it. In ancient times, when the people's spirits were low, the emperors would give them bread and circuses. In these parts, two sporadic solutions have recently provided the circus if not the bread when discontent has run rampant: a visit by the Pope or a fight with the gringos. Even the most hardheaded agnostic would have to admit that the successive visits of Wojtyla not only have generated euphoria among the people—which only goes to show that no one can beat us for being pragmatic Marxists, and that even if the opium comes from Poland it's still opium—but have created unforeseen commercial opportunities as well: hats, balloons, beach towels, deck chairs, bottles, records, and TV exclusives. But discontent is spreading, and there are no solutions in sight, not even if we had the Pope here for a whole year. The fight with the United States, well, we've escalated it into a war with the entire state of Veracruz occupied by battalions of Marines, who've penetrated as far as Huamantla and Apzaco. I know, I know: no one has to tell me we worked that one out with the gringos to stabilize and direct anti-U.S. sentiment in Mexico. Other, less generous people have insinuated that we invited the Marines in to wipe out an agrarian-socialist rebellion in Veracruz. If that was true, we would have achieved all our objectives. Those battles are already less violent than a flat bottle of seltzer—as my teacher Flores de la Peña used to say. Gentlemen, I'm offering you something better: an institution all our own. A sorceress. A witch doctor. A nurse for the poor:

(and they opened the door to her boudoir and someone pushed the poor little thing out)

a Doña Bárbara in a helicopter

(and they led her by the hand to the unbelievably expensive ladder made of white, blinding acrylic)

a woman who can fill the empty pitcher of national legitimacy: a new Mother for Mexico

(and they let her go, they left her alone, and she felt she was falling from the top of the spiral staircase down a bottomless ravine, with no sisterly hands to save her)

An ancient Mother was Our Lady Coatlicue, she of the serpent skirt

(but she managed to control herself, she shut her eyes, not knowing if she could open them again because of so much mascara, so much eye makeup, so much stardust on her eyelids, on her bedaubed eyelashes)

An impure Mother was Our Lady la Malinche, the traitorous lover of the conquistador Cortés, the motherfucker who created the first fucked mother who created the first Mexican

(and with each step she descended, her breasts shook more: in-jected, inflated, sillyconized breasts surgically manipulated to achieve the consistency, the rhythm, and the balance necessary to bounce as they bounced now even though they were squeezed and raised and revealed as they were now under the cascade of diamond chokers)

A pure Mother was Our Lady of Guadalupe, redeemer of the humble Indian: from Babylon to Bethlehem with a bouquet of instant roses, Nescaflowers, gentlemen: we've got our holy little mommy

(and so for a year and three months they taught her, swing those hips, girl, shake your ass, baby, now you're talking, honey, bend that waist as if you were the seawall in Havana, your ace is your ass, and don't you forget it, bitch)

A rebellious Mother was Our Lady la Adelita, the darling Cle-mentine, the fairy godmother of the revolution

(corseted, cinched, swaying, full of secrets only she knew, they told her, a ruby encrusted in her belly button that no one would ever see, and between her legs a white bulge and curled foam, not that slack, gawky mop she showed up with, even there they gave her a permanent and a marcelling, her vulva sewn up with golden thread and embellished with two dozen diamonds sharpened like tiny shark teeth, like hussars guarding the entrance closed to all; they told her that her temptation would be to offer hatred as a hope; that she should think that she was not real, that she'd been invented, screwed together with precious stones, a Frankedenic monster with forty-carat cathodes: the guy who gets inside you, baby, is gonna be fried, pulverized, and cut like a deck of cards)

and secret Mothers all the women from whose image we descend, but whom we can never touch: the movie stars, the devouring women, the vampire women, the great rumba and exotic dancers of our immense adolescent dreams, Ninon Sevilla, Mapy Cortés, Marie Antoinette Pons, Dinah, Rosa la Más Hermosa, Iris Cha-chachacón

(but barefoot, she'd never use shoes they told her, they ordered her, always barefoot like the little Virgin of the humble, barefoot like the Indian porters and the slaves, Holy Mother, look at yourself, as naked as a poem: you shall not return, your slave's feet will return; the people will love your feet because they walked on the earth and on the wind and the water until they found me, Little Mother, your feet went out looking and found your lost child, Mamacita, the soles of your feet were not made for the world's frivolous dancing but to ascend the calvaries of the world, your naked feet, bleeding, on a thorny path, Little Mother, bend your waist, I can't go on, but never put on shoes: think about your sons Eddypoes, Oddyshoes, Lost Children)

and supersecret Mothers all the gringas of our masturbatory dreams, Lana, Marilyn, and Ava, but, above all others, the tits of the town, teatanic Mae West from the Big Apple, when she was good she was good but when she was bad she was better, Occidental Mother, your splendid tinsel lost inside your white flesh, your secret depths: to screw you, Stepmother of the West, is to avenge our entire history of insecurity and submission, White Ass, come on your Black Prick, go on, fart so I can orient, occident, accident, crank it up blondie, your short, Daddy says so

(those lips like a scarlet satin sofa, yes, señora, that you will show—they stopped calling her girl just at the end, only señora: step out onto the balcony, señora, go down the white acrylic ladder without looking at your feet, wave without seeing anyone, señora)

superimposed on all women, gentlemen, we are finally free from the cloying sweetness of some, the nocturnal terror of others, the inaccessible distance of these, the familiar and intimate disdain of those, here is our final legitimation, our permanent prize, the fountain of all power in Mexico, the supreme edifice of machista supremacy, boys,

the perfect mix of Mae West, Coatlicue, and the Virgin of Guadalupe. A
  symbol,
The greatest human symbol ever invented:
THE MOTHER,
The sweet name where biology *acquires a* soul,
where nature *becomes* transcendent
and where sex *becomes* history:
OUR HOLY MOTHER!!!
And the minister offered his hand to the incredible apparition as she reached
  the last step:
GENTLEMEN: I PRESENT TO YOU OUR LADY MAMADOC.

He released her hand, fatigued, Jupiter without glory, devalued Pygmalion, observing in his most tranquil voice that the bureaucracy ends up creating what it conceives. Mamadoc will prove that the secret of the system *is* its secret. The important thing now is to keep up the *momentum*, gentlemen, of what we have set into motion.

"She is my gift to you, gentlemen."

She never saw him again. At one point, she actually thought she was falling in love with him. Folly, folly. They sat her in her silver Mercedes with darkened windows; and with a motorcycle escort they brought her to the National Palace, they brought her up in an elevator, they led her out to the balcony, she knew what she had to do, weep, thank, wave, pretend the people were cheering her and weeping with her and then they, the multitudes of Mexico City, in this night of castles of fire and bands and fireworks and dead stars and showers of gold, would associate their national holiday, their September 15, not with a president or liberator, all devalued now, but with her, she-who-cannot-be-devalued, the mother who returned with her slave feet, her feet searching for her children, her ideal feet . . .

What Mexican alive in the Year of Our Lady 1992, when this story of the polyphonic gestation of the child Christopher Palomar and his imminent travels around an oceanic egg takes place, could forget the supreme instant of the national destinies that my father and mother remember while they plan out my birth for October 12 next so they will win the Christopher Contest, since without Her there would be no contest: Who, I repeat, who could forget the instant in which the spotlight focused on the central balcony of the Palace on the night of flying gold, the night of September 15, 1991, when the unique cornucopia of Mexico was a castle of light and the sparkle of a fleeting rocket when the spotlight moved away from President Jesús María y José Paredes, away from his family, from his cabinet, from his bodyguards, to tremble for an instant, indecisively, and then quickly stop, white and whitewashed like the object of their desire, on Her?

She with her mountain of platinum curls and her face whiter than the moon (the same moon Robles Chacón was staring at, but *he* had created this one; how they stared at her now, the children of Our Lady the Mother Doctor of All Mexicans!) and her spangled skirt shining with green reptile scales and her chubby little feet, white, naked, now that She, like an apparition, simulated, made people believe she levitated, rising above the copper railing and showing naked little tootsies, Our Lady, her bare little tootsies posed delicately over the horns of a bull; who was going to pay any attention to the

President, who had resigned himself to this for the sake of the continuity of the system; who was going to pay any attention to the tight-lipped rage of Robles Chacón's rival, Superminister Ulises López, ready, after so many defeats, to exchange wheels for deals; who was going to pay any attention to the sullen chief of police, Colonel Nemesio Inclán, so tenacious about remaining true to his archetype with his dark glasses at 11 p.m., and that stream of green spit running out of the corner of his mouth, when this celestial apparition, the subtle summa of all our mothers and lovers, shook the national flag over the heads of a million Mexicans and cried out. Gentlemen, can't you see? she made no speeches, recalled no heroes, condemned no Spaniards, none of that! If the business at hand was to give the Cry of Dolores, Mamadoc, right here, gave her first *Cry*, as if she were giving birth to the mob that was staring at her in rapture, a shout that cracked the bells in the Cathedral, that knocked a pair of stone putti off the Sagrario Metropolitano, a *Cry* that made each and every one of the million souls down below with their tiny tricolor flags and their sugar candy and their lollipops shaped like oil derricks, believe that *She* was giving birth to all of them, that now this ceremony *did* make sense, that finally they understood what this Cry of Dolores was: it's that our little mother is giving painful birth to us, sons of a whore! And yet that shout which was so loud was also so melodic, so tender, so sweet that it seemed like a bolero intoned on a velvety afternoon by Adelina Landín, by Amparo Montes, by the Aguila sisters . . .

My father and mother went together. My father, oh so lopezve-lardian, shouted with impassioned and repugnant love to that figure who from now on would be at the center of our history:

"Prisoner of the Valley of Mexico! You don't know what you've gotten yourself into!"

Robles Chacón stared at his creation from a balcony at some distance from the system's central nervous center. He looked at Mamadoc and then at the people—his plural enemy. He thought about his own parents. He'd never seen his father, Federico Robles, a ruined banker who died before his son was born. And his mother, Hortensia Chacón, had never seen him: she was blind. And now *he* was giving to *all Mexico* a mother that *everyone* could see and who could see *them*. Now *he* was the *father* of the *mother* of *all*.

She would be forgiven everything, that was the point. The triumph of the people would be to see in her what *they* didn't have: she would have the right to have what the rich had, because she came from the secretarial pool of the SEPAVRE and was the girlfriend of a mortician and she had memorized all the boleros Manzanero and Agustín Lara had ever written, to the point that she could win one of her own contests, those famous (from now on) National Contests of Mamadoc.

She certainly could confess, and sublimate in the name of the system, all the corruption of the system: she would confess her propensity toward luxury, extravagance, ostentation; she would be forgiven this and more, but no one else would be; what in others would be a vice would be in her sincerity, popularity, admiration, matriarchal right.

Her astounded creator watched her, with her tall platinum hairdo, her décolleté flowing with diamonds, her cartridge belts crossed over her chest, her beaded bustle, her snakeskin petticoats, her bare feet, all of her as whitewashed as the moon, responding to the exclamations she aroused, trembling and weeping an instant before the masses did but persuading the masses to believe that they made her weep and tremble for their sake; and he would have wanted to say to her by way of farewell, seeing her enthroned, she all by herself assuring political legitimacy for fifty or a hundred more years, with no revolutions, with renewed hopes, that the sin of others was to have destroyed a nation to satisfy their vanity; she, on the other hand, could do the very same thing because, knowingly or unknowingly . . .

"Everything that is not vanity is pain, girl."

He corrected himself instantly: "Excuse me . . . señora."

Then the fireworks spelled out the night's message:

NO ONE SHALL POSSESS HER BUT THE PEOPLE

For which reason she yawned this morning before the mirror and her hairdresser said to her, honey, don't pucker your cunt, and she stood up, even taller than she was and mounted on the elaborate high heels she wore in private to balance out so many hours walking barefoot in public, and she gave the impudent, upstart wench a slap in the face, señora! señora! that's right, I'm señora here and you're my little maid, my little asshole, yes señora, pardon señora, and now she could remember herself as she was before all this because she had a reason and the power to do it: Minister Federico Robles Chacón, her creator, her torturer, the object of her passion, Mamadoc began to spit like a llama perched on a peak in the Andes, spitting on the mirrors which they'd finally let her look into, although they forbade her to have a son, now she understood it when she'd proclaimed this shitty contest about the shitty little Christophers, sewn up forever with diamonds sharpened like shark teeth, condemned forever to Virginity, not even Mary was required to do so much, they let Mary give birth, but not Mamadoc, Mary lost her virginity, but Mamadoc recovered hers, Mamadoc would not have a son, but she would proclaim the Son of the Republic, the odious infant who would be born on October 12 to inaugurate the Mexican dynasty of the Christophers, colonized colonists, no more need for elections, no more headaches, chosen successors, nonreelections, all over a dynasty, ingenious Federico Robles Chacón and she about to explode in rage, scratching at all the mirrors of identity, her hands sticky with reflections, her fingers smearing her own saliva over those fleeting portraits of her accumulated iconography, trapped by a bolero into feeling that, despite everything, she existed, she had a love, she was loved, that he was the one who whispered in her ear—in Lucho Gatica's voice:

> You filled my life
> With sweet disquiet
> And bitter disenchantment

that things were the way they always were, that the problem was how to deal with powerful men and powerless women, and she punching the dressing-table mirrors to pieces while her hairdressers fled in a panic and she with her bloody, smeared hands on her serpent skirts, on her rebozo with its little ball tassels, and on her powdered, depilated face, she answering the tender bolero with another tearful bolero, which she herself sang amid the ruin of glass and quicksilver and blood:

> You passed right by
> With nothing but indifference

oh, my love, my love, turn around and look at me, my love, be nice, here I am your lover girl, your lesser half, oh let me share your shadow, oh my love, she in love with him, folly, folly, she with all apparent power and no real power, she spitting on the mirrors and Uncle Homero Fagoaga staring at her behind the two-way mirrors, after having paid off the hairdressers with lots in Tumbledown Beach as a bribe so they'd secretly let him into that space prepared by the hairdressers to let in by means of moderate munificence (MMM) the voyeurs who might want to watch Mamadoc powder herself and curl the lesser parts of her body: with a kind of ecstasy Uncle Homero received the Andean spit from Our Lady of Mexico, humiliated but clean, anxiously desiring that Mamadoc land one right on his cheek, Don Homero coming with an unpublished, secret, oh so hidden and warm pleasure; caressing as well a small but growing hatred against the man for whom she made these scenes, squandering these passions: not on him, not on Homero Fagoaga, but on another man, hateful, hated: Federico Robles Chacón!

5. On Streets like Mirrors

The rivalry between the two Secretaries of State (as our Uncle Don Fernando Benítez informs us) dates from the catastrophic earthquake of September 19, 1985, a date our uncle remembers for two equally sad reasons. First came the quake, which affected everyone, and hot on its heels he heard the news of the death, far away from Mexico (in Siena), of Italo Calvino, the great Italian writer who imagined that the earth was so close to the moon that we could all go there by canoe to drink Diana's milk. He shared this grief with thousands of readers; but beyond the protective walls of his house in Coyoacán, Don Fernando also shared the grief of millions of people surprised by a physical catastrophe in which the image of the city became, as Benítez said, its destiny. And my father, to whom my in-fancies unite me every instant, repeated for posterity:

"From now on, the image of the city is its destiny."

My father was deeply pissed off at the fact that the epicenter of the hideous earthquake, Acapulco, had remained unscathed. My father was a son of Mexico City, of its history, of its incredible capacity for survival: burned down, sacked, invaded, victim of wars and occupations, plagues and famine which in twenty-four hours would have finished off New York or Los Angeles, where since time immemorial people don't realize that time is coming to an end and that the Fifth Sun is burning up and shaking the earth until it breaks it. For my father, the suffering and the resistance of the city were comparable only to those of the cities devastated by the war in Japan and Europe; he would have been interested to see New York or Los Angeles bombarded, with no food, occupied by a foreign army, besieged by a guerrilla insurrection. They wouldn't have lasted a week.

From the time he was a boy, from the time he lived through the earthquake at sixteen years of age in the house of his grandparents, Don Rigoberto Palomar and Doña Susana Renteria, and miraculously the little house on Calle Génova, in the hardest-hit zone, had come through unscathed, my father was astonished to see that everything old was still standing, untouched: Aztec pyramids, baroque palaces, Spanish colonial buildings; and that only the new, buildings hastily constructed to pocket more cash, fell down inexcusably, with a mocking rictus in every broken window, in every twisted beam. My father walked around in shock that catastrophic morning: he saw the collapse of those plaster palaces, those cardboard castles: steel accordions, houses of cards.

My young father turned on his heels on the nervous sidewalk of Paseo de la Reforma; he didn't know what to do but he knew he had to do something, a truckload of boys, some his age, some older than he, but all young, passed by, shouting above the echoing din of the earth and the chain collapses; a young, dark man wearing aviator glasses and a beige jacket held out his hand to him, and Angel, my father, jumped on, grasping that strong hand: they were going to the hospital, the worst collapse, don't get worked up, Fede, your ma's probably okay, said another boy, lightly hugging the leader of this first-aid group, which was not the only one, and as they made their way quickly that morning along Reforma, Ejido, Juárez, the trucks, pickups, vans, and cars filled with young men armed with picks, shovels, whatever they could find—their bare hands. Organized on their own, with a ferociously lucid instinct for survival, a spontaneous fan spreading throughout the city, half an hour, an hour, and two hours after the catastrophe. My father, Angel, looked into the eyes of those around him. As with him, no one had organized them, they had organized by themselves, and they knew perfectly what they had to do, without instructions from a government, a party, or a leader.

My father was really outraged that the "killer quake," as it was called abroad, or KQ, as it came to be known here and everywhere else, didn't take place in Acapulco, and later on, when he went home, exhausted, thinking about what he might do, he painted a sign and he stuck it on a branch of a fallen tree and brought it out to the front of the house, proclaiming with orange paint, so everyone could see it: DELENDA EST ACAPULCO.

Even though he was just a kid, my father took careful note of the man who had taken charge of the rescue operation at the hospital. He was nervous, dark, he never stopped adjusting his aviator glasses on the bridge of his nose, his dark curly hair was white with dust from the dead buildings, his face, his arm, his index finger were like a compass needle indicating decisions, orders, and changes in the rescue operation: doctors arrived along with lawyers, engineers, and businessmen, men who abandoned their offices and shops to form human chains to the tops of the cement mountains, the wounded chain of hospitals, hotels, and apartment buildings devoid of breath, never to breathe again. A line of soldiers formed around the hospital. Desperate people clawed the ruins, isolated cries for help (from inside and outside as well) reached the soldiers, like a chain of voices identical to the chain of arms that passed pieces of cement, twisted wire, the body of a little girl in a basket from the top of the ruin down: some pieces of cement flew against the troops and struck their helmets, wounded their hands tensely gripping their weapons: bloody fists, the world like a vast bloody fist, soldiers, victims, rescue equipment. This is what my father remembers and tells my mother. A stone hit the helmet of a sergeant in charge of a squad. Even today, my father remembers the man's greenish face, his black glasses, the stream of green saliva running out of the corners of his mouth: his invisible stare, his grimace of patient revenge.

He looked more closely at the eyes of the young man who had organized the rescue.

"Where is your mom?" a buddy asked him.

"I don't know. It doesn't matter now."

But Federico Robles Chacón would count every minute, every hour that passed until the end of this story; he accepted the idea that he would never see his mother again. Hortensia Chacón had been hospitalized the night before the earthquake. On the other hand, as the days passed, he would not accept the idea of abandoning the newborn babies who were saved one by one over the course of a week, two weeks, little girls born an hour or a night before the quake, who survived in the ruins seven or nine days after being born: terrible images of the survival of the city, of the entire nation: a baby girl crushed by a steel beam, she lived; another baby girl suckled by her dying mother, she lived; a baby boy, stuck fast, with no food but his fetal fluids, with no air but that in his fetal hemoglobin, he lived— equipped to fight, equipped to survive; I listen to all this in the womb of my liquid, prenatal tides, and I want to weep in surprise, joy, and fear: I shall also manage to survive the catastrophes that await me. My God, will I also manage to survive, like these miraculous children who survived the Mexico City earthquake?

My sixteen-year-old father marches with his homemade sign DELENDA EST ACAPULCO in front of the offices of Don Ulises López on River Nylon Street, and the short, astute functionary and financier laughs to see such a bizarre sight. The city has filled up with out- landish lunatics, religious fanatics, charlatans. Look at that loon demanding the destruction of Acapulco! he said to the meeting of the administrative council of construction and real estate, his back to the window: of course, of course, what we're going to do in Aca- pulco is just what we're going to do here in Mexico City: we're going to give full value to property, not sell it off cheap. Where did these nuts get this idea of hauling off the debris from the earthquake to construct miniparks and libraries? Kids and books on lots that are going to be worth five times more than before just because the build- ings next to them didn't fall down, and we—we, gentlemen, we, partners—are going to construct the best, the most solid and secure buildings, government offices first—we've got to take care of Big Brother first—then, frankly, buildings with commercial value, after all the government doesn't know how to keep books, identify property, or find out where anything is. We do. Ulises López stood up, we are going to evaluate—right away—every square inch of property hit by the catastrophe, with a view to taking advantage of its value and rebuilding on it, if not today then tomorrow; in Mexico, sooner or later, you can do anything because sooner or later someone who thinks like us, partners! will have more power than those who oppose us.

The homeless—thirty thousand, fifty, a hundred thousand?—dem- onstrated a few times, demanding housing, some got it, most spent time in flophouses, hangars, schools which they then had to leave, they went back where they came from or stayed on with relatives or scattered among the traffic islands in the city streets where they set up their tents and huts: immovable. Others returned to the empty places where they once had a place to live, a job, a little shop, they settled down in vacant lots, and Ulises López just laughed at them, looking forward to the day when the public authorities would agree with him in kicking them out; the financier-functionary snapped his fingers and said, a good day's work, an earthquake Mexican-style, classist, racist, xenophobic, and what's that young economist doing there, Robles what's-his-name, what? digging? he's looking for his mother, ha ha, I didn't know he had one! The eyes of Ulises López in his Shogun model limousine, of Federico Robles Chacón with a smashed piece of Sheetrock in his hands, and those of my father with his ridiculous poster against Acapulco, all met.

6

And where was I? Tell me right away before I forget, O mighty Breeder: my parents have just conceived me, surrounded by blazing beaches and crumbling towers and peaks as white as bones and the miserable hillsides, where, says my father, the human ivy of Acapulchritude used to live, hanging on like ticks to the sumptuous body, he says, although by now gone soft, wormy, of old Acapulcra, O my nubile fisher-girl whose limp hair once hung down to her waist (he says in the name of all the children of the past who went to spend happy, prepollution vacations in Acapulco), in yesteryear busy with your nets and your brightly painted boats, now betrothed to death, a courtesan in exhausted sands: Look, Angeles, look at your Acapulco like a Cleopatra about to nest the scorpion in your breasts, a Messalina ready to drink the cup of sewage, a Pompadour bewigged to camouflage the cancers on her hairy skin, ugh . . .

The Army kicked their asses out of the mountains around the bay, even out of the mountains not visible from the white half-moon of hotels, restaurants, and McDonald's (which, the upstanding citizens claimed, the guerrillas wanted, horror of horrors, to rename

Marxdonald's and force to sell *chalupas* filled with caviar instead of that classic Mexican dish cheeseburgers and catsup). All a matter of aesthetics, said a television talk-show host, because (though he didn't say this) no one meddled with the invisible, squat neighborhoods of repair shops, dust, food stands, and tents behind the barrier of sky-scrapers that came, more and more, to resemble sand: but, since they'd kicked their asses out of the visible and invisible mountains, everyone said that it wasn't a matter of public health or aesthetics but self-interest: the mountains were to be parceled off, the Icacos Navy base was sold to a consortium of Japanese hotel owners, and the inhabitants of the mountains resisted for months and months, squatting there challenging, refusing with the swollen stomachs of their children, their trichinosis, their water filled with revenge, their eyes so clouded over with grief and glaucoma that they couldn't see the magic carpet at their feet, the Acapulco diamonds over a velvety night, an aquamarine day, a blond sunset, the opulent asphyxia of toasted bodies and pink jeeps and pale condominia, and gangrenous lunch counters, and cadaveric discotheques and crab-infested motels, and neon signs turned on at midday because

MEXICO HAS ENERGY TO BURN

says my mom to my dad the afternoon of my conception: those who were displaced to the hidden lands—points out my mother from the water—behind the mountains where no offended tourist could see them, much less hear them and much less smell them, found that the promises of new homes were just words: they were screwed per-fectly by being sent from the mountains facing the sea to a swamp called Florida City because the only thing there was a cesspool with no electricity, plumbing, or roof, just some piles of lumber and prefab Sheetrock, which turned out to have been bought by the municipal president of Acapulco from the company of a brother-in-law who was cousin to the governor, who sat next to Minister Ulises López in school, who was owner of the aforementioned cement factory, uncle of the administrator of the aforementioned cesspool, may God keep him in the cabinet of our incumbent President Jesús María y José Paredes, and who will, God willing (the important people in Kickapulco support this) (moral support, you understand), within fewer than four years comply with the huge revolutionary responsi-bility of naming his successor, do it in favor of, please, svp, come on now, prego, the aforementioned Don Ulises López, preferred and proffered son (prefabricated they say over behind the mountains in Florida City) of the Costa Chica of Guerrero, where I am taking a nice bath right now, where I sense, knowing, do you know? throbbing, throbbing me, that the coral and the jellyfish surround me outside my mom's belly (thanks, Mother, for taking me in when my father fired me out of his pistol, I suspect that just for having done it, most belovèd protectress, I will always love you more than I love him, but nyahh!).

They say that the mayor of Tearapulco, Dr. Noel Guridi, received the gift of thirty coyotes trained by the governor of the state of Guerrero, General Vicente Alcocer, and he told him, don't be afraid, you've got to work over these rebels, you understand me, work them over.

And the trained coyotes went out at night with their tongues and eyes irritated and burning, bonfires of smoke and blood in their eyes and snouts, the coyotes went out to do some working over, went out with their bodies covered with mangy fur and their muddy claws on the necks of the old and dying, on the necks of the sick and the helpless, whether they were cooling off on the mountains, groaning on their pallets, creaking motionless in their huts. They were the last rebels to remain scratching the mountains with a view of the sea and the bay: the sea and the bay belong to the jet set, not to the squatters, said Governor Vicente Alcocer as he stared at his photo in *Paris-Match*.

The boy with the long face and the long snout, like that of a plumed coyote, stands up stiff and tall like a banderilla in the center of the dried-out palm grove on the heights of the old communal lands of Santa Cruz, his yellow eyes wide open. He waits patiently for what must come: the dark eyes, the wet muzzles, the copper-dust-colored fur—the nervous howls—the giggles, the animals that laugh, waiting for the full moon: he waits for them with the patience of a brother, shedding his skin, as if the time and anguish of the wait had torn him apart both inside and outside.

The boy with the ragged suit and the snakeskin belt closes his eyes when the full moon appears, so that he can be seen without having to see them: he knows he should not look directly at them, they hypnotize, they misinterpret the stares of others and their own stares are easy to misunderstand: the coyotes believe in nonexistent challenges, or they communicate them.

He closes his eyes and smells them, he sweating and they sweating.

They have gathered in a circle, as if they were having a conference. They fall silent. They listen to their leader, who is always the oldest animal. The others imitate him, will imitate him. The boy with long, greasy curls only knows that the coyote is a cowardly animal and that's why it never comes close to people.

He opens his eyes. He offers them a hand filled with corn fungus. The coyotes come closer. It's a new moon, and the boy howls. The pack approaches him and eats the corn mushrooms out of his hand. The boy feels their wet muzzles in his open palm, he pets their copper-dust-colored fur, finally looking into their dark eyes.

He takes an old-fashioned car horn out of his pocket and squeezes it: the honks at first scatter the pack, making them walk in nervous circles, until the pack leader identifies the noise with the boy, and the others follow suit.

"A coyote is just as capable of attacking the oppressed as is the oppressor. Give them music, not beatings."

He tells the people hidden behind the mountains where no one can ever see them, give them food, stop them from being afraid of you, play the jukebox for them, so they won't be so scared, then take them down to the town so they won't be afraid of cars, get them used to the noise of the port, the smell of the tourists, one day let one go into a hotel lobby and see what happens . . .

Desperate, I cling to my mother's oviduct.

The Holy Family

The traditions of all past generations
weigh like a nightmare on the brain of
the living.

Karl Marx,
The 18th Brumaire of Louis Bonaparte

1

Later my father and mother emerge from the sea and put their ears to the sand as if to listen for something far off, to listen through walls, depths, to listen for the earthquakes that are coming, to listen for the growth of the grass and the creaking of the graveyards, the noise El Niño makes moving over the sea and the trot of the coyotes coming down the mountains.

I've been hearing noises since the beginning—they resound. I dream that: wherever I am I shall be covered, masked, but still resounding, hearing, dreaming, perhaps one day I shall be listened to, but for now I only listen, listening to them through my prenatal filters, like this:

"This is my second question: what will the boy's name be?"

"Christopher."

"Don't be a jerk. I already know that: What else? Which last names!

"Palomar."

"What else?"

"I don't know what your other names are. I named you Angeles. Angel and Angeles sound good."

"Describe me today."

A green flame I would have wanted to touch when she was a girl, before and before and before, a green flame is what she looks like now, liquid emerald, daughter of the dawn (well, of this dawn: the one we managed to get): well, you're better than nothing. Tall and slender, fair but trying hard to get a tan. Black hair, cut short, shaved at the neck, raven wing and kissmequick over one eye: very twenties. Both of us dress very twenties. Hippie style's out of fashion. Today to be a rebel in fashion means to be seriously retro: I wear dark suits, gaiters, hats, scarf pins, ties, starched collars. She wears black bandeaux, gray silk stockings, shoes for dancing the Charleston. Now I've made her dress Tehuana-style to fool Uncle Homero: she in Tehuana clothes, me hippie-style; folklore and revolution, things that don't shock our relative or anyone else.

Angeles: your expression is so hard sometimes, while your flesh is so smooth and soft. I love your perfumed nape, your acid axillas, your naked feet. Angeles, my Angeles: give me things to think about at night. My Engelschen with long legs and breasts that seem immobile they're so small and so well fixed. Pale, limp, and white (now tanning under the January sun of Acapulco). She commemorated her lack of a past as well as her arrival in Mexico City by going alone one afternoon to the Monument of the Revolution to make wee-wee on the eternal flame and by declaring later in the police station when they arrested her for disrespect:

"That flame doesn't cost the government a dime. That's why I put it out."

Later she confessed to Angel that she only did it to get even, to show that a woman not only can urinate standing up if she so chooses but can even put out the sacred flame of the Mexican Revolution that way. Uncle Fernando Benítez took Angeles in when the girl turned up on his doorstep out of the blue one day in the year '91, after the national disasters in '90 that left us bereft of half the territory remaining to us, and many people from the provinces decided to flee from Chitacam, the Yucatán, Mexamerica, from the coast north of Ixtapa-Zihuatanejo, in order to go on being Mexicans. Angeles appeared before Benítez with no suitcase, without even a change of clothes, which Don Fernando liked because he didn't want to know any more about her; he said he liked to decide things once and for all right on the spot, decide about love or friendship or justice without proof or explanation. She said she'd seen him from a distance in the

plaza of her hometown and she liked the way he came right up to
people, he spoke to people to whom no one else ever spoke: she liked
that and that's why she'd come. And she'd read his books.

He told the authorities she was his niece and defended her with
all the sophistry of a good Mexican lawyer—even if he had no degree,
Fernando Benítez, like all literate Mexicans, had a jurist locked in
his bosom, just dying to get out into the world. While Angeles was
being held, Don Fernando Benítez sent his agile young ally, the
Orphan Huerta, to reignite the flame; by the time Angeles appeared
before the magistrate, it was impossible to prove that the flame had
ever been extinguished, and Benítez could declare the following: Are
you saying, your honor, that the flame of the Mexican Revolution
can be put out just like that—as declared by these two exemplars of
the best police force money can buy, even if they were in all prob-
ability a bit tipsy at the time and for all practical purposes merely
concupiscent, the miserable nobodies! The truth of the matter is that
my niece did feel an urge, that's so, was seen and chased by these
fleet-footed minions of justice, which heightened her nervousness
and its effects on her bladder, so she eliminated where she could—
but to put out the flame of our permanent revolution? With a mere
squirt of wee-wee? Who could do it? Not her, not me, not even you,
your honor!

And Angel? Will you describe him, Mom?

Also green, very much a gypsy. Tall, a boy from this new generation
of skinny, tall Mexicans. Both of us are dark and green, me with
black eyes and he with lime-green eyes. We looked at each other:
he's shortsighted, knows how to whistle all of *Don Giovanni*, and
says that I would have been a perfect courtesan in an opera if I'd
been born a hundred years ago, and if I hadn't begun reading the
complete works of Plato. The set with green covers. Vasconcelos.
The National Autonomous University of Mexico. God, it's the only
thing that lets me look at myself in the mirror and say to myself:
There you are. Your name is Angeles. You love Angel. You are
going to have a baby. What makes you think I won't read the whole
Cratylus, which is a book about names: Angel, Angeles, Christopher:
Are they the names that really belong to us (my love, my man, my
name, my son)? Or are the names ourselves, are we the names? Do
we name or are we named? Are our names a pure convention? Did
the gods give us our names, but by saying them (our own and the

others) do we wear them out and pervert them? When we *name* ourselves, do we *burn* ourselves? None of this matters to me: I intuit that if I have a name and I name you (Angel/Angeles) it's so I can discover little by little your nature and my own. Isn't that what's most important? What does it matter then that I have no past or that I don't remember it, which is the same thing. Take me as I am, Angel, and don't ask me any more questions. This is our pact. Name me. Discover me. I am going to have a son and I'm going to read Plato. What makes you think I won't, despite all the accidents that in Mexico make intellectual endeavor impossible, all the distractions, the pleasant climate, the deteriorating environment, let's take a walk, the coffee klatches, the gossip, the parties, there isn't a real summer, the winter is invisible, politics are taken care of for us every six years, nothing works but everything survives, you was born, you dies, you don' reads, you don' write nothin'. What makes you think I won't? Do you understand why I'm memorizing Plato? Those books are those men, Angel, the others, the people, the ones who did something, read, spoke, listened: Angel, I have no other connection with the others, not even with a past, not even with a family or anyone else. I have no past, Angel my love, that's why everything that falls on me sticks to me, all causes, all ideas, feminism, the left, third world, ecology, ban-the-bomb, Karl and Sigi, liberation theology, even traditional Catholicism as long as it goes against conformity, everything sticks to me and whatever sticks to me has to be good, my love, because the only thing that doesn't stick to me is respect for authority, faith in the chief, superior races, the murder or oppression of anyone in the name of an idea, history, the nation, or the leader, none of the above. I am a good receptacle, Angel, a white wall without memories or my own past, my love, but a place where only pretty things can be written and ugliness has no place. Now I leave it to you to write there with me, but don't force me into anything, my love; I need you, but don't chain me up; I follow you, but don't order me to follow you; let me make the life I never had or don't remember with you, Angel, and one day we can remember together, but I'll have no memory of anything but my life with you: please, let's share everything. Pardon my habitual silence. I'm not absent. I observe and absorb, my love. This is our pact.

Your father Angel says I feel superior to him because since I have no past I've had to enter today's universality in a flash, the universality of violence, haste, cruelty, and death. But his parents died comically, eating tacos.

What did Grandpa and Grandma do, Dad?

Your grandparents, Diego and Isabella Palomar, were inventors, Chris: in the tabloids of the period they were called the Curies of Tlalpan. I'm telling you this so you know right from the start that in this country anything you do will be pardoned as long as it serves in one way or another to justify and legitimize the status quo. Your uncles, Homero and Fernando, who detest each other, have at least that in common. Don Homero's illegal trafficking is pardoned because he does his job as Defender of the Castilian Tongue. Don Fernando's critical gibes are forgiven because he is the Defender of the Indians. My grandpa General Rigoberto Palomar's eccentricities are forgiven because he is the only person who believes body and soul that the Mexican Revolution triumphed. And my parents were given official protection for their inventions because they were the Curies of Tlalpan: two inventive and daring scientists during the period, my boy, when Mexico thought it could be technologically independent. One illusion less! For thirty years we were buying obsolete technology at high prices; every five or six years we had to turn our decrepit machinery in for new obsolete machinery, and so on and so on and so on . . . And thus the techniques for robotics and cryogenics, biomedicine, fiber optics, interactive computers, and the entire aerospace industry passed us by. One day, when you've grown up, I'll take you to see the ruins of the investments in the oil boom, son, when we spent forty billion dollars to buy junk. I'll take you to see the ruins of the nuclear plant in Palo Verde, next to which Chichén-Itzá looks like a brand-new Coca-Cola and hot-dog stand. I'll take you, my dear son, to see expensive, rusting machinery sitting in the useless industrial Gulf ports. And if you want to take a ride on an ultramodern Japanese bullet train, well, maybe it would be better for you to take a ride on the kiddy train in Chapultepec Park instead of trying the paralyzed inter-ocean train that according to its Mexican designers was going to knock the crap out of the Panama Canal. Seek in vain, my boy, the rapid shipment of barrels of oil from Coatzacoalcos to Salina Cruz, the shortest route from Abu Dhabi to San Francisco and Yokohama: seek it, sonny, and all you'll see are the cold rails and the hot illusions of insane Mexican oil-grandeur: no immortal spring, only these, Fabio, oh grief: the blasted heath between the Gulf of Mexico and the Pacific Ocean. Mountains of sand and the cadaver of a spider monkey. Long live the Opepsicoatl Generation!

But, Daddy, when did they make you?

(His parents conceived my father the night of October 2, 1968, as a response against death. At times they'd thought of not having children, of dedicating themselves totally to science. But the night of the student massacre at the Plaza de Tlateloco, they said that if at that instant they didn't affirm the right to life so brutally trampled on by an arrogant, maddened, and blind power, there would never be any science in our country: they had seen the troops destroy entire laboratories in University City, steal typewriters, dismantle the work of four generations of scholars. As my grandparents made love they could not shut out the noise of sirens, ambulances, machine guns, and fires.

My father was born on July 14, 1969. Thus, his intrauterine life took place between two symbolic dates. In that fact he sees a good omen for my own conception: between Twelfth Night and Columbus Day. But my mother balances this abundance of symbols: she doesn't even know when she was born, much less when she was conceived.)

But my grandparents, Dad, tell me about my grandparents.

I don't know if what my parents, Diego and Isabella, invented in the basement of their house in Tlalpan (where I was born) was useful or not. In any case, whatever it was, it hurt no one, except, as it turned out, themselves. They believed in science with all the love of novelty and all the fury of liberal, emancipated Mexicans and rejected both inquisitorial shadows and the sanctimoniousness of the past. So their first invention was a device to expel superstition. Conceived on a domestic scale and as easy to use as a vacuum cleaner, this manual, photostatic device made it possible to transform a black cat into a white cat the instant the feline crossed your path.

The apparatus's other accomplishments were, my boy, as follows: it reconstituted broken mirrors instantaneously by magnetizing the pieces. They used it to leap Friday the 13th gracefully and to close automatically the portable ladders under which it was possible to walk the streets (a supplemental movement deflected the paint cans that might, for that very reason, fall on one's head). It even caused hats carelessly tossed on beds to float indefinitely in the air.

They even invented the salt-jumper, which, when someone spilled salt, caused it immediately to bounce over the left shoulder of the person who made the mess. But their most beautiful invention, without a doubt, was the one that created a delightful space in the sky and clouds above any umbrella opened inside a house. And the most controversial was the one that permitted any hostess to summon instantaneously a fourteenth guest when at the last moment she found herself with thirteen at table. My own parents never understood if that saving guest was a mere specter created by lasers or if the invention actually created a new guest of flesh and blood whose only vital function was to eat that one meal and disappear forever without leaving a trace, or if there existed an unfathomable complicity between the device and certain living—and hungry—persons who, on finding out about the dilemma of protocol and superstition, turned up to get a free meal, convoked by some message between computer and consumer which escaped the control or intention of my diligent parents.

The invention of the Fourteenth Guest led in its turn to two more inventions, one metaphysical, the other, alas! all too physical. My mother Isabella, no matter how modern and scientific she might be, especially because she was rebelling against her family, the Fagoagas, could never manage to free herself from an ancient female terror: whenever she saw a mouse, she would scream and jump up on a chair. Unhappily, she caused several accidents by jumping up on rickety stools and improvised platforms, breaking test tubes and occasionally ruining ongoing experiments. By the same token, there was no way to reconcile this attitude of hers with my parents' declared purpose; namely, to transform superstition into science. The fact is that the basement of their house in Tlalpan was full of rodents; but so was the rest of the city, my father, Diego Palomar, pointed out, and if Diego and Isabella had enough money to invest in pieces, even slices of cheese to put in their mousetraps, what could the garbageman or the ragpicker put in theirs?

Moved by this scientific and humanitarian concern, which distanced them so greatly from my mother Isabella's family, they proceeded to invent a mousetrap for the poor in which the owner would put, instead of a piece of real cheese, the photograph of a piece of cheese. The photograph was an integral part of the invention, which would be sold (or distributed) with the color photo of a magnificent piece of Roquefort cheese standing upright in the trap. Excited, your grandparents set about testing the device at home, as they always did. They left the trap in the basement one night and eagerly returned in the morning to see the results.

The trap had worked. The photograph of the cheese had disappeared. But in its place my grandparents found the photo of a mouse.

They didn't know whether to treat this result as a success or a failure. In any case, they did not lose hope; instead, they derived the following corollary: if the representation of matter, its reproduction, is complemented by an opposite term, it must be possible to isolate this relationship within matter itself, seeking within each object in the universe the principle of antimatter, the potential twin of the object. To make the antimatter materialize at the instant matter disappears became the concentrated, obsessive avenue of your grandparents' genius, Christopher.

They began by taking simple, organic objects—a bean, a piece of celery, a lettuce leaf, a jalapeño pepper—and submitting them to a kind of infinite race between Achilles and the turtle. By keeping each one of those objects connected to its vital source—the root that supplies nutrition—my parents tried to accelerate the process by which the bean, the lettuce, the pepper, and the celery were ingested, while at the same time they were replaced by the accelerated reproduction of other identical objects. From integrating the process of growth with the process of consumption there was only one revolutionary step: to introduce within each pepper, lettuce, bean, or celery a principle of reproduction that would be inherent in but separate from the object in question: the Achilles of consumption would be caught every time and more and more by the turtle of reproduction acting as an active principle of antimatter.

All that remained to my parents, Isabella and Diego, to do was to apply this discovery to the natural envelope of those ingredients: the tortilla, our national and supernatural food, and announce the discovery of the Inconsumable Taco: a taco that, the more it is eaten, the more it grows back: the solution to Mexico's nutrition problems! the greatest national idea—Uncle Homero Fagoaga laughed when he learned about it—since *mole* was invented in Puebla de los Angeles by a dyspeptic nun!

They all laughed, Angeles, Uncle Homero, and his horrid sisters Capitolina and Farnesia (ages unconfessable), as they made a detailed inventory of the house that belonged to my parents and me in the neighborhood of the Church of St. Peter the Apostle in Tlalpan: a house painted in bright colors—yellows, blues, and greens—with no windows on the street but plenty of interior patios, located between a hospital from the Porfirio Díaz era and a water-pumping station: making an inventory of what one day, according to my parents' express intention, was to be mine, along with an inheritance of forty million gold pesos. It was to have been mine when I turned twenty-one.

"I can stay right here and live alone," I said, stubborn and full of the sufficiency of my eleven years.

"No, no, by Jesus, a thousand times no!" exclaimed Farnesia. "In this horror?"

"Quite horrible, little sister, but property values here are going up because of how near the paper factory is, and the diners, and the entrance to the Cuernavaca highway," Don Homero said, calculating rapidly. He may have been very academic in regard to the language, but he was also very academic in business.

"In any case, the boy should live with us so he'll be educated: he has our name, so we should sacrifice ourselves," opined Capitolina. "Poor little orphan."

"Ay, little sister," agreed Farnesia, "talking about sacrifices, how this ungrateful tot is going to pay for making me leave my house to bury his parents and come here to bring him home—you know that for me it is a sin to leave the house!"

"And you can see he doesn't believe in God."

"Proof of his bad upbringing, Capitolina."

I understand you, Angel, when you tell me that when you were still very young the first thing your Aunts Capitolina and Farnesia told you when they took you in, poor little orphan, was that you were never to mention the reason why you were an orphan, it was too ridiculous, everyone would laugh at you. What will they say if they say that they said that you are the taco orphan or something else like that? What would be left of the family honor? The merest vestiges, Capitolina answered. No, no, dear Jesus, a thousand times no!

You went to your parents' tomb doing violence to your own memory, imagining all the time that they had died of something else, of anything else, tuberculosis or cancer, a duel at dawn, drowned in a storm on the high seas, smashed up on a bad curve, romantic suicide pact, simultaneous cirrhosis of the liver, but not of indigestion after eating tacos.

Since you had to imagine death as a lie, you felt that everything around you was also a lie. If you couldn't remember your parents' death, how were you going to remember the promise of the resurrection of the flesh? How were you going to believe in the existence of a soul? Buried in a lie, they will never truly be resurrected. Cause and effect were missing. Death by Taco: Immortal Soul: Resurrection of the Flesh. Death by Zero: Zero Soul: Zero Flesh. Nothing comes of nothing!

You communicated your doubts to your aunts, and there was a family meeting with your tutor, Uncle Homero. Heretical child, your Aunt Capitolina berated you, even though you don't believe in God, as your words suggest, at least say that you believe or what will become of you? You will go to hell. Worse, interrupted Farnesia, no one will invite you to their parties or give you their daughter's hand in matrimony, heretic and remiss child, and in the second place . . . Go to church, added Capitolina, even if you don't believe, so that everyone sees you there, and when you get older, Farnesia sensibly observed, go to the university or no one will know what to call you if you aren't Dr. So-and-so: there has never been a Fagoaga who's just been plain Mister, God forbid! And when you get older, Uncle Homero concluded politically, go to Party assemblies even if you fall asleep listening to the speeches, just so people see you there. Asleep, Uncle Homero? Bah, just look at the photos of the deputies fast asleep during the presidential report: then your sacrifice will warrant their compassion, respect, and a rising career in national politics, why not? An alert and contentious deputy would be a bad thing, like that bearded tribune Don Aurelio Manrique, who, from his Potosí seat, shouted "Fraud!" at the Maximum Hero of the Revolution, General Don Plutarco Elías Calles, who was perorating in sonorous Sonoran tones from the august rostrum of Doncelles; but a sleeping deputy can quickly become a wide-awake minister, just look at the dazzling rise of that dynamic public man from Guerrero, Don Ulises López, nephew, Don Homero Fagoaga went on, oblivious of Angel's internal torments, don't doubt it for a minute and learn, little nephew: how are *you* going to make a career for yourself, my innocent little Angel?

"Three centuries of Mexican Fagoagas and we've all made careers in arms and letters, in the Church and the government, always adapting ourselves to the conditions of the times: one day with the Viceroy, the next with Independence; in bed with Santa Anna and the conservatives, wide awake with Comonfort and the liberals; united with the Empire, lawyers for Lerdo; with Porfirio Díaz for nonreelection, with Porfirio Díaz for reelection; momentarily with Madero, unconditionally with Huerta, at the orders of Carranza, followers of Calles, enemies of Cárdenas, that's right, we'd have nothing to do with *him*, even our oh so tall and noble glass of family water can overflow, we have our limits; and disciplined and enthusiastic supporters of the Revolution after Avila Camacho, when the President, revolutionary general that he was, declared himself a believer and a friend to capitalism and thus resolved all our contradictions: Learn, my boy.

My father says to my mother.

My infantile eyes, Angeles, looked at that round, redundant presence—my Uncle Homero Fagoaga—with whom I had to coexist during the years of my childhood and adolescence, as did Juan Goytisolo with the *caudillo*, Francisco Franco: to inconceivable limits, to the point that I could not imagine life without my oppressor, without his pronouncements, orders, concessions, and rules. Uncle Homero got fatter and fatter, as if he were eating for two. It was impossible to imagine him as a child. He must have had an old man's face when he was born. He knows everything. He's obsequious to everyone. The active dialectical organization of all opposites is immediately perceptible between his two cerebral hemispheres, as vast, conceivable, as all the other paired fleshy parts of the abominable anatomy of my Uncle Homero Fagoaga.

Look at him as he imperiously saunters through salons and antechambers, offices and auditoriums, churches and fashionable discotheques: the archaizing thesis runs from the totemic soles of his flat feet properly protected from the slightest contact with Mexican filth by white Gucci leather to the top of his head, involuntarily tonsured by time and Pantene massages; the modernizing thesis runs from the greasy, well-oiled strands on his cranium (that head which is the top of Don Homero's corporeal pyramid): there, in the gaze of this eminent personage (he's arrived! he's here! let him pass through! stand at attention, everyone! Don Homero Fagoaga has entered!) the illiterate masses would find that the entire Age of Reason, from the spirit of law to the cultivation of our own garden, parades through the bright belvedere of his eyes, now—we must admit it—often covered over by lashes ever shorter and more sticky, the bleariness ever thicker, his brows ever longer, his eyelids ever droopier, wrinkled, thinned out, and other disasters of the autumn of life; but the Spanish Counter-Reformation, with all its inquisitions, expulsions, prohibitions, and certificates of purity, remains in the same way Don Homero's calluses last and scratch in the same way Don Homero's uncut, mandarin toenails remain: Torquemada inhabits one of his demonstrably functioning testicles (this in spite of our liberal Uncle Don Fernando's slanderous rumormongering), and Rousseau the other: born free, his second ball knows no other chain than that of a coquettish pair of Pierre Cardin briefs; under one armpit rests the nun, the mother, the holy betrothed saint of mine; under the other, the rumba dancer, the whore, the holy whore. There is, therefore, no admirer more devout or impassioned of the singular synthesis obtained in Mamadoc; Don Homero's got gunpowder in one nostril and incense in the other; with one ear he hears the Blessed be He and with the other he hears that old revolutionary song, the *corrida* about the ballad of the Revolution, girl Valentina; with one buttock he sits at the table of reaction, with the other on the benches of the Revolution; and only in the holes and uneven centers, in the singularities of his body, which is so vast it is dual, white and flabby twice over, fundamentous and quivering in every binomial, fervent and odorous in every cotyledon of his gardenia, ambitious twice over, hypocritical twice over, a fool twice over, intuitive twice over, malicious twice over, innocent twice over, gluttonous twice over, arrogant twice over, provincial twice over, resentful twice over, improvised twice over, everything twice over, nothing twice over, Mexican to the depths of his soul, no nation was ever blessed with so much nothing and nothing of so much except the baroque mirage of a gilt altar for an unshod Virgin (thinks Don Homero Fagoaga, pinning a carnation to his lapel before the mirror and dreaming of seducing Mamadoc). Only in the holes and unmatched centers, says my father Angel, can the vital distance of so much paradox be conjugated: like a deep vein that says scratch away at me and you'll find silver; his anus a whirl of thick golden ingots that says wait and you will receive gold, don't be deceived by appearances (our Uncle Fernando Benítez closes his eyes as he flies over the precipices of the Sierra Madre toward the last Lacandon and smells the nearness of a mountain of blind gold): the inexhaustible verbal fuel in his tongue.

Because he owes his renown, above all, to his dominion over language, to an exquisite use of the forms of courtesy ("I do not offend through those with which I sit down, Marquise, if I say that your ladyship's next flatulence will figure on my bill; you just go on eating this sublime dish from our national cuisine, refried beans, slices of onion, Manchego cheese, and peas, who could want more?") and to his marvelous use of the subjunctive ("If I were to like or were not to like, I might not doubt, exquisite friend, to proceed perhaps if to do so you would have or might not have some problem alluding to your female progenitor, but only if to do it, there were incontrovertible proofs of your being bastards"), without forgetting his incomparable use of the national political language ("After the proclamation of Independence by Father Hidalgo and the expropriation of oil by General Cárdenas, the inauguration of the Road Dividers of Chilpancingo is the most transcendent act of National History, Mr. Governor") and even of international political language ("From the cosmic balcony of Tepeyac may be heard, vicars, Holy Father, the hallelujahs of the deaf genius of Bonn!"). To any word Don Homero Fagoaga ascribes some twelve syllables even if it only happens to have three: gold on his lips is transmuted into go-oo-aah-ll-dd and Góngora comes out sounding like gonorrhea.

"Learn, my boy, the Fagoagas never lose, and what they do lose they yank right back!"

Pillars of the Government, of the Church, and of Commerce, lost in the immensity of His-panic time:

> Who defeated the Moor in Granada?
> Fagoaga!
> Who defended the cross in Castile?
> Fagoaga!
> From those faggots, Fagoagas.
> From those powers, Homers!

exactly as it is written on the family coat of arms. Angel stared at the final product of that line—his Uncle Homero—and said no.

"If I squeeze, as if they were lemons, all the Fagoagas who have existed over thirteen centuries, Angeles, I swear I wouldn't get more than a bubble of bitter bile and another of flatulence, to use his term. Sorry, baby; I except my dead mom the inventor who showed her intelligence by marrying a blundering scientist who was a man of few words, like my dad."

2

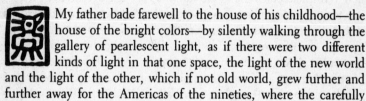My father bade farewell to the house of his childhood—the house of the bright colors—by silently walking through the gallery of pearlescent light, as if there were two different kinds of light in that one space, the light of the new world and the light of the other, which if not old world, grew further and further away for the Americas of the nineties, where the carefully framed portraits of my grandparents' heroes were hanging.

There was Ernest Rutherford, looking rather like a sea lion, tall and with a shaggy mustache, gray, as if he had just come from the depths of his cave, dazzled as he left the darkness behind, seeing in the heavens a duplication of the world of the atom.

There was Max Planck, with his high forehead right out of a Flemish painting and his narrow shoulders and drooping mustache, and Niels Bohr, with thick, protuberant lips, looking like the good-natured captain of a whaling ship, forever pacing the deck of a universe on the verge of rioting and throwing the savant into the open sea in a rowboat without oars, and Wolfgang Pauli looking like the perfect Viennese bourgeois, stuffed with pastry and the music of violins.

Perhaps Wolfgang Pauli, in his constant coming and going on the Copenhagen ferries, revived the dialogue between men and forgotten words. Like Rimbaud, said my father (as my genes tell me), like Pound, like Paz: resurrection of language.

"What language will my son speak?"

"In what world will my son live?"

"Which world is this?"

"Who is the Mother and Doctor of All Mexicans?"

"Why did they first run off and then kill the inhabitants of the mountains around Acapulco?"

"What's Hipi Toltec doing surrounded by friendly coyotes in the middle of a dried-out palm grove?"

Nevertheless, the eyes of my child-father, educated by my scientific grandparents in the brightly colored house in Tlalpan, reserved their greatest interest, their greatest affection for the photograph of a young, blond, smiling savant on the verge of launching himself down the toughest slopes of the grand slalom of science. My father always thought that if someone had an answer for all the riddles of the day of my conception, it was this boy: his name, inscribed on a tiny copper plaque at the bottom of the photo, was Werner Heisenberg, and nothing affected my father's young imagination so much as the certainty of his uncertainty: the logic of the symbol does not express the experiment; it *is* the experiment. Language is the phenomenon, and the observation of the phenomenon changes its nature.

Thanks, Dad, for understanding that, for assimilating it into your genes that come from my grandparents and that you transmitted to me. A kind of cloud of warm rain bathes me and covers me from the unruly mop of hair, mustaches, and calf's eyes of Albert Einstein, and I've been living with him from before my conception, swimming in the river of when and the three wheres of my current and eternal dimension; but when I emerge from the interminable river to see a time and a place (which are my own), the one who accompanies me is the young mountain climber: thanks, Werner, and because of you and for you my very personal Heisenberg Society formed in the uterus of my mother Angeles, the first club I ever belonged to and from whose fluffy (enjoyable!) armchairs I already observe the world that nurtures me and which I nurture by observing it.

Thanks to them, I understand that whatever is is provisional because the time and space that precede me and whatever I know about them I know only fleetingly, as I pass, purely by chance, through this hour and this place. The important thing is that the syntheses never finish, that no one save himself, ever, from the contradiction of being in one precise place and one precise time and nevertheless thinking about a time and place that are infinite, denying the end of experience, maintaining open the infinite possibilities for observing the infinite events in the unfinished world and transforming them as I observe them: turning them into history, narrative, language, experience, infinite reading . . .

My poor father: he grew up in this world, he lost it, and would take years to return to it by the most labyrinthine paths: his Sweet Fatherland, mutilated and corrupt, had to return to the universal promise of the physical wisdom characteristic of the men whose portraits hung in the pearlescent gallery of the house in Tlalpan and to the reason in the dream of heroic Mexicans, capable of being biologists, chemists, physicists, creative men and women, producers, productive, not only consumers, barnacles, drones, in a society that only rewarded rogues. The reason in the dream and not only the dream of reason: men and women devoured and devouring, chronophagous, heliophagous, cannibals eating their own fatherland. This is what Isabella and Diego, my grandparents, wanted to overcome. But now their son, my father, had lost the house of intelligence.

How long it would take us to return to the portraits in this gallery!

It's time I revealed myself before you, Reader, and tell you I have already returned by way of *my genes*, which know all, remember all, and if, a bit later, I, like you, forget everything when I'm born and have to learn it all over again before I die, who would deny that in this instant of my gestation I know everything because I am here inside and you, Reader, are you out there?

3

 And so, when his parents died, my father was brought to live with his Aunts Capitolina and Farnesia Fagoaga, sisters of his mother (and my deceased grandmother) Isabella Fagoaga de Palomar and that powerful survivor, my avuncular Don Homero Fagoaga (oh, horror). Although Don Homero did not live with his little sisters, he did visit them every day, took most of his meals with them, and in their house on Avenida Durango he honed his moralizing rhetoric and gave his punctilious lessons in proper Christian conduct. My father, between the ages of eleven and fifteen, was the principal object of this evangelizing.

It is not possible (my genes inform me) to give the precise ages of Capitolina and Farnesia. In the first place, my aunts have fixed themselves in an environment that denies them contemporaneity and that facilitates their seeing themselves as younger than all that surrounds them. While other ladies of their generation, less astutely perhaps, have sold off all the furniture, bibelots, pictures, and other decorations that at a given moment go out of fashion, Capitolina and

Farnesia have never consented to deacquisition what they inherited and, moreover, to use and inhabit their inheritance. Wrapped in antiques, they always seem younger than they are.

The house on Avenida Durango is the last remnant of the architecture that flourished during the Mexican Revolution, precisely during the years of civil war, between 1911 and 1921: in the transition between the French hotels of the Porfirio Díaz era (1877–1910) and the indigenist, colonialist horrors of the reign of Plutarco Elías Calles, Maximum Hero of the Revolution (1924–35). Don Porfirio and his gang crowned their native versions of the Faubourg St.-Honoré with mansards; Obregón, Calles, and their disciples first built public buildings in the shape of Aztec temples and then lived in domestic versions of churrigueresque churches that had been passed through the filter of the Hollywood stars. The guerrilla fighters ended up living like Mary Pickford and Rudolph Valentino. Those who remained in Mexico City during the armed struggle, with gold under their mattresses and infinite ability when it came to hoarding food and attending property auctions—the Fagoagas, for example—built these mansions out of stone, generally one story high, surrounded by gardens with tamped-down dirt paths, fountains and palm trees, their façades ornamented with urns, vines, and impassive masks, their roofs crowned with balustrades and balconies with high French doors painted white. Inside, they stuffed their villas with all the furniture and paintings they'd inherited from the turn-of-the-century, the national Belle Epoque with its landscapes of the Valley of Mexico, its society portraits in the style of Whistler and Sargent, with display cases full of minutiae, medals, miniature cups; their pedestals with Sèvres vases and white busts of Dante and Beatrice. Heavy plush sofas, carved mahogany tables, red curtains with lots of tassels, much stained glass in the bathroom, stairs with red carpeting and gilt rug stays, parquet and canopied beds; washstands in every room, gigantic armoires, gigantic mirrors, chamber pots and cuspidors in strategic locations; the suffocation of porcelain, dust, varnish, lacquer, terror of fragile, tiny things; a house of look—but-don't-touch. In their house the little Fagoaga sisters preserved a style of life, of speech, of whispering secrets, and excitation, all of it totally alien to the city outside.

Nevertheless, though they shared a style, they were quite dissimilar: Farnesia was tall, thin, dark, and languid, while Capitolina was short, pudgy, fair, flat-nosed, and febrile. Capitolina spoke in tones that brooked no rejoinders; Farnesia left all her sentences hanging in midair. Capitolina spoke in the first person singular; her sister in a vague but imperial "we." But both practiced piety at all hours, suddenly falling to their knees before crucifixes and spreading their arms at the least appropriate times and places. They were obsessed with death and spent endless nights in nightgowns, with their hair braided, recalling how Mr. So-and-so or Miss What's-her-name died. They only read the newspaper for the obituary notices, which they read with consternated glee. But if for Capitolina this activity was translated into the satisfaction of knowing about a misfortune so she could feel well, for Farnesia it was reduced to the conviction that sanctity consisted in doing more evil to oneself than to anyone else, and that this would open the doors of heaven to the inseparable sisters. Because Farnesia was absolutely convinced that the two of them would die at the same time; Capitolina did not share (or desire) such a calamity, but she would not argue with her high-strung little sister.

To go out or not to go out: that was their question. The house on Avenida Durango was for the sisters a convent proportioned to their needs. To abandon it was a sin, and only the most terrible events— like the death of a relative or bringing one home to live with them— could push them out of their home. But there were voyages out they believed—with pain in their souls—could not be postponed. Capitolina and Farnesia, it seems, had a passion: to find out what unbelievers were about to die so they could try to convert them on their deathbeds, for which purpose they dragged along with them the priest from the neighboring Church of the Holy Family.

No heretical will, no atheistic indifference, no lay prejudice, could stand between their crusading and the deathbed. They would clear paths by swinging their umbrellas, Capitolina snorting, Farnesia fainting, both advancing with their priest toward the bed where, more often than not, the Misses Fagoaga were accepted with a sigh of resignation or with saving praise by the dying person, who thus found in them a pretext to admit he was a closet Catholic and so to arrange his affairs—just in case—with the Other World.

This crusade by the Fagoaga sisters to save souls was put to the test by the staunchest agnostic among their relatives (by marriage), General Don Rigoberto Palomar, father of the deceased inventor Diego Palomar, husband of Isabella Fagoaga and my father Angel's grandfather. General Palomar, whose life ran neck and neck with that of the century, had been a bugle boy in Don Venustiano Carranza's Constitutionalist Army, and at the age of eighteen became the youngest general in the Mexican Revolution. His merit consisted in retrieving the arm of General Alvaro Obregón when the future President lost it in an artillery barrage during the battle of Celaya against Pancho Villa. Some say, maliciously, that the severed member of the valiant and canny division leader from Sonora was recovered when General Obregón himself tossed a centennial gold coin up in the air and the lost arm tremulously rose up from among the cadavers and, with immutable greed, snatched at the money.

The modest truth is that the bugle boy, Rigoberto Palomar, accompanied by his faithful mascot, a retriever named Moses, found the arm, which the dog sniffed and took up in his jaws. Rigo kept the dog from gnawing the bone. Alvaro Obregón's white flesh and blond hair made the famous arm stand out; the bugle boy delivered it personally to Obregón; he was instantly promoted to general. Out of gratitude, the brand-new boy brigadier shot Moses dead so no witnesses would remain—not even a mute one—to the fact that a dog was about to dine on the limb, which, as everyone knows, was preserved in a bottle of formaldehyde and buried along with the general, who, on July 28, 1928, a few days after his election, was treacherously murdered by a religious fanatic during a banquet held in a restaurant called the Lightbulb. Only General Palomar kept the secret of the President-elect's last words: Obregón, as he died, dragged his one remaining hand over the tablecloth, his blue eyes fading and his voice imploring, "More corn muffins, more corn muffins," before his inert body collapsed. Today, a monument to his memory stands on Avenida de los Insurgentes, in the very place where he died. Sweethearts meet there by day and marijuana smokers by night.

The guardian of all these scenes, both public and secret, General Rigoberto Palomar, was a national treasure: the last survivor of the Revolution in a political system excessively eager for legitimacy. All of which contributed to making Don Rigo—who was sane on all other matters—insane on the subject of the Mexican Revolution. He simultaneously held two contradictory beliefs: (1) The Revolution was not over; and (2) the Revolution had triumphed and carried out all its promises.

Steadfast between these pillars, Don Rigo, who grew up in the anticlerical cyclone of the Agua Prieta government, fiercely upheld secularism. Let no priest come near him: then Don Rigo showed that the Revolution was indeed on the march by committing some undescribable atrocity or other, from stripping a priest, mounting him on a burro, and leading him through town, to summoning a firing squad to the patio of his house on Calle Génova and pretending to go through a formal execution.

On afternoons, accompanied by his wife Doña Susana Rentería, Grandfather Palomar would climb up to the crest of a ridge with a stone in his hand. He would then toss the stone down the ravine and say to his wife: "Look at that stone, the way it goes on and on."

This madness of General Palomar made him part of the national patrimony: the government named him Eponymous Hero of the Republic and the PRI gave orders that he never be touched or bothered in any way, an indispensable requirement in a regime where unwritten law, as always, was the personal whim of the man in power. The fact is that my great-grandfather lived a quiet life: he dedicated himself to administering wisely the goods and chattels he'd acquired honestly and lived out his life in perfect sanity, except as regards this matter of his revolutionary madness and his strange love for Doña Susana, who was left to him in the will of a landowner from Jalisco who had supported the Cristero revolt. His name was Páramo and he'd been arrested and murdered by General Palomar's troops. His last wish was that Don Rigo take his daughter Susana Rentería under his protection, that he symbolically marry her, that he bring her up, and that he consummate their marriage when the girl turned sixteen. The girl, Susana Rentería, was only five years old when her landowning Cristero father was killed, but Don Rigo respected the idea of a last wish, above all that of an enemy, and accepted Pedro Páramo's inheritance.

He brought Susy (as he came to call her) to his house in Mexico City, where he took care of her, dressing her as if she were a doll, in old-fashioned shifts and velvet slippers. When she was sixteen, he married her. There was a twenty-year difference in age between them, so that when Susy married Rigo, he was about thirty-six years old, and Cárdenas had just forced the Maximum Chief Plutarco Elías Calles out of Mexico.

None of the people who knew them had ever met a couple more in love, more considerate of each other, or more tender. Susy learned very quickly that her husband was an extraordinarily reasonable man in all matters except the Revolution, and she learned over the years to humor him and to say yes, Rigo, you're right, there isn't a single priest left alive in Mexico, not a single piece of land that hasn't been returned to the peasants, not a single parcel of communal land that isn't a success, not a single archbishop who doesn't walk about dressed in mufti, not a single nun wearing a habit, not a single gringo company that hasn't been nationalized, not a single worker who hasn't been unionized. Elections are free, the Congress calls the President to account, the press is independent and responsible, democracy blazes forth, the national wealth is justly distributed, but there is corruption, Rigo, there is corruption, and it is a revolutionary obligation to wipe it out. The general turned the artillery of his revolution, simultaneously triumphant and permanent, against corruption, Rome, and Washington. Imagine, my tumultuous and elective genes, my Great-grandfather Rigoberto's dismay when no one could hide from him the fact that the Holy Father, the Vicar of Christ, the Pope himself (and Polish into the bargain!) was in Mexico, dressed as a pontiff and not as an office worker, walking with all due pomp through the streets, welcomed by millions and millions of citizens of the Republic, celebrating Mass and giving blessings right out in public. Don Rigoberto collapsed, took to his bed, howling against the betrayal. He preferred to die rather than admit that Article 3 of the Constitution had been violated: why had all those men died fighting the Cristeros? Why did you have to die on us, General Obregón? Where are you when we need you most, General Calles? You may fire when ready, General Cruz!

Susy called the doctors and advised the family—including Capitolina and Farnesia, who saw a golden opportunity: charity begins at home. They dragged along with them the priest from the Holy Family and my poor twelve-year-old father, so he would experience the hard reality of life. They walked in scattering incense and holy water, calling for the salvation of wayward General Palomar's soul and warning my young dad not to be surprised that, if Rigoberto did not repent of his sins, horns popped out of his head right then and there and Satan in person might appear to drag him by the heels to hell.

General Rigoberto Palomar, sunk in his soft but rumpled bed, was taking his last breaths when the Fagoaga sisters walked in with the priest and the boy. His wild, bloodshot eyes, his emaciated, tremulous nose, his palpitating throat, his half-open mouth, his entire face as purple as an aubergine, were not softened by his liberty cap with its tricolor (green, white, and red) cockade that he wore as a nightcap to cover his shaved head.

All the general had to do was see the sisters, the priest waving the sacrament on high, and the boy tossing the censer around like a ball-and-cup toy and he instantly recovered from his attack. He jumped up on the bed, cocked his cap coquettishly over one eye, raised his nightshirt to his waist, and waved a nicely stiffened phallus at the Misses Fagoaga, the boy, and the priest.

"This is the sacrament I'm going to give you if you come one step closer!"

Stunned, Farnesia walked toward Grandfather's bed, murmuring vague phrases and holding her hands in front of her, as if she were expecting a ripe fruit to fall into them or a sacrament administered to her.

"Besides . . . In the first place . . . After all . . . In the second place . . . We . . ."

But her domineering sister stretched out her parasol and with the hooked handle caught her straying sister at the same time she declared: "To hell, that's where you're going, Rigoberto Palomar, but before that you shall suffer the torments of death. I'm telling you here and now! Now cover yourself, you've got nothing to brag about!"

The old man looked at the boy, winked, and said to him: "Learn, kid. What this pair of witches needs is to feel the whole rigor of the penis. I know who you are. When you can't put up with these old bags, you have a place to live right here."

"You are going to die, you scoundrel!" shouted Capitolina.

"And in the third place," Farnesia managed to say.

General Rigoberto Palomar never had another sick day. Balancing out the shock of John Paul II's visit, he renewed his vows in the permanent revolution—there was so much more to be done!

After this experience, my father Angel was never the same. He began to realize things, some of them quite small. For example, when he kissed Aunt Capitolina's hand every morning, he discovered that she always had flour and jalapeño pepper on the tips of her fingers and under her nails, while Aunt Farnesia's hand smelled strongly of fish. The Misses Fagoaga ordered their domestic life according to purposes my father did not understand very well. He began to notice their manias. Their household staff changed constantly and for reasons Angel could not fathom. But they always called the maids by the same name: Servilia; Servilia do this, Servilia do that, Servilia on your knees svp, Servilia I want my corn-flour soup at 3 a.m., Servilia don't use rags to clean out my chamber pot, which is very delicate and might break, use your smooth Indian hands. They were more particular in this than their brother Don Homero, although they all shared that creole vice. They needed someone to humiliate every day. The sisters sometimes accomplished this by organizing intimate suppers in which they did their utmost to confuse, annoy, or insult their guests. It wouldn't have mattered to them if their guests ever returned, but the fact was, they observed, that the majority were delighted to return for more, eager for more punishment.

Miss Capitolina would fire off her irrefutable arguments:

"So you doubted the probity of Viceroy Revillagigedo? Ingrate!"

These arguments were received with stupefaction by the guests, who had never said a word about the viceroy, but Capitolina was once again on the attack:

"They make jam in Celaya and sugar candy in Puebla. Are you going to deny it! I dare you!"

The shock of the guests was not assuaged by Farnesia, who interrupted her sister's conversation with verbal inconsequentialities of all sorts:

"It doesn't matter. We shall never accept an invitation from you, sir, but we will give you the pleasure of receiving you in our salon. We are not cruel."

"Now that you mention tacos," Capitolina pronounced, "I can't talk about tacos without thinking of tortillas."

"But I . . ." the guest would say.

"Never mind, never mind, you are a Jew and a Bulgarian, judging by your appearance, don't try to deny it," Capitolina would assert, one of her manias being to attribute to others whatever religion and nationality came into her head.

"No, the truth is that . . ."

"Ah!" Farnesia sighed, on the verge of fainting on the shoulder of the man sitting next to her. "We understand the pleasure it must give you just to have met us."

"Who is that ugly old dumb woman you brought, sir?" Capitolina went on.

"Miss Fagoaga! She's my wife."

"Damn the parvenu. Who invited her to my house?"

"You did, miss."

"A strumpet, I tell you, and I'll say it to her face, strumpet, gate-crasher, vulgarian, how could you ever marry her!"

"Ah, Mauricio, take me home . . ."

"Incidentally," Farnesia commented, "and in the third place, we never . . ."

"Miss: your attitude is highly rude."

"Isn't it, though?" Doña Capitolina would say, opening her tremendous eyes.

"Mauricio, I'm going to faint . . ."

"And you just can't imagine what happened yesterday," Farnesia would immediately say, one of her other specialties being to accumulate inconsequential information and breathlessly communicate it. "It was just six o'clock in the afternoon and we naturally were getting ready to take care of our obligations because you should never leave for today what you can do tomorrow, the doorbell was ringing so insistently and we remembered the open window and we went running upstairs to find out if from the roof we could see what was going on and our cat walked right in front of us and from the kitchen came a smell of cabbage that, my God, you know we're getting too old for these surprises and after all either you drink in manners with your mother's milk or your mother learns manners, we never know and we're about to go mad!"

These suppers were discussed by the sisters with great satisfaction. One of their ideas was that only people of their social class should live in Mexico. They cherished the idea that the poor should be run out of the country and the rest of the lower orders be thrown into jail.

"Oh, Farnecita, je veux un Mexique plus cossu," Capitolina would say in the French she reserved for grand moments.

"Cozy, cozy, a cozy little country," her sister complemented her in English, and when they said these little things, the two of them felt comforted, warm, sure of themselves, just like their quilted tea cozy.

These enjoyable intermezzi, nevertheless, gave way more and more to tensions my father discovered as he advanced into adolescence: the aunts looked at him in a different way, whispered to each other, and instead of kneeling alone, grabbed him, each one taking an arm at the most unexpected moments, forcing him to kneel with them and strike his chest.

One night, some horrifying shouts woke him up, and my father ran around in confusion, looking for the source of the noise. He tripped over innumerable bibelots and display cases, knocking them down and breaking things, and then he stopped at the locked door of Capitolina's room. He tried to look through the keyhole but it was blocked by a handkerchief redolent of cloves. All he could hear were the terrible shouts of the two sisters:

"Christ, belovèd body!"

"Brides of the Lord, Farnesia, we are the brides of the Lord!"

"Husband!"

"You are a virgin, but I am not!"

"Isabella our sister was happy to give birth!"

"Surrounded by respect!"

"We give birth in secret!"

"Filled with shame!"

"How old is the boy today?"

"The same age as he is!"

"Oh, my Lord! My holy bridegroom!"

My father walked away in shock and could not sleep, either that night or any subsequent night he spent under the Fagoaga sisters' roof. At the age of fourteen, he felt urgent sexual desires, which he satisfied standing before a print of the Virgin offering her breast to the Infant Jesus. He repeated these exercises twice a week and was surprised to see that whenever he did it a sudden ray of light would illuminate his room, as if the Virgin were sending him flashes of gratitude for his sacrifice.

"A few months later, Uncle Homero walked into the Calle Durango house with all his insolent overbearing, called Servilia an 'obscene trollop,' and stood me next to her in the grand salon of the sisters' house, with both of them present, and accused me and the maid of making love in secret. Servilia wept and swore it wasn't so, while Capitolina and Farnesia shouted out their denunciations of the two of us and Don Homero accused me of lowering myself with the servants, and the three of them accused the maid of thinking she was their equal, now she's gone beyond her station, the maids always hate us, they always would like to be and to have what we are and it's a miracle they don't murder us in our beds.

"Servilia was fired, Uncle H. made me take down my trousers, and after caressing my buttocks he spanked me with one of Aunt Capitolina's shoes, informing me that he would discount from my allowance the broken glass and other damage I'd caused.

"All this seemed tolerable and even amusing since it put my Christian faith to the test and forced me to think: how can I go on being Catholic after living with the Fagoagas? I have to have faith!"

"What an incorrigible romantic you are! You have to have faith!"

"What do you mean?"

"I mean you rationalize everything."

"To the contrary, I am merely repeating the oldest article of faith. It's true because it's absurd.

"But I was dying of curiosity. Every night I spied through my aunts' keyhole, hoping that just once they would forget to block it up."

"And what happened?"

"They shouted, as I told you, we give birth in secret, the lost child, the same age as Angelito, the lost child. One night they forgot the handkerchief."

The keyhole was like the eye of God. A pyramid of air carved in the door. A triangle anxious to tell a story. Just the way it is in one of those unexpected openings in old-fashioned fairy tales: the kitchen opens onto the sea, onto the mountain, onto the bedroom. It smelled strongly of cloves. He imagined the bleeding, embroidered handkerchief with silver borders.

"Did they purposely not put it in, or did they really forget?"

My father wished he hadn't seen what he saw that night through the keyhole in the room illuminated only by candlelight.

"What happened, for God's sake! Don't turn this into a suspense story!"

He wished he hadn't seen what he saw, but he couldn't tell it to anyone.

"Not even me?"

"Not to you or anyone else."

"You say you were consumed by curiosity."

"Just imagine."

Inebriated by the smell of cloves, blinded by the fantastic theology of the candles burning down, saying I am afraid of myself, he ran out of the house on Avenida Durango and went to live with his grandparents Rigoberto Palomar and Susana Rentería in the house on Calle Génova, but he never told them what he'd seen. He swore it: he would die without saying a word, it was the proof that he was now a man; he closed his eyes and left his mouth open: a fly landed on the tip of his tongue; he spit, he sneezed.

4

"Don't go yet, Mommy, I want to know how you and Daddy met, that way I'll know everything about the holy family."

"Sorry, sweetie, but we're only in January and all that happened in April; you'll have to wait until the right month rolls around."

"The cruellest month."

"Who said that?"

"T. S. Shandy, native of San Luis."

"San Luis Potosí?"

"No, San Luis Misurí: T. S. Elote. Fix your genetic information circuits, son, or we're never going to understand each other. Which leads me directly to the finish of the tale of the wellspring of all confusion in this story and in the world: your uncle, Homero Fagoaga, who baptized you from the air at the instant you were conceived."

"Shit!"

The intrigues against Uncle Homero began one October day more than six years ago, and he didn't know it, said my father, and he, the most interested party, was completely unaware and told that to my mother when they both walked into the Pacific Ocean to wash off the shit which had rained down on them that midday of my conception, when I had just been admitted into the supreme hostel, bombarded by voices and memories, places and times, names and songs, foods and fucks, memory and oblivion, I who had just abandoned my metaphysical condition, being El Niño Child, to acquire my name, I CHRISTOPHER, but in any case, even though I had my own name, I had to begin as El Niño, look ye well your mercies, if I was going to win the Contest of the Quincentennial of the Discovery of America on the next 12th of October 1992. They said, if it's a girl we're dead ducks, so we ditch her straightaway because we're not entered in the Contest for Coatlicue or Malinche or Guadalupe or Sor Juana or Adelita, who are our national heroines, whose virtues are now for the glory and benefit of the nation incarnate in Our Lady Mamadoc. No way, we're in the Christopher Contest.

> COLON CRISTOBAL
> CRISTOFORO
> CHRISTOPHER COLUMBUS
> COLOMBO
> COLOMB CHRISTOPHE

the same in all languages, see, baby? Christ-bearer and Dove, which is to say, the two persons missing from the Trinity, the Son and the Holy Spirit, our Discoverer, the saint who got his footsies wet crossing the seas and the dove that arrived with a little branch in his beak to announce the nearness of the New Land and the one who broke an egg to invent us, but all this history and all this nomenclature depend, as you all can see, on something over which neither Angel nor Angeles, my parents, has any control, that is, that the data in my father's spermatozoid and my mother's reproductive cells divide, separate, give up half of themselves, accept this fatal sacrifice all in order to form a new unity made of two retained halves (but also of the two lost halves) in which I will never be identical to my father or my mother even though all my genes come from them, but for me, only for me, for no one else but me, they have combined in an unrepeatable fashion which shall determine my sex: this unique I Christopher and what they call GENES:

"Hey, the genes are to blame for everything," said Uncle Fernando Benítez.

"Right," agreed Uncle Homero Fagoaga, "the genius is to blame for everything. Hegel is to blame."

Thus did Uncle Fernando, tired of his in-law's feigning deafness when it suited him and always confusing him in order to wriggle out of the moral definitions proposed by the robust liberalism of the elder uncle, decide to stop speaking to Homero and instead organize the band of Four Fuckups, who at that time, says my father, must have been between fifteen and eighteen years old. All this in order to screw Uncle Homero, dog him day and night, never give him a moment's peace, follow him through the streets of Makesicko City from dawn till dusk, from door to door, from his penthouse on Mel O'Field Road to his office on Frank Wood Avenue, as if they were hunting him down, don't cut any corners, boys, my abused lads, set traps and snares for him, hunt him down.

Don Homero Fagoaga insisted on living in this uncomfortable building on Mel O'Field Road for a very simple reason: all the buildings around his had collapsed during the consecutive earthquakes of 1985, so that Uncle H.'s condo was surrounded by "fields of solitude, dejected downs": flattened lots, ranches wiped out by the city's acid rain, but his building was standing, saying to the world that where Homero lived, earthquakes were sparrow farts. This sublime and sublimated lesson did not go unnoticed, he was informed by his public-relations experts, for whom he acquired at astronomical prices the properties in the center of town that the government wanted to transform into gardens but which Ulises López sold through his front man, Dr. Fagoaga.

"I am twenty years older than you," Uncle Fernando said to him, "but I'm still on the make."

"Did you say quake? Again?" asked Uncle Homero, running to take his place in the nearest doorframe.

"Twenty years older than you, but harder in the phallus," Uncle Fernando said.

"You like Niki de St. Phalle's art? Terrific!"

"I still like to screw . . ."

"Stew? Only when the weather's cool . . ."

"No, Jimmy Stewart, you old fool," Uncle Fern exclaimed in despair. And he ordered his boys: "Chase him as if it were hunting season and he were big game, you've got to be hard-nosed and hard-assed with this old rhino! Keep an eye on him, my little Fuckups, make a fool of him. Drive the miserable old fart nuts."

It all began when the shortest (but the oldest) of the Four Fuckups, the so-called Orphan Huerta, set up his stand of overripe fruit right at the well-guarded door of Uncle Homero's condo on O'Field, singing out day and night in his soprano twang. Day and night in the shrill voice of a kid from the slums.

"Oranges, pears, an' figs," chanted Orphan Huerta in his intolerable voice whenever Uncle Homero walked through the building's revolving door, a miraculous fact in itself, according to my dad, because Uncle Homero's mass should not by rights have been able to pass through any door, revolving or stationary, open or closed, screened or screenless:

"Condomed door."

"Cuntdemned door, did you say?"

"Like the Doors without Jim Morrison, sans issue."

"I see, I see."

"You see nothing, you old fart, so stop pretending."

The fact is, they don't make them (doors, that is) that huge any-more. Uncle Homero can only get through a revolving door the way jelly gets into a jar—adapting himself to the circumstances, in a word.

"I do so love belly dancers," said Uncle Fernando.

"You love jelly doughnuts, at your age?" observed Uncle Homero incredulously.

"No, you fat slob, hegelly doughnuts," retorted Uncle Fernando, getting up and knocking his chair over backwards.

Or perhaps Uncle Homero is rehearsing to get into heaven through the eye of a needle every time he enters or leaves his house, says my mom, floating in the sea just as I float inside her in the fetal sea.

"Through the needle of an eye?" Don Homero feigned surprise.

The Orphan Huerta never allowed himself to be intimidated by the contrast between the narrowness of the door and the generous dimensions of Don Homero Fagoaga, LL.D. As soon as he saw him, he burst into his hideous chant, which sounded like a rusty knife being dragged across a plate.

"Oranges, pears, an' figs; oranges, pears, an' figs."

Uncle Homero begins to shake (like a bowlful of jelly) and offers the poor Orphan a five-cent coin from the times of Ruiz Cortines, at the same time that he corrects him:

"Oranges, pears, and figs, my boy."

He was offering him something more than five cents from the fifties, inestimable era in which the Mexican Revolution was going to celebrate its Golden Anniversary and when the peso was devalued to twelve-fifty, and even so they went on loving each other for a little while longer (the Revolution and the peso). Uncle Homero is offering the poor Orphan something more than five cents, he is awarding him a verbal mother and father, he is offering him education, without which (Don Homero says to the Huerta boy) there is neither progress nor happiness but only stagnation, barbarism, and disgrace.

"Oranges, pears, and figs, my boy."

Proper speech, that's what he offers him, the Castilian tongue in all its pristine, puritan purity, the Gothic Virgin and her pudgy acolyte: the Castilian Tongue and Homero Fagoaga LL.D.: the Ideal Couple: Don Homero nothing more than a servant of the Spanish Language, Hispaniae Lingua. He hones it, he fixes it, he gives it splendor, and he offers to the future, to the potential, to the possible Don Orphan Huerta LL.D. the possibility of being, finally, in the following order, Mother's Day Poet, Orator of National Holidays, Declaimer of the Sexagesimal Campaign, at worst a Congressman, people's tribune and at the same time elitist Demosthenes, owner of the Language: Uncle Homero licks his lips imagining the destiny of the Orphan Huerta if the boy would only give his tongue to the old man, if he'd allow him to educate it, sentence it, diphthong it, vocalize it, hyperbatonize it.

Uncle drops the Classic Tongue like a golden pill on the savage tongue of the Orphan Huerta, who stood there astonished with his mouth as open as a mailbox, filthy, the poor devil, his face darker from the grime than from his infamous genes, the scum and the dust and the mud of the no-man's-land from which the kid emanated with his head crowned with a helmet of gray felt, the ruin of a quondam borsalino, emblazoned with beer or soda bottle caps. The Orphan Huerta.

"Oranges, pears, an' figs."

Uncle Homero adjusted his balloon trousers, which were held up by yellow suspenders (one side bearing the image of the Holy Father repeated along its full length, thus holding in place the whitish softness of the lawyer's right bosom; the other side bearing the image of Emiliano Zapata, alternately wearing expressions of shock and heart failure, on his left bosom); he buttoned the only button on his *Barros Jarpas* (as our Chilean lady friend enigmatically refers to these striped trousers) and dropped the coin of verbal gold on the bottle-capped head of the Orphan Huerta.

"Oranges, pears, and figs, son."

He said it in the same voice God said let there be light, in the same voice His Son (oh Godoh!) said verily I say unto you suffer the children to come unto me. The Orphan Huerta regarded him with a suspicious eye.

But in that instant Uncle Homero was the pedagogue and not the pedophile. "Or, as the dazzling light of Spanish grammar that spoke incarnate in the voice of the illustrious Venezuelan, Don Andrés

Bello, said on a great day, the tendency to drop the final *d* in the copulative *and* before a monosyllabic word beginning with a consonant is to be resisted at all costs."

The Orphan Huerta ceased to be suspicious. Uncle Homero's grammar lesson culminated in a gaze appropriate to a hanged donkey. That's how tender were the eyes of this fatted calf. That's how stretched his baggies were by his pedophilia.

"Resisted at all costs, son," said Homero tenderly, caressing the bottle-capped head of the boy, and the Orphan Huerta tells even today how he extracted from the depths of his filthy soul all the revenge sunken into the bottom of Lake Texcoconut that each and every Makesickan carries in the mudbank of his guts, next to the treasures of Whatamock, father of the fatherland, which is to say toasted tootsies for the toast of the nation, said my daddy-o, the vacillating hero, washing off the shit, while I, pleased as punch, floated around in the ocean within my mother where I am not touched (oh, still not) by the shit of this world.

Resisted at all costs, son: Uncle Homero's skin could not resist the razor-sharp edges of the bottle caps on the boy's cap. He raised his wounded finger to his tongue (his tongue, the protagonist, the star of his prodigious body, now full of his own acrid blood spilt by a grimy gamin from Atlampa) and he looked deliberately at the Orphan, but finding no reaction to this dialectic of grammar and bottle caps and finger and blood and tongue, he ended up repeating:

"Oranges, pears, and figs."

And the Orphan answered:

"Fat old fart *an'* motherfucker."

That was only the beginning. The Orphan stuck out his tongue horribly at Uncle Homero and then fled. The supremely agile grammarian, who resembled nothing so much as a dancing hippopotamus, a balloon on a string, a sentimental elephant and the other fantasies of Waltdysneykov, that is, the Grimm Brother of our infancies, said my father while he washed the excrement from his hair, tried to chase him, but the Orphan dashed across a vacant lot next to Uncle H.'s condo and joined some other boys—his brothers, his doubles?—who also could run with blazing feet over the stones that had been burned by industrial detritus.

Lawyer Fagoaga knew that this was their style; the Cuauhtémoc cadets he called them, ancient children, unique heroes at the moment of their birth, he called them, secretly enraging my lopezvelardean father; they had blown their noses into the huge black handkerchief commemorative of Anahuac's ecocide. They were born wearing huaraches, in the words of Don Lucas Lizaur, the founder of the prestigious shoe emporium the Buskin (located at the corner formerly known as Bolívar and Carranza, today Bully Bar and Car Answer, where the drunks would call for cabs as they emerged from the bardiscotheque-boîte of our Chilean lady friend, as the reader will soon see): they were born with a layer of hide on their soles, making them able to walk the hot streets of the capital, conquered this time by her own sons, the industrial, commercial, official conquistadors.

"Oh, Mexico, favorite daughter of the Apocalypse!" Uncle Homero sighed as he watched the Orphan disappear in the burning mist of the vacant lot and join his pals. City dogs get bloody noses from sniffing the pavement, my mother says, and their paws are like shoe leather.

"What will my baby breathe when he's born?"

5. What Will My Baby Breathe When He's Born?

The pulverized shit of three million human beings who have no latrines.

The pulverized excrement of ten million animals that defecate wherever they happen to be.

Eleven thousand tons per day of chemical waste.

The mortal breath of three million motors endlessly vomiting puffs of pure poison, black halitosis, buses, taxis, trucks, and private cars, all contributing their flatulence to the extinction of trees, lungs, throats, and eyes.

"Pollution control?" Minister Robles Chacón exclaimed disdainfully. "Sure, when we're a great metropolis with centuries of experience. Right now we're growing, so we can't stop, this is only our debut as a great city. We'll regulate in the future."

(WILL THERE BE A FUTURE? wonders the placard my proud father parades along Paseo de la Reforma)

(WE HAVE BEEN A GREAT METROPOLIS SINCE 1325, says the

second placard he proudly exhibits on the streets of the posh Zona
Rosa)

"Anti-pollution devices on cars and trucks?" indignantly exclaims
Minister-for-Life Ulises López. "And who's going to pay for it? The
government? We'd go broke. The private sector? What would we
have left to invest? Or would you prefer that the gringo investors pay
for that, too? They'd be better off investing in Singapore or
Colombia!"

(INVEST IN SEOUL, SUFFOCATE REVEREND MOON, says my
tenacious father's eleventh placard as he pickets the Korean Embassy
this time)

"What will my son breathe?"

Mashed shit.

Carbonic gas.

Metallic dust.

And all of it at an altitude of about one and a half miles, crushed
under a layer of frozen air, and surrounded by a jail of circular
mountains: garbage imprisoned.

Madam, your son's eyes may also contemplate another circle of
garbage surrounding the city: all it would take would be a match
tossed carelessly onto the circular mass of hair, cardboard, plastic,
rags, paper, chicken feet, and hog guts, to create a chain reaction,
a generalized combustion that would surround the city with the flames
of sacrifice, setting loose the feathered Valkyries named jade and
moon, who would, in a few minutes, consume all the available
oxygen.

Vomited by the city, blind, dazzled by sudden light, by the accumulated goo on his eyes, by the threat of visual herpes, fed by the
garbage, swollen by the sewage, his hairy head crowned by a brimless
felt hat decorated with bottle caps, his skin discolored from disease,
the Orphan Huerta. Like a badly digested turd, he flew out of the
Insurgentes subway stop and headed for Calle Génova in the Zona
Rosa, where my father, calm and sure of himself, was parading around
with his WILL THERE BE A FUTURE? placard. The Orphan ran
blindly, like a fetus thrown prematurely into the world, the uterus
in his case a stairway, pint-sized and stoned, the umbilical cord in
his case the INSURGENTES metro line, until he slammed into the
back of a short man elegantly dressed in gray shantung, standing in
the entrance to the El Estoril restaurant. The blind but instinctively
predatory snotnose (literally dripping) stretched out his hand toward

the pants pocket and then the stomach of the bald, shortsighted, and bearded character who shouted *Miserable punk!* grabbed the kid by the wrist, made him scream (Well done, Uncle Fernando!), and quickly twisted his thieving arm around his back.

Don Fernando Benítez wore a money belt to keep his money safe, as everyone who walks around Makesicko City does, but he never stopped showing off the watch and chain that hung from the middle of his vest. It had been a gift from his oldest to his youngest lover, who had bequeathed it to Benítez when she died, like all the others, before him, thereby subverting the rule of feminine survival. He considered the watch a legitimate part of his lifetime, lifelong harvest: at the age of eighty, the eminent creole journalist and historian believed that sex was art and history. His blue, penetrating eyes wanted to penetrate the veil of grime and suffocation that covered the face of this infant Cacus, or infant caca, and read there something, anything that would not condemn him without giving him beforehand *the right to a reading*. In the eyes of the boy, he read: "Love me, I want to be loved."

That was all he needed to bring the lad to his house in Coyoacán, change his clothes (the Orphan Huerta clung to his bottle-capped borsalino, as if to remember where he came from and who he was), and no shoe could fit over his feet turned to stone by industrial detritus, his feet whose soles were made of natural rubber: foot toasties, Cuauhtémoc cadets!

"You actually look handsome, son of a bitch," Benítez told the boy once he'd bathed him.

He knew his name. "I was always called Orphan Huerta."

Where did he come from?

He shook his head. The lost cities of Mexico were anonymous cities: larger than Paris or Rome, six, seven, eight million inhabitants, but *no name*. The Orphan Huerta, he at least had a name, but about the nameless city he came from (in the *Cratylus* my mother reads, names are either intrinsic or conventional, or does an onomastic legislator give them out?), nothing was known.

Benítez understood that a language was hiding itself so as to be understood only by those initiated into a cabal, a social group, or a criminal caste, but it hid entire cities without even burying them, without hiding them in the liquid oblivion of a sewer—this could only happen in a city without a sewage system!

"We've got to give this kid an origin, he can't wander the face of the earth without a place of origin," said Benítez's wife, in a display of good sense. So the two of them covered their eyes and pointed to a spot on the map of the city they had hanging in the kitchen: Atlampa. From that moment on, they said that Orphan Huerta was from Atlampa, that was his neighborhood, Atlampa this and Atlampa that. But one day Don Fernando took the Orphan for a walk through Lomas: first the boy became excited, then he became sad. Benítez asked him what was wrong, and the boy said, "I would have preferred to be from here."

From here: he stared dreamily at the green lawns, the shutters, and the high walls, the trees and the flowers, but above all the walls, the protection. The sign of security and power in Mexico: a wall around the house.

This boy had a brother—Benítez managed to understand that after deciphering the Orphan's pidgin—but he'd gone away a year ago. When he left, he asked where the man who had done most damage to Mexico was. General Negro Durazo, chief of the police in charge of order and justice in the times of López Portillo, or Caro Quintero, himself an immoral thug who was a great success in drug trafficking, in seducing women, and who killed people with the same callous indifference as the chief of police. The difference between them was that the drug lord fooled no one, always worked outside the law, and didn't hide behind the law. The drug lord, concluded the Orphan's brother, did not do the nation the same kind of damage the police chief did by corrupting the justice system and discouraging the people. He said all that one afternoon after vomiting up that day's meager, rotten food: "I'm cutting out, bro', and I'm gonna see if I'm like Caro Quintero, who was a guy who'd try anything, who did himself a lot of good without fucking up the country in the process. Later on, I'll come back for you, little brother. I swear by this."

He kissed the cross he made with his thumb and index finger. But the day of his return never came (the Orphan measures time in terms of diarrhea attacks, senseless beatings, blindside attacks, who beat you up, orphan boy? Neither the sun nor the night is any good as a way to tell time: the Orphan can only count on the orphaned hours of the day) and the brother who stayed referred to the absent brother as "the lost child" and what was he? One day he slipped like a rat into the recently opened metro—before, he could use only packed minibuses or go on foot, and then one day it became possible to get on a train redolent of clean, new things, enter through the dust of the anonymous city and pop out like a cork into the boutiques and restaurants and hotels of the Zona Rosa:

No, Benítez said to him, I don't want you to be a young corpse: one more in this land of sad men and happy children. You've got lots of energy, orphan boy, I mean, you feel strong, right? Yessir, Mr. Benítez. Then let me show you how to survive by using jokes, humor is better than crime, right? You (we) have the right to laugh, orphan boy, all of you have at least that right, the right to a giggle, even if your laughter is mortal: wear out your power in the joke and perhaps you will find your vocation there; I'm not going to force you, who knows what kind of mind all the kids like you develop in the hells of this world?

The boy asked if someday he would find his lost brother, and Benítez took off his brimless borsalino, patted his bristling head, and told him of course, don't worry about it, lost children always turn up sooner or later, of course.

Uncle Fern was a wise man: he showed him the way with humor, without Teutonic tyranny, waiting to see what this boy was made of who'd been spit into his hands by the subway, which had transformed the Zona Rosa from an elitist oasis into a lumpen court of miracles. With whom did he hang around, to what ends were his talents put? Bring your friends home, Uncle Fernando told him, I want them to feel welcome here, and so one day there appeared with the Orphan a fat white boy with flat feet and slicked-down black hair. He said he was an orphan, too, like the Orphan, a projectionist in a theater that specialized in classics, where they showed old films. He'd met the Orphan at the entrance to the Hotel Aristos, should I tell your godfather what you were doing, Orph'? The boy with the bristling hair nodded assent and the chubby lad said, "He was beating out a rhythm with the bottle caps on his hat, he beat out a tune on the caps, just imagine what kind of talent he has, sir."

"And what about you?" asked Benítez.

"Well, I joined up with him, sir. Uh, I'm a little ashamed. I mean, I don't know if you . . . Darn, this long hair . . . I still wear mine that way, even though it's out of fashion, but I . . . Well, the fact is that I use pins to keep it in place, see? My black curls, ha ha, well, I could pick out a tune with a hairpin, and I joined up with your godson here . . ."

They gave a demonstration and agreed to see each other a lot and meet to practice their music in Don Fernando's house. The fat boy, who never mentioned his name and who evaded answering all questions about his family, expressed himself with difficulty, but now he said goodbye to Don Fernando with his brows worried and in a voice of mundane fatigue and extreme precision:

"Don Fernando, I think this is the beginning of a beautiful friendship."

He put on his dirty trench coat and went out hugging the Orphan. Two days later, they both returned with a third friend: a dark boy who was peeling and disheveled, barefoot, with a snakeskin belt wrapped around his waist. He was falling to pieces. The Orphan and the fat boy introduced him as Hipi Toltec, but the boy only said in (bad) French: "La serpent-à-plumes, c'est moi."

His instrument was a matchbox, and soon they began to rehearse together, dedicating themselves to their music. Don Fernando would walk by and look at them with satisfaction, but suddenly two things occurred to him: with each session, the musical harmony of the three boys became stronger and more refined. And he, Benítez, about to turn eighty, still had not exhausted his vital plan, his struggle in favor of the Indians, democracy, and justice, but his physical strength was indeed waning. Perhaps these boys . . . perhaps they would be his phalanx, his advance guard, his accomplices . . . They would help him bring his revolutionary plan to fruition.

One Saturday, he gave them three instruments: a set of Indian drums for Hipi Toltec, an electric guitar for the Orphan, and a piano for the long-haired fat boy. There was no need to sign a contract. They all understood they owed each other something.

"A man is nothing without his partner," the little fat boy enunciated clearly, pulling his gray fedora down over his brows.

But he immediately reverted to his normal personality, saying to Uncle Fernando, "Well . . . it's that we need . . . I mean, we aren't just three . . ." Benítez expressed his astonishment: he even counted on his fingers.

"No . . . it's that . . . well . . . umm . . . the girl's missing."

"The girl?"

"Yes, yes, the girl Ba . . . She, I mean, plays the piccolo," the fat boy suddenly declared solemnly, and then he sighed.

Benítez preferred not to ask for explanations and, humoring them, honored their tacit agreement. He bought the little flute and handed it over to the fat boy. That night, in his room, he listened to them practice and could identify all the instruments perfectly: the piano, the guitar, the drums, and the flute.

They baptized themselves the Four Fuckups.

Benítez could find out nothing about the origins of Hipi Toltec; he accepted the invisible existence of Baby Ba and he paid attention to every word the fat boy said, so tongue-tied in ordinary conversation but so sure of himself when he applied dialogues he'd learned in the theater to everyday life.

But our uncle, a journalist after all, never let up in his investigation of Orphan Huerta—where did he come from? did he escape from his lost city only because the new subway line had opened? how much was this kid going to reveal about himself?

With a kind of fortunate parallelism—Don Fernando commented—the detestable Homero Fagoaga also had a young boy, Philippine in origin, named Tomasito, only where Benítez gave the Orphan and his buddies the courage and freedom to be independent, Fagoaga incorporated the Filipino into his service as his valet and chauffeur.

At that time, a story was going around, and one night Benítez repeated it to my father and mother, so they would see that he was man enough to give the devil his due. Homero had saved the young Tomasito from a farewell slaughter ordered by the Philippine dictators, Ferdinand and Imelda Marcos, before they fell. Homero left him, so it seems, at the mercy of a U.S. officer in the Subic Bay naval base, and now he brought him to serve as his houseboy in Mexico City.

"But don't go soft on Homero," warned Benítez insistently, waving a severe finger. "You should all know that Homero owes his relationship with the Philippines to the fact that he acts as Ulises López's front man there, exporting wheat which cannot be sold in the U.S. because it's been poisoned with a chemical agent. It's exported to Mexico, where Ulises López stores it and then, through Homero, exports it to the Philippines. There it's received, hoarded up, and distributed by a monopoly that belongs to Marcos's buddies, who still can't be dislodged. It sounds very complicated, but given Ulises López's global economic thinking, it's not."

When he heard that name, the Orphan Huerta jumped up from

behind a green velvet chair where he'd been hiding and with an audacious fury he repeated: López, López, Ulises López, Lucha López, as if they were the names of the devil himself and his hench-man. They burned our houses, they said the land was theirs, they murdered my folks. Because of them, my lost brother and I fled!

My mother instinctively embraced the Orphan, and my father recited one of his favorite verses by López Velarde—the Christ Child left you a stable—and Benítez agreed that the city's image is its destiny, but Ulises López did not, there was no destiny, there was will and action, nothing more, he would repeat to his wife Lucha Plancarte de López: wherever a band of squatters would set up on their lands, they would get them out with blood and fire, showing no mercy. After all, they only lived in miserable cardboard shacks, like animals in stables.

6. *Fatherland, Your Surface Is Pure Corn*

Uncle Fernando's second revenge was to order the Four Fuckups to stand in front of lawyer Fagoaga's Shogun lim-ousine at the moment he was to leave for dinner.

Don Homero had spent an extremely active morning at his office, which provided him a perfect front for his activities: old-fashioned, supremely modest, on a fourth floor on Frank Wood Avenue, with old, fat-assed, half-blind secretaries who'd heard their last compliment during the presidency of López Mateos, folio upon folio of dusty legal documents, and hidden behind them a notary from Oaxaca wearing a green visor and sleeve garters. Don Homero had spoken on the telephone with his gringo partner Mr. Kirkpatrick, agreeing (Homero) to import from his partner (Kirkpatrick) all the pesticides prohibited by law in North America, to send them from Mexico to the Philippines as a Mexican export (our exports are highly applauded because they bring in revenue, ha ha), even though I pay you more than any Filipino could pay me, ha ha, don't be a joker, Mr. Kirkpatrick, I'll never eat a tortilla made from a kernel of corn sprayed with your pesticide. I have my baguettes flown in by Air France from that chic bakery on Rue du Cherche-Midi. Luckily there are no consumer protection laws here! It's better to have investments and a job, even if they bring cancer and emphysema!

Now our esteemed LL.D. descended from his traditional offices on Frank Wood Avenue, putting on his kidskin gloves and his dove-colored fedora and making his way through the masses that at three in the afternoon were filing along this central street, which in other eras had been known as San Francisco, then as Plateros, and lately Francisco Madero, got into his wide-bodied car through the door obsequiously opened by his Filipino chauffeur Tomasito. At the time, Tomasito was very young but sinister-looking because of his Oriental features. As Don Homero was making himself comfortable on the soft seats, he saw that the street mob had gathered around his car, their eyes popping out of their heads, staring at him, Don Homero Fagoaga, lawyer and linguist, as if he were a two-headed calf or a millionaire who followed the President's orders and brought back the dollars he'd exported in 1982.

Uncle Homero ordered the Filipino chauffeur to go on, to get out of here now, but Tomasito said in English *No can do, master,* and the multitude grew, rubbing its collective nose on the windows of Mr. Fagoaga's Japanese limo, sullying the windshield, the windows, and the doors with their saliva, snot, fingerprints, and blinding breath. Such was the massive and to him incomprehensible curiosity Counselor Fagoaga provoked. He sat, fearful and besieged, in all his obesity within this Turkish bath which his automobile had become with its windows closed to fend off a death which the illustrious member of the Academy of the Language didn't know whether to ascribe to excessive hatred, like the deaths of Moctezuma or Mussolini, or to excessive love, like that of any rockaztec idol of our times, stripped and dismembered by his groupies.

"Open the windows, my Manila-bred charioteer!" shouted Uncle H. to his chauffeur.

"Is danger master, me no likey lookey!" (En Anglais dans le texte.)

"Well, you're starting to annoy me, you bastard son of Quezón," exclaimed Uncle H., who valiantly opened his window onto the excited mob, in order, as it were, to pick out the kid with the bottle-capped head, shouting orbi et urbi, gather round, free show, the kid with the vulcanized feet held aloft by his disciples, a fat guy with limp black hair and a skinny kid who had a coyote's snout and tangled hair, shouting look at this car, the windows are magnifying lenses, hoisted right off the ground by the horrible skinned kid with the huge snout and that soft fatty with long hair who could have been, ay! Homero himself at sweet sixteen, shouting look at the Japanese car, latest model with magnifying windows, and look at the fat man inside magnified, now or never, ladies and gentlemen.

"Take off, yellow peril!" said Uncle Homero furiously to Tomasito, who was rapidly closing the window. "Take off, don't worry, run them over if you have to, I've told you already, you know the official opinion of the Federal District police force: If You Run Over a Pedestrian, Do Not Stop. Get moving, Tomasito, they're using in-quest reports as wallpaper in all the law offices and courts, get moving, even if you run them over and kill them. It's legal, because it costs more to stop traffic, make police reports, and sue people. Kill these downtrodden masses, Tomasito, for the good of the City and the Republic. Kill them, Homero said, but in his crazed eyes desire trembled. He loved them and he hated them, he saw them running across vacant lots, barefoot, unarmed, but by now used to the wounds caused by dioxides, phosphates, and monoxides; he peeked out the closed, dripping window of the Nipponese limo, and stared angrily at them, as they ran along Frank Wood behind him; in front of the curious crowd: the bottle caps, the skinned one, and the pudgy little one; he observed their three pairs of legs, let's see which ones he liked best, and their six feet which ran behind his automobile were deformed in some way, eddypusses, or Eddy Poes, says my dad now, punster supreme, feet deformed by that protective layer of human rubber which has been forming on the feet of the city kids and which is sure evidence that they spent their un-fancies in the streets, lots, in this place we call Mexico, DOA: eddypusses of lost children, running behind Uncle Homero Fagoaga's limo: the Lost Boys, Or-phan Huerta, Orphan Annie, David Copperfield, Oliver Twist, Little Dorrit, the gaseous exhalations of Mexico, DOA:

"Charge, O Horde of Gold!" Uncle Homero closed his eyes as his faithful Filipino obeyed and cut a swath through the curious bystanders—the spectacle looked like a Posadas engraving of Death on Horseback massacring the innocent. More than one nosy body was summarily dumped on his backside ("Fools!" exulted Don Ho-mero), but in fact our uncle only had eyes for that boy with the ferociously grimy mien, the one wearing the bottle caps on his cha-peau and running with his two companions . . . Nevertheless, as it usually turns out with even the obsessions truly worthy of the name, he eventually stopped thinking about them and the crowd scene he'd just endured. He was exhausted. When he got home, he went up to his apartment and asked to have a bath drawn. Tomasito ran to carry out the order and then returned, delight written all over his face: "Ready, master."

Homero tweaked his cheek. "Just for that, I forgive you all your sins, because when you're efficient, you're a wizard, my little Fu Manchu." He undressed in his black marble bathroom, coquettishly imagining in the mirrors another form for his body, one that while being the same would drive the obscure objects of his desire mad, he, Homero, a Ronald Colman with a Paramount mustache. He sighed, thankful for the liquid verdancy of the water in his Poppaea-ish tub fit for a Roman empress. Deliberately, but fleetingly, he thought that in Mexico, D.F. (aka DOA), only private comfort—not only exclusive but actually secret—existed because anything shared with others had become ugly—streets, parks, buildings, public trans-portation, stores, movies—everything, but inside, in the corners left to wealth, it was possible to live luxuriously, secretly, because it did not involve a violation of national solidarity—like having to give back hard but illegally earned bucks, or giving up $5 million co-ops on Park Avenue, or selling off condos in Vail at bargain rates, it did not involve offending those less fortunate than he who . . . He gazed with a sense of marvel at the intense green color, at the same time liquidly transparent and beautifully solid (like marble, one might say), of the water in his bath and gave himself up to it completely.

He let himself drop, with a jolly, carefree plop, into the tub, but instead of being enveloped by the delightful and warm fluidity of the green water, he was embraced by a cold, sticky squid: a thousand tentacles seized his buttocks, his back, his knees, his elbows, his privates, his neck: Lawyer Fagoaga sank into something worse than quicksand, mud, or a tank full of sharks: unable to move a finger, a leg, his head bobbing like that of a marionette, Homero was sucked in by a tub full of green gelatine, a sweet pool of viscous lime Jell-O in which Uncle H. looked like a gigantic strawberry.

"What have we here, a barrister in aspic?" guffawed Uncle Don Fernando Benítez from the door, wearing a starched butterfly collar, bow tie, and a light, double-breasted shantung suit.

"Tomasito!" Homero Fagoaga managed to scream, seconds before sinking into horror, surprise, and rage, which were even stickier than the gallons of gelatine put there by the Fuckups: "Tomasito! Au secours! Au secours!"

"Does your boss really know French, or is he just a disgusting snob?" asked Uncle Fernando, taking the stick and hat that Tomasito, the perfect though perplexed servant, handed him before he went to help his master, who was shouting, "Benítez, you Russophile! You café Marxist! You salon Commie!" His extravagant list went on, my mother noted, and every item pointed to the exact moment in which his political education had taken place and dated him.

Tomasito, after saving his master with vacuum cleaners, massage, and even corkscrews, withdrew to pray to a potted palm he carried around with him. He begged the gods of his country that he never again confuse his master with the relatives, confidants, or friends of his master, that he never again allow them to enter the domicile of his master, or that he ever serve more than one master at any one time.

Then, sobbing, he went back to Don Homero Fagoaga, prostrate in his canopied bed, to squeeze him out a bit more and beg his forgiveness.

"I think there's still some gelatine in his ears and nose," said my father Angel, but my mother merely repeated these words:

"What will my son breathe when he is born?"

"Perhaps I'd better answer your question about which language the boy will speak first. Didn't you ask about that, too?"

"Okay. Which language will he speak? That was my third question."

3

It's a
Wonderful Life

Child, girl, woman,
hag, sorceress,
witch, and
hypocrite, the devil
takes her.

Quevedo

1

My circumstance consists of certainties and uncertainties. One certainty: the boy has been conceived under the sign of Aquarius. One uncertainty: his chances of becoming a Mexican fetus are one in one hundred and eighty-three trillion six hundred and seventy-five billion nine hundred million four hundred thousand fifty-three hundred and forty-eight, according to my father's calculations, which he made as he waded into the Pacific Ocean with my mom to wash away the shit that rained on them from the sky that midday of my cuntception. First day of the c(o)untdown they called it. I call it my first swing in the cemetery, as I moved toward the ovarian reading lesson, because even though they remember now what happened that day, I knew it absolutely and totally from the moment in which my dad's microserpent knocked over my mom's corona radiata (no, not a corona corona, Dad's was an exploding cigar, a MIRV, come to think of it) as if it were made of rose petals, while the survivors I've already mentioned of the great battle of Hairy Gulch invaded the gelatinous membrane, de profundis clamavimus—but nobody was home: which of us will have the honor to fertilize Doña Angeles (no last name), wife of Don Angel Palomar y Fagoaga Labastida Pacheco y Montes de Oca, descendant of the most exclusive families of Puebla, Veracruz, Guadalajara, and Mexico City?; one in a million, the lucky little guy, the fortunate hunchback. All madly trying to penetrate, break the barrier, perforate the shell, and overcome the fidelity of this Penelope who will not invite just any old dick to dinner, only one, the champ, the Ulyssex returned from the wars, the greatest, the Muhammad Ali of the chromosomes, número uno:

YOU MEAN LITTLE OLD ME?

I, admirable and full of portents, I allowed in, bombarded by voices and memories, oh dear me, places and times, names and songs, dinners and fucks, speeches and stutterings, rememberings and forgettings, this unique I CHRISTOPHER and what they call genes.

"Hey, genes are to blame for everything," said Uncle Fernando.

"Of course," agreed Uncle Homero Fagoaga, "Hegels are to blame for everything."

Why did two men who hated each other, who were so unalike in everything, my Uncles Fernando and Homero, have to be together, colliding, interrupting each other? What impels us to do what we don't want to do, to self-destruction? Is it that we prefer an insult, a humiliation, even a crime—murder—to being alone?

My father and mother, for example, are no longer alone: they live together and they have just conceived me—ME. I will listen to them throughout this story and I shall learn, little by little, that their union, their true love, does not exclude a constant struggle between what they are and what they would like to be, between what they have and what they would like to have. I state here and now that what I have just said without breaking any rules of narrative (know it well, your mercies benz) because the difference between my father and my mother is that you'll know all there is to know about Angel at the beginning, while about Angeles you'll know a little at the end. There are people like that, and I don't lose anything by stating it outright at the start. It's more important to note the opposing forces within them: what I am and what I want to be; what I have and what I want to have. I, so solitary in the solar center of my narrative, I understand well what I'm telling you, Gentile Readers. Since I am so alone, I have to wonder incessantly: what is it I need in order not to be alone; who is the other I need most in order to be myself, the one and only Christopher Unborn?

My answer is clear and forthright:
I need you, Reader.

2

At any hour of the day, in any social class, in any of the infernal circles of this *selva selvaggia*, there are two problems: how to be alone or, alternatively, how to be in good company. But in Makesicko City, the city where my father grew up, the problem is saving oneself from pests (Angel told Angeles).

They tell me that in other countries a person with manners would never dare interrupt someone's morning work time or his well-earned leisure time without setting up a date in advance and then showing up at the exact time; they send blue *pneumatiques* (or used to until *pneumatiques* died prematurely in 1984) or at the least call. Not in Mexico. The D.F. is a village with village manners disguised as a megalopolis. "Hey, man, get over here right now." "Listen, I'm coming right over, okay?" Complete with kings, tombs, tribes, and leeches.

The most virulent form of this social disease known as the leech is the "parachutist," who "drops in" at any hour of the day or night without calling, interrupting a dinner (if it's the gate-crasher variety, it wants to be invited to join in), interrupting sex (if it's a refined voyeur and sniffs out the hours when others take their pleasure), interrupting reading (if it happens to suffer acute agraphia and feels annoyed if someone settles down to cohabitate with words).

Which language will the child speak? asks my mother insistently, and my father answers that our language is dying on us, and only because they know that will they (Mom and Dad) pardon the existence of my Uncle Homero. We just saw all that.

But for the parachuting or interrupting pest no pardon is possible: its language is pure chatter, yakitiyak, gossip, tongue-wagging, and championship bouts of chin-wagging, although these creatures often invent dramatic pretexts to justify their undesired intrusion to the victim: during his adolescence, my father Angel (he tells us) attracted these creatures (of both sexes), especially those wandering around loose in Colonia Juárez or Colonia Cuauhtémoc.

In this city, then, populated by perpetually invading hordes (si j'ai bien compris) that arrive from anywhere at any hour of the day or night without being called or desired, who knock at the door (bam-bambam, Anybody home? knockknockknock, It's the devil! Nobody home? Am I interrupting? Could you lend me your maracas? Don't you have a little *tepache* in the fridge? For whatever reason, says my father Angel: in this city, he believes that when he was a young man he was sought out more than any of his friends or acquaintances because they all still lived at home or because of inflation they all went back to live with their parents or had to rent rooms in uncom-fortable, promiscuous boardinghouses, fearful of ending up in old neighborhoods or the new, lost neighborhoods, and by contrast, An-gel was an orphan, but an orphan with a nice place; and all of them were suffering under revived nineteenth-century discipline (or earlier: the interregnum of disorder in Mexico was born with the Rolling Stones and ended with the austerity of Rollover Debts: on the crum-bling corners, the saddest song was once again the one about there being only four thousand pesos left from all the oil that was mine *ay* ayayayay; the happiest song, the one about the death of the petropeso, the death of conceit, you want a tiger in your tank?/ well money talks and bullshit walks): someone knocked on the door of his grandparents' house, a beggar dressed as a monk, asking for alms:

"Please contribute to my grandmother's funeral."

Angel's grandma, Doña Susana Rentería, pulled off her wedding ring and, trembling, handed it to the monk. Then she shut the door, embraced Angel, and begged: "Please don't tell my Rigo what I just did."

Okay, the pest rarely sets up a date and when it does it invariably arrives late; on the other hand, if it comes without warning, it always arrives (by definition) right on time: such was the case of the myriad parachutists who dropped in on my father when he was living—more freely than anyone in his generation as far as coming and going were concerned—in the coach house annexed to the house of his grand-parents, Don Rigoberto Palomar (ninety-one years old) and Doña Susana Rentería de Palomar (sixty-seven years old) on Calle Génova. Having emancipated himself from the tyranny of Don Homero Fa-goaga and his sisters Capitolina and Farnesia, my father enjoyed a unique reputation: if he lived alone—so the story went—it was be-cause he was more respectable, more mature, more trustworthy than any other boy or girl in his public school: HEROES OF 1982. The school, originally private, was founded by Don Mamelín Mártir de Madrazo (better known in financial circles as Jolly Roger), who created it as proof of his public-spiritedness. Of course, Don Mártir, the most expropriated banker in Mexico before he was kidnapped and murdered, never imagined that this last bulwark of his civic prestige would also be expropriated. They never even bothered to change the school's name, since HEROES OF 1982 by definition could apply just as well to the expropriators as to those expropriated—all the better, in fact, since those who expropriated the school would one day leave government for private industry, where they would in their turn be expropriated by the next government, revolutionarily ad infinitum. The net result was that at school Angel Palomar y Fagoaga paid dearly for his fame because pests dropped in at all hours to tell him their troubles, using metaphysical or physical anguish as a pretext: I'll commit suicide if I don't talk to someone, which actually meant: If I don't commit suicide I'll talk to someone, and by the way do you have anything in the fridge (an ocean), what are you reading (*The Life and Opinions of Tristram Shandy, gent.*), how tired I am (go to bed, baby), aren't you? (sure I am and here I come), what record should I put on (the last one put out by my favorite group, Immanuel Can't), well, Kan't you sing me something?

> The life of the turkey vulture
> is a wretched sort of life
> All the year he flies and flies
> his head as bald as a knife

insult me: slut! will you pull off my peplum, my chlamys, my fibula, strip me bare and help me with the homework? I've got such a pain right here, what could it be? I thought you might be sad—with nothing to do—screwing around as usual—as alienated as I am—jerking off, pig—on your way out, eating, sleeping, don't you like me to visit you?—is it true that they told you that you told them to tell me?—I came over so you could tell me what you mean—got any dope?—could you introduce me into your sister?—I need bread, man—lend me a few rubbers—do you guys know of anyone who might need a fireworks expert for November 2? a paid insultant?—money, man? unless you have influence they won't lend you any money at the bank, know any bank directors, Angelito?—lend me

your comb—lend me your cock—wasn't it you who had the recipe
for those tamales wrapped in banana leaves?—lend me—lend me—
could you call up—couldn't you have an Equanil sent up from the
pharmacy on the corner?—looks like the revolution starts tomorrow—
the fascist coup—the military coup—the Communist coup—lay in
lots of canned goods, Angel, let's get to the state of siege right away—
nail polish at the perfume counter, right?—where are those cold
beers, bartender? what? are you turning cheapskate on us, what happened?—could you store my mint collection of *Playboy* for me: they
just don't understand at my place, ya know?—my collection of stuffed
toys, Angelote, at my place, if my mom sees them, you know—
could I leave my Toyota Super XXX here in your patio, Angel, at
my place my dad is so strict, that stuff about moral renovation—
capisc'—let me leave my valise here in case I take a trip—my collection of Almazán posters?—my Avelina Landín records?—my book
of López Portillo's favorite metaphors?—my collection of tops?

Between his sixteenth and his twentieth year the pests pestered him
and the parachutists rained on him, as if the independence of his
generation (which grew progressively more disciplined under paternal
tutelage) depended on Angel in his house, from which it was possible
to see the Angel of Independence on Paseo de la Reforma. It was as
if that were the price of the unsettled, excited twenty years of death,
repression, opening, reform, triumph, collapse, and austerity in
which Angel and his friends had the good fortune to be born and
grow up: they saw their own coming-of-age postponed again when
they were between eighteen and twenty-two and the effective control
of their parents extended and strengthened to a degree worthy of the
most severe household of the prerevolutionary Porfirio Díaz era—
until, thought my father Angel, privileged spectator that he was, the
time for the inevitable reaction came, the helplessness, solitude,
escape, and nomadism that began after the Disaster of 1990.

But one might also say that the very illusion of liberty depended
on Angel's isle of autonomy, on that and something else: as if the
eventual resurrection (oh, vain illusion!) of the moribund city, where
by now all the worst prophecies about it come true, without anyone's
ever having raised a finger to stop them, depended on the wobbly
survival of Colonia Juárez, the only urban oasis that still maintained
a certain veneer of civilization. In the ears of Angel, in the ears of
his genes, and in the ears of his descendants in limbo, there rumbles

the sound of filthy water, pumped in and out, pestilential, a gigantic parallel to the beats and vulnerabilities of his own heart.

In the coach house on Calle Génova, my father found himself alone with a mountain of garbage and the conviction that nothing—really nothing—of all that was piled up there was worthy of being saved: the magic of the marketplace, as President Ronald Ranger liked to say, at the outset of the odious eighties, saved nothing: it destroyed everything, while making people believe that the garbage deserved to remain. And the worst thing is that Angel could not or would not get rid of the mountain of detritus that threatened to bury him in his own cave. He wouldn't deprive himself of that most eloquent testimony to the era he was honored to live through: the monument of scrap, vinyl, and old hair. Hitler's evil genius consisted in offering to the times in which we lived its most truthful prognostication—the mountains of enslaved objects from Auschwitz. Who didn't have his innocent Auschwitz in an attic, a coach house, a medicine chest, a trunk, or in his own back yard?

Thus it was that my father Angel, when he reached his twentieth birthday, one before by law what he had inherited from his deceased parents, the inventors, should be handed over to him, he came to the full realization that having grown up in a world that was proudly conservative in its economics, both in its principles and in their application, in reality he had grown up in a world of junk and economic anarchy. The truth had been a lie, and realizing it offended him greatly.

This afternoon of my creation, my genes and chromosomes begin to talk as if my life depended on language more than on the fortuitous meeting of semen and egg: listening to my father and mother speak immersed in the sea which is the cradle of life, the unique refrigerator in the burning world that incinerated all forms of life in the universe except those that took refuge and developed underwater and left, I tell you with perfect certainty, the primitive ocean inside every one of us, floating eternally in a certain sense in saltwater, because the problem, your mercy the reader should know, is not to dry out. Never, under no circumstance: if you dry out you die, like a fish without scales, a bird without feathers, or a pup without fur: pity the person who tends not the savage ocean he bears within him because it's the only thing left to him from two overlapping creations: that of the world and that of the child. I say this because I feel that my parents are speaking one afternoon from within the Pacific Ocean, about another ocean of dust: a city they will, I suppose, bring me to someday, since they talk so much about it, think about it so much, predict so many things about it, and fear it so much. For example: "Look, Angelito," his (mine, mighty, mymighty?) Grandpa General Rigoberto Palomar said to him, "the Drainage Sewer was built by Don Porfirio Díaz in around 1900 at a level lower than the city's at that time. But now the city has sunken in its swampy bed and the sewer is higher than our shit. Now it costs millions to pump day in day out so that the shit rises to the level of the sewer and flows away. If they stopped pumping for two minutes, Mexico City would be flooded with poop."

3

Angel put up with everything until the day when a pest of a different nature joined the crowd. A tall, robust, dark, mustachioed young man with the eyes of one of the guerrilleros photographed by Casasola drinking chocolate in Sanborn's in the Year of Our Lord 1915. I see him now: I'd seen him in the halls of alma mater, HEROES OF 1982, walking as if he'd spent his life pushing the cannon in the Zacatecas campaign, with his gorilla-like shoulders: invisible cartridge belts crossed his chest, an invisible, blackened straw hat covered his big head: anyone who did not avert his eyes ran the risk of meeting him in person and getting demolished. His name was Matamoros Moreno.

"What can I do for you, bro'?" asked Angel, opening the door, his ability to be surprised having early on been eradicated. An ear of green corn in *mole* rolled from the inside of the house toward the street.

"Remember me?"

"Who could forget you?"

"Do you mean that?" He bared tremendous teeth as he gazed with unfeigned lust at the pile of deflated condoms and dried-out Kotex behind Angel. "Bet you can't remember what my name is."

"Petero Palots," said my dad with insouciance, not so much out of irreverence but simply because he was unconscious of the danger.

"Whadya mean?" grunted Matamoros Moreno.

"Listen, man," answered my pop, "it's not good manners to knock on someone's door and then ask the guy who answers if he remembers your name ten years after having been in the same class with you and two hundred other assholes, staring at the map of the country while the son of a bitch of a teacher spent most of the class calling the roll. The only thing I remember is that he took sixty minutes to get from Aguilar to Zapata by way of your humble serviette Palomar y . . ."

"Moreno," grunted the visitor, while my father, after a mnemotechnical shove like that, saw once again the map of the Republic before its current shrinkage (the country abbreviated during the disaster of 1990!), and the light bulb went on in his head.

"Tabasco Moreno."

"Too far south."

"Jalisco Moreno," suggested my father timidly.

"Farther north," said Moreno melancholically.

"Sonora Moreno."

"O, it ends in o," he said, this time almost begging for recognition. "Even by name I'm macho, Palomar." He looked toward some false eyelashes someone had stuck on a mannequin head and forgotten there.

"Of course," exclaimed my young father, "of course, who could forget that name: Matamoros Moreno. You just caught me off-guard. Now, what can I do . . . ?"

Before he could finish the sentence, Matamoros managed to put one foot between the door and the jamb. "He won't jamb me," my father said to himself. "Enough is enough." But this orangutan was scaring him.

"Don't get all bent out of shape, Palomar," said the big guy, now blinking one of his tiger eyes through the partially open door and speaking in a voice that was so sweet my father felt ashamed of himself.

"Don't get upset, coward. Don't try to evaporate on me," he added quickly with a ferocity that convinced my father that his decision to make it difficult for Matamoros to get in was sound.

"Don't get upset, chum," Matamoros said after a bit, in a voice that shook my dad's soul and confirmed his worst fears.

Later he said to himself that he had always feared the day someone would ask him for an opinion about a literary text. He was well

known as a reader in HEROES OF 1982. He could recite Quevedo.
He quoted Montaigne. He was a fan of López Velarde. He had access
to the vast library that belonged to his scientist parents. His Quevedian
motto was: Nothing surprises me. The world has bewitched me. But
that it should turn out to be Matamoros Moreno who would turn
over his first literary efforts to him, who would ask for his sincere
opinion, who would assure him that he had admired him from a
distance in HEROES OF 1982 as the most highly cultured boy in
their class, the most avid of readers . . . My father sat down among
his empty bottles, his bicycle wheels, his squashed cardboard boxes,
and his collections of alien porn, to read the literary efforts of his
fellow student Matamoros Moreno.

The reader is cordially invited to fill the virgin page following with
his own version of Matamoros Moreno's text, read by my father that
afternoon when he was twenty years old. The only hints about it are
some statistics: Matamoros says "heart" twenty times; "tumescent
flesh" and "maculate flesh" appear eighteen times each; fifteen times
he exclaims "Holy Mother," attributing to this fertile lady eleven
times the expression "white hair" and only ten "little mop of cotton";
there are fourteen "blazing shines," thirteen lives scattered among
rosebushes, and twelve mad passions; only four coral lips appear in
this census.

Angel's first reaction was to laugh. But three things stopped him.

The first was that in Chapter 2, as if to arouse obligatory applause,
Matamoros said only:

> THERE'S NO COUNTRY LIKE MEXICO,
> DON'T *YOU* AGREE?

This attempt at demagoguery was strengthened by Chapter 3, which
proclaimed in lapidary tones:

> SHE DID IT FOR NO OTHER NATION

The proclamation of the Virgin of Guadalupe added religious terrorism to patriotic terrorism, my dad had objected. The great thing
about Matamoros was that his zenith was also his nadir, his alpha
was also his omega: his peak was down below; there was no fall, just
as there was no ascent; his sentences were the high point of a gorge,
never the low point of a ridge.

But the third, the real problem was telling him all this.

Or letting him know indirectly.

Matamoros, of course, had given him no address: he said he'd be back next week. The mail didn't work anymore, who didn't know that? My father calculated that a week for Moreno would be exactly one week, and when the seventh day after the Matamoorish visit came around, he hung the manuscript in a manila envelope on the outside doorknob, along with a "Very interesting" note.

He heard Matamoros Moreno's unmistakable footsteps at three o'clock in the afternoon, the precise hour at which the seventh day came to an end. He pressed his ear to the door without breathing. He heard the rustle of papers. Then the long, jailhouse footfalls going into the distance. He opened the door to see if the coast was clear. Not a trace of Matamoros, but the manuscript was still hanging from the doorknob. Matamoros had appended a note to my father's note: "What's very interesting? I'll be back tomorrow at the same time. Do a better job. And don't try to jerk me around."

My father spent a restless night. To mock Matamoros would be to put himself in physical danger. So my father Angel spent his morning between fear and mockery, mockery and fear: Matamoros Moreno was laughable; he was also to be feared. What was to be done with this supreme invader of the impossible private life of Angel Palomar y Fagoaga?

He was on the verge of asking his Grandfather Rigoberto Palomar for advice. But he did that only on the most important occasions, when there was clearly no way out. His grandfather would expect more agility from him, a more fertile imagination. It was an unwritten agreement between them. Besides, what was Angel going to do at three that his grandfather would or would not do at two or four?

At exactly three, Matamoros materialized. "Well, what did you think of my work?"

"It provokes digressive flights."

"Whadya mean?"

"I mean that the metaphysical transposition, taking control of the signifying practices, ultimately modifies all the prosodic and morphologic instances, eventually hastening the triumph of the linguistic eros, itself related to the fungous and fusive homophony of the homologous."

Matamoros Moreno stared severely at my father. "Cantinflas couldn't have put it better, bro'."

He looked with paleolithic irony toward the interior of the coach house, as if he could read the stacks of love letters written by other people and take the rust off the abandoned motorcycles. "Tomorrow I'll be back for a serious opinion, Palomar. Remember, three strikes and you're out."

Off he went, dragging his chain, pushing his cannon. My father leaned back, cursing all classmates, from the beginning of time. Because of fear and laughter he could not sleep: his nightmares about Matamoorish violence were interrupted by attacks of insane laughter as he remembered the most singular sentences penned by his classmate. Three strikes and you're out, warned his old school chum (may God protect us from them!), so here we go. But if he didn't have the guts to laugh right in his face and tell him, look, Matamoros, your prose is an exercise in involuntary humor; or the courage to say, look, Matamoros, your prose is shit, then at least he'd have the valor to confront this unforeseen nemesis a third and possibly last time. Neither scorn nor fear. Let's see what happened.

Matamoros Moreno was right on time when Angel Palomar opened the front door for him. My father could imagine Matamoros from head to toe, but he didn't imagine him with anyone else: no, Matamoros didn't need protection; he was his own bodyguard, clearly. Nor did Angel imagine he'd be with a woman, even if the woman provided another kind of protection or blackmail—how could Matamoros do that to him! No, not that. But yes, yes that. Except that the woman was an eleven-year-old girl. Dark, plump, dressed in pink, with tresses, bangs, dimpled cheeks, and black little eyes— Shirley Temple translated into Mexican.

"My daughter. Illegitimate, of course. I couldn't leave her alone. Thursdays the day care is closed. Sorry. Her name is Colasa. Short for Nicolasa. I don't like Nicolasita. So it's Colasa. Kiss the nice man, honey."

Moist, sticky, chocolatey, bubble-gummy, aromatic kiss. My father confesses he collapses—yesterday, today, and tomorrow—in the presence of girls between three and thirteen years of age. Defenseless. Victimized. Against Colasa Moreno he was nothing.

"Colasa Sánchez, sorry, after her mother. I'm not sexist. Why should she have to carry around a man's name all her life, first her father's and then her husband's? Let her have her own name, her mother's name, right?"

Angel my father was about to say that a woman always has a man's name, whether it's her mother's maiden name (a father's name, after all) or her father's name, so that the name of Colasa's mother was her grandfather's name, but . . .

"So what's the story with my stuff, buddy?"

Vanquished, my father was obliged to say that it was an unusual example of poetic prose: the pitfalls of sentimentality had been avoided with skill and intelligence; it was difficult to communicate more beautifully a feeling of so much filial goodness. Wasn't it Dostoevsky who said when he outlined the theme of *The Idiot*, WHAT?; no, that's the title of a Russian novel, okay? OKAY, get on with it man, I like what you're telling me, like it a lot, Colasa likes it too, doncha honey: yes Daddy, the nice man really is nice and very intelligent, right Daddy?: groan of agony from Angel Palomar: "It wouldn't be unworthy of an anthology of this kind of writing."

"Well, see about getting it done."

"Getting what done, Matamoros?"

"Getting it published, man. I'll be back tomorrow at the same time. Come on now, Colasa. Say thank you to the nice man. Thanks to his help, we're going to get rich and famous, kid. And something better: we're going to be happy. You're a good guy, Palomar."

As if her father were a prompter, Colasa Sánchez started to sing:

> My heart's delight's this little ranch
> Where I live content
> Hidden among the mountains blue
> With rainbows heaven sent.

It was difficult to get him out without actually shoving him through the door, without seeming impolite, assuring him that tomorrow was another day, they'd see for sure, of course, the famous anthology, yes, ha ha ha, the girl singing happy ranch, my little nest, with honeysuckle scent . . .

He didn't flee from Matamoros Moreno and his daughter Colasa Sánchez out of physical fear of such fearsome characters or because of any moral fear of telling them the truth or out of psychic fear of his desire to laugh at them: my father took the bus to Oaxaca that afternoon of his twentieth year in the month of November out of the purest compassion: so they wouldn't suffer. How could he have imagined that that damned Matamoros had left his daughter Nicolasita (it was an annoying nickname!) standing guard on the corner near his grandparents' house?

Night and day, obviously, since the snot-nose was sitting on her haunches in front of a country-style ministore, as if she were on strike, with a lantern for night work, a black and red flag, and a pot of smoking beans. The simple child was hugging an ancient, moth-eaten doll of the *charro* Mamerto, a character my father recognized from a collection of comics someone had left in his coach house.

No sooner did she see my father than Colasa let out a shout, threw the *charro* with his huge black mustaches aside, and pointed her finger at my dad:

"Stop him! Stop him! The shameless rascal is fleeing! The scoundrel is going back on his word! Stop him! In the name of heaven and justice, I implore you not to abandon a poor girl! Stop him! The coward is fleeing, stop the knave!"

Horrified, my father ran like the devil toward Paseo de la Reforma, not even stopping to greet the statue of Don Valentín Gómez Farías, as was his custom, not even blowing a kiss to the Angel of Independence. He boarded a taxi and left poor Colasa behind, weeping, her tresses standing on end. When he reached Oaxaca thirty hours later, my father was so nervous that he walked into the Church of San Felipe Neri to take Communion for the first time since he abandoned the house of the Fagoagas. He looked with the sweetest serenity at the church made—my genes swear it to me—of golden smoke. Of course, how was he to know that, expelled by the language of Matamoros Moreno, he would find in Oaxaca his own language, as a kind of faith, as a quasi-madness, and above all as an act of conscience.

He realized in that moment of peace that never in his life had he left the boundaries of the Federal District: his horizon had always been that of the valley trapped among mountains, among the steepest slopes of the tropics, and under a sheet of cold air: the least intelligent, least provident city, the most masochistic, and suicidal, most stupidly stupid city in the history of the world. He left it thinking about the insult of the pests and its mountains of garbage.

Now a pure and unforeseen thundershower in November, the sky washed clean, the earth resurrected: he was in Oaxaca.

4. *Your Breath the Blue of Incense*

"Then I fled to Oaxaca," my father told my mother, "far from Matamoorish fury. For the first time in my life, I was leaving the D.F. Searching through my knapsack for some gum, I found a letter from my Grandma Susana telling me that when I got to Oaxaca I should look up a Mrs. Elpidia, who, although she did not advertise, took in recommended guests and made food fit for a king. Also: her house was located a short distance from the plaza.

My grandmother had also included an envelope with two hundred thousand pesos in it—to cover expenses—and the complete works of López Velarde in one volume. How she knew that I was leaving when I hadn't said a word about it is something I jealously guarded in my unmentionable hoard of family witchcraft, where she held the place of honor.

I'll get bored here, I thought, but I was mistaken because the patio of Doña Elpidia's house was shaded by cool trees and contained a cage with a joking parrot in it. The old lady gave me a room with a view of the mountains and served me the best yellow *mole* in the world. I acquired a relaxed rhythm, that of my own body, my own heart: I realized that I had been living inside a Mixmaster my entire life; I learned again how to walk, stop, rest, look, and smell.

I began to live with light, not against light; with my digestion, not in doubtful combat with my own guts; sleeping and waking up at the proper times. It happened little by little: a dawn sculpting itself; an abrupt afternoon; a city of greens and blacks and golds. There was time for me to sit in the plaza and listen to the band play overtures to Italian operas. There was time for me to eat prickly-pear ice in the atrium of Santa Rita. Time to walk into churches alone. Oaxaca gave me only itself. It was something new: I was in the world and not a refugee from the world. This was Oaxaca's first gift.

About a week later I began to get nervous. I was at the peak of my sexual powers and I must confess that, in exchange for psychiatric care and furniture warehousing, I enjoyed the favors of all the broads who passed through my cave on Calle Génova. (Of this, more later.

I always associate sex with December, when the chicks in the Distrito Federal do more screwing in a month than they do in the rest of the year. Before they make their New Year's resolutions, which should be "Start screwing in January.") In Oaxaca I was afraid of losing what I'd already won, out of pure sexual distress. I strolled around the plaza, in the opposite direction from the way the local girls would walk each Saturday and Sunday. It was useless. They seemed to look away from me on purpose. I started to get bored with ices, the overture to *William Tell*, leafy laurels, and clean, trim mountains.

Even Doña Elpidia's *mole* started to annoy me . . . The only thing I could do was talk to the parrot, which I did with determination one boring, calm Sunday morning, trying to teach him some bawdy verses by Quevedo:

> *He who trusts whores is a gelding.*

But Doña Elpidia's parrot, indifferent to my classical instruction, went on repeating the same stuff—like a parrot:

> *He who eats a locust will never leave this place . . .*

And Doña Elpidia, who was about to celebrate her ninety-ninth birthday behind the door of her kitchen, was chanting, as if I didn't understand the parrot, "He who eats locust never more shall leave this place . . ."

"Does he need some locusts, Doña Elpidia?" I said ever so obligingly—and besides, I know how to take a hint.

"Yes, he does, son, and the market isn't even four blocks away . . ." she said, showing me her vacant gums.

I walked down the cobblestone street from Elpidia's house, and in the Sunday market I found lots of stands selling red crickets powdered with chili powder, and in one place I found a girl who looked like Colasa Sánchez, Matamoros Moreno's illegitimate daughter—was it the same girl? was it her sister?—who flashed an irresistible smile at me (let me remind you, Christa Balilla, that I cannot resist any girl between three and thirteen years of age). She offered me a little plastic bag filled with locusts. But when I went to take them, the girl refused to give them to me, hugged them to her breast, and wiggled her finger at me to follow her.

She led me to a tiny church that looked more like a passageway, with windows open onto the street, and only there did she hand me the bag of locusts. Then she ran off, covering her mouth with her hand.

I ate those delicious insects that crackle between your teeth before releasing into your palate the airy burn of dawn (Matamoros dixit). Then I walked into the Church of San Cosme and San Damián, perhaps the simplest I'd seen in this city of baroque frills.

It was crowded.

But there was only one Agueda.

How could I not recognize her? Normally I wouldn't have noticed a woman there praying before the Christ of the Way of Calvary, but in this Sunday crowd I believed anything and everything when I saw her there kneeling in contradictorily prestigious starched skirts and fearsome full mourning.

Of course I bit my tongue as I recognized I was quoting the poem by López Velarde I'd read the night before in my solitary bed, resisting the temptation to masturbate, imagining Cousin Agueda's fingers weaving "gently and perseveringly in the sonorous corridor." How could I not recognize her this morning if just last night, sadly, I ended up offering up to her that small, jumping, nervous sacrifice, I myself a cricket with chili on it, imagining her as I saw her now, dressed in mourning, but resonant with starch, with her coppery eyes, and her ruddy cheeks, and I wishing she would caress me as she was caressing the beads on her rosary with her fine, agile fingers.

Oh my chaste and pure soul! Agueda turned her head covered with veils of black lace just at the moment when I decided to give in to the seductions of the language appropriate to the woman and the place: to stop resisting and become that language. She turned her head and looked at me—just for an instant (telling makes it seem longer, but it all happened in an instant)—with her unusual copper sulphate eyes.

"I had, inland, an impoverished sweetheart": in those eyes that rhymed with each other I detected an infinitely modest happiness, oh my unborn son, and all my sour tedium drained from me. In Agueda's eyes I discovered not conformity but peace.

She looked at me for an instant and again wrapped her mourning in her shawl the color of ivory and mother-of-pearl. I followed her to the exit. She didn't try to avoid me. She didn't stop to say, "Do not compromise me further, sir."

To the contrary. She turned to look at me from time to time; and I stopped each time she turned, telling her that I would follow wherever she led: Agueda. Well, she went from the flagstone floor of San Cosme and San Damián to the golden glory of Santo Domingo, and from there to the temple of Our Lord of Health, which smelled intensely of flowers and the bakeries next door, and finally to the artnouveau Church of San Felipe Neri, where she settled down for a long stay. It was now five in the afternoon and she wasn't moving, surrounded by those fleurons that seemed invented by Gaudí in Barcelona but which in fact were the work of Zapotec craftsmen from Oaxaca in the seventeenth century. I began to think of the gaze of the Holy Child of Atocha dressed in brocade and red feathers more as that of a rival than as a gaze of reproach.

"Young man, we are closing now," a bald sacristan dressed in a filthy brown suit informed me I don't know how much later.

On the other hand, he said nothing to Agueda, who was still wrapped in her radiant mourning.

Since I saw she wasn't about to move, it occurred to me to hide in one of the confessionals, on the priest's side. The doors were locked and the lights were extinguished, but when I left my hiding place, I saw Agueda still kneeling there, Christopher my boy, and I didn't want to watch her become an old maid.

I approached her; I touched her shoulder; she turned toward me. All her symbols depended on her eyes: the apostolic spider, the nocturnal hieroglyphic, the enigmatic Edens of her hair, the cruel scorpions of sex; the vacuous intrigue of erotic chess.

She, too, remained silent; she left everything to my immediate memory of López Velarde's verses, names and musicality, a poet dead at the age of thirty-three, my unborn Christopher, all because he strayed from the old park of his heart in Jerez de Zacatecas to go to die in the noisy thoroughfare of the decadent, rouged, and lipsticked capital; in 1921, on a June morning, the poet Ramón died with his pockets full of papers without adjectives.

Oh, my retrograde heart: Agueda looked at me and I feared she would think all this about me: this dark, tall, green-eyed boy with the brand-new mustache is my sweetheart, my cousin, my poet Ramón López Velarde. But it didn't happen that way—that was only my imagination seeking to explain the sudden solitude of the Church of San Felipe on a Sunday night in November in 1990, when the poet from Jerez had enjoyed barely sixty-nine years of immortality.

She said nothing; but she did raise her veil over the comb she wore in her hair, thus revealing the rustic novelty of her perfumed nape. The nape was both annunciation and invitation. I had no idea that a nape, the beginning of her hair and the nakedness of her neck, could be as exciting as the meeting ground between pubic hair and belly skin. I kissed her as her clothes slid off her back and she abandoned the starched mourning shawl on her shoulders.

She knew me (or rather knew the poet): she bared only her back, shoulders, and nape; she invited me to monopolize with my kisses the incomparable smoothness of her body, she gave me the ecstasy of the chaste, acid fragrance of her armpits; of her shoulders, perfect for a copious and liquid cry; of the wingèd virtue of her soft breast; in the sleepy quintessence of her soft back: I breathing it all in, I forever in love with the smoothness and softness of provincial women, fair-skinned and light on their feet, pretty faces that never miss a Mass, young ladies with apple-shaped faces, prisoners of the glacial abandon of their beds, who so quickly turn from being intact virgins to Matres dolorosas: I would like to fall asleep in your beatific arms, Agueda, as if on the breasts of a saint.

The perfumed partiality of Agueda's body in the church infected me with the absolute. Clenching my teeth, I told her I could not desire her and only desire her, that she should give me what she had even if it were on the threshold of the cemetery, "like perfume," I whispered in her ear, "and bread and poison and cauterization."

The statue of the Virgin in the church, dressed in mourning like Agueda, was also a somber triangle presiding over the lucid mist: Mexican Virgins have feminine sex and shape, and then Agueda, who felt me kissing her back and shoulders and nape but who felt me within as well as near her underskirts, raised her feet and offered them, sliding on the pew, to my insatiable curiosity.

I took off her shoes, I kissed her feet, and I remembered verses about feet that fascinated me enormously. It is not I who return but my enslaved feet, said Alfonso Reyes the exile among us. I love your feet because they walked on the earth until they found me, said Pablo Neruda the immortal lover. Luis Buñuel in enraged tenderness washed the feet of the poor and of some young Mexican ladies in the most exciting scene of Christian eroticism on a certain Good Friday. Now Agueda's feet seek my sex, which is opportunely free of its prison of shorts and zippers, and Agueda kisses me only with

her feet, Agueda makes me tremble and I imagine her in the role of
Veronica, granting me the gift of her patience while her now tranquil,
thaumaturgic eyes watch my pleasure: for you, Christopher my son,
not yet: that time it was for her and for me because unless the father
experiences pleasure the son never will.

She gave me water to drink from her cupped hands.

She was no longer there when I woke up in the morning when
the first of the faithful entered the church.

I searched for her in the market, in the plaza, in old Elpidia's
patio, in the churches through which I'd followed her that November
Sunday. I asked Doña Elpidia, the girl who sold me the crickets and
led me to San Cosme and San Damián. I even asked the parrot, who
only said: "He who eats a locust will never leave this place . . ."

I tried to answer him again with Quevedo, almost bringing myself
down to the damn parrot's level:

> Fowl of the wasteland, who, all alone,
> Leads a carefree life . . .

The parrot was never going to learn that poem, and I was never going
to find Agueda.

I realized it that night as I strolled around the plaza:

Now the Oaxaca girls did look at me, flirt with me. As if they
knew I was their own; that I belonged to them; that I shared a perfumed
and black secret with them. As if before they hadn't looked at me so
as to force me to look for Agueda.

And the parrot's verse? And the looks and notes and instructions
of Doña Elpidia? And the girl who sold locusts in the market? Wasn't
it perhaps a perfect and logical chain that had led me to Agueda in
the shadowy Church of San Cosme and San Damián? I stared intensely into the eyes of one of the girls in the plaza: she stopped,
proud and fearful, as if I had insulted her; she hid her face in her
hands and left the circle of love, accompanied by another girl, who
looked at me reproachfully.

Dried out, crazy, or dead: that's what I told them without speaking;
the only thing I thought as I looked at them.

They fled as if condemned by my words to the clean injury of
virginity: a resignation full of thorns.

The enchantment was broken.

5. Fatherland: Always Remain the Same, Faithful to Your Own Reflection

Renewed, happy, and retrograde, my heart spent many more weeks in Oaxaca. I let Oaxaca penetrate and possess me, just as I had wanted to penetrate and possess the vanished Agueda. Slowly but surely, I purged myself of the need to hurry. I wisely reconquered the softness of Agueda's back, sitting alone on a bench in an anonymous park. I won it all little by little, my boy: the willowy bodies of the girls, their sugar lips, their loving provincial modesty, my nostalgia for the feet of my beloved, the clear Sundays, the cruel sky and the red earth, the chronic sadness, the miraculous illusions, the wells and the windows, the dinners and the sheets, the prolonged funeral rites, the prophecy of the turtle . . .

I made everything mine. Even the source of Matamoros Moreno's prose: I recognized it, I shared it; we were brothers, doubles, barely separated by the lines on an open hand: courtesy and camp. Brothers, doubles, because López Velarde transformed the commonplaces of our small-town kitsch into poetry and mystery, and that's something Matamoros knew better than I.

In Oaxaca, I even acquired the insanely heroic habit of talking to myself.

I returned to Mexico City when I thought the danger of Matamoros and Colasa had succumbed to my prolonged absence, by which time they would have avidly sought new, more promising opinions, backing, and recommendations for Matamoros's efforts.

I returned by bus, alone, repeating, repeating to myself the verses of López Velarde's *Sweet Fatherland*

surface: maize
oil wells: devil
clay: silver
tolling bells: pennies
smell: bakery
fowl: language

breathing: incense
happiness: mirror
    I looked for Agueda and I did not find her
    I looked for the Sweet Fatherland and didn't find it
    Three months later, I found your mother.

I searched for a nation identical to itself. I searched for a nation built to last. My heart filled with an intimate, reactionary joy: as intimate as the joy felt by millions of Mexicans who wanted to conserve at least the borders of their poor country: conservatives. I said I learned to love true conservatives. Bishop Vasco de Quiroga, who constructed a utopia in Michoacán in 1535 so that the Indians could conserve their lives and traditions and not die of despair. Fray Bernardino de Sahagún, the Franciscan scribe who saved the memory of the Indian past. The Indian and Spanish builders whose structures were meant to last. Resistant stone, faithful countries: was only Mexico's past serious? asked my father Angel after his return from Oaxaca, his loss of Agueda, his meeting my mother. Does Mexico's future have to be like its present: a vast comedy of graft and mediocrity perpetrated in the name of Revolution and Progress? Thus, I want the Sweet Fatherland, my father Angel ordered us to say, ordered, that is, my mother, whom he had still not met, and me, still in the most perfect of limbos: a country identical to itself: hardworking, modest, productive, concerned in the first instance with feeding its people, a country opposed to gigantism and madness: I refuse to do anything, plant anything, say anything, erect anything that will not last five centuries, Christopher, my son, created to celebrate the five centuries: beloved Angeles.

This was his resolution, mulled over in the few instants of solitude he enjoyed in his coach-house merry-go-round over in Colonia Juárez. But putting the resolution into practice presented him with a mass of contradictions. He would understand these contradictions later in February when he met his friend the fat little guy, the projectionist and lyricist for rockaztec, who explained to him that the tragedy of his life and the source of his artistic inspiration was his father, a living (when he was alive) contradiction. When he married, his father was given a horrible gift, nothing less than a vast, hideous bronze sculpture, dominating and inexorable, that contained images of Father Hidalgo, Don Benito Juárez, and Pancho Villa, together raising the national flag (executed in tricolor silk) above the Basilica of Guadalupe, on whose portals (executed in polychromed wood) hung the tricolor shields of the PRI. This gift was sent to the fat guy's father, who was an engineer specializing in public works, by his principal client, the head man at the Secretariat of Public Works, and even though our buddy's dad detested the sculpture and huffed and puffed about it the whole day, and even though its presence in the entryway of the family house in Colonia Nápoles almost caused his divorce and was certainly the source of a conjugal irritation that lasted throughout his parents' life, our buddy would tell us all that his dad would never take it away from there: suppose the Director General of the Secretariat comes around and doesn't see his present? Suppose people think that in our house we don't respect the symbols of the nation? Our national heroes? The flag? The Virgin? I'll tell you what could happen: bye-bye contracts, bye-bye three squares per diem!

But this same man, his father, as our buddy again remembers, mocked authority all day. He said he would take nothing from no one, let's see someone try to give him an order, he was a serious professional, independent, an engineer, to be more precise: he'd like to see someone try: he refused to do his military service or to pay income tax (which, according to him, ended up in the Swiss accounts of government officials); he refused to join with the neighbors to create a neighborhood patrol; he refused to get on line for movies or bread (lines? me? I'd like to see the guy . . .); he never stopped for a red light; and he never ever (it redounds to his honor) paid off any cop or meter maid: he hated all uniforms, even those of street sweepers or ushers: he would urge them to be individuals, to dress as they pleased, they weren't nuts and bolts in a machine, they were individuals, damn it, INDIVIDUALS! not rags, not doormats; he never signed petitions of any kind, never bought a lottery ticket, never lent candles to the neighbors when the power went out, never depended on anyone so that no one would depend on him, never helped anyone, never asked for help; but he never got rid of that hideous sculpture down in the entryway: he would say, what if the boss comes?; then bye-bye three squares per diem; but more than that, he never dared to touch the symbols: his individualism became abjection in the face of those domineering symbols; just as he always refused to go to a political meeting or obey a traffic light, he refused to act against any abstract abuse by the powers that be, even an abuse that condemned him and his family to walk in front of that sculptural monstrosity every day of their lives: individualist to the end, but abject to the end as well: my poor old man, our pudgy little pal would sigh, anarchist and synarchist, and that's the way we are in these parts: rebels in our private lives and slaves in our civic lives.

This is the dilemma my father Angel expressly tried to avoid. It was easy to distinguish and decide, but very difficult to do things. No sooner would he act than he would fear falling into total disorder and ending up not in a bower of bliss but in the slough of despond. He denied that being conservative meant being an "hidalgo," because hidalgos only try to prove themselves in love and war and end up with no roof over their heads and no brains left, and what turns out to be the ultimate test of hidalgos is doing absolutely nothing. And what my young father began to fear was that if he didn't watch out, he too would disappear, chewed up by the jaws of Mexico and her Institutions: he tried to imagine himself in a trashy Iwo Jima, a mock Laocoön, which the father of his future pal Egg installed in the vestibule over in Colonia Nápoles. In any case, the Canaima Option, the grand Latin American solution, was best: remain immobile in a jungle landscape, with no more company than an araguato monkey and slowly but surely let the vines cover you up. The jungle swallowed him up!

Neither was he going to carry on like a creole aristocrat with old-fashioned expatriate nostalgia for Spain, because he knew that in Mexico there have traditionally been two ways of being Spanish: being the *gachupín* with the grocery store, the frugal Don Venancio who sleeps on the counter and keeps an exact inventory of how many cans of sardines have been sold every day, or being the anti-Don Venancio, the creole *gachupín* who, in order to get a taste of what it's like not to run a grocery store, keeps blissfully chaotic account books, goes into debt up to his sideburns, and in doing so puts the nation into debt: all to show he's no shopkeeper, but an hidalgo: not Don Venancio the Sober but the spendthrift conquistador, the Very Magnificent Don Nuño de Guzmán, to bankruptcy and collapse, full speed ahead. My father had read Emilio Prados, Luis Cernuda, and León Felipe, the Spaniards who were exiled by Franco and who came to live in Mexico in 1939. These were the real Spaniards: not Venancio or Nuño, neither a Spaniard returned with his pockets full of New World gold nor a conquistador. He never wanted a Creole Camelot.

How would he be? He romantically reinvented himself as a rebellious conservative, in the same way that he would be an assassin if he could get away with it: but he was much more concerned that no one dare judge him, banking on his dishonesty, as was normal in Mexico, but banking instead on his virtue. He believed that in order to achieve his goal he would always have to do not the "right" thing but whatever he wanted to do and that would be the "right" thing. He tossed a veil over his personal failing: sensuality.

"Now tell me, buddy, what finally happened with that statue or monstrosity or whatever it was?"

"Well, what happened was that one night some thieves broke into our house—because, of course, my father refused to join the neighborhood patrol. Dad and Mom went downstairs in their pajamas, and the thieves threatened them with a knife. I saw it all from the stairs."

"Who threatened them?"

"A great big guy wearing a mask. He seemed to be dragging a ball and chain and had what looked like a dwarf with him who was also wearing a mask. My mother saw her chance, Angelito, the heavens opened up to her. She ran to where the sculpture was so she could hand it over to the thief. But the truth is that she hugged the thing as if it were her dearest possession. At least that's how the crook saw it, 'cause he apparently couldn't stand for whatyacallit in psychology, a resistance, and right then and there he cut my mom's throat . . . Christ! shouts my old man, forgetting everything he'd ever said about the Director General over at Public Works, and then screams at the thief: 'Asshole! What she wanted was for you to take the thing! She wanted to get rid of . . . !' He never got a chance to finish. Who knows what the crook was thinking, because he cut my old man's throat, too. Then he took the damn statue, helped by the dwarf. He must've thought it was made of gold or had secret drawers stuffed with dollars, God knows . . ."

One February day, my father Angel attended a session of the Academy of the Language presided over by my Uncle Homero Fagoaga. He was dressed up like Francisco de Quevedo (it was the first time he wore the disguise in public). He listened politely to Don Homero's speech in honor of the newest member of the Academy, the gongorhythmic poet J. Mambo de Alba, listened to Mr. Mambo's sublime nonsense—he praised the crisis because it enclosed Mexico within itself and kept out foreign books, movies, art, and ideas. Now we were to scratch ourselves with our own nails! To read Proust is to proustitute oneself! To read Joyce is to make a poor choice! Reading Gide is doing a bad deed! Valéry is the valley of the shadow of evil! Mallarmé is marmalade! E. E. Cummings—well! He should be condomed! Let's hear it for Tlaquepaque, coffee with cinnamon, serapes from Saltillo, Michoacán pottery, let's head structuralism off at the pass, forget nouvelle cuisine and postpunkrock, let's be like Ramón López Velarde, who, nourishing himself exclusively on the Revolution, with no foreign readings or fashions, found the essence of the Sweet Fatherland. It was the reference to López Velarde that aroused my father Angel's rage. He'd always imagined his favorite poet wearing out his eyes looking for and finding and reading Baudelaire and Laforgue, while the colorless (but not odorless) poet and academician celebrated the dearth of imported books, the closing of the cultural borders, all so we could scratch ourselves with our own nails! Impetuously, Angel leapt up from his seat, went to the podium, and grabbed both his uncle and the poet by their noses. While he twisted one nose with each hand, he declared to the stupefied audience the things he'd just said here:

I SEEK A NATION IDENTICAL TO ITSELF
I SEEK A NATION MADE TO LAST
NOTHING THAT DOESN'T LAST FIVE CENTURIES
FATHERLAND, ALWAYS REMAIN THE SAME
FAITHFUL TO YOUR OWN REFLECTION:
LONG LIVE ALFONSO REYES! MEXICAN LITERATURE WILL BE GREAT
BECAUSE IT'S LITERATURE NOT BECAUSE IT'S MEXICAN!

and my father forced everyone there, beginning with the uncle and the poet, to breathe onto a mirror:

"I knew it. You're all dead. I will not bestow the conservative tradition on a gaggle of exquisite corpses."

He was very young. He mixed his metaphors. He was sincere. He didn't know if his anarchic whims, outlandish jokes, and premeditated disorder would give him the key to happiness: Sweet Fatherland!

6

In these annals of a wonderful life prior to my conception (which makes me wonder if I'll be lucky enough to find something amusing in my intrauterine life and—and even this I don't dare hope for—later on), my father returned in February 1991 from Oaxaca, transformed, even though he still didn't know it.

He went on leading his bachelor's life, protected by his Grandparents Rigoberto and Susana. He still hadn't found my mother and took up again with an old girlfriend named Brunilda, a great big sexy girl, lively and sentimental, with eyes like limpid pools and the mouth of a clown.

He was not faithful to her, nor she to him. And they both knew it. But he had never asked her to have a drink in the Royal Road Hotel bar along with one of his other girlfriends. She, on the other hand, enjoyed those collisions between rivals, allowing the two gallants to stare each other down like two polite basilisks while she chewed on the fringe of her ash-blond hair and observed them from the depths of her twin pools.

"So you think you're terribly liberated, eh?" she would say, making catty faces from time to time. "So you think you're terribly civilized, eh? A pair of little English gentlemen, is that it?"

Photos and letters from the rival accidentally left on Angel's bed.

Now they were all together in the VIPS in San Angel, the afternoon of Thursday, February 28, 1991, neutral territory where they could explain all these things. Angel yawned. He shouldn't have done it: life in Mexico City contains more surprises than any yawn imaginable deserves.

In the ecumenical and inexhaustible taxonomy of Mexican pests, Angel gave a high place to professional wives: these women feel it's their job to promote their husbands twenty-four hours a day, to see to it that they are invited to elegant dinners, to castigate verbally any misguided critics of their divine consorts, and to imagine cataclysmic snubs provoked by the envy of others. But above all, the professional wife feels authorized to cash checks, an activity without which anything else she did would be meaningless.

Among the members of this subspecies for whom Angel felt special revulsion was Luminosa Larios, wife of the millionaire magazine impresario Pedrarias Larios, and it was not without a tremor of fatal anticipation that he saw her sit down at two in the afternoon on that same day at one of the tables in the VIPS.

No sooner did Luminosa Larios lay eyes on my father Angel than she obliterated any imaginable possibility for the couple sitting there to air out their problems. Luminosa always acted as if there were two people in the world: she, the quasi-ecclesiastical representative of her Genial Husband, and the person privileged to hear her revelations. She now began to enumerate these glories, stretching her hand with its voracious green nails toward Angel's shoulder: her husband Pedrarias had just opened—simultaneously—twenty-four gas stations in the Nations of North America, *The New York Times* had published an article by Tom Wicker in which he compared Pedrarias with early Hearst or late Luce or murky Murdoch, she didn't remember quite the way it went now (she scratched the air with her green claws so that the gold charms on her bracelets would tinkle more musically). Pedrarias had a cameo in the new Pia Zadora film, Pedrarias was received by President Donald Danger, Pedrarias may have earned seven hundred million pesos last year, but he still has a social conscience, and emblazoned across the cover of his magazine *Lumière*: SOLIDARITY WITH THE SUBJUGATED PEOPLES OF THE FOURTH WORLD VICTIMS OF THE OIL IMPERIALISM OF THE THIRD WORLD.

"What a whirlwind! What publicity!" exclaimed Luminosa in satisfied tones. "But even my husband has his limits: even though they've asked him repeatedly, he would never do the ads for those Cuban heels made by Rising Star Shoes. I mean, really! Where do they get off, making up stuff like that? It came out in some two-bit paper published in Mexamerica that nobody reads; here's the article and some other interesting clippings. Next year my husband's book comes out, an exciting, stupendous confession entitled *Epic of a Paranoid Hick in Paris.* We deny completely that we've been evicted from seven different apartments for not paying the rent, the telephone bill, or for fixing the broken furniture. And it was our enemies who made up that lie about our using towels to wipe our asses. Nothing but lies!" shouted Luminosa, bright red and cross-eyed.

With growing excitement, the lady began to pass around catalogues, posters, press clippings, photocopies of checks, magazine covers on which she appeared wearing a bikini, as if the fame and merits of her husband depended now and forever on them. The printed matter flew over Brunilda's head, messing her hair and annoying her, as her cat-like eyes showed. Then the words settled in the tortilla soup the couple were eating. And amid this avalanche of luminous publicity, Luminosa took the opportunity to mention, as if in passing, this bit of news, which changed my father's life:

"Oh yes, Angelito, I just found out that your Uncle Don Homero has disinherited you or something like that."

My father Angel did not know what to take care of first: Tom Wicker's article floating in his tortilla soup, Brunilda's horribly fulminating and disappointed stare, or Doña Luminosa Larios's infinitely hypocritical smile, fixed on her face as she cocked her little head to one side as an invitation to middle-class approval. Her Gorgon eyes were bulging because no quantity of scalpels doing any quantity of plastic surgery could erase those crow's-feet that looked like quotation marks between which she eternally recited her husband's deeds. She dripped joy at the sight of someone suffering.

The lady resolved my father's dilemmas by sensually stretching her arm, wrapped in an atrocious blouse of violet crepe, and resting her sympathetic face on one of her wrists ablaze with jewels. "Don't forget to come over at the usual time, now," she said, withdrawing her hand just before Angel could touch it, and then proceeding to play peekaboo with her napkin.

Brunilda gave my father a look of double warning that he could read easily because she said everything with looks: "You're not only ruined financially, but you publicly two-time me with this parrot who seems to have escaped from the Rocky Horror Picture Show."

Angel got up with his bowl of soup in his hands and emptied all of it—checks, clippings, and catalogues—over Doña Luminosa Larios's head. Brunilda got up impetuously, her mouth wide open.

"It's a frame-up! This lady is making up a romance!"

"Don't you dare follow me," she said to Angel. "I've got lots of options. This one just died."

For two weeks he didn't see her. Of course, he was not deprived of female companionship, since there were lots of girls eager for pleasure, especially the pleasure of escaping from the plague of their families.

"I'll tell you what's goin' on with this 'flation," one of these bonbons summarized. "There's no jobs and no megabucks,' so we all gotta stay home, Angel baby, the power elite is takin' it out on us women, man, ya'oughtta see, they've got us back in their Tyrone Power."

"Who's got the power?" asked my dad at the door, as always inventing useless passwords to protect his chaste and pure dwelling, knowing full well that pirating music and videotapes was the hottest business in town, especially because the city lacked both entertainment and contact with the outside world. Seeing old movies on videocassettes was the supreme form of entertainment in the Mexico of the nineties.

"Who's got the power?"

"Mischa Auer," answered a cinephilic teenybopper's voice. There was nothing left to do but open the door and fall into the Felliniesque arms of María de Lourdes, María Cristina, Rosa María, María Concepción, Maricarmen, or María Engracia."

"Who's got the air?"

"Fred Astaire, baby."

"Who's got the marbles?"

"Greta Garbles."

"Who set the table?"

"Esther Fernández."

He didn't open the door.

Brunilda didn't know this new set of passwords, so she never got Behind the Green Door to Deep Trope. She telephoned, but the mythomaniacal yet astute Grandmother Susana happily sent Angel on a hypothetical one-way trip to Chile. Next came letters, some love letters, some despair letters, but all unanswered letters. Brunilda was torn apart by the anxieties of sex and vanity, emotions both linked and compulsive, to say nothing of her horrible suspicion about a future devoid of inheritance.

Because one fine morning Grandfather Rigoberto Palomar appeared in my father Angel's coach house with a ream of documents, turned a blind eye to the naked piece of ass who squealed as she went to get dressed (later she complained to Angel that Grandpa had caressed her ass), and confirmed to him that Uncle Homero Fagoaga, as the documents stated it, had brought suit against his nephew Angel Palomar y Fagoaga, accusing him of being a spendthrift, irresponsible, and incapable of administering the estate of forty million gold pesos which, according to the last will and testament of his deceased

parents, he was to have inherited on his twenty-second birthday—
the new age for adulthood, according to the law, which Angel would
reach on July 14, 1991.

Angel understood the shrug and the challenging expression on his
grandfather's face: one meant fatalism, the other meant freedom, a
mixture appropriate to an old man as wise as this one, who was always
saying to his grandson that even though he could help him—although
now there was little he could do, true enough—Angel ought to use
his imagination and his own resources.

"But you know so much, Grandfather."

"No matter how much I know, I am not your age and I can't sniff
out everything you can. Your intuition is definitely better than my
knowledge."

Freedom is everything, everything, Angelillo, said the old man,
handing him the documents. Even fatalism, he said, is a way of
being free. Sometimes our will is not enough, see? if we don't know
that things can go wrong for no good reason. Then we aren't free.
We're deluded. You can count on my support, but manage your
affairs freely, with imagination, and without fear, Angelillo.

Angel had been going out with Brunilda for quite a while and
preferred ending a relationship which had no more to it than a
pleasure which, if solid, was always the same. The additives Brunilda
used to try to diversify normal sexuality—unilateral jealousy, inop-
portune encounters with other occasional lovers, letters from one
boyfriend left for no good reason in the bed of another—wore Angel
out: a romantic relationship was nothing if it wasn't a means whereby
one man could be set aside from all the rest. Brunilda imbued all
her relationships with analogies in order to avoid the harmony of
tedium; her diversions frustrated Angel's romantic intentions.

Three weeks after the break with Brunilda, my father, on a whim,
decided to go out on the town in disguise. He put on a toga and a
Quevedesque mustache and walked unnoticed by anyone from Calle
Génova to Río Mississippi, where traffic was heavier. There a boy
of unusual whiteness (accentuated by his shiny pitch-black hair) was
putting on a spectacular performance of bullfighting with cars and
trucks; his agility momentarily disguised his thick, soft body and the
fact that he resembled nothing so much as a pear.

Angel, for his part, watched with openmouthed admiration as the
boy executed a twirl around a bloody-minded taxi, a left feint in front
of an irate heavy truck driven by an albino in black glasses, a rapid-

fire series of veronicas in the face of a ferocious squad of motorcyclists. But when the fat young man posed on his knees in the path of a Shogun limousine without license plates but with darkened windows—which accelerated down the wide street as soon as it saw the boy on his knees—Angel leapt to rescue the erstwhile torero and dragged him to safety.

"You nuts, man?" asked Angel.

"What about you, goin' around dressed like the Masked Avenger!?" panted the pudgy lad.

"If it bothers you, I'll take it off."

"Who said you should take off?"

"No, not me, it. My disguise, I'll take it off."

My father pulled the cape off his shoulders and the huge glasses off his nose.

"Actually, I did all that to get your attention," panted the fatty. "Brunilda told me to tell you that if you don't call her this afternoon, tonight she'll kill herself. Swear to God."

They walked along Paseo de la Reforma to the flower market at the entrance to Chapultepec Park. Fatso explained that he was a composer; perhaps Angel knew his last hit, "Come Back, Captain Blood"?; well, he wrote that number along with the new group he was putting together, because the group he'd belonged to before, Immanuel Can't, did not respect the individual personality of its artists, required everything to be group experience, collective expression; that was their categorical imperative, laughed the overweight conversationalist as he raised the dust on the Reforma sidewalks with his big feet. He was not in agreement, he said, with that philosophy, which was too sixties; he wanted to be conservative, romantic postpunk conservative, and his motto was REWARD YOURSELF!

"Reward yourself, that's what I say. You never know what tomorrow may bring."

They reached the flower market. As Angel placed an order, Fatty recited a few stanzas of his rockaztec hit:

> Wontcha come back, Captain Blood?
> You're a great big iron stud,
> And we all need what you've got
> Adventure, honor: HOT!
> You gave it to our dads:
> Now what about the lads?

They liked each other and agreed to meet the next day for coffee. Fatty then told him that the funeral wreaths had begun to arrive at Brunilda's apartment in Polanco at four in the afternoon, one after another, purple and white, violets and tuberoses, some shaped like horseshoes, others plain wreaths, still others artistic diaphragms; suffocating, perfumed, permutated, indefatigable dead man's flowers to celebrate her announced suicide, truckloads of flowers that invaded the apartment of the girl with immense eyes and clown mouth: she wept. She tore apart her sky-blue satin robe, she threw herself on the bed, she tried to keep any more wreaths from entering the house, she dramatically fainted off the bed and onto the floor, revealing one exuberant breast, all of which only convinced the messengers they should bring her more flowers than those Angel had ordered, so they tossed a whole cartload of flowers on her, only looking for a glimpse of that trembling antenna of Brunilda's pleasures.

"When I left her, she was crying with rage. She said she'd get even by marrying your rival tomorrow. They'll be on their honeymoon starting tomorrow night in the Hotel Party Palace and they'll drink to your death."

Now my dad Angel ordered a piñata delivered the next night to the bridal suite at the Party Palace. He added a note addressed to Brunilda's brand-new husband: "At least you'll have one thing to break, asshole."

Along with the fat boy, Angel set about making the preparations for the coming-of-age party his grandparents had insisted on throwing for him in the very room where his deceased parents had been married, the traditional Clair-de-Lune Salon on Avenida Insurgentes, where thousands and thousands of sweet-sixteen-party piñatas had done service ever since the forties. The grandparents say that aside from the sentimental value of the place, Uncle Homero will be looking for evidence of Angel's spendthrift ways (for example: his recent flower purchases at Chapultepec, his numerous girlfriends, his dinners in posh restaurants, his cassette business, or the rumors of his shacking up, according to Aunts Capitolina and Farnesia, in boardinghouses, and, Holy Mother! even in Oaxaca churches after hours), but the whole idea of celebrating his coming-of-age in the Clair-de-Lune is such a cheap idea, so I-wish-I-could-afford-better that it will give you a humble air, Grandson. No, you can't hold it here in the house because anything private has to be exclusive, luxurious, and criminal.

7

 Angel and his new buddy the fat boy (whose original name no one remembered or chose to remember) spent a nervous week preparing the July 14 party. Angel convinced him not to rejoin the snobs in the Immanuel Can't group while at the same time admonishing him not to fall into the horrible vulgarity of those plebes the Babosos Boys. Instead, the two of them should use their imagination to create a new group that would synthesize those two extremes. Fatty said no problem, that he knew a fabulous guitarist/singer, a protégé of the eminent polymath Don Fernando Benítez, a guy named Orphan Huerta. In his urban rambles, he'd also come upon a grotesque named Hipi Toltec, who walked the broad avenues of the city, his long, greasy locks hanging down, his face thin and long-nosed, like a plumed coyote, wearing rags and a luxurious snakeskin belt that announced in French: "La serpent-à-plumes, c'est moi."

"He thinks he's always right in the middle of the conquest of Mexico, that he's come back and that no one recognizes him; he's a harmless nut, until he screws up the signifiers."

"Well then, fat boy, we've got to keep his signifiers straight for him."

"It's worth the trouble. He's the best drummer around. But you've got to convince him the drums are tom-toms. He sort of disintegrates as he plays. He drives the girls crazy."

"What do you do, pudgy?"

He played the piano, the maracas, and the piccolo, and—he blushed—he had to include in the group a ten-year-old girl who played the flute, any problem with that?

"It's your band," said my dad Angel with a no-problem wave, imagining the girl in that privileged age, between three and thirteen.

"We're all set, then," said Fatty. "The four of us are friends and we even have a name, the Four Fuckups. All we needed was someone to get us moving, to provide moral support. Thanks, Angel."

"You're welcome. If you like, I could even be your business manager."

On the afternoon of the birthday party, the fat boy arrived first at the Clair-de-Lune, so he could set things up, arrange the tables, put flowers in vases, clear a space for the musicians, and check out the marvelous metal egg put there by the constantly recharged imagination of the salon's directors as a spectacular device for introducing the guest of honor: they raised the egg to the ceiling, which was decked out with Styrofoam stars and half-moons, and then, once all the guests were present, lowered the egg with a trumpet fanfare to announce the arrival of the new citizen, the sweet-sixteener, or the daring society debutante.

Fatty's intention was to make sure things would go well and that my father Angel would be comfortable during the hour or so he'd have to spend in the ovoid prison where he'd wait for all the guests until the moment—11 p.m.—when the signal would be given, the egg would descend, and my dad would pop out of it in the bloom of health.

My dad's pal was deeply involved in poking a needle through the ventilation holes to make sure nothing was blocking them (not an easy task in the half light of afternoon) when suddenly two hands, not powerful but having the advantage of surprise, pushed him into the improvised sarcophagus, locked him in, and sent him up to the ceiling. It didn't take Fatty long to understand his situation: no one would get him out of there before eleven. But even that hope faded when through the ventilation holes he heard a pomaded voice say:

"Do not concern yourselves with this ovoid artifact, workers of the manual sort. My nephew has decided not to use such a worn-out symbol. I have convinced him to abandon this ceremony in exchange for a tasty and much to be preferred gift of a million pesos. To you, for acceding to my desires and withdrawing from this locale tonight, I grant a similar sum. Besides, as the Admiral of the Ocean Sea might have said to his mutinous crew: Why should I worry about one ovoid ball, when I need two?"

Then, when the workers left, dividing up those devalued pesos, the same voice shouted to Fatty, locked within the metal egg: "May you rot in there, you irresponsible spendthrift! A Fagoaga never loses, and what he does lose, he snatches back!"

This was followed by the kind of laugh a mad monk makes in his catacomb. Afterwards, hours and hours of silence in which Angel's chum, feeling rather like one of Dickens's poor heroes taking the place of his friend at the guillotine, decided to while away his time writing a novel in his head. He said to himself that the principal problem in such a project is knowing how to begin, so, since he'd thought of Dickens first, he began his mental novel with the words "It was the best of times, it was the worst of times, it was the season of Light, it was the season of Darkness, it was the spring of hope, it was the winter of despair, it was the age of wisdom, it was the age of foolishness . . ." But he shook his head. He felt something was superfluous there and tossed those pages written in the ovoid darkness into the trash heap of his mind before taking up his imaginary pen and making a fresh start. "For a long time I used to go to bed late. Sometimes, my candle still burning, my eyes so firmly open that I had no time, not even for counting burros and cursing my insomnia . . ." No, no. He began again: "In a place in La Mancha which I remember perfectly, and which is located barely twelve miles to the east of Ciudad Real, in the foothills of the Valdeña Mountains and right on the bank of the Jubalón River . . ."

No, that wasn't right either. He tried another beginning: "All unfortunate families resemble each other; happy families are such each in its own manner." Bah! He thought about the stupid death of his own family or that of his buddy Angel Palomar and wondered if with that story he could at least start a novel. But he left it for another day, because the hours were going by and he was in total darkness. Happy families: "When his father brought him to see ice, Aureliano Buendía thought that one day he would be shot." Unhappy families: "When he woke up that morning after a restless night, the insect found he'd been transformed into Franz Kafka."

In the darkness, he saw in his mind a black whiplash and thought that in reality it was the dark ghost of a perfect spermatozoon like the one that might give life to his own son or that of his friend Angel Palomar, or those of his buddies the Orphan Huerta, Hipi Toltec, and the Baby Ba, and directly below the Reader would be able to wonder, wherever he might be reading a book apocryphally entitled

Christopher Unborn
by
CARLOS FUENTES

years after the events narrated there took place, that is, as it always happens, the most rejected books end up being the most accepted books (mentally wrote the pudgy rock-and-roller), the most obscure books become the clearest, the most rebellious become the most docile, and that's the way it goes, Reader. The most likely thing is that You are a poor adolescent girl in the Sacred Heart Secondary School busily copying down in your crabbed hand some classic passage from this novel which you have stuck between your missal and a joint and that perhaps you have opened to the page where in this instant you find Yourself and I find Myself and deprived of any other guide you begin to write My Novel as if it were Your Novel, copying not the one you are reading here, that is, a new novel that begins with these words:

Prologue: I Am Created

I am a person no one knows. In other words: I have just been created. She doesn't know it. Neither does he. They still haven't named me. No one knows my face. What will my sex be? I am a new being surrounded by a hundred million spermatozoa like this one:

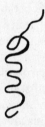

imagination engendered me first, first language: it created the black, chromosomic, heraldic snake of ink and words that conceives everything, unique delectable repetition, unique riveting that never fatigues: I've known it for centuries, it's always the same and always new, the serpent of spiral sperm, the commodius vicus of history, narrow gate of vicogenesis, vicarious civilization that God envies us: phallus and semen, conduct and product, my parents and I, serpent and egg

rather a novel in which the possibilities of all the participants are comparable: the possibilities of the Author (who obviously has already finished the novel the Reader has in his hands) and those of the Reader (who obviously still doesn't know the totality of this novel, barely its first months), as well as those of the Author-Reader, that is You when you finish reading the novel, possessor of a knowledge the potential Reader as yet does not have, the Reader who may one day read the novel or perhaps never read it, or who may know of it and intend to read it—just to distinguish the potential Reader from the kind who know it exists but who refuse to read it because they disdain the Author, are bored by him, and turn down his invitation to a ludic read, and also to distinguish the potential Reader from those completely ignorant of the existence of this book and who will never have this knowledge, those, possibly, who are already dead or as yet unborn, those who, should they be born, will never find out about, or find out about but not want to, or want to but be unable to read it; or, simply, the sinister novel, its earthly function accomplished, may forever be out of print, out of circulation or excluded from libraries because of its obscenity, its offenses against reigning good taste, or because of its political impossibility: in any case, Fatty, big feet and all, hanging in his unwanted aviary, consoles himself, the limit to what a person can read is not the same as the limit to what that person can say, nor is the limitation of what is sayable a limit to the doable: this last possibility is the possibility of literature, our pudgy friend smiled without witnesses, his superiority over the accidents and contingencies of life or over the strict propositions, so demanding of being tested, of science and philosophy: infinite possibility, common possibility of the Reader and the Reader, common possibility of Life and Death, Past and Present, of a Man and his unborn Son: to recognize themselves in the same book, symbolized by a spurt of black sperm, a spark of sinuous ink: life and opinions, peau de chagrin that consume themselves in desire and thus articulate the certainty that we all have to die our lives and live our deaths.

Thanks to this symbol our big-footed, shiny-maned Fatty could imagine everything, a son for his new friend Angel Palomar, the child's mother a beautiful, slender, dark girl who walks through a park, hidden sometimes by a tree, at other times by a balloon, come closer in the flutter of her skirts and the rhythm of her waist: a girl with . . . with a halo!: Angel and Angeles, parents of a child yet to be born, what shall we name the child? what language will the child speak in Makesicko Dee Eff, what air will the child breathe here where the air is queer? will the child find his little chromosomatic brothers and with them reconstruct their X's and Z's, probing to the very root of their chain of genetic information? well, wrote Pudgy, in the same way, a novel seeks out its novels, the ascent and descent of its spermatozoon of black ink: like the child, the novel is no orphan, it did not spring from nothingness, it needs a tradition just as the child needs a family tree: no one exists without something, there is no creation without tradition, no descendence without ascendence. CHRISTOPHER UNBORN philadelphically seeks its novelistic brothers and sisters: it extends its paper arms to convoke and receive them, just as the recently conceived child misses its lost brothers and sisters (he even misses the girl he might have been, which I give him straightaway: the girl named Baby Ba) and convokes them all blindly with a movement of his hands. This is his genealogy:

THE SONS OF LA MANCHA	VERSUS	THE SONS OF WATERLOO
Christopher (modest)		Bonaparte
son of		*father of*
Jacques (fatalist)		Sorel
son of		*father of*
Tristram (shandy of shandy hall)		Becky Sharp
son of		*mother of*
Alonso (quijada or quezada)		Rastignac
father of		*father of*
Tristram (digressive)		Rubempré
father of		*father of*
Jacques (toujours de questions!)		Raskolnikov
grandparents of		*uncle of*
Catherine Moorland		Nietzsche
		nephew of
		Louis Lambert
		brother of
		Raphael de Valentín
		stepchildren of
		Niccolò Machiavelli

Emma Bovary:
fillies who read follies
Pickwick
Myshkin:
men good as gold, caviar, beer
  cousins of
Nikolai Gogol (from the Slavic branch
  of the family)

Charles Dickens (from the Anglo-Saxon
    branch of the family)
Franz Kafka and
Milan Kundera (from the Central European
    branch of the family)
    great-grandsons of
Erasmus (of Rotterdam) : praiser of follies
    father of
Alonso (Quijano)   : reader of follies
    grandpa of
Nazarín   : do-gooder priest
Oliveira   : doubly exiles from La Mancha
                                             La Plata
                                             La Seine
        and Pierre Menard: *author of*
                Don Quijote
                The Praise of Reading
                The Madness of Reading

Erasmus: Appearances are deceptive
Don Quijote: Windmills are giants
Tristram Shandy: Digressions are the sunshine of reading
Jacques Le Fataliste: Let's talk about something else
Christopher Unborn: Okay, while the captive fat boy decided without
thinking to triumph over boredom by means of these concerns, re-
warding himself despite the situation, but resigned to writing an overly
pessimistic novel whose only repetitive element would be "It was the
worst of times. It was the worst of times. It was the worst of," the
salon was filling up with waiters, bartenders, guests, the guest of
honor—my father because he was Angel Palomar y Fagoaga happily
twenty-one years of age, and his grandparents (my greats in that
case) Don Rigoberto Palomar and Doña Susana Rentería, the members of the new band, still incomplete but which, nevertheless
(the prisoner in the iron egg felt almost as a posthumous homage),
played and sang the hit song he'd composed: "Come Back, Captain
Blood"

From the masthead you wave to us
Sailing toward the sunset

Fatso listened, half suffocated, already with a taste in his mouth that said: Baby, you're turning blue: half crazy inside the metal egg, now smelling himself, now smelling the exudates from the silver-plated copper: on the verge of shouting Help! Au Secours? Help! Aiuto! I Need Somebody! but, in the first place, no one would have heard him with all the noise of the party and, second, he was no crybaby; he was a tough little man who neither gave nor accepted explanations, just like his hero from the pirate movies:

> Bye-bye, Captain Blood,
> I'll never see you again . . .

He closed his eyes, making his last effort at a first line for a novel: "Call me Christopher." Then, as if he had spoken a magic word (down sesame!), he heard the creak of the pulleys, the movement of the cables, and the abrupt descent of the egg from the star-studded ceiling of the Clair-de-Lunatic to its dance floor.

Trumpets sounded and the band played the march from Aida. People laughed, their voices grew louder, they exclaimed. Angel laughed and said it was a mistake, what's going on? he was already there, he laughed nervously, what is all this? he was already at the party and was certainly not going to pop out of any egg, he feared the unforeseen, a fantastic surprise: a girl was going to step out of the egg! A woman he didn't know but loved, whom he had wanted to introduce to family and friends, as a surprise, as if the girl were his gift to them and they would introduce her to him, not knowing that he already knew her! not knowing that the two of them (he and she) had met in a park but had promised to get to know each other little by little, between April and August, one meeting per month, first the voice, then contact between their (respective) feet (May), then their fingertips only (June), they would clasp each other's hands (yummy-yummy) (July), and only in August, as the grand prize, would they finally see each other's face.

The lights went on in his head: Don Fernando Benítez!

And there he was on the other side of the hall, arm in arm with his wife, the two of them drinking his health.

Benítez had a gift for bringing young people together, for protecting them, taking them under his wing. Had he put a girl inside this egg for him, for Angel? Was this his supreme gift for coming of age? A dream! The idea shocked him because of its excessive pleasure and he wanted to stop the whole thing, but the workers said no way, it's in our contract that we lower the egg at eleven o'clock, without finding out about anything else and a bit drunk from the beers they'd bought with Uncle Homero's bribe, and Grandfather Rigo: get on with it, boys, do your job, let them, Angelillo, don't get into trouble with a union on top of the problems you already have with Uncle Homero's lawsuit, and the workers, in low voices: fat old asshole! today we get paid twice, whaddaya think: hatred blinds you, no doubt about it!

When they opened the doors of the ovoid sarcophagus, they found the nice boy with no air, blue in the face, disoriented and totally bald. His quondam black and shiny hair had all fallen out.

The fat boy was pulled out of the egg and brought back to consciousness by Angel, the Orphan Huerta, and Hipi Toltec, who put a hand mirror in front of Pudgy's face to see if he was still breathing. Then he put his coyote-like muzzle to the pink lips of the fat boy to resuscitate him, breathing like an animal, like a bellows. The boy came out of his faint and saw his bald reflection.

"Call me Egg," he managed to gasp.

"Our dear buddy, the Egg," said my father Angel, publicly baptizing him.

"Where is Baby Ba?" Egg asked as he came out of his stupor, and he didn't know if with that question he should begin another novel: "Would I find the Baby . . . ?"

After the guests departed, Don Rigoberto and Doña Susana listened to each one of the boys—their grandson, Angel, the recently baptized Egg, and the new friends of the rockaztec band, the Orphan Huerta and Hipi Toltec—give the hitherto unknown reasons that united them in their hatred for Homero Fagoaga.

They were highly amused to learn that each faction on its own, the Four Fuckups and Angel with Uncle Fernando as a providential intermediary, had already perpetrated myriad parallel tricks on the pesky, pernicious, and pestiferous (each group had its adjective) Don Homero Fagoaga: now they would join forces and nothing would stop them!

Fat, disgusting, *an'* a motherfucker, said Orphan Huerta, smiling, remembering and reaffirming at the same time.

The stolen communal lands in Acapulco, said Hipi Toltec truculently. Les terres communales dépouillés à Acapulco.

My parents' legacy, said Angel, while secretly repeating to himself: why Mexico City and not Acapulco, when the epicenter was on the coast? His eyes grew misty as he remembered that terrible and heroic day when he was sixteen: the earthquake of September 19. I wanted to shout from the unborn center of my pregnant mother: and what about the children of Acapulco? Would it have mattered to you that they died if you could have saved those who died in D.F.? This certainly says a lot about my father's moral sense, but for the moment I can't argue the matter with him face to face. I'm dying of rage! I'm getting carried away! How impatient I can get to be born, damn!

It isn't a person, it's a symbol, said Egg: Acapulco.

Therefore, the revolutionary grandfather Rigo Palomar concluded with perfect logic, what you should do is destroy Homero by destroying Acapulco. Perfect syllogism.

No, exclaimed Angel. Not Homero. Not Acapulco. The Sweet Fatherland.

That expression was going to hang over my father Angel like a dream he could half remember when awake, but in the meantime, things started happening very quickly: in August, my father saw my mother's face, and only when he'd seen it did he have the desire to put into effect his symbolic plan for the destruction of Acapulco which in reality turned out to be the splendid fancy of saving the Sweet Fatherland, the Good Fatherland: but this took, know it your mercies benz, something like half a year, during which time our buddy Egg wondered why he had given that purely symbolic reason, "Acapulco," instead of revealing that it was none other than Don Homero Fagoaga who had pushed him into the birthday egg. Who else could it have been? But he didn't tell on the uncle, nor did the others ask him: How did you get inside that egg, Egg? It had to have been that malignant Uncle Homero who . . . This was a mystery, and on nights of moral ecstasy Egg asked himself, Why did Jesus allow himself to be crucified knowing beforehand what was going to happen and above all having singled out Judas at the Last Supper (Would I find the Baby Ba . . . ?)? He also knew that one day, once things got moving, he would not be able to resist the temptation. He would expose Uncle Homero. Egg was not Jesus, nor did he wish to be. Besides, Acapulco was calling for them.

8

 But before we get to the New Year's party, won't you tell me how you and Daddy met, Mom?

"What a stickler for details you are! It was during April. Come on now, it's nothing to bite your nails about."

"I don't bite much of anything, Mom."

"Right. Okay, but if I tell you what you want to know now, I can only tell you as if we had met in December."

"Just the facts, ma'am."

"Okay, I met him by whispering into the ear of the statue of Benito Juárez in the Alameda Hemicycle. We climbed all the way up. No, I don't know what Angel said to the Great Hero, but what he told me—he speaking into one of Juárez's ears while I listened at the other—was: 'Listen, baby, if we manage to hear each other through the marble ears of the Great Zapotec, we'll really have made it.' "

I think I mumbled back something like, "Let's never hurt each other. We're all here together."

A fat child wearing a summer hat and holding a helium balloon came toward us out of the Alameda Park, holding the hand of a woman who looked like a skeleton dressed in a ball gown from the beginning of the century. The child, who resembled a wise, contented frog, stared up at us as we clung to Juárez's head, and then went off, still clutching Death by the hand. Actually, I don't know if we saw that or if Angel told me about it later. The next month we came back to the same place on the same day of the week even though we had not laid eyes on each other. Something else: we came back without having seen each other the first time, as if from the first moment we had promised not to look at each other until later; we spoke through the heroic marble of the Indian of Guelatao—let's not ask for more than is given us.

Q. What is a miracle?

A. Something that takes place very rarely.

Because, by the time the day came when he let himself be seen by me, we'd already spoken through the ears of Benito Juárez and gone on doing it for more than four months, meeting again and again without fixing a time or day, without even saying "See you here next month, baby"; of course, it happened that one would get there before the other, but we'd wait: how could I not wait when I didn't sleep a wink the night after I met him because I was so happy? And that was without seeing him!

My father Angel, is he a poet?

He would be if he were ugly. The day he finally let me see him he turned up disguised as Quevedo, his glasses as curlicued as his mustachios and goatee, wearing a ruff, and limping. But he forgot one thing: he didn't change his voice: "My voice was not that of the poet Quevedo, who died in September of 1645 in Villanueva de los Infantes because he couldn't stand the idea of one more winter sitting next to the fireplace where each chill convinced him that he was only living to see himself dead. Quevedo died from the cold and the humidity that came from the river that flowed directly behind his bed, denounced to the Inquisition, a courtier who remained independent, humorous and funereal, imperialist and libertarian, medievalizing and progressive, moralist and cynic—like Love "who is in all things contrary to itself." That's the disguise your father turned up in the first time he let me see him.

As contradictory as our famous Uncle Homero?

Yes, but able to use language like a great poet. I think your father did that intentionally. It was his first attempt to overwhelm Uncle Homero and his world, and the way he did it was by refusing to concede Homero a monopoly on language, by using Quevedo—no less—to taunt Homero, Quevedo, who was just as opportunistic as Homero but who was saved by his poetic genius. Of course, your father's voice was not Quevedo's.

No, it was the voice of the world remembering Quevedo, and Quevedo remembering himself, immortalized and self-immortalizing a hundred, two hundred, a thousand years after his death. It was Ramón Gómez de la Serna calling him *the great Spaniard, the most absolutely Spanish Spaniard, the immortal bestower of tone—he who gave tone to the soul of our race*, it was César Vallejo calling him *Quevedo, that instantaneous grandfather of all dynamiters*, and it was Quevedo himself requesting a place in an academy of laughter and disorder, and calling himself *the child of his works and stepfather of other people's works, as short of sight as he was of luck, given to the devil, on loan to the world, and recommended to the flesh: with slit eyes and a slit conscience, black hair and black luck, long in the forehead and rather long-winded as well!*: the portrait of the poet Quevedo was identical to that of my father Angel disguised as Quevedo, when he finally revealed himself to my mother, but my father already had an answer, a suggestion, before she could say a word:

I looked at him for the first time, and he looked at me.

"You've got a halo, baby," he said, touching my cheek.

"No, I never had a halo before."

"I think you were born that way but that you never really saw yourself."

"Maybe no one ever saw me that way before."

Then a guy carrying a glass tower on his back bumped into us; then two playful kids came along. I didn't know if his disguise was in fact Quevedo's ghost. In the ugly bustle of Mexico City, who would know about such things. And yet they exist. Even though you've got to be a poet to know about them. Know about them? To *see* them even, because, as everybody knows, that's the beautiful thing about your father, Christopher. So of course I didn't sleep all that night, out of pure happiness. The devil took me away from Plato. Or maybe he put me more deeply into Plato. "We say it was or it is or it shall be, when in truth all we can say about things is that they are."

The first thing I thought when I saw Angel disguised: he's Quevedo, if Quevedo had been handsome. Then I said to myself: Quevedo is handsome.

His name is Angel Palomar y Fagoaga, he lives with his grand-parents, but now he has met me, and I am a woman who can't sleep because she's so happy she met him. But that night we went to the Café de Tacuba to eat *pambazos* and *chalupas*, as if we wanted to sink our roots deep in the earth because we were both flying like kites we were so excited at having seen our faces, saying to ourselves in secret: *This is how he looks; this is how she looks; this is he; this is she.*

We left the café and in the freshly poured cement in front of the old Chamber of Deputies on Donceles Street, next to the house where the ancient widow of General Llorente and her niece Aura lived such a long time ago, we wrote out these words with our fingers. At the time, I had no idea they were your father's answer to the

Fagoaga coat of arms, how the Fagoagas attack Goths and Moors, how Fagoagas never lose. Quevedo hovers over us. He's our poet.

> It is burning ice, frozen fire,
> a wound that pains but is not felt,
> a dream of good, an evil right at hand,
> a brief but tiring rest
> . . . . .
> an imprisoned freedom

Then we heard the shouting, the whistles, the ratatatat, and the bombs, the boots running over the oldest cobblestones in Mexico, along that street now called Virgin Knights to the infinite confusion of Uncle H., who never did for the Castilian tongue what my Angel and I did to celebrate our meeting, leaving the signature of our love which cannot go beyond imprisoned freedom, and why bother deluding ourselves: we ran far away from the noise of the police, who could have been chasing us for having written a poem in the wet cement on Donceles, or perhaps they were chasing someone else for some other reason, but if they'd found us they would have grabbed us along with the rest (the rest? who are *the rest* in the Mexico of '92?), spreading their persecution without asking questions.

The supreme law was once again Shoot first, ask questions later.

How could I forget the first thing Angeles told me over our Benito Juárez telephone circuit?

"Let's never hurt each other. We're all here together."

"We're invincible, baby."

"I couldn't say anything more spontaneous or truthful. I could only tell you because I don't intend to be hurt by you. The others don't matter to me."

We ran fleeing from a threat that was all too real and yet absent at the same time, the worst kind, the threat that can both be and not be, strike or not strike, ask questions or not: we certainly did not have to be born, she and I, in the sixties to know that in Mexico the law remains, nunc et semper, the whim of whoever happens to be holding power. We ran to Fat St. Mary, far from the solitude of Virgin Knights, where we were saved by homeless squatters, by kids asleep on top of the hot grilles covering the subway vents next to the brotherly pelts of dogs with bloody noses. So, who told you, Ixcuintli, to go around sniffing the pavement? Around here the stones burn, but you and I, Angeles, left a sonnet by Quevedo written on the hot palm of the cement, and repression, immutable, stopped at the frontier of darkness and silence.

"Tell me, what language will the child speak?

9

Things didn't just happen all by themselves: they met several times, they talked about why they were going to do what they were going to do, was it was only to try to fuck up Uncle Homero, who had sued Angel, confiscated his house and fortune, and had in all likelihood tried to suffocate Egg in his namesake in a botched attempt to suffocate his nephew? My mother Angeles asked all this when she met the group in order to find out what she was getting herself into. Then she added: "Would you be doing this if you didn't know Uncle Homero, if you didn't hate him?" Yes! And that was Angeles's first impression of the Four Fuckups:

She thought Hipi Toltec was disturbed, his eyes weepy because he had so much trouble falling asleep, which he did by counting Aztec gods instead of sheep, and because he lived within himself and his historical confusion: "La serpent-à-plumes, c'est moi," but he had a strange notion of justice, clear and swift. At first she feared him, but eventually felt a tenderness for his mystery. She saw the Orphan Huerta pass from an unfocused resentment to a sensual enjoyment of the things that success brought when the Four Fs got famous for their renditions of Egg's ballads. The first thing she heard him say was: "I don't remember anything. I never knew my father or my mother." The second thing she heard him say was: "We've only seen milk and meat in newspaper photos." But after the success of "Come Back, Captain Blood," the single was later reissued with the songs in the album *Take Control* and another single "That Was the Year," and Orphan Huerta began to buy himself (wholesale) china-doll shoes, Guess jackets, and Fiorucci sweaters, calling them *my* china dolls, *my* Guess jackets . . . Angeles noted that Egg was observing his two comrades with compassion and understanding, although he reserved his glances of real tenderness for the invisible

Baby Ba, to whom he dedicated his most loving expressions: precious girl, chubby girl, my lollipop with curls, how's my little birthday cake today? and other cute expressions Angeles caught him making up in flagrante. Embarrassed, Egg would say things to her such as: "Children should be sin but not hurt." Or, blushing furiously: "I'm not crazy, miss; every once in a while my mind wanders, see?" But she began to realize that he was looking at her more and more as he made his cute remarks to the absent Baby Ba, that the more he looked, the more quickly he would avert his eyes or look in another direction if my mother caught him in the act. Or he'd start talking to Angel, the Orphan, and Hipi in English:

"Where you going?"

"I'll go in a while to the River Nile . . ."

"Have some fun . . ."

"Where's fun in Makesicko '91?"

"Madness is in the mind of the beholder"

"Madness is only a state of mind"

"Don't let your feelings show"

"Reward yourself!"

The band's first great hits emerged from this daily banter, and they went on to put together the thirty-million-copy-selling album *That Was the Year* in the same way. The Four Fuckups intended to debut the songs in that album at New Year's in Acapulco, where, to lay the groundwork for their apocalyptic disorder plans, they had allowed themselves to be hired by the famous French Marxist chanteuse Ada Ching for her floating discotheque, Divan the Terrible. My mother noticed that things gestate in the same way I'm going to gestate: art or a child, drop by drop, the only hair on opportunity's head is that long forelock we're supposed to grab, and to think that this hit song began when Uncle Homero F. (?) locked the fat boy in the egg, and then it gestated to the rhythm of these conversations and the band's comings and goings through the deteriorated city where only Angel had his own place but never invited his pals over so he wouldn't make them feel bad about it or so that he wouldn't bother his grandparents, who were by now quite old. The buddies had no place to live and no relatives, but Uncle Fernando lent them the living room in his house in Coyoacán and that's why they ended up involving him in their intrigue against Uncle Homero (Don Fernando didn't have to be begged, even though his mind was on the Indians up in the mountains and not on the tourists on the beaches) and with Benítez they planned their escape from Aca when . . . and with the Four Fs all the details of the destruction of the Babylon of Garbage. Angeles said nothing, Angeles only looked and tried to understand without compromising her language in the underground, carnivalized, cannibalized noise buzzing around her feminine mystery: like the Orphan, she had no past; like Hipi, she imagined herself unknown; like the Baby Ba, she thought she was invisible; like Egg, she feared she was mad; like Uncle Fernando, she aspired to be an instrument of justice, and, in her indignation at what she saw in Mexico, she felt like a composite of all of them, her comrades and friends (did she have others before? she didn't remember). At the same time, she felt strangely alienated from the man she came to love and with whom she slept in a sexual uproar; my mother tried to guess the reasons behind the terrible act they were preparing to commit at year's end in Aca. She listened to my father talk about the Sweet Fatherland, about the need for an exemplary act of cleansing, complete with biblical fury: Bye-bye Babylon, So long Sodom, Go, go Gomorrah, only a ninny could like Nineveh, So ciao to Baby, So, go, Ninny:

Babylon? You mean Baby Loan, since we've mortgaged our children's future. Of Babylon nothing remains: she looked at Angel and understood that the entire situation prior to her arrival, the crisis, the impotence, the rage, the corruption, the past, the youth—all of it was forcing Angel (explicitly), Egg (a bit less), Hipi and the Orphan (intuitively), to exorcise the demons, to upset the order, to humiliate the king, sweep out the garbage, find (Angel!) the Sweet Fatherland: Angel the postpunk, romantic, conservative who went from disorder to anarchy to the sadism of underdevelopment in order to find the utopia of the spotless fatherland: she would see him plunge into horror in order to destroy it; or would they be destroyed, he, she, all of them, by the horror which was indifferent to them?

These thoughts transformed my mother during the Acapulco apepick (simian and marine) into the most cautious and taciturn woman in the world; at times she thought she was going to win the Johnny Belinda deaf-mute contest, and, frankly, she could not foresee that her participation in the extraordinary events of the month of January would prove to be so tranquil. She would participate from now on in a silent dialogue in the hope that all of them (the band of buddies) would be able to speak together afterwards, and that triangular dialogue would go something like this:

ANGEL: I WANT ORDER
(FULLY KNOWING THAT NO ORDER WILL EVER BE
SUFFICIENT)
EGG: I WANT FREEDOM
(FULLY KNOWING THAT I SHALL FAIL)
ANGELES: I WANT LOVE
(FULLY KNOWING THAT LOVE IS ONLY THE SEARCH FOR
LOVE)

and that's why Angel marched toward disorder, Egg sought the commitment of the invisible by singing songs to the world, overcoming his inability to express himself fluently, and my mother Angeles kept silent in order not to reveal that perhaps she hated what she was doing.

"Besides," my dad said to her, "if we succeed in fooling Uncle H., we might get the house of bright colors back. That's where I spent my childhood. I love the place. I'm sick of having to see you just now and again in your Uncle Fernando's house or in my coach house. I have to live with you all the time."

He dressed her as Annie Hall (tweed jacket, man's tie, blue jeans), while he wore faded chinos, a Hopi shirt, and love beads. Both put on wigs of long, thick hair for their visit to Don Homero Fagoaga's penthouse on Mel O'Field Road. They were going to ask him if they could make peace and spend New Year's together in Acapulco.

My father had no real reason to be there, and Uncle Homero smelled a rat: he did, however, receive them. Just looking at them, he could see they were harmless. But just looking at my mother was all he had to do to suffer a shock: Don Homero Fagoaga's sexual fantasies were infinite, and my mother put him into such a state of erotic excitement that he became a stuttering teenager:

"Well . . . indeed . . . so we have a little couple here, huh? I mean, are you thinking of getting married . . . ? Excuse me, I didn't mean to imply . . . Well!"

Angeles realized that the success of the expedition depended on her, so she coquettishly lowered her eyes and touched the hand of the invincible Don Homero.

"Ah," groaned Don Homero, wagging his sausage-like finger, "aaaah, my innocent niece, I may call you niece, may I not? thank you: out of pure honesty, sacred temple, as the bard from Córdoba, Don Luis de Góngora y Argote, wrote on an amorous occasion . . ."

He carefully looked Angeles over, adding *pure alabaster, small door of precious coral . . .*

"Uncle," my mother interrupted him sweetly but decisively, "in the first place, don't change the subject on me: may we come to your house in Acapulco? In the second place, don't let that lemonade go to your head, and in the third, if you go on in that way, comparing my body to hard alabaster and my cunt to a small coral door, my husband here, your nephew, is liable to take matters into his own hands. Isn't that right, Angel?"

"Angeles! Good gracious! You've mistaken me, niece! That Gongoristic metaphor refers to your mouth, not to your, your . . ."

Don Homero dropped the spoon he used to stir his martinis: "Tomasito, fan me."

"Yes, master."

"My wife is right. Don't get out of line, Uncle Homero."

"How dreadful! For God's sake, I hope you accept my invitation to spend New Year's with me in Acapulco. You did receive my invitation, didn't you? No? How awful the mails are these days, as our invincible sovereign Philip II said when he received the news about the Armada! The rest of Europe was right to say: 'I hope my death comes by way of Spain so it gets to me late!' "

That's why all of them except for Angeles and the Baby Ba are there stretched out on the Countess Beach listening to three chicks chatter relentlessly about if it wasn't a bit much that each one went with two hunks to the Divan last night or if the vibes were good but right then they started in, ya know: Ya can take the boy outta Brooklyn but ya can't take Brooklyn outta the boy; they got all hot and bothered and tried to start necking. But the girls said enough was too much now that they'd showed what grotty chauvinist pigs they really were. Situations like that were sticky, 'cause when these nouveaus get going they don't ever wanna stop, and they chanted:

> *I don't want to live forever*
> *But I'm afraid to die*

and when they saw my dad, Egg, the Orphan, and Hipi stretched out there sunning themselves in their bulging bikinis, the three chicks said, oh sorry about that, we're not letting you rest with all our gossiping, and my father the provocateur said no, I didn't hear you, I was thinking, and they, hmm, he didn't even hear us, we seem so uninteresting to these nouveaus, and Egg, just to be nice, said yes, yes we did hear you, how could we not, everything you said was instructive, while the girls were putting on sun cream, ah, so these nosy nouveaus are real pests, always sticking in their noses where they shouldn't, to which the boys: a one and a two and a three, they began to throw sand at the bonbons, who at first laughed, then enough already, then they coughed, then they screamed; finally they were buried in the sand, and Hipi danced the deer dance over them to flatten them out and make sure they were good and dead and in complete privacy, and the most curious thing is that no one turned around to look at the scene, much less to interrupt them. A lesson that did not escape the attention of Pappy & Company.

Out of all these elements, as usually happens in artistic affairs, was born the great hit broadcast by the Four Fuckups for the New Year's parties: and with what pleasure do I transcribe them for you, from their Dickensian inspiration (a tail of two cities; hysteria of two cities; the color of Aca and Defé) up until the time they released it officially in the discotheque run by Ada Ching and her lover Deng Chopin: Here it is, all together now:

> It was the worst of times
> It was the worst of times
> The year was the jeer
> The day was the die
> The hour was the whore
> The month was the mouse
> The week was the weak
> It doesn't get better than this!

and my folks make love in the bridal suite Uncle Homero reserved for them, and she feels opulent, sensual, rich, new things, delicious things, she's afraid to feel things she's never felt before, she feels more modern than ever when luxury surrounds her and she doesn't understand why she's never been in a place like this, air-conditioned, piped-in music, unknown smells that expel the usual olfactory experiences (markets? churches? damp patios? leafy jungles? carved stones? quince, mango, laurel and silk-cotton trees?: now what is not there begins to come back to her): she is afraid to remember everything that happened before, now that she's in something that could never happen there, in a *there* she says to my father after having an orgasm, *where I* see myself moving, *light*, suddenly I saw myself a minute ago, *moving and light in the past*. What does that mean?

Neither one could answer. For the first time, she was terrified of her openness, her willingness to be everything that fell upon her and stuck to her in her newness or innocence. She'd never seen towels marked His and Hers, or sheets with Mickey and Minnie Mouse, or personal hair dryers, or peach-flavored vaginal ointments. She missed her history, and said to my father:

"Of what interest could these sordid provincial tales be to you: bastard children, runaway father, new lover for mother, exile with relatives who live far away? Of what possible interest could my past be?"

10

Let's see now: six years after Uncle Homero's green Jell-O bath, the Four Fuckups are playing rockaztec in the floating disco moored off Califurnace Beach down old Acapulkey way, and my parents take advantage of the circuntstance (as you might say) to ask Uncle Homero to bury the hatchet and invite them to spend New Year's of 1991–92 in his castellated house on Peachy Tongue Beach, where their fat relative has constructed a kind of Foreign Legion fort right out of *Beau Geste* to protect himself from whatever might happen. He gave his niece and nephew the complete guided tour this end-of-December morning, marching them past towers and battlements that shot up out of the sand, blockhouses and casemates, parapets and escarpments, and even fearsome concertina rolls of razor wire, ranks of poised, pointy lances—excellent defense against cavalry charges!

In the center of his fortress, Uncle Homero built a pool in the shape of a tongue, with a secret tunnel disguised as a drain which would allow him to escape in a minisub (How would he fit? Like a pig in a sausage, said my father; like a rabbit in a pâté, like Christ in the host, host! said my mother) into the sea, shot out like a cork, in case of emergency.

"I'm making you a gift of some beach property," Uncle Homero said one day in a tone of magnificent condescension to Uncle Fernando, some twenty or so years earlier, after the Tlateloco riots. He compounded this felonious friendliness by clapping Uncle Fernando, a small, high-strung, but sturdy little gent, on the back. "You can build a house there for your declining years." To which Don Fernando said no thanks, how would I ever defend it against the guerrilleros who'll be coming along in twenty years?

Tomasito the waiter served my mother a pineapple filled with whipped cream and then slipped directly into a reverie, staring obliquely and nostalgically toward the Pacific route of the Spanish galleons. Acapulco, key to the Orient, warehouse for the silks of Cipango, the ivory of Cathay, the scents of the Moluccas: good old Acapulkey!

My mother follows his eyes and stares at the sea as the sun goes to the Philippines. None of this distracts Uncle Homero from his task of presiding over the al-fresco dinner in the patio illuminated by the torches that Tomasito lights so that the flames and the glow of the setting sun can clash on the grand cheeks of the grand personage, as if they were fighting over the round color of the soft, saliva-drenched, cushioned tongue that slithers over lips, molars: Don Homero sighs and looks at my parents, who had felt obliged to dress in folkloric costumes. He then raises his glass of piña colada and gives instructions to Tomasito, which the Filipino does not manage to understand completely: when Uncle Homero says "More drinks," Tomasito answers, "More stinks? No, master, smell fine." Don Homero wilts and proffers his glass as if he were a blind man selling pencils. He sighs: There you see it all: four centuries a Spanish colony and all they have to show for it is pidgin English. Pigeon, master? Pigeon make too much shit on head. Shit on head, eh? Well, as the patient Filipino public servant, Don Manuel Quezón, said on a memorable occasion, you must have fallen out of your crib and landed on your head!

To which Tomasito immediately responds by feigning a yawn, checking his watch, and saying good night, as he serves Uncle H. a slice of Gorgonzola, following the ancient Mexican custom of serving cheese before dinner.

No! I said head, not bed. My God, this is the end of language as communication: no one understands me. With that he drank down his piña colada in one gulp and instantly felt, as our friend Ada Ching (whom the reader will meet shortly) would have said, "soulaged." He was admiring my parents' outfits: my mother dressed Tehuana-style, with a sleeveless blouse and skirt made of virtually transparent cloth, and my father decked out in railroad-worker blues, complete with red neckerchief: who knows what images of sin and revolution, Demetrio Vallejo and Frida Kahlo, folly and finality, passed through the carefully combed, plastered-down, parted-down-the-middle mind of Our Relative; his manner, from the moment he opened his door to them, had been, come to me, you innocent doves.

He said this was just not his day as far as servants, local or imported, were concerned. Nothing, decidedly nothing, had gone well for him from the moment one of these somber servants crossed his path, he sighed. Nothing at all had gone well, belovèd niece and nephew, but he felt better, like Perón safe-at-home, as Don Eduardo Mallea had so wittily written. Mallea, who maintained the proud purity of our language with Argentine passion from his bay of silence. He (Uncle H.) was happy to have his niece and nephew here with him on vacation, all useless rancor dissipated, no bad memories, once again one big happy family as Tolstoy or Tolstuá (his name can and should be pronounced both ways) might have said; ah Federico, Federico, you were the last poet to say Understand me for I understand you, now, as you can plainly see, no one understands anyone and this is my challenge, my mission: as Antonio de Nebrija the gram-marian said to Queen Isabella the Catholic, Language is always the companion of Empire and Empire (he pointed to himself with a butter knife) is one Monarch and one Sword: Tomasito, pour out the nectar.

Instantly, the Filipino snatched off his own bow tie and tried to fasten it onto our stupefied uncle, whose imperial discourse died, along with his fallen glass, on the cement of the tiny island. You said pull off necktie, massssster. Moron, monkey from Manila, let go of me, get that thing off my neck. He sneezed, swallowed, gagged, his round red eyes darting toward Angel and Angeles, and he saw what he did not want to see: no one got up to pat him on the back, to fill his glass, or to attempt the Heimlich maneuver on him. Angeles = dark eyes, those of a child who has never been treated tenderly,

Angel = green, serene eyes, like a lake, green how I love you green, the black night spread its mantle, the mist rose, the light died: dark eyes and green eyes full of what Don Homero did not expect to find there in response to his call for aiuto! help! au secours! auxilio!

"Ah," coughed our uncle, "ah, hatred persists, as the enlightened Venezuelan despot Don Juan Vicente Gómez said once in a jocular mood—when he publicly announced his death in order to arrest and then punish those who dared to celebrate it, ah yes, so this is the way . . . ?"

He pounded his delicate fist into his open palm.

"I have right on my side, nephew. If I sued you for being a spendthrift when you turned twenty-one, it was not, as God is my witness, to increase my own personal fortune, but to save yours, that is, what remains of it after your father, my poor brother-in-law, embarked on that mad enterprise, the Inconsumable Taco."

"Leave my old man out of this, Uncle H. He's dead and never hurt a fly."

"Ah, my little sister Isabella Fagoaga is also dead. And a dark day it was when she linked her destiny, as the superb Chilean bard Pablo de Rokha said, in a rare metaphor, to that of an enemy of the national economy like your father, Diego Palomar. An inconsumable taco! A taco that grows as you eat it! The solution to the problems of national nutrition! The greatest idea since the invention of *mole* in Puebla de los Angeles by a dyspeptic nun!"

Tomasito tried once again—at the worst possible moment—to serve our uncle a Cointreau on the rocks with Pepsi-Cola ("Your Merry Blizzard, massster!), but Don Homero went on, carried away by the inertia of his eloquence, evoking beaches piled high with fish, first nervous, then dead, then rotten, what does it matter, millions and millions of lost proteins on the exuberant coast of our shrinking (ay!) national territory, while this deluded Don Diego Palomar was fabricating an eternal taco, because his genes carried him away, just as Ganymede was carried aloft by the eagle . . .

"No speak evil, master!" interjected a shocked Tomasito.

"What, you Rabelaisian monkey?"

"Rabble east?" queried the perplexed Filipino. "No, master, no rabble here, east or west! Only *very* fine people, yes?"

Don Homero regained his composure: "Now, where was I? Yes, your progenitor, Don Angel Palomar, perpetrated a frontal attack on the entire concept of supply and demand, on national progress itself, a taco with a mortgage is what I call it, but it was mortal for the only two people who ever dared ingest such a poisonous dish, your father and mother, may they rest in peace."

He breathed deeply, he swelled up, his eyes seemed to pop out of their sockets, and he instantly closed them, fearing some new Filipino gaffe, may he rest in peace, as he recovered the beauty of the artificial oasis (was there ever a natural oasis? Homero thinks not; creation was born subverted) constructed by him at Port Marquee Bay in Paramount style—shady islets surrounded by crystalline brooks that babbled among coconut and date palms, and a band of araguato monkeys trained to throw coconuts from the high branches of these not so tristes tropiques: Aaaaaah! Someone's going to interrupt him, the Filipino, Angel, or Angeles, may they rest in peace, one of them is going to say something, but no, they are strangely quiet for people their age, for people so famous as jokers and (above all) rebels, why are they so quiet? why are they letting him speak so badly of that pair of obtuse illuminati, Diego and Isabella Palomar?

And so, in the silence of niece and nephew, Homero Fagoaga savored a triumph which he knew was Pyrrhic. He was defeated in victory, ay Tomasito, you would have to take out of the white pocket of your fine Filipino shirt a black-fringed photograph of Elpidio Quirino, the deceased Father of the Islands. Just what Uncle H. had feared. He did not have to open his eyes to say:

"I, as your testamentary tutor, had and still have the obligation to bring your excesses to heel, to put order in your life, to force you to think about your wife, and also, perhaps, if God so ordains it, your child, your children!"

"Tartuffe," murmured Angeles, almost biting her champagne glass out of rage, "may God not so ordain children because they all get a share in the inheritance, and then what will you get, you old hypocritamus? Tartuffe! Tartuffe!" She began to raise her voice, but she fell silent because Tomasito entered just then with the dessert of the same name, and Uncle Homero did not become enraged with him because he had not caught Mom's allusion to Molière. He simply exclaimed:

"Both of you must learn, please allow me to say so, the virtues of our national dialectic, which, once we've assimilated it, makes us the Mexicans we are because we are progressive because we are revolutionary because we are reactionary because we are liberal because we are reformists because we are positivists because we are insurgents because we follow the Virgin of Guadalupe because we are Catholic because we are conservatives because we are Spaniards because we are Indians because we are mestizos."

"And are you a member of PRI, Uncle Homero?" asked my mother without looking at him, looking instead at the sea, looking Homero, looksee, lacksee, lackadaisical. Oh mère, oh merde, Homère.

"At your service," the avuncular personage says automatically, but Angel and Angeles fall silent because Tomasito enters a second time to serve the Tartuffe (or to serve the Tartuffe the Tartuffe), and Uncle Homero declares, as he looks up at the black sky as if to show he knew how to be a good loser and to celebrate such a happy reconciliation worthy of other embraces in the state of Guerrero, Acatempan, he invited them to spend this New Year's Eve in the floating discotheque Divan the Terrible unless

they would prefer to stay here and fight the night away over the legal problems related to the suit for being a spendthrift

they would prefer to let Tomasito babble, since he was quite capable of filling an entire night with vaudeville at the slightest semantic provocation

they would prefer to return in indignation to Mexico City because Uncle H. had spoken ill of Angel's father

they would prefer to spank Uncle Homero for being naughty

they would prefer to drown him in the pool of his tropical fortress

the dessert had been poisoned by Uncle Homero

the dessert had been poisoned by Angel and Angeles

Tomasito got drunk in the kitchen on Merry Blizzard and forgot to serve dessert

Angeles memorized Plato's *Cratylus*, which she'd studied in the classic university edition with green binding published by

Homero had drugged Angel's drink and, naked, would chase his delectable niece along the beach

Homero had only drugged Angeles and ordered Tomasito to tie Angel up so he could watch his wife being raped by his satyr uncle

the Three Wise Men entered Don Homero's coastal compound mounted on camels

it rained unexpectedly in January

all of them just went to sleep.

4

Festive
Intermezzo

1. I Don't Want to Serve Anymore

Angel and Angeles arrived at Ada Ching's floating disco at approximately 10 p.m., singing the John Donne One by Mao Tsar. The breeze was rattling the inflatable rubber Byzantine cupolas, and He—Don Homero Fagoaga Labastida Pacheco y Montes de Oca—insolently posed on the deck as if the sea, the moon, the distant shore, and the great globe itself owed their existence to Him alone. He was once again in public, performing, exhibited for the delight of the unfortunate masses, perpetually fanned by Tomasito: Io non voglio più servir!

But then, with terrifying ill-will blazing in his eyes, with a gesture of permanent hatred, he looked at the three boys who helped him up from the launch while Angel and Angeles pushed his buttocks up from below. He stared at the lads with rancor; first he saw the three pairs of legs, let's see which ones he liked, and four of the six feet were in one way or another deformed, eddyfeet, yes Eddy Alien Toes says my pundit pop, feet deformed by that protective layer of human rubber that has been appearing on the feet of city kids: some feet shredding as if charred (Uncle Homero averts his eyes in disgust), others white and milky like those of Uncle H. himself (disgusting,

disgusting!), still others svelte, golden brown, firm, well shaped, ed-
dypolinean, in that case, and on those lawyer Fagoaga fixes his hungry
gaze, raising it slowly without seeing all he wants. To calm the
Filipino, my parents hummed the aria *Io non voglio più servir* sung
by the servant of Don Joe Vanni, the capo of the Sevillian mafia,
and the lawyer Fagoaga absorbed the detestable though desired presence of those cabaret waiters dressed in extraordinary bikinis stamped
with the lamented effigies of Joseph Stalin and Mao Zedong. The
waiters wore huaraches, the one with the nice legs was strangely
familiar: his face was fighting to get out of Uncle's drawer of deliberately forgotten things, where the boy was wearing a brimless, bottle-
cap-encrusted borsalino on his filthy black head of stiff hair; Uncle
H. felt as if he'd seen him, fleetingly, before, where, where, David
Campo de Cobre? Lost Boy? Olivo Torcido? If you twist the olive
branch in fields of copper, you will only create a pip of a problem.

He looked homerically at the face of the Orphan Huerta with a
confused feeling of desire and hatred he simply could not repress.
He did not even see the faces that corresponded to the other two
pairs of legs, the chubby ones and the tattered ones, nor did he hear
what one said to the other, listen, bro', where's the girl, and the other
answered that he hadn't seen her and the bottle-capped one don't
worry, Baby Ba will turn up when she feels like it, all that matters
is that she does her flute accompaniment for us.

Homero was both inconsolable and uncontrollable, almost attacking the Orphan Huerta bodily; the three boys scattered and only two
pairs of hands were left clutching Uncle Homero's equally tiny hands.
Angeles thought they were even smaller in proportion to the fagoagean
hulk that weighed in at three hundred and ten pounds; my Uncle
Homero's Vienna sausage-pink hands blended with the yellow lemon-
colored hands of the little man whose smile was as tenacious as his
grip and who refused to let go of our uncle and kept him from pursuing
his object of desire with passion and hatred.

"I'm the psychialtlic pianist, Deng Chopin. I takey velly good care
patients by coming down hatch next to galley storage cupboard. I
telly you maybe you need selvices."

"Well, as the Procurator Pontius P. once asked on a memorable
occasion—where can I wash my hands around here? Oh yes, please
decamp instantly, oh Mongolian minihorde," said Don Homero, not
deigning to look at the little man.

But Deng Chopin (short hands, indefinite age, long fingers, shaved head, dark eye shadows, redolent of opium) refused to release him and forced our relative to bend over until his cheeks brushed his Sino-Polish lips.

"Only fool or drunkard no see water when in ocean," said Deng. "Set me free. I do not understand your argot," said Don H., but he could not break that iron grip.

"Oh"—Deng Chopin smiled—"must go on deck, hear noise of lain or voice of God. Rust mean tears, and preasure is seed of pain because pain is seed of preasure."

In his uncomfortable and undignified pose—he looked like an elephant kneeling to hear the advice of a mouse—Homero, his eyes ablaze with the sparkle of awakened desire, inquired, "Preasure? Pleasure?" he asked, confirmed, and desired. "Pain? Is that what you said?"

"Ah, I see you understand. Mouth is door of disaster. No speak more." Deng scurried away with the rapid steps of a Mademoiselle Butterfly (maid in Japan), summoning, with a mandarinesque wave of the hand, our panting, polecat-scented Uncle Homero, who once again saw the Orphan Huerta pass by, this time with an electric balalaika in his hands:

"Careful," murmured Deng. "Even Devil handsome when only fifteen. Better you come me, Homelo. Lemember, good deeds stay at home; evil deeds travel around world."

Homero followed Deng through a hatch. Angel and Angeles glowed, phosphorescent in the tropical night, looking from the deck of the floating disco at the nocturnal world of Dockapulco, itself dominated by this ominous symbol: a gigantic pleasure raft with four Byzantine onion cupolas made of rubber and inflated with gas, all floating over a sea of oil (don't put your hands in the water, Mom and Dad; all of Neptune's waters could not wash your oil-blackened hands clean) (WELCOME TO BLACAPULCO GOLD) itself floating on the liquified shit of an Imaginary Fatherland: Oil of Olé! Welcome! It is here where all the oil pipes, the wells, the refineries, the motor of progress, the circulation of our wealth, the end of mortmain disgorge: an Acapulco discotheque! Welcome! WE HAVE ENERGY TO BURN and the sewage from one hundred hotels, shit, piss, bottles, orange peels, rotten papaya skins, chicken bones, Kotex, condoms, tubes from various kinds of cream, the creams themselves, the bubbles from bubble bath, used gargles, the liquid, oily equivalent of what Angel had in his garage on Calle Génova was bobbing around on the black waves.

"Welcome!" shouted the owner, Ada Ching (fifty-five years old), "and merci, merci," Ada thanked Angel and Angeles for having sent her the Four Fuckups, "a success," gestured Ada, as she cheered on the arrival of the New Year's celebrants, the launches, the fashionable gondolas, and the humble rowboats bobbing around the disco. She was dressed in a slate-blue tunic and elephant trousers, which hid her imaginably tiny feet. "Most esteemed guests," Ada Ching said breathlessly to Angel and Angeles, gently pushing them toward another hatch on the ever more crowded raft, "great keeds, these minettes, thanks for envoying them to me," she said: Ada Ching, the last remaining supporter of the Sino-Soviet alliance, armed with a portentous French accent which enabled her to communicate with reporters from Le Monde, the only people interested in her case, as personal as it was peculiar, and "come along, my infants," she said to my parents, "did you know that your ongle, your oncle sent his valet to find out if there was a sadomaso cabaret here in Aca? Since we're here to serve our customers because the customer has always reason, well, just regard, sacred blue! Enter please the cathedral of S & M! Formal attire required: Rubber, Leather, or Skin!"

The dark cabin Ada Ching led them to was fitted with a two-way mirror through which they saw Uncle Homero, on his knees, entering through a narrow little door, a comfortable enough passageway for his Sino-Polish host, but not so for this fattest of sausages, sweating away on his knees. Uncle Homero stands up, brushing the sawdust from his knees; Deng Chopin's sadomasochistic cabaret looks like a stable—it's filled with cows. Homero pinches his long, thin nose between two of his fingers as he stands there amid the slaughterhouse gear, looks at his knees smeared with manure, then sits down at a table. Deng, with a napkin over his arm, takes his order, what you rike, Mr. Homero? I would like lobster, says Don H., In that case, you'll have a steak, asshole, says Deng, delivering our astounded uncle a smart slap in the face, and from behind the tail of a cow leaps a blue dwarf wearing an orange-and-black banner from Princeton University, who sits down on the aforementioned fat knees of Our Relative. And what does this mean? asks Homero, seeing that the painted dwarf is staining his white safari jacket blue. It to piss you off, asshole, answers Deng, and next to my folks in the penumbra of the mirrors, Ada Ching repeats, biting her nails in excitement: "Pour t'embêter, pauvre con," as she admires the performance of her lover, the psychiatrist/pianist.

Now Deng takes up a yoke, hangs it around Don H.'s fat neck, and orders Homero, "Down on all fours, fatso," and hangs water bags over his back, slips a girth around him—he's agile, that mandarin, remarks my dad—puts the bridle over Our Relative's sweaty nose, encloses his double chin with a halter, and then attaches a crupper. Delighted with the President of the Royal, who can still use his tongue and whines with pleasure, Deng Chopin ties a cowbell around the neck of Don Homero Fagoaga, President of the etc., and orders him to moo, and mooooo he does, moooooo, mooooooooo, longer and longer. The Chinese whips his buttocks and then, nude, as if in an all-too-tangible dream, the Orphan Huerta appears, no longer dark-skinned but golden, covered with golden dust, his buttocks golden, likewise his erect phallus, which Homero, on his knees, spattered with cow shit, yoked, stretches his arms out to touch, and he moos, moos as the naked Orphan sings in his usual voice: The ox shits, the cow shits, the girl with the biggest tits shits, and he drops a little golden nugget, round as a lump of Klondike gold right in front of Uncle Homero's bridled face. He stretches out his hands, invincible Uncle H. Take the excremental gold of your obscure object of desire, Angel and Angeles urge him on from the immobility of the mirror, try to eat it, you coprophagic old man, rub it into your muzzle while the Orphan passes and disappears like a dragonfly, and with each movement of his impossible and humiliated desire Uncle makes the cowbell ring and moos and his voice, tremulous from longed-for humiliations and defeats rises whining, through clangs of the bell, through hatches, and between planks, to the deck, where it blends in with the voices of the musicians, moooo, moooooosica. The pretty girls dance to the sound of the bells, For Whom the Belles Toil, moooo, moooooostery, mooooouerte, the rockaztec on deck in counterpoint to a distant subterranean bellow made by the humiliated, beaten Relative, trembling from unfulfilled pleasure, kissing the feet of the diminutive psychoanalyst, and on deck, the Orphan Huerta, now on the bandstand with his electric balalaika, Hipi Toltec with his tom-toms and teponaztlis, Egg at the synthesizer, and a wind section consisting of a flute. Pop and Mom, now that you are fixed in your decision not to confuse humiliation with death, don't give humiliation prerogatives. Angel, don't confuse humiliation with non-existence, don't let yourself be seduced, my love, by the cruelty that makes the victim know who his executioner is and thus satisfies executioner and victim: Uncle Homero deserves only death, the most radical disappearance, although he does not know who gives it to him. Angel and Angeles come up on deck and join the dancers on the floating discotheque and the flute solo accompanied by the singing of the Four Fuckups:

> Serpents are better
> When feathered
> —See their eggs fly!
> And after they shed
> Their skins
> You can bake them
> In a pie
> Baby, baby, in a pie
> Reptiles in the sky!

No no no listen to me, please, don't just change the subject, tell me if you can hear that little refrain, the only melody in this cacophony they call rockaztec, tell me even before I'm conceived if there isn't a cute little girl with chestnut hair pulled back and parted down the middle, wearing a white percale dress, who's playing a flute in the Four Fuckups band, but my parents' invisible, hasty glances do not see what I can see before being born. They do not listen to the flute I listen to from my perfect limbo.

they hear the rockaztec of the plumed serpent,

they see Egg, his face growing paler by the minute, our belovèd buddy is losing his face, he has no more face, it's not his fault, let's restore his face to our great buddy Egg, to whom we owe so much, merely our lives, says my father, all our lives, I would say, because if my father had suffocated inside that metal egg because of Homero, he would neither have met my mother nor created me,

they see Hipi Toltec falling to pieces, sprinkling tiny shards of skin about as he dances on the bandstand, his snakeskin belt and his conchshell at his lips, a combination Tezcatlipoca and Mick Jagger,

they see the Orphan Huerta leading the band, a rearview mirror

tied to his head so he can see what's going on behind him, see himself
from behind, see the world in a 360-degree pan, ah my BARRO-
CANROLL, ah my rockaztec, how they shout when the Orphan sings
    Reptiles in the sky!
with his shrill but erotic voice and Hipi with his low, phantom-like
voice, and Egg without a face, much less a voice
    (and Baby Ba's flute: Only I hear it)

> *Serpents are better*
> *When feathered*

the grand dionysian delirium out of doors in Acapulco, under the
luminescent, sick sky. Angel and Angeles make their way through
the throng and pick out the faces that dominate the color sections of
the ever more numerous newspapers and the ever more sporadic
gossip spots on TV, Mariano Martínez Mercado, the handsomest,
most marriageable (excuse me, I meant marketable) young man in
the National Organization of Commercial Kingpins (NOCOKS),
creole with violet eyes and an aura of beige elegance: wearing, of all
things, a mess jacket, can you beat that? to come to the Acapulco
Raj from the sulphurous metropolis, the D.F., starched shirt-front,
wing collar, black tie, black trousers with red stripe, and now barefoot
in order to greet the well-bred, dark-skinned little girl dressed as a
Carmelite nun, who seems to have been dipped in tea, how else
could she have touched the infinitely brittle skin, so thin a sigh would
tear it, of Mariano M. M., the most etc., but she doesn't even look
at him, the upstart, he might be turning cartwheels, but she doesn't
look at him, she merely allows her bare foot to touch the naked foot
of Mariano, dazzled by the light and by this naked contact between
his white foot and the unshod nudity of her lost girl's foot:
    anonymous and naturally barefoot—she is dressed as a Discalced
Carmelite, she looks at you, Dad, looks behind Mariano and looks
at you, beyond the very tall, very thin, very blond, and very snooty
gringo that you, Mom, recognize as D. C. Buckley, of all the species
of carnivorous hymenoptera, the best-acclimated Wasp in our country, the favorite emissary in Mexico of the Liberal and Independent
Republic of New England and Adjacent Islands, the autonomous
entity that in the early nineties united libertarian tendencies, protests
against abuses of human rights, gay rights, lesbian rights, without

gagged, controlled, or disinformed press, New York and its islands, Long, Martha's Vineyard, Nantucket, where abortion is a right but where no rights are aborted: the last refuge in the world of habeas corpus and due legal process represented here by the last Lector of Lawrence and Lowry who believes in Mexican sensuality here not in the incestuous drunken brawls of the Four Islands (Manhattan and), D. C. Buckley is dancing touching toes with a street girl who usually hawks corn candy and other sweets on the Acapulco docks, as the owner of the disco, Ada Ching, tells my folks, that's what he asked for, a daughter of nature to be his escort for the night, pure, a tabula rasa, a room without furniture, untouched by the oracles of sibylization, a nobel sauvage, understand, mon Ange? someone who could scrape the grime of Chicago off him even if it meant a case of Chilpancingo crabs

and now she makes her entrance, this then! the blue foot! fools, get those spots on her, the queen of the jeunesse dorée of the capital, look at her, Angel, the golden girl, she abandoned the sun just to console the stars down here, what an honor, what a privilege, drenched in sequins, sweet sixteen, it's Penny López, the daughter of the minister Don Ulises You Know Who, author of the key slogan of Mexican industrialization, the one you see written on every mountain, every wall, in the sky itself, dragged by blimps and engraved in skywriting on the clouds:

MEXICANS: INDUSTRIALIZE:
YOU WON'T LIVE LONGER, BUT YOU WILL LIVE BETTER

and she passes by right next to you, accompanied by her governess, Miss Ponderosa, her two bouncy bodyguards, and her usual companion, the young Brazilian diplomat, Decio Tudela, dressed like Tyrone Power (of short memory) in *The Rains Came*, oo-la-la! I danced with Tyrone Power in La Perla cabaret, How long ago was that, mon Ange? where are the snows of yesteryear, and oo-la-la Decio Tudela's wearing exactly the same outfit as Mariano Martínez Mercado, except that Decio has a red turban, like a maharadish, and one of two things is going to happen: either they will start fighting or they will make the mess jacket de rigueur for nocturnal visits to discos. But now excuse me, if I don't get the FUBARS rolling again there's going to be sikhening melee here.

My dear parents: I tell them that the dark little girl who was dipped in tea wearing the caramel Carmelite habit dancing with Mariano Martínez Mercado is looking at her escort as if he were Cervantes's Glasscase Licentiate and her low, fearful eyes only see my father. The golden Miss López rests her eyes like two dark butterflies on my progenitor-to-be and then looks elsewhere without paying him any more attention. But my mother Angeles does indeed pay him more attention and stares at him. I was still hanging around my dad's egg pouches, but I can say to the reader straight from the heart, the fact is that my very life depended on that stare, look here your mercies benz! I'll never forget it.

Ada Ching on the bandstand, bathed in a glow of mercury vapor, asking her clientele what it was you desire, my minettes, what do you wish my infants. You know Ada! Ching! all shout in chorus, except the ones you know straightaway to be nouveau hicks who have never been here before, like the tea-stained dark girl who never takes her eyes off my dad Angel. What do mes minettes want to see? That ass with class, drop those pants! And on those delectable half-moons shine forth two tattoos: on the left cheek of this Norman Magdalene we see the ruddy countenance of the Great Helmsman, swimming across the broadest part of Ada Ching's gluteus maximus as if it were a milky Yangtze; on the right cheek, Breton bread, emblazoned for all the world to see, is our dear uncle, smiling Steely Joe, with his pipe in his mouth, pointing toward Ada Ching's delightful curves as if he were asking for a light: with a coquettish gesture inherited from the improbable memory of Renée St.-Cyr, Ada Ching pulls off her blouse and pulls up her drawers; D. C. Buckley begins shouting Moon-Ah, Moon-ah, and the Four Fuckups pick up the rhythm of the M's—after all, that's what everyone's here for—and mooooooo groans Homero from the bowels of the beached rubber galleon, mooooo, M, My M's, they sing

My Mexico My Mortification My Muerte My Mordida Marina Mystery Malfeasance, and each one takes the M the Musicians assign and each one shouts back his own M toward the altar of the moooo-sicians, Hipi at the drums, Egg at the synthesizer, the Orphan manning the balalaika, Ada shaking her breasts and panting out the rhythm into the microphone, Mictlán, says Marianito, and all of them repeat it in a roar, both funereal and joyful, Malediction, says Decio, and that too is chorused, Marina Mystery. Mordida, Ma-macita, Merde, interpolates Ada, Muck, the Fuckups, Mystery,

Mother, Malinche, Mortification, and Mustang, Miramón Mariano looks with indifference at Decio the pestio, and Mariano Monkey Mendicant, Machineguns Mexican M's, all together *não*

My M's Muddy Murdered Miraculous Monks they sing, they answer, they shout, the boys and girls mixed, mestizos, mixed, all together *não*

Mixing bowl Mesalina Monk Mortification Mortar Mamá, Máaaaamá, Mammary, Mamado . . .

Penny's bodyguards have their hands on their holsters, an instant of terror flew over one and all like a foamy angel soaring over the bobbing heads in the disco Divan the Terrible, Penny herself did not seem to understand what was happening as she danced the rockaztec called MEXICAN M'S with Decio

the pop style of the nineties, Penny López choruses the new series Mesa, Maraca, Martyrdom, Mixtec, Matamoros Matamoros. When he heard that name shouted and sung by the band and the dancers, my father Angel stopped, thought something (what it was, Reader, I don't know; I'm not omniscient, all I know is what my genes have set aside for me since the days of Mock the Summa), I say that he got an idea, this was the night of the loose ends, the unfinished suggestions, the unkept promises: it was his fault, his and only his, he wanted to be free and available for the great event set for Epiphany, and everything unrelated to that day made no impression on him, his mind was an opaque veil For whom the veils soil except for What's Going to Happen on Epiphany:

He looked at Penny: the audience was urging Penny to take off her shoes; she was the only woman who hadn't done it, and now she did, no hands, lifting her leg, her thigh, showing her thigh under her sequined skirt, along with a downy crease, a nosegay of quince, a tiny coin made of moist copper. My father looked at her but she took no notice of him. The tea-dipped girl did look at my father, but he took no notice of her. My mother Angeles looked at my father; he wanted to take notice of her but he thought something, an idea occurred to him, Matamoros, a seed of concern, hostility, enervation. He felt the arm and the iron hand seize his own.

He looked down. Deng, impassively sad, observed him. My handsome father, my tall father who could not be a poet because he was too handsome (says my mother, forgetting Lord B, the young Percy B. S. and John K., the divine Alfred de M. and old Ezra P.), had

the delicacy to bend down while Deng Chopin stood on tiptoe. All
he said to my father was this, but this was all my father heard under
the waves of music and happy shouting:

"Have you ever been in Pacífica?"

The tide of people separated my father from the fine, long, extended
hands of Deng Chopin.

It's my mother who only has eyes for the dialectic of eyes. She
looks at my father Angel and says to herself (she says to my genes)
that for him there must be three kinds of woman. First, the ones like
Penny who look elsewhere and don't take any notice of you. Second,
the ones like my mother who do take notice of you and look at you.
And third, the women like this dark little girl dressed as a Discalced
Carmelite who look at you but who actually look through you at
someone behind you: the demon, the angel. She was not jealous of
Penny. She was not sad. The dark little tea-dipped girl scared her.
Her little breasts were bouncing under her scapularies.

2

I declare that my mother's black eyes are a beach that
changes only so that it will look even more like itself.

I declare that my father's nearsighted yellow-green eyes
are a sea devoid of progress or being: my father changes
constantly but always remains the same.

I declare that my father and mother meet in the dance, but that
they know this is just one more ceremony for postponing death.

I declare that she, silent and astonished, suddenly feels light, elsewhere, running through a garden of modest statues and walkways of
smoke, my mother laughing, delicately treading on the grass with
her silk slippers, my mother discreetly raising her crinoline, my
mother feeling the thumping of her skirt hoop on her pubis and the
starched brushing of her ruff under her chin. My mother is blind: a
green handkerchief covers her eyes, and she laughs, not knowing if
she is being chased or if she is chasing someone: ballads, gallantries,
old-fashioned games.

I declare that she does not know how she came to be in this garden
or why she glides with such agility through the past, she who re-

members no past at all: my mother appears and disappears among the cypresses, distanced from the boomboomboom of her heart in the Acapulco night and the rockaztec and the barrockanroll but the handsome gentlemen with forbidden faces listen to her more closely than she listens to them: they hear the rustle of her green taffeta, the game of the blind doubles is brought to conclusion awkwardly, rapidly, head over heels: forehead to forehead, he and she, without seeing each other: both blindfolded, they embrace, they kiss under a sky of green flashes in an old-fashioned garden of smoke and symmetry:

I declare that he tears off her blindfold, and she looks at him and screams: dressed completely in black, my father with his ruff and his white cuffs brings the round, the game, to a successful conclusion with the capture, but she looks into my father's eyes, and in them she sees a man she knows and doesn't know, she knows him in the past and doesn't know him in the present, a man simultaneously young and old, innocent and corrupt, barely a novice in matters of love and at the brink of satiety, one foot in the bedroom and the other in the cemetery. A caddish gentleman, he embraces her, tears off her blindfold (it's the San Silvestre dance at a tropical port; it's the San Silvestre in a Fragonard landscape; it's the San Silvestre dance in an Andalusian patio), and she, horrified, stares at a man with forbidden eyes, covered by another blindfold: it doesn't matter, by the mere mute movement of his lips she knows what he is saying: I love myself through you, and I could only love you if in touching you I would touch all the women in the world: Can you offer me that? Can you swear to me that you are all the women I desire? Can you convince me you are Eve restored for me? Can you swear to me that your love will send me where I want to go: to hell?

I declare that she tears off his blindfold, and he screams in horror: she's been branded on the forehead with a hot iron. It's possible to read her forehead. Her forehead says: SLAVE OF GOD.

I declare that she has not existed in the past. But she has been in the game.

I declare that he takes her by her perfumed nape, bares her shoulders, picks her up by the hips so the crinoline opens like a rustling bud. He takes her by the feet, he raises her by the feet, he shows her to all those dancing, holding her up like a candy statue.

I declare she is dressed in green and he in black.

I declare they are on a barge floating on the Thames and on a floating discotheque in Acapulco. The fireworks go off.

I declare that she is annihilated by this violent manifestation of a past she does not remember.

I declare that he is frightened because he sees the burning seal on my mother's forehead.

I declare that he asks her, Did you see, Angeles? and each time he does it he swears he sees my mother's eyes change: they change color or place or perhaps they only change intention, which is like changing color or place: each time he embraces her, an icy, blue, clear, foamy splinter of ice passes through my mother's eyes.

I declare that my father takes my mother's hand in order to resist the temptation to kiss her perfumed nape, the acidity of her underarms, the oven of her tiny feet.

I declare that my father says to her, Angeles, give me time to get to know you.

I declare that when he touches her she screams: Death is a long way off!

3

 Behind Deng Chopin he emerged, hahaing and hungry, Uncle Homero Fagoaga, just when the dance was breaking up in exhaustion; Don Homero collapsed listlessly onto a curule chair screwed to the deck opposite the table covered with a paper tablecloth where Angel and Angeles were sitting. Behind him, as rigid as a statue, Tomasito took up his place. Uncle turned his veiled, febrile eyes, like those of a wise tortoise, upward, where the scarlet sails decorated with Chinese ideograms were fluttering in the ominous silence of the tropical night; peering through the masts, he could see the Byzantine cupolas that marked the dominions of Ada and Deng.

Let's get cracking! Mrs. Ching imperiously ordered the musicians, I pay them more than anyone so they think they have the right to rest between sets, no way! see what the gentlemen and the lady want: no, Homero imperiously said to Hipi Toltec, who was arranging the table, no, not a fourth seat: don't sit down, Tomasito, fan, Tomasito, you shall dine when we get back to the house.

"Yes, master."

"Io non voglio più servir."

Our buddy Egg looked under the table, asking in a complaining voice, "Baby Ba, where are you? Don't hide anymore, sweetie, come out so we can give you some candy . . ."

Our homeric uncle looked at this bizarre waiter, who was as white as an egg, as hairless as an egg, depilated to the point of avarice, depilated till death us do part, and then he looked at the other waiter: he was shredding, his skin was peeling off right before their very eyes. When the waiter with the porcupine hair and the bottle-capped hat approached the table of our suspicious Uncle Homero, Uncle H. simply did not look at him: he smelled him, he smelled the sweat and grime the boy had had the misfortune to possess since birth. Where? Tell us now, little orphan boy, little boy lost, an irrepressible tide of repulsion seemed to drown our uncle's eyes: "Why is it that we have to be served by these stinking inferiors?" he exclaimed, his rage, his age, this page at its highest pitch. "What we're paying for here in crisp dollar bills is a fine meal beautifully served by people as elegant as we are! Why do we have to go on putting up with being served by our inferiors? Don't we have enough power to be served by our equals?" he shouted in a delirium to which the imperturbable chanting of the waiter with the bottle-capped hat served as a musical accompaniment, while his peeling colleague went on setting the table, while the fat one was down on all fours looking for the girl, and while the selfsame bottle-capped Ganymede waited patiently to take the order of the Palomar y Fagoaga family.

"Now then, boy," said Uncle Homero, lolling on the curule seat opposite my parents, perpendicular to the nocturnal breeze fanned by Tomasito, and beneath the rubber cupolas floating on the rolling sea.

"Wha' chu' wan', sir?" said the boy in a nasal, whining voice.

"Wha' chu' wan', sir?" he who gives purity and splendor to our tongue mimicked him in atrocious disdain. "Now then, boy, bring me a dry, straight-up twist of lemon."

"Oliver Twist?" inquired my father.

"This is no time for silly jokes," said the President of the Academy severely, focusing his eyes ambivalently on the waiter/crooner. "Don't mess around, you damned darky." (The waiter with the sleepy eyes and the whisk-broom hair, naturally, screwed up his order completely, bringing him a lemonade and straw along with a Canada Dry, instead of a dry martini. Uncle Homero swept the lot off the table onto the floor, scattering cherries and olives to the four winds, and said to the waiter, "Down on your knees, slavey, mop up that slime, you mountain monkey, then come back, use your brain, if you can, cretin, and then bring me, let's see if you can get it right this time, what I ordered, you poor illiterate donkey, and learn how to serve a gentleman!")

He paused as if to congratulate himself—you've rarely been in such great form, Homero—and then stared with redoubled fury at the waiter, who was bent down, picking up the cherries and olives: where did you stick your fingers before you put your cherries in my lemonade, slimebag? Just as I thought, as that great Argentine educator Hugo Wast remarked to his intimates, implacably remarked as he took his place in the Argentine military cabinet, this is no time for modesty, there can be no doubt, I repeat, no doubt that he's scratched his testicles or picked his nose or wiped his tushy before he touched and served my food. Don't you ever think about things like that when you eat in a restaurant?

He raised his voice so that everyone could hear him clearly, above all the filthy boy, who was now bringing him a sumptuously arranged pineapple sorbet.

"The boss lady sends it to you," said the boy, trying to overcome the powerful chortles of our robust Uncle H. "Compliments of the house, is what she said."

"Learn how to serve a gentleman, you grimy slavey!" intoned Uncle Homero. "Hold on there, servant, you used condom, you demented lollipop!"

Don Homero looked the waiter up and down: he was no longer sporting his bottle-cap hat, just his tangled broom, as if he wanted to upset everyone's concept of zoology by wearing a sea urchin as a toupee, standing there with his arms crossed after serving our uncle his sorbet, while Homero surveyed the chaos the floating disco had become that New Year's Eve.

He raised his spoon to attack the sorbet: "People like me are used to living with beggars but not with proles. No one has a greater sense of honor than a Mexican beggar. When you offer a nickel to an authentic beggar, he responds by refusing to take it: 'A man's hunger is his castle.' An authentic beggar is a poor man in the classic style, that is, with no place in the world to rest his head, but possessing the whole Spanish-American code of honor intact."

With his nervously avid nails, Don Homero incised the poor tablecloth, on which alternated pop icons and the faces of Steely Joe and Mighty Mao.

"These waiters, you see, and *this* one in particular, are crooks, thieves who work by night and lurk in the shadows, bandits disguised as waiters. They don't ask you for money honorably the way beggars do, certainly not! they mug you, my dear niece. They're con men, they rile up the people who are happy in honorable poverty and organize them into unions. They embitter them with their utopian ideas, and they end up by stealing private estates, saying they were communal lands during the times of King Cuauhtémoc. They produce nothing, they scare off tourists, they ruin the nation, and they should be jailed, the sooner the better. This is my social philosophy, as we are entering, my dear niece and nephew, 1992, which promises to be quite a turbulent year. For ages now, we, the gentry, have defended ourselves from the Indians and the peasants—after all, we've been in charge of them since 1521. But these filthy brutes who pop up out of nowhere, how are we going to dominate them?" he asked with some anxiety.

"What I mean to say"—he was going into high gear—"is that we have to kill these scorpions, as the poet Horace says, *ab ovo*, that is, in the egg, before they can do any damage, and destroy the crows in their nest before they peck our eyes out: look right over there at that lost boy (he stabbed at the Orphan Huerta with his spoon). In him you can see the arrogant bureaucrat, the demagogic redeemer, the implacable ideologue, the Salvador Allende *in potentia*, why have you stopped fanning, you Luzon poltroon? Look at him and suffocate him, as the martial statesman from Chile, General Augusto Pinochet Ugarte, said recently, and he is a man who, by fair means or foul— but in either case to our great relief—continues to be the supreme leader of that southern nation."

Having said that, Uncle Homero finally stuck his spoon into the pineapple sorbet, as if it were a mound of frozen gold: even his desserts were Klondikes over which he assumed he could exercise a patrimonial right of conquest: he sucked and slavered noisily, belching, until he actually seemed likable, after all, doesn't all the world love a fat man?

Nevertheless, the noises Don Homero made drowned out the lovable innocence of the archetypal glutton because they sounded like erotic provocations, with all kinds of uncontrollable squints and lip-licking directed either toward my mother Angeles or toward the sullen boy with tangled hair and golden legs, legs now adored by Uncle Homerosexual. But damn it all to hell, where the devil had he seen that boy before? How beautiful his niece was! Angeles, bah! There was nothing angelic about her, and she only went by that name because Angel decided they would both have the same name, because Angel and Angeles sound good together, but our fat uncle knew something better: at night he'd crept to the window of the bungalow where the two slept and he heard them screwing, so, as far as being angelic was concerned, well, for him she was a devil and that was that.

Diabolical Angeles, he whimpered hopelessly, seriously attacking the ice cream, and how deliciously the velvety sorbet stood in for other pleasures, other tongues!

Only in the instant in which he finished the ice, eating mechanically but with his eyes fixed on his dreams, did Don Homero look down. It was then he realized that the dessert was resting on an artifact which was not a pineapple hollowed out to receive the cold joy of his palate, nor was it a crystal vessel cut with elegant, starry facets in imitation of a pineapple made of ice; no, it wasn't even a vulgar tub of the kind used for the washing of plates (oh, how Don Homero wished he could be excused from the disaster he felt to be so imminent by exercising his oratorical skills, by using language, divine language, his reason for being). No, it was what now shone metallically and tasted acridly, and sagged soddenly: he had eaten pineapple sorbet ladled into the brimless, bottle-cap-encrusted hat of, of, of this waiter! Of that bastard boy who befouled his life night and day! The Orphan Huerta emerged triumphantly from the drawer of forgotten things where Uncle H. stored every disagreeable event that had occurred during his exceptional life, oranges, limes, and lemons, or was it apples, figs, and pears? Don H. stood up trembling with rage, but the waiter with porcupine hair had already scampered out of range, while Tomasito reproached him, "Say 'yes, master,' " and Orphan Huerta shouted from a safe distance 'Yes, Mother, yes,

Mother,' and lawyer Fagoaga clutched his hands to his throat, shouting for help, poisoned, his windpipe blocked, old Coca-Culo caps, rusty metal Orange Crotch, Cerveza XX—like my potential genes— rows of lances like those I have on my beach to defend me from intruders, especially mounted cavalry, especially surly servants, nouveaus who think they have the right to be there, Indians in revolt, HOLY JESUS, oh, my poor tongue pierced by bottle caps, my reason for being and the being of my reason: my tongue cut to ribbons! my palate cleft by base metals which will cause me to speak in a high-pitched nasal twang like that odious runt, oh my good taste, my savoir faire, ruined forever!

Tomasito fanned his master with his usual tenacious patience; Deng Chopin, immutable, appeared through a hatch to see what was going on; Uncle Homero slipped off the curule seat to the deck and the owner Ada Ching approached to calm, to thank him—it was an honor for the floating discotheque Divan the Terrible to receive the President of the Academy of the Language as well as Angel and Angeles, whom she counted among her most favored guests. This was no time for anger, because in a few minutes it would be time to celebrate the New Year of 1992, perhaps the year chosen for the renewal of alliances, the Third Rome and the Middle Kingdom, culture wresting control from ideology, ha! only culture would survive the ups and downs of politics, and culture was dancing, carnival, Saturnalia, it was the moment to celebrate. Uncle Homero only wanted to throw himself on the Orphan Huerta, to embrace him, to kiss him, to kill him, to fuck him, to beat him, Orphan Huerta once again on the bandstand with Egg and Hipi Toltec. Suddenly, a drunken D. C. Buckley but sat down on Uncle Homero's lap, Buckley arguing in a high-toned Massachusetts accent, Let us hang on foah deah lahf to the planks left aftah the sinking of the Anglo-Saxon *Pequod*, which has dragged us with its bloody hahpoons into a hunt foah all the illusions of the twentieth century: it is impossible to save ouahselves in this rush to disastah, impossible to be modahn without participating in Annglo-Sexon populah cultcha. Uncle Homero, despite the weight of the ultratall gringo, groped for a napkin wide enough for his belly and resigned himself in despair to using the edge of the tablecloth: thrust now between the African white hunter's stained blue tunic and his smoked Hamingwegg stomach.

"Be ernest about that," said D. C. Buckley . . . or about a cetacean implacably hunted down by the furious Ahab . . .

"Oh, you movie dick," said Buckley, tickling Don Homero's sleeping little dicky bird, whose proclivities lay in another direction . . .

"W. C. Fields forever," sand the rockaztec band of the Four Fuckups.

"Bathroom Campos!" giggled the drunken Buckley, inebriated with English and Spanish calambours, punnish the spinning spunning Spanish language! while Don Homero sighed in resignation, telling his niece and nephew that he in no way opposed the myriad puns they might create because he hoped that the Castilian language would digest them all and emerge triumphant from this test, that it would reach the beach of the twenty-first century alive, overcoming, digesting, excreting the Anglo-Saxon universe, and he remained there staring, embracing the unknown D. C. Buckley, staring at the bikinis of the musical waiters and the white buttocks of Ada Ching.

They would never remember in which moment the sad year 1991 ended and slipped away unnoticed, undesired like a thief in the night as Don Homero would say, the certainly fateful 1992 of our five Christophercolonized centuries:

My mother Angeles looked uneasily at my father Angel looking at the cinnamon-colored little girl who was dancing between Decio and Marianito made into brothers in their desire for classist intermingling and racist risk and partying with the people, the Acapulco Slumming Party, desperately seeking ménage à trois with innocent and telluric Mexican girly bathed in tea,

who only had eyes, nevertheless, for my dad,

who looked with a desire my mother wished to deflect (which she could not) to the sweet-sixteen dancer Penny López,

who looked at no one: she was dancing.

4

And that first dawn of the New Year, which arrived amid a premonitory silence, while the diminutive Sino-Pole delicately licked the foyer of her vagina while with tiny, equally delicate nibbles he removed the odd pubic hair and then dug in like a playful kitten to sniff her clitoris, Ada Ching said yes, Shorty, time for fucky-fucky, who knows, it could happen any time, the world may change forever, and we'll be celebrating Russian Easter and Chinese New Year again. I don't want to miss my chance if it comes around, my naughty little chinky, yes, my little golden nugget, yes my little yellow pearl, I've been waiting for it for twenty-three years, just imagine, when I was a girl of twenty-three and we got the terrible news that Moscow and Beijing had broken off relations, that's right, make love to your Ada, your Sada, Bada, attaboy, that was a long time ago, I'll make myself a beauty for the soirees to come, but now you see: no one even remembered to celebrate the New Year, it came and no one noticed, but come on now, make me remember my tongue with your tongue, goose tongue, your Ada of Provence the sea the sun, your final flower of the Albigensian tree, your heretical survivor of the criminal crusades of Gaston de Foix Gras, lick my culo you dirty little coolie, stick your tongue up my anus, you polack peking piggy, you and I we sure are going to celebrate the Year Four Twenties and Twelve, so that I am cleansed of all mortal desires, so that I am empty of all lust and so that there remains nothing of my body drained by your yellow tongue except my spirit, my words, my purified ideology, and a body white at last, clean at last, washed spotless, my dengchowprick, all my garbage swept away by the broom of your tongue, my chinaboy, and I finally free of the sin of the evil God who gave me guts and tubes and blood and excrement and the lewd buttocks that I show up onstage every night to that mob des cons, but without ever renouncing my political principles, all that in order thanks to you and your immense sex— as big as you are small, my putto—to reach the good God of justice, name of a name of a Lenin, name of a name of a Chou, Albigensian of a Marx who are waiting for me at the end of the long tunnel of my impatient, bored flesh, century after blasted century that finally join together in the telescope of pleasure, in the telescunt of history, yesterday's millennia and today's millionaires, apocalypse in the tenth century and pocky lips in the twentieth, you and I the last of the Albigensians, long-fingered dwarf, yes, try to screw me so you can be pure and we two can reconstruct the last chance for the proletariat, who've been dragging themselves from millennium to millennium, through the mud of history, that's the way, just with your hands and tongue, I'm coming, I'm coming . . .

"What did you say to the fat old man, my little cabbage?"

"That it possible we all inside nightmare of bat."

"And to Angeles?"

"Brind man no flaind snakes."

"And to the garçon Angel?"

"You know where is Pacífica?"

"Do you think that it was enough for them to see the fat uncle humiliated?"

"No, no. They want kir him, not him suicide serf."

"Well then, my little Papa-God, we won't get out of this one alive."

"Wolk of priest to save humanity, not save humble skin."

Ada Ching looked at herself in the cabin mirror with a sense of misgiving and of having lost her way.

"I was really beautiful. When no one loved me. Not this painted-up, fiftyish old monster. Ooooh, they called me La Fellini when I was young. Until they finally understood the task I'd taken on and respected me."

Deng Chopin looked at her with supplicating eyes. She caught the reflection of that glance and began a vigorous brushing of her red hair—almost burned to a crisp, Was it by Breton hot combs? Norman ones? Or Provençal?

"Don't look at me that way. Throughout my childhood I had to put up with the humiliation my parents suffered after the Molotov–Ribbentrop pact. Then in the sixties I myself had to say that it just wasn't so. Beijing and Moscow have not had a fight, they are the bastions of the proletarian revolution. If Beijing and Moscow separate, there will be no revolution, no proletariat. No one could sacrifice that power, Sacred Blue!"

She put down the brush. Deng stared at her intensely.

"Well, what do you say, chinaboy?"

He shook his head in the negative and sadly looked at the sheets.

"And to the world then, what do you say to the world, my sublime dwarf?"

"When people talk you about it, paladise, when you living there, it hell. I tell it to you, World. But you undersand it, Universe."

"And to me what do you recount, my adored rekeket?"

"With one hair from woman possible to lift elephant."

"Papa-God!"

"Papa-papa, papagoda!"

"Ayy, now my little yellow pearil, wouldn't you like me to take you inside, my dove, my dive, my divinity?"

"Yes, Ada Ching."

"Well, how does it feel to want? Put your glasses back on and read something from the Palace of Pleasure and stop screwing around because you know very well that you don't get into my pussycat until the Sino-Soviet alliance is reestablished. That's that."

"Tomollow maybe we dead."

"That's no reason to throw out one's principles."

"Nothing glow 'less seed planted, even death."

"Alors, a fallen bud never returns to its branch. Bon soir, mon Chou."

5

 Well now, we were saying that sexual cells enter the sea to meet, to fertilize each other, without all the complications (my genes have been warning me about them for eons) that surround the simple conception of a human being and the philosophicomoralhistoricoreligious ceremony of copulation (I know all about whole eras of genes but only a little about gentlemen and ladies, after all): coral and jellyfish enter the sea to fertilize themselves and to peer through the corrupt water of the hotel drain and the turbulence caused by El Niño at the mountains where the people can no longer live, available now only to tourists and unsleeping advertisements: All the neon lights in Aca are lit, wasted during daylight hours:

WE HAVE ENERGY TO BURN!

Nobody else. Never again. Around here, yes, the coral and the jellyfish reproduce by external fertilization (listen, Reader, I'm going to talk about something your honor knows nothing about: about what I am: a sperm that left its ancestors behind and defeated his little brothers in the race of the charros of ire and who now has found the hot egg and is distributing his X's and Z's) and the sexual cells (I'm talking about my family history, living now and certainly external, which for me is a short, secret history unless your mercies deign to inform me starting now and from the outside, to which purpose I concede exactly one page to add whatever you might want, now or never, before I take up my discourse again, recapitulating, as follows):

Reader's List

Christopher's List

* (the two of them on Pichipichi beach washing themselves off in the sea after creating me)
* (Uncle Homero flying diarrheically through the skies of Acapulco, fleeing from the guerrillas)
* (Uncle Fernando flying through the skies of the Chiticam Trusteeship in a helicopter toward the Lacandon forest)
* (Mamadoc foaming at the mouth and spitting at the mirrors because she has understood the reason for the Christophers Contest: to deprive her of children and to invent an artificial dynasty for Mexico)
* (Federico Robles Chacón remembers how he saw his creation, the Mother and Doctor, conquer the people and

on seeing her from a dark balcony, without even daring to think of her as a human being: his statue, his bronze Galatea with wig and tricolor skyrocket

* (My parents on the beach remembering what happened days before during the New Year's celebration that led to my conception)
* (Ulises López nervously choosing between consulting his Hindustani guru at Oxford University or defending himself against the plots of Secretary Robles Chacón, his political rival, plots which will keep him from becoming president. He finally opts for forgetting economics and politics and thinks only about squash)
* (I demanding from my new existence, which they don't even suspect, that they explain to me how and when, the place and the time in which all this takes place, what space is, what happens within the within and outside the outside and within outside and outside within)
* (In the old El Mirador hotel: its shape
* (They answering my demands before I make them by pure intuition. I already adore them!)

* The first thing Professor Will
Gingerich noted when he arrived
at the New Year's cocktail party
on the terrace of the Hotel
Sightseer (originally El Mirador)
was that all
that of layered terraces: the guests were made of glass.
He didn't blame his headache for this
illusion. Aspirin should be delivered
with the Acapulco sun. But now the sun was
not shining. Night had fallen. His herd of
gringos had met to get to know each other
before
before beginning tomorrow's Fun & Sun Toltec
Tour.
Each one had stuck a badge on his chest with his
name and address on it. Damn! So why weren't they
looking at each other? He observed each of them
looking at the badge of the person standing next to him
just as that person looked at his, smiling in a happy
but absent way and avidly seeking the badge of the next
guest. Their eyes pierced the badges as if they were panes
of glass framed so they could see the Vermont landscape in
winter. But here, behind the glass, there was only more
glass. All of them wanted desperately to leave behind the
next traveling companion and meet another one, who was also
made of glass, all of them waiting, innocent and crystalline.
An Acapulco waiter offered him a Scarlet O'Hara. Will Gingerich
took the glass with its brittle stem and felt nauseous as he tasted the
cloying liquor flowing around drunken strawberries. He looked into
the thick, bovine, impenetrable eyes of the Mexican waiter: his body
was as square as a black die, so thick that no glass gaze could ever
penetrate it. Professor Gingerich breathed deep and remembered that
he ought to be introducing himself and looking after his flock. He
slowly strolled across the terrace balanced high over the rocky, sonorous sea that night.
"Hi, I'm your professional guide."
He didn't have to tell them his name because he, too, had it
written on the chest of his faded windbreaker, which also had Dartmouth College Vox Clamantis in Deserto 1769 inscribed on it. The

inscription was too light for anyone to decipher. He would bet on it. No one looked him directly in the eye. No one in fact did read the faded inscription. And he was not going to tell anyone that he had set himself up as a tour guide in Acapulco because Ronald Ranger had destroyed higher education in the United States with the speed of the fastest gun in the West. Among the items the President had certainly read on the hit list for budget cuts were two exotic subjects, Spanish-American Literature and Comparative Mythology. The President had wondered what earthly use they could have and marked them as definite cuts from the federal aid package. Gingerich consoled himself thinking that it was worse for the insane because the President had also eliminated federal aid for mental health: he had appeared on television with a statistical chart which showed beyond the shadow of a doubt that cases of mental imbalance had diminished sharply in the United States during the previous twenty years. Aid for an illness in decline was no longer necessary.

Will Gingerich did not want to think of himself as a victim of America in the eighties or announce it to his heterogeneous flock. Besides, the sixty-year-old couples who comprised it were not looking at him, even if they did squawk their appreciation, Oh, how exciting! as they read his badge. If only they were as excited about the age and prestige of Dartmouth College. But they neither read the inscription nor asked Will to translate the Latin.

"A voice crying out in the desert"—an index finger accompanied by a modulated, serious voice stopped him smoothly.

Will Gingerich stopped his wandering eyes in order to match his interlocutor with a body. Certainly it was something more than a finger and a voice. Gingerich shook his prematurely balding head. He was afraid of falling into the same malaise that possessed his flock. In front of him he saw a person who was not invisible. Will was on the point of introducing himself in a positive fashion: "Yes, I am a professor of mythology and literature at Dartmouth College." But it seemed an insult to the institution.

He didn't have to say a word, because his interlocutor had begun a unilateral evocation: "Ah, those white Dartmouth winters. Really a white hell, which is what José Clemente Orozco said when he went up to paint the frescoes in the Baker Library during the thirties. Did you ever see them?"

Gingerich said he had. He realized that the person speaking to him had not started this conversation because he thought Gingerich had bought his jacket at some university souvenir stand out of nostalgia, or a desire to impress.

"That's why I took a job at Dartmouth. Those murals are a strange presence in the cold and mountains of New England. Orozco would be normal in California because California looks more and more like an Orozco mural. But, in New England, it was a pleasure for me to write and read protected by the murals."

"For you, the murals were de luxe bodyguards."

"Yes." The professor laughed. "Orozco is an artistic bodyguard."

He could not refrain from carefully scrutinizing the tall, thin man dressed in a tasteful combination of open-necked shirt, sports jacket, white trousers, mahogany belt with heavy buckle, and blucher moccasins, doubtlessly purchased from L. L. Bean. In one hand, and with no sign of nervousness, the man, who introduced himself as D. C. Buckley, held a Panama hat, which from time to time he comically twirled on one finger.

Buckley raised his other hand to a thin, hard-edged face, like the one in the old Arrow shirt ads, and ruffled his hair the color of old honey. He couldn't be more than thirty-five years old, Gingerich (who, at forty-two, felt old) estimated, but his hair was old, prophetic, as if an ancient Seminole chief had lent it to him.

"Look, old salt," he said to Professor Gingerich with the immediacy of the eternal frontiersman, "I suspect you've satisfied your primary obligations by this point. I'd rather be nonallusive, and I hope you wouldn't think it illiberal of me (at least) when I assure you that your flock will not be needing your services for the time being."

He posed and paused, looking at the sheer cliffs of La Quebrada, which were so highly illuminated by spotlights and torches that they ended up looking as if they were made of cardboard.

"First, they'll numb their tongues and palates with these appalling cocktails until they're quite immune to any kind of culinary offering. Later on they'll eat—because they've demanded it, and, because they've demanded it, the trip organizers have provided food—baby food: pureed things, bottled dressings, vanilla ice cream, and cold water—and after a while they will be ready to fix their distracted gaze on the divers who plunge off the cliffs. The heights they dive from will be the main attraction, not what takes place in the heart of the Acapulco boy who, like you, only does what he must in order to eat. Don't you agree?"

Gingerich said it wasn't hard to guess that a university professor working as tourist guide in Mexico had to be doing it out of sheer necessity. "But," he hastened to add, "at least I'm trying to kill two birds with one stone.

"I came here because I'm finishing a monograph on the universal myth of the vagina dentata."

"If it's universal, why did you want to come here specifically?" asked Buckley critically.

"Because this is where the Acapulco Institute is located," said Will, as if the institute itself were a universal myth. He blushingly realized he'd been talking like a pedant and added, "The Acapulco Institute has amassed all the documentation relevant to this myth, Mr. Buckley."

"For God's sake, call me D.C."

"Sure, D.C. You can understand why this field is not one that gets much support. Government opposes it. And the women who keep the cult alive would have anyone who even hinted anything about it killed."

"My favorite detective, Sam Spade, says that only a madman would contravene the sentiments of a Mexican woman. The consequences, to put it that way, would be dangerous; illiberal at least."

Buckley signaled that the dialogue was coming to an end by twirling his Panama hat: "If you agree, my dear professor, we can kill one stone with two birds, ha ha. I'll accompany you to the Acapulco Institute if you go with me to investigate vaginas, dentatae or otherwise, to be found here in Acapulco, ha ha!"

And he clapped his Panama hat on his head at a rakish angle.

In D. C. Buckley's swift Akutagawa coupé, they drove down the steep and twisted road from La Quebrada to the bananafied stench of the seawall road. Gingerich consulted his faithful Filofax with the seal of Dartmouth College embossed on its cover: the Acapulco Institute was on Christopher Columbus Street, between Prince Henry the Navigator and Ferdinand and Isabella Street, in the—the only name missing—Magellan district. The Mexicans were exploiting the didactic aspect of street names to the maximum, the professor noted, and then dared to ask D. C. Buckley what brought him to visit this country.

"You know, old salt. It's possible, as Henry James wrote, to be faithful without being requited."

Buckley said all that without taking his narrow and always unperturbed eyes off the twists and turns of the highway.

"No, no," said Gingerich, amicably shaking his head. "Don't think I'm some romantic gringo looking for the golden age and the noble savage."

"It would be illiberal of me to think anything of the sort, old salt," said Buckley. "I'm a native of New York and Adjacent Islands. I'm a member of the Anar Chic Party of the North American Nations. And though you might not believe in primitive man, that's what I'm looking for here: an immersion in primigenial sensations, but with primitive woman, ha ha. And you, to which of the nations do you belong?"

"I left Mexamerica when it became independent. I'm too frugal to be from New York and the Islands, and too liberal to be a Dixiecrat. I think I have too much imagination to be part of the Chicago–Philadelphia Steel Axis, and I know I have too much of a sense of humor to sink into the hyperbole of the Republic of Texas, so I joined up with New England."

"Have you ever heard of Pacífica?" Buckley twisted his mouth.

"I don't know if I have any right to. In any case, I'm afraid."

"Well, here we are. But there's no sign of your Acapulco Institute anywhere."

"No, they don't exactly advertise. You have to go straight in."

"It's open at night?"

"Only at night. That's what the pamphlet says. I've never been here before."

They got out of the Akutagawa. The Acapulco night smelled of dead fruit. They stopped in front of a decayed building. They walked up some stairs, holding on to the rusted railings for support.

"At least the ventilation's good," said Buckley, brushing the reddish dust off his hands.

Buckley was alluding to the fact that the stairs went up past stucco pilasters badly in need of painting and windows devoid of glass; but then the deep blue of the windows made the night seem even darker. They stopped in a hallway whose only light came from a solitary, immobile bulb that hung over a nondescript door.

"Nothing worthwhile in Mexico is announced anymore," Will Gingerich explained. "But the institute does send its pamphlets abroad."

He knocked at the door, involuntarily letting himself be carried away by a forgotten jazz phrase.

"Is this proof that the institute is not worthwhile?" insisted D.C. courteously.

The door opened, and a man of perhaps thirty-two years of age, tall, powerful, wearing a large mustache, with eyes like the chief of an unconquered tribe photographed by Mathew Brady *c.* 1867, stared at them with no expression whatsoever on his face. Because of the heat, he was wearing Bermuda shorts. Despite the heat, he wore a thick turtleneck sweater. The professor gave his name and introduced D. C. Buckley as his assistant.

"Matamoros Moreno, pleased to serve Quetzalcoatl and you." He nodded his huge head, and D. C. Buckley felt a tremor run down his spine: he, who had come to Mexico following the tracks of D. H. Lawrence, to receive this gift . . . and so out of nowhere! He thanked the professor for his liberality with a glance—thanks, old salt!

But he had no time to say anything because Matamoros Moreno ushered them in with a gesture of hospitality, closed the rachitic door of the Acapulco Institute, and shuffled into the naked space as if he were wearing a ball and chain. He slumped his gorilla shoulders and sat in a metal chair facing an *ocote* table finished in red lacquer.

The professor sat down in the other metal chair, with D.C., modestly adapting to his role as assistant, standing behind him, tall and distant from the terrestrial eyes of Matamoros, who even when sitting seemed to be pushing a cannon uphill. With no preamble, Matamoros said, "As you know, the ancient myth of the vagina dentata only survived in sixteenth-century texts thanks to the missionaries who took the time to listen to the oral histories of the conquered and wrote them down to use them in the Indian colleges. But those texts were soon destroyed by the colonial authorities, both civil and ecclesiastical, because they were deemed lascivious and impure."

He paused, perhaps to show himself under the light of another bulb that deepened the shadows on a face that was threatening in its immobile simplicity. That face, D. C. Buckley said to himself, merely announces the danger of his body: anyone who doesn't avoid those eyes runs the risk of not avoiding the body and of being demolished by it. Buckley decided to avoid both.

"The text and the illustration I possess"—now he looked only and terribly at Gingerich—"are the only ones on the vaginal myth saved from the estate of Don Fernando de Alva Ixtilxóchitl, the Indian prince transformed into a writer in the Spanish language, even though he descended from Prince Nezahualpilli of Texcoco."

Like a cobra about to strike, Matamoros stared fixedly at Will Gingerich. The professor made a face of the kind he only remembered making at muggers in obscure residential streets in Cambridge, Mass., where he was assaulted sometime around 1985. Matamoros's face simply expressed one thing: that payment was required for his information. But Gingerich said nothing—even a fish wouldn't get into trouble if he learned to keep his mouth shut. Buckley, too, remained silent. His eyes had wandered a few minutes before from Mr. Moreno and were seeking the swift, hidden eyes lurking in the darkness of the Acapulco Institute.

"I make two conditions for showing you the documents, Professor," said the president of the aforementioned institute in very grand, very Mexican style.

Gingerich did not ask; he merely waited.

"The first is that you try to publish what I've written in some prestigious magazine in the neighboring republics to the north."

Matamoros's eyes were nothing compared with his tremendous teeth, which he was now showing. Buckley did not see them because he was looking at the doe-like eyes of a woman in the darkness, behind a door with opaque glass panels, a door that led to . . . ?

"I will certainly try to do that, Mr. Moreno."

The professor cleared his throat and then went on in the face of Don Matamoros's obstinate silence, "Of course, the publishing crisis in North America even affects the most powerful publishers, as you no doubt know. It will be very difficult . . ."

"I don't give a fuck about any crisis," said the fearsome Matamoros. "You figure out how to publish my stuff—with a powerful publisher or a weak one, I don't care. You swear you'll get me published, my dear professor, or you will never find out about the myth of the vagina dentata in Fernando Ixtilxóchitl."

"In that case, I swear," said Gingerich serenely.

"And if you don't"—Matamoros Moreno smiled through his knife-sharp teeth—"may the fatherland call you to account."

He blew his nose noisily, then looked at Gingerich, his handkerchief still covering his nose and mouth.

"And if the fatherland doesn't call you to account, rest assured, my professorial friend, that your humble servant will."

Gingerich swallowed hard in order to be able to say, "And the second point, Mr. Matamoros?"

"No, pal, it's not a point, it's a *condition*."

Gingerich could not withstand Matamoros Moreno's stare. He concentrated on the mustache of the director of the Acapulco Institute: it was not merely a bushy mustache; it was a bush. Matamoros soaked his mustache and covered his ears—it was the only way (said the professor) he could free himself from the din out on the terrace. Was he blind as well? Gingerich then realized that Buckley was no longer in the room.

The citizen of New York and Adjacent Islands was not looking at or listening to this supposed exchange between mythographers. Buckley had stealthily followed the doe's eyes, which slowly but surely had withdrawn from behind the door with glass panels.

"*Condition*, of course, Mr. Moreno," Gingerich agreed, swallowing again.

"This is it: once my work has been published in North America, you personally will take a copy, with the cover, *The Myth of the Notched Cunt* by Matamoros Moreno, clearly visible, and you will seek out, wherever he may be, a certain Angel Palomar y Fagoaga, Mexican citizen, resident of the capital. You will find him, Professor, somehow and you will force him, in your presence, to eat the paper on which my ideas are printed."

"Page by page?"

"Ground up like confetti," answered Matamoros with a truculent gesture.

"But I don't know this Angel Palomar person."

"You'll find him."

"May I delegate this function? Umm, to my assistant, for example? (Where are you when I need you, you Gothamite bastard?!)"

"You have to do it yourself. You have to be there."

"What if I'm not."

"There are other professors willing to accept my conditions. Here's a letter from the University of El Paso, for instance . . ."

"I accept," said Professor Gingerich hurriedly, his mind on the honor of Dartmouth College.

D. C. Buckley followed the little doe in the darkness, smelling her, stepping on the coffee-colored clothing she tossed onto the tiles, while Will Gingerich avidly read the document Matamoros Moreno set before him like some special treat. Despite his impatience, Matamoros's eyes never left the professor. Buckley touched the girl's shoulder. It was as smooth as a glass of eggnog with cinnamon. He touched her face. He dared to bring his finger to her mouth. She nipped Buckley's finger and laughed. The New Yorker got used to the darkness. The naked girl got into a barrel, and invited him to join her. She opened her mouth until it was incredibly wide and cleansed the sky of storm clouds. Buckley lowered himself into the barrel next to her.

"And you are like the bored maguey; you are like the maguey; soon you will have no juices," Gingerich read hastily. "You men have impetuously ruined yourselves; you are empty. In us, the women, there is a cave, a canyon, whose only function is to wait for what is given us. We only receive. You, what will you give us?"

"That's enough," interrupted Matamoros. "This is only a taste. Now read my things. But you must think I'm a boor. Colasa! Pour the gentleman a cup of coffee!"

But Colasa did not answer, and Matamoros laughed and said that the girl had suddenly taken up star counting as a hobby. Gingerich looked around for D. C. Buckley, but said nothing about his absence; Matamoros Moreno had forgotten about the assistant. Had he really forgotten about him, wondered the professor as he walked back down to Christopher Columbus Street with the sample of the myth in one back pocket and Matamoros Moreno's manuscript in the other. D. C. Buckley's Akutagawa was still there.

"I saw you dancing last night at the Divan," whispered Buckley into the girl's ear. "You looked as if you'd been dipped in tea."

Colasa Sánchez brought her warm dark body closer to the gringo's white cold body.

"Why don't you say anything?" asked D.C.

The girl sang, *My heart's delight's this little ranch/ Where I live content/ Hidden among the mountains blue/ With rainbows heaven sent,* and stared at D.C. for a long time. Finally she told him that there was a boy at the disco, tall with green eyes, dressed Hippieteca style. His wife was in Tehuana costume and they were with their fat uncle. Didn't he see them?

"I have the vague impression that there were lots of people there."

Oh, she thought that place was like a club; the owners, the frog and the chink, were giving out free tickets to poor boys and girls to promote class confrontation, that's how they explained it to her so she would go. It was terrific that the gringo had noticed her, now he was on top of her, it was terrific that she could count the stars, he couldn't, he had his back to the sky down at the bottom of this barrel: couldn't they both go find that boy she was talking about?

"What do you want to tell him? What do you want to give him?"

Just what I'm giving you, said Colasa Sánchez seriously, come on now, gringo, I'm moist and ready for you, come inside your sweet little girl, I've just had my thirteenth tropical birthday and all for you.

D. C. Buckley unbuttoned his fly, and Colasa opened her legs as if they were tea leaves and stared at him with the eyes of an anxious deer. D. C. Buckley's member slowly felt around the entrance to Colasa Sánchez's body, took aim like a bullfighter's sword about to make the kill, and pushed its way in with strength and a single, brutal motion. The white teeth in Colasa Sánchez's vagina shattered on D. C. Buckley's infinitely hard phallus. The gringo laughed with pleasure, while Colasa wept for the same reason.

Later he took her brusquely by the nape of the neck, twisted her black hair, and said all right now count all the stars, and don't leave out a single one.

6

This is the novel I am imagining inside my mother's egg. I was certainly not going to be put in the shade by my parents's buddy Egg. Of course, little Christopher: if the earth is round, why shouldn't a narrative also be round? A straight line is the longest distance between two words. But I know that I am calling in the desert and that the voice of history is always about to silence my voice. But that's all over with, and anyone might think I'm telling all this twenty years after my birth. But if the reader is my friend and collaborator, as I wish and am sure that . . . he will not stop to figure out whether this novel is narrated by me *ab ovo* or twenty years after (either in Horace's fashion or à la Dumas). What-

ever his premise, he will contribute something of his own, he will
be an auxiliary, an external, respectful chronicler of the conscientious
inquiry into my internal gestation and of what happened before it,
because no event comes without its accompaniment of memories: in
this you and I, Reader, resemble each other; we both remember, I
with the syntony of my genetic chain, in the world exterior to my
own: what I don't know how to remember, you can remember for
me; you know what happened, you will not let me lie, you remember
and tell me that . . .

7

 Gingerich returned to the Sightseer on foot and found a
small group from his flock still drinking at the bar decorated
with ship helms and dolphins next to the sea cliff. The
tourists looked even more faded than they had before; as
they age, North Americans lose color, even those with Mediterranean
blood turn as white as talcum powder, their faces white as sheets
until they die.

"Where are you from?"

"How much do you make a year?"

"When's the last time you moved?"

He was tired, sweaty, and unwilling to answer the indiscreet questions asked by these happy, drunk, and old farts. No, philanthropy
had not come to the rescue of higher education, Gingerich told them.
President Ronald Ranger should have been sentenced to spend the
rest of his life watching Robert Bresson movies or listening to someone
read him select passages from the *Quixote*. The tourists could not
understand what he was talking about, and behind his back one
gestured that Gingerich must be mad.

Buckley saved him. He walked in, saying, "Hi there, Pastor Gingerich, what news from your lambs?" and ordering a double Scotch
in the same breath. He then dropped into the sofa-rocker next to the
professor. In his hand, he carried a wooden device in the shape of
a phallus—it was battered, bitten, bristling with splinters, but still
erect.

"The myth is alive, Mr. Shaman. Take it. It's a souvenir. And now let's get some sleep. Tomorrow I want to go to the beach."

8

 At 9 a.m. on Monday, January 6, 1992, complaining about the duties entailed in this kind of meeting—comparable in ways to military training or obligatory sugarcane harvesting—the Antillean critic Emilio Domíngez del Tamal, known as the Sergeant because of his long record of denunciations, detective-like snooping, and thundering excommunications, carefully wiped the green sauce off his thin lips and caught sight of his pale reflection in the bluish windows of the tropical dining room, an imitation aquarium made of thick smoked-glass panels.

The Sergeant, the colors of passion dripping out of his mouth (ancient hope, eternal envy), grimaced and straightened his guayabera over his body, which was so thin he could only be seen from the front. He was getting ready to give his celebrated lecture on the responsibility of the writer in Latin America, a rhetorical jewel that had been his bureaucratic launch pad and in which he first enunciated abstract, philanthropic, and utopian goals, linked, naturally, to concrete historical-material realities and to prophetic warnings aimed at those who did not write for the people and who, therefore, were not comprehensible to the Party, and who, therefore, were ridiculing the representatives of the people incarnate in its leadership elite more than in its artistic elite: How could such things be allowed? the Sergeant would ask with rhetorical astonishment, standing before the crowds at the First Congress of the Newest and Most Recent Literature. Since when has the artistic elite paid the salaries of bureaucrats, since when!? This is a realistic question, an honest question; left adrift on the literary market, artists like him, who sacrificed their poetic inspiration to the Revolution, would not survive, so they stopped writing in order to advise, influence, perhaps govern, no, long live the governing elite because it pays the poet a salary, and not the public or people, which is incapable of understanding him. What am I saying!? But the Party and the state understand his silence, they appreciate it, they pay him for it, they reward him for it: because, although Domínguez del Tamal never writes a word, he is perfectly capable of demanding in no uncertain terms that everyone else write in such a way that the Party and the governing elite understand them: to demonstrate my sense of responsibility with regard to the people and my fidelity to the Revolution, I now read my list of art-for-art's-sake snobs, CIA agents disguised as lyric poets, ingrate formalists who have turned their backs on the nation, francophiles!, structuralists!, aaaaah, the pleasure of denunciation replaces the pleasures of fame, sex, or money: I shall sacrifice myself for truth and let no one accuse me of having an impoverished imagination: in nine months, the exact time nature grants for human gestation, Sergeant del Tamal went from Vademecum of the Opus Dei looking to heaven, to Falangist looking to Madrid, to Christian Democrat looking to Rome, to Social Democrat looking to Bonn, to being unaligned and looking to Delhi, to Directed Democrat looking to Jakarta, to Tito Communist looking to Belgrade, to Marxist-Leninist looking to Moscow: all in nine months, I tell you! Imagination! Imagination! and Protection! Protection!: the Sergeant paused for an instant, looking at the roll with which he was about to dip into his huevos rancheros, and in that piece of bread he found the moving memory of his Latin American Catholic origins: oh, indivisible sacrament, how I need you, he confessed to his roll that morning, oh divine prostitution, possession of the body of truth and the word in my mouth that hungers for dogmatic security, oh Latin American with five centuries of Catholic Church, Inquisition, and dogma behind me, how can I abandon you in order to be modern, how can I deny you without setting myself adrift in the storm, oh Holy Trinity, oh Holy Dialectic, oh Papal Infallibility, oh Directive from the Politburo, oh Immaculate Conception, oh Proletariat, Fountain of History, oh Path to Holiness, oh Class Struggle, oh Vicar of Christ, oh Supreme Leader, oh Holy Inquisition, oh Union of Writers, oh schismatic heretics: Arians, Gnostics, Manichaeans, oh heretical Trots, Maoists, petit bourgeois, Luxemburgists, oh mystic ladder, oh democratic centralism, oh protecting cupola, oh Thomistic scholasticism, oh socialist realism, oh bread of my soul, oh matter of my bread, oh oh oh

Sitting across the room from the Sergeant, finishing his breakfast of waffles with pecans, the eminent South American critic Egberto Jiménez-Chicharra, fat and olive-complexioned, all beard, oil, and melancholy eyes. He looked toward the Acapulco beach and mentally

reviewed the structuralist darts he would hurl with deadly accuracy
that morning against Domínguez del Tamal: but despite the lecture
on synchrony that was pouring between his cerebral hemispheres just
as the Log Cabin syrup was pouring over his frozen, hard waffles
smeared with unmeltable margarine, he could not erase the sense of
delightful nocturnal obligation which would force him to choose
between the handsome Jamaican poet and the rough Argentine novelist who had seduced him, literally, with a lecture whose referent
was, d'ailleurs, ailleurs, the otherness of a literature that was being
produced, metonymically, at the level of syntagmatic structure, but
which also, semantically, in successive preteritions constituted sub-
stantive constellations without any sacrifice of the aforementioned
preterition. Using his fork, he sketched out a tiny diagram in the
syrup he'd poured on his waffles; it faded, only to be replaced by
palindromes and palpitations that raced through his feverish mind.

Emilio and Egberto caught sight of each other. Emilio was the
first to look away and move toward the exit that led to the hall where
the First Congress of the Newest and Most Recent Spanish-American
Literature that Never Grows Old and Always Astonishes, only to find,
to his disgust, on the other side of the bluish windows a line of
caryatids out in the open air, women as svelte as Sergeant Censor,
with long white necks, twist the neck of the swan of sex, there is no
socialism with sex, said Emilio to himself: it was as an article of faith.
There is no capitalism without decadence, smiled the flabby Egberto,
uncomfortable because he insisted on wearing his corset in the tropics.
Deo Gratias both, both finally Catholic, both believers, frightened
of being bereft of their Church, of their sins, the spice of their life,
both of them staring at the gringa models with swan-like necks, in a
phalanx on the sand, in the water, draped with blue, red, lilac,
pistachio organdy, posing with their arms raised and their armpits
shaved as smooth as ivory, wearing straw hats, the Acapulco touch,
they who had not the slightest trace of heavy religious traditions,
holding on to their hats with one hand while the wind, what wind?
both literary critics asked themselves, when this January heat lowers
your blood pressure and sentences you to drink cups of coffee (Emilio)
or to stay in a tub of cold water with the door open and one of
Madame Kristeva's old books leaning against the bar of Palmolive
just in case (Egberto), but those girls were fluttered by a wind that
made the patresfamilias walking on the beach with their kids toward

the playground tremble until naughty little Pepito, who was snapping his towel at a tropical parrot, said look, they're blowing air onto those gringas, hahaha, they should have hired me to fart at them, shut up you little bastard, is that why we brought you on vacation here where the peak season never peaks, oh come on now honey, stop complaining, we'll have a good time and look how nicely they make the wind blow on the pretty gringas with those breeze machines that flutter their clothes, when you gonna buy me some rags like that, hon, why do I always have to go around with Salinas y Rocha clothes when all the other ladies in the neighborhood take their little trips to Mexamerica to buy outfits in the Laredos and Juarazo. Because they're smugglers and bitches, said her husband. What pisses me off, sweetie, is seeing these models surrounded by beggars, cripples, blind people, and hawkers trying to sell decorated gourds and embroidered blouses, as if there were only Indians in this country, look at them photographed for Vogue, holding serapes and things made of onyx: little burros, ashtrays, and bookends of Mexicans asleep with big sombreros over their eyes, the whole world's gonna see that, Matildona, they're gonna think that's what we're like here, so where do you get off with wanting to make a trip to Mexamerica to buy clothes, that's why when you get there they look you up and down as if they were doing you a big favor to sell you their shit, because they think you just that minute walked away from your corn grinder, that you're married to some slob who sleeps off his siestas under a big hat on a street full of lost burros and nopal cactuses, just like that, is that what we've progressed for? is that why we became dignified, clean members of the middle class? well, what about it?

"Calm down, Rey," said Matilde to her husband, and the three of them—father, mother, and son—entered the vast Acapulco amusement park, but at the gate the guard told Pepito that the parrot was not allowed, that it was dangerous, an insane animal, and the little bastard gave him the finger and ran in anyway, even if Matilde and Reynaldo stopped for an instant to contemplate the entryway, whose arch was made up of gigantic plaster whales, Moby Dick ballerinas, which Matilde said were very cute and Reynaldo said he was shocked at her lack of ignorance since anybody knew that this was the posthumous creation of David Alfaro Siqueiros, his 3-D Acapulco polyforum, ah, said Doña Matilde as they walked into that implacable paradise unblemished by a dot of shade, all cement and still waters, completely dedicated to the cult of sunstroke.

They walked toward plaster islands decorated with pirate ships, squirting fountains, hoses, jungle slides reached by bamboo and sand ramps that rise to Tarzanish heights and from which you slide down, ass to the burning tin, here comes someone down said the kid as a vulgar girl cools her steaming backside in the pool where a young, thin, dark-skinned life guard wearing a racing suit and a cap decorated with bottle caps on his hairy head waits for her, he's got to protect himself from the sun, poor guy, out here the whole damn day in the sun to help the kids who slide down, but Pepito is now running, followed by his breathless parents, to the gigantic pool, the sea in miniature, the Pediatric Pacific, which is calm one minute and the next, to the accompaniment of an air-raid siren, becomes artificially turbulent, full of waves higher than their heads, and Pepito is happy, that's what he's here for, Mati, yes it is, Rey, look how much fun our son and heir is having, it was worth all our sacrifices, don't say it wasn't, you didn't go to the Laredos so the kid could come to Aca, right? oh Rey, don't go on like that, you'll make me cry, forgive me, honey, you're right, you're always right, don't worry, Matilde, we're going places, they'll always need accountants, some because they've got dough, others because they don't, some because they make a lot, others because they lose a lot, but I'm telling you they all need accountants. What's that, Rey? What, sweetie? That noise, I mean it isn't normal.

That's exactly what the folks on the Sun & Fun Toltec Tour were wondering—go on cooperating out there, Reader—as they breakfasted in the Coastline Burger Boy, whose mercury vapor lights blinked and then darkened to the color of the omnipresent Log Cabin syrup: that noise is not normal, mused Professor Will Gingerich, lecturer attached to the tour, young and nervous, and eager to communicate his thesis, even at this time of smiling pancakes from smiling Aunt Jemima. We North Americans always try to get to the frontier, the West, that was the source of our energetic optimism, there will always be a new frontier, we joyfully look for it within the American continent, sadly outside the continent, and hysterically when we use both up: Isn't there any other place left? Is the whole world California, the end of the earth, the shaky cliff over the sea, the San Andreas Fault? And the ground here in Acapulco is shaking too, but with a frisson the Richter Scale doesn't register: That's just how a herd of buffalo sounds, said a sleepy old man from the Wisconsin flatlands as he lit up his old corncob pipe: but what they saw first were not buffalo but three swift camels racing along the beach, mounted by an old man, a black, and a Chinese, all scattering golden nuggets and thick perfumes: oh, typical Mexico—fiesta, carnival, joy, but the V*ogue* model asked if she might wash her hands after four hours of posing, and when she pulled the chain at the beach club, a tide of shit came bubbling out of the toilet bowl. The model wrapped her green tulle around her, patted her nonexistent stomach, right, that shit was not hers, certainly not hers; she tried to open the door, the lock, naturally, did not work, a strange beach boy, fat and hairless, had removed the handle, the shit tide rose, gobbled up her beribboned, silver Adolfo slippers, wet her infinitely discreet Kotex blemish, her flat tummy, swirled in her belly button and her pursed asshole, she had no time to scream, to escape.

Mariano Martínez Mercado woke up in his room in the Mr. President Hotel wrapped in the arms of his rival, Decio Tudela, both extremely satisfied after a night of shared marijuana that compensated for Penny López's refusal to leave with either of them. But Marianito wondered about the discomfort of his nightmare, the lethargic stench of his room, which was not solely the burnt-straw-mat stink of marijuana; he got up, dizzily untangling from between his legs the bottoms of the Brazilian tropical pajamas Decio had lent him—barely a suggestive loincloth—in order to feel his way blindly to the air-conditioner controls. "Shit," he said to himself, "it's busted." Then he went to the window, but the window would not open, and a label stuck to the greenish glass informed him:

THIS SUITE HAS BEEN CLIMATE CONTROLLED FOR YOUR
C   O   M   F   O   R   T
DO NOT OPEN THIS HERMETICALLY SEALED WINDOW

and amid the growing cloud of smoke that poured out of the air-conditioning vents with an aroma of burnt mustard as suggestive as his carioca topless pajamas, Marianito fell to his knees, scratching the glass and recalling his not so distant childhood, as if he had lived it a thousand years before and not merely fifteen: he remembered the signs under European train windows, as though they were decal Madeleines:

E PERICOLOSO SPORGERSI
NICHT HINAUSLEHNEN
INTERDIT DE PENCHER EN DEHORS

In the words of Eugenio d'Ors, Against the rules to pinch the whores,
he inexplicably chanted, looking out the window at the full length
of the coffee-colored stain on the bay, like the juncture of the Amazon
and the Atlantic Ocean, he said to the Brazilian, but Decio Tudela
was no longer moving, Decio Tudela was dead, suffocated, and
Marianito cried out in horror and pleasure when he touched him,
still warm, and decided to die hedonistically, that at least, seeing the
dead and naked body of Decio in the bed. Marianito gently spread
his legs and said he was going to give meaning to his life with an act
of mortal pleasure, a gratuitous, erotic culmination, he left his whole
vain and frivolous life behind him in that instant: he was going to
affirm sex even in death, above and beyond death: there would be
witnesses, yes sir, because they would be found this way, coupled
like dogs, like this, in a perpetual ecstasy, oh, a huge dark-colored
tub was invading the purity of the sea, a coffee-colored flow, a vomit
of all the garbage from the hotels and restaurants in the half June
moon between López Matthews Avenue and Witch Point. Jogging
along the public beach of Little Sunday, where he would surely find
the supreme justification for Lawrence & Lowry's ultra-Mexican for-
mulas, D. C. Buckley could not appreciate things in exactly the same
way Marianito had in his death throes, but he was the first to see
and suffer the worst.

The steady trot, controlled, not rapid but worse than rapid because
it was so controlled, like an infernal drum, distant at first. D.C.
stopped jogging, cocked his ruddy ear: the noise came down from
the hills, crossed the street that ran along the coast, now it had become
a trot over sand, horrid, eerie. Would D. C. Buckley survive thanks
to his Yankee communion with savage nature, the landscape of evil,
according to the precepts of Larry & Lowry? The long, blond, chro-
momacaronic Wasp asked himself this in a fleeting presentiment
while thinking about the group of North American government functionaries and military men vacationing in the Last Breezes Hotel. As
they were taking their preprandial dip in the saltwater pool of the
Shell Beach Club, they discussed the current dearth of bad guys in

the world: without reliable adversaries, we can't know who we are. What would become of us without a Bad Guy—Nazi, Commie, Chinese, Korean, Bulgarian, Cuban, Vietnamese, Nicaraguan. The United States can't survive without enemies, even though we have the source of all evil: Russia, the Evil Empire. At the same time they played pat-a-cake with their little feet, noting that between pats there was not only a ludic will and a strange love but also little patties of shit. Then, above their heads, above the seawall, above the beach umbrellas, indifferent to everything that held it back, as ferocious as a Campuchean defoliation, as inexorable as a Chilean putsch, the grand wave of poop sent with unparalleled energy by the reversed currents of El Niño from the coasts of Chile and Peru buried Professor Vasilis Vóngoles, a Romanian expert in Mexican affairs in the State Department, General Phil O'Goreman, commander in chief of Panama Canal defenses, Ambassador Lon Biancoforte, North American representative in the neighboring republic of Costaguana, and Mrs. Tootsie Churchdean, North American Ambassador to the Ministry of Colonies in Washington. The wave surprised all of them, cocoloco in hand, gardenia-scented straws in their mouths: it buried them in the Suzukis, the Hondas, the Honduras, the Guatemalas, and the Nicaraguas they had forged: the tide swept away Professor Vóngoles's glasses and D. C. Buckley saw them from afar, before anyone else, in that morning's repentant fog, the derelict, diplomatic specks in the sea, while on the beach the disciplined trot, the dark eyes, the wet muzzles, the copper-colored skin: all the dogs of Acapulco fell silent: they were going to hear their masters, their atavistic fathers: D. C. Buckley thought quickly: in California he'd been told never look a coyote straight in the eye, they hypnotize you, feign indifference, walk slowly, go into the water, perhaps they won't dare follow you.

He never had a chance: the coyotes went right for him, all intent on attacking a single part of his body, carefully protected but also exhibited in its sleeping eloquence, exhibited to the admiration of the beaches and the savage dark girls on the beaches: the pack of coyotes assaulted Buckley's sex behind the curtain of a blue Speedo bathing suit, they devoured the carefully folded Kleenex Buckley used to augment his admirable priapic dimensions, they dined on the nervous, shrunken flesh, they tore it off in one piece, and Buckley fell flat on his face in the sea at Little Sunday Beach, thinking that a few days before he had escaped Colasa Sánchez's vagina dentata and that her tight, skinny little ass had been a whirlwind of foam and blood.

9

The coyotes run along all the beaches, from Little Sunday to Tamarind, to Califurnace, to El Ledge, to La Countess, but they do not always attack. Nor do they even stop every time, as if they know where they are going. They all follow the oldest, and he follows the ragged boy who nurtured and trained them so tenderly during all those months. Like a banderilla of tattered skin planted in the center of a red coconut grove at the heights of the communal lands of Holy Cross, the boy, his eyes closed, invokes the most secret genealogies, the most perverse atavism: the children of wolves, river of wolves, Guadalupe—where the wolves ford the river—Matamoros Moreno mutters silently, as if he were pushing an entire artillery train, followed by the blossoming Colasa Sánchez, seeking out his enemy: my father, Angel Palomar y Fagoaga, seen in the disco the previous night by Colasa. But the coyotes are faster than Matamoros, faster than the cars, they turn away from the beach and head for the street in order to avoid the gigantic tidal wave that bites the very nails of the beach to the quick, and the bald fat kid at the municipal pumping station gives the order to all the allies of the Four Fuckups, those who had been run off the hills, their relatives and friends: Pump the sewage back to the bathrooms, give it back to the places from whence it came, the toilet bowls and hotel kitchens, block up the pipes, let shit return to shit.

Faster than the cars, the coyotes: panic seized those in traffic-bound cars when they understood that they were cut off, surrounded by ferocious beasts, windows closed tightly, horns silent out of fear, like the dogs that silently watched the return of their savage ancestors. The pack poured in through the service entrance of El Grizzly Hotel in the same way that the papayas injected with prussic acid, the pineapples spiked with copper sulphate, and the Mirinda lemonade blended with santonin had poured in from delivery trucks earlier that same morning. The Mayor of Acapulco Town Council, Don Noel

Guiridí, pauses in the heat to have a lemonade, reaches his arm through the window of his navy-blue Ford LTD, and receives the opened bottle without even looking at the Mirinda. Delighted, he drinks, checking over the keynote address he is about to give at the Literary Symposium. Our Don Noel is not only the standard-bearer of the PRI's revolutionary revindication in the port of Acapulco, but also a qualified literary critic, thus demonstrating that belles lettres are not estranged from the political fray, a man who is transported in a luxurious limousine wearing (the reason why he is so fatally thirsty!) a scarf, earmuffs, and a camel-hair overcoat, because of his mania for trying to convince people that Acapulco is not in the tropics but is actually a spa with a wintry climate where the human mind comes alive and ready for literary creation: the figure he cuts, even more than his speech, constitutes an attempt to add an unpublished chapter to the history of Ice at the Equator (such was the monomania of the monograph he was prepared to read that morning: the Venezuelan novelist, and quondam president, Rómulo Gallegos sent an Indian downriver along the Orinoco to Ciudad Bolívar to eat ice cream for the first time in his life; Gabriel García Márquez took a child to experience ice in Macondo; Sergio Ramírez Mercado causes it to snow in a fictional Managua just so the pro-Somoza ladies could show off their fur coats; and cotton snowflakes fall on the spectators during the production number "Flying Down to Vigo" in Carlos Diéguez's film *Bye-Bye Brazil*), but instead of all that, he begins to shout ay, I'm seeing everything green; he loses control and urinates a purple liquid; he becomes delirious, trembling, he falls unconscious, then dies. His horrified chauffeur rapidly raises the car's pitch-black windows. Then the coyotes attack the armored car and for once are frustrated.

On the other hand, inside the hotel, one coyote leaps at the throat of the eminent Antillean critic Emilio Domínguez del Tamal at the exact moment he is finishing his habitual lecture with the words The peoples of our nations demand this revolutionary commitment from the writer and is awaiting the usual counter-statement from the no less celebrated South American critic Egberto Jiménez-Chicharra with questions such as what about preterition? And diachrony? And epanidiplosis? But this time the words of the Literary Sergeant are mortally tasted by the coyote's saw-like canines, since Chicharra decides to express his scorn for del Tamal by skipping his lecture and sinking instead into his bath, which is bubbling with wonderful lemon-colored Badedás bath salts. He leaves his book of structuralist criticism on a book stand next to the tub and leaves the door to his suite open as well, open to chance, danger, and sin, said the eminent critic to himself, even though he was frankly annoyed that homosexuality was no longer a sin for anyone and merely one more practice among so many others, tolerated by all, denounced by none. He wanted homosexuality to be a sin again, that it be the vice that dares not speak its name, not an activity as neutral as brushing one's teeth. Why did the idea of sodomy as a sin excite him so much and leave the young men cold? he wondered, when through his bathroom door, like a miraculous dream, came, fleetingly and busily, a naked young man, covered in gold dust, his whisk-broom hair covered by a horrid rimless borsalino decorated with bottle caps but oooooh what a penis and what a hard little ass . . . The Orphan Huerta said not a word; at the same time, he dropped a hair dryer, an FM radio, and an electric mixer (all three plugged into a transformer) right into Chicharra's bath; he died fried without responding to del Tamal: a silent critic, a thankful Angel would sigh, but the same was not to be said for Matamoros Moreno, who violently strode toward the congress, followed by his daughter Colasa, in hopes that he would have his works published by one of the participants, perhaps with a prologue by Sergeant del Tamal and perhaps with an epilogue by Jiménez-Chicharra: father and daughter hear the repeated sound of the song "Flying Down to Vigo" played on a broken phonograph, but it does not rain cotton flakes, here what is coming down is darkness, their blood freezes, and Matamoros says to Colasa:

"If I find out that this opportunity was also stolen from me by that punk Palomar, I swear, Colasa, I swear to you I'll . . ."

He had no time to finish; outside, the phalanx of coyotes once again advanced toward the sea, pushing the phalanx of *Vogue* models toward the water's edge; the coyotes howled and the models shrieked, and there were no more photographers to be seen.

The symptoms of arsenic poisoning are convulsions and leg cramps, vomiting and diarrhea; the throat dry and closed; unbearable headache; precipitous fall in pulse rate, cessation of breathing, finally collapse of the frozen bodies (snow in Managua, ice in Macondo, refrigerators in Ciudad Bolívar, Flying Down to Vigogogo! Forever/ Forever!), and those on the Fun & Sun Toltec Tour exhibited quite a few of those symptoms. They lay there over the counters, on their backs on the tile floors, clutching a handful of straws in the Coastline Burger Boy; Professor Gingerich, overly absorbed in his theory of frontiers, had eaten nothing and walked out onto the avenue trembling with fear, abandoning the death that had been injected into plastic bottles of Log Cabin syrup: he looks at the desolation around the Tastee-Freez, the Kentucky Fried Chicken, the Denny's, the VIPS, the Sanborn's, the Pizza Huts, all overwhelmingly silent while their neon signs finally fall dark and the howls of the coyotes are followed by their almost human laughter, a cross between the laugh of a hyena and an old man, the laughter of clowns and witches.

The coyote's laugh, if you've never heard it, sends real chills down your spine: Gingerich sees groups of the beasts on the hilltops, gathered in circles, as if they are holding a meeting before attacking the lost, helpless gringo tourists in their pink jeeps. The coyotes pour down crags and hillsides; no one on the coast road can move now, the animals are much faster than any old taxi or new Mustang: a knot of silence, no one dares to blow his horn out of fear of attracting their attention, so the traffic jam stretches from the new hotel Señorita Mariposa on the site of the old Navy base of Icacos to Elephant Stone Point on the Caleta peninsula, and at the amusement park the noise of the squirting fountains and hoses and the artificial waves isolate the happy families from the horror around them. Don't tell me that all this isn't cuter than the beach, more comfortable and modern, says Reynaldo, who imagines himself in the Cathedral of Amusement for Suburban Man, Eden Regained! Matilde, who is very Catholic, follows him intuitively because in nature it's just like that, well, you know, that's where Adam and Eve sinned, right? Our First Parents were chased out of there by angels snapping towels, just like Pepito snapping his towel at the parrot, who now reappears as a bird of ill omen, screaming on top of the slide: Bastards, It's All Over, All Over, Bastards, which Pepito had taught his little parrot at night under the covers. Soak Your Ass for the Last Time, You'll Be Drinking Through Your Ass Soon, My God, make him shut up, Rey, what will people say, at least no one knows it's our son or our parrot either, said Matilde who prefers to look toward the pool, where the waves were beginning to stir again and her Reynaldo, what? Because the parrot from his forest perch is screeching Matilde Rebollo is a Whore and Reynaldo Rebollo is a Faggot, ay ay ay, Matilde starts to faint now for sure, everyone would find out, her husband stopped her, the fat matron gets away from him, falls into the pool, and there she becomes entangled with the insecure bodies of those of her class enjoying their tropical vacation, amusement paid for out of savings, mindful of advertisements, and the considerations of prestige: both of them, Reynaldo and Matilde Rebollo, hugging in the pool, amid one hundred and thirty-two other bodies defined by centuries of monastic pallor or canefield ringworm, and our Pepito, where, for God's sake, is he? why don't we see him? why can't we get out of here? How slippery this is getting, Rey, the waves are getting higher, isn't it too much now? Why don't they stop it? Answer me, Rey, but Reynaldo was dragged to the eye of the cyclone along with the other one hundred and thirty bodies submerged by the artificial waves that kept them from moving freely, tossed like corks, less than corks! The pounding of water on their heads, once, again, again, and again and again, the machines manipulated by the Orphan Huerta down in the underground control room, the cascades of broken glass hidden in the slide water, the screams, the astonishment, and once again the silence.

The cockroaches checked out of the hotels of Acapulco that morning, the coyotes moved in to devour the asphyxiated bodies, the bodies with dilated pupils, clenched teeth, foam-covered mouths, and that smell like almonds; and the cadavers with acid guts, burning tripes, metallic tongues, and blue vomit. Behind the pack, the dispossessed from the hillsides reunited by the Four Fuckups along with Angel and Angeles, who told the homeless: Do unto them what they did unto you: Acapulco belongs to two nations, tourism below and squatters above, okay, now come down, and this young fellow here, Hipi Toltec, has been training the same coyotes they used against you.

Angel, an old connoisseur of garbage, had laid out, as if he were setting up an open-air market, bottles of Heinz ketchup, Cap'n Crunch and Count Chocula cereal boxes, bottles of relish and rancid mustard, rubbery bread, and plastic chickens, McDonald's murderous hamburgers, the sickly concoctions found in gringo refrigerators, open bags of North American garbage food, chips, Fritos, Pop-Tarts, gobstoppers, smurfberry crunch, pizza-to-blow, and the spilled syrups of Coke and 7-Up and Dr Pepper, and side by side with the most grotesque examples of this antifood of suicidal madness—the balloon, fart, prepared, and greasy heart foods of the North—he put deodorants like Right Guard, the soaps and shampoos of Alberto VO5, Glamour and hairspray and Dippity-Do jell, and capillary dye, Sun In, tanning creams made by Sea & Ski, and the most secret element of all, vaginal ointments—lemon-scented, strawberry, raspberry—menthol condoms, eucalyptus suppositories. All so the coyotes could smell them, know one from another, and attack those who used, digested, sweated, wore, put up with, or who were all this. All this escapes exclusive receptacles to join the shit in the sea and the national refuse of fried-food stands and plastic Virgins of Guadalupe, sumptuous *zapote* rinds and soda bottles used as nesting places for small mice and snakes; the garbage of the North comes out to join the garbage of the South and the coyotes are trained and fed by Hipi Toltec with pieces of his skin. Egg took charge of poison and gas logistics, the Orphan Huerta was responsible for drains and pumping stations, to say nothing of (he had a personal interest in it) the destruction of the amusement park: he spends half an hour looking at Pepito's castrated cadaver, his balls cut off by the glass sent down the slide, and the Orphan, a crooked grin on his face, stands there watching him: so you had a mom and dad, did you, you little bastard, so you lived in Nouveau Heaven, and had your little vacations in Aca, so you had lots of Ocean Pacific swimsuits and lots of rubber balls, well now you've got glass balls, you little bastard!

The entire spectacle was conceived and directed by Angel and Angeles Palomar, as were the mottoes, especially the gigantic sign that now at midday is burning brightly on the decrepit walls of the last Sanborn's in Acapulco:

SHIT MEETS SHIT
SHEET MEATS SHEET
LONG LIVE THE SWEET FATHERLAND!
LONG LIVE THE CONSERVATIVE REVOLUTION!

5

Christopher
in Limbo

1. *Your House Is Still So Very Big*

 While all this was going on in Acapulco, Don Fernando Benítez was flying over our mutilated nation: from up above, he saw it as an island in a gulf of shadows.

Then, as they landed, he understood that he was in a dry, silvery valley, surrounded by dark ravines that left it in eternal isolation.

The helicopter landed on a mesa, and Don Fernando thanked the pilot, an employee of the National Indigenist Institute. The pilot asked him if he was sure he didn't want him to come back, but my Uncle Fernando Benítez said no; perhaps he no longer had the strength to climb all the way up here, but getting down would be a different matter. Right, said the pilot with a crooked grin, going downhill's always easier.

The inhabitants of the mesa gathered together when they heard the noise of the propellers and dispersed without making a sound as soon as the chopper landed. Perhaps they thought the pilot would be leaving instantly to return to the Salina Cruz base, and that they, living at this isolated altitude, could return to their normal life.

The wind came and went, ruffling their tattered clothes.

A high, burning sun returned. The Indians looked at him without closing their eyes. But the wind did make them close them.

He saw a people in rags.

When the pilot from the NII disappeared into the distance of the southern Sierra Madre, my Uncle Fernando walked quickly toward the group of Indians which by then had begun to scatter. He raised his hand in greeting, but no one responded. In more than thirty years of visiting the most isolated and inhospitable places in Mexico, he had never seen such a thing. Uncle Fernando had spent half his life documenting Mexico's four or five million Indians, those who were never conquered by the Spaniards, who never allowed themselves to be assimilated into the creole or mestizo world, or who simply survived the demographic catastrophe of the conquest: there were twenty-five million of them before Cortés landed in Tabasco; fifty years later, only one million were left.

My Uncle Fernando looked at them respectfully, with his intense, ice-blue eyes, as fixed and piercing as two needles behind his round, gold-framed glasses. He took off his worn straw hat, which was wide-brimmed and sweat-stained—his good-luck charm on these journeys that took him from the Tarahumaras in the north, who were tall and who would run like horses over the roofs of Mexico, to the sunken remains of the Mayan Empire in the southeast, the only place in the world where each generation is shorter than the previous one, as if they were slowly sinking into the sinkholes of their forests.

He always said and wrote that all the Indian nations, from Sonora to the Yucatán, had just three things in common: poverty, helplessness, and injustice.

"You are no longer owners of what the gods bestowed upon you," he said in a low voice, stretching out his hand toward the first man to come near him that morning on the sunny, cold plateau.

But the man went on.

My Uncle Fernando did not move. Something he could not see told him, stay right where you are, Benítez, don't move a muscle; easy now. The clouds that surrounded the plateau like a cold foam moved one flight lower and shredded in a hoary wind that combed through the dried-out fields. The men in rags took up their wooden plows, shook their heads, shrugged off the potbellied flies that tried to land on their faces, and began to plow, they were slow but they seemed to be working more quickly than usual—they raised their faces to the sun and groaned as if they knew that midday would arrive today sooner than ever—with clenched teeth, as if enraged about the time they'd lost. The noise. The wind murdered by the helicopter.

My uncle did not move. The groups of ten or twelve men plowed in perfect symmetry, they plowed as if they'd erected and then decorated a sacred talus; but each one of them, when he'd reached the edge of the field with his plow, awkwardly butted against the rocky soil and the twisted roots of the yuccas and had to make a huge effort to get his plowshare free, turn the tiller around, and plow in the opposite direction—as if he'd never seen the obstacle.

The rest was pure clockwork: the sun was the minute hand, the rhythm of work, the noise of feminine hands slapping the tortilla dough. The only irregular element was the passing of the hasty clouds that fled toward the sea; the wail of the babies clinging to their mothers, almost ripping off their old rebozos, the ragged blouses that had once been white, stiff, and embroidered—even the roses on an Indian blouse ended up wilting in these parts, my uncle said to himself: in other villages, kids are like little animals, free, daring, and happy; in Mexico, who knows why, kids are always beautiful and happy; a country of sad men and happy kids, said Fernando Benítez to himself without knowing why, at this the stroke of noon, surprised by the formula that came into his mind and which he wrote down in his notebook in his minuscule, illegible scrawl.

The children here cling to their mothers, incapable of leaving them, and the women shoo away the flies that drink up their babies' eyes.

He put the notebook in one of the pockets of his guayabera and shook his head, in just the way the Indian farmers shook the flies off their faces. He shook his head to free himself of that formula which kept him from understanding the mystery, the ambiguity of this land inside Mexico, the seed of Mexico, but so totally alien to the white Mexico with blue eyes, of the *Nouvel Observateur* and *Time*, and BMWs, toothpaste, toasters, cablevision, periodic checkups in Houston clinics, and the imminent celebration of the Quincentennial of the Discovery of America—a fact totally unknown by the men, women, and children he was contemplating: an undiscovered population unaware that it had ever been discovered, a date, an enigma imposed on it by others.

The men, women, and children he was contemplating.

And now hearing: they began to wail something in a language my uncle, abandoned on the insular crown of the mountains, had never heard before, something like Zapotec, he thought, he was going to write it down, but he realized he shouldn't lose even an instant in writing, that his eyes were his uncertain guides, helped powerfully by the thick dioptric lenses in his glasses, but they, too, after all were bathed by light, not permanently separated from light, screw that, not yet, he said to himself: my Uncle Fern, a bantam rooster, a fighting cock, almost eighty years old, sprightly, short, but straight as a die, loaded with memories, romantic adventures, diabolical jokes, and bragging arrogance: my Uncle Fernando Benítez, whom your worship the reader will get to know very well because in my prenatal life he was my firmest ally and the nemesis of my horrid Uncle Homero Fagoaga, who in the very instant of my conception excrementally plowed the air over the Bay of Acapulque.

Now my Uncle Fernando was listening to that impressive music wailing, which had no other purpose than to greet the sun at its zenith: the Indians, high noon on their heads, the blazing sun of the tropics, a desert in the clouds, first close to their hands, then to their naked shoulders and burned faces, finally as straight as an arrow aimed directly down onto the top of those heads, covered in black, straight hair, the heads of the Indians of the mesas.

They stopped. Time belonged not to them but to the sun.

It was only an instant of raised faces and hands stretched forward— not to protect themselves from the sun but to try to touch it. From wherever they might be—the fields, the entrances to their adobe shacks, a sonorous well like the bell missing from the church in ruins, here there was no priest, shopkeeper, teacher, or doctor (in the modern sense, noted my uncle scrupulously)—the men, women, even the children helped by their mothers tried to touch the sun without averting their eyes from it. No one protected his eyes. Midday passed as it had come: an instant now lost forever.

The cloud banks around the plateau came down another step. Now it was possible to see the other side of the extremely deep canyon, to see another frozen plateau on top of one of the thousands of extinct Mexican volcanoes.

Another tribe had gathered there, right at the precipice. My Uncle Fernando walked as far as he could, until the tide of clouds kept him from going any farther. The people on the other shore were too far away; he could not hear what they were saying, although he could guess what their gestures meant. Dressed in white, with starched, shining shirts and trousers, these were a different people, not the abandoned tribe my uncle had perhaps just discovered—why not? as astonished as Cabeza de Vaca must have been when he discovered the Pueblo Indians—but a people who had connections outside their village: they were waving their arms as if they wanted to bridge the gap between their village and this one: they stretched out their hands. They were smiling, but there was anguish in their brows: they didn't want to frighten him, that's all.

He turned his back on them. It made no sense to push them into an impossible communication. They would say nothing to each other. He sat down to eat the tacos wrapped up in napkins he carried in his knapsack; a drink of water. He listened. The music from the throats of the tribe lingered on, hanging sonorously on the mountain peaks for a long time after silence had returned to the earth, interrupted only by the punctuation of a baby crying. He looked. The gesture of the hands greedy for sun remained sculpted in the air an instant longer than the flesh that had made it. The silence was stronger, more persistent than the wails of the baby; but even more powerful was the image of this place that he began to free from all similarities with anywhere else.

When afternoon began, the ten- or twelve-year-old boys turned out to guide their elders in the plowing and sowing: they stumbled from time to time because they still did not know how to set the pace with their fathers, but the boys guided their fathers in the same way a father helps his son take his first steps. All, young and old, leaned on the plow staffs, long or short, that also served to split the earth. And the small boys—he saw and understood immediately—cradled their mothers.

He smelled. In the mountain afternoon, near and secret smells displace the vast cargo of the passing wind—its storms and errant flowers. As the sun sinks in the distance, the earth withdraws into itself, snuggles under its covers and smells itself in its intimacy. The men left their plows, picked up their torches, while, heedless of the bright light of sunset, the boys lit them and the men then instantly raised them on high.

On the distant side of the canyon, the Indians crossed themselves and went down on their knees.

On this side, the women, feeling the smoke in their noses, stood up with their infants. They all walked toward the dusty spot that could pass for the center of the village.

It was only a dry mound, with that smell of old excrement left out to weather, forgotten even by the flies that live in the fields. But here the mountain of shit was sculpted, arranged—by whom? Who was the witch doctor responsible for this coprologic stele? Where was he? First the entire village silently knelt before it, their hands joined, and now, for the first time in the whole day, they closed their eyes and took a deep breath: they didn't chant, they only breathed rhythmically, in unison, they breathed in the smell of shit, the strongest smell of the body, thought my uncle, the one that displaces all the rest and confirms our physical existence: the soft metal of the body, its offering to the gods: shit is the gold of our body, shit in the same way that gold is the excrement of the gods, their feces which are our riches.

My old Uncle Fernando felt himself to be mortal and stupid. His spirit suddenly waned, as if flowing through a sieve, and he tried to rationalize the absurdity of the body. Only symbols, allegories, or ideas could be more grotesque than the body and its functions: symbols, the allegories, or ideas superimposed on the body in order to alleviate it of its own mortal horror. He felt his bowels loosen and only barely managed to control himself. There where he could no longer imagine it urinating, shitting, fornicating naturally, without a perturbing symbol that said to his body: You need me because you are mortally absurd.

He knew of a Polynesian tribe for whom all deaths were murders. The shock of death did not violate our lives but rather our immortality.

They stayed there worshipping the little mountain of poop for an hour, breathing deeply, and then, in perfect discipline, the children first, followed by the women, then the young men, and finally the oldest (ninety-two altogether, counted my Uncle Fernando, the same number of people as years had been used up in the century), they all went to the mound, dropped their trousers or raised their skirts— if they had them; if not, they shit right through the holes in their garments—and gave their offering to nature, giving back to their absent gods their treasure. Thus they added to the height of that olfactory monument, the temple dedicated to the living senses of this tribe of sleepwalkers.

Night fell fatally, and the Indians, once again leaning on their plows, had to return to their domestic chores, eat hunkered down next to their dying fires, all in silence, alien to my uncle now as always, my uncle who for them had never been there, this man who traveled and wrote books invisibly, that's how he felt it that afternoon on the dry plateau in the uplands: they never saw him or greeted him. The invisible author.

He approached them without touching them, one after another, afraid he would awaken them from an ancient dream (and some felt the nearness of his breath, they grunted, walked away, dropped a piece of blue tortilla, some drew together, embraced as if fearing the nearness of an implacable ending; one grabbed up a burning branch and began to beat the shoulders of the wind, to burn the eyes of the darkness). Up until then, my uncle, with his mannish humors, his breath, his distant cosmetics, did not approach any of them; no sooner did he do so than he disrupted everything. They smelled all the difference, they extinguished the hostile fires, unnecessary in any case for seeing things at this hour of the day, got into single file, hands on each other's shoulders, as if they'd been practicing this rite (or defense) forever, each Indian with his hand on the shoulder of the one in front of him, forming a circle that would capture my uncle as if he were a wild animal. They smelled him. They knew how to use their sense of smell. Nothing was stronger than smell for them, nothing more venerable, nothing more certain as a fact of the world beyond the shadows. No odor was stronger than that of shit. Not even the smell of creole historian.

Noise displaced smell, the helicopter blades overwhelmed the olfactory presence of my uncle, even that of the scatological mound. No animal had ever dared to climb up here. Pumas or ocelots knew what awaited them here. Did anyone give better beatings than these people? On the other hand, today, twice, an eagle . . . Nothing was faster or stronger than the machine piloted by the man from the NII, who descended to the confusion of the tribe, opened the door—never ceasing to chew his gum—and told my uncle that he was sorry to have disobeyed him, but that he had had to inform his superiors that Professor Benítez intended to spend the night in the mountains with an unknown group of Indians, that the information reached President Paredes, and the President himself gave him the order to go back and get him. How had it gone? asked the pilot as his helicopter, which never again landed on the lands of that tribe, levitated.

In the air, flying toward Palenque, under the aegis of a special permit that allowed them to fly over and land in the Chiapas–Tabasco–Campeche Trusteeship, my Uncle Fernando felt afraid of himself, afraid of his historical curiosity: he had the anguishing feeling that he had interrupted something, perhaps a sacred cycle that sustained the life of that lost tribe on that mountain which was like an island on the moon; he feared a catastrophe. His own was sufficient. His own fear was enough for him.

The permit granted by the Trusteeship administered by the Five Sisters stipulated that the Mexican national Fernando Benítez could land in Chitacam territory for the purpose of interviewing the last Lacandon Indian, before, as the document put it, "it was too late." He feared, as he flew over the mountains of Oaxaca, that today he had just precipitated the disappearance of the last ninety-two members of the tribe of eternal night.

Could it be, he wondered, staring at the inglorious sunset, that from now on each year there would be one Indian less in that tribe of hereditarily, willfully blind people who were born with the sense of sight but who had it devoured by the larvae of those flies which were their only company, all victims of their isolation? He could not find out; but from now on he would imagine it. An invisible author for an imaginary day.

Mexico—what remained of Mexico after the Partition—was dying without Mexicans—those locked within the confines of the emaciated Republic—ever getting to know each other. Without ever getting to know what was left of the fragmented fatherland.

The tribes separated by the canyon never shook hands. But one tribe could see the other, and one would never see its brothers.

Don Fernando Benítez was on the verge of vomiting out of the helicopter window, but a strange vacillation, one that secretly seemed to warn him against the horror of symmetry, calmed him.

"Do you believe in the Virgin of Guadalupe?" he asked the pilot.

"The what?" the pilot answered (the racket, the earphones).

"I say that only a miracle like another manifestation of the Virgin of Guadalupe can save Mexico."

"No, we're going to Palenque," shouted the pilot. "Not to Mexico City . . . The Presi . . ."

Fernando Benítez closed his eyes and patted the shoulder of the young pilot.

Incredible! All solutions seem irrational except one: believing in the Virgin. Our only rationality!

Then something extraordinary occurred: afternoon renounced night and on both sides of the canyon there exploded in midair, as if they were trying to reach the helicopter, race with it, or damage it, bouquets of skyrockets, green and blue fireworks, hysterical, colorless lights, luminous sheets and then bunches of liquid silver and castles made of piercing air: a night full of red, acrid, and miraculous gunpowder: my Uncle Fernando, his eyes closed, did not see the night of the Mexican fiesta, that astonishing night and that astonishing fiesta, born of plundering and absence: fans of fire, towers of liquid metal, the wealth of poverty, rockets and castles that came out of who knows what invisible hiding place, out of who knows what savage squandering of money; harvests and carpentry, pottery, masks, looms and saddles: all of it set on fire here at the instant of the communication between the two shores, a communication he either could not or did not know how to accomplish, savings wiped out in a blast of powder; wealth existed only for that: to dazzle the eyes of the white, nostalgic village, for the glory of the sense of smell of the blind, ragged village: finally they had shaken hands, surrendered all their wealth to one instant of irreparable loss: the fiesta.

He opened his eyes, and the sun had still not set.

He looked outside the cabin and found eyes identical to his own. He shook his head; it was not a reflection. It was a bird. It was an eagle with the head of an owl, and a collar of rainbow-colored feathers, tied up like a chignon, as flowery as a ruff; the harpy eagle that was flying throughout the entire New World, from Paraguay to Mexico, celebrating all by itself the discovery of which the Indians were ignorant. Fernando Benítez saw those eyes and the dogged flight of the eagle, parallel to that of the helicopter: flying like two arrows, both of them together that afternoon in the Sierra Madre. In its powerful talons, the harpy eagle was carrying a living monkey, its shrieks drowned out by the noise of the motors.

2

There are two movements, my mother says her Platonic tome says: that of all things, which eternally revolve around themselves without changing place, and that of things that wander eternally, things that move, Angel my love, far from this secluded shore where I already shine one month after my conception in the immobile center of my mother, and I concentrate in myself the two movements of which they speak outside of me. They are desperate to understand what has happened between January and February, I who arrived in the impetuous gush of my father's errancy, and I now feel that I am hanging on for all I'm worth to a wet, hot cave from which I never ever want to leave, Mommy, I beg of you, don't say what you're saying, let everything spin endlessly around you and me, both of us together, not errant, not displaced, not . . .

The two of them cuddle in Uncle Homero's grand, uninhabited, and silent mansion on Peachy Tongue Beach, and each one agreed with the other, never again would so many significant occasions come together at one time, New Year's Eve parties, the beginning of the year of the Quincentennial, the Literature Congress, Uncle Homero's vacation, the vacation of the military and diplomatic high command in Washington—a break before masterminding the destabilization of the new enemy, Colombia—and Penny López's vacation, eh? My mother winked and my father feigned ignorance, self-confidently adding Ada and Deng's disco. It's better to prepare things with a will, is what I say (said my mom), than to leave them to that Mexican, weeeelll, let's see how it falls and if it does happen, good thing (she said, interpreting my father's will). She decided to contradict him only in order to maintain a modicum of independence within her willing acceptance of her tight union with my father. Which is why she said:

"I want to enjoy the supreme availability. I don't want to earn money, organize a trip, or even plan what we do in a single day. I'll bet you someone will do it for me."

My father laughed and asked himself if everything that had taken place in Aca a month ago had been merely gratuitous. We can always imagine what could have happened if everything had gone well, but we always had to be sure that chance would get an oar in now and again; that's why she would like to understand better what she still doesn't know and not to think that it was only a joke, but by the same token that it was not just an act of perfect will: not even a getting even, she says to him, not even an act of meting out justice, which someday may separate you from me, and deprive us of our love, my love.

Angel: "Why? I really wish jokes or gratuitous acts could be a way to get justice, why not, Angeles?"

Angeles: "Because the twentieth century is soon going to die on us, and I refuse, whatever the justifications, to equate justice with death, what about you?"

Angel: "All I know is that what we had to do here is either all done or should be all done." My father spoke in muffled tones: he'd put his head between my mother's legs, as if he were looking for me.

Angeles: "As Tomasito would say, till no see, no believe."

Angel: "Unfortunately, everybody in these parts thinks just the opposite. They say that if you want to believe you're better off not seeing." My father raises his head. "Why didn't the Filipino carry out the final part of the plan?"

Angeles: "I have no idea. What was supposed to happen?"

Angel: "At 15:49, Hipi and the Orphan enter Uncle Homero's house."

Angeles: "You mean here, where we are right now the day after Candlemas, February 3, 1992."

Angel: "It was a Tuesday. Tomasito opens the gate for them, knowing that at that time Uncle Homero is always in his sauna next to the pool."

Angeles: "Then the guys from the band and Tomasito burst in on him, so that Uncle Homero realizes he's been betrayed."

Angel: "Homero shouts, 'You Judas, I never should have confided my security to a scion of that damned colony named after my King Don Felipe, as the universal Argentine genius Don Manuel Mujica Lainez might have said!' "

Angeles: "And perhaps he remembered what Uncle Fernando said to him when Homero offered him a lot here twenty-four years ago: 'And how do I defend it from guerrillas?' "

Angel: "Perhaps he did. Why not? But perhaps Tomasito had an attack of conscience."

Angeles: "What do you mean? What are you getting at?"

Angel: "What I mean, Angelucha, is that after all, Tomasito owes his life to Uncle Homero."

Angeles: "You knew that and you went ahead anyway?"

Angel: "How can there be risk if nothing's left to chance? Uncle Homero, to prove his humanitarian, philanthropic, and liberal credentials, took in Tomasito when he was a boy, when UNICEF put him up for adoption after Marcos's last massacre in Manila. Would you like to tell the rest? Please do."

Angeles: "It was when Ferdinand and Imelda were desperately trying to wipe out the opposition. They couldn't sleep because they were making up crueler and crueler repressions. Now you pick it up, silver tray. Up and at 'em, oh genius!"

Angel: "Then Lady Imelda goes bananas and announces to Ferdinand: 'Last night I dreamed that fifteen years ago a boy was born who was going to plocraim himself King of the Luzons: you were Herod and I was Herodias and we went out to kill all the boys born yesterday fifteen years ago to rid ourselves of these redeemers, using the slogan "Better Deads Than Reds." ' The Mindanao death squads went out to hit all fifteen-year-olds."

Angeles: "And Tomasito was saved from that death thanks to Uncle Homero, who just happened to be in Manila . . . Are you kidding?"

Angel: "He *just happened* to be in Manila because he was funneling a few hundred million Mexican pesos through the Philippine stock market. The money he'd kept from the tax man he'd picked up from the sale of a subsidiary of the International Baby Foods Company that was supposed to bring foreign investment to Mexico and did just the opposite—but it still had to have a Mexican as the majority shareholder. That patriot just happened to be our trusty uncle, who, to be sure, is hard to imagine as a straw man, but he turned up one day with a check from the Mexican branch of INBAFOO, payable to the Philippine branch. The price paid for the Mexican subsidiary was minuscule, but no one in Mexico or the Philippines ever saw a centavo, not the public treasury, not the consumers, not even the brats who eat that shit, but, you guessed it, the Board of Directors and Preferred Stockholders of INBAFOO in the Republic of the Sun Belt, in the capital of the said republic, Dallas, did indeed see some centavos. How'm I doin', babe?"

Angeles: "Super, Angel. Your uncle's your major theme."

Angel: "And that's how Homero appropriated all that humanitarian publicity and ducked all the attacks on him for being a go-between, but the fact is that Tomasito hates him, too, but he must also love him, because if, on the one hand, Homero did save him from the Herodian fury of the Marcoses, on the other he knows that the kids who didn't die in the massacre did die of gastric hemorrhages after eating the little bottles of slime distributed in the Philippines by the Mexican branch of the conglomerate."

Angeles: "So when he heard Hipi and the Orphan knocking on the gate outside Homero's house, Tomasito began to have doubts."

Angel: "Just imagine that his fate could have been this one: having his head cut off by a machete in the pay of Imelda."

Angeles: "And, instead of that, here he is living like a captive prince in a golden tropical cage, so how could his heart not start beating double-time and he not begin to have his doubts?"

Angel: "But it may be that Tomasito, paralyzed by doubts, mulling over his own salvation compared to the death of his little brothers, consumers of the baby food made by Homero, just went back to his room to let things run their own course, just as you say: the supreme availability, someone else will do it for him . . ."

Angeles: "Or maybe Tomasito, letting his gratitude get the better of his doubts, instead of admitting the Four Fuckups, cuts them off and then the Orphan Huerta gets mad and shoots Tomasito . . ."

Angel: "I'm telling you we've got to calm that boy down. Sometimes he goes too far."

Angeles: "Aroused by the noise, Homero leaves the sauna naked, puts on his guayabera just when the Orphan was overcoming the resistance of the doubtful Tomasito, overcome this time by an aberrant fidelity . . ."

Angel: "Then Homero puts on the parachute, gives rapid orders to the man driving the motorboat, and escapes by flying, he passes over our heads, shits on us, and disappears into the thick air of Acapulco."

Angeles: "If that's so, then where is Tomasito?"

Angel: "I don't know. Where are the Orphan, Hipi, and Egg?"

Angeles: "And the Baby. Don't ever forget the Baby. I don't know where she is, either."

In this and in other sparkling repartee, my mother and father spent the first month after my conception in Uncle Homero Fagoaga's silent, abandoned house. That adipose Icarus left them, devoting himself to an avian life and, of course, adding his own small contribution to the epidemic in Cacapulco.

Angel and Angeles did not open the doors of the fort. No one, by the by, ever knocked. Tomasito decamped, leaving a full pantry; Uncle Homero had prepared his mansion, since 1968, for a prolonged guerrilla siege.

Thus it was that my father tried to transform the besieged house (in their imagination, of course, nothing beyond that) into a phalanstery = he said to my mother that without discipline they would not survive and that his own conservative revolutionary plans would be frustrated. Punctuality and discipline: my mother made no objection when, at seven o'clock in the morning, they prolonged the postures of their pleasure by going down on all fours and mopping down the tropical terraces of the mansion that belonged to the fugitive Don Homero.

This news was only lived by me and with pleasure during this long month. I communicate them to the readers. You should know that during the first week I floated freely in the secretions of the oviduct until I set up camp permanently in my mother's uterine cavity. At that time, I, Christopher, was a cluster of well-organized cells, with defined functions, learning the classic lesson, innocent that I was, about the unity of my person—confirmed by the diversity of my functions. Well, if each and every one of the cells that emerged from the fertilized egg has the same genetic structure and therefore each and every one preserves, latent, what my hair color will be, the color of my eyes, not all give these factors equal importance: only the eye- and hair-pigmentation cells concern themselves with a function that is, nevertheless, inscribed in all the other cells.

But after the second week of waiting for the nonexistent news about what transpired on Twelfth Night, when the Three Wise Men are supposed to come, I already thought myself the Wisest Man on Earth (a melodic gene informs me), then bang, my situation becomes so precarious that I almost, dear Reader, never got to tell this intriguing story which has no set ending (because it had no set beginning) because, between being pissed off and pissed on, I began to show myself for what I was, or rather for what purpose I was:

I was a foreign body within my mother's body, a splinter that would normally be rejected by the wounded skin: a button, a ring, a watch, swallowed by mistake: I forgot, Reader, about national contests, Ma-

madoc, and Uncle Homero, and I defended myself as best I could,
I scrambled up into my spaceship and I launched myself into intrauterine star wars: I ate my mother's mucous membrane, I penetrated
my mother's circulatory system, devouring her oxygen and food like
a desert rat, I excavated, Reader, a hole within my mother's hole,
until my oh so poor, fragile, and frugal existence became, through
my will to survive, part of her body and life: I *buried* myself in my
mother, Reader, I caused myself to be swallowed by my mother's
matrix against the rejecting will of my mother herself (an unconscious
will, but a will nevertheless) until I felt the surface of this recondite
cunt close over my head like a beneficent roof (just like the Cupola
that the government, says Uncle Homero, is building over Mexico
City to purify the air and then distribute it equitably among the thirty
million inhabitants), until I felt that I was expanding, that I was
triumphing by cannibalizing my mother, who was unaware that a
tiny Saturn was inhabiting her guts, taking up all the free space of
that dear curlicue, until I felt, oh benign Reader, that the maternal,
generous, flowing blood was drowning me . . .

(My father, feeling the need for the constant company of my mother
and surprised by it, he who had always lived on a sexual merry-go-
round since he had escaped the nets of Capitolina and Farnesia until
he abandoned the flashy Brunilda, wanders Uncle Homero's house
during the afternoon, melodically shouting Angeles, Angeles, I'm
back from the beach: he enters a long gallery that faces the sea and
at the end of it he sees her, on her knees, her shoulders bare, wrapped
in a towel from the waist down, her head hanging before her and in
front of her, on a white towel, arranged as if they were a surgeon's
tools, a whip and a crucifix, a high, pointy, penitent's cap and a sign
painted with red letters which she hangs around her neck and which
hangs over her glacially unprotected breasts: I AM THE WORST
WOMAN IN THE WORLD. Angel is about to shout something, but
even the name "Angeles" freezes on his lips. Was it really she? The
afternoon light is uncertain and treacherous. He thinks she has seen
him in comparable situations hundreds of times and has never made
him feel vulnerable: she, who has accompanied him in everything
he's decided to do from the time they first met, does not deserve to
be interrupted by him. He stares intently so that he will never forget
the scene.)

3

While these portentous events were transpiring here inside, just think, your mercies benz, that outside in the cosmos my parents spent the four, five, now the six weeks that separated them from Twelfth Night waiting for news that never came.

What did people know?

What were people saying?

What did they think the Acapulco catastrophe meant?

Mom and Dad had begged the Four Fuckups: inform us by Arabian telephone (what in Englatl you call smokesignatl or popocatele), smoke signals, or anything else, of any news you have: nothing.

They asked Don Fernando Benítez: tell us where we can rendezvous with you in the mountains: nothing.

My folks spent long hours contemplating the crackling, gray, striped blackboard of the Sony television set: nothing.

Nothing about the Acapulcalypse. Nothing that would precipitate, which was my parents' secret intention, a national crisis which would shake up the predictable, pleasant normality of Mamadoc's contests, which during the days of our confinement followed one on the other with all joy and inexpressible collective enthusiasm:

First Week: National Prize for the Best Oral Description of the Fifty-Centavo Silver Coins Quality 0720 [no longer in existence (neither the coin nor the quality)], nicknamed El Tostón;

Second Week: National Prize for the Inhabitant of the Central Plateau Who, Overcoming His Natural and Genetic Disgust, Eats the Most Fish in a Week;

Third Week: National Prize to the Lady Who Returned the Lost Wallet of Don Wigberto Garza Toledano (Native of Monterrey), While Traveling on the Niños Heroes Subway Line;

Fourth Week: National Prize to the Citizens Who Confess in an Act of Civic Courage without Precedents to Having Been Supporters of Benito Coquet, Donato Miranda Fonseca, Esequiel Padilla, Emilio Martínez Manautou, Javier García Paniagua, Aarón Sáenz, Angel Carvajal, or Francisco Múgica in Past Internal Conflicts within the Institutional Revolutionary Party (PRI).

It was as a function of this last contest, held during the first few days of February, that my parents (and I along with them) became most upset—when we least expected it—by the announcement that, in the first few days of March, Dr. Don Homero Fagoaga Labastida Pacheco y Montes de Oca, after a month of reflexive reclusion in his beach home and careful preparation in his offices on Frank Wood Avenue, had announced his candidacy for the office of Senator from the state of Guerrero. His campaign would kick off with a mass meeting in the town of Igualistlahuaca. The citizens of Guerrero were cordially invited to view the event on television and to express their support for the PRI candidate. Dr. Fagoaga is a distinguished son of Guerrero, as irrefutable documents clearly prove, and in order not to put off for twenty years the democratic opportunity of today, and in order not to be excluded by main force, as were Benito, Donato, Emilio, and . . .

Angel and Angeles exclaimed in one voice: "But Uncle H. is strictly from Mexico, D.F. He's never set foot in Guerrero, what did Guerrero do to the boys in the capital to deserve this punishment, etc., as we've been saying for decades: Angel and Angeles got over their spontaneous indignation and awaited the next newscast with bated breath.

Angel closed his eyes and said to my mother that they must be totally befuddled by the success of the operation, the failure of the operation, by all of the above = he shook her by the shoulders in order to shake himself.

"It's all make-believe. We forget that from time to time. I get carried away."

"Let go of me, Angel."

"The idea of passing from chaos to despair with no transition scares the hell out of me."

"Being a conservative anarchist is a little stupid, honey . . ."

"Nihilist. What I am is a nihilist. And I'm afraid of what I am, I swear. I want to restore certain values, not to be left with no values at all."

"Calm down. That's not what you are."

"Well? What are we going to end up being—unintentionally?"

"There will be many obstacles, what you want won't be easily achieved, all that stuff about the Sweet Fatherland, your . . ."

"I'm afraid of ending up as what you're saying, the opposite of what I'm trying to achieve. Everything always ends up like that, the opposite of what we set out to do."

"Terrorists. My Uncle Fernando, who lived through that era, would call us terrorists—if he knew."

"He doesn't know a thing. He thinks it's a joke. Better a joke than a crime."

"Was all that a crime? Tell me. I have no past. I learn everything from you. Everything I get from you sticks to me, even my need not to be like you!"

"Angeles, it's taken for granted that in the nineties we young people all have the right to an adventure of this kind, it isn't a statute in any constitution, it's like what going to a whorehouse or getting drunk used to be; terrorism is a rite of passage, nothing more, it has no importance . . . Everybody does it. Remember when the Spanish kid García poisoned all the people in his father's restaurant? Or when Baby Fernández put dynamite under the altar of the Infant of Prague and set it off during twelve o'clock Mass?"

"Sure I do. I like what you're saying. I don't see any problems in it."

"I hope you see some problems in this damned news blackout!!"

"There's something that worries me even more. Everything turned out too perfectly. There wasn't even a blink between cause and effect. It's as if we started gambling with ten pesos and the possibility of winning a hundred and instead we came home with a million."

"We're some mean fuckers." My father laughed unwillingly. Then, genuinely afflicted, he hung his head—not without first kicking the Sony, which fell onto the marble floor, shattering and scattering gray glass, sorry, Angeles, those are just words—terrorist, nihilist, conservative, left-winger, sorry: I'm a guy who's always pissed off, understand? pissed off that I've spent my whole life, since I was born back in 1969 until now in 1992, desperate because I'm so mad and so impotent, I never had the slightest optimism about "openings" or "booms" or "renewals," guys my age just felt hemmed in, desperate, pissed off: at least being pissed off is something, right? Better than trading in your pesos for dollars, making jokes about the president, blaming the gringos for everything we don't do, sitting down to wait for the next president to announce his successor, transferring hope every six years despite all the evidence to the contrary, demanding that others do what we can't, saying the people lack all confidence, that there's no leadership, that there's no this, there's no that . . . Shit, Angeles, at least I get pissed off and only much later will I ask myself your horrible question, which is breaking my balls, as if it were a good kick: does justice justify murder? Ask me again some other day, don't forget about it, don't throw it out with the trash, please. Think the worst of my moral sense."

"What do we know, Angel?" asked my mother, stroking my father's hand. He hesitated, then answered:

"About what we did, nothing. They're not going to say a word. At least not until it suits them. And if they're not saying anything now it's because it suits them to keep quiet. Remember the President's favorite motto: 'In Mexico you can do anything, as long as you can blame it on someone.' "

A half-opaque light passed through my mother's eyes.

"You say you're conservative, and I say I'm left-wing. But we both know that labels don't matter. What does matter are concrete acts, okay? But did we really do what we did, Angel of love? Are you sure? *Are we both sure? Did we really do it?*"

Ever since their first night in seclusion, she was answered by the wailing voices of the professional mourning women, who were always hired to come down from the town of Treinta up in the mountains to lament the daily but sporadic deaths that occurred in Acapulco.

These new dusks belonged to their most dolorous, their longest choral chanting: it seemed to be born at the bottom of the sea, and my parents heard it every night without speaking, because it reminded them that not only tourists, literary critics, government functionaries, and millionaires died that day in Aca, but waiters and chambermaids, taxi drivers, and cashiers: but Homero Fagoaga did not die, and now he's a senatorial candidate, we're fucked . . .

These bastards *are not thinking about me in the slightest.*

They know nothing about my shock: expelled by my father, rejected by my mother, against both of them I've set myself up in the womb and I myself am creating the placenta, sucking blood and food through the sponge that I'm weaving onto my mother, who has been invaded now by my new being: I, the accepted parasite, the guest who devours his mother to stay alive, taking refuge there for nine months, thinking now that this pair of nuts is following the noise of the hired mourners, which has supplanted that of the coyotes, that I'm already a disk about one one-hundredth of an inch across which is rapidly growing from button shape to tiny needle shape with head, trunk, and umbilical cord. What else matters? I'd like to ask them noisily about all this that happens without anyone's knowing it. Or about everything that you endlessly discuss, what's happening with everyone's knowing about it.

Beginning in the third week, when the nice lady who returned the wallet belonging to Don Wigberto Garza Toledano (native of etc.) was given a national prize, I was already a well-established embryo beneath the surface of Mom's uterus, I eat away at things and grow in search of food, I expand the very cavity that received me, I fill the empty spaces, creating my own head and my own tail.

But then they endanger this entire enterprise by hiking up to the highest peak on Uncle Homero's property, a crag that dominates Acapulco's two fronts, Puerto Marqués and Revolcadero Beach on one side, and the entire bay on the other, in order to make sure that Acapretty was destroyed over a month ago, on Epiphany, and that even if the newspapers and television do not reveal it, the Professional Mourners from Treinta certainly do, as do my parents' eyes (the remains of the discotheque float like a gigantic condom; the crepe worn by the models trapped on the rocks at La Countess beach flutters in the air), and their long strides to the top of the crag make me fear a Christophalypse consisting of hormonal deserts, hunger, thirst, the prelude to a rain of blood that kills me and washes out the cloaca which I will have become, dissolved, unformed, again: inform.

My parents go down to the beach where I was conceived, staring at the smoke and dead fury that was Acapulco, the Babylon of the poor, chosen to exemplify in the mind of the nation ALL THAT IS NOT THE SWEET FATHERLAND: standing on the hilltops, they hear the melancholy sirens, and my father reminds my mother that one day he returned from Oaxaca transformed—a different man, disconcerted by the melancholy of having lost what he'd just won.

On the beach where they created me and over which Uncle Homero flew, my father writes on the sand:

Fatherland, your surface is a pothole, I mean

Your sky is stagnant smog

The Baby Jesus granted you a palace in Las Lomas and a ski lodge in Vail

And your oil deposits were a gift from a devil who lives

on the spot market in Rotterdam, I mean

A little wave came and washed it all away.

Angel and Angeles found Tomasito's body in an advanced state of decomposition in a canoe that had lodged between two rocks on Pichilinque beach.

Piercing his back was a black spear, fantastically wrapped in green feathers: a jungle spear.

Angeles: "Just a minute. Homero and Tomasito weren't enemies: they were allies."

Angel: "Homero thought Tomasito was his enemy, so he killed him when he fled."

Angeles: "The Four Fuckups found out about Tomasito's betrayal and they killed him."

Angel: "Tomasito was just one more victim of the slaughter that went on in Acapulco."

Angeles: "What Tomasito died of was his death."

Angel: "Everything happened simultaneously. One event happened neither before nor after but right next to or between another two events:

TOMASITO AND HOMERO
FRIENDS

TOMASITO AND HOMERO
ACCIDENTS

TOMASITO AND HOMERO
ENEMIES

Angeles: "Nobody died; they all went to the beach . . ."

Angel: "You and I are walking arm-in-arm along Peachy Tongue Beach."

Angeles: "Animus intelligence!"

They freed the canoe, set fire to it, and launched it on the tide, where it floated toward Manila, the Pacific, Tomasito's home . . .

Then it happened that out of the seas of smoke and blood and arsenic and mustard, enveloped in the distant fog of panting coyotes and mist the obscene color of pureed cockroaches, there emerged a body that swam and panted like a coyote but which was tenacious in its decision not to sink in those waters polluted in saecula saeculorum: the smoke rose from the burst cupolas, ashes rained down like grotesque green and yellow chewing gum over the sea from the floating disco Divan the Terrible: and the diminutive figure of a tiny man's tiny yellow hand seized the prow of the black canoe where the cadaver of the Filipino servant Tomasito was lying, and emerged from the seas of smoke and blood and arsenic and mustard, falling prostrate like a Pekinese puppy at the feet of the Filipino.

4. All Citizens Have the Right to Information

 INFOREADER: They haven't spoken, they haven't done anything beyond what they've already said and done, they haven't lived beyond what they've already lived, and what about me? When they started imagining probabilities, alternatives for the story, without remembering, first of all, that they've already made me and, second, that I myself possess a thousand alternatives, they drive me nuts and make me want to cut out, to leave my mother's ovary without returning to my father's testicle:

They say I will be a boy and be named Christopher, they've gone so far as to decide that for me, the assholes, but suppose I turn out to be a girl? Are they going to Herodize me the way Imelda did with Tomasito? They realize that the probabilities of my being a Mexican boy named Christopher are about one in 183,675,900,453,248 and that all it would have taken was a turn of the genetic screw for me to be an armadillo, and you know, I like that idea. It sounds good, a lost, friendless armadillo with no obligations on one of those misty hilltops down which we tumble, or a jolly dolphin, making love at ten miles per hour over the blue Pacific?

"Have you ever been in Pacífica?"

Why does my dad always ask himself that same question? He'd be much better off thinking that, thanks to me, lost unity will be reconstituted, lost time found once more, all because of little old me, my respected progenitors, your information divided, get it? understand what I'm telling you?

"Is information really power?" asks my dad, and I start trotting along like a burro, wishing I could tell him that his sperm only had half of my vital information, and my mother's reproductive cells only had the other half, and then

I ARRIVE

and just for being myself I gather together all the NEW information, oh what a glory, to know it now, from this moment on, I combine the total number of chromosomes that my father and mother can give to a new being so he will be new and will not be they, even if they have engendered him, and so that one day I can return them what they lost, their memory, their prophecy, their complete being: so why are they mistreating me like this, bouncing me along a ridge on top of a burro in a rainstorm, with night coming on? What did I ever do to them? We barely know each other and already they start fucking me over!

What do they know?

INFOTEL: Someone called Uncle Homero's house in Acapulco, saying he has a radiogram from my Uncle Fernando Benítez transmitted from an NII helicopter to the presidential antenna in Mexico City and from there to the private telephone of Dr. Fagoaga, LL.D., in the Pearl of the Pacific, the Mecca of Tourism, the Oriental Port of the New World, the Bay of the China Galleon and the Manila Galleon:

"Have you ever been in Pacífica?"

This is what the message says to my nephew and niece Angel and Angeles Palomar: I expect you on the 22nd of February, the anniversary of the day President Madero, the Apostle of democracy, was murdered, in Cuajincuilapa, all communication between the D.F. and Aca inexplicably cut did you know Homero is a candidate question mark yours Benítez.

What do any of us know?

Wake up, children, wake up, said Grandpa Rigoberto Palomar in an alarmed but serious voice, wake up, today is Saturday, the 22nd of February, and they pulled the blanket off the still-sleeping President Francisco Madero, they took him, surrounded by bayonets, out of his cell, they put him in an automobile along with Mr. Pino Suárez, they stopped the car at the gates of the penitentiary, they made them both get out, they shot each one, a bullet in the head, at 11 o'clock p.m.: Wake up, children, we have to go to the Revolution.

What do I know?

The day of the great uproar, the blind young Indian, wild from the intensity of the invisible noises and smells, took the virgin girl he'd been sniffing after for over a week with a dizzy delicacy: it was after the girl's first visit from the sticky sorceress, and the smell of blood both repelled and attracted him. She said nothing, she allowed herself to be touched, and she herself touched the man's smooth hot cheek with pleasure.

INFOGENES: This only I know: That in the vertigo of my Uncle Fernando Benítez's visit to the people up on the plateau, a blind boy was created at the same time that I was created in Acapulco.

The right to information: this only I know. Grandfather knows which day it is in history, Uncle Fernando knows what days those are in the calendar. But my parents, do they know anything?

INLOCOPARENTIS: They must not even be aware that they've created me; they just couldn't be so cruel, such children of their own genes that they have created my death without even acknowledging my life: acid and arid, irritated and insecure, scraping against everything around me, everything that comes to me in this seesawing around (seesaw my eye, something between a gallop and an earthquake!), which in reality is a throbbing racket for one who was conceived on the beach under the palm trees and who now knows he is in another place, savagely transported in one jump to a restless, volcanic, thorny landscape: one day they'll tell me about it, and I'll visualize it, even though I know it right now, I know that (it's my darkest secret) one day I'll forget it because your mercies should know that no one is willing to give a child the supplementary days to which he has a right: nine months extra, winning the lottery and getting a Christmas bonus all at the same time, nine months more than the adults, but the adults say, how can this be? They think that it's enough to recognize that

WHEN WE'RE BORN WE ARE ALREADY NINE MONTHS OLD

which means we possess an intolerable advantage, namely that we have the power to impose the laws of our infancy on them and there is nothing they fear more even though they won't admit it: what I'm dreaming is, what is is what I dream, what I want I touch, I touch what I want, what I desire exists, what exists is what I desire, I have no reason to work, intrigue, screw other people, covet my neighbor's property, what for, when all I want I have right here at hand, can you see this your mercies idem?

There is nothing more subversive than instantly turning desire into reality, and that's why they try to surround us unborn types, and later, when we're children, they limit us, surround us with schools and jails and churches and programmed vacations and calendar holidays and economic whorehouses erected between a child and the object of his desire, which would be Christmas in July and Two-Year Vacations and Around the Day in Eighty Worlds (which, for Julio Cortázar, would be July in Christmas), and the Garden of Delights—no, all pleasures deferred, we have to conquer it all by means of obedience the discipline of work austerity abstinence Calvinistic savings and the banishment of fantasy from the desert of reality instead of the fantasy of banishment from the desert of reality, Satan: look, says my old and interminable chain of genes to me, look where we've gotten to since puritanism took over the world, pretty well fucked up since Simon Peter, say my chromosomatic chains, and Saul-Saul-Why-Do-You-Persecute-Me imposed his rules of abstention after abstention, says my father on foot behind my mother trotting along on her burro through the Sierra Madre, riding the burro along the steep, curved, almost virgin paths that go, says Uncle Fernando, who is guiding us, from Acapulco to the Sierra, not even Cortés knew about these routes, adds our uncle, who knows all of them, and says put on your ponchos here comes a cloudburst and the peaks grow gray suddenly, crowns of misty iron, fleeting heart flutter in the sky: my mother's nearby heart also beats faster and my father recites out loud, almost sings, scolding the storm that whips us and is about to take revenge on us, say I thoroughly saturated by the Acapulco excesses organized by my mom and dad, by the contradictions I already perceive between their condemnations of puritanism and their indiscriminate extermination of vice in Acapulco: did two young homosexual lovers deserve to die merely because they went around wearing mess jackets à la Tyrone Power? Did Egberto deserve to die because he was a fag or because he was a critic? And Emilio, because he was a puritan or because he was intolerant? And the models, because of the pleasure they gave or for the money they earned? Ada and Deng because . . . ?

"What are you talking about?"

"Nothing, nothing at all," said my father and he looked for an instant at the mask of his Uncle Don Fernando Benítez, who would be turning eighty in a few days and who still walked energetically through the tropical highland storms, leading us on foot through mountains he knew better than the back of his hand, Don Fernando Benítez's creole mask, his blue eyes blurry from the storm that beats against the lenses of his gold-plated wire-rimmed glasses, his slightly bulbous nose distilling the essence of the squall that drips off the ends of his handlebar mustache bathed in the idem, his mouth a rictus of sad wisdom:

"You two asked me about Pacífica, but do you know where I've just been? Doing an interview with the last Lacandon Indian. But guess what happened? The last of the Lacandon Indians interviewed me instead."

He groaned and furrowed his brow, raising a hand to the imaginary knot of an imaginary tie. He says the Indians are all we have left; they are our ghosts; for thirty years he's been interviewing them, defending them, going to the most remote places to see them before they disappear, oh of course, saying to Mexicans, we owe loyalty to the world of the Indians, even if we disdain them, exploit them, because it's the loyalty we owe to death. He gets excited about the idea, he stops a moment, just for theatrical effect, damn but we've become just as eccentric, just as fragile, just as condemned to extinction as they have, why don't we recognize the fact?

"Killing an Indian is like burning down a library."

He roared out a lament that conquered the storm and echoed through the sierra:

"Oh, God, all of us are Lacandons!"

"So no one in the rest of the country said anything about Acapulco?" asked my mother Angeles, insistently but serenely. I suspect that she hasn't got the remotest idea that I'm bouncing around like a marble in these boondocks she's carried me to.

"No." Uncle Benítez shook his hat-covered head, turning his back on them once again and stubbornly maintaining the pace. "Nobody knows a thing about it."

Our Uncle Fernando Benítez made his nemesis face, and I registered what happened in the seed of what would soon be my cerebral cortex: "Killing an Indian is like burning down a library," and we've already got more than two hundred pages written, one movie hour, two TV hours (including commercials), several oppressive nightmares because it's all over, and nevertheless we persist in reliving it every twenty-four hours: Father and Mother, my genes tell me better get used to it, Chris, that's Mexico for you, live one more day so you can live on that day the seven centuries since the advent of the Heagle and the Herpent.

Please, your discriminatory worships, please do not ask to know what my parents and Uncle Fernando Benítez see at 2 p.m., three days after their climb up the sierra, the southern mommy, in the storm, three days after sleeping in shacks Don Fernando knows and in Indian villages which take him in with astonished recognition, as if they were getting ready to visit him quite soon and don't bother coming out here to see us, Quetzalcoatl: cold, high nights I remember (I shall remember), the smell of burned forests, the grunting of hogs running around freely and the soulful laugh of the burro who is sadly, happily sure we don't understand him simply because he doesn't speak to us. Now we descend to the flatland, where the sun and shadow are equally long at all hours of the day, sculptures made of air, astonished at their own existence (we are in Guerrero, at the corner of Oaxaca, says my father; let's go to the market in Igualis-tlahuaca, I'm hungry and they make delicious grasshoppers in red pepper there and then they say he who eats grasshopper never leaves this place):

Better look at what's written on the hillsides:

MEXICANS: INDUSTRIALIZE
YOU WON'T LIVE LONGER, BUT YOU WILL LIVE BETTER

The saying that made Don Ulises López, Penny's father, remember?, famous. My mother threw the rebozo that had been covering her head over her shoulders, good old Penny sure does get around.

MIXTEC: ACT RESPONSIBLY!
VOTE DIALECTICALLY!

but my father says look at the farmers on horseback, riding at a controlled pace, wearing grimy straw hats, the bridles black with sweat, the red tulips, the blue sky through the leafy laurels, the burros laden with hay, the light rain, a three-minute sprinkle, the noise of the rivers hidden underground and the vast rose-colored fields, a valley of rolling heather and the sudden end of the rain.

No, says Uncle F., you don't have to look so far away, just look over there at the gangrenous walls of Igualistlahuaca, Guerrero:

CITIZENS OF GUERRERO STATE
VOTE FOR A MAN WHO'S REALLY GREAT
VOTE FOR PRI, VOTE FOR HOMERO
HE'LL MAKE A FUTURE FOR GUERRERO!

and if any doubts remained

INSTITUTIONAL REVOLUTIONARY PARTY
Today at 2 P.M.
Igualistlahuaca Arena
DON'T MISS THE BIG WRESTLING MATCH
His Honor, Homero Fagoaga, Senatorial Candidate
Mass Meeting Outside Igualistlahuaca Church

ROBIN VERSUS BATMAN
Eight O'clock Sharp
A five-fall match
It all begins at 2:00, right in front of the church
Citizens Unite Behind Homero
Fagoaga, He's Our Man
Bluedevils versus Ungrateful Pussy
FAGOAGA, HE'S OKAY!
HIT A HOMER WITH HOMERO!
CITIZENS OF IGUALISTLAHUACA: WAKE UP!
GET BEHIND THE INTERNATIONALIST SOCIALIST PARTY
LUXEMBURGIST FACTION OF
LIEBKNECHT TENDENCY
OAXACA PLEKHANOV CHAPTER
FIGHT FOR THE VICTORY OF THE DICTATORSHIP OF
THE PROLETARIAT!
ALL UNITE AGAINST HOMERO!

HOMERO: THE LANGUAGE CANDIDATE

Yes, I, Homero, am your homer, I win the game and save hometown honor for the forgotten masses of hometown Mexico, intoned His Honor Homero Fagoaga, from the bandstand set up in front of the Igualistlahuaca church. He insisted on it, my debut, my maiden speech, if you'll allow me to play the coquette with you, brother Delegate of the PRI, maiden speech in the language of Shakespeare means a virgin speech, ha ha, see, just imagine for a moment, after all that this tongue, bequeathed to me by the glorious hand mutilated at the battle of Lepanto, has been through! By which I mean, metaphorically, you've got to understand the subtleties of our maidenspain prosody, that is, you've got to understand the language of Spain, Mr. Delegate, made in pain, because Pain Is Spain, Mr. Delegate, the Spanish tongue taken as a perpetual and painful wedding night of proper discourse, and since the local Delegate, a bucktoothed, myopic lawyer from Cuajincuilapa, baptized, of all things, Elijo Raíz, was staring at him in incomprehension, Homero said to himself, humm, out in these boondocks there isn't a single shyster, graduated from some music school or other, who doesn't think he's potential Benito Juárez: now they're going to see what it means to use language to fascinate the multitudes, right now! He demanded and was granted permission by the local PRI to give his first speech, his virgin speech, his maidenspich made in Spain maiden's pain Maiden Spain and Mad in Spain in the plaza outside the Igualistlahuaca church, with the street and the market in front of him and the altars behind, demonstrating in that way, candidate Fagoaga explained to his crosseyed interlocutor, that in the Party of Revolutionary Institutions all Mexicans should coexist, rich and poor, chauvinist and xenophile, reactionaries and progressives, after all Mr. Delegate, what was the meaning of our national political system if not to overcome, once and for all, the fratricidal confrontations between liberals and conservatives which in their nineteenth-century avatars condemned us, as they did our sister republics of Bolivaresque destiny, to swing back and forth between anarchy and dictatorship, self-perpetuating despotism and savage hatred, worthy of Shakespeare's Verona: the Mexican Revolution, Mr. Delegate, reconciled the Masonic Montagues of the Scottish Rite with the Capulets of the Yorkish Rite, it overcame Mexico's Sicilian weaknesses and the Balkanic lethargy of Latin America and only erred in its rhetorical opposition to the banners of Christ.

"But now," said Uncle H. as he swallowed an armadillo in green *mole* sauce in one of the incomparable culinary retreats lining the Igualistlahuaca plaza, "it falls to us to reconcile secular faith with divine faith, the sacred with the profane."

Who could forget the visit of the Polish Pope to Mexico fourteen years before, the most spectacular entrance into the capital since that of Hernán Cortés, when, sotto voce, the most prudent strategists in national politics said to themselves, as they peeked out from behind the thick brocade curtains at the Seat of Executive Power at the seven million souls who awaited, who followed, and who surrounded the Vicar of Christ in the Zócalo and the Cathedral:

"All the Holy Father would have to do is order them to seize the National Palace. They would do it, your honor, and nothing could stop them. Am I right?"

"Well," Uncle Homero directed his beautifully enunciated prose against the difficulties of a bit of crackling (overcoming that recalcitrant tidbit, of course), "the time has come for us to reconquer the sacred for the Revolution. Let us stop, Mr. Delegate, being fools and playing at anticlericalism. We've recaptured everything in order to achieve our heart's desire, National Unity: left and right, bankers and field hands, now also, thanks to our August National Guide, even our Ancestral Matriarchy. I warn you, let us capture the world of the sacred before it captures us. I warn you, Mr. Delegate from the state of Guerrero, Coreligionist in PRI, Don Elijo Raíz: there is an Ayatollah in our Future. Now let's finish up this crackling!"

A parrot squawked on the shadowed portal of the plaza, and Homero, flying on metaphoric wings, swallowed his plum dessert in one gulp, eagerly thinking about the Mixtec–Zapotec homeland.

5

And so it was that at midday Don Homero Fagoaga ascended the bandstand erected in front of the old rose-colored church in Igualistlahuaca, equidistant, our budding national figure, from the two towers and from the bell towers worked in pale cut stone and watered-down marble. Uncle H. standing before his microphone, surrounded by sixty-three local PRI hierarchs, the tribunal festooned with banners that repeated the slogans of the day, Don Homero surrounded by small-town orators eager to be seen with the future Senator but also with the sixty-three hierarchs, one for each year the Party had been in power, to think there are men sixty-three years old who have never seen any other party in power, murmured Uncle Fernando indignantly as he led my parents Angel and Angeles (and, as a bonus, me as well, though none of them knew about it at the time, they'll only remember me retroactively, retroat-tractively—really acting retro is what I understand it to be), who were now entering the crowded square, she on the burro, he wrapped in his poncho, heading toward the tribunal where Uncle H., saved from the Acapulco furies right under the noses of my impotent parents Angel and Angeles, lets himself be loved by the PRI ephebocracy, the young men who make sure his microphone is set at the proper angle, who smile at him by smiling at the sun, and who seek their own rapid, not to say meteoric, rise through the hierarchy of our civil church, the P–R–I, their black eyes already shining with the dream of being Pope, cardinal at least, what about archbishop? okay, bishop would be enough, deacon if there's nothing better to be had, sacristan sounds good, altar boy's better than nothing, Swiss Guard, whatever, whatever your mercies say as long as they're not left out in the cold, and his honor Homero Fagoaga glowing amid the am-bition of the young men and the fatigue of the old ones, ayyy the survivors of heighty campaigns like this one, height million height hundred heighty-height glasses of Hi-C, mountains of black *mole*, horse meat, barbecued pork with everything on it, skin and hair, civic parades and social nights dancing polkas with fat ladies, in town after town, village after village, survivors of phantasmagoric cam-paigns—the sexennial Mexican presidential nonrace—for president and senator, the triennial races for the Congress, biennial races for local legislators and municipal presidents, all of them bewitched by this need to campaign, to become president, as if they were going up against the Italian Communists, the English Tories, and the French Gaullists: bah! exclaims Uncle Fernando, whose speech my mom is recording amid the Mixtec Mass this morning for the future reference of my collective unconsciousness, only the gringos beat us out with a single party that pretends to be two parties. The only truly authentic slogan should be:

ELECTIONS COME EVERY SIX YEARS,
BUT MISFORTUNE IS ALWAYS WITH US

Sixty-three years, my dear niece and nephew, what do you think of that, and no end in sight, said Uncle Fernando: not Hitler, not Perón, not even Franco, only the U.S.S.R. beats us and now not even them because now we have a PAN president, which allows the PRI to blame the opposition for everything and to govern with more power than ever, and for that very reason Don Homero Fagoaga adjusts the microphone to the height of his multiple chins, warms up his delivery, the crowds gather, curious, trucked in, bribed, a hundred pesos, a taco, lemonade, a beer, a brass band, you name it, things might get screwed up if you don't come, let's see now about your property-line suit, let's see, let's sue, let's sewer: with a great sense of satisfaction, Homero scanned the multitude of Mixtec citizens spread out in front of him, standing there on the pavement stones next to the sickly pines and laurels near the church and beyond the gates out to the unpaved street and the market tents of opulent misery. He looked at the heads of the multitude of varnished straw hats, the heads of the women crowned with green, blue, and scarlet silk, their tresses tied up with orange and lilac wool, four thousand, five thousand heads carrying traditional offerings, with earthenware pots balanced on their heads, heads offering tomatoes and herbs, grasshoppers and onions, and the nervous little heads of the children, first running like porcupines but finally they too, the happy children in the land of sad grownups, captured by the sinuous words of Don Homero Fagoaga, who was comparing the Guerrero sierra "to Italic Latium and Hellenic Attica, glorious sites of humanistic honor, cradles of democracy, crucibles of society where a metaphysical tremor made men and mountains, children and stones all speak in one voice to repeat with the immortal tribune, quaestor, and consul, my model in action and speech, Don Marcus Tullius Cicero, of Arpino, mens cuisque is est quisque, which in the glorious language we speak thanks to the Hispanic Motherland, to, of course, no discredit to the Autochthonous Motherland, which I see here exemplified in its roots of impassioned telluric tremor, means the spirit is the true being and where, oh citizens of Guerrero, would that truth be more profoundly true and scientifically rational and precise than here in the Mixtec homeland, ever fertile cradle of the glorious motherland—MEEXXXIIICCCOOO: Civis Romanum sum, the glorious tribune exclaimed with pride but without arrogance and here we can repeat, Civis Guerrerensis sum, because if indeed the uncle of Augustus declared his modest and for being modest moving preference to be first a son of his village and second a son of Rome, it was not merely for that reason that he stood a model for legions of his admirers then and now, but above all looking forward to, anticipating, the Mexican meritocracy that our Revolutionary Institutional Party offers with equal opportunities for all, for each and every one of you, to rise, as the Well-Deserving Don Benito Juárez rose, from illiterate shepherd to the Presidential Throne, from being first in place of honor in Rome and saying to his people: You have Caesar and his fortune with you!"

He cleared his throat, was offered a turbid glass of *tepache*, his microphone, which the vibrations of his mighty word and the pulsation of his potbelly had pushed far away, was readjusted, a little old drunk raised his bottle of Corona Extra and shouted out Long Live Don Porfirio Díaz and Homero: oh, fellow sons and daughters of Guerrero, let it at least be said of Homero Fagoaga that he serves both you and Our Lord in Heaven (pregnant pause): there is, fellow voters, fellow citizens, friends, brothers in the Lord (significant pause), and coreligionists of the Revolution (hasty conclusion: con brio), *no corner of the world that smiles on us more than this one*, as the ancient bard Horace said of his native Venosa.

Uncle Homero paused with a distant but fierce blaze in his eyes: irritated at the stupidity of the people hired to plaster the walls of Igualistlahuaca with posters and how they'd confused the hour, the name, the theme, and the message of his sacrorevolutionary oratory with a vulgar wrestling match between Batman and Robin, and what, by the way, could be further from his five thousand listeners, Homero suddenly said to himself, the Match or Cicero? No matter, he sighed: a Mexican can make do with anything because he can be anything: the PRI not only allows it but makes certain he can. But in that briefest of instants in which the local Party hierarchs thought some things and the candidate thought others and Uncle Fernando, my dad, and my mom, and I inside her (a mere figment of the collective unconscious inside the spirals of history, the vicious circle) felt ourselves pushed, first pressured secretly, then little by little pressed by a human, incomprehensible power that could not be located in any one individual and even less attributable to that grand no one which is everyone, finally trampled, tossed by the multitude of Mixtecs who moved forward with impassive faces, devoid of laughter, devoid of hatred, devoid of tears, with their unmoving terra-cotta features, as Uncle H. would say from his bandstand, with a blind determination and an enthusiasm that was frightening precisely because of its silence, a quiet horde of Mixtec Maenads moving toward the bandstand occupied by Uncle Homero and the Sixty-three Hierarchs: can you guess what happened next? They didn't applaud, they didn't throw tomatoes or grasshoppers at the distinguished personages on the dais: they just moved, advanced, my father later said, in the same way the waves, the clouds, all the beautiful and terrible things in this world, move, as Homero opened his arms to receive the love of the masses which would waft him on to a senatorial bench, from this dump to SOMEWHERE OVER THE RAINBOW! oh, my Uncle H., in what moment did you realize what the Sixty-three PRI Hierarchs had begun to guess, the worst, seeing that silent mass, hardhearted, devoid of emotion, moving toward him with the fatality of the six-year term, with an imperturbable resolution that was open to any and all interpretations, and Homero asked the young coffee-cup-sized orator on his left, whose name was Tezozómoc Cuervo, LL.D.:

"Did they like it?"

"My dear sir, see for yourself."

Homero sighed in the face of this native political dexterity and turned to the hierarch on his right, an old man with a pear-shaped body and loose suspenders, famous in local circles as the first and foremost supporter of President Calles in the state of Guerrero, Don Bernardino Gutiérrez:

"Tell me: why don't they clap?"

"They don't know how."

"Then why don't they throw tomatoes and onions if they don't like my speech?"

"It isn't a matter of their liking it or disliking it. To the contrary."

"You mean they didn't understand my Latin allusions, is that it?"

"No, sir. They didn't understand anything. Not one of these Indians speaks Spanish."

Don Homero had no time to show shock, fury, or disdain, much less to get on his horse and hightail it; impossible to know if it was excessive hatred, outrage, or fascination, or perhaps a love incapable of showing itself in any other way, that was moving five thousand Mixtec men, women, and children from the Guerrero mountains who, beyond communication, incapable of communication, reached the bandstand, stretched out their hands, pulled down the tricolor paper flags, the tricolor rosettes, and the PRI posters, then the eyeglasses belonging to the state delegate from Cuajinicuilapa, bucktoothed and myopic, the daisy in the lapel of the m.c. and the old politico's suspenders, which snapped back against his feeble chest, and that's when the panic began: the hierarchy turned its back on the people and went running into the church, shouting sanctuary, sanctuary!: the trembling candles were extinguished by their stampeding feet and their screams and my father, still wearing his rain poncho and with his face covered by four days' growth of beard, led my mother, still on her burro and wrapped in a blue shawl and with me in the center of the universe, and the Indians gave way, they let us pass and my father made a sign with his hand and said come here Homero, you shall pass through the eye of a needle because that's exactly how wide our mercy is: but virtue is measured in magnitude, not things, and of course our Uncle Don Fernando translated these holy words into Mixtec and all of them stood aside without uttering a word, like the waters of the watermelon-colored sea while the sixty-three hierarchs locked the church doors, and braced themselves against them to add to the bolts the weight of each one of their sixty-three years of political predominance, and Don Bernardino Gutiérrez, first and foremost supporter of President Calles in the state of Guerrero, exclaimed that you can't get milk from an ox but that when it's time to fry beans what you need is grease, and Elijo Raíz, LL.D., who came in in 1940 with Avila Camacho, added that it all had to end the way it began, in the bosom of the Holy Mother Church, hallelujah, amen, push, pull, and national unity!

6

Curiously enough, the first things we feel, even as mere monozygotes inside the maternal womb, are the fluctuations in the exterior dynamics that surround us and in which our mothers participate; for instance, the apprehensions entailed in our flight from the holy places of Igualistlahuaca when we were going against the tide of the masses who listened to my Uncle Homero's discourse as they pressed up against the locked doors of the rose-colored church with its double cut-stone towers, against which doors sixty-three leaders of the Revolutionary Institutional Party of Guerrero were pushing with all their might, shoulders, hands, hips, and backsides to keep the aforesaid masses from entering, since those masses had just scared them out of their wits by moving without them and they didn't understand (nor did we, the group running away) whether what the citizens, the faithful, the plebes, the helots, the great unwashed, the redskins (each of the sixty-three was muttering what he really thought about them as he pushed against the splintering door), wanted to show was a great love, a concentrated hatred, or an explosive despair devoid of hatred or love.

The first things we feel: the bustle, the ambition, the obstacles— other bodies—that impede our own movement, my mom's and mine for instance, our tensions, our fear of everything around us that moves with or against us, said my mother and I. Don't, your worships, jump to conclusions because I was there and you weren't, as we were once again on burro or on foot heading for the hills and the mountains that Uncle Fernando knows like the back of his hand, as he heads for Malinaltzin, he tells us, because there is very little landscape left and even less land left in this land of ours: where are we Mexicans going to walk around? North of the Temazcal is off-limits because there's a war on there, east of Perote is out of bounds because that's where the oil is, north of the Infiernillo is out of bounds because that's where . . .

"Pacífica is . . ." says my father in a low voice, but Uncle H. was not listening, neither to my father nor to my Uncle Fernando, as he snorted in rage astride the longest-suffering burro in burrodom: the rotund personage whines and regurgitates, not even listening to what my father and my other uncle, Don Fernando, are saying.

"Oh, Lord, what could I have done to deserve this humiliation, I, saved twice in the same year by my nephew Angel to whom I have done so much evil? Oh, I beg forgiveness, a thousand times I beg forgiveness."

Homero Fagoaga slipped off his burro as they went down a moun- tainside and kissed the feet of my father—ramrod-straight, bearded, green-eyed, and Guelfish. Forgive me, nephew, I am in your hands, you saved me from the Acapulco mob by sending Tomasito to warn me in time so I could escape by speedboat and parachute instead of using the minisub I had prepared (they didn't take my etc. into account) . . .

"It was Tomasito who warned you?" groans my mother.

"Precisely. And because of his loyalty the heroic son of the ar- chipelago died, died, I say, at the hand of pimpish types whose faces and manners I seemed to recognize," said Uncle H., staring at us with eyes that said I'm holding a royal flush too, but we're all pals here, right? "Who will ever be able to explain what makes some people completely loyal?" he added, wagging his tremendous Tartuffesque jowls. "Tomasito is dead!"

"And you are alive, Uncle."

"Thanks to you. And I had time to prepare my campaign and call my plane from Mexico City, so that I could keep my appointment with our well-beloved Mexican soil. Now you have saved me from those monolingual aborigines, oh how can I ever pay you for doing me such favors?"

"You miserable fat slob," interrupted Uncle Fernando, "what are you running away from?"

"My best speech, dear oh dear, the one I'd worked over most, the one I'd virtually chiseled out of Parian marble, the most eloquent, the most erudite, my most heartfelt one as well, lost in the face of five thousand sandal-wearing plebes who didn't understand a word! Mexico in a nutshell, my dear, dear relatives! Everything for nothing and nothing for everyone! But doubt, doubt is what's consuming me! Did they love me? Did they hate me? Please, don't take my doubt away from me!" said Homero, standing up with dignity.

"The one thing there can be no doubt about is what your buddies from the PRI will be thinking about you, you pudding on legs," Uncle Fernando declared.

"Bah, after all that confusion they'll understand my reasons just as I'll understand theirs," said Uncle H. with diminishing haughtiness, as he mounted his burro with bizarre agility.

"Well, my dear Uncle, it seems to me that even as we speak the tribe has probably already chopped up the hierarchs who vainly sought refuge in the religious sanctuary. Dear me, yes, Uncle. The purest tamale. Just you think about that."

"All sixty-three, nephew?"

"But of course, Uncle."

"Elijo Raíz, the delegate born in Cuajinicuilapa?"

"Ground up fine."

"Don Bernardino Gutiérrez, first and foremost supporter of President Calles in the state of Guerrero?"

"Ground up fine."

"But just yesterday, as we were leaving the airport for the hotel, I asked him, listen, Don Bernardino, you who've been in national politics since the days of General Calles, how have you managed to survive and adapt yourself to so many changes, fluctuations, and shake-ups? Think of me as a humble apprentice and let your experience illuminate my hope. Then Don Bernardino stuck his index finger in his mouth and stuck it out of the car window to tell which way the wind was blowing."

"That's how to do it, son."

"Gelded like a hog."

"And the young Tezozómoc Cuervo, pristine orator, formed like a jug and of coffeeish hue?"

"That boy, as Don Bernardino would say: now he's a busted jug."

"Good God, what have I set into motion?" whined Homero Fagoaga.

"The beginning of the end, you miserable swine," interjected our guide, Don Fernando, without bothering to turn around to look at him as he drove the mules back the way we came.

"The end of the PRI?" asked Homero, about to fall off again.

"You look pale."

"Deflated."

"Oh! Ah!" The burro bucked, sending the not so future Senator flying through the air.

Homero hung on my father's neck, who later said it was like being hugged by a gigantic vanilla ice-cream cone with chocolate sauce on the verge of melting.

"Hide me," said this would-be Senator Fagoaga, desperately but alertly: "Don't let them take their revenge on me, I'll do anything you ask, but don't abandon me to the revenge of the PRI!"

He stretched out his arm. "Fernando, my friend."

"Will you be quiet, you miserable swine?" Our Uncle Fernando turned to face him. "You are going down in history as the man who destroyed the PRI! Damned if that isn't historical irony! You, Homero Fagoaga, illustrious member of the PRI . . ."

"At your service!" exclaimed Homero, almost standing up, like one listening to the national anthem, but then fell instantly on his knees and begged to be hidden in the old house in Tlalpan that had belonged to my father's parents, the house of bright colors near the Church of St. Peter the Apostle, the house the wicked fat man had ordered seized and sealed in his lawsuit against his nephew's prodigality, but which was, said the finicky creep, the last place anyone would think to look for him. Hide me there, no one would ever think to look for me there, the enmity between him and his relatives was well known, and thus he could respect the devout modesty of his sisters, Capitolina and Farnesia, the last two certified virgins in Mexico. Sure, and put up with Uncle H. in the house in Tlalpan, which would remain sealed, cut off from profane eyes, where no one would look for him, in such proclaimed modesty, within such a frugal space . . .

"And what do we get out of it?"

Uncle Homero, on his knees, spread his arms like a penitent.

"I'll stop the suit that would declare you, my nephew, Don Angel Palomar y Fagoaga, prodigal and irresponsible, I'll pay all court costs and damages, I will return the Tlalpan property to you, I will free up the gold pesos legitimately inherited by my aforesaid nephew after the perfectly legitimate, sudden, and undeniably accidental death of his parents, Don Diego Palomar and Doña Isabella Fagoaga de Palomar, my sister, the couple who came to be known as the Mexican Curies before the accursed taco crossed their scientific path. What else do you want? More?"

"You are going to resign publicly from the PRI, Homero."

From then on, my mommy is going to tell to anyone who might care to listen that the shock of our Uncle Homero Fagoaga was eclipsed and simultaneously magnified by the afternoon glow in the mountains, that shock of the earth as it looked at the clouds, the shock of the clouds as they looked at the cut stone, and the shock of the stone as it contemplated itself in the light, and the shock of the light as it found the flashing expanse of the field of heather. Nothing in all that could match the historical shock painted on our uncle's face.

In the oleaginous eyes of the man kneeling before his detested saviors, in his equally oily syllables, in the very posture of his defeudalized abjection, which contrasted with the indifferent splendor of invisible nature, my mother managed to distinguish a plea for compassion, destroyed, of course, in the act by Homero's words:

"But, Fernando . . . Fernando . . . I was born with the PRI, it's the source of my national pride and my personal destiny, Fernando: I can't conceive of life without the PRI, I am oriented, synchronized, plugged into the Party, I owe my language, my thoughts, my ideals, my deals, my schemes, my opportunities, my excuses, my acts of daring, Fernando: my entire existence, right down to my most intimate fibers, I swear to you, to the PRI and its system, I am Catholic because I believe in the hierarchy and the sweet dogmas of my political church; but I am a revolutionary because I believe in its slogans and its most archaic proofs of legitimacy; I am conservative because without the PRI we head directly to communism; I am liberal because without the PRI we head directly to fascism, and I am a Catholic, revolutionary, progressive, and reactionary millionaire all at the same time and for the same reasons: the PRI authorizes it. Without the PRI I wouldn't know what to say, think, even how to act. Just think: when I was born, the Party was only three years old; it's my brother! We grew up together; I don't know anything else! Without the PRI I'd be an orphan of history! Can you really ask me to give that up? Have mercy! Without the PRI I don't exist! The PRI is my cradle, my roof, my soup, my language, the nose I smell with, the palate I taste with, my eardrum, the pupil of my eyes!"

Homeric pause.

"Can you really ask me to give that up? What else?"

Don Fernando Benítez, wrapped in his corn-husk mantle, with his head bare and his old, muddy, scuffed boot resting on the lowered nape of this conquered Gaul, our Uncle Don Homero Fagoaga Labastida Pacheco y Montes de Oca, LL.D.

"Yes, you filthy barnacle bloodsucker, there is something more."

"More, more?" whined Homero.

"This you will have to do and confess, Homero, to pay for your sins. You shall believe in liberty and democracy, Homero. You will go forth to fight for them whenever I order you to do so, Homero. You will have faith in your fellow citizens, the faith no one has ever wanted to have in them. You will give this disdained land the chance to be democratic, Homero."

"But it has never been democratic!" exclaimed the hollow-eyed Don Homero as Don Fernando ground his cheek into the mud with his boot.

"You will have to do it despite all evidence to the contrary, you coward. The important thing is that you believe it without proving it, that you confess it, admire it, and defend it: Mexico can be a democratic country! With your powerful arm on our side, Homero, we shall undo all the wrongs of our history in order to proclaim to all, blessèd age and blessèd century."

I'm inside my mother, but my mother can't know it yet, and nevertheless one day I'll know that she doesn't say anything out loud that afternoon because in a strange way she feels that she's trying to confer an impossible dignity on things with her silence, my mother says in secret, staring at Uncle Homero, submissive to the insane demands of Uncle Fernando, who stands, as small and nervous as a prancing fighting cock, bald and pink, with his handlebar mustache and his blue eyes, his tiny glasses in a creolized Franz Schubert style, expert on Indians, and author.

"Get down off that burro, Homero, and do me the honor of leading me to Malinaltzin!"

7

Don Fernando paused triumphantly and told the humiliated Don Homero and my parents (and me, hanging on as best I could, unrecognized by them just as they are not recognized by Nature) that in memory of this victorious campaign for democracy we would all take refuge in the baroque beauty of the Malinaltzin church, which the Indians had built, and thus unite— this was our Uncle Fernando's permanent intention—tradition and modernization, culture and democracy. He turned his steps and his trots toward the church, but soon they discovered that the sacristan wasn't there, that he'd gone to the state capital (Chilpancingo) to drink up a good tip given him by a tourist who'd come yesterday, and so who had the keys? Don Fernando asked one of the locals, So-and-so, and where might this person be? well, working on the highway, breaking rock and laying asphalt, why didn't they get someone to stand in for the sacristan? who knows, go ask him yourself, and they walked and trotted toward the highway under construction on the outskirts of the village, this miserable hamlet, which is a vast brown hole dotted with puddles, which were its only amenity and distraction. Its walls were made of sad mud, a lament of dry adobe, and on them the opposition had plastered slogans denouncing Don Homero and his party.

MIXTEC PEOPLE, AWAKE!
HISTORICAL MATERIALISM
MEANS VICTORY FOR THE PROLETARIAT

cheek by jowl with:

CHRISTIANS YES! COMMIES NO!
VOTE WITH THE SYNARCH FALANGE AND
CROSS OUT THE ATHEISTS!

and just beyond the usual fucked-over faces, my mother sends me effluvia of vibrant acid, all to this drop of tremulous life, this tiny Mercury without wings that I am, beyond the walls and among the puddles and dogs are the men, women and children, the mass of fleas, hunger, sickness, self-centered pride, and abysmal ignorance of what really matters in the modern world and equally abysmal knowledge of what no one can any longer touch, listen to, understand. My mother orders me to say, not you Homero, not you Fernando, not you Angel, not I, not you, Reader, not even you, my own future offspring.

From a distance, they caught sight of the workers busily paving a stretch of the access road to the highway: the mounds of gravel, the barrels of tar, sieves, and an ancient leveler that ecumenically announced its passage in a series of steam hiccups.

"The time has come!" exclaimed Don Fernando Benítez, sitting astride his burro, to Don Homero Fagoaga, who was docilely leading him along by the reins just as my father Angel was leading my mother Angeles through the rose-colored fields of heather in this provincial place where he had learned to love a land which he had not given up for lost, doubtless because between strolling through the garden and sitting immobile in church he'd learned to talk to himself and in doing that he'd heard for the first time: don't give me up for lost; wipe off my makeup; I know how to endure.

"The time has come!" repeated Uncle Fernando energetically.

"The time for what?" Homero asked in consternation.

"The time for you to prove your loyalty, villain."

"I don't understand what you mean," said Uncle Homero, regaining a measure of his tottering conceit.

"You most certainly do: you are going to go up to that group of workers we see in the distance and you are going to speak to them, Homero, not in official jargon but in the language of democratic truth."

"What do you want me to tell them?" asked Homero with less irony than resignation.

Don Fernando scanned the horizon.

"I'm willing to bet they're not unionized. In these parts, they subcontract some jobs and the worker is not protected in any way. Bah, the economic philosophy of that skunk Ulises López has spread and now people think that the democratic way to do things is for each worker to make his own contract with the boss. You must convince them in socialist-style talk of their need to join together and bargain from a position of strength about salaries. Get going, you rat."

Don Homero's protests were useless; the group made up by my two uncles, my father, and my mother (and I, bouncing along without anyone but your worships knowing anything about it) went trotting along in the classic style toward the workers, who stopped working when they saw them; someone whistled, laughter rang out, and a huge, powerful, dark man got down from the leveler. The machine ground to a halt, either as if the man had been pedaling it and simply stopped or as if it simply refused to go if he weren't driving it: the image was that the man, who was wearing a wide-brimmed straw hat pulled down over his eyes, its brim turned downward so that his face was always in the shadow, was consubstantial with the machine he drove. A centaur of our national machinery.

The other workers were all wearing old khaki, as if they were in uniform. And, just like the man who got off the leveler, they, too, wore old hats to protect themselves from the sun. My mother squeezed my father's hand, trying to tell him something's going to happen, I have a feeling, this is no joke, I swear I suddenly feel more afraid than I did in Acapulco, as if all that had been a joke and now being here with these people was not.

But there was no time for any more hunches. Uncle Homero, following Uncle Fernando's irrevocable command and showing the agility he only revealed on grand occasions, ran toward the leveler recently abandoned by the somber, powerful man, who was walking as if he were dragging a chain and cannonball. Still agog, Uncle H. clambered up the leveler, on the side facing a row of dried-out agave, slipping and sliding, squeezing himself over under and around the driver's seat and finally posing on the outside stair.

Two things happened: first, our admirable relative, as soon as he realized he was once again on a speaker's platform, recovered all his flatulent self-confidence; second, his traditional lordly bearing was comically undermined by his having to cling to the iron handle on the outside of the leveler so he wouldn't fall into the fresh tar above which he was swinging while the members of the work squad nudged each other. Don Homero launched into the second speech of his nerve-racking electoral campaign: he always knew to whom he was speaking; in his bosom and in his tongue all opposites came into harmony; Fagoaga never loses, so: Comrades!:

"Just one look at your callused proletarian hands tells me that only a divisive, murderous faction could detour you away from the route of workers' internationalism. But I am here to remind you that in the proletarian struggle the real enemy is the enemy within, always the one inside us."

He glowered in a sinister way at the workers; one of them put his index finger to his temple and made a circle with it. My father tried to interrupt with a shout, as if he'd been impelled to do so by Angeles's foreboding: "We've come about the keys! Who's got the keys to the church?" he shouted, trying to speed things to their conclusion.

But Don Homero Fagoaga, master of distraction and fraud, would not allow himself to be distracted or defrauded, especially after what had happened in Igualistlahuaca.

He went on intrepidly: "The front line of the left-wing parties is made up of groups so divergent that they will never manage to form a single party unless we first search our bosoms for the vermin hidden there whose divisiveness will ultimately succeed in chaining us to the chariot of the upper classes who, even though they have been conquered, nevertheless cannot resign themselves to disappearing forever from the stage of history. But as soon as you unite, expel the turncoats, discover and break up the network of traitors and provocateurs that exists right here among you"—and here Uncle Homero's ill-fated rhetorical impulse caused him to point his finger at *this* man, *that* man, the *other* man, all of whom raised their eyes from their tacos, left their bottles in peace, and wiped their mouths (which were smeared with dark plums) on their sleeves—"because, comrade, we don't know if *you*, or *you*, or even *you*, comrade, have the perverted intention of sniping against the working class and the revolutionary movement." And now the first plum splattered against Uncle Homero Fagoaga's already ill-used jacket, another plum to the stomach, plum to the knees, plum to the backside when Homero uselessly tried to retreat. A final plum caught Uncle Homero right in the face, a black flower splattered along his nose and cheeks while our brave Uncle

Fernando walked right up to the man standing with his arms crossed and his face covered by the brim of his hat, the man Fernando had intuitively singled out as the leader of the group.

"Tell this bunch of jerks to knock it off. All we came to ask you to do is form a union if you haven't already done so, so you can better defend the rights you should enjoy under a democracy."

"We don't need any union," said the man slowly.

"You work by subcontract and for a lump sum, so don't let yourselves be exploited."

"Now listen up, you old jerk," said the chief impatiently, "get off our backs."

Barely had he spoken these fierce words to my bantam-rooster Uncle Fernando when Fernando was all over him with two punches that were so well delivered to the aforementioned leader that the surprise of the attack knocked off his hat and revealed his face, which looked like a photo of a guerrillero. Surprised and angry, my father instantly recognized the face as that of his literary pursuer, the frustrated author Matamoros, father of Colasa Sánchez. However, that discovery was itself obliterated by a rapid series of events: first, the plums were replaced by stones and Uncle Homero did a belly flop into the freshly poured tar; this was followed by an outcry from the twelve workers, who cursed Homero up and down for ruining their day's work; then some of them picked up sticks to defend their leader Matamoros and beat Uncle Fernando; still others were busy kicking Uncle Homero out of the mud pond the tar they had poured and leveled that morning had become, which tar was to have been the road President Jesús María y José Paredes would have driven over two days later, thinking that a highway had been built linking Chilpancingo to Malinaltzin, even though the President knew full well that the funds allotted to the project had been divided in not precisely even lots among the state governor (50%), Minister Ulises López (20%), the contractor (another 20%), and a few other local officials (5%), leaving only 5% for actually building the national highway. So the President will certainly be the most surprised of all to see, when they point it out to him from the governor's swift Fujiyama limousine, that a highway really does exist, but these poor workers, what do they know about all this; all they know is that their job won't be finished on time and all because of this miserable, fat, progressive or synarchist or sonofabitchist tub of shit, and others are looking at my father, who has rushed to defend the octogenarian Don Fernando, who is shouting to Matamoros and his gang:

"Calm down, boys, I swear I never slept with your sisters."

"It's only because you're an old asshole that I don't beat you to death," said Matamoros Moreno truculently. "I wouldn't care even if you were my father, damned old fool."

"I could have been your father, but I didn't choose to be," said Don Fernando Benítez, at the crest of a wave of sarcastic dignity, all of which only made the men beat him all the harder, while the others were tugging Uncle Homero out of his lake of pitch and then tossing him, all three hundred pounds of him, until they let him fall in a death cry that blended with Uncle Fernando's peremptory threats, just as my father arrived to rescue them like a knight in shining armor. He and Matamoros glared at each other, eyeball to eyeball, as they used to say about nuclear confrontations, and Don Fernando blared out:

"Unions! Democracy! Justice!"

To which the workers, laughing their heads off, responded:

"Food, Clothing, Shelter, wherever they come from, wherever they are, a place to sleep, a girl to sleep with!

All eyes turned toward my mother sitting on her burro; then they saw Don Fernando stumbling blindly along the highway looking for his glasses and shouting, Miserable rats, all we did was bring you a democratic message, left-wing pep talk, poor lost people, degraded people, foul mongrels, scarecrow beggars, and poor Homero was lying black and sticky in the tar.

The eyes of the work team turned toward their leader and Matamoros gave them permission with his eyes. Four of the workers pinioned my father, the rest grabbed my mother. A red, foreign light, unrecognizable, alien, belligerent, so strong and so horrible, so without even a by-your-leave, so long and oiled and without ears like a garrotted worm, as ruddy as someone totally drunk, that only I could shout to my own inner self, I don't know you, I don't know you, you are not the same one who approached Guanahaní, who upset Fernandina, who took Veragua, who took Honduras, who collared Tabasco, who landed in Puerto Rico and tossed me into my first voyage of discovery, into my infinite sailing in the uterine sea, twinkle, twinkle little star / how I wonder what you are, but she didn't care whether I felt like a foreigner in the bosom of my own gestation,

I exiled within the womb of my own mother, my golden age: kaput, my noble savage: ciao, ciao! my happy age all fucked up: this is where the age of iron took its toll, and the bubble of my conception was burst by these detestable times of ours and the enclosure law closed up throughout my refuge, pushing me inside, until I hit my head against a wall: this was a refuge no longer; it was a desert; no longer a cloister; it was an avenue passed first by a strong man who seemed to push me, my mother, and the world as if we were cannonballs; then the rest, less strong but more avid, each one taking his turn to visit little Chris: my debut in society, 1992 style, the reminder that we are not alone, see? the bastard solidarity of my destiny if by chance I still believed in the illustrious solitude of my destiny: welcome to Christopher's egg, afflicted working masses of Mexico!

Matamoros Moreno released my father Angel Palomar and buttoned his fly.

"To make up for what you did to me, bastard. For having laughed at my literary first steps. For having refused to help me get published. For having snubbed my precious little girl Colasa. You didn't give a shit about me, right? Well, let's see if you forget me now! All that's left now is for the gringo to make you eat my book on the vagina dentata, that's the last detail, stuck-up bastard shitass!"

Then he made a gesture that my father be beaten until he stopped moving, until he lay there in the middle of the highway that would never be finished because tomorrow the President would see the paved strip from a distance and appearances are enough because in Mexico appearances are not deceiving: my father stretched out there with his trousers tangled around his knees, a burning pain, and the feeling that he was talking by himself, dreaming by himself, walking by himself.

Matamoros and his gang tramped noisily away along the road to Malinaltzin. One of the workers took the time to throw the church keys to Don Fernando: "So you can cleanse yourself of your sins, you shitassed redeemers!"

My father remained lost in his own thoughts, his eyes closed, not daring to look at his Angeles. Don Fernando, on the other hand, still searching the field for his glasses, could still shout: "Miserable bastards! Save yourselves, then!" and Don Homero could only groan, making an obscene gesture with his finger: "Take your democracy."

It began to get dark and I suppose that everything calmed down.

I held on with something like a desperate fatigue to my mother's flesh, she watched Angel get up in silence and pull up his trousers. But without knowing that I inside her, more than ever intimately bound to her, listened to her, she wondered what Angel would or could say out loud. What could anyone say out loud now, in this year, in this land?

It was nighttime in Malinaltzin and the village seemed asleep; but a presence that could not be silenced, more eternal than the Creator himself, continued to dominate the air: the loudspeaker in the plaza in front of the church, a copied tape that copied itself over day and night without stopping filling the infinite silence of the town with noise. The loudspeaker became the second nature of the abandoned villages of Mexico. Angeles my mother wondered if someone heard it or if it were by now as natural as breathing. Who tries to hear the beat of his own heart?

The mariachi band was playing furiously when Uncle Fernando, with his broken but recovered glasses, opened the doors of the Malinaltzin church.

> *My happy little ranch, my jolly little nest,*
> *My little perfumed nest of garden flowers*
> *Where dwells the one that I love best,*
> *Her black cherry eyes glow in my little bower.*

"What can anyone say out loud?" repeated my mother.

8

 What? What, indeed? I try to answer her, I who am gestating right along with language because if I weren't I wouldn't be able to say any of the things I'm saying: language gestates and grows with me, not one minute, not one centimeter before or after or less or more than I myself. You, selective readers, have no more proof of my existence than my words here, growing with me: my words grow eyes and eyelids, fingernails and eyebrows, just as my body does. I want to be understood; for that to happen, I myself must understand. I want to understand what's being said here, outside of me: language, *invoked* so much by Uncle Homero, *applied* so much by Uncle Fernando, *used* so much by all. What I do is *share* it: what my genes tell me is that you are language. But what kind of language am I? This question is my vicohistoricoribonucleic spiral: I am vicoized, in flagrante devictus, convict: St. John the Baptist Vico, the only saint I pray to. Everything, before any anecdote lived or heard or repeated here (Who knows the order these things should be in? You do, sublime Reader, father and son of mine, oh!), is language, but the languages I listen to, that of Uncle Homero as well as that of his enemy Uncle Fernando as well as that of my father, are, how shall I put it? *preallocated* languages (is that the right way to say it? located beforehand? *locos* from birth? ideological or ideo-locos?), that is they are languages and they are always already there, not only do they precede me, unborn as I am, but they precede as well those who speak them, they are languages that precede them-selves and in the very act of speaking them (which, for that very reason, is the act of repeating them): they are official idioms, my Uncle H.'s is unabashedly official, and he brags about it; but the moving democratic discourse of my nice old Uncle F., and the reasoning in three verbal tempos of my belovèd father A. (before: Sweet Fatherland; today: hard fatherland; later on: new fatherland), aren't they also, in a certain sense, preestablished modes of discourse, preestablished by their liberal or conservative tradition, by their blind necessity (which is their tender summons) to be shared by others? But when they are, won't they also turn into official discourse? Isn't every language approved, applauded, understood by many people, because of that, what I call official discourse: but doesn't the mere idea of official discourse signal an immediate need for another lan-guage, one that is not directed at many but at the few, to one of you and not only to all of you, to me and not only to us, when the balance of language tilts more to the plural than to the singular, and more to us than to me, to all of you and not only to one of you, when the opposite occurs? My mother speaks very little: gentle Read-ers, you may have noticed it, and if her silence continues, my pro-genitrix will break the world silence record. She's simply devoid of language. She's empty of words (she communicates me in silence or communicates it in silence, but it turns out that I, mere sleepyhead that I am, happen to be bedded down in her soft womb, whether she knows it or not: I listen to her, I hear her marvelous silence: her silence speaks to the other, the one who is absent; she receives what the world prints on her language, but a marvelous compensation leads her always to find the antonym of the word given her: her discourse shares my father's discourse, but it completes it as well). She does not speak. I only listen. It isn't the same. But something links us. She creates me, but I create myself as well. She comes toward me. I go toward her. Her son. My mother. I see the world through the life she gives me. But she also sees it through the life I give back to her. We will never be the same, we will never be a union, we shall always be a difference: mother and child, we shall celebrate not our union but our alterity! We are the mirror of our languages. I shall be within hers to say what she cannot say. She shall say what I cannot say. Gentle Readers: pray for me, pray that I do not forget (as I shall forget so many other things the instant I am born) the lesson of language I've learned in my mother's womb. Allow me on being born to know not only my language but the language I leave behind, so that for ever and ever in my life I can always say not only what I say but what she says: the other: the others: what I am not. And I hope to God the same thing happens to them! Today I am accusing no one. I know as well as they (Homero, Fernando, Angel, and Angeles) that all languages have antecedents (as Egg proved in his egg), that before ceding, on being said they become present: I sail away from my mother's verbal softness! What's dis, Cadiz, the port of departure? Enough is enough. Throughout this, my monologue (involuntary, I assure you), I should allow all exterior voices to clash like storms within my solitary discourse (listen: here you can hear the politico, the lover, the ideologue, the comic, the powerful, the weak, the child, the intellectual, the illiterate, the sensual, the vengeful, the charitable, the personage, but also history, society, language itself: the barbarous, the corrupt, the Gallic, the Anglic, the latic, the pochic, the unique, the provincial, and the Catholic: listen your mercies, please, pay attention!), I request the presence of this blast of voices in the chamber of my own echo in the hope that one day, today and tomorrow (or yesterday: who knows?), my own voice will cross the verbal universe like a storm, the dialogues and monologues that belong to *them*, to YOU, out there, others and yet nevertheless here as well, inside, equal: I shall send these messages from my fleshly catacomb, I shall communicate with those who do not hear me and I shall be, like all minority, silenced authors, the rebellious voice, censured and silent in the face of the reigning languages, which are, not those of the other, not those that belong to us, but those of the majority. I'm telling them to you, as silent as a fish on the bottom of the sea. Silent and not only from a minority but, God help me! a minor! Think then, oh sublime, sublimating, sublimated *Reader*, that, having said what I just said, this person speaking with you will not hesitate, within seven tiny little months, to keep the silence of the absolute, catacombish minority of infancy (in-fancy) and that, instead of those high genetic intentions, he will be reduced to saying goo-goo, if he's lucky be/a: ba and, now at the apex of his eloquence, here comes the A, with its little feet spread wide, here comes the U, like a little umbilical cord for you to skip rope with, tell me if all this isn't enough to drive a person mad! What iniquities we children must suffer!

9

 Uncle Fernando Benítez, a Catholic in his youth, can't remember if in fact that night was the first time in sixty years that he'd prayed; in any case, just talking (even to oneself) was a prayer in this, the last Indian church in Mexico: Malinaltzin, fruit of a desperate nostalgia in the soul of a conquered people: a temple of aboriginal dreams transformed into forms and colors.

Kneeling below the lemon-and-gold garlands in the vaults and clutching the gold-and-green carved railings with both hands; wrapped in this vast mirage of flowers, our uncle closed his myopic eyes: the earth seemed as fleeting as life itself. For Fernando Benítez, reality was animated by the past. He stared at the eternal season of flowers created by the Indians in this church. Our ancestors die on us before we are ready to live without them. Then they come back as ghosts, because the gods have fled. The Indians are our ghosts: these are the sentences he repeated in my mother's ear, and this is her question:

Does life become stronger because of that?

Because they don't know what to say to each other after what happened, she speaks to me: this for me is the important thing: she knows her period is now four weeks late, she knows that in a couple of days she will know for certain, but she doesn't know that my body, arched forward, my great big head, which is all forehead and brain, the curved tube which is my heart, the sprouting buds that are my legs and hands, and *my constantly open eyes—I still have no eyelids,* are focused on her, trying to hear her and understand her, just as she, at a distance, hears and understands her Uncle Fernando, in exactly the way I would like to hear her, more than ever in this night in which I have convinced myself that I don't yet exist outside her no matter how different I am from her; she saved me from the thick lances that came in to smash against my half-finished little head with their own blind and hungry sconces; the fact is that she spoke to me and said that she didn't know how to tell Angel that what he'd heard here today was old and useless; the ideas were blockaded by an out-moded vocabulary (blockabulary?), and that all the speakers, from both sides, were talking in terms of absolutes because only in the absolute could beauty, the good, and politics get mixed up together; but only art can really tolerate the absolute; the common good and politics cannot: when the good and politics aspire to be absolutes they demand our blind, romantic, unconditional commitment, with no criticism allowed, and that, she told me, me a more powerful im-minence than many realities, was the same for both factions: being absolute, well, that was easy; what was hard was to be relative in everything, as relative as the world, science, love, memory, life, and death: who is alive? my mother Angeles asks me, because tonight she does not know how to ask my father, who is silently holding her, lulling her, and soothing her.

At the risk of being misinterpreted, she only tells my father the same thing she told him the first day they met: "Let's never hurt each other. We're all here together."

And she took him by the hand. He had the impression (he told her later) that she was talking to herself. Who could hear her? he wondered.

"And I said to myself that with you I could be apart."

"I said we failed, Angel."

"I can't hear you, baby."

"What a pair. You aren't supposed to scream in church."

"But there's nobody here but us."

"Are you sure? What a pair. We've been together for ten months.

I've gone along with you in everything. You said the system is a total chaos, and that we're going to answer it first with tiny chaoses. . . ."

"What else can you do in the kingdom of Mamadoc but create chaos, honey?"

"We failed."

"What's that?"

"I said we failed, Angel."

"What's become of your halo? It went out, Angeles. They really worked it over."

"Angel, listen to me: Don Homero Fagoaga the millionaire never committed any crime against us like the one that proletarian, the head of the work gang, committed. What do you say to that, Angel? Are we going to kill the proletarian?"

My father did not answer, but she closed her eyes and squeezed his hand. It was the moment in which she had to confess the lateness of her period to admit that I existed: she had to do it in that instant or she would have lost my father and me: whose son would I be, if in that instant, in the Indian church of Malinaltzin, she didn't recognize me: of what member of Matamoros's crew? I had to have been made before that: on the beach at Aca, on Twelfth Night, Year of Our Lord 1992, so I could win the Christophers Contest, so I could not be the product of a rape in the Guerrero sierra: I had to be born for her, in her mind, in her voice, from that moment on, in that instant which is the instant in which she recognizes me: she recognizes me because she desires me and she desires me because she needs me and she needs me because she imagines me. It was there she mysteriously found out about me, poor little me who was still between being and not being, conceived for barely two weeks, freely floating in my mother's secretions, in the depths of the uterine cave, but no longer just any old lump but an organized system of extremely active cells that are dividing up the job. And you desire me, imagine me, even name me, Mom, although you cannot know if I'm
going to be a stranger who will be cast out in
your next menstruation and in that case
ciaoaufwiedersehenseeyoulaterbyebyesalutututut and then on to another pleasure bout and once more bambambam let's see if now yes but I don't want to get lost, Mommy, after all we've been through together, after what's been set in my genes, what you've had me learn, do something so I won't be lost, now that you've just recognized

me in this instant while a spark of fiery blood flies from your womb to what someday will be my brain, and from my existence, which already is and is not yours, to yours, which already is and is not mine.

MOMMY!

MRS. ISABEL DE LOS ANGELES PALOMAR
HOME ADDRESS:
TLALPAN, MEXICO, D.F.

WE ARE PLEASED TO INFORM YOU THAT YOU ARE PREGNANT, AND THAT WITHIN EIGHT MONTHS, GOD WILLING, YOU WILL GIVE BIRTH TO A SON
STOP CONGRATULATIONS STOP
SIGNED

Christopher Unborn

10

 As rubicund as a rose, Uncle Homero woke them up. The light was pouring through the high cupolas, illuminating the sumptuous nave of the grand Indian church made of wood and polychromed stucco.

There were no authorities around because yesterday, throughout the state of Guerrero, the masses had seized control of the local offices of the Revolutionary Institutional Party (PRI).

Here in Malinaltzin they took over the van with the two huge loudspeakers attached to it the Party used for propaganda purposes— it was a U.S.-style van translated into Mexican by decoration: a setting sun glowing between two volcanoes, Popocatepetl and Iztaccihuatl.

In their hysteria, the masses knocked off one of the loudspeakers. A matter of slight importance. In order to bring himself into harmony with the group, Homero decided that the van, deprived of one of its ears, would henceforth be named vango.

They would return to the capital.

The van stood outside the church, and Angel would drive it.

Uncle Homero approached the representatives of the Mixtec community as they were eating an early and frugal breakfast, but this time he abstained from speaking to them in Latin or hyperbaton. He asked for the Indian who spoke Spanish and told him—winking an ironic eye and licking his sweaty lips, that's our unc—who was with us and in what battered condition: he identified Don Fernando Benítez, the Protector of the Indian—a Bartolomé de las Casas who traveled by helicopter—and then asked if they would lend them the van, not a great deal to ask for a person of the importance of Don Fernando Benítez!

Who, in person, got up, put on the glasses broken during the skirmish with Matamoros and his men, looked at Uncle Homero in a neutral fashion, and declared before exiting the sacred space: travel is broadening but constipating.

Homero's eyes filled with pious sweetness and he knelt down at the altar, where he buried his face in his hands, as if in profound prayer. The light in the church changed. An intense perfume spread from the stucco flowers; a mist of incense drove away the kneeling figure of Uncle Homero and pushed Angel's body closer to Angeles's, both covered by this sacred fog—a ceremonious mourning—which did not prevent my father from kissing my mother's nape and feeling a desire to weep on her shoulder: a copious, liquid weeping. She took my father's hand and told him just what she said the first time they'd touched, I couldn't sleep all night, because I was so happy I'd met you.

It all happened in a flash; Homero approached my parents and lowered his voice to a whisper; now they, who had lived under his protection in Acapulco, had to know the whole truth—he said—before they returned to the capital and protected him.

"It's a very serious matter," said Uncle Fagoaga, playing the part, so natural to all Mexicans, of political conspirator. "It is imperative," he went on after a hiatus punctuated by penetrating looks and pregnant pauses, "that *the three of us*, relatives after all and all well-born, that we all come to an understanding."

He took a deep breath and let the cat out of the bag: the federal government wanted to kill off Acapulco in order to clean it out; if it didn't, it could never touch its vested interests, drugs, alcohol, the peasants pushed off the communal lands, the squatters expelled from the peaks, the unlicensed condominia, the graft involved in contracts arranged with foreign companies that excluded members of the federal government, and all of it flowing into the pockets and building the power of Don Ulises López.

That was the first thing.

Second, the federal government was at odds with the mayor of Acapulco and the governor of the state of Guerrero, who were rabid separatists. The myth of Acapulco, the tide of dollars that rolled into it, our most important source of foreign exchange since we lost our oil, the value of land, all of it: the federal government was not going to allow all that to go on slipping through its fingers just so it would finance a separatist stunt. The only problem was that even though the mayor and the governor wanted to separate from the Republic of Mexico (or what remained of it) they had nothing to join.

The third—Uncle Homero was now going full tilt—is that it was the police, who took orders only from their chief, Colonel Inclán, who had put Operation Knockapulco into action. They let the revolutionaries out in the hills and, according to what they've told me, a gang from the capital set a pack of hungry coyotes on the city and poisoned a few tourists. Which was of no importance. The troublemakers and the gang, whoever they may have been, unwittingly did the job of the federal police. On their own, the poor jerks wouldn't have been capable of poisoning a parrot. The important thing is that, under the pretext of reestablishing order, the Armed Forces entered the city and saw to it that both the rebels and the local authorities were taken care of.

"A brilliant maneuver!" snorted the ineffable Uncle Homero. "No one knows for whom he works, as the intrepid labor leader Don Fidel Velázquez once said in the marble halls of the IOO in Geneva. The central government, once again, liquidated the local leaders, and Minister Robles Chacón, to whom I tip my hat, practically eliminated his rival, Minister Ulises López, who until now I esteemed highly. But as Don Bernardino Gutiérrez, first supporter of President Calles in the state of Guerrero, says, every once in a while you've got to wet your thumb and stick it out the window to see which way the wind's blowing!"

But the last straw was this: our government is such a benevolently back-stabbing government that it never told a soul about anything.

Acapulco has disappeared from the face of the earth, and there is no information available. Or, as Minister Ulises López said in better times: Information Is Power. No Information Is More Power.

That's the whole story: anyone who tries to find out anything gets stonewalled.

CBS could air a program in New York called "Whatever Happened to Beautiful Acapulco?" and it would never be seen in Mexico.

In these parts, anyone who has questions knows he'll never get answers. And no one's going to dig too deeply: after all, there's something comforting (even though we might not want to admit it) about knowing that something no longer exists or no longer is where it was or where it existed. The same thing happens in our collective conscience: unexplained disappearances weigh lightly on our individual consciences. Ruperto the canary, our sickly Aunt Doloritas, or, for that matter, the sunny port of Acapulco. Bravo!

And since no one except you and me—alas! not even faithful Tomasito, who died doing his duty, fighting against that lowlife mob—no one, not to mention the canary or poor Aunty, survived the Acapulco catastrophe, on this radiant Mixtec morning, as the Colombian bard León de Grieff said during a fleeting visit, I am authorized to tell you that if you keep your mouths shut about what you know or have guessed about this matter, you may return in peace to Mexico City with me, all three of us, it goes without saying, keeping a low profile in terms of our activities, our notoriety, our very presence, as Senator Patrick Moynihan said when—Ireland in the clutches of Luther—he stood in as social coordinator at the White House during the term of President Dickson Danger, before the Watergate Waterloo!"

He took a breath of air and gazed in puzzled joy at his niece and nephew. Then, sighing, he lit a candle to St. Anthony.

"But why are you so down in the mouth, children?" he asked, turning his back to them. "You look as though you'd seen a ghost! Come on now, let's forget our little differences, remember your promise to put me up until sufficient time passes for my merits again to outshine my possible defects, just think that the tropical paradise of our dreams, Acapulco, where we had such a wonderful time, has not disappeared and that it will return in all its former splendor in such a way that it will benefit the federal government and not a mafia of local bosses and that, as you know full well after having spent almost two months there, my tropical Fort Zinderneuf was not and will not be affected by mobs of soldiers, or gangs of chain-swinging delinquents from Mexico City; and so, up, up, and away, as the ebony-hued singer Dionne Warwicke, with her opulent figure and her silky voice, said as she boarded a TWA L1011. Don't lose your serenity!"

At that moment, Don Fernando Benítez rejoined them, zipping his fly, catching Don Homero Fagoaga's last word, and noting Angel's and Angeles's gray faces:

"I don't know what this mound of flesh told you, but don't let yourselves be taken in by his siren song."

"La Serena," responded Homero with equanimity, "is the capital of the province of Coquimbo, as Don Miguel Cruchaga y Tocornal moderately asserted."

"The Siren!"

"La Sirena"

"Lazaretto!"

"Lazarillo!"

"The chippy!"

"The cherry!"

"The cheerio?"

"The cherry-nose!"

"Santa Claus?"

"Satan's Claws!"

"An insanity clause?"

"An Oedipus rex!"

"An Eddy Poe nose?"

"No Goody Two-shoes!"

"Las Sirenas!"

"Las Serenas!"

In these and other delightful torts and retorts Uncle Homero and Uncle Fernando whiled away the hours as our Van Gogh rattled out of Guerrero toward (you guessed it) what was once the place where the air was clear, city of palaces, and the marvel dreamed of in the stories of Amadis of Gaul.

But that will be the matter of my next chapter.

6

Columbus's Egg

All is perpetual flux. The
spectacle of the universe merely
presents a fleeting geometry, a
momentary order.

Denis Diderot

1. Potemkin City

The city is the poetry of passion and movement; quietude is part of that poetry; it is rare; it is definitive; in fearing it we fear disguised death.

My father composed these sentences in his head as he realized he was returning for the second time in his life to the capital he had only left on two occasions: when he found his country in Oaxaca and when he lost it in Acapulco. On the first occasion, he'd left the provinces bearing two fears: that of not finding anything in its place when he went back to look for it; that of having too easy a time finding another woman instead of Agueda or those shadows of Agueda, her cousins with invisible shoulders and enigmatic hair: the "governesses of his heart" whom he exiled from his life when he exchanged glances with them, glances in which he imagined them all dried out, mad, or dead.

My mother Angeles has fallen asleep leaning on my father's shoulder as he negotiates one curve after another on the old abandoned road from Apango to Mexico City. But I do not sleep: my eyes, you know, are open all the time; my eyes are transparent within the opacity of the maternal womb; my eyes still devoid of veils read my father's words: this is something only we recently conceived types know; later on, even we forget it; but now we are too close to the origin: the pleasure and pain of that first expulsion flooding down the long chain of genetic information. What are my father's thoughts as he takes heed of the faded signs DANGEROUS CURVE 600 FEET AHEAD compared to my DNA as it loses itself in the night of Aztec and Andalusian centuries crisscrossed by Moorish and Hebrew flashes! Well, it's like Uncle Homero's tongue as he sleeps there in the back of the PRI propaganda van!

For which reason I am well positioned to inform you, Reader dear, that as he drives, my father looks at the signs but he also looks at my mother's nodding head, her hair parted down the middle, and the hint of spectral whiteness to be seen in the part itself, and he knows that, despite everything, he was not mistaken about the resolution of his second fear; there are women we see just once and see completely and others we only discover little by little; Angeles was one of the latter: he never fully discovered her; she was not the López Velarde-style woman, nor Agueda or her mourning-clad cousins: Angeles was modern, intellectual, independent, and left-wing: but as with those numinous cousins, he never fully found her, and in this movement in which he knew where things were (Agueda in the San Cosme and San Damián Church, Angeles in the Alameda Park) but things were transformed, they ran away, they reappeared enriched, they turned over their golden fruit and fled once more with the hope but not the certainty of a return. He wanted to find the harmony of the contra-diction that nibbled at the apple of his life: to be a modern Mexican conservative. Thus, to find Angeles without finding her completely was never like returning to a place, experiencing the comfort of recovering it there, but knowing that he would never completely know it or understand it. This, said Angel Palomar, my father, to himself, was the secret of his soul.

And she, asleep, loving, raped, both of them raped by Matamoros Moreno, physically raped, immediately abused, not from a distance by money and power, not emblematically, as by poor Uncle Homero, who was now awake and arguing interminably with Uncle Fernando in the rear of the van. And what about her? Did she know all his secrets, understand them, keep mum about them in order not to break the harmony? The idyll of their meeting, the secret surprise:

"I couldn't sleep all night, I was so excited after I met you . . ."

"And what about me, babe? I was there too, remember . . ."

And what about her? Before her, before Agueda, women always came to my father, sought him out, he didn't look for them: but they were an urban nuisance: spongers, droppers-in, pests: the problem, ultimately, was always how to get rid of them; he only tracked down two women in his life. Angeles, asleep now on his right shoulder, smelling of resin and earth; Agueda, asleep on his left shoulder, as if she'd flown in through the open window smelling of dust and incense. He wondered if they knew that the ferocious promiscuity of this man who tracked them down so monogamously was only taking time out, that it was like a latent infection, a moral herpes that made him confuse the economic and political disorder of Mexico with amorous chaos: how long could the contradiction between social disorder and erotic fidelity last?

Placing his life at risk, he closed his eyes for an instant in order the better to smell my mother's hair, and prayed that he would never fully understand her; that there would never be a third desire in his life: that he would never again be tempted to include his erotic life in the collective disorder of which he was a victim and which he wanted to judge and damage for that very reason. But my mother Angeles had her own dream, unknown to my father. He had met her in a garden in the heart of Mexico City. On the highway, she dreamed that she had never left that garden; as in some ancient book illustrated with the romanticized image of nineteenth-century childhood she'd seen in Angel's grandparents' house, the curious little girl opened the window of her cabin to see the forest and venture out into it, but the forest had another door to a garden and that garden yet another door to a park and the park led to a jungle and the jungle to the sea, which was the most mutable garden of all. He thought he found her in a park. But he didn't know that she had always lived in parks. And that it was an illusion to think he could find her anywhere else. My mother has not just been found by my father because the garden she lives in has not been completely explored by him; but he doesn't know it yet. The doors of that storybook might be the lock on the door to Aunt Capitolina and Aunt Farnesia's bedroom.

She woke up when they were on the bridge over the Atoyac River in Acatlán and a barrier forced them to detour uselessly to Puebla and avoid—for what reason no one could tell—passing through Cuernavaca. She opened her eyes and saw the ineluctable and elemental signs of human life: women on their knees washing clothes at the river (women on their knees to enter the church, to make tortillas, to prepare to give birth), a boy happily urinating off the bridge, an angry man tugging at a mocking burro (patience is the burro's irony), another boy's white funerary procession: a distracted potter spinning his wheel just as God idly gave a single spin to the universal top.

Then the first walls painted on the shores of the desert:

IS GOD PROGRESSING?

The mutilated van rolled along like just one more tumbleweed past the agaves and the yuccas in the high desert, all of them hoarding water, as if they knew what was waiting for them as soon as the car dove into the sudden black hole that seemed to swallow everything around it—in this case, the backed-up line of cars and the multitude on foot, some barefoot, others wearing huaraches, all poor and fine, with the aristocratic bones of misery piercing the skin of their faces, arms, and ankles: the jammed-up cars and pilgrims who wanted to enter Mexico City through the eye of a needle, a genuine and not even slightly metaphoric Taco Curtain, said Uncle Fernando Benítez, one that completely surrounded the capital, with strategically located entrance points at Texmelucan, Zumpango, Angangueo, and Malinalco: but the Malinalco entry is closed because the son of a governor or mayor—no one bothers to remember—seized by force of arms all the land adjacent to the new highway from Yautepec to Cuernavaca and no one knows if the complaint lodged by the people from the communal land, who haven't seen a miserable endomorphic peso, has been taken up by the authorities, or if the highway is being built, or if the son of the governor or mayor ordered it closed forever, let's see anyone try to get through: who knows? who knows? who knows? and what about us, how are we going to get through the inspection held at the Taco Curtain, especially now that a powerful fourteen-feet-high Leyland eighteen-wheeler is getting in front of us. its driver staring ferociously out the window at my father, still driving the Van Gogh, challenging him to pass the long line of vehicles ahead on the curve, not caring that there is an armada of wheezing buses coming from the other direction. My mother wakes up instinctively at that moment and, along with my father, stares back at the truck driver, a cut-off albino about twenty-five years of age, dressed in leather, wearing gloves decorated with chrome-plated studs, clearly visible because the albino grasps the truck's gigantic steering wheel so ferociously. The albino stares at us ferociously (they say) through his black wraparound glasses, the kind worn by blind singers (felicianos we could call them, charley rays, wonderglasses): what's ferocious about him are his white, high, curving, mephistophelian brows. My parents see the pictures of the Virgin, Mrs. Thatcher, and Mamadoc as well as the portrait of an unknown Lady, all surrounded by votive lamps inside the cab, while, outside, the truck's jukebox-style lights go on and off, and on the roof a light spins around, throwing out even more multicolored lights.

"Let him pass," my mother says. "Truck drivers don't care who you are or whether you live or die. In my town . . ."

She stops talking; the noisily insolent truck went ahead of us. The truck had the right (or wrong) of way and showed it in its open back door, which revealed its refrigerated interior, where the cadavers of steers swung back and forth on bloody hooks; fresh cow and calf carrion, fresh pig heads and trotters, shimmying gelatines, brains and liver, kidneys and lamb heads, testicles, sausages, loins, breasts, the albino's armada gets ahead of our van, drowning out the joyous exclamation of Uncle Fernando: "A Soutine!" drowning out everything with the prepotency of its mission: all of that was going to feed the monstrous city of thirty million people: we, if we were lucky, were going to be fed too, and if we were on the highway, it was because there was no other way to get to the city: first the roads were left to rot when it only cost ten pesos to go from Mexico City to Acapulco by plane, but then the creaking planes stopped working because there were no spare parts and inspection was totally inadequate, airports without radar, colonial backwardness, less than what you find in Botswana, whined Don Homero!

The truck armada passed us laughing, giving us the finger, all of them with their doors open and their hacked-up wares hanging out so we could see what they were carrying and why they had the right to pass us, put our lives at risk, and enter Mug Sicko City before we did, they were carrying the red, chilled death just to bring life to the pale, suffocated life of the capital; they were the long-haul drivers, a race apart, a nation within the nation, who possessed the power to starve people and link the remotest parts of the squalid, disconnected territory of the Sweet Fatherland. A decal on a fender proclaimed:

TRUCK DRIVERS WITH THE VIRGIN

Their cargo would be our lives: we let them pass by and just miss smashing head-on into the Red Arrow that was coming from the opposite direction, and we waited our turn, exhausted, paralyzed, inching along just to have the privilege of reentering the Federal District by means of the highway, without having Uncle Homero—which would have been the easy way to do it—take out his PRI identification, which he cannot do because he has to keep a low profile for a bit, and Uncle Fernando can't appeal to President Jesús María y José Paredes without bringing Uncle H. to grief, and as for us, well, it's better no one knows where we're coming from or what we did in Kafkapulco in what seems a century ago now—time flies, time flees, time fleas, time flies, tempus fugit!

"Eheu, eheu, fugaces!" sighed our fecund Don Homero Fagoaga, as if he were reading my intrauterine thoughts. My parents turned around to see both uncles: Don Fernando had his head in his hands and was muttering, his eyes turned upward: "Oh, Lord, please, please free us from our relatives, Lord. What a nightmare! This is the last straw."

Homero Fagoaga was decked out with two lustrous pitch-black tresses tied up with tricolor ribbons; he'd shaved off the tuft of hair he wore under his lip, rouged his cheeks, powdered his brow, smeared his lips scarlet, and restored the sparkle to his dying eyes with the help of some Maybelline; naturally, he had no need to powder the milky whiteness of his bosoms and his bare arms, given the rather small size of the blouse embroidered with carnations and roses he'd managed to squeeze into, although it was true he did have to tighten the red rebozo around his waist and, finally, work his way into the tiny red velvet slippers and shake out the beads on the wide skirt of the *china poblana* outfit he'd tricked himself out in.

Dear niece and nephew, please don't look at me that way. You know how curious I am: well, this morning I was poking through the chests and armoires in the Malinaltzin sacristy. I found no white vestments, no stoles, no bodices, but I did find this proudly national costume. Think what you like, imagine what you please. I'll simply repeat the famous words of the onetime chronicler of this magnificent city—which, it seems, is keeping us at arm's length for the nonce—Don Salvador Novo, when a press photographer discovered him sitting at his dressing table: "I feel pretty, and witty, and gay."

He hummed a tune from *West Side Story* and delicately stepped out of the Van Gogh to deal with the ill-featured but well-armed cop who was about to question us. He swirled his beaded skirt even more: Uncle Homero needed no crinolines to stand out in a crowd. The width of those homeric hips was such that the design of the eagle perched on the nopal devouring the serpent did not flaccidly hang down from his waist to the ground but virtually flew, proudly unfurled over Uncle Homero's ass.

"I'm coming, I'm coming, if I don't that eagle's gonna lay an egg!" exclaimed the policeman. With a graceful gesture, Homero pushed aside the cop's submachine gun and, with his eyes as bright as street-lights, said, "I can see you're happy to see me, Mr. Policeman, but let's not get carried away; come on now, put your little gun away!"

"Got a pass?"

"A pass?" swaggered Homero, his hands resting on his hips. "A pass for the queen of the bullring, the empress of the arena, Cuca Lucas, who's needed no pass to get into Buckingham Palace or the White House?"

"But it's that . . ."

"Don't say a word. Our national honor has been carried through the world on my songs, young fellow. Neither the world nor love has ever closed its doors to me—so do you think you'll be the first?"

"But it's that we've got to know where you're coming from."

"Where *do* my songs come from," said Homero in a singsong voice, "and where *do* they go: to praise the singularity and the beauty of the fatherland!"

"We've got our orders, miss."

"Madam, if you please."

"Okay. Madam."

"Don't bully me now, young man. Put that gun away. So you want to know where I'm coming from, do you now, dearie? From my little farm just beyond the wheatfield there."

"And what about your friends here, ma'am?"

"Friends? You could treat me with more respect, handsome."

"Ma'am, the law . . ."

"The law, the law, handsome! Papers, license plates, influence, friends, isn't that what you mean?"

The representative of the law looked sadly and apprehensively at Uncle Fernando's handlebar mustache and his broken glasses. "I'm her agent," said the loyal Benítez as the cop closed his eyes. Then he opened them in curiosity at the resort shirts and blue jeans my parents were wearing: "We're the lady's musical accompanists," said my father. "I play the guitar and she plays the violin."

"Okay . . ."

"You can believe me, Mr. Policeman," said Homero, climbing back into the van. "Thanks to me, the glories of Mexico are known throughout the world. Why, because of me, people know that only Veracruz is beautiful, how pretty Michoacán is, that there is no other place like Mexico, how pretty the morning in which I come to greet you is, that I'm a guy from the borderland, hurray for Ciudad Juárez, hurray for Chihuahua, and my pretty country! and Granada, a land I've dreamed of . . ."

"Okay, okay . . ."

The cop closed the door behind Don Homero's ass—including the eagle in repose—just barely resisting the temptation to stretch out his hand, resisting the reflex action of firing his machine gun.

"My, how pretty Taxco is, that cute little town with a saintly face! Toledo, the shining star of the world is what you are! Matamorelos the handsome, with your superb orange groves, and Puebla is just the frosting on the cake, that's what Puebla is!"

"Enough, ma'am . . ."

"Din-din-din go the bells of Medellín; ay, Jalisco don't give up; Querétaro, rétaro, rétaro, don't hold me back, 'cause here I come!"

"All I'm gonna say now is get the fuck out of my sight, ma'am, get going 'cause you're blocking the way . . ."

"The way to Corralejo, my beautiful Pénjamo, you shine like a diamond . . ."

"Stop, ma'am!" shouted the cop in a flood of tears.

"Don't stop, nephew, step on it now!"

"Ma'am," sang out the cop, "I want to hear more about Pénjamo, that's where I come from . . ."

"Step on it and don't lose your nerve, Angelito! Just what I was afraid would happen . . . !"

"Oh, honey, don't do this to me, it's breaking my heart!"

"Will you get going, you idiot!"

He could hear the weepy voice of the trooper—"a girl from Cuerámaro told me I looked as though I came from Pénjamo"—and then he entered the gray-skied world, near to where Hernán Cortés had his private hunting preserve on Peñón de los Baños, plastered up

with signs advertising beer, lubricants, and cockroach poison, while
Angel stuck his head out the window trying to find a way through
the wheezing jalopies and Angeles began to cough: her eyes vainly
sought the birds of Moctezuma's aviary, the quetzals with their green
plumage, the royal eagles, the parrots, and the fine-feathered ducks,
the flower gardens and fragrant trees, the pools and cisterns of fresh
water, all of it built in cut stone and stuccoed over, and instead they
found the monumental series of one-dimensional façades of famous
buildings and statues and bodies of water all lined up at the entrance
to the city to raise the spirit of traveler you have reached the place
where the air is etc.: the Arc de Triomphe and the Statue of Liberty,
the Bosphorus, and the Colosseum, St. Basil's, the Giralda, the Great
Wall and the Taj Mahal, the Empire State Building and Big Ben,
the Galleria in Houston (Texas) and the Holiday Inn in Disneyland,
the Seine, and Lake Geneva, all lined up in a row, in hallucinatory
succession, like a vast Potemkin Village erected in the very porticos
of Mexico City in order to facilitate self-delusion and so we could
say to ourselves, "We aren't so badly off; we're at least at the level
of; well, who knows, we're as good as; well, who said we didn't have
our very own Galleria Shopping Mall and our own Arc de Triomphe:
who says this is the only great metropolis without a river or a lake;
who would dare say it; only a bad Mexican, a sell-out, someone green
with envy . . ."

But as they stared at this hallucination, Angel and Angeles knew
(Don Homero was rubbing off his makeup, removing his wig; Don
Fernando refused to believe what he was seeing through his glasses
broken by Matamoros Moreno's thugs) that this one-dimensional
cardboard prologue to the city was identical to the city itself, that it
wasn't a caricature but a warning: Potemkin City, Potemkin Land in
which President Jesús María y José Paredes heads a government in
which nothing that is said is done, was done, or will ever be done:
dams, power stations, highways, agricultural cooperatives: nothing,
only announcements and promises, pure façades and the President
goes through a series of ritualized actions devoid of content which
are the content of TV news programs: the President of the Republic
ritualistically distributes land that doesn't exist; he inaugurates mon-
uments as ephemeral as these painted backdrops, he pays homage to
nonexistent heroes: have you ever heard of Don Nazario Narano,
hero of the Battle of the Coatzacoalcos Meat Packing Plant? About

the child heroine Malvina Gardel, who gave her life for our sister republic wrapped in a true-blue sky-blue Argentine flag? About Alfredo Mangino, who donated his entire bank account—in dollars—to the tune of $1,492, to the nation during the 1982 crisis? About the oil worker Ramiro Roldán, who ripped off his wife's ears and cut off her fingers so he could donate her earrings and rings to the National Solidarity Fund to pay our foreign debt? About the Unknown Giggler, who died laughing sitting in front of his television set and seeing all the aforementioned acts of heroism and seeing functionaries in mansions surrounded by stone walls in Connecticut and condos next door to the Prince of Wales and Lady Di in Trump Tower on Fifth Avenue, and in Parthenons over the sea in Zihuatanejo, receive the life savings of Mexico's poor?

The President of the Republic has declared war on make-believe countries and has celebrated totally fantastic historical dates. Did you know there is a battalion of Indians defending, even as we speak, the honor of our nation against the outrages and insults of the dictator of the neighboring Republic of Darkness? Did you know that the seasoned veterans of Squadron 201 from the Second World War have bombarded, just to humiliate them, the haughty despots of the tropical dictatorship of Costaguana? We've run out of the patience necessary for a Non-Intervention Policy—what the hell!

And, fellow citizen, how is it possible you missed the August 14 celebration, the anniversary of the date Mexico City and Calcutta were declared Twin Cities? And what about September 31, Fatherland Plus Day, February 32, the day we Mexicans celebrate You Can't Do That to Us Day: or You Can Have Your Leap Year; I'll Keep the Five Proud Extra Days in the Aztec calendar! Don Homero is about to begin singing yet another gem from his patriotic songbook:

> I'm a real ol' Mexican, my land is a tough one,
> An' I swear by my manhood there's no place on earth
> Prettier or tougher than my land . . .

But all of them (including Homero) flee from Homero the bard of the vinous smog, they fly far away from the van that coughs as often as its crew, they arise now with their mental cameras and zoom back to a far-distant point in order to reenter the Mexican metropolis, the most densely populated city in the world, a city with more people in it than all of Central America, with more than there are Argentines between Salta and Cabo Pena, or Colombians between Gorgona island and vibrating Arauca, or Venezuelans between Punta Gallinas and the Pacarima!

2. *Taking Wing with the Crippled Devil*

The truth is that the biggest city in the world, the city into which, in waves and successive seismic shudders, entered faceless Aztecs in 1325, Spaniards disguised as gods in 1519, gringos with their faces washed by Protestantism in 1847, and French, Austrians, Hungarians, Bohemians, Germans, and Lombards with the prognathous face of the Hapsburgs in 1862, the city of the priest Tenoch, the conquistador Cortés, General Scott, and the Emperor Maximilian, always deserves a spectacular entrance. My Uncles Homero and Fernando, my parents Angel and Angeles, and I, mere layabout that I am, Christoham, have no other choice but to imitate the first narrator of all things, the first curious individual, the crippled devil who still remembers his angelic wings, mere stumps now it's true, but stumps that rise in flight through a power God does not know, which is that of telling stories: and on this afternoon of our return to Mexico City (okay, okay: I'm here for the first time, but my genetic memory is only the scientific name for my innate sense of déjà vu) the buzz of creation is coming in loud and clear, the interminable hiss

s
 s
  s
   s
    s
     s

of the original bang: creation can still be heard, I say, above the ashy scum of the city, and there is nothing strange in the fact that we all try to fly toward it, my parents hanging on to the mutilated wings of the crippled devil, Homero still dressed in his *china poblana* costume, holding on to the demon's scarlet, pointed tail, Fernando clinging to the black, broken cloven-hoof of the genius of storytelling, I, disoriented, because I don't know if I'm still swimming in the ocean inside my mother's womb or if I'm swimming in the corrupt air, which nevertheless is better than the black hole we flew out of, saving ourselves from the sensation of sinking into a fetid swamp: from above we see millions of beings crowded against the entrance to the Taco Curtain, we see the one-dimensional façades of prestige, against which crash the dark waves of peasants fleeing from violence, crime, theft, repression, and the mockery of centuries: for them we invent the illusion of a city of opportunity and promotion, a city equal to its television screens, a city of blond people advertising beer, driving Mustangs, and stuffing themselves in supermarkets before taking a well-deserved vacation in Las Vegas, courtesy of Western Airlines and Marriott Hotels: they prefer the illusion of the city to the barren fields where they were born: who can blame them? Now they want to enter the city which is just as barren, violent, and repressive as the land they left and they don't know it or they do know it (from the air, we look at the city decked out in dust) and they go on preferring it because the more of them who come, the more the image of the beer, cars, supermarkets, and vacations will be blotted out.

Off we go into the wild gray yonder, hanging on to the wings, tail, and hoof of the only angel interested in telling a story, the curious fallen angel who only has his imagination left to raise himself up, and we're flying over a city whose roofs, faithful to his own tradition, the devil begins to lift: the roofs of Mexico, D.F. (hold on tight, little Christopher) (the crippled devil coughs, spits, spits some phlegm on the posh Zona Rosa, phlegm that lands smack in the center of a bowl of stracciatella soup in a restaurant located on the Génova mall and which is eaten as if it were floating egg yolk) (the limping devil scratches at the thick air with his free hoof; Don Fernando is clinging to the other and the dust from the free hoof falls like snow devoid of temperature on the Nueva Anzures zone, upon which all the locals bring out their Christmas trees): FLYING DOWN TO VICO!

The crippled Lucifer of storytelling simultaneously raises the roof of one house in Bosques de las Lomas and another in Santa María Camarones: we did not see, in the first case, if in fact we used our eyes (and mine still lack the veil of eyelids), any material or physical movement inside that mansion surrounded by nationalized banks or, in the second case, inside that shack trapped between railroad tracks: in the mansion we saw a naked couple embracing, but the physical reality was the desire to suppress the difference between the two of them and their fear of being changed or changing; in the shack we saw another naked couple embracing and they were afraid of staying inside the shack and they were afraid of leaving the shack: prisoners within, exiles outside: Mexico City.

We rose so high, so very high, that my mother was afraid of smashing against the dome which, according to what Uncle H. said in Aca, was being built to dole out to each and every inhabitant of the city a ration of pure air, and she screamed out in fear, but Uncle Homero laughed in the heaven of heavens because the dome was a lie, an illusion, another governmental placebo: all they had to do was announce one day that it was being built and announce on some other day that it was finished for everyone to breathe more easily: like an aspirin posing as a vitamin, and this is the snake oil that brings the dead back to life: we did not, therefore, smash into the arc of the nonexistent dome, but the devil laughed at what Homero said and dropped us, and we fell coughing and spitting into the black hole that swallows all, we dropped like meteors tearing through the layers of pollution (only Homero's fall was slowed, because of his full skirts). From a distance we saw a tourist attraction: a bulldozer half buried in a lake of cement next to some hastily abandoned mansions patrolled by howling dogs, we scraped our noses against the extravagant slogans of the past peeling off walls more eternal than words:

WE ARE ALL THE S
O
L
U
T
I
O
N   ALL OF U
S

myonlyreligionismexico

and we flew like a flash over the thousands crowded together who had not been allowed to enter the city and then we lost our bird's-eye view of the closed city, the concentration of wealth, migration, and unemployment; the capital of underdevelopment: Mexico City here I come! and when we could make out the noble cupolas, real and solid this time, of San Juan de Dios and Santa Veracruz, opposite the Alameda, where my parents met, I realized, if not what my destiny would be, at least what my vocation was:

I shall attempt to decipher the perennial mystery of names
I shall fight untiringly against the unknown
I shall irreverently mix languages
I shall ask, speak familiarly, imagine, finish just to start a new page
I shall call and answer relentlessly
I shall offer the world and its people another image of themselves
I shall undergo a metamorphosis while remaining the same:

CHRISTOPHER UNBORN

3. Time

Time flies: barely had the eternal devil lifted the roof of my parents' house in Tlalpan and dropped us all inside (all of us: Uncle Homero dressed as a *china poblana*; Uncle Fernando with his slicker and his broken glasses; my parents with beach shirts and blue jeans, and I Christopher inside my dear mother Doña Angeles Palomar) when we all felt that time was different: we were inside the capital city of the Mexican Republic, where, by definition, everything is faster, above all time: time flies, leaves us behind: time weighs on time itself, it drags, because, as my dad says to my mom, who's making us be modern: before, time was not our own, it was providence's own sphere of influence; we insisted on making it ours just so we could say that history is the work of man: and my mother admits, with a mixture of fatal pride and responsibility, that if such is the case we must make ourselves responsible for time, for the past and the future, because there is no longer any providence to coddle our times: now they are our responsibility: we must sustain the past; invent the future:

"But only here, today, in the present, only here do we remember the past, only here do we desire the future," my mother tells my father as she caresses his cheek the night of their return to the city; cleansing herself of the filth of the road, simple things, enjoying them the way they enjoy them (for my recovered happiness), without accepting that something broke on the road from Malinaltzin and now she is going to wait until after they make love to tell him:

"I'm quite certain."

Six weeks have gone by since my conception; menstruation is more than four weeks late and I'm already floating in all my splendor— I'm fully half an inch long—convinced, deluded that I'm still in the ocean, giver of life and origin of the gods, with no more ties to terra firma than the umbilical cord and with no clouds on my horizon except the dark cloud that will be my circulatory system, still alien to my body, still distanced from, outside of, me, in the placenta, sucking blood and oxygen, filtering out waste; if this is my new ocean, it's only a sea of blood that threatens to blind me:

My skin is thin and transparent.

My spinal cord is phosphorescent.

These are the lights I use to fight the strange tide of blood that envelops me.

My body is arched forward. The umbilical cord is thicker than my body. My arms are longer than my legs: I would really like to touch, caress, embrace; I don't really want to run: Where would I go? What place could be better than this one? Have I learned of anything out there better than this place? After all, home is where you hang yourself . . .

I am my own sculptor: I am shaping myself from within with living, wet, malleable materials: what other artist has ever had available to him as perfect a design as the one possessed by my hammers and chisels: the cells move to the exact spot for building an arm: it's the first time they've ever done it, never before and never again, do your mercies benz understand what I'm saying? *I will never be repeated.*

Nothing could be more dynamic than my fetal art, ladies and germs, just like that a foot appears, and at the same time five condensations on my hand that will be my bones and fingers: feet and hands detach from the trunk (but I don't want to run away; I only want to touch); and my cheeks, my upper lip all join in the work: my nasal cavity sinks so it can take part in the development of my palate; my face begins to take shape; the cells on both sides of my trunk start moving in twelve horizontal currents to form my ribs; my future muscle cells emigrate between my ribs and under my chest, the subcutaneous tissue stretches backward and forward, the cells on the external layer of my little body begin to form my epidermis, my hair, sweat glands and sebaceous glands: do your mercies know of any combined action more perfect than this one, one that is more exact than the dancing little feet of the Rockettes, the southern flight of ducks from Canada in October, the perfect rainbow the butterflies form in the hidden valleys of Michoacán, the Wehrmacht goose-step, or the deadly aim of General Rodolfo Fierro: the precision of a parachute battalion, of a triple-bypass cardiac operation, of one of Le Nôtre's gardens, or of an Egyptian pyramid?

My blood pulsates rapidly, it runs toward the forest of my nascent veins; a tunic falls over me, like the shroud over the city we saw from the air:

My eyes are about to close for the first time!

Can you understand this terror?

Do you even remember it?

Until now, weak and unformed, at least I had my eyes wide open, always wide open: now I feel as if had gone to sleep inside my white thin tunic, as if a weight against which I have no strength were covering my eyes little by little:

My time changes because I don't know if from now on I will not, deprived though I am of sight, know anything about what's going on outside, nor will I be able to connect my genetic chain with the simulacrum of vision: I'm going to accelerate a time I thought eternal, mine, malleable, as subject to my desire as are the fragments of information supplied by my genes: now my eyes close and I am afraid of losing time; I'm afraid of turning into a being who only bursts into different times without knowing with whom or with what he'll meet whenever he makes one of his sudden appearances: I close my eyes, but I am preparing to substitute desiring for looking: I want to be recognized, known, please Mommy, swear you'll recognize me, Daddy swear that you're going to recognize me: don't you see that I have no other weapon but desire, but that there is no desire that achieves that condition if it is not known and recognized by others and without knowing that you know that I am condemned to the unsavory condition of unknowing: I could have been conceived in Untario!

Without my desire reflected in yours, Pop and Mom, I shall succumb to the terror of the fantastic: I shall be afraid of myself until the end of time.

4. *The Devil's Wells*

And I begged them: Please give time and tenderness to your little Christopher. Tell him everything that happened in the time between our arrival in the city and the third month of his gestation.

Which is to say, once we'd moved into the one-story, rainbow-hued house whose balcony faces the plaza and a hospital of the Porfirio Díaz period, near the symmetrical stairways of the Church of San Pedro Apóstol, the Campidoglio of underdevelopment, the Place Vendôme of the Parvenus, the Signoria of the Third World, our basic situation was this:

First, Uncle Homero Fagoaga, whose political instincts were infallible, decides to hide out in my parents' house until he finds out what the official reaction is to the events surrounding the electoral riot in Igualistlahuaca; it's likely he'll be blamed for that outburst, which could be confused with either love or hate, depending, but in Mexican politics you're better off not depending on depending—Don Homero pontificates, having seated himself, as if by divine right, at the head of the table during all three daily meals, with a view of the aforementioned hospital, wolfing down pastry after pastry—and should only skate on thick ice, like that old supporter of President Calles, Don Bernardino Gutiérrez, who wouldn't make a move without finding out which way the wind was blowing. In other words, don't take a step without having your sandals on, especially if you're in scorpion country, and he fully intended to spend two months in retreat here, at least until the beginning of May, when the combined festivities of the Virgin Mary and the Martyrs of Chicago might just allow him to show himself in public with the assurance that the politicos would recognize his liberal merits, which would shine once more, while his conservative defects would be forgotten. Was there anyone in our political world who hadn't at one time or another done the same thing?

When my incredulous and gaping father and mother stopped listening to him in order to eat a slice of coffee cake, they noticed that Uncle Homero, who never stopped talking for an instant, had devoured the mountain of powder cakes my mother had delicately arranged on a blue platter of Talavera ware. Now Don Homero was dunking the last bit in his hot chocolate and was asking my mother Angeles if she would be so kind as to make him another cup—but it had to be freshly ground chocolate, comme il faut, to give the Aztec nectar its aromatic foaminess. A chocolate stain occupied the place once reserved for Don Homero Fagoaga's mustache, only now beginning to reappear.

My parents, malgré their recovered lovemaking, and despite as well their happy certitude that I was on the way and could compete in the national Little Christophers Contest, had a secret fissure in each of their souls, one they preferred not to reveal. It was no longer the Matamoros Moreno horror; I think that event actually drew them closer together. It was, rather, the terrible suspicion that in this country at this time and in this history everyone was being used. The Spanish tongue, lawyer Fagoaga admitted during the long meals in which he made his domestic appearances, did not possess expressions as well-wrought to indicate in laconic fashion a colossal joke as did that lapidary French possessive:

Tu m'as eu

or its no less terse Anglo-Saxon equivalent:

We've been had.

You just can't say these things because in Spanish (gigantic wink from Uncle Homero) they have an excessively sexual charge: Don Homero strongly suggested they not comment in public about the events that transpired in Guerrero, in return for which he would himself keep silent: he had seen nothing at the highway construction site; they had seen nothing at the Igualistlahuaca riot and the events that followed: Don Homero was not tossed in a blanket; they weren't raped. Everything that happened in Acapulco resulted from the government's clever maneuvers.

Thus, the increasingly infrequent visits by Uncle Fernando Benítez to remind Don Homero of his promise to sally forth and defend the honor of Lady Democracy as soon as his retreat was over were deflated not only by the obese academic's understandable desire not to be the object of a routine extermination at the hands of the uncontrollable and ignorant police force run by Colonel Inclán but by my parents' lack of support:

"But are you really going to let this beached whale rot here for another month?" exclaimed Benítez. "If you keep this up, I'm going to disown you."

Whenever he bothered to notice the look on their faces, Uncle Homero would tell them not to worry, that he would keep his promise to withdraw his suit about Angel's prodigality, so they could live in luxury until the end of their days. Ah! in life everything was exchange, give to receive, receive to give, according to the law of convenience, and when my parents sat down at the table, they found there was nothing to eat: Fagoaga had swallowed, as if his mouth were a rapid, cannibalistic straw, the chicken in red sauce my mother had prepared with her own dainty little hands. All that was left were the bones and a sigh of satisfaction made by Don Homero as he wiped his lips with a king-size napkin. My parents were still afraid, given the absolute whimsicality of Mexican public decisions, of an unexpected change in the rules of the Little Christophers Contest; but no, the national contests sponsored by Mamadoc followed one on the other, undisturbed. During the month of March, for instance, quiz shows called the Last of the Last were broadcast almost every day: at the end of the show, a representative of Mamadoc would personally hand a prize (a sugar skull with the name of the winner written in caramel over the forehead) to the Last Fan of Jorge Negrete, a decrepit gentleman who in his wicker-seat wheelchair would pedomaniacally play the first bars of "Ay Jalisco Never Give In," or to the Last Supporter of President Calles in Mexico (a title won, foreseeably, by Don Bernardino Gutiérrez, previously mentioned as the First Supporter of President Calles. Don Bernardino took advantage of the prize ceremony to hurl veiled accusations against the Cristeros who might be hiding in the ranks of the Revolution, nefarious types who with their intention to reconcile things that were simply unreconcilable—the flowing, crystalline water of the temporal with the heavy, priestish oil of the eternal—undermined the foundation of the Party of Revolutionary Inst . . .). Uncle Homero nervously turned the television off, taking Don Bernardino's words as a direct allusion and a certain index of the officially low fortune of our relative, who sighed and pulled a tea cozy over his head.

Sitting immobile for an entire month in front of nationalized television, my parents and their Uncle Homero Fagoaga resembled catatonics awaiting the reliable news that would galvanize them and pull them out of this TV-induced hypnosis.

Uncle Homero Fagoaga, his Turkish slippers resting on an old telephone book, drowsily pointed out that the government was constantly creating false news items they broadcast as live action: just look, he said, languidly pointing one morning, at that police agent, caught by the cameras just at the precise moment he is refusing to accept a serious bribe from a North American tourist arrested for drunk driving, who is now compounding the felony by trying to bribe a representative of the police force; look now at those pictures of retroactive justice being meted out to government functionaries who got rich under past regimes; look now at that auction of bibelots, paintings, and racing cars for the benefit of the people, look at these ceremonies for the transfer of private parks to public schools and the return of tropical golf courses to members of rural collectives: every single event is false, it's all made up, nothing of what you're seeing is really happening, but it's all presented as a fact freshly caught by the camera. Now look, Mamadoc in person just dove into Lake Pátzcuaro to save a group of pure-hearted girls who were bringing little headache poultices of onion and rose petals to the statue of Father Morelos in Janitzio because, in their gay naïveté, they thought he suffered from perpetual migraines—after all, didn't he have a handkerchief tied around his head all the time? Well, in the enthusiasm of their ingenuous fantasy they capsized their canoe, which, by the way, dear niece and nephew, allows us to admire the cathedral-like figure of Our Mother and National Doctor in her lacy bathing costume of Copacabana design, and this, dear niece and nephew, is happening right now, at 12 noon, March 18, 1992, as President Paredes enters the Azcapotzalco refinery to celebrate fifty-six years of nationalized oil production—switch to the other channel, Angelito —and to remind us that our lack of sovereignty over the black gold is transitory. By paying the nation's debts, oil is still serving Mexico, and Mexico faithfully keeps her currently pawned word to the International Monetary Fund: it doesn't matter who administers the devil's wells, as long as Mexico gets the benefits; and now a word about the construction of the famous dome which is to purify the atmosphere of our capital and distribute the pure air fairly among its thirty million inhabitants, but you, dear niece and nephew, already know by experience that this is just one more trick to give a longed-for distraction to our people, and when some innocent demands an explanation about the construction from some functionary, that bureaucrat knows just what he has to answer:

"As the Lady says, it's part of a Strategic Beautification Plan."

They sit there for a month watching TV. My mom makes trips to the market to buy the food my Uncle Homero gobbles down. We are visited, infrequently but cathartically, by Uncle Fernando Benítez, who would often arrive at around 5 a.m., pounding on the door. My alarmed parents would discover Don Fernando on the threshold, dressed in a trench coat, a Stetson pulled over his eyes, and pointing a flashlight into my parents' bleary eyes:

"Proof that we live in a democracy: if someone's knocking at your door at five in the morning, would you think it was the milkman?" At other times these visits would end with a heated exchange of noncommunication between Fernando and Homero:

"Immanuel Kant."

"But Cesare Cantù."

But the sign just doesn't come. What is not a contest is a news flash, and what is not a news flash is a subliminal ad, which runs for a fraction of a second every fifteen minutes: the defining motto of Mamadoc's regime:

UNION AND OBLIVION
UNION AND OBLIVION
UNION AND OBLIVION

And then the television goes back to running contests and celebrations, because, as our Mother and Doctor reminds us, not a day goes by, not a second passes, without something worthy of being celebrated in it, Bach is born, Nietzsche dies, the sun comes up, Tenochtitlán is conquered, black thread is invented, the last time it rained in Sayula, finally we hit a whole new level of

UNION AND OBLIVION:

They created a brand-new prize for the parvenu poet Mambo de Alba for *Not Having Written Anything* during the year 1991: Literature Is Thankful; the contest about the Last Mexican Revolutionary was voided because there were no contestants; President Jesús María y José Paredes, from the PAN party, impulsively declared that the PRI, after recent local events (our Uncle H.'s heart if not his dessert almost flew out of his mouth), reaffirmed its respect for the most absolute pluralism and admitted the existence of splinter groups in its very bosom which, if the citizens of Mexico so desired, could become authentic political parties.

To add spice to this political pizza, President Paredes, in a master stroke, renounced his membership in the right-wing National Action Party (PAN)—just to set an example—and then declared, in absolute impartiality, that he was joining millions of voters like himself who had to debate very seriously in their heart of hearts a decision pregnant with consequences: to which party do I wish to belong from now on?

This took place at the end of March. Then there was a long silence, until April 2, when President Paredes asked at a joint session of Congress meeting to honor Porfirio Díaz (UNION AND OBLIVION), whose name was inscribed that same afternoon in gold letters in the Congress, why citizens were so slow about massively joining the new parties, upon which Representative Hipólito Zea, deputy from the ninth district of Chihuahuila, stood up to exclaim emotionally, spontaneously, and brilliantly from his place:

"Because we are waiting to see which party you join, Mr. President!"

And that shout was followed by another from Representative Peregrino Ponce y Peón, Senator from Yucatango:

"Your party will be our party, Mr. President. Just tell us which way to go, so we can be with you!" added the peasant leader Xavier Corcuera y Braniff, deputy from the twentieth district of Michoalisco, and "Please stop torturing us, Mr. President," tearfully whined the deputy from Tamaleón and representative of the actors' guild, Ms. Virginia Iris de Montoya.

Genuinely moved, the President answered amid an impressive national silence:

"You just can't make a snap decision in a situation of such transcendence as this one. I cavil. I ponder. I consult the core of my Mexican being. In September I will reveal my decision. But let it not be an impediment to anyone else's decision: let everyone freely choose the party that's best for him."

This time, Uncle Homero rose from his semirecumbent position, the tears in his eyes reflecting those of our President, and from his lips came forth this exclamation, one of his favorites, almost as an involuntary reflex, the essential expression of his political being: "At your service, Mr. President!"

But knowing himself to be excluded, for the moment, from these events of historical transcendence, his candidacy for the Senate suspended (he hoped) but not nipped in the bud, he had to limit himself to lucubrating in the void, like the proverbial man on the street who has no access to well-founded rumors, political breakfasts, high-quality gossip, unnamed sources, and other funds of solid information: what does this declaration mean for the fortunes of the National Action Party (PAN), to which until this very moment President Paredes said he belonged, having won the election under its blue-and-white banner? Might the situation have so bettered that the Revolutionary Institutional Party (PRI) could once again take control of the executive responsibility and symbolism, without piling the blame of all our problems on the back of the opposition? What part would Mamadoc play in all this as the central symbol of unity amid this inter- and intraparty squabbling? Would her creator Minister Federico Robles Chacón lose power because of what happened to her? Does this decision mean a return to power of the most eminent emissary of the past, Minister Ulises López? Enigmas, enigmas that Homero, in despair, could not resolve, which made him once again sink into the contagious languor of pure spectatorship; and what, he mused, were the majority of Mexicans if not spectators for those endless contests served up by national television, betting on every conceivable thing: how many miles is it from Acaponeta to San Blas, how many tortillas were sold in the month of March in the state of Tlaxcala, be the first to call, we will give a prize to the first caller to our studio, the first letter, the first coupon; how many miles are there on the odometer of the Red Arrow Mexico City–Zumpango bus number 1066, manufactured by Leyland and sold to Mexico because it was spewing out clouds of carbon monoxide, nicknamed *Here's My Sword, Follow Me, Men?* Hold on! Looks like Leyland's getting a corner on the prize market: the driver who's brought most merchandise into the City of Palaces in a single day has also won himself a prize. (There appears on the screen an albino boy dressed in black leather, said to be named Gómez, long-haul trucker; he disappears from the screen as quickly as he appeared.) They all saw the entire nation immersed in prizes, tests, anniversaries, which don't leave them a free minute, as they await the grand prize, the perpetual superlottery of Makesicko Shitty: useless, exhausted, dead—but about the Mexican middle class we can at least say that it was never bored: this was its solution and its paradox: UNION AND OBLIVION and yet one more subliminal message that each afternoon blinks on all the TV sets and which says, redundantly:

CIRCUSES AND CIRCUSES

and further transcending Roman demagoguery which promised, besides, bread bread the doctor's dead, the blessèd smell of the bakery, but who likes bread without butter? yeah, but what about circuses and circuses? Ah, sighed Don Homero, the meaning of Catholic carnival was to abolish terror, even if our relative Benítez would say that among our Indians it's the devil who organizes the carnival.

Don Fernando Benítez rapidly sketched out a map of the republic on one of the blackboards in the Tlalpan house. He made Don Homero Fagoaga, dressed as always in red-striped pajamas and barefoot, sit down in front of it as if he were the class dunce.

"Where are we?" asked Benítez, marking an X with green chalk on the blackboard.

"In Tepatepec Hidalgo," huffed Homero, "prepared to give our lives so that the peasant organization shall be respected."

"And now?" asked Uncle Fernando, marking another spot on his map.

"In Pichátaro Michoacán. We've just walked into Pichátaro to defend the workers' cooperative."

"Look—and don't shut your eyes, fatso—where's this?"

"I'm in Cotepec de Harinas, struggling to have the municipal election respected." Homero stood up with his eyes closed and grabbed Benítez by the throat. "I'm going to send you to jail for life, your honor"—Benítez shaken about by the furious Uncle Homero — "for allowing yourself to be suborned so you'd be on the good side of the stronger party"—and Benítez slams his elbow into Homero's paunch. "It's you who's going to prison, your honor, because unless the judiciary is independent everything else is an illusion." And Benítez raised his miner's-boot-covered foot to squash Homero's bare toes. "Listen here, your honor," snorted Homero, hanging on to the neck of the semi-asphyxiated Benítez, "we Mexicans can practice democracy without any need for hit men, or crimes, or bribes, or hucksters!" and Don Fernando had doubts about what to do: "Do I allow him to go on living out my teaching with such conviction, or do I stop him from strangling me?" He stopped doubting and let his miner's boot fall on Homero's bare toes, the fat man shrieked and sat down in his dunce's seat once again, rubbing his smashed toe. Benítez straightened his tie and went on, coughing from time to time:

"You shall walk the byways of Mexico untiringly, shedding those extra pounds, ready to give your life so that in Tepatepec Hidalgo the peasant organization shall be respec . . ."

My father, an apostle (though now he was somewhat reluctant about it) of disorder, then imagined a diabolical play in which laughter and fear would coexist perfectly: the humor would not annihilate what is individual in terror, only what is finite in it. My mother did not understand this, later on, in bed, my father pointed toward a photo from the Cristero war, taken around 1928, which they had tacked up next to their bed: a religious guerrilla wearing a felt hat, open shirt, vest, riding trousers, and boots with spurs, stands against a wall and waits for his death. The government rifles are already cocked. But he holds a dry cigarette in his stained fingers and bends a knee forward as if he were expecting his girlfriend and not death (and who said what?) and he smiles the way no one has ever smiled. Baby, I swear: can you imagine yourself smiling like that when you're about to die, when they're going to shoot you? Could you do it? Would you like to try? She said no; things like that were macho myths, magic ceremonies for jerks; she wasn't interested in dying, with or without dignity.

He says how hard it is to die.

She says how hard it is to be free.

And that's what he wants too, he says, but if he has to take his revolt to the edge of life and not the edge of ideology, that means taking it to the edge of death (he says to my mother in secret this dry night of mid-April the ***est month under the sheets that isolate them from the part of their space occupied by Homero Fagoaga: during the day he swills, at night he snores, he's always pushing his way in, what a pain this uncle is!), but she repeats, I do not accept death, even with dignity: if you die on me you'll create a void in the world, a woman's left alone and anything can be pulled in to fill her void; she said she didn't want a void left by him and he answered that she mustn't forget she's expecting a son; that—he laughed— should fill all her voids. But, without wanting to, he dreamed about something (he dreamed when he pulled away from my mother and fell asleep with his knees touching hers) that walks into a discotheque bathed in the cold light of the spots and covered with sequins: she has eyes like two cloudy butterflies and as she dances she raises her leg and, without wanting to, reveals her thigh under her short skirt, a crease of down, a moist little copper coin: my father dreams, without wanting to, of her.

In the meantime, my eyes close. But my ears open.

My mother dreams while she's asleep (because sometimes she dreams while she's awake, the divine diviner): she's already missed two periods, sleeping like this with her hair down, hiding her light-olive-complected face, sleeping deeply with me now, breathing deeply, hot under her arms and on her nape and between her legs: hot and me there all complete now, as if to make up for my sudden blindness: all complete now in myself, small, I don't need anything more, too many cooks spoil the broth: I am already a tiny little person who from now on will do nothing but grow and perfect my functions: do you know my heart's been BEATING for a month? That my muscles have begun their exercises? My mother wakes in surprise; she wants to tell my father Angel; she smiles and keeps her secret; I feel happy knowing she's happy, and in the marvelous pool she's given me, I, out of pure pleasure, do a few aquatic flips, like the little seal that I am: but I am already beginning to acquire my human face, and my priest-like hands invite prayer and peace. My face is human, I say, but my eyelids have closed up tight. And I don't know if I'm going to fall asleep or if I'm going to wake up. But if I say all this it's because I want to convince myself quickly that I am becoming the artist of my own creation, and I say this big fat lie only to protect myself from the suspicion that my father can believe I am not his son, that I am no longer his son or that I was never his son, after that gang of thugs had free run of my mommy's guadalcanal: now I depend more than ever on her convincing him that I was made before then and that what happened in Malinaltzin doesn't affect me, but suppose it affects him, suppose it turns him into a Mexican macho, and even if he was buggered by Matamoros Moreno himself, in this sibylization it's the men who are priests and their auguries say permit all and forgive all men all things, but the women, the eternal vestals, no way: is that how it's going to be? Well then, I'm already screwed, Readers, and for that reason my fetal scream in this instant of my return (all right, my arrival) in Makesicko Seedy is:

Give time and tenderness to your little Christopher!
Sing ballads to one another!
Remember one another!
Screw yourselves into Siamese twins!
Love each other, Mom and Dad!

5. *Ballad of the Cruellest Month*

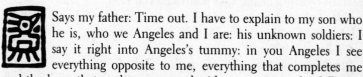 Says my father: Time out. I have to explain to my son who he is, who we Angeles and I are: his unknown soldiers: I say it right into Angeles's tummy: in you Angeles I see everything opposite to me, everything that completes me and the hope that we become equal without ceasing to be different: I say to you give me things to think about at night which is exactly what you are going to ask of me: the most important thing we can think about each other now is that I believe in you because I believe that the good should recur someday, it cannot remain behind, and only if I accept that, my love, can I admit that I am not what I would like to be. Help me, Angeles, to be what I want to be even if it is something very different from what you want, that would be good: say something just for me, don't just stand there immobile and silent, and she (my mother, that is) will smile and say Angel we met each other when we were very young and incomplete, I'll give you what you ask of me, we can form each other (share our formation) after we know each other: would it have been better to meet when we were already mature?

I interrupt the ballad of the month of April; or perhaps I merely add a voice to the dialogue, turning it into a chorus: Mommy, remember you swore that in April you'd tell me how you and my daddy met, don't let the month go by without telling me: Mom!

"Angeles. I found you because I looked for you. That afternoon on the Juárez monument was no accident."

"You think not?"

"I want you to know for a fact that I did not find you by chance or because I lost Agueda or because you are so different from Agueda that I perversely came up to you . . ."

"It doesn't matter. Our first meeting happened; it's done. Why bother bringing up that moment so often?"

(Is she saying it to him? Is she saying it to me?)

"It's that only by remembering it can you understand that if I lose you or if we separate, I will look for you again: I'm leaving nothing to chance, my love . . ."

"Okay. Now we live together, perhaps we'll have a son in October; for the moment we're performing together. Okay. What page of your book are you on?"

"Look: on the page where Plato says that we're living in the post-Marxist, post-Freudian, and post-industrial era."

"We've had enough wise Jews already, now we need a few asshole Christians. Go on quoting Plato."

"What about death?"

"Isn't it a long way off?" My father laughed.

"That's why I love you, because you're a mass of contradictions."

Angel romantically reinvents himself as a conservative rebel. He would be an assassin if he could get out of himself completely. He can't. His memory won't let him. We would all be assassins if we had no memory. Memory reminds us: Cain. The Tiger of Yautepec. Caryl Chessman. Dr. Crippen. Goyito Cárdenas. But you just can't say to crime because of memory I will not make you mine. I want Angel to be able to say that no one would dare judge me betting on my dishonesty or on my virtue even though I do as I please and not what people think proper. I want a world (with me, Angeles) in which the proper thing is not to do the proper thing but what we please: doing what we please would then be the proper thing. Is it possible? Angel is not what he'd like to be. I want him to need me in order to be it. I know that all this is impossible. But I'm going to enjoy it while it lasts and I'm going to try to make it last, without his finding out about my secret: I am in love with my love for Angel, I love loving him, I don't want him to find out. Angel, on the other hand, is going to find out that love is a matter of pure will: we love what we want to love. Understanding that is going to make him very sad. But for a while he won't have the power to fight that power: he'll love whatever he wants. Angeles will be in love with her love for Angel. Angel will be in love with his will to love. When Angeles understands this, she'll want his will to be to love her, to concentrate in her all the

power of his will to love. This cannot happen, gentle Readers, until
Angel unfurls his will to love, imagining that the variety of the will
is the proof of its existence; he will confuse the will to love with the
different kinds of love and the different kinds of love with the imagination of love. Poor guy: he'll have to eliminate the different kinds
so that imagination and love really see each other face to face, kiss,
screw: the singularity of sexual love between man and woman is that
we see each other's face and animals turn their backs on each other
to screw; you and I, my love, can look into each other's eyes but we
are like animals in that we can never see ourselves as others see us
making love: are we good for love or are we bad? How can we
compare? How can we know? Is it true when she says: you screw
divinely, Angel, who taught you? Is it true when he answers: you
taught me everything, aren't you the one who screws like a queen?
Why do my parents say these things? to screw around? to dominate?
or because it's true? to love each other more? can people love each
other without dominating each other? screw around without screwing
up? My father's love takes place within what he is and what he
believes: He loves my mother as part of what he wants: an order.
And he knows very well that no order will ever be sufficient. My
mother on the other hand (we're in April, the ***est month) loves
love but knows very well that love is only the search for love. How
the hell can they understand each other? She proves to him that she's
right: no order is sufficient if the value is to love and to love is to
search for love. He proves to her that he is right: love cannot be part
of an established order, it questions it and passes it by and transforms
it every time two lips touch two lips and one hand stretches out to
touch a sex as if it were its own that belongs to another: domination
has begun, Angeles, it's inevitable that you women generate guilt,
that you persecute us so that we feel guilty, the bitches are not happy
unless they see us accepting that we are guilty and for that reason I
accept what happened in Malinaltzin: I won't make you take the
blame today so that you never make me feel blameworthy and let's
be that way, my love, the first happy couple in history hip hip hurray!
hip hip my rib!

"Is it true or not?"

And Angeles: if you accuse me of something which I think but
don't do, I cannot deny it. That isn't guilt. But desiring even if it
isn't carried out, is that blameworthy for you? Don't just sit there

without speaking, say something. Angeles dreamed she urinated and urinated until she refilled Texcoco Lake, and refloated the damned dried-out city, restored its canals, its water traffic, its liquid death. Angeles dreamed that they returned to Mexico City and lived again in the house of bright colors and I asked them, please:

Give time and tenderness to your little Christopher.

What a lack of imagination! They don't listen to me.

6. Hollow-Eyed and Made Up

I don't know if I'm going to sleep or waking up.

But my big old ears grow and listen.

I hear someone say that the domestic situation has become impossible. My parents have never been examples of Calvinist parsimony; no matter how postmodern, post-industrial, enlightened, conservative, Freudian, Marxist, or ecologist they declare or have declared themselves to be over the course of their brief and disturbed existences, Angel and Angeles are Catholic–Hispanic–baroque prodigals, spendthrifts, anachronisms: it's impossible to be modern without being Protestant, even if you happen to be Catholic, Angel muses again as he watches Uncle Homero devour the groceries of the young married couple in the house of bright colors: he wouldn't dream of asking permission or saying thank you or offering to raise a finger, that is, until my mother says to my father Angel one April morning:

"I've just smashed the last piggy bank, honey. What a pain. What do we do now?"

In a certain sense they exempted Uncle Homero because, after all, he did say that he would withdraw the suit against Angel, and, in this world of great expectations and perpetual illusions which is Mexico '92, that means that the kids (my parents) had in their possession forty million in gold pesos. Just like that. The fact is that the cupboard was bare, and they, looking seriously into one another's eyes, declared the primary truth: we've got to get jobs. The secondary truth was that, without the help of the Four Fuckups, they didn't stand a chance in the job market.

Their logical conclusion, after hearing what Uncle Homero said in Malinaltzin, was that their buddies, Egg, Orphan Huerta, Hipi Toltec, and the Baby Ba (despite the fact that she was invisible) had perished in the hecatomb arranged by the government in Acapulco and blamed on the victims.

My parents were vegetating as they watched the alternative reality offered on television, when suddenly two things happened. The Last Playboy Centerfold Contest, a hard one to win because that enterprising Chicago-based magazine hadn't yet given up the ghost, not even in the face of the puritanical reaction of the eighties (monogamy, condoms, herpes, and AIDS), not even in the face of the change of generations, not even in the face of geographical distances—statistics proved they'd photographed more than 80 percent of the cunts on the planet. No: the magazine had defied age and, some suspected, would defy death itself. But the file of dead beauties in the safes facing windy Lake Michigan, in the iron-steel axis that ran from Chicago to Philadelphia, was closed to public scrutiny, even as the photos of naked crones began to be peddled around in a very discreet fashion. Who would win? The postmortem centerfold of the divine Swede, Lola-Lola, sitting astride a gravestone, or the venerable grandma of the bobbing breasts, Doña Sara García, posing naked as a jaybird?

Neither. This hot April night, a woman barely fifty years of age, well preserved, pretty, although with thick Andalusian ankles and without a jolly Cuban ass, square in the waist and with a cinched-in bosom, her hair tightly curled, red—a grownup version of Little Orphan Annie—a plunging neckline that went nowhere and revealed nothing, forcing the viewer (in this case, my parents and my uncle) to concentrate on the strange glimmer of her teeth, inlaid, overlaid, and plated with silver and gold even if they may have been rotten, turns out to claim the title of Last Playboy Centerfold.

"Clown of a whore," she said. "It's not that I haven't had anything to eat, but there's going to be some hair pulling if my rights are not recognized, you bunch of stinking ragpickers. I won't move from here, even if the cops come to cart us off to jail. Shit! Long live Chile!"

"Concha Toro!" exclaimed my father. "The woman who took my virginity! The Chilean bolero singer!"

But the picture, which really did not seem posed, quickly disappeared, and in another television studio someone was handing the prize for the Last Flower Child to none other than Hipi Toltec, while the announcer explained that they had first intended to award the prize to the oldest hippie (there were lots, since someone who was twenty in 1962 was fifty in 1992: no matter how fragile he looks, Mick Jagger is going to reach his fiftieth birthday, and Paul Mc-Cartney can indeed ask in a trembling voice "Will you still need me / Will you still feed me / When I'm sixty-four," which is how old Shirley Temple will be this year, along with Gabriel García Márquez and Carlos Fuentes). So, since there is really no one more out of it than someone who was a flower child in the sixties, they chose instead to give a prize to the youngest, the person who personified the prolongation and not the extinction of a nostalgic tradition

OBLIVION AND UNION:

Hipi Toltec, shredding, took the little sugar skull and said the contest organizers had made an error, he was neither a hippie nor young: he was the plumed serpent who had finally returned to demand

UNION AND OBLIVION:

The channels turned into scrambled eggs: both the video and the audio; a bolero sung by Concha Toro and a rockaztec ballad sung by the Four Fuckups got blended into the audio and mental confusion of the TV managers, but my parents turned off the set, left Don Homero sitting there with his mouth hanging open, got dressed in their own style, my father in a three-piece black suit, tie and tie pin, starched collar, patent-leather boots, spats, white gloves, stick, and bowler (models: Adolphe Menjou and Ramón López Velarde); my mother in the tragic style of the early twenties, which looked so well on her: black satin top and skirt, to which she added languid tulle veils that turned her outfit into a dark cascade from her bare knees to her covered ankles; a black satin ribbon went around her forehead, leaving her wild, frizzy hair unfettered (models: Colette and Pola Negri), and free at last from having to feign, to vegetate, to stare endlessly, they walked out (the switches that turned them on, their inspiration: Concha Toro and Hipi Toltec) into the city because the city, after all and legitimately, was calling them, waiting for them, offering them these two solid moorings in a world left adrift, because:

"Where do you think the Bulevar is these days, baby?"

7. *You Live Day to Day, Miracle to Miracle, a Lottery Life*

Would they find the Bulevar? They'd been out of town since December, and since March they'd been locked in with Uncle Homero in Tlalpan; the Bulevar changed location every week, sometimes every twenty-four hours; it was never the same twice, but it was always everything: the place to meet in the capital, the place to see and be seen, the Plateros, the Madero, the Paseo de las Cadenas, the Zona Rosa of yesteryear, but now with this scandalously wonderful singularity: where that meeting place was no one knew, as secret as language (the new languages) it mutated every day, every hour, in order to remain ungraspable, uncorrupted by writers, orators, politicians, or any other manipulators.

The dripping sky is one of the constants in Mexico City; it rains incessantly, a black, oily, carboniferous rain that darkens the grandest neon signs; the sensation of a veiled dark sky in whose fogs fade the skeletons of the buildings, many of them unfinished, many just rusted steel beams, truncated towers, the temples of underdevelopment, skyscrapirontemples, others mere canvas, like those at the entrance to Puebla, others just cubes of cardboard dripping acid rain, but very few real, inhabited structures: the city lives by moving, permanence has become secret, only movement is visible, the stands along the old Paseo de la Reforma, fried foods, fruit stands, wilted flowers, black candy, sweetmeats, burro heads, pigs' feet, maguey worms (perpetual humidity of the city, immense breeding ground for mildew, moss, rotten roe, peevish ants ready to be eaten), and the files of figures bent over devouring the tacos sold along Reforma in front of the tents illuminated by naked bulbs and burning mosquito repellant. But these details can only be seen with a microscope because from above (the view our happy foursome had as they entered the D.F.) the city is an immense, ulcerated crater, a cavity in the universe, the dandruff of the world, the chancre of the Americas, the hemorrhoid of the Tropic of Cancer.

Since the earthquake of '85, tens of thousands of the homeless have taken over the traffic-circle islands and medians along Reforma and other main, divided arteries: shacks and pup tents, little shops and stalls: with each passing day the capital of Mexico looks more and more like a hick town. The somber but comic outfits Angel and Angeles are wearing, very twenties, as they drive the Van Gogh along Paseo de la Reforma, are an answer, a conscious and collective answer made by all young people with some spirit left, to the ugliness, the crudeness, and the violence around them.

The neon sign on the pockmarked façade of the theater in the Social Security Building blinked AFTER THE FIESTA THE SIESTA, and Angel and Angeles followed a horse-drawn coach shaped like a seashell. Who could be in there, behind those drawn curtains? Angel and Angeles exchanged glances: what they were thinking was probably what everyone who saw that coach right out of Cinderella's nightmares thought: wherever that pumpkin on wheels is going is where the party, the Bulevar, the place, the sacred oasis of crime and cathartic violence is, for sure. The crowds grew larger as they went along Constituyentes, but it still wasn't the Bulevar, they instinctively knew it. The packed, pallid throng tossed mango skins into the faces of those they didn't like. Many young men walked quickly, without looking at anyone, all of them with bags hanging over their backs. From her window, an old lady was throwing flowerpots full of dirt and geraniums down onto the street, indiscriminately smashing the skulls of the passersby. No one even bothered to look up at her; no one looked down at them. They all wear identification labels on their chests (blouses, lapels, sweaters): name, occupation, and existence number for D.F. It rains ash. The ID cards neither fade nor come loose. The slow collapse of all hydraulic systems—Lerma, Mexcala, Usumacinta—have been compensated for by the constant acid misting caused by the industrialization of this high, burning, and enclosed valley.

"The problem is water," said Don Fernando Benítez to Minister Robles Chacón. "You make people think it's the air just to distract their attention from the real problem, then you make up this Disneyland story about the Dome that's going to protect us from pollution and give a fair share of pure air to every inhabitant of the city. You miserable rats lie and lie and lie! The problem is the water, because every single drop of water that reaches this city costs millions of pesos."

"Don't you worry about it, Don Fernando," answered the minister in a calm, friendly voice. "We know how to distribute our reserves and how to ration out that precious liquid. How are your water tubs doing, tell me. Have you had any problems? Haven't we taken care of you just as you deserve?"

"Like everyone else, I'm saving as much water in them as I can, so my tubs are just fine," said Benítez despondently. Then he quickly recovered his fighting spirit: "And how's your mom?"

"Blind and buried," said Robles Chacón unflinchingly.

"Well, let's hope you have enough water to keep the flowers on her grave alive," said Benítez before leaving.

"We forgive writers all their excesses! Ah, legitimization, history, all that's left!" The minister resignedly sighed. He looked incredulously at his feet and called his aide-de-camp, the statistician he kept hidden in the armoire:

"Let's see now"—Minister Robles Chacón snapped his fingers explosively—"get out here and catch me that rat, and make it snappy! A rat in the office of the Secretary of Patrimony and Vehiculi . . . But get a move on, you jerk, what's your problem?" shouted the minister to the little man who'd emerged from the closet at the sound of that betitled and superior snap, and who then skulked his way through the furniture bought in Roche-Bobois, hunting for the rat and explaining that Mexico City has 30 million human inhabitants, but it has 128 million rats. He fell on his knees and stretched his hand under a table made of aluminum and transparent glass, a model people in the luxury market called the New York Table—they inhabit sewers, Mr. Secretary, drains, and mountains of garbage, every year they contaminate more than ten million people with parasitosis—he looked at his own white hand under the glass, floating under the transparent crystal, the hand gesturing in its search for the invisible rat—and other intestinal ailments.

"And they consume thirty tons of corn and other cereals every two weeks. These rats are murderers, sir, but they themselves die mysteriously when they eat certain grains that cause the death of the very rats that eat them."

"Stop hiding in your damn statistics. I'm telling you to catch this specific rat that's gotten into my office, damn your soul!" shouted the minister.

But the statistician lacked the strength to get up, so instead he put his head under the New York Table and flattened his nose against the glass, moistening it with his breath.

"Mounds of dead rodents have been found, dead from eating imported corn. And the cats, coyotes, and other animals that eat those dead rats also suffer serious sicknesses."

"Then aren't those grain importers taking part in the deratification campaign?" inquired Robles Chacón.

The diminutive statistician dressed in his tuxedo cleaned his breath and drool off the bottom of the glass table in the French office of the minister:

"No, sir, because rats breed every twenty-one days."

He got to his feet with difficulty, adding, as he smoothed his hair into place, "Perhaps the importers simply contribute to the . . ."

"Statistics, no moral judgments," said the minister to the statistician as he slammed the closet door closed in his face and sat down to chew on a Minnie Mouse lollipop.

The city lights up and goes out like a Christmas tree without presents.

"What a national hangover!" someone shouts from the intersection of Patriotismo and Industria.

"Pay the bill. And nobody take off without paying the bill!"

"But the bankers already done it, gone from Mexico to Grand Cayman, cash in hand."

"What about that banker Don Mamelín Mártir de Madrazo? Made everybody think he was kidnapped so he could send his ransom money to the Bahamas."

"And all that foreign money poured in here poured out again to safe countries."

"Let's hear it for safe Paraguay."

"Oil glut."

"Foreign debt."

"Population explosion."

Bodily functions are going backward. The smell of the people in the swirling mass at the corner of Tacubaya and Avenida Jalisco, where the Hermita building is slowly turning into sand, is like flatulent breath, an anal breathing. Everywhere there are more people than fit. The roofs have become a second plateau, surrounded by dark abysses, canyons where the dark rain drips. Signs of antennas and tubs are barely visible now. Horrified ladies wrapped in rebozos run with their shopping carts filled with bank notes, they form lines, there are neighborhood guards (adolescent boys with clubs and lengths of pipe) who protect them on the long lines leading to the tortilla vendors and pharmacies, the crackling stands. A shout from a grocery store in Mixcoac: "We only sell sugar for dollars." A mango skin splatters against Angel and Angeles's windshield.

"Devastated city."

"Screwed city."

Angel points to the old men in threadbare shit-colored jackets and ties playing guitars at stop lights,

only once in my life did I love anybody

and they run huffing and puffing, their Buskin shoes worn through, their Arrow shirts frayed, their High Life ties stained, to pick up the thankyoumisterlady as they doff their old Tardán borsalinos now devoid of band (in their melted brains the advertising slogan of their youth and of national promise rings out incessantly: From Sonora to Yucatán/ Gentlemen all wear hats by Tardán/ Twenty million Mexicans can't be wrong: when the entire nation had fewer inhabitants than the capital in 1992: 1932), clean old men spitting on the windshield then cleaning it off with the remnants of towels purchased at the Iron Palace before the lights change. The Mixcoac stones reflect and project what's left of the daylight. Along Avenida Revolución, a barter economy flourishes: underwear for combs, marjoram for tobacco, brass knuckles for Barbie dolls, condoms with feather crests for pictures of the Sacred Heart of Jesus, two Madonna cassettes for a sack of beans: I worked in an office, I was a student, I was a pharmacist, I imported grain, I was a chorus girl; now all of us are on the Street, check-out clerks in the black market scatter along Altavista toward Insurgentes, in the little plaza in front of the Obregón monument the hoods set up their illegal, swift, the-hand-is-quicker-than-the-eye games, under the walnut shells, in between the curtains of the deeds of the Revolution, in the confusion of pots, papier-mâché Judases, funny money only worth what the market says it's worth today next to the graffiti smearing the monument of the Hero of Celaya.

LENIN OR LENNON?

The street theater for the city of thirty million people spreads toward San José Insurgentes, flamethrowers, shoeshine boys, lottery vendors, car washers, strolling musicians, beggars, people selling all kinds of things, mix with clowns, dancers, people giving recitals in the eternal night.

"So, what did you assholes expect?"

"Don't delude yourselves."

"So, what did you bastards expect?"

"We killed the water."

"We killed the air."

"We killed the forests."

"Die, damned city!"

"Come on and die: fucked-up city, what are you waiting for?"

The people push their way along Taxqueña, yo asshole watch where you walkin' man / fuckin' old lady whut you need dat cane fo'? Give it here so ah can play golf wit' yer doggy's head / look dis cripple Nureyev's pushin' / why you wanna get in front of me, lady, go fuck yourself old fart / yo blindman len' me your glasses chuck dat nonseer in front of dat truck getta moveon fuckers he look like a wad o'phlegm someone done stepped on / a car stops at the intersection of Quevedo and Revolución / got to get movin' / who's stoppin' / dis meat wagon don't move / a thousand vendors suddenly surround the car it doesn't move anymore / it's a whale beached in an asphalt gulf on which descends the interminable banquet of things to buy an asphyxia of secret languages offering useless objects and unserviceable services hyperbolically described:

"Here you are, sir, awzom chewing gum."

"Yo, I'm the kool kat wit the winning ticket."

"I swear man, dese cigs is the real thing."

"Take a look, lady, genuine humongous bras."

"Check it out, man, look at these galoshes here."

"Wanna learn to French kiss, got da bes' book right here, man."

Angel and Angeles stared at the rows of young people with no future, the long rows of bored people on guard before the nothingness, expecting nothing from the nothingness, Mexico City, decrepit and moribund and the street theater set up on tubs and broken-down trucks representing everything, reason and unreason:

AFTER THE FIESTA THE SIESTA

Step inside, step inside, just see how the oil prices plummeted

THE OPEC-AND-ONE NIGHTS

Step inside, step inside, see how the border was closed to wetbacks

TALES FROM THE TACO CURTAIN

Right this way to see how Mexicans bred until they exploded demographically

NO SECTS PLEASE WE'RE CATHOLIC

Right here on the big stage, ladies and gentlemen, events in Central

America, or how President Trigger Trader made the worst prophecies
come true just by saying them out loud

WELCOME TO SAIGONCITO

Ladies and gentlemen, don't miss these scenes of virile violence
in which President Rambold Rager widens the war to include Mexico
and Panama

IF I PAY THEM THEY ARE MY FREEDOM FIGHTERS

Step inside, don't miss the extraordinary comedy about the rise in
import duties

IS THAT A GATT YOU'RE CARRYING OR ARE YOU JUST HAPPY
TO SEE ME?

Right here on the big stage: in 3-D and Cinerama, back up your
optimism with the complete history of our foreign debt, or how we
beat out Brazil and Argentina in the race to disaster!

AFTER THE FIESTA THE SIESTA

and from car to car along the Beltway, the shouts of the city of gossip,
the nation of rumors:

"The peso's dropping to thirty thousand per dollar."

"Did you hear that Mamadoc got fed up and is quitting tomorrow?"

"What I hear is that it's Mamadoc *and* the President."

"No, what Mamadoc wants is for Colonel Inclán to fuck her."

"Get out, man, where'd you hear that?"

"I've got a brother-in-law in SEPAFU."

"He's lyin', man."

"That minister Don Ulises is a wife-beater."

"They say he broke his wife's legs."

"How'd you find out?"

"Ask the lady herself, there she is coming out of Sanborn's."

"They say President Paredes took a billion pesos to Switzerland."

"Who told you that?"

"They say it came out in the *Gall Street Journal*."

"Since when do you know English?"

"I've got people to translate for me. But it's box populi, box dei."

"Didya hear that Mamadoc had a copy of the Petite Trianon built
for her in El Pedregal?"

"Some people saw Don Ulises López in Las Vegas."

"Yeah, and he lost three million dollars in one shot playing
baccarat."

"And we don't even have enough for a trip to Xochimilco."

"I hear Robles Chacón can't get it up, and that's why he loves power so much. Just like women."

"Colonel Inclán's really a queer."

"And Mamadoc's a transvestite."

"No, man, she's supposed to be Julio Iglesias wearing a wig."

"Wrong, man. It's that old group Menudo under one big skirt."

"Yeah, I hear she only likes to sleep with dwarfs."

"Robles Chacón's a junkie."

"Apparently the Minatitlán wells went dry, but nobody's saying anything."

"Wheredya hear that?"

"My brother-in-law has access to Pemex."

"Well, someone told me that Guatemala just occupied the entire state of Chiapas and nobody even noticed."

"No way. My nephew was just drafted and he says the real war is with Australia over the Revillagegedo islands."

"Right. It's about that nodule thing."

"Whatsat?"

"Instead of oil, it's nodules now, didn't you hear?"

"Never heard of it."

"With these manganese nodules, man, we're gonna take off again."

"All have to do is administer our wealth!"

"But President Jomajeezus wantsa sell the islands to the Vatican."

"No way. Who toldya?"

"I got an uncle who's a sacristan in the Basilica."

"I don't believe anything anymore."

"I'm telling you tomorrow they're gonna announce another nationalization."

"But there's nothing left to nationalize."

"There sure is: the air."

"But who wants it?"

"They're gonna make a window tax, just the way Santa Anna did."

"Tomorrow they declare a moratorium."

"You'd better get your savings out while you can."

"Sell everything."

"Spend it all."

"The whole thing's going down the tubes."

"How many people are here?"

"Enough."

and along Emita–Ixtapalapa an army of impostors and con men besieged each other, besieged each other trying to make deals, if you want to get into Los Pinos / I was just named superintendent of the Tuxpan refinery / I'm on my way to be ambassador to Ruanda-Urundi / I'm writing Mamadoc's memoirs / the President has commissioned me to / the IMF has ordered me to / I have the job of bringing Dr. Barnard to operate on private individuals, just sign here / I've been offered a corner on the U.S. corn crop / the Rockerfeller Foundation has assigned me the job of distributing scholarships in Mex / would you be interested in spending a month free at the Ritz Hotel in Paris? Just sign here / I'm selling a condo in Beverly Hills at a hundred Mexican pesos the square yard: just sign here / the New York production company PornoCorno would be very innarested in offering you a contract, baby: just sign here /

The women selling shrimp tacos in the snack bar for Churubusco Studios note:

"Look here now, Sadie, my only contribution to the crisis of confidence we're suffering is, as Don Paul Volcker declared recently, the U.S. deficit undermines confidence there, too."

"Can you imagine, Frannie, the U.S. is asking for loans of $100 billion out of foreign savings accounts every year now, isn't that incredible?"

"Well, Sadie, all I know is that when the dollar's high it means high interest rates."

"Frannie, you just said a mouthful. Gimme another shrimp taco / and the Van Gogh plods along the Tlalpan causeway, where the dwarfs, eccentrics, and scribes the provinces export in large numbers to the capital in order to raise cash meet and offer their services to their urban clientele. The van stops in the little plaza of the San Pedro Apóstol Church, about one hundred and fifty feet from the house of bright colors. The seashell-shaped coach drawn by horses also stops there: the meeting place was their own house, it was here the Bulevar was to be today, they'd gone around a big old circle, everyone making a sincere effort to keep up a certain style, to restore the romantic image, make dark suits, high hats, feather boas, crinolines, Nankin trousers, embroidered vests, ostrich feathers, suffocating chokers, and Derbys fashionable, today they're parading here, they can't avoid all the urban gangrene, but they do avoid some of it, yes, the carriage doors open and out tumble the Orphan Huerta (very much changed), Hipi Toltec (with a tiny electric fan in his hand), and Egg asking Baby Ba not to get left behind, now baby, we're almost there, look: Angel and Angeles, our buddies . . .

"Serbus!" shouted the Orphan by way of greeting.

"In ixtli, in yóllotl!" said Hipi Toltec.

"Animus intelligence," answered my mom.

"Buffalo," synthesized the Orphan.

"We thought we'd never see each other again," said my dad.

"You thought the Four Fuckups were F.U.B.A.R.?" said the

```
            u  p  e  l  e
            c     y  l  c
            k     o     o
            e     n     g
            d     d     n
                        i
                        t
                        i
                        o
                        n??
```

Orphan

"As a matter of fact, I did," said Angeles.

A group dressed in green began clubbing the horses pulling the coach, first beating them to their knees and then continuing to pound them until they died, always shouting Equus, equus, the horses of the conquistadores. As they rolled over, the two Percherons tipped over the conch-shaped carriage.

Angel was the only one who looked. Without turning his head, Egg said: "There's this competition to get included in the frieze on the Monument to the Heroes of Violence."

"So they didn't kill you in Aca?"

"Níxalo; draftearon us for to clinup Aca."

"Under what conditions?"

"Jus juan: that we not sing for a whole year so people'd think we died wit de udders in Aca."

"Ce Akatl!"

"Wich mean dat da Babosos Brudders gonna teikover da calpulli."

"Disisdapits."

"Bulook: der's no competencia in the mágica of da marketa except da Immanuel Can't."

"Parvenus an home boys facetaface."

"Awzom!"

"Don' spase out, Orphan, an stop wit da self-flagellation, 'cause der's broken glass anstoff."

"Laic yunó."

"Cheesis, man, ay mus eet seben time ahuic Damningo Loonys Madness Mercolates Hoovers Bernaise an Savagedog."

"Good buddy."

"Ay too mus tacofy from damningo to savagedog."

"Baby Ba says she's hungry: won't you invite her to your house for dinner?"

"We ain't got much."

"Except for Uncle Homero."

"You forget it's the first of May: he's gone with the wind."

"We saw him from here: he gone."

Alone in the house of bright colors, Don Homero Fagoaga said to himself: "This is my chance." For the first time he found himself without Angeles, who, though she did sometimes go out shopping, would leave him with Angel, who never left the television set alone; but what a time to choose to abandon him: would that missionary Benítez pop in again to catechize him about democracy? Alone and permanently dressed in red-striped pajamas: the owner of Pichilinque and Mel O'Field and Frank Wood harbored the feudal suspicion that his sister Isabella Fagoaga and her husband the inventor Diego Palomar were not as disinterested and spiritual as it seemed; aside from the forty million gold pesos that Isabella left her son Angel, there had to be something else, Homero felt sure of it this morning; he had investigated bank accounts, stocks, CDs, but had turned up nothing: there had to be a hiding place in the house, money, jewels, papers, something.

Like a teenager who takes advantage of the fact that parents and servants are out of the house to get out his pornographic magazines and excite himself, exciting himself above all with the prospect of the imminent return of those guardians and punishers, in the same way Homero threw himself into exploring the house of the Curies of Tlalpan, crammed with blackboards and portraits of famous scientists and mousetraps. Homero immediately went down to the cellar to find the family treasure, where the first thing that happened to him was that a mousetrap caught his pinkie, and the pain, the anger, and the humiliation of the uncle were so great that he came charging back upstairs, knocking over blackboards and smashing a prehensile mousetrap against the photo of Niels Bohr, as if only a human face deserved the reaction of this rage, but barely had the trap hit the glass covering the photo when the fragments reassembled themselves instantly and once again covered the benign face of the Danish scientist, who looked like the benevolent captain of a whaling ship. Don Homero fell over backward, tripping over a stepladder that instantly folded up, allowing a pail of black paint to fall on a white cat that just happened to be there searching for the house's celebrated photogenic mice; and the cat, now transformed into a black cat, jumped on top of a cabinet and knocked a box of salt onto Homero's shoulders. Homero grabbed an umbrella that happened to be handy in order to protect himself from the rain of objects, but as he opened it, a rainstorm hidden inside it fell on his head, and Homero in despair threw himself on a bed where there happened to be twelve top hats, which, because of the homeric obesity, snapped open, forcing our startled academic out of bed, and making him run through the halls in hopes of destroying all the other photos of scientists, but he found the frames empty, the glass all broken expressly to cut his feet, and at the end of the corridor, he found a long banquet table and twelve men sitting at it, dining by candlelight: as they had in the Sun & Fun Toltec Tour of Acapulco, under the tutelage of Will Gingerich, each guest had a name tag on his chest: E. Rutherford, Cambridge; N. Bohr, Copenhagen; M. Planck, Berlin; W. Heisenberg, Göttingen; W. Pauli, Vienna; R. Oppenheimer, Princeton; A. Einstein, Princeton; E. Fermi, Chicago; J. D. Watson, Cambridge; F. Crick, Cambridge; L. de Broglie, Paris; L. Pauling, Berkeley, and as soon as they saw Homero they all politely stood and invited him, in a friendly way, to join them and take the last seat at the table: number 13, shouted our uncle, horrified, turning his back on them, running away, tripping over blackboards, paint cans, umbrellas, top hats, cats, mice, and mousetraps intent on pinching his naked toes: he fled out into the street, in pajamas, barefoot, and those who saw him thought he was a madman escaped from the nearby Tlalpan sanatorium or perhaps an escaped convict, what with those stripes on his uniform and with no shoes on, Sadie!

8

They decided to look for jobs while everything that had to happen did happen, meaning that I had to be born on exactly October 12 in order to win the contest, and after that, watch out, baby, but how was the contest going? Did anyone know anything? Even so, it would have to be checked out and in the meantime all of them would have to stay together in the Tlalpan house, unless it turned out that our miserable Uncle Homero had flown the coop merely to order the police to keep anyone from living in it while he mended fences with the PRI, God knows what goes on behind that feverish brow. In the meantime, everybody is here in the tits of the family, so to speak—Hipi still disintegrating, portable electric fan in hand; the Orphan changed forever, my mom says that now he looks like Charlie Chaplin when Chaplin was young, an amazed look on his face, all eyebrows, with a tiny black mustache and kinky hair, and complaining that without the income from rock-aztec he won't be able to dress in style.

Woe is me, he complains as he strolls through the secondhand clothing stores with their wares hanging in huge stalls along the streets of Ejido with the monument to the Revolution in the background and under its dome dealers in products whose importation is strictly forbidden, blackmarket clothes that aren't even in style but were ten years ago; woe is me, complains the Orphan, followed by Egg and Baby Ba among the clothes hangers on the avenue, succulently ca-ressing the tweed and leather, the glittering hobnails, and the soft cotton of the gringo T-shirts, all forbidden because of a year of abstinence imposed by the government on the Four Fuckups. Our buddy Egg stares nostalgically at the brands of internationally pro-duced consumer goods sold illegally but right out in the open under the dome of the monument to the Revolution, the things he'd like to buy Baby Ba so she'd look better, and he limits himself instead to serving her in secret: he makes her bed, he puts her to bed, he tucks her in, he gives her her favorite Cabbage Patch dolls: that's how we know he's got a past and what fucks me up about these fucked-up types is that I have just as much past (genetic info) and they, the

Orphan most of all, don't have any past, and Hipi only the past he's
invented, which isn't even his: je suis la serpent-à-plumes, sure,
buddy, with that fan in your hand.

One day, my mother (with me inside her, remember) goes out
with him because Hipi wants people to think he's got a girl and that
she's even going to have a baby. My mom is for the idea and does
him this favor and he brings us to his parents' house, which is on a
roof and surrounded by water tubs near Balbuena and the Puebla
highway: a shack whose walls are tubs and a crowd of people there
you can't even see because it's so dark, but Hipi kisses all of them,
talks to them in Nahuatl, repeats that greeting of his "in ixtli, in
yóllotl" and my mother repeats it in Spanish (my mother would like
to be minimally rational in this era in which we live), "a heart and
a mind," gravely curtsying before the shapeless old men and women
wrapped in ponchos and serapes and old newspapers in the shack in
the lost, nameless city built on the garbage belt, but surrounded by
gadgets which, we suppose, Hipi Toltec brings them from his ex-
peditions, because he gives his electric fan to a little old man as
wrinkled up as a prune, a real prune, and the little old man carefully
piles it next to his Mixmaster and his Sanyo icemaker and his Phillips
TV set and his Sears toaster and his Machiko Kyo hair dryer and his
Osterizer microwave oven and his Kawabata alarm radio, all stored
there in that smoky, sepia-colored darkness devoid of electricity,
which doesn't even get light from the street. And my mother wonders,
will they go on accumulating the trophies this prodigal son brings
them forever? Like Columbus or Cortés returning to the Court of
Spain loaded with coconuts and maguey, hammocks and rubber balls,
gold and precious woods, feathered crowns and opal diadems, they
thank him for it, he kisses their hands, they pat his long, greasy,
straight hair, they all speak Aztec and say, my mother thinks they
say in any case, things that are very poetic and beautiful:

"Ueuetiliztli!" (Old folks!)

"Xocoyotizin!" (Young pup!)

"Aic nel toxaxahacayan." (We shall never be obliterated)

"On tlacemichtia." (There everything was stolen)

"Olloliuhqui, olloliuhqui!" (How the wheel of fortune spins!)
and with enormous satisfaction they look at my pregnant mother,
they look at the center of my mom, where I launch into an Olympic
dive, but when we get back to Tlalpan I still cannot understand Hipi's

world as a past (I want everyone to have a conscious past so I can be born a bit better) but as something very different: he has a secret family and in it there is only a memory of silence.

Something similar is going on with the Orphan Huerta (with all of them in fact, these are their pasts, barely what passes by, nothing more, my tranquil genes tell me, the past is only the past), but the Orphan at least talks about a brother who disappeared, the Lost Boy, he calls him, and about a grandmother who lives in Chicago, where she forgot her Spanish and never learned English: so she became a mute: a memory of silence, I tell them again, this time captured between the successive infernos of wind and ice and a suffocating purgatory: Chicago, City of the Big Shoulders, says my mother, reciting something or other, and the light of reverie goes on in the eyes of all present—Egg, Orphan, Hipi, the invisible Baby Ba (who suddenly I want to see more than anything in the world, convinced suddenly that only I will be able to see her: but in order to do that, I'll have to be born, to be born and see her, it's not true she's invisible, I convince myself because no one sees me either, nor do they pay me the slightest attention, unless I kick or jump around or take swan dives in the stomach of Chicago and Lake Michigan).

There was lots of talk about Chicago in those May days because that's where the Orphan's grandma lived, condemned to silence. But there was another reason as well: Uncle Fernando passed by the San Pedro Apóstol house with two Indians, a couple he said he'd met during his excursion in February to a land of blind people, and we saw this strange couple with light eyes and dark skin, standing like two flexible statues in the doorway of the house of bright colors, I don't know if they were blind (I've already said it: they don't see me, so how can I judge those who are also not seen and who just accumulate, if your mercies would care to do the arithmetic: Baby Ba, Hipi's smoking family, now this couple my parents tell me are handsome, strong, with a strange determination in their clouded-over eyes).

Uncle Fernando speaks for them, but my parents say the couple's silence is even more eloquent: there is no one better, no one more intelligent in this country than this couple and people like them, no one, not the financier Don Ulises López, not the minister Don Federico Robles Chacón, not the academician Don Homero Fago-aga, not my father, the sensitive and tormented conservative rebel, not the serene and (she tries to be reasonable!) reasonable mamma mia on the left, who is so silent at times in order not to interfere in the obvious results of everything that's happening, all of them together are not as intelligent, as determined as this pair of Indians who got married the day of the great noise and the night of her first moon, creating another child at the same time I was created, giving me an invisible brother who would never be seen by his parents, created (remember, Reader) in the final moment of an incomprehensible, noisy, incomparable day in which all times went mad and no one could tell whether he was awake or dreaming.

Uncle Fernando returned to the sierra of the blind people, and this couple, who had used his earlier visit as reason for marrying and making a child, recognized the smell (unmistakable, that odor of creole historian) of his return, they stuck to him like glue, repeating again and again a word they'd learned only the gods know where (*Chicago, Chicago*), and Benítez said to them, "Not *Chicago, Chicago*, no, you stay here, this is your homeland, you're needed here, you'd get lost in the world, and two months later here they are, she pregnant, both of them blind, Indians, monolingual, idol worshippers, mythomaniacs, shamanic, syncretic, and, all in all, screwed up, how does that sound for a collection of handicaps, eh? What more can I say? And by saying *Chi-ca-go*, full of determination, magically willful, here they are and no one's going to stop them: they are going to escape from the vicious circle of their rural, age-old poverty, they are the most valiant, most stubborn, craziest people in the world: and they have created my brother, the child who was conceived with me! They are going to break with their fate. Will it be worth the trouble?

I don't really understand what's going on, I admit it. Don Fernando reasons and fights; they say "Chicago"; it's cold; that's where the Orphan Huerta's grandmother is; if they insist, well here's her address; but they're asking for trouble.

In bed, my father says to my mother:

"Quetzalcoatl went east."

"Cortés came from the west."

"Wetbacks go north."

"The dead go south."

"Those are the cardinal points of Mexico, and no one can escape them!"

9

My father needs a compass to find his way through the city:
he's like a navigator in the Unknown Sea. The group has
decided that if they're going to survive, all of them will have
to find work in a city overflowing with the unemployed;
suspiciously, no one knows anything about Uncle Homero, and Uncle Fernando, who lives off a modest university pension and the
success of his books in Poland and Yugoslavia (he's piled up millions
of zlotys and dinars he never expects to see, but he does consume
the income in pesos of thirteen Polish and Yugoslav writers in
Mexico), has dedicated himself to sowing panic in D.F. parking lots.

Example: he materializes and announces he's the parking-lot inspector. People think it's Jupiter turning up at the Last Judgment:
they all run, hide, pour water on the heroin, flush the grass down
the drain, pretend they know nothing about the smell of marijuana
in the air, and even though everyone knows that in parking lots, in
trunks, motors, and under seats is where drug trafficking takes place,
only Don Fernando takes the bull by its moralizing horns and tells
people he's an incorruptible inspector. No one ever saw such shock,
and sowing moral terror is all our Uncle Fernando desires: the point
is not to accept any bribe, so that his activity benefits neither himself
nor us.

"In any case, with us bribes have become very exclusive. Before,
there was a certainty and a democracy to them—they were available
to all. In fact, the only human right won by the Mexican Revolution
was the right to corruption, which in El Salvador or Paraguay is the
privilege of a minority, but which in Mexico belongs to all, from the
president to newspapermen, to the cop on the beat—and anyone who
isn't corrupt is an asshole. In any case, in Mexico bribery used to be
natural, as it had been since the Aztecs and the colonial period: why,
in the court of Carlos III of Spain, bribes were called "Mexican
grease." But nowadays, dear niece and nephew and you FUBARS
here present, functionaries refuse the first bribe and play to see who'll
give more, they make scenes—How dare you, sir! International Baby
Foods offered me double that, the Emirates Baksheesh Corporation

triple that, what an idea! Come now, you can do better than that, sir. They even use an international vocabulary nowadays: the pure and simple bribe is called the perquisite or baksheesh, kickbacks are called pot-de-vin. Even the bribers have begun to put on airs; now they choose those they want to bribe and don't try to buy off just anyone. There are categories, what did you think, eh? Anyone who bribes a transit cop is committing a serious breach of Mexican etiquette. Bribing a customs agent brings a total loss of face. Bribing, real bribing, takes place only if you bribe the Cardinal Primate, the President, Minister Robles Chacón, Mamadoc, or, extraterritorially, the North American President, Ronald Ranger (if in fact he really exists and isn't merely what he always was: a photo opportunity, a fleeting TV image no one could hear because his voice was drowned out by the roar of the helicopter whisking him away for a weekend at Camp Goliath, just one more decal on vans with Colorado oasis windows, a hologram!). Okay, let's see you bribe the Iron Lady, Emperor Akihito, Bishop Tutu, or Mother Teresa. Now that's bribery, not some flea-bitten congressman, the cop on the corner, or the customs officer, forget it!"

This being the situation, my father took his compass and, together with my mother (me inside her) and the Four Fuckups, organized first their jobs within the generalized unemployment in order to survive until we won the Christophers Contest in October, when we'd live it up and up and up, oh don't be perverse, universe, or as Dad says, "Avoid the mess, avoid the mess . . ."

This is what they managed to do in the merry month of May:

Egg was hired as a TV weatherman for the Tlalpan district, but he was fired because his powerful resolve led him to scorn storms, hurricanes, earthquakes, and other forms of excitement that traditionally and officially were suggested to make the programs more pleasant. He was content to say, "The weather today is the same as it was yesterday," or "Yesterday's weather was a little better than tomorrow's will be."

Fired from this job, he managed to get a job as cleanup man in the Sanborn's on Avenida Universidad. When the restaurant and the stores were finally empty, our buddy Egg would first clean up all the trash and mop the floor, and then he would take down from the book rack a volume published by Alianza Editorial in Madrid (prohibitively expensive books) and would sit down to read in the solitary café until

dawn. He thus became something enormously secret: the Sanborn's
Reader. Without knowing it, he took the same book that Angeles, my
mother, never finished reading: Plato's *Cratylus*, that dialogue where
all they talk about is names: What is a name? Does a name exist because the thing demands to be named? Is a name merely a caprice? or,
perhaps: Was it God who named us?: Egg and Angeles, that book connected Egg to the world of Angeles and neither one knew it.

Hipi Toltec was, successively, a tobacco spitter and fire-eater out
on the streets, dresser (or tailor) for fleas, fireworks expert, and a
walker of elegant dogs. But he contaminated all the dogs he touched
with rabies; one of his skyrockets went so high that it proved con-
vincingly that the dome was nothing more than a fairy tale; the fleas
abruptly formed a union; and his longest tobacco expectoration hit
the license plate of Don Ulises López's black Transnational limo and
no one could ever get it clean: what Hipi spits, I think, is the liquid
equivalent of the fire in the Fifth Sun.

The Orphan Huerta began by going to Cuernavaca as a pool digger,
but he gave up the job because every time he finished digging, it was
dead bodies instead of water that flowed into the hole, right on his
head. He didn't want to find out any more about it, so he went back
to Mexico City, where his new look, that Chaplinesque air of innocence, guaranteed him a certain success as a house sitter. That's
how he came to be taking care of the immense house that belonged
to Don Ulises López and his wife Doña Lucha, when they went to
Taxco on vacation in May. He also informed my father that Miss
Penny López, whom we thought killed in Ada and Deng's nightclub
in Aca, was alive and kicking (that's kicking, not screwing): all alone
in her mansion in Las Lomas del Sol, under the protective eye of
her somber duenna, Ms. Ponderosa.

Dad filed that precious bit of information and offered his services
to SEPARVE, which was looking for a translator of Mexican sayings,
since—to everyone's surprise—they'd found a European market for
Mexican folk sayings: such was the hunger for certitude and wisdom
in the Vecchio Mondo.

Among the most celebrated of my pop's exports are these, which
were received with open arms, even in London and Paris:

You left me whistling on the hill
A qu'elle est naine ma fortune, que est-ce qu'elle grandira?

Thou hast made me muffins with goat's meat!
La prudence, on l'appele connerie
Here only my fried pigskins crackle!
Aux femmes, ni tout l'amour ni tout le fric
We only visit the cactus when it flowers
Faute de baguette, mangez des tortillas
Don't call me uncle, we haven't met yet
Les amours à la distance sont pour des cons à outrance

This clean industry (except when Angel had to translate "Aguacate maduro, pedo seguro" and came up with "Art Is a Fart"), devoid of problems (even "rosario de Amozoc" had illustrious equivalents in "Donnybrook" and "Branlebas"), yielded a nice income which, in accordance with the Tlalpan pact, my father divided up with my mother, Egg, Hipi, the Orphan, and (possibly) with Baby Ba, not to mention your humble servant.

At the same time, my mother was hired by the Secretariat of Culture, Letters, and Literacy (SECULELA) to devise ordinary-language versions of Shakespeare that could be understood in the proletarian neighborhoods (are there any other kind?) in the D.F., DeeEff, DeeFate, DeeForm, De Facto, Defecate, Dee Faculties. Her greatest success was her translation of *Hamlet*:

"To be or what?"

But then she had to revise everything because perhaps she should have begun:

"To be here or not?"

Not all members of the group knew such success. The Four Fuck-ups were deeply demoralized by having their musical vocation frustrated, enervated by their absence from the space preemptively occupied by and divided up among the affected intellectuals in the Immanuel Can't group.

> *The critique of reason puuure*
> *For madness a sure cuuure*

To say nothing of the crude, gross violence of the Baboso Brothers:

> *Last night as I watched yer daddy screw yer mom*
> *Ah jes had to puke my guts up, the grits an' eggs an' ham*

which was all you heard on the radio from morning till night, while the Fuckups had to hide their great nineties lyrics under a bushel for a year:

> *If ah stay, ah'l jes forgit her,*
> *So it's better that ah go.*
> *Oh, Lady Disdain, do not*
> *Let me be your Swain:*
> *If ah stay, ah'l jes forgit her,*
> *So it's better that ah go.*

which they composed at night, exhausted, in the Tlalpan house, at which, one day, the following note from Uncle Don Homero Fagoaga inevitably arrived:

> Doubtlessly Distinguished Niece and Nephew:
> I saw you both leave the house on May 1. I observed your costumes and listened to your comments. I thought that since we'd all taken refuge under a common roof, to which all of us had a right, that at least, juris tantum, we'd all spoken the absolute truth about what happened in the recent past. I must confess my disillusion. You two, with perfidy and with an eye to profit, caused yourselves to pass for old-fashioned hippietecs with long hair and blue jeans, using the slang of the sixties in order to deceive my habitual sagacity and make me think I was dealing with naïve greenhorns from the age of Mick Jagger, Janis Joplin, and Chic Guevara. But it was all a huge hoax! You both are part of the reactionary avant-garde of rebel conservatism! You look for your fashions in the first half of the century, before any gringo left his poop on the moon, forever changing the balance of the universe! I've had to suffer lots of shocks in my life, but none of them has put my understanding of the world into such a crisis as this trick of yours. You may expect my revenge. Pack up your gear, because that house won't belong to you for very long!
> Effective Suffrage. No Reelection.
> (*signed*) Homero Fagoaga, LL.D.

Hipi and the Orphan said they should get ready for the siege of Tlalpan: Homero would only get them out by force, and before that happened they'd pour molten lead on him and shove a stake up his ass, even if it gave him infinite pleasure, but Angeles my mother said that what really surprised her was the idea that Uncle H. had managed a reconciliation with the Party and the government (the rest was a pretext) and would screw up the Christophers Contest: that would be his greatest perversity, it had to be stopped. So, one morning in May, my parents, dressed in the most conservative and old-fashioned way, took the Van Gogh and the compass and set out (I a marble within) to find out the status of the contest and to enter it in proper form now that there remained no doubt whatsoever that Angeles, as Capitolina and Farnesia would say, was "in a family way."

10. More Rumors Than Pennies in a Piggy Bank

 The Palace of the Citizenry, in the northern sector of the city, was the symbolic end point—when it was built—of the Pan-American Highway and was flanked on both sides by statues of the Green Indians. From there, a causeway, surrounded by recycling water, ran to the vast central island, where, no joke, an eagle perched on a cactus devoured several serpents every day. If the eagle was replaced every so often, it was something no one ever checked or even desired to check.

From that central island a dozen stairs descended to the tunnels, where, in an asymmetrical arrangement, the barred windows opened for the business that more than justified this multimillion-dollar structure, erected by the government of President Jesús María y José Paredes in the midst of our ongoing crisis.

ALL CITIZENS HAVE THE RIGHT TO INFORMATION
ALL CITIZENS HAVE THE RIGHT TO COMPLAIN
ALL CITIZENS HAVE THE RIGHT TO GIVE UP

Dressed in black, he flourishing his walking stick, she flouncing her mourning veils, Angel and Angeles walked down a stairway to the tunnel and, before doing anything else, got on the INFORMATION line. Their first order of business was to find out how a couple went about entering the Columbus Day contest for 1992. Two hours later, a man with his hair combed forward to cover his baldness, dressed in the old-fashioned bureaucratic style, wearing a blue eyeshade and sleeve garters, listened distractedly to my parents' request:

"Gosh, there are sooo many contests . . ."

"Yes, but this is the Christopher Columbus Contest, arranged for October 12, 1992—this year . . ."

"Of course, but, you know, there are lots of contests every day . . ."

"There certainly are, but there is only one Columbus Contest . . ."

"Are you sure of that, sir?"

"Of course I am, and so should you be, if you know what you're doing . . ."

"Now don't you get nasty with me, young fellow . . . Next!"

"The next person is my wife, who will ask you the same question: about the Christophers Contest . . ."

"Didn't you just say Columbus, the Columbus Contest is what you said a moment ago. Have you changed your mind?"

"Christopher or Columbus, it's all the same, Christopher Columbus: don't you know who he was?"

"Look, if you get smart with me, I'll slam this window shut right in your face."

"Let's see you do it . . ."

"I'd just be dumping you on one of my office mates here, sir, and that would not be kind."

"Knock off the crap. The Columbus Contest, announced by Mamadoc on October 12, 1991 . . ."

"Didn't you say that it was for 1992, this year? How can anyone help you if you can't say things straight?"

"The contest will be held in 1992, but it was announced in 1991 by Mamadoc . . ."

"Trying to use influence on me now?"

"It just so happens that she announced the contest."

"You know what happens to people who threaten to use influence around here? Have you ever heard of moral renovation?"

"I was just a kid when that came out."

"And now he insults me for being old, what a lack of respect!"

"Look, sir, all I want to know is how I can find out about this contest, I don't want to have anything to do with you . . ."

"Very nice. Now he calls me an incompetent. Keep it up, son, keep it up. I want to see how far this insolence of yours will take you."

"With all due respect, sir, where can I . . ."

"Now listen, I have a name, why do you keep calling me sir, it's as if you called me buddy."

"Okay, what's your name?"

"Use your imagination."

"I don't have any left. You used my last drop when you wore out my patience."

"In that case, go over to the personnel office and find out what my name is so you learn how to treat a public employee with respect."

"But all I . . ."

"Soon you'll be calling me that guy or damned old baldy there behind the bars, that's what I expect from you, come on, why don't you call me a miserable bureaucrat with smelly feet standing there all day like a jerk, careful when you call me a jerk, sonny, or I'll have you thrown out of here, hey, security, get over here, this guy's threatening me, what else am I going to have to put up with!"

My parents, still followed, like it or not, your mercies, by the cloud of suspicion resulting from the Acapulco caper, stepped out of line and headed in the opposite direction, looking for another information window. They actually and respectfully dared ask a middle-aged guard with a sweaty upper lip, wearing a gray uniform and a strange French kepi, sitting in a wheelchair next to a staircase: "Information about the Christopher Columbus Contest, please?"

"Take this staircase," said the crippled guard.

"Thank you."

My parents started to walk toward the stairs.

"Just a moment," said the guard.

"Yes?"

"Are you going to go up or down?"

"I don't know. We're going to the contest office, and you told us . . ."

"This is a down staircase."

"Okay, is the contest office upstairs or downstairs?"

"That depends."

"Depends? Depends on what?"

"On if you go up by going down or if you go down by going up. There's a big difference."

"Where is the contest office?"

"Don't change the subject."

"I don't want to change the subject, what I want is information . . ."

"Well, why didn't you say so? The information window is right over there, where that gentleman with the blue visor is standing . . ."

"Let's go over this again calmly, sir. You told us that we should take this staircase. Now tell me: should we go up by going up or go down by going down."

"Now we're getting somewhere."

"Well?"

"It all depends."

"On what, now?"

"Well, before you get to the stairs, there's the door."

"I can see it. I'm not blind."

"Well, tell me if you think you're going to go out the door or enter it."

"Go out, go out, no question about it: go out."

"In that case, go down three levels and on the left you'll find the Columbus Contest office."

"The Columbus Contest?" suspiciously asked a lady who looked like one of the Bergen-Belsen jail guards in an early-forties Warner Brothers movie: hair pulled back, chignon, pince-nez, shadows under her eyes, lips like Conrad Veidt's, high collar, scarf, and cameo with the profile of Hermann Goering painted on it, and the Ride of the Valkyries playing insinuatingly on the Muzak:

"Mozart," said my mother.

"What?" The lady sitting there narrowed her serpent's eyes as she carved an Iron Cross into the wood with the knife she held in her hand.

"We would like to know where to sign up for the Christopher Columbus Contest set for the twelfth of Oct . . ."

"You've come to the right place."

"What do you know." My father sighed, putting on his pince-nez so as not to be a step behind the receptionist.

"Who is going to have the baby?" said the bureaucrat directly.

"I am," said my mother.

"It will have to be verified."

"Certainly."

"Dr. Menges!" barked the lady. "Another one for the Götter-dämmerung!"

A man with black-dyed hair, twitching cheeks, and blue, slightly crossed eyes appeared behind a white hospital screen. He himself wore a white gown, black patent-leather shoes, and brick-colored gloves. He smiled.

He asked my mother to come into the space behind the screen (I inside, trembling with fear), my father tried to follow her, but the lady stopped him.

"Spread your legs," said the doctor.

"Isn't my verbal statement enough? I had my last period almost two months ago and . . ."

"Spread your legs!" shouted the doctor.

"Think the rain will let up?" my father asked the lady with the chignon.

"Don't try making small talk with me," answered the lady.

"So sorry, but when do you think World War III will break out?"

"Don't get all gemütlich with me, I'm warning you."

"Me? I wouldn't dare. I'd rather listen to you."

"What do you want to know?"

Suddenly a light went on inside my dad's head: "What law governs the activities of this office, what is, shall we say, its Kantian categorical imperative?"

The lady in charge answered with great seriousness: "Everyone can do whatever he pleases as long as there is someone to blame."

Angeles screamed horribly when the doctor brought a white-hot branding iron with a glowing swastika on its tip close to her labia: the entrance, meine Damen und Herren, to Ali Baba's cave, where the final treasure is ME; my mother gave the doctor a kick in the jaw, and as he fell to the floor he shouted that this baby is not Aryan, this baby should not be allowed to enter the contest, this baby has the blood of slaves, gypsies, Indians, Moors, Jews, Semites, he mights, he did go insane, screaming his head off, and we fled. We ran up the three levels, we saw the guard in his wheelchair, abandoned, unable to move, soaked in his own urine, asking us: "Where are you going, folks? Stop! First ask me! You can't go that way! That window is not for looking out but for looking in!"

My parents and I (more upset than ever, more even than when I

was visited by the proletarian, carnal cylinders in the Guerrero mountains, I horrified by what I saw, oh my, oh innocent, impure me,
in the lightning flash of the instant in which my mother spread her
legs and the doctor's beswastikaed branding iron approached my
exit—would that aperture be useful only as an entrance and not as
an exit?) ran toward a fountain of light, and I, only I, saw in the
burning swastika a pair of hypnotic blue eyes, a pair of eyes that was
also a sea of eyes, wave after wave with the same eyes, as if the air,
the ocean, and the land were made of blue, hypnotic, cruel eyes:
my father in his haste collided with a man, and my out-of-breath
mother fell into his arms in the grand marble corridor of the Palace
of the Citizenry. The man blushed, held her so she wouldn't fall,
but actually offered her to my father with a strange sweetness that
said, I don't want her, she isn't mine; is she yours?

The tall, thin man with huge black eyes, bushy eyebrows, a full,
thick, black head of hair and the long, wolfish ears of a Transylvanian
vampire, Nosferatu from the silents, begged her pardon for his clum-
siness. He was looking for the exit.

"I'm looking for the exit."

"I think it's over there," pointed my father.

"I've been looking for it for years," added the man, wearing a
celluloid collar and a black suit, vest, and thick gray tie, without
listening to us.

He went on to say, with just a faint gasp of hope, that he never
expected to find it, but that he would never give up trying.

My parents passed in front of the window where the employee with
the blue visor was standing. He was saying to a fat, dumpy little
fellow of indeterminate age: "I've already told him that you can't go
because you're drunk, but what does it matter to you if you go
tomorrow?"

He raised his eyes and caught sight of my parents. "You again?
Now what do you want?" he shouted. "Do you want to know everything? Everything? Everything?"

11. I'll Believe in You as Long
as a Mexican Girl

The twenty-odd days they'd spent in Mexico City had transformed my parents. My genetives tell me that when we live
with someone we don't notice the passing of time, until one
day we exclaim, just look at the old geezer! when did your
clock strike midnight, man? but the guy was only a kid just the other
day! and then we catch sight of ourselves in a smoky mirror and we
realize that we, too, have not managed to save ourselves from the
ravages of . . . Well, all I know is that my mom, as soon as she got
to Mexico Circus, began to cough, her nose began to run, she started
blowing her nose all day, she sneezed, things I sense and convulsively
resent, you tell me, dear Readers, if I'm not right, there's no one
closer to her secretions than I am and I say this eternal postnasal drip
is polluting my swimming pool. She coughs and the Richter Scale
in here hits 7.

I'm inside her and that's how I know what no one else knows: my
mother Angeles may occasionally seem passive, but inside she's extremely active, who's going to know better than your humble servant,
when the coconut inside her spins at about a thousand m.p.h. and
the best proof is all of what I've been saying, because if she weren't
my intermediary, I'd be quieter than the Congress during Gustavo
Díaz Ordaz's administration. All I want to say on this occasion is
that thanks to her I know that she sees my father Angel, twenty-two
years of age, when they all return to Mexico, D.F., and says: "He's
young. But he looks tired. He's going to inspire too much compassion.
No chick will be able to resist him."

There was solid evidence that something was happening. Because
there were certain interesting earnings to be had in foreign exchange.
Because of this proverb translation business, my parents had the
pleasure of making incursions into the gigantic Tex-Coco-Mex-Mall,
which was divided into the four arms of an enormous cross, Mall-
efic, Mall-feasance, Mall-function, Mall-formed, where, on the bed
of what in ancient times was Lake Texcoco, all the luxury, the elegant
consumer goods, the chance to go shopping without getting on lines,

abundance: my father says it's something like the foreign-currency stores in Communist countries—if you don't have dollars, don't bother coming in.

Angel goes up the escalator in the Nuevo Liver Puddle, which happens to be going down: he has his hand resting on the rubber handrail. He doesn't lift it, not even when (much less then) he sees a woman's hand, which is coming down. He touches it. Sometimes the feminine hand pulls back. Sometimes it doesn't. Other times it squeezes. Others it touches lightly. Others it caresses. And other women, no sooner do my mommy and I look the other way, return to the scene of the crime and leave tiny pieces of paper in my father's predisposed hand. My father once again applies the eternal motto of the eternal Don Juan (which he is): Let's see if it's chewing gum and if it sticks!

Which doesn't mean that amid this florid May, as my mom's tummy grows (and I, too, inside her), my father was not assailed by the anguished desire to know if he was getting old without having experienced sexual plenitude, if he'd let opportunities slip away, even if the sense of the contradiction between his ideas and his practices held him back. His renascent sexuality, was it progressive or reactionary? Should his political activity lead him to monogamy or to the harem?

Ultimately he concluded that a good screw explodes all ideologies.

She forgives him everything, the jerk (I say), because, says the egghead, jealousy is an exercise based on nothingness: the other is not there, she refuses to see it (her): the other woman. What is there, finally, is jealousy and its object: which is invisible. What matters to her is that he comes to her at night and says forgive me, I'm not perfect, I want to be something else, and I still haven't reached it, help me, Angeles, and she, the dumbbell, really loves him, since she sees in him everything that is opposite to what she is, everything, therefore, that completes her. But, for all that, she does not give up the hope that after a time they will be equals.

"Give me things to think about at night," she said to him one day, and now she can't complain. He's giving them to her, by the ton. She does not know if little by little, instead of being fascinating, she is becoming fascinated by Angel and my father's problem of creating a program of rebellion and personal creation and not being able to purge out the temptations that deny and smash that program. This fascinates Angeles, but Angeles ceases to be fascinating for him and she does not realize it and I don't know how to communicate it to her. She doesn't know how to say anything other than this hint of a reproach:

"I hope you're not going to say someday that you wished you were like everyone else."

Angeles, my mother, knows how to radiate an admirable confidence. People say that she and my father met when they were very young and incomplete. She thinks the two of them can shape each other, share their formation, and get to know each other. She's an optimist. That's why she admits that sometimes one wins and sometimes the other. It's a game they have both accepted ever since the two of them were raped at the same time by Matamoros and his cohorts in Malinaltzin: there they both lost, but they both won the ability to accept what happened one afternoon in the month of March without blaming each other. Only in May did they begin to compensate for that sublime nobility and to make barbed little comments that meant, this time I win, this time you lose, since even Angeles's intrinsic nobility, when it notes Angel's peccadillos, becomes a figure of speech: this time I win because I'm noble and understanding. Then he lets her know that he will not feel blameworthy unless she shows a little outrage. What sickens him is precisely all this nobility of soul: my mom as Gerald Ford—let's pardon everyone in sight so we can be home in time for cocktails. But if my mom shows the slightest disgust, then my father starts talking again about women as the creatures who created guilt. Then she gets indignant and says to him:

"Draw me a picture of them."

"I'm better at telling," says Angel and he puts out the light, and I'm left disconcerted. But, after a while, one or the other (and this is where they really take turns, punctually, mathematically) brings his or her cheek close to the ear of the other, one looks for the other's little foot (like a hamster), one (him) slips his fingers into her luxurious mink triangle, one (she) has already taken the measure of the bag where the golden nuggets are stored, and we're off and running: the sheets get hot, the pillows are fluffed up, and my old friend the guy with no ears is already inside his home and I happily greet him: Ahoy there! Animus intelligence!

How much time will pass before each one refuses to see him- or herself in the mirror of the other, before each one refuses to know through the other if he or she is getting older, if he or she still makes love well, if he or she should go on a diet, if he or she is taken seriously, if they really do share memories? Who knows, Reader! Better turn the page on this chapter.

7

Accidents of the Tribe

. . . the city is an accidental tribe . . .

Dostoevsky
The Diary of a Writer

1

Médoc d'Aubuisson, the López family's cook, was the only survivor of the final explosion, attributed to the Princes of Turenne and the Abbesses of Tooloose (POTATOS), the legitimist terrorist organization that blew up the ancient Le Grand Vefour restaurant, which had occupied a beautiful corner of the Palais Royal in Paris since the times of the Duc de Choiseul.

The reason the POTATOS gave for their attack was that Le Grand Vefour was serving meals to functionaries from the neighboring Ministry of Culture on the rue de Valois and the ministry was the brain behind red, antimonarchist propaganda in France. Farewell Vefour, welcome Médoc: the survivor's celebrity caused Doña Lucha Plancarte de López, wife of the ex-Superminister Ulises López, to demand the services of the chef de cuisine: how the girls would howl when they found out!

Fought over by the bourgeoisies of Peru, the Ivory Coast, and the Seychelles, the emir of Abu Dhabi, and, last but not least, the Republic of Mexico, Médoc accepted the last offer because of one special circumstance: his great-great-grandfather had been cook for Princess Salm-Salm, Maximilian's lover in Cuernavaca during the ephemeral Mexican Empire. Besides, one of Médoc's uncles, a hit man from Marseilles, emigrated to El Salvador and founded the death squads there. Médoc wanted at least to be near his American past, but he accepted only after making outrageous demands: these meteques from Las Lomas del Sol would not only pay him in dollars and in New York (twenty thousand per month) but would also unquestioningly accept his menus and would purchase the raw materials he required from wherever they were to be found—be it Roman truffles in season or Chinese ants from the tombs of Qin Shi Huang— at whatever the price; once a week the lady of the house (Doña Lucha herself) would prepare and serve him his meals, only so that insidious comparisons be established, and although Médoc had the right of veto with regard to the persons the Lópezes might invite to eat his delights, he absolutely ruled out dinners for more than eight people.

This last stipulation frenetically frustrated Doña Lucha's ambitions; after all, if the lady wanted to have the best chef in Mexico (excuse me: the world), she also wanted to offer the most lavish and well-attended parties.

"Order sandwiches from a hotel," Médoc told her when Doña Lucha weepingly explained that the imminent celebration of her daughter's Sweet-Sixteen Party—her daughter Penelope López, the celebrated Epic Princess of Mexico-in-Crisis, the Debutante of Fashion in a Society with Nothing to Debut and Fashion Like No Other in the World—would require at least five hundred guests, well chosen to be sure, but five hundred nonetheless.

Having pronounced the statement recorded above, Médoc went on vacation in the Club Med's Cancún barony, abandoning the López family to its own devices not only as to the creation of a suitable menu but also as to the composition of a guest list of five hundred young boys and girls who would celebrate Penny's birthday with her. Yet another problem: the political plague that surrounded Minister López after the meteoric rise of Federico Robles Chacón and his creature, Mamadoc, made it improbable that what was left of the jeunesse dorée of 1992 would attend a celebration in the ghetto (also golden) of Las Lomas del Sol. The result would be a serious loss of prestige for both mother and daughter.

Enter Ms. Ponderosa, dried-out and galvanic, the purest Castilian stock, skinny as a rail but with the thickest of ankles, a Portuguese mustache to complete her Iberian physiognomy, and a whiff of garlic to give the lie to her appearance of implacable, Inquisitorial, Counter-Reformation austerity. Ms. Ponderosa pointed out, first, that for a real Castilian any goat will do for roasting and, second, that both the twelve-thousand-odd newspapers and the innumerable television stations in the city were constantly announcing a new public service called TUGUEDER, whose spokesperson, a charming boy with an egg-shaped head, was offering to those who desired to leave the labyrinth of solitude a matchmaking service (Ms. Ponderosa blushed), and that, third, his service would eliminate the possibility of party failure during the current crisis by guaranteeing that the number of guests required by the hosts would be there.

"We don't even have a cake; *I* don't know how to make cakes," mooed Doña Lucha. "Do *you*, miss?"

Ponderosa triumphantly said she did not: "But here in the fine print it says: *Birthday cakes specially made by Baby Ba.*"

"But who runs this organization? Does it belong to anyone we know?"

"It says here the president of the company is named Angel Palomar y Fagoaga . . ."

"Labastida Pacheco y Montes de Oca!" exclaimed Doña Lucha, who knew the Mexican Gotha by heart: "The best families of D.F., Puebla, and Guadalajara!"

"If you say so," Ponderosa commented dryly. She withdrew—without turning her back on the mistress.

2

 Like a ghost, Ulises López wandered through his darkened house in Las Lomas del Sol. During the day, ablaze with mercury vapor lamps, incandescent spots, and multicolored strobes, the mansion looked like the Duty-Free Shop in any international airport. Every one of the mementos of petroseventies opulence was piled up there for all the world to see: French perfumes, German cameras, Japanese computers, Yankee recorders, Swiss watches, Italian shoes. All of it, felt Doña Lucha, should be on display, because, as she never tired of saying:

"My money is my money and I have absolutely no reason to hide it from envious eyes. I do as I please!"

But at four in the morning the owner of the house flitted like a phantom from his severe mahogany-furnished bedroom with velveteen-covered walls to the preposterous Guggenheim staircase, to the cement garden, to the pool in the shape of the map of the U.S.A., with the stars and stripes painted on its bottom, from there into the private casino and to the cockfighting pit, muttering to himself about his career and his fortune, without knowing that Federico Robles Chacón, his archrival, had given the cook Médoc d'Aubuisson a farm with fruit orchards and a shooting range in Yautepec in exchange for which Médoc would put a tiny grain of sugar into Don Ulises's breakfast papaya every day. The grain of sugar was actually the last word in computers invented in

– – – – – – ((Pacífica)) – – – – – – –

Once ingested, it registers a person's murmurs and most secret thoughts for twenty-four hours, transmitting them to a data bank in the office of Robles Chacón, where they are deciphered and processed by a Samurai computer, providing Minister Robles Chacón with infinite delight and inside information. However: since the microchip enters with the papaya, it also leaves with the papaya, so it must be replaced every day. Médoc will not scant his duties just because he's going on vacation in order not to have to feed five hundred parvenus. Into the ear of Ms. Ponderosa, Médoc has whispered his promise that she will abandon, if not her virginity (of which she was deprived a long time ago by a powerful Spanish Civil Guard), then at least her current solitude as soon as he (Médoc) returns

TUGUEDER (flashes the neon sign in the Ponderosa noggin)

if she will slip the daily grain of sugar into the master's papaya.

In a solitary cockpit at four in the morning, we find a sleepless Ulises López, who can only vent his rage against Federico Robles Chacón through a sentimental review of his own career: he was born a poor boy on the Pacific coast of Guerrero, but even then he was thrifty, a pack rat of a boy who saved everything, who found a use for everything, and that's how he made his way: When no one else had toothbrushes—call Ulises! When someone needed a top—call Ulises! When a bus needed a nut—call Ulises! When a nicely stuffed box of votes for the PRI would win an election for the Party—call Ulises! And when Ulises requested admission to high school in Acapulco, law school at Chilpancingo, the doctoral program at the National University, and postgraduate study at USC, he got what he wanted because Ulises López always had something someone else needed: that was his secret, and that was his way to the top:

"I made my money following the national rules of the game," he would say, and no one ever doubted the truth of that statement. From low-level jobs he rose to high-level jobs, but in all, low or high, he maintained or solidified his power base. Guerrero, where he achieved favorite-son status, was indispensable to him; then national private enterprise; foreign relations—U.S. finance and business; then national government and the PRI. All this was well known and fairly normal. The difference was that Ulises embodied this pattern at a unique moment in Mexican history—between 1977 and 1982, when more foreign money entered the country than had come in during the previous 155 years of our independence. During the oil boom, everything was expensive in Mexico except the dollar. Ulises realized that before anyone else. He founded the famous Theta Group (of which he was the only member) and took over banks in order to lend himself cheap money he used to import the torrent of consumer goods he sold at inflated prices in the status-conscious middle-class market; he deposited hundreds of millions in rival banks and then abruptly withdrew the money, causing his competition to collapse; he created financial empires within Mexico and abroad, vast labyrinths of paper within pyramids of noninsured credits and companies backed only by documents based on the country's oil promise, taking advantage of low interest rates, petrodollar loans, and the rise in the cost of raw materials; he deposited carloads of profits in European and U.S. banks, but he was the first to stand up and cheer when López Portillo nationalized the banks and denounced the money exporters in 1982. What the hell: the people he denounced were standing right there with him, wildly applauding a denunciation the President—in a theatrical act unprecedented since Santa Anna staged a coup d'état against himself—directed toward other people and himself. Eventually, Ulises said to himself, and he said it with full confidence, I'll be paid back for the loss of my banks and then I'll send my money safe and sound to Grand Cayman; and that's just how it happened. Now a cayman is a crocodile, but even a crocodile (like Don Ulises) can suffer the odd setback: he took a nasty hit because of his paper speculations, but by 1989 his 1982 losses had been paid back. Smack in the middle of the crisis, he realized that the foreign shareholders in his Mexico Black Gold Mutual Fund (a dummy subsidiary of the Theta Group) had bought ten million shares at twelve dollars per share in 1978; now they were worth two dollars each. To compensate for that loss, he became the first Latin American to enter into the greenmail racket—green, green: how I love you green, green cells, green stocks, green dollars, and green dolors: the loans that broke us were asshole loans made by asshole banks to asshole governments, said Ulises; we could have broken the international banking system by suspending payments, but we didn't dare; they screwed us because we were honorable men and we forgot that the United States never paid its astronomical debt to English banks in the nineteenth century. I'm delighted—Ulises jumped for joy, clicking his heels (I'm faithful to capital, not to the fatherland!). Transformed into a greenmailer, Don Ulises was the star of a kind of financial fraud that worked like this: he'd buy a huge amount of stock in a famous transnational corporation, announce that he was about to take it over, thus sending its value into the multinational stratosphere and thereby forcing the company to buy—at a very high price—the stocks belonging to Ulises López in order to retain control over the corporation and to silence speculation. Using this method, our astute Guerrero magnate earned $40 million free and clear in one shot and could thus repair his fortune, damaged by the collapse of the paper empires—well, not damaged all that much, muttered the squatty, rapidly pacing Napoleon of the business world, after all, as Don Juan Tenorio was heard to say, time does eventually run out on you, and therefore there is no debt that can't be negotiated so that you don't have to pay in propeller-driven pesos what you contracted to buy in supersonic dollars; we've got lots of things to sell in Mexico, beginning with twelve hundred miles of elastic and continuous frontier, then moving on to revalued earthquaked property expropriated by the government in 1985 and renegotiated by Ulises in 1989.

Don Ulises López's principal task during the Crisis of 1990, when he was named superminister, to supervise (from a very advantageous position) the de facto dismemberment that de jure disguised itself as condominiums, trusts, limited concessions, and temporary cedings, in which the Yucatán was handed over to Club Med, the Chitacam Trusteeship was created for the Five Sisters, the existence of Mexamerica was sanctioned, and no attention whatsoever was paid to what was going on in Veracruz or on the Pacific coast north of Ixtapa.

Nothing brought more fame to Ulises López than these deals, disguised in euphemisms like "realistic acceptance of interindependence," "patriotic adaptation to dominating forces," "a step forward in nationalistic, revolutionary concentration," "patriotic contribution to peaceful coexistence," etc., and whatever the individual's party affiliations, there was something for everyone.

For his many efforts, Don Ulises was rewarded during the Crisis of the Year '90 with the portfolio of SEPAFU (Secretariat of Patriotism and Foreign Undertakings); some people said that his business successes were balanced by his disastrous tour as minister, while others said he was rewarded with a brilliant portfolio for his business disasters. Our brave Ulises remained undaunted: from the Super Economic Secretariat he announced his market philosophy through all the media:

In public: "It does not matter who makes money, just as long as everyone pays taxes."

In private: "I'm willing to lose all the money in the world, as long as it isn't my money."

In public: "Public service is the only justification for holding power."

In private: "Like sex, power can only be enjoyed when it needs no justifications."

In public: "We are all involved in production."

In private: "This country is divided into producers and parasites. I had nothing in Guerrero. I made myself into what I am today out of nothing. No one ever gave me a free tortilla."

In public: "When all of us get our fair share, production goes up."

In private: "The government should only help the rich."

In public: "The glory of our nation is forged by one hundred million Mexicans."

In private: "The glory of Ulises López is forged by one hundred million assholes."

In public: "As the poet says, no one should have too much when someone doesn't have enough."

In private: "Who needs a Jaguar or a Porsche to survive? I do! For whom is having a thirty-ounce bottle of Miss Dior a matter of life or death? Do I really have to answer that?"

Publicly or privately, Ulises and his policies were an open secret: Ulises and his pals got rich because the nation got poor; he made money thanks to bad government; oil ruined us but it set Ulises up; the government is tearing the country to pieces; foreign banks are tearing the government to pieces; Ulises tears all of them to pieces.

"Put me in jail for theft!" Ulises shouted with haughty bitterness at the invisible roosters that night he paced the empty cockpit. "Cut me down! And then wait for someone with my genius to pop up! All aspects of human nature are reborn, demand to exist, to grow, to bear fruit: ALL OF THEM!"

But, in a flash, the nefarious Robles Chacón usurped all the wisdom, the capacity for intrigue, the talent for scheming, the rhetorical skill, the balanced exchange of favors, and, in the same way, replaced the contradictions and the discredit, the lack of results and the animosity of the people toward Ulises López's administration with a politics of symbols: Mamadoc, the contests, Circus and Circus, all with such spectacular results that Ulises, locked away in his mansion, sleeplessly pacing his cockpit, drinking coffee at all hours of the day and thinking how to take revenge on Robles Chacón, on that monster Mother and Doctor, on his former financial rivals who had accommodated themselves to the new situation. Ulises López believed in self-affirmation, and his shout into the night was this:

"I was a shark and I'll be a shark again!"

All of the above meant absolutely nothing to Ulises's distinguished wife, Lucha Plancarte de López—as long as it did not affect her lifestyle, which for her was everything. An essential part of that style was foreign travel, and when her husband announced that from then on they would only travel to Querétaro and Taxco, the lady almost had a fit:

"Why? Why?"

"We just can't offend the middle classes, who are unable to travel because they have no foreign currency."

"Well I, thank God, am not middle-class."

"But you will be unless you watch out. The time is just not right for conspicuous consumption, Lucha. I'm not a cabinet minister anymore, and I don't want to give Robles Chacón any pretexts to get even with me."

"Maybe you should be thinking about getting even with him, dummy."

Doña Lucha López was tall, outspoken, dark, with a good figure, curly-haired wherever she had hair, with an ass like Narcissus' pond—deep enough to drown in, her husband said when he met her—and Tantalus tits—because they always bounced away when his fingers came too close. She had been known as a femme fatale in the city of Chilpancingo when the two of them went out dancing during their courtship, and Ulises had to protect himself from the train of punks and would-be Don Juans who would follow Lucha's silhouette to the movies, to cabarets, on vacation, and when they went out for a snack. But Ulises made his first million before the others and that determined her choice: she tall and graceful, he short and nervous. They didn't waste time on a honeymoon: he de-femme-fatalized her; she de-Don-Juanized her Chilpancingo lover boy and then they de-sisted. She put on weight, but always maintained—Ulises would say to himself—"a divine skull." As long as she lived, she knew how to sit as if she were posing for a portrait by Diego Rivera. She was involved, even though her husband knew all about them, in a series of compensatory escapades, the price, he admitted, he had to pay, as he ate his daily papaya, for his own escapades with power and money:

"I only use those who would use me or who do use everyone else. If I exploit them, it's because they also exploit; if I'm tricky, it's because everyone's tricky. Everyone wants exactly what you and I want. Power, sex, and money."

"But not in equal quantities, dearie."

She wanted sex and money, power she didn't care about. As long as she felt young, she made herself the leading lady in a labyrinth of illicit love affairs, secret meetings, motels, threats, escapes, daily excitement, and above all the adventure of knowing she was being followed by a dozen or so thugs and private detectives working for her husband and none of them could ever find her or bring proof to poor Ulises. That captain of industry decided not to take revenge until the time was ripe; in the meanwhile, he would enjoy the dis-interest of their sexual relations and the interest both said they had in their daughter and in her place in Mexican society.

The crisis ruined everything. Lucha never forgave Ulises for having given up on the trips abroad. Neither the mansion in Las Lomas del Sol nor the cook from Le Grand Vefour could compete with the emotion Lucha felt when she walked into a great department store in a foreign country.

"Are we or are we not wealthy Mexicans?" she asked in murderous tones as he ate his daily ration of papaya with sugar and lemon—without which the diminutive tycoon suffered dyspepsia and intestinal irregularity.

He did not respond to this recrimination, but he did share it. Ulises López's reward to himself for his childhood in Guerrero and his dynamic ascent in Mexico City was a dream populated by waiters and maîtres d', restaurants, hotels, first-class plane tickets, European castles, beach houses on Long Island and Marbella: oh, to enter and be recognized, greeted, kowtowed to, in the Plaza-Athénée and the Beverly-Wilshire, to call the maître d' at Le Cirque by his first name . . . For Don Ulises, these compensations, nevertheless, put him in a state of perpetual schizophrenia: how to be cosmopolitan in Rome and a hometown boy in Chilpancingo? he didn't want to lose either his provincial power base (without it, he would have no political support) or his international standing (without it, he'd have no reward of any kind for his labors).

Our little Lucha, on the other hand, had fewer refinements than her husband: for her there existed nothing beyond stores, stores, and more stores, especially U.S. malls; the reward for being proudly rich and Mexican was to spend hours obsessively patrolling the Galleria in Houston, Trump Tower in New York, the Hancock in Chicago, the Rodeo Collection in Los Angeles, and Copley Place in Boston: hours and hours, from the moment they opened until closing time, Lucha Plancarte de López walked more miles through those commercial corridors than a Tarahumara Indian through his mountains.

"That's why we made the money in the first place! And now what happens? I hate your guts!"

With these words skiing over the fissures and grooves in his cerebral cortex, Ulises went back into his bedroom, laid himself down, and instead of counting sheep, repeated: I did lots of favors, lots of favors were done for me, returned to me, there was never a contradiction between my interests and the interests of the nation, it's all favors, I do the nation a favor, the nation does one for me, I'll do it back, how will I get even with Robles, how will I get even with, how will I get zzzzzzzzzzzzz and Lucha, on her side, was trying to get to sleep by reading, at her husband's entreaty, López Velarde's *Sweet Fatherland*. Learn something, honey, he'd say, don't always look so dumb, you're Ulises López's wife, don't forget that, and all that seemed true to the lady, but what stuck in her craw was that line about "The Christ Child bequeathed you a stable," an idea that instead of making her relax set her to hopping around, subliminally reminding her that Christ was the God born in a manger (they always pop up where you least expect them!) and literally reminding her that a mob of squatters left over from the earthquake were building mangers on her property. Bullshit, said Doña Lucha Plancarte de López, wife of the eminent financier and minister, stables for Christmas Eve, fine, God bequeathed to me my house in Las Lomas del Sol, 15,000 square feet, a tennis court, black marble toilets, the bedrooms lined with lynx to rub up against cozily before making whoopee on the water bed with a melodious musical background by the great composer Mouseart piped in and my televised scale that electronically tells me my weight and the image of the ideal figure to which I get a little closer every day: size 12 here, girls, so drop dead! Besides, think of all we did for our little Princess Penny to make her existence cute: a heart-shaped Jacuzzi, a ballroom right here with three hundred of the latest cassettes, a little casino where her friends can have fun with backgammon tables, roulette wheels, a screening room done in red velvet, a stable of ponies to pull cute little coaches when Penny rides around the garden dressed up as Marie Antoinette, she says, although to me she looks like an elegant little shepherdess, and a track for dog racing, a cockpit, a little heated pool in the shape of the States, a modest copy of the first floor of Bloomingdale's, modest because we don't want to cause any fuss, what with the crisis, and we almost never travel anymore, but it does have shopgirls imported directly from the U.S. and a perfume counter that, my God! makes my, my . . . my nose twitch! So have a good time with your stable! Me, I'll take my cash, my property, my little girl who speaks English, my greenbacks to travel with once in a while even if it's to Mexamerica, my little group of girls to laugh with and have a good time with and a few drinks, or more than a few—who's counting? Stables: not for this filly!

My parents spent half of June running from one government office to another, from the SECULELA, which was where Angeles composed her Mexican versions of Shakespeare, and where, naturally,

the contest ought to have some cultural impact. They were sent back
to the Palace of the Citizenry, where the same old man in the blue
visor read them the following regulation:

"You cannot enter the contest unless you present the child first."

"But how can we present the child when he hasn't been born yet?"

"No way around this regulation. It says right here that only those
who present their child can enter," all of which led them to the
SEDECONT (Secretariat for Demography and Birth Control) to see
if they could find an explanation for this requirement, but all they
found there was the same old man who worked in the morning at
the Palace of the Citizenry, with the same cripple in his wheelchair,
eternally sitting in his own shit with no one to help him, acting as
doorman. My parents, more fatigued than desperate (and Angel thinking: in any case, she'll have the baby, contest or no contest, quincentennial or no) (and Angeles saying to herself: this contest is
essential to Angel's free, unstructured life, the contest gave him a
goal; without it, I wonder if his adventure and his faith, his love for
anarchy and his ideology of order will all be compatible . . .), decided
that to cover all contingencies they ought to earn more money by
means of new jobs and enterprises, and that explains the birth of
their parallel activity in

TUGUEDER

A Service That Brings People Together
and Organizes Brilliant Parties
Get Yourself Out of the Labyrinth of Solitude!

"Do you know any lonely proletarians?" asked Egg, explaining why
the project was a sure thing. "You don't, right? Only the rich are
going to need this service, mark my word."

Baking Services Under	Service Director:
the Direct Supervision of:	Angel Palomar y Fagoaga
Baby Ba	

Meanwhile, Angel went on translating sayings, Angeles translated
classics into street talk. Orphan Huerta hired himself out to the various
newfangled political parties that had sprung up in the wake of President Paredes's free-will reform: he became a political cream-pie

thrower, an essential figure at all political rallies. Hipi Toltec, because
he looked like a magician, sold pills that let you dream your favorite
TV program, and Egg along with Baby Ba devoted themselves exclusively to TUGUEDER.

"Bet you can't guess," said Egg one June afternoon to Angel. "I
just got a call from the house of Ulises López. They want us to
organize a birthday party for their daughter, Penny."

Egg paused as he was writing down a list and looked knowingly at
Angel: "Remember her dancing at Divan the Terrible down in Aca?"

How could he forget her? Egg watched the reverie pass through
the gypsy (if myopic) eyes, streaked with Moor and Aztec, of his
friend Angel: even if Penelope's golden butterfly eyes had merely
fluttered over him that New Year's Eve, his own were fixed on his
memory of her that night: he'd only seen her once, and for that
reason his visual memory was charged with nostalgia; she was more
beautiful, more brilliant than if he'd seen her every day and, above
all, more beautiful than if she had noticed him *even once*: ah, the
golden girl, who abandoned the sun to come down here and console
the stars, said Ada Ching that night (rightly, for a change), and it
was then Penny's eyes had settled like two dark butterflies on my
father, only to move on, never to return. She danced, lifted her leg,
showed her thigh under her sequined skirt, and a down-covered
crease, a slice of quince, a tiny, moist copper coin which suddenly,
tonight, my father desires more than anything in the world, as he
spontaneously rejects my mother, the contest, and me, desiring more
than anything else a night with Penny, his penis in Penny, penetrating
Penny, forcing Penny to look at him with her butterfly eyes as they
come at the same moment, all for the promise which in that instant
passed through his mind, filling his with color fugues, red and blue
circles that light up and go out, futuristic, energetic murals shot into
the void, all in the name of his resurrected passion for Penny López,
the daughter of the minister, and all because feeling nostalgia, living
on nostalgia, on the unreachable becomes intolerable for my father,
a kind of death in reverse, a waiting for the past in order to die in
it, an impotent dissatisfaction with what is already dead and gone.
A catatonic nostalgia for the films of Constance Bennett or the records
of Rudy Vallee or Schiaparelli's dresses or fin-de-siècle postcards from
Baden-Baden was possible, but so was a violent nostalgia to recover
Fiume, annex the Sudetenland, or manifest your destiny to Texas

and California: my father didn't want nostalgia, he wanted Penny and he wanted Penny to want penis, and when he desired all this, we (the contest, Mommy, and Baby Meme) faded into the background, although my father did feel enough remorse to admit the faults in his stable character, which was conservative, traditionalist; damn, man, he dared to say aloud to Egg, everything conspires against what I want to be; and that's how it would be if you wanted to be just the opposite, our buddy Egg said with a smile in his eyes; I can't stop playing the lover boy, even though it means putting my balls on the line, said my father in silence (I know he said it because later on he said it aloud to my mother):

"This is my worst contradiction, babe. I want to be a conservative without retiring as a lover boy."

"What contradiction are you talking about?" my mother answered him. "Don't fool yourself. You're right smack in the tradition. Don't think that playing around is some kind of progress."

In any case, Angel cut out a color photo of Penny López from Nicolás Sánchez Osorio's society page in *Novedades* and pasted it over an article by Philip Roth in a copy of *The New York Review of Books* that Angeles refused to read for fear of contracting even more ideas. My father trembled with the thrill of the risk he was taking.

But the rift occurred later on. Now it was time to organize for Penny López's June 15 Sweet-Sixteen Party in the house of the magnate and ex-minister, Don Ulises, and his wife, Doña Lucha: five hundred guests of the highest quality was what the lady had requested; there weren't that many, said Egg seriously. High society had either collapsed or run away a long time ago; only the ones who are really in love with power are still here because there's no way they can exercise it from a Jacuzzi in Malibu, and besides, my mother reminded them, this Ulises guy is really a pariah and no one is going to want to become one too by going to his house. Then Pater Meus had a luminous idea: Concha Toro! The Chilean singer still existed. She'd appeared on TV for having won one of the Last Playboy Centerfold Contests, how long ago was it? They sent Orphan and Hipi out to wander the streets for the entire day, and twenty-four hours later they produced her c.v., which Egg translated from Anglatl slang with his renowned mental agility:

Concha Toro
(née) María Inez Aldunate y Larraín
in Chillán, Chile,
on January 6, [year blotted out]
aka Dolly Lama
Aristocratic family
Family ruined by the collapse of the
nitrate market
Education: Santiago College
Emigrates to Argentina as a young
woman
Proclaimed High Priestess of Sexual
Ultraism
Emigrates to the U.S.A.
Enters conga line with Xavier Cugat's
orchestra
Sings celestial choruses for M-G-M
movies
Dancer, chorus line of *42nd Street* road
company
Backup girl in Las Vegas Dionne
Warwicke and Boy George show
Success in Mexico singing boleros
Hostess at SIMON BULLY BAR
Supervises Home-Delivery Theater
services

"Perfect!" shouted Egg. "Who wants to interview her?"

"She took my virginity," said Angel, my father.

"That lets you out. We want this deal to be totally professional, no personality factors, I'll talk to her," said our buddy with totally uncensored enthusiasm.

And my father reasoned that he already had enough on his mind with his soul divided between the presence of Angeles and the potentialities of Penny to allow himself the luxury of nostalgia for a woman who had to be in her sixties by now: let Egg arrange the Home-Delivery Theater in the López house to help Penny celebrate, while my father attempted to work out—though he knew he'd fail—the two anguishes he was feeling that June:

Could he rely on the contest as an avenue to the future?

Could he be faithful to Angeles without letting Penny get away this time?

The first anguish (and how rapidly you run, dear Dad, from disorder to despair!) got even more serious when, on his eleventh visit to the Palace of the Citizenry, he found all the employees abandoning the place: feverishly shredding documents, packing up books and typewriters, taking down the official photographs of President Paredes and Mamadoc, sweeping up the dry leaves that had invaded the corridors with a preternatural taste of autumn. The man with the visor was no longer in his window, nor was the crippled doorman in his place, Dr. Menges and his companion, the lady with the Goering cameo, were being taken out, quite stiff, on stretchers: their blue faces and their necktie-length tongues suggested a sinister end; and the operation was being directed by a face that Angel fearfully recognized as that of the implacable Colonel Inclán, chief of the metropolitan police. Who could ever forget his black glasses, his skull-like face, his greenish complexion, the green spittle running out the corners of his mouth, his hoarse voice giving rapid, precise orders:

"Quickly, or you're all dead."

I suppose that my father's anguish resolved itself into a single desperate action: to speak to Inclán, to ask him about the contest, about what was going on with it; but when the colonel saw him running up and shouting What about the contest? he started to draw his pistol, as did his squad of bodyguards. Angel trembled, but he didn't know if Inclán could see him through his black glasses. Show me your ID, my father was about to say, shitting in his pants, where's your badge! his exquisite cinematic memory demanded of this Indio Bedoya of *Treasure of the Sierra Madre* fame for the nineties who was foaming yellow at the mouth as he repeated incessantly, his hand resting on his gun, caressing the grip:

"Only shoot when it's really necessary. Count to ten. Remember how you were taught. We don't want any more Tlateloco Massacres. Count to twenty. Don't call this asshole an asshole. He dares mention the Mamadoc contest to me! He dares to mention Robles Chacón's symbols to me! But don't kill this asshole. Not yet. Offer him a friendly hand. A friendly hand. The paraffin test for my friendly hand. Take my friendly hand. Take it! Take it!"

Angel grabbed the hand of the Supreme Policeman, ominously

backed up by his coterie of green-uniformed Janissaries, the cold of that superdry palm burned him, the gray, steel-sharp fingernails scratched him slightly. He sought in vain heat, sweat, or hair: like the skin of a crocodile, Colonel Inclán's hand had no temperature. It wasn't even cold, Angel said to himself, as he released it and withdrew like Ponderosa before her mistress—not daring to turn his back on Inclán in the half light of this cement Tenochtitlán where the colonel, immobile, devoid of temperature, surrounded by his assassins, muttered No violence, friendly hand, friendly hand, with a voice that grew more and more horrifying and thick. He was swallowed up by the Aztec night and the living eagle perched on the cactus outside began to fly against a red sky, but a few yards up he was stopped by the chain around his leg and after a bit he roosted on a parabolic antenna. But he never released the serpent he was carrying in his beak. Angel turned and ran.

3

 "Life," Samuel Butler once wrote, "is like playing a violin solo in public and learning the instrument as one goes on." Our buddy Egg, dressed in his morning coat and striped trousers, cravat, and pearl tie pin, remembered that quotation as he tried to rehearse the seven-piece orchestra hired for Penny López's Sweet-Sixteen Party by the amalgamated forces of the TU-GUEDER service and the Home-Delivery Theater service of Concha Toro, alias María Inez Aldunate y Larraín, alias Dolly Lama. This combo, which crawled out from under God knows what rock, couldn't understand Egg even with the sheet music our buddy composed right under their noses, and the musicians whiled away their time tuning their instruments. Although the five hundred low-caliber guests constituted a crowd, they certainly didn't make a party: their costumes were depressing, folkloric or cosmopolitan, following the standards set in Mexican movies during the forties. There were people in *tehuana* and *chinaco* costume, society ladies with concrete beehive hairdos wearing gowns cut Greek-goddess style from the Eisenhower era, gentlemen wearing tuxedos and white vests that were too long or dinner jackets with white, very wide piqué ties, gentlemen wearing golf trousers and ladies wearing white foxes and pillbox hats inspired by the Maginot Line: the entire wardrobe supply of Churubusco Studios, the storage bins and inheritance of Virginia Zury and Andrés Soler made their phantasmal appearance chez Ulises López, his wife Lucha, and their daughter Penny, the day she turned sixteen. The ballroom in the mansion in Las Lomas del Sol turned out to be too small to hold—that's how Doña Lucha began a society column she was writing in her head—the darling couples from our jeunesse dorée, accompanied by their distinguished chaperons, who looked like (Ulises held back his disgust) extras in some film starring María Antonieta Pons and, as it turned out, that and only that is what they were: Concha Toro's Home-Delivery Theater gave work to thousands of old extras from Mexican movies. None of this seemed to bother my dad Angel in the slightest, because that night he only had eyes for the guest of honor, the adorable ingenue, Penelope López, who appeared wearing a miniskirt and a gilt breastplate, long golden legs, and high, stiletto heels. She was a bit dazed by the mob, and stared through the guests as if they were made of glass. The truth is that all they were doing was occupying space, adding to the body count, filling the ballroom that was enlivened by a combo that never managed to play a single number, tuning up endlessly, led by our truly desperate buddy Egg: what did these guys have against his music? why didn't they play it? and with Penny on her cloud and Angel unable to make eye contact with her.

Mrs. Lucha Plancarte de López was instantly attracted to my dad Angel (descendant of the best families); she stalked up to him like a panther, led him to the punch bowl, and spoke to him about people like us, you know what I mean, young man, aristocratic Mexicans of means. She then gave him a detailed description of her first visit to Bloomingdale's, an event of transcendent importance in her life, and she gave another detailed description of the suite she usually took at the Parker Meridien in New York in, alas, other times, the bubble having burst, but she (after taking my father's arm, little Lucha's hand hidden in my father's armpit) could survive any crisis with a little tenderness and understanding. Mrs. López's verborrhea enveloped my father Angel: she never stopped talking about trips abroad, and when she'd exhausted that theme she went on to relatives, illness, servants, and priests—in that order.

"I can't stand any more of this idle chitchat," my father said to her brutally.

"Last night I went to see a property of mine which had been illegally occupied by squatters," Mrs. L. P. de López said suddenly by way of response. "I brought along my gunmen, and we set the whole place on fire. No one got out of there alive, son. Who is your confessor? Like to see some photos of Penny when she was a baby?"

She scratched my father's hand. With a cigar in his mouth, Ulises López watched the crowd moving through the hall. From a distance, saw how his wife approached my father Angel, saw the anxiety with which Angel tried to penetrate Penny's vacant stare, when the circle his extremely active mind was about to draw was broken by an apparition: a Chaplinesque boy, his eyebrows raised in astonishment, was helping another boy, this one dressed in snakeskin, to carry the stupendous birthday cake to the round table which had been set up in the center of the hall. They set it down, put in the sixteen candles, asked Penny to make a wish and blow them out, which our Valley (Anáhuac) Girl did, blasting away with an unexpectedly bullish snort. The candles went out without a whimper, everyone sang Jappy Burtay Two Jews (without musical accompaniment; the combo was still tuning its instruments), Orphan Huerta and Hipi Toltec cut the cake and served slices to the guests, first, of course, to the guest of honor and her proud parents. Out of the corner of his eye, as he was raising his first forkful of chocolate cake with vanilla sugar icing and strawberry filling to his mouth, Don Ulises saw a cinnamon-tea-colored girl, her dark skin visible through her transparent raincoat and clear-plastic gloves, enter the hall with the expression of a lost shepherdess on her face, dripping the acid rain of the June night at exactly the moment in which Ulises, Penny, Lucha, and everyone else bit the cake and spit it out, shouting, vomiting:

"It's made of shit! This cake is make of shit!"

And the girl with sharpened teeth and transparent clothes shouted—in English: "I'm a lollipop!" Then she fainted.

Don Ulises offered my father Angel a brandy snifter of Ixtabentún-on-the-rocks while my elegant pater, the shit having been kicked out of him by the López family thugs, was drying the blood on his forehead with pink Kleenex. López confessed that the color scheme of the salon had been chosen by his wife, Doña Lucha, to replicate certain of their common associations from the time they were courting and would go to the movies together—you know, with little sisters, popcorn, and everything.

"Ha," laughed the illustrious politician and financier, currently in the Republic's reserve forces. "She calls those chairs Blue Angel Marlene, the upholstery is Rhonda Red, and carpeting is Garbo Beige. Isn't she sweet? Isn't she incomprehensible?"

Angel accepted the drink: he needed it after the beating he took ("So you run the TUGUEDER service? you muddahfuckah! yer gonna need that shiteatin' grin!"), and when Angel touched Ulises's hand he compared it with Inclán's: What? Had everyone with power in Mexico stopped sweating? Did they ever go to the bathroom? How could they spend nine consecutive hours going from place to place, giving speeches, and constantly attending meetings of the PRI without having to pee or sweating? He looked at his host's amiably cold eyes and filtered them through the edge of the glass so Ulises's features would melt in the sickly-sweet tide of the liquor; it didn't work; Ulises emerged the winner.

"But I love her deeply, young man. Do you understand me? I'm being honest with you because even though you offended me seriously I admire your nerve and your initiative, even if it all goes into dirty tricks. But, going back to Lucha: as long as I'm with her I can be generous, even magnanimous. Want to know something? Every day, in the penthouse above my offices on River Nylon Street, there's a banquet all prepared for a hundred people, with galantines of turkey, pâté de foie gras, Gulf shrimp, carré d'agneau, cakes (real ones, ha ha ha, what a card you are!), whatever you could want, ready for a hundred people, whether anyone comes or not, and at five o'clock in the afternoon, whatever is left over is distributed to the neighborhood beggars. You see, when I'm with her I can be generous . . ." repeated Don Ulises, dreamily. "I'm afraid that without her I'll get stingy and that's why I love her, keep her, and worry about her dying."

Ulises made a peculiar face—coyness, modesty, or some combination thereof.

"For me, my wife is still the girl I tried to seduce with flowers and chocolates when I got to Chilpancingo from the coast."

He affectionately patted Angel Palomar's knee with his open hand, and said that my father in all likelihood knew lots about him; most of what he knew was true, and he would admit it proudly. What in fact did people say about him? The worst things! requested Ulises. And Angel told him: "That you are an out-and-out thief." Ulises López said with equanimity that he would prefer a great statesman who was a thief but who would make Mexico into a great nation to an honest statesman who would lead it to ruin: unfortunately, what we've gotten over the past few years have been thieves who ruin us as much or more than the honest ones, but I'm not talking about trying to balance the honest ones off against the thieves or throwing out the baby with the bathwater, Ulises went on, and that's why mediocrity, envy, and resentment had conspired to freeze him out. But he was biding his time; a great politician, he said that night to Angel, has to be an abstract, immoral con man who manipulates the passions of others while he puts his own on ice.

"I like your initiative," he repeated, concentrating his tiny, mandarin eyes on Angel. "Too bad you don't know how to focus it. Take a lesson from me tonight, kid. Listen to my rules for getting to the top in Mexico. First: remember that your ruling passion has to be money. The others are private passions and whatever you do in private is your own business. Make use of the best and the brightest. But never tell them what use you're making of them. Don't talk much. Think a great deal. Remember that he who has power is great only when he wants power. But if that interferes with the possibility of being rich, it's better to be rich than to be great. The problem is to have both dough and power, although it's always better to have money without power than power without money because money is power: you don't really need more. Understand, then, that it's not a bad thing in Mexico to be a crook: what's bad is not being a big enough crook. Always keep that in the back of your mind as you're stating for the record that immorality in the management of public funds will in no way be tolerated any longer and then toss a couple of jerks from the previous administration into jail. Remember that in this country you can make hay for half your time in office on the sins of your predecessors. During the other half, make sure you get ready to be accused, asshole. Ha, ha!"

Don Ulises guffawed over his own witticism, and once again patting Angel's knee, he concluded: "See, kid? I put all my cards on the table. Now it's your turn. I noticed you like my little Penny."

"I go where my peenie takes me," said my father cynically. "If you really want me to be frank with you . . ."

"I'll tell you again: I like the fact that you're a wise guy, but you've got to focus your energy. Just imagine if you were my son-in-law . . ."

Angel's eyes clouded over with emotion, not because of Ulises but because of Penny.

"See what I mean? I'm putting all my cards on the table."

My father understood perfectly. This was a second invitation for him to come across with something, but he refused to give in to the temptation to fall into Don Ulises's most obvious trap. The old master still had a couple of cards up his sleeve. He repeated that he was sincere but he could be cold and calculating. He had just repeated that his maxim in terms of political action was "Don't talk about anything, but think things over again and again." His conversational style was a chess game in which Ulises, in all sincerity, could always say afterwards: "I knew it all along. You can't surprise me."

Even so, Angel sighed as he looked at this Machiavellian figure. I'm me, my young friend, in Ulises López there exists a sentimental, generous man, a man in love. He pushed a button and one wall took on a glassy opacity.

"How could I not be in love with my wife?" Ulises asked uselessly. "She's much better-looking than my daughter. Just look at her."

He pushed several buttons and the lights went down in the salon, but those near the screen (or was it a whorehouse mirror so he could look in from this side without being seen from the other?) brightened. On the other side appeared Lucha Plancarte de López yawning. She was wearing a pink silk robe with white feathers fluttering at her cuffs and collar. She brushed her teeth. Then she took off her robe and stood there in a scarlet lace monokini, her big bouncy breasts decorated with enormous black nipples that looked like black plums. Doña Lucha rinsed off a tiny razor and began very carefully to shave her right armpit, which was covered by a black stubble. She did the same with her left armpit, but this time she cut herself. She winced and then used spit to close the cut. Angel was fascinated by the trickle of blood that ran out of the decidedly gray underarm. Then Lucha studied her extensive bush, which rose in baroque curls almost to her navel and spread out on both sides like a golf course, as Don Fernando Benítez would have said. Doña Lucha swiftly soaped up the perimeter of her pubic lawn: with one hand she shaved herself, while with the other she gently caressed her labia. Her husband said to my father, "She isn't alone, ha ha, look," as she stuck her finger into a jar of (wine-flavored) Celaya jelly and then spread it over her clitoris, "she isn't alone": a Siamese cat impatiently watched the lady's every movement and in a flash, as if trained to do so, jumped into its mistress's lap and began to lick her recently shaved skin, cleaning it of any traces of leftover hair.

Suddenly, Doña Lucha stopped touching herself, stood stock-still, and stared at them, stared at my father (at least that's what he thought), stared at them through the mirror with all the emotions in the world crossing her face, rage at being discovered in an intimate situation, surprise that her husband was accompanied by that young man, desire for that young man, envy for anyone in the world who was not alone, jealousy toward herself, and the solitude of her own lasciviousness, invitation (But for whom? Ulises? Angel? Was she looking at both of them? Was she looking only at Ulises because she was used to putting on this little pantomime for him and found him standing there with a strange man next to him? Was she looking at Angel, expecting to find him alone as she had promised Ulises and instead finding the two of them there united against her? Or were the two of them—she smiled for an instant—desiring her? Or were they laughing at her, and she tossed the ill-favored cat off her lap). Perhaps she wasn't looking at anything, didn't know anything, and her stares were only a solitary, ruinous deception? Every passion in the world had flitted across Doña Lucha's face except one: shame. She raised a finger dripping clit jam to her lips as she looked at them. Ulises turned off the screen. The reader is free to choose.

Someone knocked at the door of the Dietrich–Garbo–Fleming salon.

"Come in, Penny," said her father.

The girl walked in without looking at Angel.

"Show this young man to the Gloria Grahame bedroom," said Don Ulises, without giving Penny, who wanted to interrupt to say, "But Mommy sleeps next door," or Angel, who perhaps might have wanted to say, "But I have a pregnant wife at home waiting up for me," any opportunity to protest.

Ulises's eyes said: "I already knew it. I guessed it. You don't surprise me. But obey me."

4

Emotion clouded my father's eyes, his reflexes, his very equilibrium as he walked ahead of Penny López down the spiral staircase in the Guggenheimic house in Las Lomas del Sol. He never turned his back on her, turning it instead toward the steep staircase that led to the bedrooms. She never looked at him, disdainful to the end, the bitch, he walking bowlegged, backward so he wouldn't lose sight of her for an instant, so he could explain to her, tell her what he'd been thinking since New Year's Eve in Aca, now that her sweet-sixteenish presence was within range, touchable, perfumed, so near and yet so far. She stared past him, and when he stopped right in front of her to force her to see him, she said something he took, to soften the blow, to be what Penny must have said to every man in her life, to him too, *okay*, but not only to him:

"You can look, but you can't touch. You're poor, ugly, and a boor. You're not for me."

She went on ahead, but he thought that if he didn't do something right at that moment, he might never see her again, he might never be able to tell her what he was bearing inside, never mind that she wouldn't understand a word. Angeles, my mother, now she would certainly understand, and I inside her, but of course! And if I know all this, Reader, it's because the same thing my father Angel hastily told Penny López that night when the Valley (Anáhuac) Princess led him to her guest bedroom, he repeated on his knees and quite slowly to my mother some days later, when Angeles and I within her went to live in the house of Dad's grandparents Rigoberto and Susana, leaving my father to his freedom, and he didn't even have that because Uncle Homero, once again in favor with the Powers That Be (when he discovered that he'd never been hated by them and that they'd been anxiously searching for him everywhere, oh where oh where has our little Homero gone? which is what the PRI delegate asked who met him at the door of his house when the quondam candidate for Senator appeared and threw a tantrum when he realized they always waited for him there and that he'd spent all that lost time with his insane and unappreciative niece and nephew), returned with a squad of blue-uniformed thugs, agents of the district attorney's office, and a team of lawyers to sue for the return of the house of bright colors in Tlalpan. But before that there occurred the following, which I faithfully reproduce for your lordships, more precisely, look at the dangers a fetus runs when everyone forgets he exists and, if they do remember, merely add it to a list of errors. So I exist and I exist as an error! A gigantic error, gigantic luck, an ephemeral and fleeting apparition in the infinity of a bubble—I—who managed to squeeze his drop of liquid out of creation at the exact moment that it coincided with the strange, improbable temperature of some moist drops in the improbable warmth of love, and what the fuck do all these accidents matter to the great prestellar cloud that is immutable, eternal, infinite, and I tell you parents of mine and universe what I, hidden here, know all on my own:

ONLY ERRORS MAKE MIRACLES POSSIBLE

I am already another, Christopher or Christine, it doesn't matter, I am as different as if I had been created a dolphin or an armadillo, I am already different and already unique and even if I come from you I am no longer you, I am myself and I am different and I am everyone. You forgot that, right? I am another, I am everyone, my poor little life pierced with pins is the triumph of life, as triumphant in my own environment as stone mountains, obstinate cacti, or the coyotes that came down to eat gringos and literary critics. I am Myself. I rest, breathe, sigh. And you? Go right on fighting:

"Penny López," my mom repeated that night, quickly adding with anger and sadness: "Why do your eyes shine like that when I mention her name?"

"What? Oh, I thought she was dead—so did you. That's all."

"Listen to me and stop reading that newspaper."

"It's not a *newspaper*. It's *The New York Review of Books*. I get it sent by contraband from Sandy Ego. What do you think of that?"

"Cut it out. Don't change the subject on me. Remember: we went to Aca to finish off people like her."

"Her? Who do you mean?"

"Penny! People like her! Symbols, man! But what are you so interested in . . . ?"

"I'm reading an article by Philip Roth, that's all. *Writers of Newark, Unite!* You have nothing to lose but your baseball gloves . . . !"

"Bull. Listen to me now: why are you getting so nervous?"

"It's what I was saying: what women love to do is make men feel guilty. It's your mission in life."

"The mission of all women?"

"Right."

"But not of all men?"

"No. Not us. Men are loyal and sincere with each other. We never say bad things about our friends."

"Know something? I wish I had a notebook to write down all these things we say to each other, but only if it could be in ancient Chichimeca. What bull!"

"Not at all. What you want is for people to *know* what you accuse us of. Don't kid yourself."

"And what would you accuse me of?"

"Me? Nothing. I'm merely alienated by the means of reproduction."

"Is that a fact? Well, just think about this baby that seems to be weighing so heavily on your mind . . ."

"I never said anything like that!"

"You did!" she shouted, pulling out her rollers, sitting there against the headboard while Einstein sadly stared from the wall, sticking his tongue out at her.

She throws the rollers at my father, and they go crack, crack, crack against the open pages of *The New York Review of Books* and drop down onto my father's lap, piling up on the fly of his pajamas.

"Just think that I could have had this baby *by myself*, that I could have gone to a sperm bank for famous people and had my baby without your famous contest!"

"The contest!" my highly distracted father suddenly remembered. All he'd been thinking about was conquering Penny López during my mother's pregnancy.

"That's right, I could have gotten sperm from Don Ulises López, your little Penny's daddy, or Minister Robles Chacón, or Julio Iglesias, or Duran Duran, or from Pope John Paul himself, or maybe even from Einstein, sticking his tongue out at me there on the wall. He must have left a little come behind in the refrigerator! Ozom!"

"You wouldn't win the contest, big mouth, because the rules say the baby has to be the child of the *parents* that enter . . ."

"The mother always knows the child is hers, the father *never* knows: *voilà!*"

"What are you trying to say?"

"I'm not trying to say anything: I'm saying and I repeat and I reiterate and I proclaim: I had the child without you. I don't need you for anything, and besides, the child belongs only to me, no one can prove that it isn't mine, but no one can prove who the father is, and it isn't you, bastard, it isn't you," said my mother, kneeling on the bed and beginning to throw whatever came to hand at my father's bobbing head, the six volumes of *The Indians of Mexico* by Fernando Benítez, Luis Echeverría's *Charter of the Rights and Obligations of States*, a souvenir ashtray from Tlaquepaque, Fernando del Paso's *Palinurus of Mexico*, and Carlos Fuentes's *Terra Nostra*, finally revealing the color photo of Penny from *Novedades* glued to the page of the *New York Review* article by Philip Roth = jealousy finally made visible, jealousy focused on the palpable object of desire, the blind stare of hatred, all her tenderness and understanding now forgotten, the chalk scattered all over this house filled with blackboards, the photo of Albert Einstein sticking out his tongue, the chamber pot with flowers painted on it left behind by Uncle Homero, my mother shouting I could have had it alone! only the mother knows that the baby is hers! consummating the break with my father that perhaps he wants even more than she, showing to me at this early stage of life how delicate dreams are and how easily images are destroyed: leaving me unsheltered, an orphan of the storm, just when I need them most because, as I listen to them, I realize that the world is always an act with two performers, equally determined by the one who moves and speaks and the one who hears and receives: my body.

my body
is the system
with which I am going to answer
the physical world, I shall answer the world
by creating the world, I shall be the author of what precedes me,
by answering it, no matter what they do, whether they love
each other, hate each other, separate, come together,
I shall have to answer with my body and my words,
answer the world they are creating for me
creating, *careful!* as soon as I appear
I shall create their world
for them

by answering that world they have created for me. They will not escape without paying the price, they shouldn't even dream of getting away with it, their action, whether it's fighting or being happy, maybe they think that as soon as I appear I will no longer intervene with
word and flesh
to create my world beginning with them, by thus changing their world which they still don't imagine me affecting, their ridiculous squabbles, they don't have a clue, poor jerks!
Here I come!
Careful!
There will be three of us in the world and you will never again be able to act or speak exactly as you did today! just *be careful*, I'm telling you!

—. . . nothing, Penny was saying as they went down the ramp, 'cause my mom
is one tough bitch and she like says to me better learn now for when you grow up, like you give one of these parvenus an inch and he'll like give you six back, don't turn your back or your front on any of them, yesterday Mommy set fire to the shacks those squatters set up on her property and I think they all went up in smoke like a barbecue and today she like asked Daddy to have my chaperon Ms. Ponderosa shot at the garden wall because she was like the one who made the deal with your service, the gay old freak, the ya know reeall ahhshole, and had all those reeally yuucky mummies come as guests, well I mean, ya know, I mean ooooh, and then that cake made of shit, I mean that was uh like uh soooo grotty, ya know, but I like went down on my knees and begged them not to shoot her and my daddy decided it would be better just to send her back to Segovia, that's worse than death, must be like Chilpancingo, where my poor daddy came from, and like here's your bedroom, young mán, sleep tight now, and don't even think of trying anything with me, I'm out of your range, scuzzbag, buzz off.

Angel watched Penny López's bouncing little head as if in a dream, as it gradually disappeared with its shiny carrot-colored curls, her tiny painted eyebrows and her eyelids coated with gold dust, her eyes of oneiric depths and her face alive with twitches that turned out to be its saving grace: it was, en fin, an isthmus of beauty and emotion, or, as my father punned to himself: her strawberry lips, her cute little perfumed ears, pierced by orchid-shaped earrings, her pneumatic gait—Michelin legs, Pirelli thighs, Goodrich (of course?) ass, pulling out of his life: he walked into the aforementioned Gloria Grahame bedroom, named thus, said my film-loving father to himself, because it looked like a set from a fifties film noir: anemic Art Deco, devoid of personality, conceived to rebuff any ideological identification either with President Eisenhower or with Senator McCarthy: a bed with a satin spread . . .

My father, say I in imaginary complicity with him, fell into a slough of frustration, incompetence, and reduced social, moral, and sexual scale: Penny communicated all this to him, but here he was, the conservative rebel, the window washer of the filthy building that was Mexico in '92, the purifier of the once Sweet and now Debauched Fatherland, on his knees in front of this pretentious bonbon from Las Lomas del Sol, and what else: well, the old boy reacted—how could he not if he was going to supply himself with a measure of self-justification. Out loud he said:

"I am going to screw Penny! That's why I'm here!"

"But, honey, why don't you just screw me?" said a voice through the door while invisible but inflammatory fingernails scratched with a singular, invitational rhythm.

Angel put his face close to the door: he smelled a whiff of seafood mixed with Joy de Patou.

The door opened and his expected, unwelcome, but exciting neighbor appeared in all her glory, which she'd mail-ordered from Fredericks of Hollywood: a transparent black peignoir whose wide sleeves were trimmed with raven feathers, the neck idem, and underneath, a pastry-crust bra, just waiting to be ripped off, layer by layer as if it were a biscuit, and stiletto-heeled, black-velvet slippers, black stockings held up by a garter belt, beneath which the lace panties split right over the jackpot, where was embroidered:

FOND HOPES!

When my father gave the same explanation to my mother that he'd earlier given to Penny López on that corkscrew staircase, the words were the same, gentle Readers, but it all sounded different. For example, all that about leaving my mom because she was his ideal woman and he needed Penny to keep his rebelliousness alive, his hatred, seemed insanely funny to us, because where did he get off coming around telling us that he was leaving for ideological reasons when it was nothing but sex. It was like adding a tiny lie to the huge lie that he said he was struggling against. I don't know how aware my father Angel was that his rebellion was merely a romantic pose, which is what my mother thinks; but she tells him his explanation doesn't matter because for her he's always been a different sort of man and that therefore she naturally sees him that way, a different sort of man, and she doesn't have to come up with complicated explanations.

In all this, Angeles fears that Angel is using her own desires against her, without understanding that she shares them with him; this is what hurts us most in my dad's betrayal (what else should we call it?)—setting yourself up in the Gloria Grahame bedroom in the López mansion and enjoying the favors of Doña Lucha without realizing that my mother's words were not idle talk, that she was with him even in this business but that she couldn't tell him for fear of humiliating him:

"I didn't sleep all night I was so happy I met you"—hoping that he would answer her with her words, which he had picked up in order to make them belong to both of them:

"I was there too, remember?"
and culminating with something like a chorus in which, poco fa, my own little voice chimed in:

"Let's never hurt each other."
But nothing like that happened. She was left alone with a great big belly (with me inside it), while we knew nothing about Mr. Angel Palomar y Fagoaga except what he told us the afternoon in which he put on his big sincerity act and sprayed us with his absurd pretexts, without realizing (the jerk) that my mother's halo, which he said he was defending, was quite extinguished, battered, worn out. The worst thing my father said to us was that they had created me with the contest in mind but that she was certain the contest was nothing more than a fraud perpetrated by the government, and if the contest was in fact a farce, the superbastard went on, then it didn't matter that he was abandoning my mom and me. Was the reason for getting pregnant the contest? This particular insult, which to me seemed unpardonable, my mother took quite serenely, and although he never became so rude as to tell her that Penny was nothing more than a passing fancy and that she should let the sickness run its course and he would be back by August or September, in any case, before she gave birth, she actually accepted both maternity and solitude, even

though I shouted to her from the vast silent echo of my six months of conception: "When a woman's left alone, a vacuum is created, and anything can fill it!" But perhaps she didn't believe that I was filling it to the brim (I adore her!). She could understand the fear in a man who doesn't dare abandon his wife because he feels unsure about conquering (not loving, merely conquering) another woman, and she preferred that he take a chance, that he not get frustrated— taking the risk that he might not return at all. But if he came back, she would accept him again, hoping that he would realize it was she who let him go. That was her way of loving him: letting him go.

To me this seemed like the dumbest thing in the world, a hare-brained idea that was unworthy of my mother and me, so from that moment on I decided to work by means of the mysterious powers I might lose the moment I was born, so that my mother, belly and all, with me and all, would make an instant cuckold of my father Angel. Like a real Boy Scout, I started looking around, and quite soon, without my having to persuade him in any way, the correspondent turned up, although in a very peculiar way. You can't have everything.

As I was saying, she was left alone with me swelling her belly while he lived the rebellious illusion of penetrating the sanctum sanctorum of the López family. What a blast! as Doña Lucha López would say. But, by the way, how do we know now what's being said and in what way? Easy: the Lópezes sent Ms. Ponderosa off to Segovia on a fatal Iberia flight which naturally crashed when it reached Barajas Airport in Madrid: poof! and there goes the dream of a lifetime and the secret of the chaperon—to whit: to be possessed passionately by the chef de cuisine Médoc d'Aubuisson (during whose absence these tragedies took place), through force majeure that microchip-in-Ulises's-papaya business was interrupted. To sum up: when Don Ulises told Doña Lucha that the sugar they sprinkled on his papaya gave him double his normal sexual strength, the lady stole the tube of granules and served them to my dad every day at breakfast; my errant progenitor's internal information ended up in the Samurai computer of the disconcerted minister Don Federico Robles Chacón, who at first couldn't understand what the fuck was going on with the truculent Don Ulises, why the functionary and financier's mind was sending him bizarre messages such as:

• How long does passion last? How long does hatred last? I would

like to carry on my rebellion to the edge of life, not to the edge of
ideology

• I am afraid of going mad. I am afraid of going sane
• What's harder: being free or dropping dead?
• I looked for a nation made to last, like the stones of the Indians
or the Spaniards: was only Mexico's past serious?
• I am a romantic, postpunk conservative.
• Does Mexico's future have to be like its present, a vast comedy
of theft and mediocrity perpetrated in the name of progress?
• My heart is filled with an intimate reactionary joy: as intimate
as that of millions of Mexicans who want to conserve their poor
country: conservatives.
• I WANT ORDER FULLY KNOWING THAT NO ORDER WILL
EVER BE ENOUGH.
• I am going to reinvent myself romantically as a conservative rebel:
am I betraying myself by screwing Mrs. López and desiring her
daughter?

It was this last sentence that finally convinced Robles Chacón that
his Samurai was not telling him Ulises's thoughts, that he would not
be betraying himself by screwing his wife, although it might be the
case if he really desired his daughter.

INCEST IS BEST BUT ONLY AS LONG AS YOU KEEP IT IN THE
FAMILY, flashed the Samurai in immediate dialogue with Federico
Robles Chacón. He turned it off and said to himself: Who can be
eating those microchips disguised as sugar which I had intended for
my rival Ulises López?

5

 Reader: Think about us. Don't abandon us like that, just
because your prurience has been tickled by my father's adventures in the López household. Stop. Think. Remember
that she and I are left here alone. She with her abdomen
weighed down by an intense increase in blood circulation, in pain
because of the expansion of her uterus, as heavy-breasted as a cow:
look on her and sympathize with her irritated nipples and her colossal
appetite, her weight increasing, hormone production in her placenta

increasing, all her glands stimulated, tired, sleepy, ferociously nauseous, imagining banquets of foie gras and couscous, goulash and
Aztec ants, and no one there to go out and get them for her, with
this absence without leave of that bastard, pater meus, who has
decided to drain his life to the bottom (the ass!) before becoming a
pure and idealistic man. When? On October 12 next? And as if that
weren't enough, I'm here robbing the poor thing's calcium, milk,
almost half her iron (I want ostrich eggs with truffles!), and she
threatened by the loss of all her teeth! Shit, gentle Readers, just think:
why in the world did my mother have me? Why did hundreds of
thousands of millions of mothers have all the sons of bitches born
after Citizens Kane and Able? That's the way it goes: no going backward: I'm in my fifth month since conception, and I can use my
little feet to swim, tap out secret messages, dance in the water, and
kick: until this month I paddled in the water without touching her;
from now on, on top of Angel's infidelity, the poor lady has to put
up with kick after kick on the walls of this homeland of mine: my
mother thinks she's got Moby Dick in person inside her, the poor
dear lives in the bathroom, tenser and tenser, with vaginal secretions,
hemorrhoids, cramps, upset stomach (my father doesn't give her love,
so she uses Maalox instead), her hands, feet, and face all swell up,
she gets hypertension, she has difficulty breathing, she's bloated,
thankful she has no wedding ring because she could never get it off,
she feels hot at the oddest times, sweats, would like to eat but also
to put on talcum powder, toilet water, smell fresh, she is constantly
afraid she smells and doesn't realize it, a secretion dries on her nipples,
she'd would like to squeeze a tub of Suzy Chapultepecstick onto each
of them, God help me! and there I sit or stand or float uselessly inside
her, goddamn Olympic swimming champion, the poor man's Mark
Spitz, yippie, and tell me, your mercies benz, if all that wouldn't
make you think twice before trying it!

Which is why I ask you, Reader: now more than ever, don't abandon us! Understand that your reading is our company, our only
consolation! We can put up with everything so long as you hold our
hand! Don't be cruel! Go on reading!

6

What would my father remember, ultimately, of his stormy but forgettable affair with Mrs. Lucha Plancarte de López?

Just this: how on the first night she told him it didn't matter what her husband Ulises had said: take a good look at her now while she's naked. She didn't know if Ulises had actually said that, and she would never tell Angel if she'd seen them spying on her from the star's water hole. She asked him to believe that she had surprised him ogling her, she made him her lover, but she didn't demand that he kill her husband in exchange for her favors. The idea would never have occurred to Angel if she hadn't repeated it a hundred times: I would never demand you kill my husband for having incited you to look at me while I was naked. But the truth is that at least half the ideas that feed a love affair belong to neither partner and come instead from the couple; the bad thing is that the same is true for destructive ideas. What was great about Doña Lucha was that her vagina had a life of its own, it was more self-propulsive than, say, a dog, its movements were like those of an open mouth (a banal comparison, I know), but also like a gloved hand, an undulating, down-filled duvet, a bowl of boiling hot fudge, a swirling Jacuzzi, Seabiscuit winning the Kentucky Derby, the emotion of the Quartetto Italiano playing Haydn's *Emperor*, to say nothing of the peregrinations of the wind god Ehécatl when he met the sea goddess Amphitrite right in the middle of the Sargasso Sea and above sunken Atlantis: wow!

And the way they sat down, night after night, the Scheherazade of Las Lomas and her innocent Sultan, to tell each other stories about street violence, encounters with the police, armed robberies, ecocidal horror stories, the criminal drip-drip-drip of toxic waste, truck exhausts, water and air contamination: and how hot that made them, she hotter than he, but even he got really hot (Doña Lucha knew it perfectly well) when she brought out a blue-velvet album and showed him the outline of Penny's foot when she was a baby, the list of the presents she got when she was baptized, who came to the baptism, and especially the lock of the little girl's hair, pasted onto the blue page and decorated with a blue ribbon. Doña Lucha's excitement grew:

"Look, Angel, here's the proof that she had light hair when she was a little girl, look, it just isn't true what those gossipy bitches say, I never bleached her little twat, I never straightened her hair down there, which is what my enemies say. Penny's light, she doesn't have kinky hair, she doesn't have any of that half-breed blood from the Guerrero coast like her daddy, she took after me, and my pa was an honest businessman who emigrated from Zapotlán in Jalisco, where the French left behind a ton of kids during the Empire, and they're all fair-haired, don't you believe me, Angel honey? And then she asked him to look at her mons veneris, with its thick bush, almost wavy it was, but he should screw her as if she were a black rumba dancer, what the hell, she knew how to move her hips like the best Afro dancer. Alas, but my father, no matter how much he tried, he could not ascend with her to the febrile climax that marked my conception nor attain the anticipated glory he would have with Penny. Finally he reached the point when, with Doña Lucha, it just wouldn't get hard unless he had Penny's childhood curl right before his eyes.

One night, when she received him sobbing and he didn't even bother to ask why, she blurted out:

"Are you married?"

"No."

"Your wife'll like that news."

That night, after Doña Lucha sucked him dry, wore him out, left him mere skin and bones, Angel became desperate because he realized his sacrifices were not bringing him any nearer to that eagerly desired night with Penny. So, toward the end of June, he set about making the lady feel old and decrepit, by reminding her every once in a while about how old she was (forty-eight, fifty?), by tricking her into betraying herself by recalling the remote past, setting traps for her so she'd admit having learned how to roll her hips studying the belly dancers at the Tivoli during the fifties, that she'd learned to sing boleros listening to Agustín Lara in the wee hours of the morning in the old Capri cabaret in the Regis Hotel. He tried to get Doña Lucha to hate him by forcing her to do hideous things like sitting her in front of a mirror and having her make faces, or no dickie ce soir, or making her take out her false teeth in front of him, or having her make herself up as a gargoyle by painting on thick, pointed eyebrows, emaciated lips, creases in her forehead, and hollows in her cheeks, forcing her to pull out chunks of hair so he could have it as a souvenir, to limp around the room and give herself diarrhea by forcing her to share huge amounts of papaya and granulated sugar, which she secretly served him, hoping that the aphrodisiac would bring about certain effects and unintentionally sending multiple incomprehensible and garbled messages to Robles Chacón's computer, overloaded to the point of saturation because when Chef Médoc returned from his vacation, confirmed with a sardonic smile that the Sweet-Sixteen Party was a failure, did not weep over the premature disappearance of Ms. Ponderosa, but did anxiously hunt for the minicomputers in the shape of granulated sugar to start serving them again to Don Ulises, he had to ask for a new supply from his secret Maecenas, Robles Chacón, who in this way learned that Ulises was no longer using sugar on his papaya and that instead the not very secret lover of Mrs. López did and that he was a certain Angel Palomar y Fagoaga, the nephew of the newly resurrected senatorial candidate for Guerrero, Don Homero Fagoaga, and that there was something fishy about this whole deal, or as Don Bernardino Gutiérrez, first supporter of President Calles in the state of Guerrero would say, even the lame are high-wire walkers in this country.

"Come on now, ma'am, hate me a little!"

"The worse you treat me, the more I love you. And if you were to treat me nicely I would love you even more. There's no escape for you, Angel, my cherub!"

"All right, all right. I think about your daughter when I'm inside you, like that idea?"

"I just love the thought of it, my little cherub! The mere idea gets me hot! Come over here!"

"Your husband let me look at you naked, ma'am, should I remind him of the fact? Don't you hate him?"

"I love him more than ever. I owe having you to him!"

"I hate you, ma'am, you disgust me, you're like Miss Piggy with all that cellulite, terminal halitosis, your ass looks like a dish of cottage cheese, you've got dandruff, and you've always got little pieces of tortilla stuck in your teeth!"

"And, despite all that, you still get hard! You love me, you love me, don't deny it!"

In effect, that was my priapic father's problem: his masculine vanity was stronger than his disgust in potentia, and even if he didn't want to, precisely because he didn't like Mrs. López, he would think about other things, about the unreachable Penny, about my mother when she excited him, and all that got him ready for Doña Lucha, who, as she said, didn't give a damn about what made it hard just as long as it stayed hard.

"Look! It's hard as a rock! Again! Don't you ever get tired?"

"It's not hard because of you, I swear."

"Well, I don't see anyone else in this bedroom, do you? There's only me, your worn-out but loving old pelican!"

"I think about other women."

"Let 'em eat cake! You're locked in with me."

"I am not. I can leave whenever I please."

"There's the door, cherub!"

"You know very well that my passion for your daughter won't let me leave."

"Well then, why don't you go conquer her?"

"You know very well she won't give me the time of day."

"She doesn't give anybody the time of day."

"I know it, and that's why I'm going to keep on screwing her through you."

"Well, charity begins at home, lover boy!"

"Mein Kampf!"

"I do as I please!"

7

 The current Servilia served tea (was it a Lapsang Suchong smuggled in by their little brother Homero from Mexamerica and/or

Pacífica?)

to Capitolina and Farnesia, who were dressed in robes that made them look like cocottes in a Feydeau farce: all silk, wide sleeves, feather boas at neck and cuffs, velvet slippers. Both said that at least during breakfast in their shared boudoir they could dress with a certain frivolity (man does not live by religion alone; nor do women). Their multiple social obligations forced them to be ready for last rites, wakes, and funerals, so they wore black almost all the time, because, as Capitolina was in the habit of declaring:

"Mourning is what you wear on the outside."

Morning was also the time in which they exchanged their most intimate confidences, but this particular morning in July of 1992, ten years after the catastrophes of the López Portillo era (the greatest of which, for the two sisters, had been the flight of their nephew Angel Palomar y Fagoaga, on whom they'd set their fondest hopes), there was malice in the eyes of the decisive Capitolina, which, if not unusual, was more energetic and, at the same time, more restrained, hungrier to show itself and implacably astonish the younger sister, who was usually plagued by vagueness:

"Besides . . ." was the first word either uttered that morning, and naturally it was Farnesia who said it, but Capitolina simply cast that penetrating and intelligent look on her that seriously upset the younger sibling.

"How silly, I'm falling asleep," Farnesia suddenly said in order to cover up her lapse as she sat in her favorite love seat and covered her eyes with a dark hand, which resembled nothing so much as a dark swan. Capitolina slowly sipped her tea (reclining in very very Madame Récamier style in her favorite chaise longue, her chubby little feet crossed) and stared with indecipherable intentions at Farnesia.

"You seem upset this morning," said Capitolina inquisitorially. "What's wrong? Tell me!"

"Oh dear!" Farnesia sighed. "It's something you already know about."

She swiftly got up out of the love seat, threw herself at the feet of her sister, and rested her head on those knees Julien Sorel might have envied.

"Swear," said Farnesia, forgetting for once her habitual use of the first-person plural, "swear, Capitita, that when I'm dying you won't let the old ladies into the house to go through all my boxes and chests."

"Is that what's bothering you today?"

"Yes." Farnesia sobbed, with her head nestled in Capitolina's lap. "Today and always."

"Are you still afraid that someone will discover your secret?"

"Yes, yes, that's what we're afraid of!" Lapsing into her usual form of address, Farnesia wept.

"Aren't you even more afraid of dying without sharing it?"

"Oh dear, wouldn't that be a gift! We don't have any right to hope for so much: to have a secret and nevertheless be able to find someone worthy of sharing it with!"

"We almost had it with little Angel when he was a boy."

"Almost, little sister, almost. But there you have it . . . In the first place . . ."

"Of course, of course," interrupted Capitolina, taking her sister's head in her hands and forcing her to raise her face. "And what if I were to tell you that we can achieve that desire?"

Farnesia's huge, round, dark Kewpie-doll eyes opened questioningly.

"Now I'm going to tell you what should be upsetting you most this morning, little sister. Our nephew Angel is going to have a child."

"With whom, with whom? Do we know her? Are they married? Tell me, tell me . . . I'm fainting from curiosity, in the second place and finally, I'm fainting!"

"Don't faint, Farnecita. Her name is Angeles. We don't know her. They aren't married. Now get a hold of yourself: he's abandoned her to chase after that nouveau-riche Penelope López who lives in one of those brand-new developments where they just put in the septic tank yesterday."

"But tell us more!" said Farnesia breathlessly.

Miss Capitolina Fagoaga had never had such an opportunity for drama before, so she played it for all it was worth, standing up (so suddenly that Farnesia's head bounced off the Récamier armrest), walking toward the high French window in the house on Durango Street, and playing with the curtain strings, closing the curtains bit by bit until the boudoir lay in darkness.

"More, more . . ." (The shadows were swallowing Farnesia's voice.)

Capitolina paused majestically, her silhouette barely visible in a thin line of light.

"Sister: we have managed to defend this home against all the horrors of the past fifty years."

"And we're still young and vigorous, we can . . ." said Farnesia without finishing, jumping back into her love seat.

"That's not the problem. We have to ask ourselves who is going to get custody of the child when he's born."

"Well, of course it would be his mother . . ."

"And did you bring up your baby when it was born?" said Capitolina ferociously, snapping open the curtains so that the light would blind Farnesia, who covered her eyes, burst into tears, and said, "Things were different in those days, I was a Fagoaga Labastida Pacheco y Montes de Oca, with a name, a position, a family. How was I going to raise an illegitimate child, how . . . ?"

"But our nephew's trollop can?"

"We're living in different times, with different people," whimpered the younger sister, her face entirely covered by an organdy handkerchief with raised embroidery pierced by an arrow and with the initials FB.

"You are an incorrigible romantic," Capitolina said, dropping the curtains and walking toward Farnesia. "You still have that ridiculous handkerchief with your lover's initials on it."

"That's why I don't want anyone poking around in our drawers when we die," she said in her highest voice.

"That's not what I'm talking about!" Capitolina shouted this time. "That's all over and done! He never renounced the child, he begged you that if you didn't want it, to give it to him, it was you who made it disappear, don't you remember? What did you do with your son, blockhead?"

"Don't scream at me, Capitita. I forgot! I swear that I forgot . . . I mean, we forgot, no, no . . . I mean that you must have known . . . it's my way of speaking . . . no, I didn't kill him, I swear, I gave him to, I don't know who it was, I don't remember, all I remember is that I put a silver chain around his ankle, one that could expand and grow with him, and our names, Farnesia and Fernando, there's the key in a jewel box over there, that's why I don't want . . . we don't want, isn't that so? . . . anyone poking around in our . . ."

"Don't be a fool and don't take me for one. You must have given the child to Servilia."

"To whom?"

"To whoever was the maid then. Don't you remember?"

"How can I when they all have the same name? Who was Servilia in 1964? In any case, it's our secret . . ."

"You wanted to share it with Angel."

"Yes. You know why." Now it was Farnesia's turn to stare directly and maliciously at her sister. "You know what we were going to ask him for in exchange for our secret. You know very well."

"That's not what matters here. What matters is something infinitely more important." Capitolina rose majestically. "What matters is that we get all we ever wanted—in one fell swoop."

"A child to share our secrets," said Farnesia, stretching out her hand to touch her sister's. "A child to replace my own, sister, and to replace Angelito, who abandoned us . . ."

"Especially a child of our own blood, who should not grow up on the street, whose mother is unmarried and whose father abandoned him. In a word, a Fagoaga!"

"Yes, yes, we should educate him ourselves," exclaimed Farnesia.

"Don't give me any of that Commie propaganda," her sister answered her haughtily. "You don't give education. Education's something you drink in your mother's milk. Our religion is all we need!"

"Excuse my lack of ignorance," said Farnesia humbly. "How silly, I must be falling asleep . . . you know."

"All right now. Try to understand our plan: we are going to get custody of that child. I've found out he'll be born in October. We're three months away from the delivery date. We have time."

8

The reader ought to know that in point of fact my father did attempt to escape the vicious circle of love that locked him in Lady Lucha's arms, promising that one day he would obtain Penny's favors. He accosted her at various times throughout the day—while she was playing roulette in her private casino, or sitting in her red velvet movie theater watching the complete films of Shirley Temple, or swimming in the heated pool in the shape of the United States. But the girl had a gift for never looking at him and thus fanned the flames of his almost medieval desire, as if he were a knight frustrated by the inviolable distance between himself and this maiden imprisoned behind drawbridges, chastity belts, and within the improbable purity she had constructed around herself.

One desperate day, he entered her room only to find she was not there (she always seemed to be *elsewhere*). He rubbed his cheek with a towel she had tossed aside, smelled her hairbrush; his unsatisfied passion was so strong he even wished to find one of Penny's used tampons so he could put it under his pillow, just as he'd once left a condom filled with his semen under Penny's pillow only to see it later floating in the garden pool, blown up and with Superman painted on it.

One night when he hid behind the curtains in Penny's bedroom to watch her sleep, he discovered some of the small secrets of this princess who would not allow herself to be touched by princes, plebes, or anyone else: Penny smelled herself! He saw her in bed amorously, slowly smelling first her armpits, then the hand which she'd held between her legs for such a long time, then her pinkie, which she'd hidden in her anus, and then came her farts. These tiny peals of thunder, fully audible, were jealously swept up in her little fist and instantly brought to her nostrils and absorbed there in a spasm, her eyes closing delightedly, her mouth agonizing in ecstasy; she gave her farts more than she gave him, her unknown lover! A gas got more affection than he did!

This discovery drove my father Angel right out of his foreseeable—monotonous but promising—game plan. And so he arrived, not in a bad mood, but distracted and ill-humored at the dinner table around which, perversely, the three members of the López family and my father gathered to enjoy Médoc d'Aubuisson's opulent cuisine.

"Perhaps at the end of summer we'll go someplace nice for a vacation," said Don Ulises without conviction, trying to initiate a trivial conversation.

"Where?" His wife arched her plucked and painted eyebrow. "To your native Chilpancingo? to the floating gardens of Xochimilco? Or might we venture to the far reaches of Pachuca, Hidalgo?"

"Patience, sweetheart," said Ulises to Lucha, patting her hand. "Things will straighten themselves out, I promise."

"Bah," grunted the lady. "Things will only straighten themselves out if Mexico is annexed by the United States. How I wish it would happen! Then I wouldn't have to go abroad just to go shopping."

"Don't be frivolous," Ulises sweetly chided her. "The reason you say that is because they are organized and we are disorganized. In the long run, we'll only be saved if we're governed from Washington. All the rest is nothing but outmoded patriotism."

"Well, I'd be happy with being Puerto Rico," said the lady. "It's better than nothing."

"Oooooh, I get so mixed up," said Penny. "I don't, ya know, like to traaavel, no way, because I never know where I aaam, or, like, what the name of the place is. I'm reeelly dumb in, like, geography, even though I went to the Ibero-American School."

"Well, where *haven't* you been, Penny?" asked my poor father, as innocent as a lamb.

"Oooooh, even I can answer that one. Almost nobody's been there, like, what's that place with the reeely funny name,

Pacífica,

is that, like, what they call it? How come we never go there, huh?"

A frozen silence from Doña Lucha, a kick under the table from her father's short leg, a sudden curiosity in my father, who, in that instant, felt tired of this passion, this comedy . . .

"Have you ever been in

Pacífica?"

he asked with the same innocent expression on his face, repeating the question put to him by Deng Chopin in the defunct Acapulco boîte, Divan the Terrible.

No one answered, and my father will swear that something happened there that he could not explain but which did explain Don Ulises's invitation to visit him in the Salon of the Stars (Marlene! Rhonda! Greta!), where, with no preambles, forgoing all etiquette, not even asking him to sit down, with not a hint of political caviling or philosophic evocation, the millionaire said to my father:

"Let's see now, Palomar. You've been here over a month now. You must be wondering why I brought you here and why I've kept you on."

"Don Ulises: I came here to get your daughter, not your wife."

"Yeah, yeah," said López impatiently, "I confess I need sexual collaborators for my wife. Her nymphomania wears me out and you're certainly not the first stud to dirty her sheets. But let's get to the point: you haven't been able to seduce my daughter. Want me to hand her to you?"

My father didn't know if the polite thing was to say yes or no. In the confusion that overpowered him, he could only say emphatically: "A pleasure."

This non sequitur, like a lapse in synchronization between the actor's lips and the sound of the words, did not correct itself over the course of the dialogue between my father and Ulises:

"You'll be able to take a break from my wife and all her demands."

"An honor to meet you."

"But you will not even be able to touch Penny with a rose petal."

"My name is Angel Palomar y Fagoaga."

"Unless you do for me exactly what I'm going to tell you to do."

"After you."

"I need a seraph to do my dirty work for me."

"Hello."

"What you did so well with my wife, I want you to do with my rivals."

"Happy to meet you."

"My business rivals. My rivals in the government. I want you to take advantage of your good looks, your social connections, your aristocratic pedigree, all of that, to open doors that will not open for me or my family, I want you to seduce wives and daughters, discover secrets, communicate them to me, and when necessary, to humiliate all these people and lead them to bankruptcy, and—why not?—get rid of them if necessary."

Don Ulises jumped up, almost did a flip, clicked his heels noisily in the air, and landed on his feet, while Angel said, as if talking in his sleep:

"No, I don't believe I've had the pleasure."

"See, Angelito, I've always had something that someone else has needed, and today that someone is you."

"Would you mind passing the salt?"

"Depending on how well you perform for me, little by little I'll get you into my saintly daughter's good graces. What do you say?"

"How nice! It's been such a long time. Really, it's been ages!" exclaimed my stunned father as he withdrew from the presence of Don Ulises and instinctively stepped into the garden for a breath of air. In the distance he spied something shining in the darkness. He allowed himself to be led to that light. It emanated from the Bloomingdale's replica. He approached the revolving doors, pushed them, then mounted the half-flight escalator. As he regained his composure, he thought nostalgically about the days when he felt free to intertwine his fingers with a woman's forbidden hand going up or down an escalator. He loved women he didn't know, longed for those he hadn't yet discovered, wondered if he'd used up my mother, if he knew her completely by now, if she thought he was an imbecile, wondered if he'd perhaps worn out Doña Lucha as well, although he was sure she'd worn him out, but that he still had to know if Penny could be worn out or could wear him out and why not ask her directly since there she was, in the facsimile of this Cathedral of López Delights, the first floor of Bloomingdale's. Penny was seated at Bloomie's perfume-and-makeup counter, her back to him, hiding that brilliant face illuminated by two butterflies on her eyes, gold dust on her eyelids, strawberry hearts on her lips, her nostrils fluttering, her little ears perfumed by Miss Dior, her insinuatingly cleft chin, that slightly sluttish beauty he had admired, desired, been obsessed by ever since New Year's at the Aca disco. Now she was sitting there, presenting him with her bare shoulders, wearing a striped T-shirt, her waist and ass covered by a tweed miniskirt, a whore, yes indeed, that's how he wanted her, a little half-breed from the Guerrero coast, fed for generations on rice and beans and fried plantains, squid in its ink, and Larín chocolates. Everything her mother had revealed, the farthest thing from Palomar y Fagoaga Labastida Pacheco y Montes de Oca and the best Mexico City, Guadalajara, and Puebla families: Penny López with her back to him, a pencil in one hand and a tissue in the other, and he, gawking at her, awkwardly crashes into the Estée Lauder counter, knocking down a row of bottles, and she, surprised, drops the pencil and raises the tissue to her mouth as she spins on her seat and allows herself to be seen without makeup, clean-faced, devoid of her tropical bordello glitter: Penelope López Plancarte without makeup, her face washed clean, was (my father almost fainted) the very image of a nice little prim-and-proper Mexican girl, with centuries of creoles behind her, early Masses, and lonely nights, late suppers of eggs and beans and vermicelli soup, corn-flour porridge for breakfast, centuries of church candles strained through her blood, and he knew how to tell all of them apart genetically: Penny López without gold dust and butterflies on her eyes was a pale, clean-faced nun, barely distinguishable from the nuns that the high-bourgeois girls of Mexico imitate so they won't look like the whores who are the other alternative in their reality: Penny López was one of them, like them, barely inclined to erase her resemblance to them. She, too, derives from the legion of ghosts with bloodless lips and suspicious eyes, rice-powder skin, holy-water-rinsed hands, rosaried fingers, scapulary breasts: devout bourgeois flesh hidden for five centuries of colonialism in convents, far from the sun, in somber houses with humid patios and masturbatory bedrooms: women with dead cells and the scar of a hair shirt on every freckle: he saw her like that, bloodless, pale, traditional, and in a dark flash he saw Agueda in the Oaxaca church, the mad Agueda's dried-up or dead friends in the Oaxaca plaza, saw my mother Angeles materialized among the balloons and trees in the Alameda, the woman he desired or deserved or fatally loved in a kind of desperate lottery in which his real wife, the one he should have loved madly, had still not been born or had died four centuries earlier, in a bordello in Seville or a convent in Quito: what would he say to an ideal woman that wouldn't be this absurd phrase that he repeated to the terrified Penny, poor little Penny surprised in flagrante in her monastic, colonial, genetic nakedness:

"I dreamed about words," my father said to her.

She covered her face with the tissue, like a Veronica, and told him through the paper: "My daddy gave me uh like permission for you to uh kiss my ass. But nothing else, right? Careful, prole, just the cheeks, okay?"

She stood there saying over and over "Just the cheeks, okay?" while my father slowly exited the brilliant sphere of Bloomingdale's and walked into the cold night of the high-altitude tropics, toward the gate to Don Ulises López's mansion, toward the chilled and hunched-over figure waiting for him there, on the other side, always in the street, always patient, protecting herself from the acid drizzle with her tiny clear-plastic parasol, her boots, her gloves, her see-through raincoat. Colasa Sánchez shook hands with my father through the gargoyled gate, and she told him I've been waiting for you, I knew that someday you'd come out, I waited and I'll do whatever you tell me to do.

Ulises and Lucha felt something the night Angel my father abandoned the house in Las Lomas del Sol in the company of Colasa Sánchez; they felt something when they heard Penny sobbing in her bedroom, something they hadn't felt, neither together nor separately, for a long time, something that led them like sleepwalkers out of their respective rooms and up the serpentine staircase into each other's arms, to an embrace they hadn't shared in years, since . . .

"Chilpancingo," said Don Ulises with his Lucha in his arms.

"What are you thinking about?" she whispered, trembling, in his ear.

"I don't know. Unimportant things. It wasn't an ugly town. On the contrary. It was a pretty town, with pine trees along the streets and pure mountain air."

"Are you thinking that we could have been happy if we had stayed there?"

Ulises nodded his shiny head. "I always liked picking you up at your house. You lived, let's see now, on . . . ?"

"The street was called Heroínas del Sur. That's what put the idea in your head to start producing drugs in Chilpancingo . . . The name of my street! The street your pure little girlfriend lived on, Ulises!"

"We'd walk along Avenida Juan Alvàrez, under the pines, to the movie, holding hands. I'd bring you flowers."

"It was in the national parks that you began to plant poppies, Ulises, remember?"

"You were so pretty, Lucha. All the boys were after you."

"And now they all get me."

"I took you out of Chilpancingo, I made you into a queen, I gave you a castle, all so no one would take you away from me. Just look. All the money in the world hasn't kept me from having to share you with other men."

"And I thank you for the favor, shorty. I really mean it. You don't hear me complaining."

"Lucha, wouldn't we have been happier if we'd stayed in Chilpancingo all our lives?"

"You've wondered about that too, Uli?"

"Yes."

"Well, keep thinking about it: your whole life in one of those flea-bitten towns. Your whole life. All of it. No change. Always the same, always the same. Always the same thing, what you call monotony, Ulises! I just don't see you there. Can you see me there?"

"Yes."

"I'm not the girl I used to be. And you're not the same either."

"Let me love you tonight."

"Thanks, shorty. I feel real lonely tonight, I really mean it."

Penny listened to them, poking her head through the half-open door of her bedroom, upset, doubtful, just as she was when they traveled and she never knew where they were, if it's Monday it must be Andorra and if it's Tuesday it must be Orchids, listening to them talk in voices that were not those she knew; now they were strange, melancholy voices, or could that be tenderness, or whatever you call it? Talking about pine trees and parks and secluded plazas and a church that was so white it blinded you just to look at it, that invited you in to relax in its shade: Mom and Dad holding hands. Penny almost began to cry, and wondered if a little white house surrounded by pines on Heroínas del Sur Street in Chilpancingo was worth more than this monstrosity, with its replica of Bloomingdale's, its dog-racing track, and its pool in the shape of the U.S.A. Poor Penny; she let her head fall and felt affronted by something that had nothing to do with these places or with her. The way in which that boy saw her when he finally saw her as she was. No one had ever looked at her like that—not with desire, but with shock and disgust, with revulsion. She could really go for a boy like that. She could not say to him, "I'm not for you." She heard her parents making love and realized that the boy was no longer there and that she could not imitate Lucha and Ulises.

9

As soon as they found out that Angel had abandoned Angeles, the Four Fuckups returned, one by one, like birds to the nest to be near her in the Tlalpan house: when the Orphan Huerta and Hipi Toltec, Egg, and the invisible Baby Ba got there, they found the door sealed by the district attorney's office; there were no windows, but through the wrought-iron grating the friends could clearly see that no one was there.

Feeling abandoned themselves, they stood there in the middle of the street, the very image of bewilderment. Then Egg, who was a man (to his misfortune, he would say to himself) with a memory, put two and two together and told the others that when Angel had run away from the Fagoagas he had found sanctuary with his grandparents, Rigo and Susy. Angeles had no doubt done the same thing.

"Come along now, girl, don't lag behind, honey, we're going to look for our pal Angeles," said our buddy Egg, and perhaps it's time that I reappear after such a prolonged absence and take this opportunity to tell your lardships that in this my sixth month of gestation there begin to mount up pros and contras with regard to my making my sudden but expected appearance next October, adding my existence to the thirty million citizens (or the dirty million prolecats in the powwow, as the Orphan would say in his slang), and from now on I shall try to note down in two columns, like a bookkeeper—*Debit* and *Credit*—the reasons why I should be born and the reasons that discourage me right off the bat from doing so. Okay, Egg's reference to Baby Ba is perhaps, I will admit this, the most powerful reason I've come across yet for someday appearing.

I have the feeling that she's waiting for me, that she'll look at me when I'm born and fall in love with me, and that I will be the only person able to see her, even if I can't talk to her, not in the way the aforementioned Egg now feels able to declare to my mother: "At last I can say it, Angeles. I love you very much. Before I couldn't, as you know, because Angel was my best friend. But I've loved you ever since I met you. I looked at you while I played the piano in the boîte in Acapulco, and you looked at your husband, and your husband looked at Penny López: I, your friend Egg, have loved you from that moment!"

Our buddy Egg's soul is tormented (mildly) by love and by the fact that he doesn't want to create any class differences between himself and the Orphan and Hipi, who have never been in the house of the Palomar grandparents and who don't have the same sort of background as my father and his friend.

But when they finally reach the house on Calle Génova and are let in, they find Angeles and your Humble Cervix (invisible still) in the coach house, where my father grew up surrounded by useless mementos. What joy, what a quantity of hugs, how many tears, unusual in my mom, how many hand squeezes and kisses on the cheeks, what a lot of running around by Grandfather Rigoberto greeting everyone and what a lot of bustling around in the kitchen by Grandmother Susy, who promises to bring glasses of eggnog and quesadillas with sauce, and sopes in green sauce, and salted guazontles, Aztec ants dipped in egg like freshwater pearls, and maguey worms fried and crunchy wrapped in warm tortillas with guacamole, what a party, how happy everyone is, the best I've ever had, the hottest, the most loving, the most fraternal, after all that horrifying "fun" in Aca and Igualistlahuaca, and the streets of Mexico Shitty: Grandfather and Grandmother sing a few corridos, Hipi dances a dance dredged up from the beginning of time, as monotonous as the night or the rain, and the Orphan, forgetful as usual, has to invent

a tune and hope the others join in, as in fact they do, Hipi and Egg
(and Ba, invited by Egg to take part while I dream about her) make
up lyrics for the Orphan Huerta's song:

> *Old at twenty, no good, no plenty*
> *Half are under ten*
> *At thirty, one foot in the grave*
> *Twenty years of age!*

"Búfala!" says Hipi Toltec.
"What a fresh set!" comments Egg, worn out.
"Cool, coolísimo," exults the Orphan Huerta.
"Animus!" says Angeles.
Then they all tell my mother she can count on them, that they
are her buddies; no one mentions Angel or reproaches him for any-
thing, what the hell, you know how complicated life is, man, and
nobody's going to cast the first adlaistevenstone; they kiss her, begin
to leave, don't want to, but
"What are you going to do now?"
"I'll go in a while to the River Nile . . ."
"Have some fun . . ."
"Where's fun in Mexicalpán, man?"
"Guwhere whasi' B-4?"
"Don' le' yur filins chouenlai!"
"Abyssinia."
"Humongous . . ."
"Awzom!"
"Serbus!"
"In ixtli!"
"In yóllotl!"
A gigantic error, gigantic luck, a fleeting apparition: I rest, I
breathe, I sigh.

10

Only Egg stayed behind with my mother that night of our happy reunion in the grandparents' house, and he smilingly told her that his usual verbal come-on with women was to talk to them about ecology or about the effects of television on children, but that he suspected that this time it wouldn't work.

My mother only smiled at him as she had so many times over the course of their relationship: Egg, my father Angel's best friend. That's what I am, he said, reading the situation, or whatever I take it upon myself to be tonight now that we're all alone, right? (And me, bastard, what am I? air? a streamer?) It's that friendship is perhaps the first true form of eroticism, I mean that you see a friend's body and you love it because you love your friend even though it would never occur to you to go to bed with him, his body becomes erotic for you because not only does it not occur to you to have sex with him, but above all it would *never* occur to you to have a child with him, and you see a body that is useful for something more than reproduction and that's the most erotic thing in the world: imagining a body, desiring a body, without its being useful for reproduction. Egg said that was how he loved my father Angel—well, he'd let the cat out of the bag, the name, to see what might happen—and now suddenly he wasn't there and it was as if a wall or a screen had disappeared and now he could see Angeles for the first time, without the separation that had always stood between them.

She was in the process of reproducing, my mother said silently. (Thanks, oh protectress; hip, hip, hurray!)

But he desired her for something other than reproduction, he told her. And he insisted: "Angel is my friend and will always be my friend. I want you to understand that."

"You mean you love me now for what he did?" asked my mom; note by the way that she didn't say "what he did to me" or (even better) "did to us."

"No," answered Egg, "I love you so that I can be with you. Not because I'm sorry for you. Not at all. But I don't want you to be alone. I don't want you to have to give birth alone. I want to guarantee that the child wins the contest. And that no one takes it away from you." This last he added out of pure intuition, irrationally.

She simply looked at him, caressed her belly, and said: "There's going to be an earthquake tonight. I know it for a fact. The Angel on the Independence monument is going to fall off its column. I don't know what kind of premonition this is, Egg, or if we should wait. Last night I dreamed about bats, lots of bats filling the sky, and that I did understand. I said it was a premonition about the world to come. In my dream I followed the bats—they were squeaking, blind, with big ears, and only they knew where to find food. Only they knew."

I give an intrauterine jump out of pure shock. Surprised in flagrante labore! My job is to send nightmares to people! I confess that ever since I began this sixth month I've been doggedly sticking people with nightmares! I had to start at the beginning, so I hit Mom first. A direct hit! I just found out now! How should I react? Should I be happy? sorry? Must I test my power by turning these words into realities? I'm getting French waves: cauchemar! I hear the clattering hooves of that old English night-mare! And the Spanish word for it hits me like a plumbeous plumb, its brows knitted, its jaw fixed, muttering Castilian obscenities, and in a perennial fit of pique: pesadilla! What shall I do with this language of mine but bring it up-to-date, as I just did; Mom: dream about bats—they'll come squeaking back to you; Mom: dream about an earthquake and a fallen Angel: it'll all happen, I swear to you.

But she is already saying, not caring that I have just acquired this power by realizing that I have it: "I feel surrounded by all the things not used up by haste, poverty, or indifference."

"All the things Angel left here?"

"No, no, only that. The parks. The past. The ugliness of the city, it doesn't matter. The real ugliness is oblivion."

"You may be right."

"I'm sorry, Egg. Thanks, but I just can't."

"Friends?"

"Forever."

"Nothing more?"

Yes, WORDS, she said, she who believed in words and didn't waste them, who had a terrible fear of these verbal carnivals in which all of us have put her, but with good intentions, you do see that, don't you, Mom? We want to attack all official, finished, used-up languages, all the phrases that try to pass for good taste, every classical verbal image, right in the nuts, I say, laughing my head off, totally gross, implacably clownish, so that all those present who hear this know that nothing is stable anymore, nothing is perennial, not even Spanish pique, that everything's mutable, mutating, imperfect, unfinished. Mom, listen to me, no prohibition, no norm, life turned upside down, life in drag, wearing only a crown made of gold paper, let me be born laughing, Mommy, let me live my unborn novel, which is like a vast sacred parody, a scandalous liturgy, a eucharistic diablerie, a banquet, an Easter festival, the union of body and soul, head and ass, word and shit, ghost and fornication, Mom, and now it's beginning to shake around here, and I do a delightful front one-and-a-half because the earth in these parts trembles as if it were floating on water, oscillating, and I sway, I swing and sway with Sammy Kaye—or without! And my oh so astute mom grabs on to Egg, who says thank you God for your telluric decisions and we're on our way through sette e mezzo on the Jaroslav Richter Scale, wailing away on the geological Steinway with Ludwig van's *Emperor* and the tremor does not stop and the open-beaked eagle drops its serpent out of its mouth and tries unsuccessfully to get loose from its chain to set out on an impossible flight, and Hipi gets the snake leftovers to make himself a belt avec and Julio Iglesias deigns to give an autograph to the Orphan without having to be asked twice in the trembling suite of Hotel President Grasshopper Hill, Josú, since the world is falling down once again and it's more important to die signing your own name and Colasa Sánchez's cunt incontinently and infinitely opens in front of the astounded eyes of my father Angel who was getting ready to eat pussy but who instead sees shark teeth lining the sweet treasure of Miss Colasa, daughter of the ineffable Matamoros Moreno, while the golden Angel noisily falls onto Paseo de la Reforma, its gigantic metal wings smashing the shops and stands on the traffic circle where Tíber intersects with Florencia, finally ending up such that its head—blind eyes and sensual lips—faces directly toward Chapultepec Castle, quietly but repressively taken back that very afternoon by the forces of order under Colonel Inclán, who at this very minute is inviting President Jesús María y José Paredes to stroll through the castle's belvedere, where he thinks what he always thinks, namely, that what this country needs is a dictator-for-life, that the drama of Mexico is that it has gone too long without a traditional, recognizable tyrant who would attract adherents and concentrate hatred and who would end, once and for all, this damn symbolic dispersion. Then the tremor begins, and from Chapultepec it is easy to see how the Angel of Independence falls and the colonel wonders if he should take it as a sign, almost a command: he looks at the ex-PAN president, who in that shocking instant loses all sense of ideological relationships and, in the face of this visible portent, falls quickly to his knees. But the colonel makes him stand, pulling him up by his lapels, no one should see you that way, Mr. President, no one, and the President says to the colonel: "I don't want power anymore! I can't carry the burden! You take it!" And the colonel, with his green beard and his dark glasses, craftily and slyly says:

"No, Mr. President, thank you, but Don Benito Juárez would turn over in his grave if the Army were to take power again in Mexico, no, Mr. President. The respect for civilian authority in the Mexican Army is sacred."

"This is a portent," says President Paredes, quieted down somewhat, although he has always been terrified of earthquakes. "Just like the warnings to Moctezuma in the year Ce Acatl. What do we do if there's a revolution?"

"Don't worry, Mr. President. I'll take charge of bringing you your daily quota of dead men. All contingencies have been planned for. Neighborhood by neighborhood, street by street, wherever we find them: your daily quota of dead men. The revolution will be stopped dead in its tracks."

"Thank God!" Don Jesús sighs.

"He's always on the side of those with power."

He leaves the colonel, with the green saliva oozing out from between his parted lips.

Unknown to these men of power, far away, invisible to them, Mamadoc in person is looking directly into the Angel's golden eyes, and she tries to read in them a warning that the fallen statue does not dare to communicate to her. Capitolina and Farnesia hug each other, full of anguish, thinking that death is coming for them, they have left so much undone, who will take care of the unborn child? They will perhaps die together and that makes Capitolina happy, but Farnesia weeps bitterly, thinking that everyone will come to go through her drawers and leaf through her secrets. Don Fernando Benítez is not daunted by earthquakes, and he bangs his fist against the door of Don Homero Fagoaga's penthouse. The owner quickly, fearfully, and nervously opens the door, fleeing but wrapped in a towel, and Fernando rebukes him, you've gone back on your word, you fat faggot, you have not defended democracy, you have not protected your niece and nephew, you've besmirched your honor! Well, now you'll go out with me, you miserable stewpot, to combat those who get rich from the toil of the masses, you will come, you filthy barnacle, to walk with me along the roads of Mexico, losing all your extra pounds and ready, with me, to give your life so that in Tepatepec Hidalgo the right of the peasants to organize is respected and so that in Pichátaro Michoacán the municipal election is not tampered with!

By the force of his insults and threats Fernando drives Homero back into the apartment, miserable lump, bloodsucker, fixture of waiting rooms, survivor of the United Front of Asslickers (UFA), with a good condom the world would have been spared your lamentable presence. He went on attacking the fat man and stripping him now that he had no Tomasito to defend him, although the lawyer screams, Tomasito! Au secours! and the implacable Don Fernando Benítez: you will have the faith in your fellow citizens no one has ever had and you will see that from below, my fat and greasy relative, if we allow them to, Mexicans will practice democracy without gunmen, without crime, without bribes, without orders and abuses. Don Homero Fagoaga cornered, shouting back to Benítez, sure, sure, this mass of lazy good-for-nothings, this irresponsible people, you'll see what they'll do if you leave them alone, what they'll do to you, to us, just what they did on the Malinaltzin highway! they'll beat us to a pulp because we're the enlightened minority that for good or ill has made this poor country despite its flea-bitten, passive, asshole masses, stupefied by incest, liquor, genes, the hopeless race, the damned race, the ra . . .

Cornered now, Don Homero, who entered this story flying through the air under a parachute, now leaves it tumbling off his balcony over Mel O'Field Road and onto the vacant lot, across which on a distant day he chased Orphan Huerta with conflictive intentions, the Orphan (pears, lemons, an' figs!) and now, with the threatening Fer Ben (Fer-de-lance!) in front of him, demanding all these horrors of

him, the naked lawyer and academician falls, naked, from the tenth
floor of this bouncing building down toward the trembling earth,
clutching his immense Cannon towel, imported of course! He does
seven flips in the air, his naked body just like mine inside Mamma
Mia because the tremor does not stop and finally she is holding on
tight to Egg, my father's best friend, our buddy Egg, and he has an
uncontrollable attack of the giggles, finally hugging my mother Angeles filled with me and I, Reader and Friend, ready to take over this
text, if not the entire world then at least the novel, amid the noise
of a golden Angel that falls and Egg who says to my mother: "Look.
Your halo had gone out. Now it's on again, and I Christopher, I
with no weapons but my stubborn battle against the unknown, my
irreverent mix of languages and my decision to put them all into
play, the conflict and the cause: I tell myself that when the Mexican
earth shakes and when the Angel of Independence falls and when
the bats fly in search of the food that remains, that History is faster
than Fiction (here, in Mexico, in the New World!) and that it's time
to get a move on, no more holdups, to the month of August and
what awaits us in it, pushing forward, toward the conclusion, toward
my Na-ti-vi-daddy! my Mother-Ni-Dad!

But sleep, which is memory set free from action, gets between reality
and my desire, and this is the dream of the grandparents the night
of the earthquake and the fall of the Angel and the visit of the Four
Fuckups to the coach house, where my mother and I take refuge,
and the dream is this:

11. *Fatherland, Always Be Faithful to Yourself*

Ayayay, Grandfather Rigoberto Palomar woke up screaming: a nightmare. It's just a dream, Grandmother Susana
Rentería lying at his side consoled him; it was nothing. An
uprising? said Don Rigoberto, astounded. No, nothing but
your balls, laughed his wife. Ay, my little innocent girl, said General
Palomar, my great-grandfather, to his wife my great-grandmother,
sixty-five years of age, merely because he was ninety-one, and do
you remember, Susy?

"You're not going to tell me you dreamed about me, are you, Rigo?"

The lady smiled, pausing, and caressed her husband's silky-white mustache.

"Because remember you said it was a nightmare."

He covered her with kisses—on her hair, on her cheeks, on her lips, until one of the sleeves of his brown-and-white pajamas tore open at the shoulder and the two of them laughed. She asked him to take off his pajama top and sat on the edge of the bed to sew it up, swinging her legs, which were too short to reach the floor, *her ideal feet*.

Don Rigoberto, a skinny old man, wrapped his arms around himself as he sat next to her on the edge of the bed. She sighed. "Tell me your dream, Rigo."

Now, my innocent little girl, let me see. I was about twenty and I was in President Benito Juárez's personal guard up in the northern part of the Republic. We were being chased by the French and the Mexican traitors who helped them. Two years of travel, Su, imagine what that was then, on worn-out coaches and carts pulled by oxen, all loaded with the national archives, and Mr. Juárez with a sort of portable desk in his black carriage, where he wrote and signed things.

Just imagine, my pure little girl, from Mapimí to Nazas to San Pedro del Gallo to La Zarca to Cerro Gordo to Chihuahua and from there across the desert to the far north. Every day fewer and fewer soldiers, less water, less food. Juárez put up with everything because when we began the journey he told us: "We'll never have a chance like this again in our history," and whenever we got tired, Susana, or whenever we started wondering what the devil we were doing there pushing carts loaded with old papers through mud holes and up mountains, we remembered his words and we understood them very, very well. The opportunity granted us was that of saving Mexico from a foreign invasion and an Empire imposed on us by force of arms.

The opportunity to defend a legally constituted government, which for the moment consisted of some old archives and a desk on wheels. I don't think our fatherland was ever so poor or so beloved by Mexicans as it was then. Have you seen, sweetheart, how ugly this country becomes whenever it is wealthy and arrogant? Well, you would have seen it beautiful in my dream.

What did I have to say in those days, honey? Nothing: I was a poker-faced lancer protecting the President, who one day decided to redistribute the Church's wealth, to make people respect the laws of men so they'd be better at respecting the laws of God, and to take privileges away from the Army and the aristocracy. Just like that, the roof fell in, and all the furies in heaven and hell were loosed on the land. He defeated the conservatives, but the conservatives left him saddled with a foreign debt of fifteen million pesos, which was 'the price of some bonds bought by French bankers in exchange for a pound of Mexican flesh. The bonds had no real value. The debt, for which France demanded payment, did. Juárez suspended payments. Napoleon III responded with an invasion and an Empire. Looking at Don Ben, you could see he was so serious, so worthy of his position, so—how to put it? Susanita, he was, well, so sure of his role in history. And since he didn't doubt for a minute that despite all its sorrow Mexico would end up being an independent and democratic country, he never doubted it was his job to make it so, no more, no less. I really wanted to ask him, listen, Don Benito, and if you're not here, will this country collapse, will it go on fighting, or what? I don't know how he would have answered. Lots of people thought they did know: that he thought himself indispensable. And since he was heroic, poor, and a firm believer in the law, there was no one who could argue with him. There was something else: he was a model husband and father. He protected his family; he sent them to the United States to be safe; he wrote his wife and children, punctually and lovingly. Excuse me, Susy, but I was starting to get upset: I saw him sitting like an idol inside his carriage, imperturbable, dressed all in black, frock coat, trousers, vest, a Zapotec idol dressed up—as what?

From looking at him so much, I ended up saying to myself, listen to me now, sweetie, that this man was disguised as something he loved and hated at the same time. Why was he so different? Sometimes he'd let it out in conversation; he'd been an Indian boy, a shepherd in Oaxaca, illiterate and without the Castilian language until he was twelve; between the twelfth and the twentieth year, just imagine, my dove, that farm boy, dispossessed heir to a spectral culture, as old as it was dead, Susana, that boy, lost in the light of a magic simplicity, learns to look on his past as an irrational night, can you imagine that, honey? A horror from which he'd have to save all Mexicans: in ten years he learns to speak Spanish, learns to read and write, becomes a liberal lawyer, an admirer of European revolutions, of U.S. democracy, of the law-loving French bourgeoisie, marries a white bourgeois lady, dresses up as a Western professional man, and just when he finds himself armed with all the writings and laws of Western civilization, boom! Susy, that same world he admires so much turns against him, denies him the right to modernize Mexico, denies Mexico her independence, and I wept for Benito Juárez, I swear I did, angel, when I understood that: the man was sad, divided, masked by his great contradiction, which from then on would belong to all of us, to all Mexicans: we would feel uncomfortable with our past, but even more so with our present. We would be in permanent disharmony with our modernity, which was supposed to make us happy in a flash and which only brought us disasters. How Mr. Juárez stared sadly on that desert he was rapidly leaving behind, where nothing was his, not a cactus, not a yucca.

And there I was wanting to tell him, let yourself go, Don Ben, don't hold it all in, I, your most screwed-up lancer, tell you this because I love you and I spend my time looking at you through the window of your carriage, I look at you as I bounce along to the lean and hungry trot of my horse and you lurch along to the broken and violent rhythm of your carriage; the ink spills, Mr. President, the papers are covered with blots, your top hat slides over on your head, but you are impassive, as if you were presiding over a court in Poitiers when you're right here with us, surrounded by mesquite and Apache feathers; just look over there, look at what Durango is, what Coahuila is . . . Christ!

The first time I saw him break down just a little bit was when common sense told him, listen here, you simply cannot go on carrying the archives of the Republic from the presidency of Guadalupe Victoria to yesterday as if they were nothing more than a bundle of love letters: Don Benito, we're talking about tons of paper here, even if you think paper creates reality, as do all the blessed shysters of our Holy Roman juridical tradition, there is a limit to human patience: the papers are going to drown us, are we going to lose the paper war the way we lost the War of the Cakes in '38 against these selfsame frogs? I swear his mask cracked a bit when he resigned himself to leaving the archives hidden in a cave in the Sierra del Tabaco, over in Coahuila. He bade farewell to those papers as if they were his own children: as if he had just buried each and every piece of paper, each of which for him had a soul.

He never closed his door. It was one of his principles: the door would always be open so that anyone who wanted to see him could come in. Also so that people would always see he had nothing to hide.

He was as clear as crystal. At times he went so far as to take the liberty of sitting down to write with his back to the shacks, the old ruined mission buildings, the houses of friends of his that happened to be on this road which we thought was the road of exile—but no, he'd say, it was merely the desert, which is not the same thing. The point is that for a lancer under orders to protect him, he made my life very difficult because of his self-conscious acts of bravado, fitting for a national leader destined to be immortalized in marble.

On one occasion, right in the Chihuahua desert, he got tired of writing all night and watched me guarding the open door that faced the desert, me half asleep because it was just coming on dawn, but leaning on my lance, which was firmly stuck into that hard earth. He smiled and said that the gray brush surrounding us was wiser than men. That at dawn I should look over the rise punctuated by bushes spaced out perfectly with an almost legal symmetry, like that of a good civil code, he said. Did I know why it was laid out that way? I didn't. And he said that the bushes kept their distance from each other because their roots are highly poisonous. They would kill any plant that grew next to them. We've got to keep our distance in order to respect each other and to survive. That is the foundation of peace, he said, and he quickly walked over to sit down again, to write something rapid, short, and assuredly lapidary.

No, I would have wanted to say to him, it isn't that I want to see you going to the bathroom, wiping yourself, or expelling a gas, Don Benito, or even picking your nose, Mr. President, nothing like that, but something that would not harm your dignity or mine, that's it, I would like to see you brush your teeth, Mr. Juárez, or shine your boots, because don't tell me you don't do it yourself, here we are rolling around among cactus and scrub and you don't have a valet, as Maximilian does, but you always have shoes shinier than those of any Austrian archduke: how do you do it? Would you lose some of your dignity if you let yourself be seen shining your shoes, sir?

We celebrated Columbus Day, October 12, 1864, in the city of Chihuahua, and President Juárez spent it reading back issues of newspapers written in English that had arrived from New Orleans, God knows how, but he had memories of that port in Louisiana where he'd been exiled by the dictator Santa Anna and had earned his living by rolling cigars in a tobacco factory (oh, Lord, and now his beloved papers were all rolled up in the Sierra del Tabaco, he thought ironically) and he learned English, just as his children were learning it now in schools in New York.

One item caught his attention: a gringo named E. L. Drake had discovered a new substance by digging sixty-foot wells in western Pennsylvania. According to the article, the substance was extracted from the wells from deep deposits of sedimentary rocks. This material, which occurs both as a liquid and as a gas, read Mr. Juárez, can be readily substituted, in either form, according to Mr. Drake, for whale oil, which is growing scarce, and can supply bright, cheap light to modern cities. Mr. Juárez nodded his dark head, thinking perhaps about the candle stumps that he had to use in these northern villages in order to write at night.

He talked about the discovery with other guests of Mr. Creel in Chihuahua, and an engineer said that the part about light, while certainly important, was not as significant as the use this famous "petroleum" (the name given the new substance) would have in locomotion, in steam engines, in trains, and in factories. In that instant, Susanita, I saw a vision pass through the usually impenetrable gaze, as if he were imagining himself swiftly traveling through the desolation of the Republic, free of the trammels of terrain or climate, both of which were so rough, sweetheart, so hostile to men.

He shook his head; he exiled his dream. If the important thing was to recover the Republic inch by inch, slowly, in love and poverty, perhaps Don Benito Juárez, cutie, managed to imagine himself, why not? flying by plane from Mexico City to El Paso, Texas, with a stopover in Chihuahua; but then he would have lost the country: the idea was to show that the country was ours, that here we were, and that like our native briars we had very deep roots and thorns all over our branches: let's see anyone try to pull us out, let's see who was going to come live with us in this penury, not in this fiesta. That was the unrepeatable opportunity as he saw it: "We'll never have another chance like this in all our history." Not the oil, Susanita, but dignity. Can you imagine Don Benito Juárez getting rich on the oil boom of the seventies to take off in a Grumman jet to Paris to have a good time, Susy, with a stopover in Las Vegas to play a little poker in the Sands Hotel? Not a chance.

But let's go back to my dream. My dream started filling up with death. You'll see. First he found out that his favorite son, Pepe, was sick. All the intuition, all the atavism, all the innate fatality surfaced in this Zapotec disguised as a French lawyer. His Indian fatalism told him, Susy my dear innocent girl, that Pepito was already dead and that no one would tell him so he wouldn't suffer, already they were treating him like a statue. You should have seen him then in Chihuahua, honey, fearful about his kid, the son he called "my delight, my pride, and my hope." He fell apart; he said he lost his head and filled his letters with smudges. Then he pulled himself together; but I saw him as a victim of what he thought he'd left behind forever: the Indian sense of fatality. His will took over. He went back to being his old self. No one wrote to him from home. The mail system, an accident in a situation full of accidents.

When his premonition came true, Susana, all he did was walk around like a ghost repeating, as he strode through the halls of Creel's huge house in Chihuahua:

"My beloved son is dead . . . my beloved son is dead . . . Nothing can be done about it!"

I felt that Pepe's death precipitated one disaster after another; for later on, Mr. Juárez, right in the same house, received the news of President Abraham Lincoln's death, and then in July the French launched a general offensive against Republican resistance in the north, and in August we had to leave Chihuahua for the border— but that's as far as we could go, captured in Mexico, cornered in Mexico, but never outside of Mexico, he said, never an exile who could be accused later on of having abandoned his country:

"Don Luis"—I heard him say to his friend Governor Creel, who was urging him to save himself by crossing the border—"you know this state better than anyone. Show me the most inaccessible, the highest, the most arid mountain, and I'll go up there to die of hunger and thirst, wrapped in the nation's flag, but I will never leave the Republic."

We went bouncing off again, in the carriages and with the carts, through sagebrush and cactus, the sun on our heads and the rocks under our feet . . . What can I say? Well, one night in a village in the Chihuahua desert, when I was on guard duty, posted behind a wall of crumbling adobe, he closed his door. He's going to sleep early tonight, I said to myself. But soon after I heard him weeping. I didn't dare to interrupt him; but I had the same duty the next day, and when I went to my post with my lance, which wasn't standing as straight as it once did, Susy, I said to myself, well, if he doesn't cry again, we'll forget about it. Well, as Talleyrand said to Napoleon, look, even me, the one in charge of the door, doesn't spend so much time looking into the street; in other words, I'd stay out of his business. But if the old man cried again . . .

"Is something troubling you, Mr. President?"

"No, Rigo. It's nothing."

"In that case, excuse me, Mr. President."

"What is it, Rigo?"

"You know I don't meddle . . ."

"Yes."

"But why don't you talk to me a little?"

He wasn't a saint, he had no reason to be one, he was happy being a hero, and there are lots of heroes we never hear of, heroes who don't have streets named after them or statues put up in their honor: but of what use is a saint? That night he told me about his love affairs, about the children he'd had out of wedlock, about his son Tereso, who was ugly and brave and who was fighting like his father against the invaders; he told me about the poor suffering Susana— like you, my love, the same name, did you know that?—his invalid daughter in Oaxaca, condemned to virginity, drugged to alleviate her pain, and my own for my grownup daughter, what? far away, in pain, my strange daughter captured in an artificial dream: Susana . . .

I told the farm girl to come in, not to be modest, that everything was all right, she knew it, and Mr. Juárez, too; he should look at her the way I, Rigoberto Palomar of the Second Lancers Company of the Republic, looked at her, nothing more, nothing less; we were at war, but we didn't stop living because of that; he should look at her rosy cheeks and her black eyes, her hair streaming down to her waist, and her shape like a newly turned vase; she has a name, it's Sweet Names, that's her name, I rustled her starched blouse, she's barefoot so she won't make any noise, one day not so far off she's going to die because her hands prophesy mourning, I wanted her for myself, Mr. Juárez, but I'll give her to you, you need her, we need for you to have a night of illicit love, Don Benito, tender, sweet love like a stick of cinnamon, and as strong as an earthquake, which is so close to the life from which it comes that to you it might seem, because it gives itself to you so readily, like an answer to death: go to it, Mr. Juárez, screw this farm girl, get rid of your melancholy, win the war, reconquer the country, love this girl as you loved your dead son, as you love your invalid daughter; this is as good a thing to close the door for as going to the bathroom or opening it to receive friends: don't turn into a statue on me, Mr. Juárez, you're not dead yet.

I closed the door on them, Susana, and even though I ran the risk of being punished, I abandoned my post. You see, my innocent girl, I didn't want to hear a thing. That night was his alone; he deserved it more than anyone. I hoped he was happy, but I didn't want to rob him of even an instant of pleasure. So I began to think about sad and impossible things, Susanita. Suppose Mr. Juárez wins. The Republic will be poorer than ever. How can it ever pay the debts piled up by the conservatives, the Empire, the war? How can he rebuild the country? Oh, Lord, I said to myself, closing my eyes in the cold desert, which was like a bedroom at the bottom of the sea: if only Mr. Juárez had that gringo Drake's discovery in Pennsylvania to light up all the cities in the world like glowing coals! Oh, Lord, if instead of owing fifteen million pesos to the French, Don Benito Juárez had received $15 billion a year for exporting liquid fossils! That's why I screamed, Susana. I had that horrible nightmare.

"Don't worry, Rigoberto. Your dream will turn out all right."

12

When the earth calmed down, my mother Angeles tried to calm down with it and to speak rationally. While our buddy Egg strolled around my father's old coach house playing the guitar, she said that when a woman's left alone a vacuum is created and that anything can be pulled in to fill it; she did not want Egg to be a mere fill-in, so she thought it was better that he hear her out and understand her point of view. When I met him— she told us—I told him I didn't sleep all night because I was so happy I met you. And it was true: Angel made me happy by creating me. He didn't find me: he invented me, he made me his by inventing me. I didn't sleep, I was so happy, because Angel met me exactly the way I met myself and exactly when I met myself; neither before nor after. I don't remember anything before him. I don't know who I am, where I come from, nothing.

"Let me confess something to you. I saw him as young and rebellious. So I instantly appropriated everything I thought he liked—feminism, left-wing politics, ecology, Freud and Marx, university exams, every opera ever written—the whole deal, whatever I found at hand, as if it were in someone else's closet. Imagine how surprised I was when he turned out to be a conservative rebel! No way. There was no way I was going to change my symbols just for him, Eggy boy.

"I decided it was better for us to complement each other, so I kept my mouth shut, the better to enjoy making love without understanding too well about making ideology. Love, love, love, Egg, ideology, ideology, ideology, and at the same time, running neck and neck with all this, my question: what is the meaning of all these things we do? It may help him to see in me everything that is opposite to him, to see at the same time everything that completes him. And he even shares with me the hope that we will become equal by being different (the ideal?). At what moment will Angel pass from nonsense to despair without having picked up something positive in the process? What are all of us afraid of, going insane or going sane? Who really loses, who really wins in all this? And who will leave the other one first when both of us realize that nobody can live only in rebellion without ending up in despair? You need something else, I swear, I swear, buddy, something else, and I swear that I tried to find it, quite rationally, I tried to believe in Angel, seriously, in his ideology, only because I want to believe that the good things in this world should be repeated someday, not be left behind, not necessarily rendered obsolete by progress. While you play your guitar, think about this: can progress kill your song because it is your song each time you play it, Egg, an event again and again, with or without penicillin, with television or without? Does what you play go on being an event, while infections do not and the pictures you see at home do? Art is a continuous event or a continuity that takes place: I would have wanted to communicate that to Angel in order to save him from his *either/or*, you know, his madness or reason, stagnation or progress, his world of dramatic possibilities which he likes so much and which does him such damage. I agreed to have his child in order to bring this idea to reality, the idea of the continuity of happening between the nonsense and the despair that will devour my poor Angel if he doesn't understand me. Even if he ends up doing it alone, without me, just as long as he understands me."

"You are lovable," Egg said in English as he stopped strumming. "With a little humor and intelligence, I think you'll survive all the disasters of Mexican life. That's why I love you. You are totally lovable."

"Animus intelligence!" she shouted, but she realized that her exclamation was a reflex action. So she looked at our friend, an interrogatory expression on her face, her head turned to one side. She told him that he, too, was a survivor.

"The only kind of genius that exists in this country is that of survival. It's lost everything else. But it survives."

What about him?

He took my mother's hand and remembered that after his parents' death, when he had no friends, no money, neglect, not caring, and ignorance possessed him for a time. He realized what was happening, became terribly alarmed because he could look at himself as if he were someone else. Then he wrote his first hit, "Take Control."

What about her?

She was afraid. She was afraid that things would happen and we wouldn't notice and that we would only realize that the most important event in our lives had already taken place when it was too late. She also dreamed that a vine sprouted out of her vagina.

"We all have days when nothing goes right. Options, movements, not being what people see, not seeing what's there, believing I do know, knowing I think everything is a mistake. I've been like this for thirty days. Help me, Eggy, please, help me, little buddy. I swear I'll be eternally grateful to you.

"Help me get my halo back, buddy. Don't you see it went out on me?"

That's how August began: the step toward the eighth month of my gestation.

13

Dear Reader, you may remember that in the month of March Angel and Angeles saw the Chilean bolero singer Concha Toro on one of the National Television Contests, presenting herself as the Last Playboy Centerfold, and that in June Egg went to interview her at the Simon Bully Bar to request the services of her Home-Delivery Theater, which participated— with what disastrous results, we all know—in Penny López's Sweet-Sixteen Party. The reader may also recall that Angel refused to do that chore because Concha had taken his virginity sometime during the mid-eighties at the solemn insistence of Grandfather Rigoberto Palomar (a revolutionary general at age fifteen), who could not tolerate the idea of having a virginal fifteen-year-old grandson in his house.

Since the Four Fuckups did not want personal matters interfering in their apocalyptic projects (perennially frustrated, as your lordships fully realize), Egg went to see the dear lady, but Concha Toro's appearance, her fame, and her life story impressed him so much that he blurted out that he'd been sent by Angel Palomar y Fagoaga, did she remember him?

"Of course I remember him, such a well-hung kid, remembered his name just like that, step right in, son, place's a mess, I know, but last night we, uhh, had a little fight with the cops, you know, and the police almost locked us up. But there's wine, and avocados, and peaches and white jam left over, so just help yourself. No one ever called Concha Toro a cheapskate, especially when a hungry poor boy like you turns up. The question is, what are you hungry for, son?"

She asked that last question with a lowering of her eyes that had driven several (though, it must be admitted, recent) generations of senior citizens wild in the velvet basement of the Simon Bully Bar, the entrance to which, a long, smooth red tunnel, was like a velvety, deep vagina—not unlike that of Concha herself.

Egg looked her up and down: she wasn't what she used to be, and if she was never really a knockout— her real charm was her coquettish

Chilean savvy, not her beauty—she was not really faded either: she was a strange palimpsest in which all the stages of her life coexisted in a kind of transparent simultaneity: Concha Toro! Née María Inez Aldunate Larraín y Cruchaga Errázuriz in Chillán, Chile, the night of the terrible earthquake of 1939, which destroyed the city and sank half the coast, from Concepción to Puerto Montt, into the Pacific. She grew up in the shadow of Siqueiros's murals in the school the Mexican government donated to Chile after the disaster: the powerful white and black punches delivered by the native heroes Cuauhtémoc and Galvarino made a profound impression on her tender aristocratic mind. At school she saw revolution and melodrama, while on her father's estate she saw reaction and drama: agriculture in southern Chile was the last refuge of her family, which had prospered early on, in the days when Chile was exporting nitrates, a business that covered late-nineteenth-century Santiago with mansions and the resort cities of Viña and Zapallar with chalets; nitrates paid for trips to Europe and wild spending sprees. The bubble burst in 1918, when the Germans invented synthetic nitrates, but the family managed to save the estate from the general economic collapse. So off they went, to do to the peasants what they'd already done to the nitrates: exploit them. The difference was that they couldn't export peasants. How María Inez laughed when the ineffable President Wrinkle Wrecker requested that the United States export farmers and keep the harvests at home! That's exactly what the Aldunate Larraín y Cruchaga Errázuriz family would have wanted to do, but who would have wanted to buy these flea-bitten scum, shitasses, drunks, thieving rats, with no balls whatsoever! Don't make me laugh!

María Inez resolved her conflicts by giving herself at the age of fourteen to a well-hung peasant boy—as well hung as my father Angel Palomar, I suppose—with the improbable name Randolph Pope. She immediately crossed the Andes at Puente del Inca, went to Mendoza, and from there to Buenos Aires, where this highly intelligent Chilean girl quickly got the lay of the land, changed her name to Dolly Lama and won a tango contest singing with Aníbal ("Dicky") Troilo; she read Borges's *Other Inquisitions*, disguised herself as Miriam Hopkins in *Dr. Jekyll and Mr. Hyde*: perfumed and platinum-haired, she was able, one night in the Armemonville pavilion, to seduce Jorge Borges, the blind guardian of the fragrant clove that a young Patagonian maiden stole from Magellan's circumnavigating ship in 1521 and instantly hid in what elegant Buenos Aires gentlemen used to call "la leure de sa nature": María Inez, alias Dolly, obtained the famous fragrant clove of Magellan in exchange for a sensational screw with Borges, and armed with the Illustrious Clove and the Illustrious Blind Man, she was proclaimed Priestess of Sexual Ultraism in a ceremony held in the Ateneo Bookstore. Immediately afterwards she accompanied the writer to Memphis, Tennessee, where the author of *The Universal History of Infamy* asked the poet Ossing (probably a descendant of Ossian) to lead him into the waters of the Mississippi—up to the ankles—and then give him a drink of Mark Twain's river. Dolly felt she'd done her duty as far as Latin American literature was concerned when she overcame the stupefaction of the citizens of Memphis, who were astonished to see a river of industrial waste and wet garbage pass by, by offering old Georgie a glass of Coca-Cola, which the Illustrious Blind Man drank slowly, interjecting from time to time: "Ambrosia, ambrosia!"

With her clove but without her poet, Dolly Lama emigrated to Hollywood, joined Xavier Cugat's Catalonian–Cuban orchestra, and began a successful career as a backup singer, which enabled her to sing booboopidoop behind Dionne Warwicke in Las Vegas, to whine ohohohuhm-huhm narcotically and orgasmically behind Diana Ross in Atlantic City, to shake spasmodically and masculinely despite having put on a few too many pounds and years in order to establish a contrast with triumphant androgyny behind Boy George and the Culture Club in Radio City Music Hall and Madison Square Garden. At age forty-five, she decided that she'd closed a circle by traveling from Old George to Boy George without ever having left the Culture Club and with more metamorphoses than a Kafkameleon. Fearing that a closed circle could become a vicious circle, she traveled to Mexico, invested her savings in the bar on the corner of Bull Bar and Car Answer, changed her name to Concha Toro, and finally found her true genius, her destiny, the synthesis of her life in the resurrected bolero, the bolero disdained by Mexican modernity, by the youth of the postpunk rockaztec of the early nineties, conserved by Saldaña and Monsiváis as a museum piece, a musical Tezozómoc wrapped in moth-eaten cotton: she came on the scene in one of those unexpected, genial, unsuspected, and purifying conjunctures and restored to the bolero what Homero Fagoaga could never restore to the Spanish language: brilliance, fame, emotion, incalculable splendor. The impoverished, abandoned middle class, its men nostalgic, its women longing for certitude, filled the agora of the Simon Bully Bar to listen to Concha Toro's boleros, because boleros are music to listen to while holding hands, reviewing the vocabulary and the sentiments of our intimate Latin American kitschiness, the yeast in our melodramatic optimism—my father is listening to the bolero "Tropical Path":

> With her night after night I strolled to the sea
> To kiss her lips so fresh and so free
> And she swore to love me evermore
> Never to forget as we kissed on the shore
> Those nights of our love by the sea

Disguised as Quevedo, alone in Concha Toro's cabaret, suspended between the vertices (or vortices) of my pregnant mother, demythified Penny, and resigned Colasa, my father is listening to boleros a certain night in the year of the Quincentennial of the Discovery of America: and he rediscovers the New World of the bolero, the degraded but never renounced utopia sprinkled with water that falls from heaven: the utopia of the islands, of Eldorado, of the Indian monarchy. My father looks around him, as he listens to Concha (whom he does not recognize) sing, at the captivated ruins of the once-upon-a-time prosperous middle class as they collectively regain paradise—the tropical path—by means of the operations of the heart: that is the bolero's impossible project: the precious language of the fin de siècle adapted to the sentimental necessities of the bedroom, the beach, and the bordello:

It was a captive kiss of love on a hand that had the look of a lily in a book the flutter of a dying dove	I was the enchanting butterfly in the garden of your life I was the princess from on high who relieved you of your strife
by Luis G. Urbina	by Agustín Lara
"Metamorphosis" (Poem)	"Captive" (Bolero)
recites my father and	sings Concha Toro and

defines:	*evokes:*
"*Melodrama is comedy*	"*I don't know if there's love*
without humor."	*in eternity, but there, as here,*
	on your lips you will have my
	taste."

My father, staring at Concha Toro, whispers under soft, diffused lights (they, too, like dying doves, enchanting butterflies, torches quenched by destiny, burning kisses) the immortal words: *Hypocrite, nothing but a hypocrite, queen of perversity, you made a fool of me.*

Something unforeseeable began when old people started pouring out of old-age homes to hear Concha sing boleros. *Time* put her on its cover under the rubric *The Darling of the Senior Citizens*, and night after night the entire overaged populace of Mundet, Actors Guild, Gray Power, and the Adolfo Ruiz Cortines Gerontoclub, all on the wings of the purest nostalgia, set impossible rendezvous in the velvet-lined basement of the Simon Bully Bar: a tide of little white heads, bald heads, freckled heads, and, at times, the very coquettish little blue heads, would flow in and out, sentimentally nodding, nodding approvingly when they heard lines like:

> *When silver threads appear while you're still young*
> *Like the moon reflected in a blue lagoon*

The bad aspect of this gerontocratic emigration was that the enchanted old folks refused to go back to the home; they got a second wind in Concha's bar, and there was no way they were going to cut themselves off from their refound youth; they stood their ground on the dance floor and in the aisles, overflowing all the way to Car Answer, and just when the police, following the inveterate habit and Pavlovian reflexes of Colonel Inclán, were on the point of dispersing them with clubs and gas, Federico Robles Chacón, having at that time joined the cabinet as an answer to the Crisis of 1990, decided to end repression as a solution and to use symbolism as euphemism. His suggestion was to set up the old folks in their own neighborhood, on some lots along the Toluca road, where they'd build their dwellings and their lives, and he would promise to bus them in every night to hear Concha. The lots, by the way, were supposedly the property of the wife of Superminister Ulises López, assumed to be the cause of the crisis because of his friedmaniac monetary remedies. When Minister Robles Chacón was asked if he knew whose property those lots were, his only comment was:

"I know. What about it?"

He forgot to say, "All the better," but his subordinates understood him. It turns out that this maneuver was the model for others with even more important consequences: the federal disbursement office pointed out that the closing of old-age homes meant a saving of such-and-such millions of pesos, and Ulises López, grasping this particular proof, turned it, as happens so often in politics, into a general principle: Ulises put the ball right back into Federico's court by ordering the closing down of insane asylums; thousands of patients in psychiatric clinics and mental hospitals were deinstitutionalized between 1990 and 1992, under the pretext that they were costing the government too much money. But the insane had no Concha Toro to entertain them and no Bully Bar where they could congregate.

Artist that she was, Concha Toro regarded all these disturbances as matters of political corruption that were of little concern to her. But her great success hid a profound emptiness in her life: Concha Toro didn't have a man, and looking at herself in her dressing-room mirror—there she was, in her fifties, and with only her Pekingese Fango Dango for company—she said to herself here I am, a good old Chilean girl, a wanderer worse than a Jew, who's been around the world, who's got all the success in the world, but who's far away from home and without a man to love her!

She looked into the mirror and she liked what she saw, she saw herself in her red sequins, a long dress to cover up her fat Chilean calves, makeup to emphasize her Chilean sea-green eyes, radical décolleté, lots of powder, snow white, a few well-placed beauty marks, her lipstick heavy in order to cover up her bad Chilean teeth, the result of drinking water from the mountains that flowed swiftly to the sea without calcium: bad teeth, but only a traitorous dentist could tell the world María Inez's real age: María Inez!

She spoke her own first name near the mirror, her hot breath misting up the glass: Chile, she chanted, asylum against oppression, embroidered field of flowers; pure, oh Chile, is your blue sky: far away, with no return, Pinochet in La Moneda palace forever. Bah, Concha Toro reacted. She forgot her aristocratic childhood, the estate, the Aldunates y Cruchagas in her genealogical tree, and repeated:

"I look at myself in the mirror. I see myself dressed this way, with my red sequins and my satin pumps, gold dust in my hair and my lips in Joan Crawford style: that's what my oldies come to admire, that's what I give them, that's what I grab on to, even if the others stand head and shoulders above me: they need my sincere vulgarity and sentimentality as much as they need a shopping trip to Houston.

She looked at herself, she liked what she saw, she sighed, Concha Toro, she walked out on the stage near the bar and sang:

> *You walked past me with cruel indifference*
> *Your eyes didn't even turn toward me . . .*

They loved her, she loved herself. She told a famous joke:

"When sex is good, it's good. But when it's bad, it's still pretty good."

The old folks laughed and elbowed each other: *Maybe tonight . . . ?* Singing that night under the submarine lights, blue and shimmering, and afterwards back in her dressing room, alone with Fango Dango, once again before her mirror, she analyzed her personality, her success. What had gone into it? Her success was loving to love, loving to be loved, but making clear with the cruel lyrics of the bolero that her tenderness was merely a crack in her indifference: loving but without giving herself up,

> *You walked past me with cruel indifference*
> *Your eyes didn't even turn toward me . . .*

What she wanted was what her frozen, banal, pedantic family with aquiline noses and pink skin and cruel gray watery eyes disdained the most: a Latin friendship, complete, abusive, sticky, immortal, cliquish, noisy. She gave Fango Dango a vicious kick and his howling filled the empty cabaret, but then she hugged him, petted him, begged him to forgive her, and, as she did on all other nights before turning out the light and getting into her nineteenth-century, canopied, red damask curtained bed, she wrote with lipstick on the mirror:

SHIT, LONG LIVE CHILE!

14

Concha Toro's life of wandering and change suffered a new transformation—perhaps the most important of all—the night of May 10, 1992, Mother's Day of the Year of the Quincentennial, which for her evoked her beloved southern seas.

She was singing sweetly, her eyes closed:

> *Through the palms that peacefully sleep*
> *The silver moon cuddles in the tropical sea*

And just when she opened her arms to her audience of senior citizens and opened her eyes to say:

> *. . . my arms open hungrily, looking for you . . .*

her eyes met those of that young man, much younger than she, eyes that from that moment on she could never escape, not even to save herself, because, as Concha knew, anyone who looked away from those eyes ran the risk of being demolished by them. Concha Toro trembled, stopped feeling nostalgic about Chile, felt for the first time she was in Mexico: that face, that mustache, those teeth that came directly from the movies she'd seen as a girl in the Cine Santiago: Pedro Armendáriz, Jorge Negrete, Marlon Brando as Zapata . . . !

> *In the night the scent of flowers evokes your perfumed breath*

sang Concha with her eyes closed, but when she opened them the wandering light of the bar fell on the woman sitting next to that mexaphysical guerrillero, and no, he had not brought his white-haired mom to celebrate Mother's Day; he'd brought a strange girl, strange but very young, dressed as a Carmelite, her bosom covered with scapularies, her complexion the color of cinnamon tea.

> *I feel that you are near to me,*
> *but it's a lie, an illusion*

sang Concha Toro, née María Inez Aldunate Larraín y Cruchaga Errázuriz, alias Dolly Lama, full of despair and bitterness. Then she fainted, right onstage.

When she was a kid in Chillán she'd always wanted to play hooky, cut class, fool around, and now she was being carried piggyback, as if she were on vacation, by the only person in the cabaret strong enough to do it. A man was carrying her from the stage to her dressing room, but in her dreams the cowboy Randolph Pope was once again carrying her in his arms to a spot behind the wheat field on the riverbank where he was going to deprive her of what he wanted most and she needed least: now a tall, powerful, dark, ultramustachioed man was carrying her as if he were pushing a cannon up a hill: she clung to the man's neck passionately, and when he deposited her in her nineteenth-century bed, she, instead of singing a bolero, recited the most beautiful love poem, the most memorable love poem, and, she said to herself, the most Chilean love poem as well:

> *I loved her, and she, at times, loved me as well . . .*

The tall powerful, dark, ultramustachioed man said:

"I, too, wanted to be a writer."

"What happened?" whimpered Concha.

"The envious frustrated me."

"You don't look frustrated to me," said Concha coquettishly, as she looked at the girl dressed as a nun.

"This is my daughter Colasa."

"Ah!" sighed Concha, with no frustration whatsoever.

"I had her when I was very young."

"Colasa Sánchez, at your service, ma'am."

Ma'am stared with an intensity worthy of the bolero "Think About Me" at the girl's father. "And what's your name?"

"Matamoros Moreno, putting both of us at your service," said the man. Concha Toro fainted again.

Don't forget now, dear Readers, that in the meanwhile, no matter how many things go on out there, inside here we aren't exactly sitting around killing time: add up all the things that have gone on outside: love, disasters, jokes, trips, politics, economics, language, fashion, myths, customs, and laws, and compare all that with my simple and essential activity: my hands, for example, have grown more rapidly than the arms they're attached to, they first appear with the fingers looking like buds; the last phalanx has emerged from the palms of my hands, my fingertips have formed, little tiny nails have appeared on all my fingers and toes, and the transparent and cartilaginous skeleton I had in my first four months is now bone and I move my arms and legs energetically: I have little accidents, I scratch my face with my nails unintentionally; I have pleasures: I suck my thumb incessantly; I make discoveries: I can touch my face.

Ah, my face: there is no greater accomplishment in my small organism! I couldn't envisage a greater visage! First, I have a cranium, which is the refuge of my brain. It was made of transparent skin; in the seventh week a huge vascular tide spread toward the crown to protect and feed my little, recently born brain, which is now floating in a fluid bath (never let it dry out, your lordships!) and absorbs all the catastrophes outside my delicate mechanism (and you tell me if there haven't been lots of them in these first seven months of mine!). How strong my subcutaneous tissue is getting! How the bones of my skull grow, moving toward the crown, but without fusing with it, in order to maintain the exquisite flexibility of my shell, granting me a malleable head which will permit my brain to keep growing: when I'm born, my noggin will not be as large as it will be someday—if I live that long!

But I was talking about my face: I can touch it with my hands! Do you realize what that means, your mercies? I have a face and I can touch it with my hands! My face, which at the beginning was only a bulging brow above my future mouth, soon was focused over the window to my dark soul, my eyes: a retina appeared which became dark, pigmented; a lens and a cornea. The eyelid formed little by little. My ears were very low. My brain shone under my translucent skin. My eyes closed. But they were enormous, and there was a long distance between them. Thick lids covered them. I am blind, ladies and gentlemen! My closed eyes are awaiting eternity! But they are not closed because I am asleep. Just think: I close them but I'm not asleep. My closed lids are merely protecting my eyes, which have not yet finished forming yet. I've taken the veil. I grasp even more firmly on to my umbilical lasso, just as Quasimodo clung to the bell rope at Notre Dame. I never get tangled up no matter how much I swim, no matter how many times I ring the bell: can you hear me, Mom? I can hear you! I hear the world better than ever! I hear your heart, Mother, boomboomboom, it's my turn and my dance, and when I hear your pals' band play rockaztec, believe me, Mom, I only hear, redoubled, intense, the rhythm of your own heart and that of my gestation in your womb: *boomboomboom*.

8

No Man's Fatherland

We return to nationality out of love . . .
and poverty. Prodigal sons of a fatherland
we don't even know how to define, we begin to
observe it. Castilian and Moor, shot through
with Aztec . . .

Ramón López Velarde,
"The Fatherland as Something New"

1. Thunderclap

In August the highways of the Republic of Mexico began to echo with rumors that were both expected and unusual: the federal turnpikes, the toll roads, the *frigüeys* as the jeunesse dorée of the Ibero-American School called them, had been maintained in (Egg is telling my mother, educating both of us in the process) a sort of autonomy with respect to the other realities of the nation. To drive on one of these highways, the Pan-American to Mexamerica, the Christopher Columbus to Oaxaca, the Transistémica to the Chitacam Trusteeship, was like heading into a country that belonged to all and to none, a free territory. The highways of the nineties are buffer zones in which all the weight of the newly mutilated Sweet Fatherland resolves itself in a kind of rapid, fleeting freedom—a swift and ephemeral freedom, but a freedom nonetheless. The highway knows no obstacles, like an arrow piercing the air.

At the end of the eighties, CB radios were brought into Mexico from the North, allowing truck drivers to communicate with each other on the superhighways. This further fomented the movement of contraband, drug trafficking, and highway prostitution. Egg told

Angeles (and me) that CB culture in the U.S. had developed its own slang, which our long-haul truckers rapidly adapted to the needs of rural, desert, and mountain roads, the yellow basalt and the dusty trees of the Mexican Republic: soon we, too, had our Smokeys, plain brown wrappers, Tijuana Taxis, and bubble-gum tops—called bubble-gómez here. Bubble Gómez also happened to be the name of the young leader of the truck-drivers union. Bubble Gómez, an albino, drove a spectacular eighteen-wheel Leyland seventy-two feet long, with jukebox lights around the windshield, fog lamps on its roof, exhaust pipes that could create darkness at noon in Vulture Gulch, pictures of the Virgin of Guadalupe, Mamadoc, and Margaret Thatcher on the dashboard directly opposite the leader's light eyes, which were in turn covered by fabulous wraparound sunglasses. The albino was also surrounded by opaque glass as he drove his British behemoth, which was equipped with the Whistler, the indispensable radar detector he used to warn his colleagues: listen up: speed trap at kilometer 13, pass the H to Chotas, who'll be coming in the other direction, slow down. The CBs were used for more innocent activities as well: three putas are waiting for us at the Palmillas Tamps diner . . . Or let's all sing and beat the boredom of crossing the Stinko Sierra, or get the dough ready for the Tijuana Taxis who'll be waiting for us at the La Chicharrona exit.

The unfortunate drivers who had no CB or radar were picked off by the Smokeys at strategic points along the highways: they were novices, naïfs. But when it happened to Bubble Gómez himself, one night just a few yards from the Mexamerica border, in Corralitos, Chihuahua, and near the Nuevas Casas Grandes airport, the news spread like wildfire over the CBs, from Palmillas, Chihuahua, to Palmillas, Querétaro, and to Palomaras, Oaxaca, from radio to radio and truck to truck: the Boss has been nabbed!

Bubble Gómez was caught by a plain old Smokey in Chihuahua!

Bubble Gómez's immediate loss of prestige (he must be an asshole!) combined with the general bewilderment (who can take his place?). Instinctively, the drivers tried to find the answer using their CBs, and the answer was waiting for them on every channel, repeated by every voice, running now from south to north, from Palomares Oax to Palmillas Qro to Palmillas Chih, the message was repeated insistently, the slogans offered by a velvety feminine voice, sometimes a virgin's voice, sometimes a whore's voice, listen good buddy in Nuevo León or oye buencuate in Hidalgo. Quite exciting, quite attractive the woman's voice, whoever she is, and again and again that message, which had never gone out before and was now coming through every truck radio:

WHEN YOU DON'T BELIEVE IN ANYTHING,
WHAT DO YOU HAVE LEFT?
YOUR HOLY LITTLE MOTHER!

which became personified, as it should be, in:

TRUCK DRIVER, WHO PROTECTS YOU?
YOUR LITTLE MOTHER THE VIRGIN!

and since there was not a single one of these trucks that in addition to its CB and its radar detector did not also have its picture of the Virgin of Guadalupe and often even a blessed rosary hanging right under that picture, sometimes even a candle burning in front of the dark image, the slogan caught on, since the truck drivers heard the word and instantly saw the picture and the picture told them that the word was true and that outside the truck there was nothing more than tumbleweeds and cactus or ravines or bare bluffs: outside, desolation, and here inside, fellow traveler, the comforting warmth of a woman's voice and a message for you:

Blessed are those who drive alone night and day along the highways of Mexico, exposed to all kinds of danger, victims of corruption and immorality, chased by the Smokeys and the Tijuanas, adrift in a sea of stone, dust, and thorns, blessed be the long-haul drivers because they can carry the good news in all directions:

OUR VIRGIN IS NOT ABANDONING US!
OUR DARK LADY KEEPS WATCH OVER US!
OUR LADY OF GUADALUPE SHALL RETURN!

and then in every diner along the way, in every tollbooth, in every melon, crackling, or tepache stand along those endless roads, a woman waited to surreptitiously pass every driver a cassette and the drivers were already prepared to hear that sweet sexy voice, which was now explaining more, saying more "to all those who feel adrift in modern society, hello and good news: Salvation is coming! Don't lose hope! Our little Mother is thinking about you and is sending

you an emissary! You will recognize him when you see him because
you will recognize the son of our Mother!" Cassette after cassette
announced the blessed news:

TRUCK DRIVER: THERE'S AN AYATOLLAH IN YOUR FUTURE
PASS IT ON

and the woman's voice: "Blessed be all those who have rolled through
this world and faced its dangers. A truck driver is the favorite son of
the Virgin. Blessed are they who walk through this world in time of
danger." The truck drivers began to communicate their opinions to
each other, to feel they were a chosen people, to join together so
that what had been prophesied would happen: they were chosen for
what was going to happen, the Virgin was speaking to them—they
were told by a man's voice, rough and assimilable, that complemented
the modulated, sweet, and sexy voice of the woman who swallowed
her *s*'s in a Caribbean drawl, that they were the Comanches of the
Virgin, they galloped over deserts and mountains like the brigades
of the Virgin of Guadalupe. They didn't have horses, but they had
something better: their trucks, their Dodges, Leylands, Macks, like
roaring chargers, their diesel sorrels, the Comanches of Guadalupe
crossing the fatherland in all directions, tying together
THE NATION OF GUADALUPE
which had been separated and mutilated: Comanches! Remember,
said the sonorous and Mexican voice of the man, Coahuila never
belonged to the central government: it was Comanche territory! Texas
never belonged to the Americans: it was Comanche territory! The
Comanche nation is the nation that moves, unites, takes over land
by running over the land. Comanche truck driver, spread the news
far and wide, take it as far north as Presidio and as far south as
Talismán: knock down the false borders, truck driver, you are the
Comanche, the Man of Silver, the Knight of Guadalupe in 1992!
They all came together on August 15, the Assumption, where the
voices convoked them, thousands of drivers rolling in from north and
south, from both coasts, from all the scattered borders of Mexico,
gathered first in the Zoquiapan truck stop at Río Frío and from there
to the Cuatro Caminos Bull Ring at Ciudad Satélite in Mexico,
D.F., taken by surprise (and silent) attack by the motorized Comanches, curious, excited, committed, catechized, touched to their very
roots, with their rolled-up sleeves, their bulky sweaters, their scratched
boots, and their newly whitened Adidas, their elegant T-shirts, their

beer bellies, their tight blue jeans, their underpants stuffed with Kleenex in front, their rippling muscles, their baseball caps, and some, the coquettish ones, even wearing white gloves with rhinestones on them which they'd bought in the Michael Jackson Shops along the border: they were all there and her voice (though she remained invisible) announced over the loudspeakers that HE was coming, THE AYATOLLAH OF GUADALUPE, AYATOLLAH MATAMOROS, THE MAN they'd all been waiting for, exactly as they'd imagined him, because he was the very image, the dream, the personification of Mexican machismo: tall, powerful, dark, big mustaches, with flashing eyes and an angry expression, but also a flashing smile, his head tied in a red scarf worthy of the Servant of the Nation, the liberating Generalísimo José María Morelos, in his Mexican cowboy suit, which was all black except for a huge silver cross over his chest and an old-fashioned cape which the man took off the way Manolete took off his bullfighter's cape, and then began the whistling, the jokes, yo it's Mandrake the Magician, giddyap cowboy, but the Ayatollah Matamoros stood his ground in the very center of things and looked at them as no one had ever looked at them, fearlessly but with fraternal tenderness, looking straight into their eyes, no "I'll look down," no "I'll look aside," without the eternal Mexican way of looking: suspicious, crafty, traitorous, ill-meaning, insincere, resentful, double-meaninged: he wasn't afraid of them, he looked straight at them, and the voice of the woman they knew and loved for her voice, and whose voice they thought was that of the Virgin herself, told them, "Love him, this is my son, follow him, he walks for me, listen to him, his words are mine."

Ayatollah Matamoros spoke and his voice fused with that of the Madonna and he reminded them that Mexico was the second largest Catholic nation in the world, the largest in the Spanish-speaking world, 130 million Catholics, not 130 million members of PRI or PAN or Communists or peasants or ragpickers or functionaries or anything else: *only 130 million Catholics could equal 130 million Mexicans*, that was *the only equivalence*, that was the force, that was the reason, and nevertheless, despite all that, the Ayatollah Matomoros exclaimed in his hoarse, moving voice: THERE IS NO NATION!

THERE IS NO NATION!

and he told them

WE WANT A NATION!
WE WANT A COUNTRY!

all culminating in the phrase

LESS CLASS AND MORE NATION

and they shouted back what he said in chorus and now he asked them: Where are we? What should be our idea? And they supplied the slogan that would link the nation to its Prophet:

WE ARE ALL HERE!

We are all here, the long-haul truckers roared, gathered in the bullring and proud of having invented this unifying slogan, and their "We are all here" was a "We already exist" and "There is a country" and "There will be a nation" and "The Virgin will come to help us so that we, Brothers, can help the country": Go out over all Mexico, organize those you find in the name of the Nation of Guadalupe and the Ayatollah Matamoros, who is, listen carefully now, the YOUNGER BROTHER OF JESUS CHRIST, who wants for our Mexico

> *Guadalupan nationalism! Your kind!*
> *Catholic morality! Your kind!*
> *Holy Little Mother! Your kind!*
> *New energy! Everybody's kind!*
> *New Faith! Our kind!*

shouted the Ayatollah and all answered in chorus, on foot, inflamed by the mission. No one had given a hoot about them before, no one had ever preached to them before, except some Protestant missionaries who gave them decals that said I DRIVE WITH JESUS, but they forgot to include the Little Mother. That's why they all carried their polychromed picture of Mamadoc, most loving Mother of all our appetites. But who was this holy woman standing next to the Ayatollah, this hatchet-faced Indian woman, hair pulled straight back, a severe bun, without a speck of makeup: savagely melancholy eyes, lips as straight as an arrow, like a blessing, like a promise, dressed in black, no shape, her head a shiny porcelain skull, her body a furrow of age-old suffering, early deaths, lost children, absent husbands, hands simultaneously cold and boiling, red from washing so much, from grinding so much, dry and yellow from burying so much, from praying so much?

The August rain poured down, but they all went on chanting the slogans with the Ayatollah in the center, his arms spread wide, and the rain running off his face like tears and the voice of the Woman, of the Mother, she never wept, begging her sons:

> Organize and move the nation of Guadalupe!
> Carry the message! Carry the message!
> One hundred and thirty million Mexicans!
> One hundred and thirty million sons and lovers of mine!
> Follow the Mexican Ayatollah!

Who am I? asked Concha Toro with a trace of skepticism and a degree of shock as she sat before her dressing-room mirror, rapidly transforming her "look" and her makeup (actually: her lack of "look" and cosmetics, her Gothic and Araucanian nakedness) into her usual character, the Chilean bolero singer, in order to stand before the nocturnal audience, but already imagining, day after day, her reappearance as Galvarina Donoso, the sorceress, the mother of the Ayatollah.

Damn fool idea! It surprised her to see in the mirror how easily her Basque and Irish ancestors disappeared from her face and how the essential Araucanian face of Chile reappeared.

However, she did feel that something was missing from what she saw. As she scrutinized the mirror in front of her and was surprised not to see the number of the beast 666 appear, or the seventh cup filled with the wine of God's vengeance, or the gathering (in the bullring, in the cabaret, on the highways) of the One Hundred and Forty-four Thousand just men called for by St. John on Patmos.

That frightened her.

However, she did see a lost but serene woman clearly reflected in the center of the jungle.

2

The Ayatollah Matamoros's first order was: NO MORE MONEY! He put his power to the test: he triumphed: the carts Made in Whymore full of devalued paper money (the Mexican peso plummeted to 25,000 per dollar in August) were exchanged for barrels of oysters made in Guaymas: all it took was for the long-haul drivers to refuse to accept money in exchange for goods in the markets of MonteKing, GuadalaHarry, or Makesicko City.

"I'll give you this load of Sheetrock for a load of pineapples."

"I don't want your hardware. How about you take my wire and give me your steers?"

The pineapple sellers and the owners of the steers exchanged the wire and the Sheetrock for a delivery bike or for labor to build an outhouse, the drivers ate some of the pineapples and slaughtered a couple of steers, but they exchanged the rest for bricks, which they brought from Pachuca, where they had too many, to Zihuatanejo, where they didn't have enough: Federico Robles Chacón realized what was happening, a political genius had organized the most mobile sector of the Mexican populace, the long-haul truckers, and in one stroke had eliminated the money economy and restored the barter system: Why? The minister was scratching his head in his SEPAFU office: Why? before asking himself Who? From the terrace of his ministry he could see the bonfires of paper money burning all over the city, people of every class throwing bills of all denominations into the fire, but the poor more than the rich, the poor having no doubt whatsoever about the worthlessness of the paper, which wasn't even good for wrapping things: yesterday's newspaper, a brown paper bag—these were worth more than currency; the poor knew the value of the barter system better than the rich, they knew how to set it up and how to present things as if they were sumptuous gifts and do it all by means of an incredibly swift army, the nation's truckers. Why didn't it occur to me before! Federico Robles Chacón slapped himself across the face to release his fury, and the official statistician hidden in the closet heard that sadistic slap-slap and decided to stay right where he was, so those slaps wouldn't reach him, and besides, he didn't understand what was going on, not only in the city but in what was left of the country.

From his office, Federico Robles Chacón could see the desperate outskirts of the city and observe the repetition of the nightmare that every millionaire, government functionary or not, and every government functionary, millionaire likely as not, had been having obsessively for over a decade: on the fringes of the suffering city, the outskirts of the lost city's garbage dump and the sand dumps and the caves and cardboard houses of the anonymous cities inhabited by millions of people as anonymous as the places in which they lived, the shit city where seven million animals and three million human beings defecated right out in the open so that thirty million people could breathe the shit dust, an army of the miserable was waiting for the order to march on the downtown fortresses of power and money. No one had anticipated a Zapata-style agrarian revolution, never again; and yet it would have been easier—said Minister Robles Chacón to President Paredes as the President distractedly played with a new kind of ball-and-cup game made of a tiny barrel of oil and a drilling rig with a hole in it—to manipulate peasants than these marginalized urban masses: the peasant had a history, a culture, his past was known, as was his face, his little wiles; but these new people had no history, no culture, no face to recognize: they were the forgotten, and no one had ever had to fight with them, manage them, defeat them while making them think they'd won, the way the agrarian rebels had been taken care of. What are we going to do?

The President was frustrated because he couldn't get the oil drum into the hole; perhaps for that reason he said calmly, "Turn the troops on them, that's why we have Colonel Inclán."

"That's the last option, Mr. President."

"So they tell me." He sighed, the toy dangling from his hands. "But just explain to me why, Mr. Secretary: for years and years I fought in the opposition with the secret desire to be president and turn the troops on people whenever I wanted instead of having them turned on me. Now here I am and I find out that troops are the 'last option,' that I should avoid it so as not to have a rerun of Tlateloco or a Corpus Christi and lose everything. Look here: I'm in PAN, I have to govern through PRI cadres and I can't tell the Army, 'Get

out there and kick some ass.' Tell me now, is it worth being president
if I can't do this?"

"Mr. Paredes," said Robles Chacón after looking at him for a long
time with incredulous severity.

"Yes?" said the President, alarmed that someone, especially a Minister of State, was not calling him "Mr. President."

"No one forced you to be president," said the minister, not in an
absolutely conclusive tone, but in one that invited a response that
never came, which gave Robles Chacón yet another victory.

3

The fact is they didn't have faces: they had numbers, mass,
vague labels; they were the insane released from sanatoria,
bands of eunuchs from Jalisco, desperadoes from Hidalgo,
clowns from Nuevo León, rogues originally from Puebla;
but now they were not attracted by the mirage of the city, consum-
erism, jobs: now they were called by that macho voice that told them
through the thousands of cassettes carried by the truckers to every
corner of the country:

THERE IS A NATION! WE ARE ALL HERE!
WE ARE THE NEW NATION!
LET'S BE GLORIOUS!
REAL MEN AREN'T ASHAMED TO PRAY
FOR THE FATHERLAND!

Know something? Matamoros Moreno said right at the beginning
to Concha, now rebaptized for the sake of the grand campaign with
the sonorous Chilean name of Galvarina Donoso: Did you know that
for the first time in my life I've discovered that there's a huge number
of poor people, a freaking mountain of screwed-over jerks who hate
themselves?

"Better late than never," answered Galvarina. "If I didn't know
that, I'd be a damned fool, but they've stopped believing that the
blonde in the beer ads would be waiting for them when they got to
the city: one blonde coming up, son! These boys ain't so stupid!"

"You took the words right out of my mouth, ma'am. You always know everything, and that's why I adore and respect you: just what I was thinking, and now put it in a song. I swear you're terrific!"

Which is what Concha Toro did: "One song coming up," as she would say, and she transformed the driest political ideas into bolero lyrics, songs people could hum all over the roads of Mexico: "The sky on this earth may be ever so high / The sea may be ever so deep / But nothing can keep our love from the Virgin / who watches over our sleep . . ." Or: Save us! Save us, Ayatollah: we ask you now as before / we wandered full of anguish and suffering: no more, Ayatollah, no more! / beautiful Ayatollah, you're our heart's delight / thanks to your message, we'll make it through the night!

No one knew exactly where these jingles came from, the scattered drivers could not have invented them, but they were everywhere, they upset some people, excited others, angered still others, and made everyone stop and think. Egg told my mommy all this when he visited her. He never gave up: he was bald, and they never paint hope bald. Egg himself was fed up with his new job, which was as a salesman for Souvenir Portraits, which is to say, tapes which the customer could have made of himself while alive which could then be put in the coffin so he could speak to his descendants. All you had to do was push a button.

"A terrific idea, but nobody wants to leave even a memory of himself anymore. Neither the deceased-to-be nor his heirs-to-be want to survive in any way. They hate themselves too much."

"So turn it around and offer them total oblivion when they die. Nothing, néant," said my mother.

"Oblivion insurance!" exclaimed Egg: "People hate themselves."

(A lie, I'll never be like that handsome devil in the ad driving his Meiji-Maserati, I'll never wear that Bill Blass blazer made in Hong Kong, I'll never fly to Tokyo on the Concorde, the chicks will never be all over me because I put Yojimbo in my armpits, I'll never be accepted by the Diners Club, the Blonde of My Dreams will not be waiting for me at Indios Verdes when I roll in from Pachuca in overalls looking for love, fortune, and glory in the city: it's not true, exclaimed Orphan Huerta as he painted election ads on the walls for the election of August 31, which came before the President's address to Congress on the first of September.) (President Paredes had reduced the year's electoral calendar to two days: on the first you voted, on the second you applauded, and in the meantime we had lots and lots of National Contests to amuse us, and the Orphan worked painting walls for President Parades):[1]

CANDIDATEIZE YOURSELF
FEEL LIKE A CANDIDATE!

slogans that summarized the President's obsessive philosophy: there should be no former presidents, only candidates; the most important obligation of a president in 1992 is to choose his successor and then die: did he really believe it? Is that why he walks around so slowly, so desperate at times, so taciturn, so given to playing ball-and-cup and delegating decisions to Minister Robles or Colonel Inclán?

People hate themselves because they can never be what they've been told they can be, my father Angel had said when he fled from the threat of Colasa Sánchez's vagina dentata and realized, sadly, mediocrely, with no glory whatever, that he'd been left without either dark or light meat: poor Daddy—no Colasa, no Penny, not even my poor knocked-up mommy! The Orphan Huerta paints slogans on walls and it bores him so much that he succumbs to the amusing vice of memory and wonders about his brother, the Lost Boy. What a laugh! He starts playing with words as if he were writing a song, a song no one will ever sing: Lost Boy, Copper Field, Twisted Oliver, Little Lord Fartalot, Eddy Piss, Eddy Poe, Eddy Feets, and he looks at his own torn-up feet, feet burned up since he was a kid because of having to walk, with no memories, through the garbage dumps of the city: Where ma brudder at? Suddenly, painting walls and else-where with English names: Little Dorrit, Copperfield, Oliver Twist Again Like We Did Last Summer, said the Orphan Huerta tapping his toe as he painted walls.

He has the sensation he's surrounded by phantoms and he does this work mechanically as he dreams. The Orphan Huerta has the overwhelming sensation he's surrounded by water, that he's falling, brush in hand, into a vast liquid dream: the city once again floats over its lake, the placid skiffs ply the canals laden with flowers— geraniums and zempazúchiles and wild roses, the ahuehuetes, grand-father trees, lend their shade to those on foot and the weeping willows

[1] The fortunes of President Jesús María y José Paredes can be read about in the novel, *The King of Mexico; or, If You Move You Won't Come Out in the Photo.*

moisten their branches like green handkerchiefs in the clean river waters: the Orphan Huerta opens his eyes and looks at the white wall devoid of destiny before his abandoned eyes: the dead lakes he sees, the canals transformed into industrial burial grounds, the roasted rivers, a burning shield of cement and black wax devouring what it was going to protect: the heart of Mexico.

The Orphan Huerta, full of the rage and bitterness accumulated in his twenty years, scratches the white wall, leaving in it a wounded trace, his fingernails bleed, his signature is blood: a sign on the clean wall, a destiny for me and mine, a scratch on the clean wall of destiny, damn it to hell!

The old tree falls, fulminated by old age, and my father raises his eyes from his sad job. Now he has neither wife nor home. ("I know how to give fags the whipping they deserve," his grandfather had him told by the Orphan Huerta, he'd better not turn up on Calle Génova, Angeles would have his son, me, the great-grandson of General Palomar, the grandson of the scientists Diego and Isabella; my Great-grandmother Susy would take care of me, my father'd better not turn up around there, let the faggot go live with the Fagoaga sisters, go ahead.) (I'd take you in with pleasure, and you know it, his Uncle Fernando Benítez told him, I'm not a pharisee, I'm telling you this with a grief that keeps me up at night and that perhaps someday you will understand and I may be able to explain to you: not yet, patience is an art and you, my little friend, are a talker, a poseur, a kid with a lot of gravy and no meat, in sum, a miserable rat; take stock of your life before you go on, and you'll see that nothing of what you have done has much weight; it doesn't glow with talent or move us with its sincerity. Come see me when you decide what you are going to do. For the time being you're nothing but a poor fool: all your nonsense did not get you to revolutionary happiness, only to reactionary despair. Look: the only thing I can do for you is lend you the van the people in Malinaltzin gave us, the one you called the Van Gogh. You can live in it and get around in it: it's roomy and fully equipped—after all, it was acquired for the PRI political boss in the Guerrero mountains. You can pick it up tomorrow at my house on Lerdo de Tejada. I'm leaving. There is no salvation in this city: people hate themselves too much here. Ask my wife Georgina for the van; she has the keys; she's just come back from her commune in China and she'll give them to you. I wish only pure, good things

for you, Angelito. I hope we all come out of this imitation apocalypse
in good shape: I'm going to spend a month with the Huichole Indians,
because I'd rather see what happens when the sacred moves, I'd rather
see it at its origin than in its final phase. After all, boy, the sacred,
before anything else, is a celebration of origins. Here the only thing
we're going to see is force disguised as religion. We shall start out in
the realm of the sacred and we shall end up with a government of
priests. The only constant in all this, Angel, is the sacralization of
violence. I shall watch it all from the mountains, so I don't lose my
perspective the day this apocalypse wears itself out. Farewell,
nephew!)

Discouraged, my father wondered what he was doing in this tourist
business in which he was now working, located in the ruins of the
Zona Rosa, itself infested with muggers, addicts, CIA agents who
specialized in neutralizing Central American leftists, and waiters
without jobs standing in long lines outside of restaurants. What was
he doing, he, Angel Palomar y Fagoaga, a young man people used
to say had ideas, imagination, daring, a sense of humor, erotic talents,
even tenderness, even love, what was he doing here now sitting in
a dark and dilapidated attic on Niza Street at the corner of Hamburgo,
spending his time making up lying slogans to make national and
foreign tourists think it was possible to get anything in Mexico, that
Mexico was a cosmopolitan center, that Mexico was a constellation
of international attractions: my father inventing things all day long,
solitary, bored, and scornful even of himself:

SINATRA!
FAREWELL CONCERT IN THE
ACAPULCO CONVENTION CENTER
SEPTEMBER 15, 1992
(BALONEY)

THIS IS IT, THE TOWER IS HERE!
TOUR D'ARGENT IS OPENING ITS ONLY FOREIGN
BRANCH RIGHT HERE IN MEXICO!
GUESS ITS LOCATION AND WIN
A FREE ESCARGOT PROVENÇAL!
(LIE)

FINALLY: ZIPPERS THAT ACTUALLY WORK!
FOR YOUR LUXURY BAGS!
DON'T PUT UP WITH MEXICAN ZIPPERS ANYMORE!
VISIT THE MARK CROSS STORE ON POLANCO STREET:
ZIPPITY-DOODAH-ZIPPITYAY!

(FALSE)

while in the streets of the shocked city the thing he'd vaguely foreseen was happening, the thing he'd wanted to start was now in full swing, not like that carnival in Acapulco organized by the government that made Angel and his buddies think that they, the puppets, were pulling their own strings.

Now Angel heard that noise, riding alone in the Van Gogh through the strangely awed city, as if it were on the eve of an eclipse, hunkered down like dogs who smell the nearness of death, which only they can see—and which they see before anyone—in black and white, the only colors dogs can see; a city beaten and angry: Angel saw rise up among all its things (just as Angeles said, my Angeles, what a fool I've been, and then the silly ass choked up) that were lost out of haste, poverty, and indifference, he saw rise up the signs of ancient newness; and suddenly the invisible enveloped him. Everything that had always been there and the new as well, all gathered together at last: the roar of tens of thousands of long-haul trucks entering the city at night from all directions, all driven by those men convinced they'd been born to drive and that today at last their work was their destiny: chosen to move an entire country and to enter the city this way at the vanguard of the desperate, the disinherited from all the slums: all moving at last toward the heart of the city, millions and millions of faceless people, people with no future, with nothing to lose, the misery of all the nameless slums mixed with the despair of those who had lost everything, the newly unemployed, those permanently displaced by earthquakes, police fired for corruption, bodyguards out of work, warriors and condottieri of the future in search of their chance, all behind the brightly lighted trucks, their loudspeakers blaring:

COME TO ME!
WITH FAITH!
TO CONQUER MEXICO!
FOR THE FAITH!

FOR THE VIRGIN!
YOU IN DESPAIR!
YOU OUT OF A JOB!
YOU WHO ARE HUMILIATED!
YOU WITH NO ROOF OVER YOUR HEAD!
COME TO ME!
WITH THE HOLY MOTHER!
TAKE YOUR FIRST STEPS!
TO THE NATIONAL PALACE!
TO POWER!
NO ONE CAN OVERCOME THE NATION OF GUADALUPE!
ALL TOGETHER!
COME TO ME!
YOU WITH NO JOB!
YOU WITH NO JUSTICE!
YOU WITH NO HOPE!
COME TO ME!

The truckers gathered in the Zoquiapan bus depot, on Río Frío, distributing torches from their trucks, a river of flames flooding down Santa Fe to Paseo de la Reforma and from Contreras to the Pedregal and from Peñon de los Baños to the Zócalo and then scattering confusedly, unforeseeably, in all directions in the city, the city as vast as an inexhaustibly curious spiderweb, sweeping everything in its path, devouring everything, creating an enormous, unexpressed doubt: was this mob creating or destroying? was it cleaning up or swallowing up? or had the time come when the two functions were indistinguishable? The supermarkets were the instinctive objective of the mob. My mob of Guadalupe! shouted the Ayatollah Matamoros from the roof of his black truck, his head tied up in the scarf evocative of martyr priests, headaches, beggar thieves. Saintliness and death, torture and violence all shone at the same time in the Mexican Ayatollah's black eyes and white teeth, and his mob invaded all the supermarkets in the city. The immediate recompense: Kellogg's gave them cornflakes and Chocokrispis, Heinz its ketchup, Campbell's its soups, Lipton its tea, Nestlé its coffee, Hardeez's its sauces, Coronado its jams, Adams its Chiclets, Del Monte its peas, Clemente its pickled chiles, Ibarra its tuna, Bimbo its bread, Mundet its Sidral, French its mustard, and Buitoni its raviolis. Like a liquid painting by Andy

Warhol the supermarkets emptied through the hands of Matamoros's mobs: IT ALL BELONGS TO YOU, IT'S ALL YOURS, IT WAS ALL TAKEN AWAY FROM YOU, TAKE IT BACK! THE VIRGIN BLESSES YOU! the voice of the cassette rang out, the voice of the truth, a voice that was real even if it was on tape, a persuasive voice, there among the stolen chickens and the steaks laid over the eyes of the poor the way Veronica laid her cloth over Christ's eyes and the eggs snatched up with passion, then bobbled, and then smashed on the floor. Matamoros's voice splits the air, the light, the corrupt velocity of the night lighted up with mercury in the galleries: Aurrerá, SUMESA, Commercial Mexicana; like an animated Warhol picture (and my father in the middle of this fiesta of plunder, driving the van without knowing if what was happening was good or bad, was able to think of my mother, wish she were sitting next to him, confess that he would have wanted to have her there with him, how could I sacrifice you to my vanity, to the conquest of Penny López, and end up sucked dry by her mom, Mrs. Dracula! Man, are you an asshole, Angel Palomar y Fagoaga: alone in the multitude, he wished he could take my mother Angeles's hand and ask her forgiveness), and instead the cold hand that seized his belonged to a very young but very emaciated face under the funerary lights of the supermarket, the shadows of fear under those eyes, the sunken cheeks, the deep creases at the corner of her eyes and mouth: and she was only thirteen years old! Colasa Sánchez grabbed my father's hand in the middle of the chaos in the invaded supermarket and implored him:

"Let me be your girl again."

"No, Colasa."

"Pretty please?"

"Frankly I appreciate my John Thomas too much. I didn't know how much I loved it until it came up against your nether teeth, baby."

"Let me be your rug."

"Sure, a bear rug with nice sharp teeth."

"Your dog. Let me be your dog."

"Right, my little pit bull."

"Just a shadow between your life and mine."

"But you bite! Your bite is definitely worse than your bark!"

"All I want is to adore you. Let me."

"What happened? I thought you hated me."

"I did, because you killed my gringo."

"*I* killed your gringo?"

"That tall, really handsome blond. You set the coyotes on him. He really knew how to screw me, even if he had to use a stick so I wouldn't bite him. All I did was splinter the stick."

"So that's how it works?"

"We all work things out the best we can."

"But even if you don't hate me anymore, your daddy sure does. But it's okay, any port in a storm!"

"But who says I don't hate him, too?"

"Why would you?"

"Take a good look at me, my love, just look: I'm totally screwed. He didn't give me anything I need to get married: no dowry: no plane tickets, no toothpaste, no parabolic antenna, nothing! An outcast bride, that's me!"

"Castrating, too."

"There have been other devouring women," she said in falsetto, the poor, bored girl. "They called other women that and they made a big deal of them!"

"That was metaphoric devouring."

"Well, look here, my boy. I see you're all alone. You don't have to put a thing in me, I promise, no inserts, no deserts. There are other ways of making each other happy. Let me be your barnacle. Let me hang around with you. I swear I won't be a bother. I know people. I know the country. You know my little defect. We'll need each other. We don't have anyone else!"

My father admitted the validity of these arguments, and against his better judgment, he accepted Colasa Sánchez's company during the revolution taking place that night and in the days to come. It was a way of resigning himself, without being alone.

4

Without asking permission, the Toluca road parachutists—
the homeless who had "parachuted" into vacant lots or
abandoned buildings—took a detour through Las Lomas
del Sol and hurled themselves against the fence around
Ulises López's mansion: We want the slut! they shouted, We want
the slut! and Ulises's bodyguards started shooting, surprised when the
fence fell, but when all is said and done, the philosophy of the good
bodyguard is "Do you really think I'm going to give my life to save
the boss?" And away they ran, while the squatters shouted, Burn the
bitch who burned us, death to the murderess, and inside the house
astonishment and confusion scattered one and all: the smell of flames
wafted into the nostrils of the superminister in his office, and he said
to himself, well, here it is, what we always feared, and he tried to
prepare a convincing statement, assume a dignified pose. What would
he say to them? What would he do, he couldn't hide, he couldn't
be a coward, but could he be brave and clever simultaneously? Ulises
López was profoundly confused; he was the master of doing what he
shouldn't do and his political success consisted of doing nothing but
disguising it as action in order to conceal his only real activity, which
was piling up cash: what was he going to say to these deadbeats who
were coming up the Guggenheim-style staircase shouting and waving
their torches: Listen, I only appropriated what was superfluous, not
what was necessary. I left that to you. Listen, I was once poor like
you and now just look at me; no, not that; and not the stuff about
being a self-made man, no one ever gave me a free tortilla. No: how
would he explain to them that in reality he, Ulises López, the nice
millionaire from Chilpancingo, in reality had done nothing, that
everything they saw here was, well, like winning the lottery, something undeserved, something as unexpected as a miracle, an answered
prayer; no, that wouldn't work (the noise got closer) and they would
never understand that his passivity was more subtle, exemplary, and
refined: Ulises *got to be* a millionaire and *got to be* a minister knowing
how not to do things and by *not doing them*, but who would forgive
that? Who would answer his most secret question now that their fists

were beating on his mahogany door, those questions that followed him wherever he went, hanging over his head like the sword of Damocles: Do I deserve to be admired by others? Do I deserve to be loved? Do I perhaps love and admire those who love and admire me? And the admirable mahogany door (thanks to my architect, Diego Villaseñor!) did not break under their fists, so Don Ulises had time, he was going to tell them, Look now, there is no contradiction between public and private interests, my interests are the interests of the people, of the nation, of the fatherland! Then he was shocked to see the spears piercing his door, the pointy pickets of the fence around his house, and now they were splintering his fine door, with an oceanic roar succeeding every thrust.

He'd give them back as good as he got: "Stop! You don't need a chain saw to cut butter! Everybody in Mexico has been through this office! They did me favors! I did them favors! What do you want from me? Everything's possible when we have peace!"

He was babbling; but how was he going to respond when the door fell and Ulises López saw the detested faces. He could not dissemble, he hated them, hated them for being dark-skinned, filthy, smelly, toothless, their hair a mess, resentful, vengeful, slow on the uptake, thick-bodied, out of fashion, screwed from the time they were born, he hated them and was going to do nothing to get on their good side. Are you kidding? he was going to shout when they threw themselves on him after admiring him a second and seeing that it was really Ulises López, the one from the posters and the electoral photos, and the TV news: at the exact instant their lances nailed him to his bookcase, right between the complete works of Vilfredo Pareto and the campaign speeches of Homero Fagoaga, Don Ulises was about to shout these last words:

"I was a shark and I'll be a shark again!"

Dragged along by the mob, forced to get out of the Van Gogh and join them, with Colasa hanging on to his shirttails, bewildered and tormented, and, ultimately, fascinated when he realized where he was, at the foot of the majestic, Guggenheimic staircase of the López family, my father watched her descend: the crowd with its lances and torches in hand stopped and Lucha Plancarte de López descended, for once as majestic as her staircase, wrapped in her rose-colored peignoir with matching boas at cuffs and neck and her stiletto-heeled

shoes tipped in pink satin and with tassels on their toes and a gold
orchid around her neck and her robe tightly fastened at the waist and
with her breasts like a bull's horns, proud, tauromachic, poised for
the last corrida, and with her sulky cat in her arms, the cat that licked
the hairs off her cunt: like Gloria Swanson in *Sunset Boulevard*, that
same crepuscular videocassette image is what my father saw in Lucha
López's insane dignity, Lucha, who had attacked the squatters' camps
on her properties on the Toluca road, setting them on fire, and now
she dared to face retribution, the eye-for-an-eye, Asiatic revenge of
Hammurabi right here in Las Lomas del Sol, in the high fortress of
her security and comfort. For an instant her eyes met those of my
father, who had screwed her so well for more than a month right
here, and only then did Doña Lucha seem to lose her nerve, but in
her eyes my father saw only a fleeting nostalgia for pleasure. What
remained permanently, like a longing that became more and more
real with each second, was a small-town street shaded by pines and
lined with white houses, tranquil plazas and cool mountains: Chilpancingo, Chilpancingo bore Lucha Plancarte de López to her death
with dignity, perhaps the only moment of dignity she had in her life,
and Angel, my father, covered his eyes when they set fire to her boas
and her satin and Colasa Sánchez next to him hugged his waist and
began to cry. The spoiled cat screeched as well and jumped in flames
away from his mistress.

The Ayatollah forbade nothing: it was forbidden to forbid, as it
was in Paris in May '68. Now the Ayatollah was going to prove it
right here in the house of Superminister Ulises López and his wife
Lucha Plancarte de . . . and their little girl the prom-queen Princess
Penélope López. The crowd drew aside to let him pass, between the
pincushion corpse of Ulises and the charred body of Lucha, and he
ritually intoned sacred chants, having been trained and advised by
the Pygmalionish Chilean Concha Toro:

"Liberated from time! Liberated from the body! What will happen,
brothers and sisters, if they are set free? What will they do with their
time? What will they do with their bodies?"

He didn't see Angel, but in Ulises López's devastated house everything was happening simultaneously, theater in the round, theater
without footlights, theater and its double; then, on that same staircase
of death, appeared the deluxe chef Médoc d'Aubuisson wearing a
liberty cap and a ripped shirt, singing "La Carmagnole" as loud as

he could, Ça ira, Ça ira, les aristocrates à la lanterne, but no one knew French or had ever heard of the Bastille, so they beat him up, and next to my father a familiar hand pulled on his sleeve, and my father twisted around in the crowd; it wasn't Colasa anymore, she'd been displaced, disappeared, swallowed up by the tide: it was Homero Fagoaga! Homero Fagoaga alive, dressed strangely, wearing a hat with bells and a ruff that reminded my father for an instant of his favorite, forgotten poet Quevedo:

> Into the water, swimmers,
> Swimmers into the water.
> A well-shaved shark
> Is in these parts.

In addition he had on a Roman toga that wrapped his slightly thinner body, as if death itself could not take ten pounds off him, not even that, the phantasmagoric Uncle Homero. My scourge, my nemesis! My disaster! whimpered Angel Palomar, desperately seeking even the support of Colasa Sánchez amid the mob that was now completely out of hand. In the pool shaped like the U.S.A., scores of people were urinating, adding their tears to the sea. At the dog track, the racing hounds were first set free and admired, then compared with the mutts from the Mexican slums that dragged their teats around, castrated, tangled in their own filth and sickness, their eyes infinitely covered with grime, and, as a result, the greyhounds were abominated, damn hounds probably eat better than we do, throw gasoline on them, set them on fire, they lived better than we do, kill them! And in flames the greyhounds, following a strange instinct, kept on running around the track, will-o'-the-wisps, and smoking muzzles, barking until they died:

"Weeds never die, do they, illustrious nephew? As the Maiden of Orléans said or might have said on a rising occasion to the one who had a better time of it than your beloved Princess Penny, hahaha. Look at the Ayatollah! Remember him? Remember him from the Malinaltzin highway exit? Remember how he beat us up? Remember how he screwed your pregnant wife? Hahaha." Homero was laughing in a new style, professionally, festively, as if this were his new role: to laugh. "The best is yet to come! It was I who put this idea into the head of Our Guide!"

The Ayatollah? Our Guide? His schoolmate Matamoros Moreno?

Could a frustrated writer reach any height in Mexico? Hadn't Uncle Homero died when he fell from the balcony of his penthouse as a result of Uncle Fernando's efforts?

"Tell that nearsighted fool of a dwarf that it would take more than a second-string pseudo-Mazatec witch doctor to finish off Homero Fagoaga Labastida Pacheco y Montes de Oca!" said Homero, pointing to himself with an eternally sausage-thick finger, disabusing his nephew once and for all of the illusion that he was dealing with a ghost that resembled his deceased uncle. "Destiny is more unexpected than any logic, more of a bastard than luck itself, and wider than any individual life," he proclaimed now, with the burning grey-hounds as a backdrop. "Listen to me and just see if you can contradict me: under my balcony, a little circus had set up, and the circus had a tent that broke my fall and then tore, dropping me nervously but safely onto a flexible, playful safety net, and I bounced around in it for about a minute and a half, as naked as the day I was born, my distinguished if rather diminished nephew, and the audience laughed, applauded, and made so much of me that the owner of the circus, a certain Bubble Gómez, an albino ex-truck driver whose lifelong dream was to own a circus, signed me up right on the spot, as Lana Turner, the never-to-be-forgotten starlet, might have said when she was discovered at the marmoreal soda fountain where she was in-gesting a cloying ice-cream soda—cherry—and wearing a very tight sweater; he introduced me to his patrons, the Ayatollah Matamoros and the singer Concha Toro, now transformed into Galvarina Don-oso, of Chilean and aristocratic origin, as that mad geographer Don Benjamín Subercaseaux was apt to invoke on nitrate evenings of cuecas and lilacs, as in turn might have been said by . . ."

"And what about this getup?" said my father, recovering the floor. "You look like a fifth-rate Rigoletto."

"Momus!" exclaimed Uncle Homero. "I am King Momus of this stupendous carnival!"

"Stupendous? They've emptied the supermarkets where you used to sell your poisonous baby food! They've ruined you, you barrel-assed old fart!"

"Careful with the insults now." Homero Fagoaga laughed, pointing with his sausage finger in a superior gesture. "The oven's not ready for cakes like that; now try to translate and export that proverb." He laughed with even greater pleasure.

"My oven is no place for your muffins. How's that?"

"I mean: all sacrifices are worthwhile! My protectors have proclaimed me king of laughter!"

"Mock-king, you fool."

"As you wish, Angelito: but my scepter is real in a revolution that is, after all, carnivalesque, a revolution of mad laughter, finally, my anarchic but idiotic nephew, finally! A horizontal Mexican revolution, everything for everyone and everyone for everything, here in the land of the vertical Aztec Empire followed by the vertical Spanish Empire followed by the vertical, centralized, patrimonial, and pyramidal Republic, the inversion of the hierarchy." Homero Fagoaga laughed loudly, pushing my father all the time toward the replica of the first floor of Bloomingdale's, where the holy mob was touching everything without understanding what those things they'd never seen or even dreamed were, perfumes, and more perfumes, Estée Lauder, Givenchy, Togarama, dresses and more dresses, Saint Laurent, Valentino, Cio Cio Sanel, riding clothes, clothes for hunting in Africa, sailing off Cape Cod, mountain climbing in Tibet, vaginal spermicide with the color and taste of strawberry, grapes, carob, camellia, cherry. How do you use this, how, when, what for? They passed alongside the destructive fury that broke and burned everything in Penny's personal sanctuary, where Penny stopped looking like a nun and started looking like a whore, but where was Penny in all this? "The inversion of the hierarchy!" Homero Fagoaga laughed, disguised as the King of Laughter, Prince of Comedy, Lord of Levity, Sultan of Smiles: Ah, what laughter, what crazy laughter! To think they began with me, you all begin with me, little nephew, you and your grimy proletarian friends and your pregnant, well-fornicated little wife— fornicated by my Luminous Guide—you began by making fun of me, oranges, pears, and figs, of course, hahaha, magnifying glass, Shogun limousine, remember? Jell-O baths, anything goes to make fun of Homero Fagoaga, sadistic Chinese and cow yokes and bottle caps in my dessert, why not, killing my Tomasito, even that, the destruction of my electoral campaign, my humiliation by that ragged bum Benítez, ha! my genes and not his Hegels are going to win, not your gelatines: laugh at me now, fools, laugh at the King of Laughter and the inversion of hierarchies and see what's before your eyes, beloved nephew, look carefully and remember that

FAGOAGA NEVER LOSES
AND WHAT HE LOSES HE SNATCHES BACK!

5

Matamoros Moreno rehearsed his every gesture in front of Concha Toro's dressing-room mirror; the singer showed him how to turn movement into ritual: she taught him how to look at his audience, raise one arm or both, take a step forward then stop dramatically, smile, throw his head back, get angry, speak, be silent. Matamoros went through the extremes of pride and trampled humility in front of that mirror, where Concha Toro purged herself of her own histrionic frustrations. Little by little, Matamoros Moreno, who in Concha's company had discovered a surprising new kind of lovemaking, full of nuances and refinements (even secrets) he had never known before, transcended the gestures and the rituals and persuaded himself in his innermost being that what he was doing (outside the dressing room, for the public, for the people) was the external manifestation of what he was within: a solitary man who had stored up a power that was only now revealing itself. His gratefully accepted sexual encounters with Concha-Dolly-María Inez (for which she was thankful, now that she was fifty, or perhaps a bit older) revealed to Matamoros the dark and blind energy he had held in reserve, which only now burst forth. The only condition was that he believe what he said: the Ayatollah Matamoros had to speak, move, and be seen with a total faith in what he said, the way he moved, and in how he looked. He would tell the masses that followed him that "faith is faith. It can't be proven, insulted, judged, or even jailed." Let them think about this; just in case, he said during the weeks in which he had hastily, secretly gathered together those bands of official thugs—those falcons—who had been scattered after their last operation way back in 1972, a police corps disbanded ever since those remote days of moral renovation, bodyguards left unemployed in the wake of the exodus of the rich to Houston, Miami, and Los Angeles. But he had to convince even these swine that now they had to act out of faith, that the policeman or bodyguard who joined the movement had to do what he did for something greater than they had ever done before: like the thieves and fire-eaters, like the beggars and squatters, they all had to seek and feel the same thing:

"Why follow me? So you can become new again. So you can save yourselves. So you can have good or bad luck as long as you have a destiny. Don't just sit there like a bump on a log!"

He had to believe it himself so that they would believe it: that's what he learned in the amorous tricks of the Chilean big Moma who was so wise, so sexy, and such a mistress of sexual secrets the brutal Matamoros had never practiced. In her arms, he discovered the absolute realization of everything he had written and tried to publish through his double-dealing fellow student Angel Palomar y Fagoaga, whose doom Matamoros had already pronounced: it would be a slow death, by inches, in the Grand Inquisitorial tradition: he'd already screwed Palomar's wife, he'd already beaten Palomar's relatives, he'd already buggered Palomar himself, just so he'd learn something about length, thickness, and nightmares that become reality. Matamoros was sure that he could achieve his own destiny, but that destiny included two things: to achieve total revenge on Angel Palomar for having frustrated his literary ambitions, and to prove before the entire world that he, Matamoros Moreno, was worth more than Angel Palomar: the proof would be that the people would follow him and not Palomar, dream about him and not Palomar, would love and hate him, not Palomar. Matamoros Moreno did not shudder as he came in Concha Toro's mouth because he had to be believed and followed, but in the instant when he was dropping his load between Concha's teeth (thinking as he did so about his little daughter Colasa, as a black counterpoint to the act he was involved in, a dream of the act: father and daughter), in that instant he told himself that no one would believe in him or follow him if he didn't believe in himself . . . Matamoros followed by Matamoros: the demon of hope could move the world, accompanied by its acolytes, passion and ambition, only if in that moment Matamoros Moreno realized (he gave himself: ceded) that "I have another man buried inside me, oh pretty Mama, there was another man with me and I didn't know it; why didn't you tell me, Mommy, don't you love me?"

After that internal and external orgasm, Matamoros Moreno could say what he wanted and he convinced all the unemployed, the lumpen, the deformed, the mad, the bodyguards and cops, the rockaztec groupies, he convinced everyone, intellectuals, housewives, Hipi Toltec and Orphan Huerta, even Baby Ba, who left Egg in the company of my mother and went to follow the Ayatollah. And what about me, Baby, don't you love me anymore?

"Don't let your hatred rot inside you. Get cracking. Look over there. Look at the city. It belongs to you."

"The Mexican hero is neither proletarian nor Communist. He belongs to Guadalupe, and in my hand, brother, I hold a power that is neither of the left nor of the right, but one that reveals my own nature, natch."

"Stop living a life of anguish. Join us."

"What do you get by slicing each other up? Get cracking."

"Don't hate yourself. There are better things to hate. Look at that house. Look at that store. Look at that car. Why don't they belong to you? It's up to you. Take them!"

"Blessed are those that walk the face of the earth in its dangerous moments!"

"Mexico should drown herself in the ocean of confusion in order that it be reborn on the beach of hope."

"I want a world in which prayers come true! Come with me, old woman, pray as you walk, pray."

They believed everything because he believed it: in bed with Concha, he let the other penetrate him while he penetrated the woman. His body resists. His body tells him that it is going to go mad just so that the other man inhabiting him can come out of him. He resists: his skin has always been his own, there was nothing behind it, nothing more inside. Yes: another man is emerging from within him, but his body resists and his mind resists even more: you will not be a saint, you will be a criminal and a madman. But the other man is already his spirit. He didn't realize that the spirit within him also had a body. This didn't matter to the body of the other man: he fed on the environment, on tension, on fear, on the frustration, self-loathing, disillusion: all this fed the spirit of the other within him, and the funniest thing is that it transformed bad tensions into good tensions. During the long nights of cabaret and sex with Concha Toro, when, after the pleasure of music and sex, they prepared the cassettes that Colasa—terribly diligent, animated (perhaps more so than her father) by a desire for vengeance against that fop Angel Palomar (an object of terrible hatred, you've turned out, oh, padre mío!)—brought early every morning to the Trucking Center, whence they were scattered all over what remained of the Honorable Republic of Mexico, the tension of resentment, frustration, the colossal screwing that was Mexico and Mexicans humiliated and handed over to disgrace from birth until death, became passion, dream, hope, movement. Only one thing remained the same; the spirit moves because of the tension surrounding it: it yearns for catastrophe.

Matamoros Moreno let the other come out to fuse with him in body and soul. That's how the Ayatollah Matamoros was born.

He was born to impress and defeat my defeated and insignificant father, Angel Palomar. Dear Dad, what's happened to you? Why don't we share our imagination any longer, you and I? When are we going to get together again, dear old Dad?

Thus he dragged all of us into his passionhope.

That same man, whatever he might be and however he might be, was now in a brilliant space of lights and reflections from silver and crystal, holding down a girl on the perfume counter in a replica of Bloomingdale's seeing herself reflected in the thousand mirrors and the thousand eyes of that night. This ritual was expected of him, the spiritual guide was the carnal guide, the revolution did not exalt the spirit at the expense of the flesh: sex was part of the passion and the hope of the revolution for all, in which the perennially frustrated desires of Mexicans would be gloriously brought to fruition: Screw the boss's daughter! Fuck the unreachable princess! Nail Don Ulises López's daughter! Bring the impossible close to the possible in one ferocious and vibrant blow! Matamoros Moreno owed it to himself and owed *this* to all those who stared at him that August night in Las Lomas del Sol: to take off his cape, unbutton his fly, take out his rod, and bring it closer to the open legs of the valley-girl princess, who managed to murmur at the edge of the deaf-mute idiocy that would afflict her from then on:

"You can look but you can't touch. You're ugly, poor, and a prole. I'm not for you."

That *I'm not for you* was the code murmured and repeated by everyone, which made everyone participate vicariously in Matamoros's pleasure taken on Penny, who began to scream more, more, more, don't take it out, don't come, wait for me, more, more, more, she staring and the luminous guide looking at my father, the terrible joke jabbing him like a spear is the stare of my father hugged, naturally, by Uncle Homero Fagoaga, giggling: "A penis for Penny!"

6

Colonel Inclán raised his fingers, knotty as mesquite roots, to his eyes, threatening everyone with something no one had ever seen: the eyes he always hid behind those pitch-black glasses. Neither Secretary Federico Robles Chacón nor President Jesús María y José Paredes had ever seen Colonel Inclán's eyes and the two of them trembled slightly at the prospect. The mere idea of facing his gaze frightened them, and the colonel knew it. With a smile like a death's-head, he dropped his clenched hand: *If not now, when?* Hadn't he told the President that the time still hadn't come? Well, now it had! The damn bodyguards weren't worth a shit, they'd all either run away or joined up with the Coca-Cola or aymapepper or whatever that faith healer was calling himself, but they'd been killing the colonel's best people, there were cops hanging off the lampposts, goddamn it! How far were they willing to let this thing go before they started shooting, how far, Mr. President, how far?

Colonel Inclán and Federico Robles Chacón exchanged ugly looks: Robles Chacón quietly stated that his generation had grown up in a flood of unpunished crimes that undermined the very thing they were attempting to strengthen: the Mexican State, the Party of the Revolution, and the controlled working class. The public image of the president, the PRI, the CTM, turned to dust just as their power was turned to mush by the memory of October 2, 1968, when the students were killed in the Tlateloco massacre, or by Corpus Christi in 1972, when they were again slaughtered on the Alvarado Bridge, or by May 10, 1990, when the strike by Mexican mothers was broken up when the Perisur mall was turned into a free fire zone. All that had to be paid for, said Robles, because the system no longer knew how to do with the opposition what it had always done, namely, to coopt it and to incorporate it into the system. These failures were very costly because they were debilitating both internally and externally: the mutilated fatherland was the price they paid for internal political inability and was not the result of external diplomatic ability.

"You're a fast talker and you think a lot," said the colonel, "but

I want to know what to do with my machine guns now that the time is ripe to use them."

"You go out and get hold of that Matamoros guy," said Robles Chacón.

"What are you going to do, son?" exclaimed the President, who saw in Federico Junior the resurrection of Federico Senior, the man who had launched Paredes's political and financial career back in the forties.

Inclán answered for him: "I'll bring you your nut, and then I'm going to go to bed, hugging the pillow where my mom—may she rest in peace—laid her head down for the last time before she died. All right: calm down, gentlemen, there's light at the end of the tunnel. Let me sleep on it. But . . ."

The colonel stalked ominously out, and Federico made his point once more to the President. The chain of crimes must be broken: we need imagination and memory. I offered a symbol as a sacrament between memory and hope, said Robles to the President: were they the saviors? What do you think, Mr. President? Didn't we win the game down in Acapulco when those asshole kids saved our butts from the Guerrero political crisis or when we liquidated Ulises López's (may God have mercy on his soul) power and the colonel's mom? News travels fast. Power remains. Or it should remain. Mr. President, be careful. This is a key play.

They didn't speak for a long while, and then the minister said: I don't know if you understand me, sir, and frankly I don't care. I have to talk. I have to say something: one thing in particular. Almost seven years ago, I was a young volunteer during the September 19 earthquake. We didn't need the PRI, a president, or anything else. We organized almost by instinct, I mean, all the young people in the neighborhood, or several neighborhoods. We took scooters, vans, pickups, whatever we could find, shovels, picks, bandages, one guy joined up with us carrying a bottle of Mercurochrome. What moved us that day? The sense of solidarity, a humanitarian feeling, the need to save our neighbors. We realized they were our neighbors! Do you understand me, sir? That morning, the man next to me was my fellow man. I was another fellow man. We went beyond institutions. But once the heroic moment passed, we went back to wondering what moved us that day. And our answer was something else. We acted because we were a generation of educated Mexicans, forty years of education, of reading, going to films, talking with everyone, studying Mexican history, whatever; it all came to the surface that painful morning. Civil society transcended the state. But it was the state that created civil society. That is our political conundrum, sir. We owe too much to the revolution to trade it in, no matter how old, smelly, or ugly it's become, for adventure, whim, nothing. They say the system coopted me. I was a volunteer facing up to what was judged to be the disorder of a fearful government devoid of imagination. Today I'm Minister of State in a government that is neither better nor worse than all the others: your government. Our country's history is its frustrated youth. But, despite everything, that's what a mature country is: a corrupt country. And yet, sir, no matter how much I justify myself honestly, because you listen so to me patiently, sir, because you were a friend of my father, I want to tell you that the only good thing I ever did in my life I did that morning of the earthquake. I would exchange all my current power for the satisfaction of digging at a mountain of rubble and pulling out a little girl buried there alive and only a week old.

7

This—but these are not his exact words—is what Minister Federico Robles Chacón said to the Ayatollah Matamoros Moreno when they brought him to Robles Chacón's office at the intersection of Insurgentes, Nuevo León, and the Viaduct:

"It all depends on you—we can postpone death and fulfill our destiny. Look, Mr. Holy Man, you're not the first of your kind around here, don't believe it for a minute, and all of you end up the same way. Open your eyes: you reach into your hat for a paradise and you pull out a hell."

Matamoros looked at him with that carbonizing gaze, like a black diamond, the one that had proven so effective on stage. But the rational Robles Chacón decided that Bela Lugosi's cinematic stare was much worse: where does he get off with this Dracula bit? At the same time, he did not want to laugh at Matamoros; Federico Robles Chacón did not laugh at losers, especially when they still had direct control over a mob on the loose all over the city. Besides, why plead with him? What the Mexican Ayatollah had to understand was that the surprise effect of his movement had passed, the spontaneous fiesta was over, the López family had been murdered in exemplary fashion, taking the rap for all the families of government functionaries who'd gotten rich in the past seventy years.

The cops who should have been hung had been hung.

The supermarkets that should have been looted had been looted.

The permissive instant had passed, and now—the minister gestured toward the city—now look, Mr. Holy Man, and don't play dumb: there are five helicopters flying over your divine mobs; each chopper contains two machine guns; the elite battalions of the presidential guard are posted on every corner, surrounding every plaza, standing guard on every rooftop with their M-16s in their hands. Take a good look at how long an insurrection can last in Mexico, Mr. Holy Man! But you've managed to wake up a savage Mexico and what I'm offering you is the chance to be useful and glorious as opposed to being useless and dead. Look, Mr. Holy Man, I'm making you a proposition: let's talk it over. You give me something, I give you something. What do you say?

How many chances do I have to give you the right answer? asked the Ayatollah, bruised and blackened by the flames, but smiling like an idiot, his teeth arranged like corn-on-the-cob, and bound up with who knew how much myth, fable, and atavism.

Three, smiled the Secretary of State, nowhere nearly as charismatic but far more astute.

I want the entire cabinet to parade through the streets, from the Zócalo to La Villa, each minister carrying a cross and singing the hymn to the Blessed Sacrament.

Okay, said Robles Chacón. You, in turn, will have to use your people to kidnap all those who have drained the country of dollars and hold them until they return the $300 billion they've taken out of Mexico since 1975. He said it affably.

I'll go along with that, muttered Matamoros Moreno with a sly sparkle in his eye, a gesture of craftiness that the Chilean María Inez, Dolly, Concha, Galvarina would not have allowed him to make had she been there next to him, dangerous, dearest, don't go too far, don't stretch your luck too far, it would be damn silly to . . . But the Ayatollah had already allowed that other man he had within to push his way out and fulfill his destiny. For a fleeting instant he saw himself from outside, as if he were looking at someone else, and he did not see two men, only one, although he could see a wider destiny than that allotted him by circumstance: he was an orphan, and that already meant having half a destiny or a destiny like no other, Matamoros said to himself. He never knew his father or mother, only the orphanage, his scholarship, the Heroes of '82 school, his frustrated literary vocation, his early love affair with a woman who was as anonymous as he was (he could no longer remember her face) in a dark place and the woman always in the dark, saying don't try to see me, don't ever try to see me, because if you do I'll stop being excited: an intensely anonymous woman, no, there will be no melodramatic revelations here, Colasa Sánchez is the daughter of Anónima Sánchez, Nobody, Personne, the Daughter of Sánchez, no one had a daughter with her, he always knew that the daughter would be his and with him, a young stud of a father at fifteen years of age, a writer frustrated by the envy of Angel Palomar, a man hallucinated by the idea of myth as immediate substitute for imagination. Myth is ready-to-wear imagination, as his Chilean girlfriend jokingly said: the tribe's imagination. His daughter Colasa incarnated it, she was no fantasy, myths lived and Colasa had a vagina dentata. She should have, to be transformed from an invalid into a valid political and economic asset. They should have made a fortune with that thing. It didn't turn out that way, but there can be no doubt the idea illuminated Matamoros Moreno's imagination. From a hilltop outside Acapulco, he saw the anarchic destruction of the port, and he told Colasa: "Not that way, not that way." Myths were something else, not anarchy but love, the desire for order, morality, knowing what could be counted on, understanding that the oldest traditions were the only ones that had survived and that could unite this people and make it love itself, make it feel noticed, respected, the center of its own history. Traveling around the country with his gang of workers, he of all people reduced to such a thing in the Mexico of the nineties, totally devoid of direction, when it was every man for himself and survival was the name of the game, one day here, the next somewhere else, juggler, or bricklayer, what did it matter as long as you had something to eat today, who knew what tomorrow would bring?

Matamoros Moreno fixed his terrible eyes on Federico Robles Chacón, who trembled less under those eyes than he had hearing the laughter of the mad monk on the radio and who felt that mass of people behind him, agitated, furious, gathered at the intersection where the SEPAFU offices were located, under the interminable acid rain, in the morning that always looked, as it did now, afternoon, and he told him what he had to tell him in order that he carry his destiny one step beyond, one step forward. One more step had to be taken in order to fulfill Matamoros Moreno's duplicated destiny, Matamoros, the screwed orphan who stood Columbus's egg on its end: one hundred and thirty million Mexicans are Catholics, not Communists, not PRIists, not PANists, but Guadalupeans, and thousands of people had followed him who were just waiting for someone to tell them that and to lead them.

Federico Robles Chacón scrutinized the man opposite him (he didn't dare think of him as his prisoner: Mexico was not Jerusalem and this man was not the Nazarene, nor was the minister, God forbid! Pontius Pilate) and tried to read his thoughts, to guess his feelings in that instant in which he awaited the second demand of the Mexican Ayatollah, who had invaded and interrupted Robles Chacón's project of national symbolization, his creation in the lab of a symbolic form that would replace the need for repression, sublimating it. That's why he had invented Mamadoc. He believed deeply in the ability of an enlightened minority to govern Mexico. He had no illusions, what little this country had achieved was due to a series of elites that had drawn the line, forced into submission or defeated the savage majority, that majority without direction, that barbarous majority, so much so that when they triumphed they put minorities as obscurantist and brutish as themselves in power: the anarchic ghost of Santa Anna, the nation's leading man, the cockfighter, the lady's man, the stud, transformed into a plebeian dictator, a clod, grotesque, a lackey to foreign powers, he haunted the history of Mexico like an evil omen that was constantly to be taken into account: keep the plebes out of power, no matter how noble a Zapata or a Villa might look, to preclude a reincarnation of Santa Anna. Enlightened minorities, always, right- or left-wing, conservative or liberal, Lucas Alamán or Dr. Mora, the men of the Reform: a liberal minority; the men of the Porfirio Díaz regime: a positivist minority; the men of the Revolution: a meritocracy that was much more broadly based than its predecessors, more porous, more permeable: Robles Chacón and his father, who in past centuries would have been peons chained to peasant debt, the hacienda system, and the whip, if they'd been born in 1700 or 1800, in . . . But instead they were born with the Revolution, they made it, they inherited it, and they governed instead of being governed. The price they paid was becoming themselves an enlightened minority. If they had been an anarchic majority, they would never have governed.

And now they found themselves face-to-face with the newly resurrected masses, who were once again on the move. Not for the first time, recalled Robles Chacón, not the first and not the last, but this time it was he who had to face them and the Ayatollah Matamoros. Robles Chacón knew it only too well; he read Matamoros's theatrical wink, so dramatic that it had to communicate his intention: that was his strength and his weakness as well. Matamoros Moreno was going to act out—to the death if necessary—the role he had created for himself, the role the mob had conferred upon him. He would take his chances, he wouldn't come to terms without some sort of drama, he wouldn't accept negotiation without some tragedy. Robles, son of Robles, knew it because of his millennial Mexican genes, he knew it and it tasted like bile to him because this necessary drama was going to force him to do what he did not want to do, it was going to put Mexican history to an unnecessary test, but one that was absolutely necessary for the Mexican Ayatollah's melodrama and for sacralized violence.

What I want to know, said Matamoros, is if you are really capable of murdering my people. That's my second question.

It was asked with impavid security.

The minister lowered his eyes, closed them, prayed that these things weren't really happening, that some dramatist somewhere was dictating these words to his character Matamoros, but that they weren't really his words and that he'd take them back, have second thoughts instantly. But the Ayatollah repeated, I want to know if you are capable of massacring my people, all those people supporting me down there on the street. He said it because that's what his character was supposed to say and he wouldn't have said it if that hadn't been his role.

Is that your second demand? said Robles Chacón, in total calm.

Matamoros nodded his head, still wrapped in the red kerchief, which was soiled with ash and fresh blood.

Robles Chacón simply placed his left hand on his right wrist and pressed one of the golden buttons on his wristwatch. Button, button, who's got the button? he thought, mournfully and unconsciously, leaving every level of his consciousness open to what was going to take place despite him, despite all his philosophy and politics.

Like a thunderclap in reverse, the staccato buzz of the machine guns preceded the flash of the fire burst of death and blood. Matamoros, shouting, hurling himself against the windows in the minister's office, smearing his fingerprints all over the blue glass that filtered the corrupt glare of the sun in the city "where the air is clear," saw his people rising up down there in the crowded intersection of Insurgentes, Nuevo León, and the Viaduct, his people! those who had followed him and who were there shouting freedom for our guide, set Matamoros free! He saw them fall silently like flies, the noise more and more distant, echoing through the valley morning, and the fire, by contrast, growing, mustard-colored, spreading throughout Colonia Hipódromo, toward Tacubaya and Lomas Altas, down Baja California and Colonia de los Doctores, along Parque Delta and Xola and Colonia del Valle, up Patriotismo and Colonia Nápoles, blotting out the high rose-colored sunglasses of the Hotel de México and the glass temples of the Mexican National Airline Building, fogging over Siqueiros's acrylic murals: the brownish scum hid the dying from Matamoros Moreno, the long-haul truckers and the devout little old ladies, the angry young men, the unemployed office workers, the bankrupt store owners, the deinstitutionalized lunatics—all invisible, machine-gunned, dead, their destinies now complete, at least more so than those of Matamoros Moreno and Federico Robles Chacón.

The minister didn't blink an eye. The Ayatollah shouted, save my girlfriend! save my daughter! save . . . !

Robles Chacón just laughed. So many requests! The lover, the daughter, what about that albino truck driver, a lost grandma, who was Colasa's mother? who were Matamoros Moreno's parents? the poor little orphan boy, son (of a bitch) of the morning, do you suppose that his unknown parents might be among the dead? Did he think that before he opened the doors to this bastard of a country, this savage Mexico, this sleeping tiger, did he think about that and about all those who, in addition to his daughter and his lover, came to his mind? Did he dare to condemn the albino, for example? Or was Matamoros Moreno incapable of thinking about death in the singular, was he incapable of saying "Colasa's death," "Galvarinaconchadol-lymanés's death," "the albino's death," was that it? That's what Robles Chacón icily said to him as he imagined all those victims. But Robles Chacón did not fool himself for an instant: he, Federico Robles, fils, was the principal victim of this day of blood, just one more on a long list of bloodstained days, wasn't that right? Can you only imagine collective death, the death you asked me for, you bastard?

We know everything, said Robles Chacón, after a pause. He smiled. Didn't you want to save that overstuffed Judas, Don Homero Fagoaga, your King Momus? How many of your people did you want to save? All he had to do was push a button on his Mikado wrist radar to show that he could sentence all of them to death . . .

The minister let the Ayatollah stew in his own juices for an instant and then he protected him with his own arm, a buddy's arm that he put around his shoulders in order to hug him close, the minister would give him anything, not one more murder, if the Ayatollah agreed to appear on the night of September 15, 1992, on the balcony of the National Palace, at Mamadoc's side, not one death more if he did them the favor of illustrating and incarnating the reality of national unity. The Ayatollah would not have to request amnesty for those who might not accept the deal or call him a Judas, and Robles Chacón didn't point out that those who might not respect the deal hadn't been taken into account: it was not necessary to worry about these details, there was no reason to humiliate anyone, facts are facts, I'll put myself to the test: the Ayatollah looked down on the bloody intersection, the people running for their lives, the weeping, the wail of ambulances, scattered shots, and the noise of water being sprayed over everything, as if a gigantic oilcloth throat couldn't manage to swallow all the dirty water running over the surface of the bloody city.

That water pump was like the city's heart, my father said to himself, and in a bakery he found Hipi and the Orphan happily distributing loaves of bread, rolls, Campeche cakes and powdered-sugar cookies, crackers, and pastries to the mob, who would have taken them even if our two friends weren't there giving them out, but the two of them were so happy to be taking part in things, as if they were washing themselves clean of all the grime and disaster of Aca, and the ma-nipulation they'd learned of later, and now they thought they were acting on their own but this time for everyone, and they shouted to my father, join in! we need more bakeries like this one! they laughed, it was their mission: let them eat bread!

Angel Palomar shook his head.

Would they meet later with Egg and Angeles over at his grand-parents' house?

Who knows, let's see, my father shrugged his shoulders.

8

 On the night of the Ayatollah, Mexico City once again witnessed everything it could bear: only the memory (extinct) of the fall of the Aztec capital or the forgetting (voluntary) of the memory of the earthquake of September 19, 1985, could be compared to this new disaster. Nevertheless, amid the smoke and blood of the defeat of Tenochtitlán or in the thick of the devastation of the collapse and burning that had put the capital into mourning seven years before, no one ever saw two figures like these, who are now running in a low crouch, their heads covered with woolen shawls, virtually smeared along the leprous walls, between Avenida Durango and Calle Génova; they stop on every corner, look around, move along if they detect no danger, retreat if they see or suspect any.

"I know that all we've ever wanted is peace and quiet," said Capitolina, delicately—but showing her disgust—detouring her sister around a mass of slaughtered animals in front of the aqueduct on Avenida Chapultepec.

"Peace first and finally quiet, and in the second place . . ." began Farnesia, but her sister interrupted her, excuse me Farnecita, excuse me, little sister, for exposing you to this violence, I who have so faithfully tried to fulfill my promise to our dear parents that I would protect and defend you. Careful now, don't step on that dead cat . . .

"In the first place, let's set the record straight, finally zero catastrophes, in the third place no crisis," whimpered Farnesia.

"We thought things would always turn out that way . . ."

"Just as our dear parents taught us . . ."

"May they rest in peace . . ."

"In peace, amen, in peace!"

But stealing a look filled with palpable fear at the city of quickly dug trenches overflowing with dead bodies, the rows of men hung from the lampposts along Paseo de la Reforma in front of the Social Security Building, the burning of the fried-food stands along the avenue and the shacks of the jugglers and fire-eaters on the traffic islands, the Fagoaga sisters finally looked at each other out of the corners of their eyes and burst into raucous laughter until they had to quickly cover their mouths, the small and decisive Capitolina with her pudgy little hand, the tall and tremulous Farnesia with her black shawl: they had always imagined the worst—a lie, a lie: they had always fervently desired the worst: accidents, sickness, revolution, earthquakes, death . . . And here it was! No one would escape! All of them ground into dust! This was the finishing touch to a decade of disasters, and it's true the sisters both believed what their wise and experienced older brother, Dr. Homero, told them: all that was needed was a little push, barely a flick of a fingertip to cast down the abysmal metropolis: its destiny was now its image, there was no need for any soothsayer to cut open a bird, and columns of fire, weeping women, or mirrors that reflected the stars in broad daylight were all unnecessary.

How many times had the Misses Fagoaga made a dinner unpleasant by warning an unwary guest:

"If I were you, I wouldn't eat that, sir."

That's how they survived.

Until today. Bankruptcy and devaluations didn't touch them: they had property, savings, and high interest here, dollar accounts across the frontier. The earthquake of '85, which flattened their neighborhood, providentially left them unscathed, as it had their brother Homero: God loves the Fagoagas! The evidence speaks for itself! Until today, until today when death became general not out of error or natural catastrophe or divine will, now death was policy, enacted from above, and Capitolina was realistic enough to imagine that not even they would survive the disaster.

An ambulance, its siren howling, passed along the deserted avenue. It was dawn, the hour chosen by the Fagoaga sisters to carry out their final mission. Walking rapidly in fits and starts, feeling their velvet slippers grow thinner and wetter as they walked on the dust of the footpath soaked with blood and Coca-Cola, sighing, they crossed

Florencia Street, until they turned onto Génova and headed toward the modest one-story residence that belonged to General Rigoberto Palomar, which was protected by the kind of iron gate found on garages, which might make the uncertain visitor confuse the house where Angel my father grew up with a vulgar shop.

The dawn negated the death of the Mexican vespers.

The morning light blazed like a pearl in a pigsty.

The air of the tree-covered mountains and the snow-covered volcanoes whisked away the layer of dust, along with the smell of blood and garbage. But soon the crystal would break again; the mask of sickness would reappear.

Capitolina and Farnesia approached the door of the general's house. General Palomar opened the door before they made even the slightest attempt to enter or knock. The old man had put on his belt, strapped his .45 around his waist, and clapped his red liberty cap on his shaved head.

Capitolina said: "We want to see the girl."

"What girl?"

"You know, the one amorously linked with our nephew."

"Does she have a name, so far as you vultures know?"

"Angeles, someone said it was."

"Well, and what do you spinsters want to find out?"

"Nothing, General, merely to ascertain the degree of her pregnancy."

"We have only come to say hello and then we'll be on our way," said Farnesia, taking note of the murderous light in my great-granddaddy's eyes.

"We have come for her," declared Capitolina, "so that she may deliver the child properly and so that the new member of our family may come into the world protected, loved, and in a Christian cradle."

"Are you saying that the devil would get him here?" Don Rigoberto laughed quietly.

"Well, that's what my little sister and I fear most."

"You'd turn him into a holy little hypocrite of a pharisee son of a bitch like you two . . ."

"Sticks and stones, General, sticks and stones!" Capitolina shrugged her shoulders. "Humph!" chimed in Farnesia.

"And in the process you'd have yourselves named heirs of the heir, the Palomar fortune would come to you, you pair of grave robbers."

"Our considerations are of a purely moral nature!" Capitolina shook her finger directly into the general's nose. Farnesia, who had eaten an extremely early breakfast in order to fortify herself for the day's vicissitudes, tried to copy her sister but gave up when she realized that on her finger there glistened a few drops of rich blackberry jam, so she quickly licked her finger instead.

"Moral my ball bearings!" shouted the general, but just then there appeared behind him, her shoulders trembling with cold, his wife, Doña Susana Rentería.

"Tell them the truth," said Great-grandmother Palomar serenely.

"You tell them."

"Angeles disappeared yesterday in the riot."

"You're hiding her from us!" Capitolina managed to shout before the general slammed the door in their faces. Farnesia, standing on the sidewalk, burst into laughter, a laughter that did not seem to be caused by the events but rather by the absence of any cause, a distant torment, a foreseeable humiliation, as if the immediate cause, the disappearance of my mother Angeles with me (quite frightened, I might add, your mercies), meant absolutely nothing to her.

Capitolina silenced her with a slap in the face: "Sniveling fool."

The elder sister turned her face toward the Paseo de la Reforma, and the younger, shocked, ran after her, wrapped in her shawl, laughingly observing that the destiny of an unmarried woman is to be a leader of monkeys in hell.

"A tour guide for monkeys!"

Both thought the same thing; both felt (I shall feel, I shall know when I feel, I shall feel when I know, I shall know) the immense pain of the lost child (that's why I feel and know: all of us fetuses are like the Corsican brothers for all those who have been born or who are about to be born): the lost child, one more, again without a child, women alone, empty houses, lost children.

They took each other by the hand and felt like dying.

Where can my child be, with his bracelet around his ankle? whimpered Farnesia.

Where can the child about to be born be? sighed Capitolina.

Where can *I* be?

9

The din of the loudspeakers was only made worse by the lugubrious silence that weighed on the city that September 1, 1992. Buoyed up by the acclamations of Congress, President Jesús María y José Paredes stood at the tribune of the National Assembly and released these messenger pigeons—or were they doves of light?—one after another:

The threats to the nation had been extinguished; the obstacles to Mexican progress had been overcome; the extremist riot had been violently repressed because it was born of violence; but the heroic actions of the police, whom we salute here and now (ovation; Colonel Inclán stands at attention, does not smile, is wearing his black glasses, the green spittle runs down his chin; he sits stiffly down), protected us from having to surrender our civil government to the armed forces: neither anarchy nor tyranny, only Mexico! Her institutions saved! Her revolution permanent! Neither order without liberty nor liberty without order, neither progress without tradition nor tradition without progress, neither justice without authority nor authority without justice! exclaimed our Chuchema at the climax of what was in effect a chiasmic delirium in Mexican politics, and he exclaimed it so loud over all the loudspeakers of the Mexican Republic (or what's left of it) that even I, within the maternal womb, heard it: Let us honor Colonel Nemesio Inclán (second ovation; this time the man in black glasses, either modest or annoyed, who knows? doesn't even stand up), who subordinated his personal ambition to the triumph of institutional order; glory to the Lady, Mother, and Doctor (she is not present; she is looking at herself in the mirror; she only shows herself to give the cry, to proclaim a contest; she neither steals nor shares the show: she, the Lady Pharaoh, works alone!), who held on high the symbols of the nation threatened by chaotic licentiousness disguised as freedom for the majority which so crudely sought to wrest from the Mexican people their own symbols, conquered with so much difficulty over five centuries of national experience. President Paredes, after excoriating the duped and criminal anarchists, topped off his speech by assuring one and all that the time for reconciliation and unity had come. He admitted that the nation had been threatened; he revealed to the astonished nation that since last January the United States Military Command (Caribbean) had asked permission to land twenty thousand Marines at Veracruz to carry out maneuvers that would put pressure on the totalitarian tyrants of Costaguana and protect the oil refineries of the Chitacam Trusteeship, threatened like mere dominos by the red tide but essential to the strategic health of the free world. Permission was granted in accordance with the prior commitments of Mexico within the Modified and Reaffirmed Inter-American Rio Treaty (MORE-RIOT), but when the time allotted for the maneuvers had passed, the twenty thousand Marines had refused to withdraw from the state of Veracruz, saying that they'd never actually been there since not a single one of them had remained longer than 175 days in Mexico, and that they would, according to the treaty, have to be there for a minimum of 180 days in order to be considered fully transferred from their home base in Honduras. How could the Marines pull out if, legally, they had never arrived: rotated, transferred quickly to the neighboring Republic of Shadows, relieved by replacements who in turn never remained the full 180 days. There were twenty thousand Marines in Mexico, but there were not twenty thousand Marines in Mexico: what were we going to do? And those nonexistent Marines had already advanced to Perote and scattered in the mountains, and even though President Rambolt Ranger had assured President Jesús María y José Paredes (with whom he maintains a most cordial relationship) over the red hot-line telephone that the Marines are on their own, not under orders from Washington, motivated exclusively by their autonomous decision to defend democracy wherever and however they can, it is also true that the U.S. President does not want to disavow them publicly as long as they are objectively serving the interests of the United States and the will-to-greatness of the people of the United States, and President Paredes is announcing today to the Congress that, despite all, it is incumbent on Mexico to expel those troops, which are, after all, an invasion force, to which end it is essential that the national unity be renewed, and what better example than the one proposed by the President in this moment in which all of us (even me in my ultrasonic and impermeable cabin) are listening: this is no time for selfish party politics, we must all militate in one single party, the Party of Mexico!!

"Which one, Mr. President, which one?" Peregrino Ponce y Peón,

Senator from Yucatango, dared to shout, interrupting the executive's discourse.

"Don't torture us any more, Mr. President, tell us which party it will be," said Doña Virginia Iris de Montoya, deputy from Tamaleón, who also represented the union of actors.

To which, deeply moved, the President answered as the entire nation fell into a collective hush: "I have always been, I am now, and I shall always be, even when I have said the contrary, a faithful militant in the Revolutionary Institutional Party (PRI)."

The legislative body of the nation leapt to its feet, cheering the President in his moment of glory; they drown out his final words, the PRI, the only party, the only power, with which, out of patriotic zeal, all other lesser parties should fuse. That is what we hoped for from you, shouts Hipólito Zea, deputy for the ninth district of Chihuahuila, standing tall, thank you for showing us the way, Mr. President, shouts the peasant leader Xavier Coruera y Braniff, we are with you to the death, Mr. President, long live Mexico, long live the PRI!!!

Minister Federico Robles Chacón lowers the volume on his VCR when the applause explodes. Night has fallen, and he has reviewed the President's speech for the thousandth time, he has estimated its effect, he savors the defeat of the pro-Yankee faction headed by Ulises López. Now the magnanimous minister can receive the Pasionaria of the defeated movement, the lover of the frustrated Mexican Ayatollah:

"Send in Madam Toro," he says to his tuxedo-clad toady.

Yes, Matamoros Moreno is dead, Robles Chacón brutally informs the woman, who walked in dressed as if for a Ramón Pereda movie, circa 1945: a strapless evening gown with red sequins over strawberry satin and in her hair—especially black and massive, thanks to a stuffing of store-bought hair—quetzal-feather aigrettes. Mesh stockings and supremely pointed, rose-colored velvet shoes with stiletto heels complete the outfit.

Yes, Matamoros Moreno is dead: Robles wants to get this off his chest and erase all illusions, all hope. What he doesn't explain is that he tried to save the Ayatollah's life but that Colonel Inclán demanded it: he demanded nothing else, just as Juárez had demanded the death of Maximilian despite Victor Hugo's plea, that's what he said the colonel did in order to save the nation and deliver a definitive message to the mob, the idea here is to cut off a few heads so they don't cut yours off, he said, with his eyes veiled by his black Pinochet-Huerta glasses, with his mouth dripping green slime. But after a few seconds of silence she merely chants "Baby Love." It was a political crime, declares Robles, who tonight wants to be totally sincere in order to be able to look himself in the eye tomorrow. The feathers hide Concha Toro's face, her head hangs down, lost love, because, madam, it was the response to another political crime, her feathers hang so low that the quetzal tail threatens to blend with the false eighteenth-century quill pen set in the bronze desk set on the secretary's escritoire. That's why it was a legal crime, long live pleasure, long live love (sings Concha née María Inez, her head hung low), because the country has already suffered enough from natural causes and acts of God for it to have to suffer a political, anarchic, bloody torment, oh love, if you could see how desperate I am because you aren't here with me, an earthquake can't be stopped, oh! but a revolution can.

"I am not going to tell you that I'm sorry."

"Can it be true that sin has its price . . ."

"Excuse me?"

"How high a price I'm paying for loving you . . ."

Concha Toro sang with the melancholy voice of those who sing unaccompanied, thereby doubling their solitude.

"Madam, please . . ."

"Leave me, sir." She hung her head even lower. "I must pay my tribute to my man now; in the moment in which I find out his fate. This is my requiem for my man, a little song, now, okay . . ."

"I would prefer you learn the truth from me personally."

"And I thank you for it. You should hear the lies people are telling!"

"Why are you singing here in my office?" he asked in his rational way, his arms crossed, devoid of the elegance of intuition.

"Ay, señor, do you want me to sing at his grave, when the government isn't going to give me back my sweetheart? Don't you think I know it, damn it all!"

Robles refused to feel anything. He asked her if there was anything he could do for her. It went without saying that she had been granted a full pardon, the government was magnanimous and understood that she had only followed him out of love, and she might also ask for anything she might want.

"Except Matamoros's body."

"It's very strange," said Concha Toro after a moment. "When I found out that my man would never be coming back, I began to dream, I dreamed about a wild bull in a ranch down in my part of the world, in Maule, I saw him running in the fields and then suddenly fall down wounded, can you imagine that? How silly, wounded and castrated by the wind from the mountains, the wind slicing up my bull, the wind like a knife and a meat hook turning my bull into steaks. And you know what happened then?"

Robles looked at her courteously.

"I felt real nostalgia for Chile. It hit me in the face, right during that dream of horror and the blood of that night, an aroma of plum trees in bloom and lilacs and the salty coast and rivers flowing into the sea with a wreath of kelp. Sir, I want to go back to Chile, that's what I want!"

She looked at him with languid, liquid eyes. "Please, sir, send me back to Chile!"

"It's impossible."

Robles did not lower his eyes.

"But it's that . . ."

"Madam: there is no Chile."

Robles forced himself to go on telling the truth without circumlocutions. It was a sure method, without complications; on him there could be fixed an entire symbology; symbols don't grow on symbols, symbols only grow over realities, the sage statesman reminded himself. The painful silence of the Chilean singer had the liquid eloquence of her big gray sad eyes, where there was room for all the rain of Temuco.

"Sir," said Concha after another long pause (Robles Chacón was armed with patience: he only wished someone else had shown it before making a show of power), "we Chileans are big globetrotters, but at the end of our lives we always come back to Chile, don't tell me any more of your cruel stories, sir, I'm begging you, have a heart . . ."

"I'll tell you again, madam: Chile no longer exists."

"But the tortures . . . the house of the bells . . . Pinochet in power until 1999 . . ."

"Tales made up to make people think nothing changes. I'm sorry."

"What happened to my country, sir?"

"What do you think happened? A horrible earthquake, the Pacific fault. All of Chile sank into the sea. The whole country, from the mountains to the sea. From La Serena to Cape Horn. It wasn't anyone's fault: like a sugar cube, Chile dissolved in the sea."

"What about the desert up north?"

"Peru and Bolivia split it between them."

"Well then, I can go to the desert!"

"The Peruvian Army shoots all the deluded Chileans who disembark in Arica or Antofagasta. Don't delude yourself, madam, really."

"Always the Army! Always the Peruvians! Shit! Grant me another favor, then. Please, where is *he*? Let me bury him? Take care of his grave, sir? At least make that one exception?"

"We cannot tolerate the existence of a site for pilgrims to gather. Are you going to celebrate his death year after year by visiting his grave? You can understand that . . ."

He did not finish his sentence, but his gesture was definitive. Concha Toro in that instant must have remembered every pose, every fatal gesture of every femme fatale that ever appeared on the silver screen.

"All right." She pushed her aigrette back with as much style as Marlene Dietrich when she played a spy standing in front of the firing squad. "Don't give me anything but the truth, Mr. Minister. Tell me if my man triumphed or failed."

Robles Chacón knew the answer, but he preferred to leave Concha Toro with a margin of doubt. "That wasn't his problem, madam. He neither triumphed nor failed. He had a destiny. That is, he triumphed and failed at the same time."

"Ah." Concha's eyes shone. "That's good. We all learn something. I'll remember that, what you've just said."

"That's fine," the minister answered, not yielding anything, but impatient.

"I" (she mixed haughtiness and tears in a strange way) (she mixed the affirmative tone of her voice with a broken, soul-wrenching cry) "also learned something. Your country, too, Mr. Minister, was also swallowed up by the sea. Mexico doesn't exist any longer either. It has no future. There will be no progress. It'll be screwed up until eternity. You can't accept that. Screwed up for all time. You don't want to accept that. You cover it up. My man made you see the truth. That's why you killed him."

"That's your opinion," said Robles. He bowed before her and gestured to the toady at the door to show the lady out.

Concha Toro walked down the staircase of honor in the ancient viceregal palace of New Spain, which had been built on the ruins of the Emperor Moctezuma's palace: the rulers in that palace now were the de facto triumvirate: President Paredes, Colonel Inclán, and Federico Robles Chacón, who stared blindly at Diego Rivera's murals celebrating Mexico's national glory. Tonight the epic was coming to a close, and in its place, for Concha Toro, there was only a broken heart and some coral lips singing to an absent man I swear to you, enchanter love, little love, lost love, that I shall never forget you . . .

No more epics, the last epic: Rivera's murals would be sold a few days later to the Chase Manhattan Bank in partial payment for interest due, and then transported, yard by epic yard, to Rockefeller Center, where they'd been expected for more than half a century.

Galvarina, Concha, Dolly, María Inez put on her lipstick, took off her uncomfortable stiletto-heel shoes, and walked out barefoot between two files of soldiers, thinking (it's you who communicate this news to me, Reader) about her reopening debut at the Simon Bully Bar, timed so that this faggot Giuseppe Birthday in the Guadala Harry's Bar wouldn't beat her to the punch, mentally choosing her numbers and telling herself how that frog Ada Ching would really turn green if she could see me now, alive and kicking and getting ready for a new season! Life is a cabaret!

10

 Like the plague entering the village mounted on the bony spine of a serpent: that's how I felt in my eighth month of gestation, carried away, tossed in the air, victimized by this original and intolerable fact: for the first time, Reader, I feel I'm being taken somewhere I don't want to go, and this feeling opens my eyes to another fact which until now I was unaware of: I am afraid of not being what my genetic plan has determined for me and instead being determined by outside forces, all those phenomena that my intelligence (private, interior) has been observing (with the urge to communicate them to your worship the reader; even though you, too, are outside, you lack, perhaps for that very reason, the perspective I give you) and taking note of (out of the pants-wetting fear that I have that I am going to forget all this the moment I am

born and that I'll have to spend the rest of my life remembering and
relearning what I once knew), all these exterior details separate from
my own self (I count on you to remember what I'll forget on being
born, *please*, Reader, course and recourse with me!), all that circumstance (that famous pair: Ortega und Gasset), all that setting,
take me over, nullify my will and my intelligence. Here inside, tell
me things that gratify me immensely: for example, that the only
source of my innate structure is my genetic information; that no
matter how far back I go, I shall never find another source of what
I am except that information; that my genes configure me:

```
        I am your daddy        and        I am your mom
        and grandparents and
                              great-
                                   and great-great
                              and
                                   all
                                   your
                                   lineal
                                   d
                                     e
                                       s
                                         c
                                           e
                                             n
                                               t
        as                                          diversified
      l      t c
      p      i
```
```
            e  │  g
            v  │  n
            o  │  i
            l  │  v
            v  │  l
            i  │  o
            n  │  v
            g  │  e
```

100yes, but within, always from within, always thanks to the previous
genetic constellation: no, I say to myself now that I'm bouncing

around in these boondocks, the garbage (I smell it, by God, that's *all* there is here: rubbish, decomposition, mountains of garbage, an implacable circle of garbage, a chain of garbage, linked by a network of plastic and rags), only today, only here, I swear to your mercedes that this horrifying doubt has presented itself to me:

If I'm not the son of my genes, then must I be the (bastard) son of the environment? my heritage, instead of being the one I know, within, might not my heritage be the one I do not know, outside? What a hungry fear!

Eight months after my conception, my little body is a model of
equi .... librium
ex .... libris
I feel how my body responds, adapts itself to the changes out there: from the waters of the Pacific Ocean that washed us when I had barely been conceived and baptized in shit to the sweet tranquillity of my great-grandparents' home, I've adapted to everything, even to the worst: the journey through the Guerrero mountains, the carnal attack of that scoundrel Matamoros, even the murky whirlwind of El Niño wasn't able to interfere decisively with my slow but certain development!

But now, Reader, now I feel for the first time that I'm being deprived of everything necessary for life; now the air, water, earth, voices (corrupted sound) have conspired in an alliance of insults, and I cannot adapt myself to that. Something's going on here that seems to have been preestablished so that I can't breathe, digest, see, hear, or speak: the insult is way out of proportion! My genes have determined (I know it for a fact!) that I will have chestnut eyes and that I will walk upright, but now that we've reached the place they've brought us to (you see that I include you in my story, Mom), I think that can change, too: we're surrounded by a death sentence, or at the very least an accident sentence, or a defect sentence, sentences so implacable, so fearsome that I would like to scream from the solar center of my gestation: CUT ME LOOSE FROM THE D.F.! I'm going to walk upright and have brown eyes! I'm going to breathe and drink and shit and screw and hear like a normal person!

The environment is not going to kill me, my genes are going to be more powerful than this vile concatenation of garbage!

I think my mother must be having the same thoughts, except that her fear is greater than mine: we've been taken from the grandparents' house, supposedly because of the days of violence, by this so-called Hipi Toltec, who has promised to bring us to a safe place where my father Angel—conciliatory, loving, and, above all, alive—is waiting for us; but as we make our way, we are surrounded by everything but security, and if I can identify and tolerate the violence of the times we're living through, I already know that all history is ephemeral.

FLYING DOWN TO VICO!

(A mental flash from Mamma Mia's roof: even the passage of History is a passing thing: there is more time without time and more history without history than avec: time before time: not time, time that doesn't know it's time, time incapable of imagining itself, history that isn't even prehistory because it doesn't conceive history: death of what precedes us in the absolute origin; why not then, thinks Angel, the death of a future without us; she rebels and desires my father, desires his company, his being with her, my padre mío.)

Hipi, on the other hand, brings us to a place of violence (of permanent history: is this hell? So burning hot, dry, stinking, beyond redemption, eternal, as eternal as paradise?). (My God, sighs my mother Angeles, when will you forgive the devil so that all this can come to an end. Let Lucifer ascend to your place so that your authentic grace shines forth: God has forgiven the Fallen Angel! Hallelujah, hallelujah: there is no more temptation, fear, or doubt about divine goodness; we all know it now because Lucifer appears seated at the right hand of the Lord; so don't we all believe because seeing is believing? Is it the case that we don't have faith because we have certitude? Is there faith only when we know it is true because it is impossible?)

FARE FEAR STARVING STRIVING

I was saying that even she, Angeles my mother, with her bare feet sunk in a corrupt mud (she'd abandoned her black low-heeled pregnant woman's sandals in a puddle of dying grass and liquid shit), is beginning to wonder, here, in the misery belt, whether the environment can force the genes to change me into another individual unforeseen in my DNA: something innate and even comforting tells me I shouldn't regard my genetic inheritance and my environment as enemies but as allies that divide up the work and that mutually support each other: the nature of nature consists in never working alone; nature and all things that nurture it act within previously established limits; but this nature of the Mexican city, this città dolente, has gone way out of proportion:

QUASIMODO CITY

SAMSAVILLE

HUITZILOPOCHTLIBURG

a misshapen and bloody cockroach, I receive you like the eucharist this violent morning, sacrament of dying, plague communion: I haven't been born yet and you already threaten to transform me: I'll be a scientific exhibit, numbered and classified, like the Mexican salamander: under different conditions, I'll take on different forms; if I had remained in the waters of Kafkapulco forever, I would have developed scales and gills and a tail for swimming; what will I develop if I stay in this neighborhood of garbage and thieves, this cemetery for automobiles where Hipi Toltec has brought us after the night of the Ayatollah, claiming that my father had sent him to get us? Will I be like the Orphan Huerta, rubber feet, leather soles, the Little Rascals, David Copperfield, Oliver Twist, Little Dorrit of D.F., Eddypoe, Eddyfuss?

My class intelligence, genetically uncertain, rebels against all this: I am not now nor have I ever been a plebe, a lumpen, or a vulgar swine: I am Don Christopher the Classy, you might as well know it here and now, your Mercedes-Benz, no matter who it hurts, and now I remember a smell, I recall a sound, we've left the sick air in order to enter the sickness of the air, what a misty jail, how close the zinc ceilings are and the cement water tubs, burning and hostile like a bath in lava, how close we are to a ravine in the garbage belt that surrounds the city, what a mass of people there, people who are invisible but who are kissed, spoken to, and greeted by Hipi:

"Ne netilztli!"

"Xocoyotzin!"

"Ollohiuhqui, ollohiuhqui!"

"Cíhuatl!" Hipi points to my mother.

"Xocoyotzin, ixcluintli!" An old man points to my mom's belly, to me!

"Toci, toci." Hipi points to my mother and then points to himself.

They speak a bit more, and then Hipi tells us that his family is happy he's gotten married and that very soon he will have his first child. Amid so much misery and slaughter, they are happy to see that life goes on. Welcome to the wife and soon-to-be-born son of our young pup Xipe!

The old folks offer us their house along with all the electric appliances Hipi has been bringing them over the years: let the offerings be ours, translates the flayed boy. He asks my mother to sit down near the old folks, between the smoke and the stench, and to make ourselves comfortable, because we will be staying here until the child is born.

"Ixcluintli, ixcluintli," the old folks say, announcing our evening meal, raw, smoky dog—without hair.

"We greet the young son of the gods who is about to be born."

Take note, your mercies, take careful note, dear Readers: these oldsters are referring to ME when they say these things. THEY REFER TO ME! Just think how frightened I am, trapped you know where, consulting my genetic chain like a madman to see if something was condemning me to be born in a hut belonging to some tipsy Aztecs and to incarnate, who knows? the sun, sacrifice, and who knows what the fuck else! NOTHING, Readers, exactly NOTHING. If a kind of proto-Quetzalcoatl is going to be born in this miserable hut, it isn't going to be me, maybe my fraternal twin, born from my mother at the same time as I will be but formed from an egg different from mine, fertilized by another sperm than the one I call my own: ladies and gentlemen, I feel around in the fetal night that surrounds me to see if this fraternal twin, dizzygothic (gothic and dizzy!), is within reach, coexisting near me in the womb of Doña Angeles Palomar my mother, and if it's that way, just understand, because of what might happen later, that this dizzygothic twin was not created by the same father who created me, that we inhabit different placentas and that the only thing we share is the same time within Mom's womb: only that, nothing more, not paternal origin, not destiny in the world, he is not the OTHER CHRISTOPHER, in any case he's probably the other Hipi Toltec, and good luck to him: so keep your eyes open, gentle Readers: listen to what I say, watch out for my face, my gestures, my words: we've been getting to know each other now over hundreds of pages, don't fail me now, in the moment of truth, of Baby Ruth, of the Bambino! Anagnorisis is what it's called: recognize me, it all depends on you, so when Hipi and his paleototonacs come to claim me: I am Christopher Palomar, not the (bastard) Son of the Gods!

11

No sooner had Grandfather Rigoberto Palomar slammed the door in the faces of the Fagoaga sisters than his spirits began to soar: he turned to face his wife, Doña Susana Rentería, leaned against the door, closed his eyes, and tilted his aged head back.

"Su, dearest Su," said the old man, with his eyes closed.

"What is it, Rigo? Here I am."

He opened his eyes, kissed his wife passionately, and smiled as he stepped back. "Do you remember when your father handed you over to me and you were a little girl and I'd tuck you in every night?"

"And you were thirty, but you liked being called 'old fellow' by a girl because in those days all the young men wanted to look old so people would take them seriously. You were such a young soldier."

"Things go in circles! It's the same now. Look: Angel and Angeles dress the way you and I did when we were young."

"Fashions that come to us from the North," said Doña Susana Rentería. "Don't pay any attention to it. Twenty years ago—remember?—everybody wanted to look like a teenager."

"Ah, those barbarians to the North!"

They laughed at all this, looking tenderly at one another. After a moment, she took him in her arms.

"Did you hear the President?" Don Rigo asked her. "We have to fight again. Of course, nothing is perfect, Su, and I'll tell you again that I'm not mistaken. It doesn't matter to me that Mexico is all fucked up, but what does matter to me is that Mexico exists. We shouldn't give up on the country just because it's in a bad period. To reform a country you have to have a country. I know people think I'm crazy, but just tell me if you and I could have had a better life than being taken for lunatics by everyone and only being crazy on a single point, which I chose, while being sane on all the rest. If I weren't insane about the Revolution, they wouldn't let me be sane about the rest, namely the love I have for you, and the skill with which I manage my affairs, and how well I know how to use my leisure time and have friends. It's a concession, sweetie."

"I understand you, old boy. Nothing is perfect."

"Su: when I was a boy, there was nothing here but a little boastful elite and the mass of peons. I'm right; we didn't fail, my madness is reasonable. What had to be done was done; this country had no roads, no dams, no telephones, no schools, no industry, no freedom of movement. All that we accomplished. You say that nothing is perfect. Ask those who came after us why they were so irresponsible with what we created, those who worked from 1915 to 1940, when I was young and you a little girl. Anyway, the problem with a revolution is not to betray it. It's not going through with it for fear of betraying it."

"What are you trying to tell me, old man?"

"Susy. Once again, I have a mission in life. I don't have to lie to myself and say that the Revolution is not over. You heard the President. The Yankees have invaded us! We have to defend the fatherland!"

"Let me remind you of a mission a bit closer to home. Our granddaughter has been kidnapped. Along with our unborn great-grandson."

"What do you think I should do, Susana Rentería?"

"General: delegate and give orders. You're too old for these fracases. You're over ninety. Behave like a commander-in-chief."

"I thank you for your wisdom, Su. What orders should I give?"

"Egg knows where this Hipiteca person, the boy with the peeling skin, lives. Angel should rescue his wife. And if he doesn't, well, then he should owe the favor to his friend. That first. Then you can order Angel to fight in Veracruz and redeem himself for all the idiotic things he's done. Get your priorities straight, General."

"How talented you've always been, my dear girl!"

But all their attempts to find Angel were useless. Don Fernando Benítez was incommunicado, out with the Huicholes, taking a bath in the Golden Age. The Simon Bully Bar was closed, and no one knew where Concha Toro or her dog Fango Dango was. The piano player and barman in the new club that had opened across the street, Giuseppe Birthday, said that he was new in the neighborhood, that he knew nothing about any Chilean woman, and that he hoped the general and his wife would have a libation in his new bar the Lady of the Camels: Quench Your Thirst Here. The López mansion had been looted and its inhabitants (Ulises and Lucha) murdered, although the girl (Penny) wanders around the U.S.A.-shaped pool tossing in sunflower petals and muttering:

"You can look but you can't touch. You're ugly and a plebe. If it's Thursday, this must be Philadelphia."

Dear Readers:
Only my genes, the current seat of my intelligence, can assure you that my vision, activated perhaps by a dream or one of my mother's desires (I dream of you without wanting to, Angel, I desire you without dreaming of you, without knowing why. You receive the seed from both of us, my son, dream and desire, my son), is capable of dreaming of desiring and of seeing my father in this particular instant: I cling to that intelligence, which, after all, I inherited from him and her and not from the stinking environment where I'm suffocating in this shack that belongs to Hipi Toltec's family. (One hundred genes determine intelligence! superior intelligence dominates inferior intelligence! eighty percent of the differences between individuals are genetic! neither race nor country of origin nor social class nor climate nor pollution: intelligence is what counts.)

I mean that I feel sure of my genes, you see, and my genes feel sure of me. This mutual confidence allows us to see what others only imagine: by illuminating my genes, I see my father from the kidnapped belly of my mother:

On the highway out of the black hole called Mexico, D.F.cation. My father and Colasa Sánchez look from Paso de Cortés, where the Van Gogh gave up the ghost, out of gas, sick, deaf (the other loudspeaker fell off). They look toward the swamp of toxic waste and contaminated water. Angel realizes that for her all this is normal. The city under the persistent acid rain is not something different. But culture and nostalgia have set my father apart. But she doesn't know that the city is the cramped waiting room of eternity. Perhaps she doesn't even know that her father is dead. My father feels remorse for having abandoned us, although his feeling grows weaker when he looks at the external city (the extreme city) and its distant rumbles of hunger, crime, and violence: the persistent dripping that he cannot locate continues to pursue him; she is pursued by her own vulnerability: she's run after this young man—my father—since she was eleven years old, she obeyed the homicidal orders of her father Matamoros Moreno, she owns the only vagina dentata in America the

Toothyful, and nevertheless here they are, the two of them, chilled to the bone this early September night, looking at the city's deceptive lights from the Paso de Cortés. He slips his jacket over her shoulders, protects her, accepts her, and the two of them feel that being a loving couple is more difficult but also more important than having no ties. Angel covers and protects Colasa because he remembers my abandoned mother (and perhaps me!) and he feels guilty. But Colasa doesn't know this and accepts Angel's tenderness with a little shudder of pleasure that is also not without its tinge of guilt. She wanted to kill this man she desires. She's loved and hated him since she was a girl, when she set herself up in a striker's tent outside his door on Calle Génova. Today, on this cold, sad night up on the heights, she is going to have to decide. If she gives herself to him, she destroys him with her teeth. If she doesn't give herself to him, she will have to sustain love in some other way, without physical contact, and she doesn't know how that can be done, but she fears that he does know and that he'll go back to Angeles and keep her as a mascot. What problems I make for myself! Colasita exclaims, hugged, protected by my father, covered by my father's 1920s-style jacket this cold night in the mountains, but she doesn't have time to express her doubts or make decisions, and for one reason alone: this city of death should, despite everything, live. The fog lifts suddenly and the caravan of lights blinds the night: it's the armada of long-haul trucks that travel in the darkness to fill thirty million bellies in Mexico City. They enter the city with their ephemeral cornucopia of fruits and vegetables, meats and cheeses and chickens and lobsters and fowl and oysters and beer, but Angel Palomar and Colasa Sánchez want to flee from the city. To flee because he feels guilty, overwhelmed, no compass, his reasons forever scattered (he tells Colasa: I've lost my reasons, understand? and she says no, that she doesn't know what he's talking about, but it doesn't matter because it's so nice being together, the two of them, keep talking, keep talking. Once I went to Oaxaca and I found my reasons; maybe I ought to go back; in any case, I ought to get out of here, I wanted to confront Mexican society and Mexican society defeated me; and do you know how, Colasa? *by not paying me any attention, Colasa!* And she: But you talk so pretty, gosh), and all the trucks entering the city: only one is leaving, going in the opposite direction. They are doubly blinded by the clash of lights, like blind men fencing, the beams of light from the powerful headlamps of the trucks crossing each other and Colasa squirming free of the arm of my protective father, Colasa always excessive and impetuous in the middle of the highway exposing herself to death, my father shouting to her from the shoulder of the road, Colasa, be careful, you're crazy! and the enormous wheels of the only truck abandoning the city, an eighteen-wheel Leyland, fourteen feet high, with a revolving light on its roof, brakes to a screeching halt in front of the small figure still dressed as a Discalced Carmelite.

"What the hell was that! I can't see a thing! I almost killed you, you idiot!"

The driver's voice screams from the truck, he leans out a face that looks like a made-up clown; it's a white skull wearing enormous black glasses. Irritated, he takes off his baseball cap and shows his hair, which has no color, not even white.

"Help, help a poor devout girl, show mercy, sir, says the clown Colasita Sánchez, kneeling before the albino driver, the girl bathed in scales of mercury, and the driver opens the door, helps her to her feet, while she points to my father: "And my friend, too. Won't you give us a ride? Jesus, Patron of the Needy, will love you for it!"

12

Inside the border checkpoint between Mexamerica North and Baja Oklahoma, the immigration agent, Mazzo Balls, stares attentively at the infrared screen that detects heat from human bodies. Tonight the screen is blank. No heat waves activate the detection device and none shows up as a ghost-like image on the screen. Nevertheless, Mazzo Balls's sixth sense tells him that there are ghosts crossing the forbidden frontier tonight, just as there are every night. The exception does not prove the rule—a maxim they taught him in his training course for interdicting illegal aliens. The invasion from the South is constant, unstoppable, a flood. It takes place at all hours.

Tonight would be the first night in his entire three-year tour of duty (a solitary posting in this no-man's-land out on the Texas plains) in which he would not detect at least one Mexican, Honduran, or Salvadoran trying to sneak into Baja Oklahoma, not happy with the nice reception arranged for him in Mexamerica, that version of the

Polish Corridor between Mexico and the United States, which supposedly declared itself independent from both countries, although in reality it served the interests of both, absorbing eighty percent of the illegal aliens that used to sneak into Texas, California, the Midwest, and the Great Lakes states . . .

Agent Mazzo Balls was the most zealous enforcer of the final version of the Simpson–Nobody law, which, in exchange for metaphysical control over the U.S. frontier, sanctioned fines and prison terms for employers of illegals. Foreseeably, this punishment was applied indiscriminately to anyone who employed dark-skinned workers, whether they were U.S. citizens or not, and ended up (also foreseeably) forcing every traveler to carry first an identity card, then a passport, and finally being able to move only within hermetically sealed zones—just like South Africa. Blocking the entrance and employment of Latin American laborers into the United States not only heightened the social crisis in Mexico and Central America but brought about the collapse of the labor market in the United States. The absence of Hispanic workers in hospitals, restaurants, transportation, farming, and manufacturing left a horrible vacuum which, contrary to the laws of physics and the baroque (noted our Uncle Fernando Benítez with a bitter smile), was not filled by anyone: no one wanted those jobs, but everyone had to take a step down as far as getting loans, good salaries, and jobs was concerned, in order to disguise the labor shortage.

All this (Don Fernando would have wanted to warn the city and the world) had to contribute to pauperization and the current disintegration of the States in the Union, with no one winning anything: how could Uncle Fernando explain all this to the pair of blind young Indians who one day turned up at the house of the blackboards on the way to their chimerical goal: Chicago, the city of the big shoulders, far from the fatality of poverty, sickness, and tradition, breaking the circle of their age-old destiny. Don Fernando foresaw a catastrophe for the young couple (the girl, remember, your mercies, made pregnant at the same time as my mother, she bearing a baby who would be my contemporary, olé!).

Now I foresee: the day we meet Uncle Fernando again, he will tell us what probably happened: Mazzo Balls cannot believe that the greasers have skipped a night in their attempt to slip through the rat trap, which is emblazoned with a huge sign in Gothic letters:

VOTE WITH YOUR FEET

and just to give himself the satisfaction, he orders the service helicopter to take a look and see if there aren't any illegals crossing the
border. It'd be a miracle! A peaceful night! Silent night, holy night!
hums Mazzo Balls, his Miller Lite in one hand, his unlit Marlboro
dangling from his lips, his feet perched on the console, and his favorite
TV program on: *The Forsyte Saga*. The series transports him to
another era, like a fairy tale: how Mazzo would have liked living in
Edwardian England, with butlers, kitchen boys, and parlor maids
running up- and downstairs all day long!

But it wouldn't be tonight: the helicopter takes off and the pilot
radios an urgent call to Mazzo Balls, listen, shithead, did your detector break down on you? What made you think there weren't any
Spics? I put on my night-vision glasses, the ones activated by moon-
light, and I hope you realize that it's a clear, starry night, and I'm
following two, a man and a woman, I'll describe them to you since
your fucked-up screen can't pick them up: the two of them are wearing
straw hats, white outfits, all ragged, both barefoot, the miserable rats,
they're carrying something that looks like a supermarket bag, or it
might be a shoulder bag, hanging down on one side, they're staggering
as if they're drunk, scratched up by the wires, as if they don't see
them, do you hear me, Mazzo? It's the first time in my life that I
turned these searchlights on greasers and they don't automatically
look up or get scared shitless when they see me with my black mask
on and my robot eyes, they think I'm Darth Vader, hahaha, dazzled
or covering their eyes with one arm, listen, fat man, this time we're
going to arrest them, right? What do you say, jerk-off? And Mazzo
Balls flushed with rage and shame and said into the microphone no,
you know that it isn't worth the trouble to arrest them, and we don't
have the funds to pay for the gas to send them to Norman, but we
do have funds to pay for the gas in this stupid chopper? asked the
pilot. That's right, answered Mazzo, that's the way the funds are
distributed, you have gas, you get the good part, stop complaining,
the highway patrol doesn't have a cent. Well, I'm a son of a bitch
if I don't feel like giving away my gasoline so we can capture this
pair of savages, you should see them, Mazzo, they look like Powhatan
and Pocahontas or something like that, we would have wiped them
out around here years ago, savages, barefoot, they don't seem to see

me, Mazzo, but they sure do hear me, she's got her hands over her ears, and he's waving his arms around as if he were scaring off a horsefly or a swarm of bees, listen, Mazzo, check it out, he thinks I'm a bee, hahaha, buzzbuzzbuzz, how did that song about the flight of the bumblebee go? an old radio program used it as its theme song, buzzbuzzybuzz, hahaha, I'm gonna drop down and really scare 'em, they don't seem to see me, these stupid Indians, but they know I'm here, uh-oh, her ripped skirt's blowing up, Jesus, she's knocked up, the slut, they can't stop screwing and having kids, these pigs, the woman's disgusting, she must be eight months gone, her gut's almost as big as yours, Mazzo Balls, hahaha, that swollen, Christ, but not from Miller Lite, like you, but with one more little brown greaser, another shitass who's here to take the food out of our mouths and steal another American's job, walkin' in here like it was their own home, Jesus, the woman's stuffed with another little easy-livin' fucker! they're takin' rocks out of their bag, rocks, haha, they're gonna chase me away with rocks, Mazzo! rocks against the chopper! Who do they think they are, Sitting Bull? Viva technology! Listen, Mazzo, this is getting cute, I wish you were here, I swear this is the best battle I ever saw since they cut off General Custer's balls at the battle of the Little Bighorn, did you ever see Ronald Reagan in *Santa Fe Trail* on the Late Show? haha, well I'm gonna get even for Custer, I'm gonna blow away this pair of Indians, I've been asking for a license to kill for over a year now, but I'm takin' matters into my own hands here, haha . . . Mazzo, they hit me on the head, Mazzo, can ya see me? Mazzo, the rock's blinded me, what an eye that guy's got, can't ya see me, Mazzo? If only the Congress had bought you an infrared 'scope like the one they have at Sandy Ego so you could see at night, track down the illegals, see them under the midnight sun, Mazzo, Mazzo, I'm comin' down, they're . . . Mazzo, do ya read me? . . . Mazzo . . . ?

Sitting on his splendid backside, Mazzo Balls looked through his window at the desolate frontier and saw the helicopter drop swiftly, then spin madly, and crash in a ball of fire.

Just before the crash, Mazzo looked at his screen for any sign of the couple: they produced no heat whatsoever. But the helicopter certainly did—the needles were jumping off the scale, and the screen filled with an orange glow.

One day, Uncle Fernando Benítez will tell us that on the Baja

Oklahoma frontier a strange man received the blind Indian couple, doffed his bowler (although they could not see that courteous gesture), and with his other hand straightened his starched butterfly collar. With a gesture of his gloved hand and an innocent sparkle in his big black insomniac and persecuted eyes, he said: Welcome to the Grand Theater of Oklahoma.

Then this tall, thin dark man, who resembled a question mark, pointed to a place far away on the plain where a mirage appeared, that is, it had to be a mirage: a circus tent, a papier-mâché Arc de Triomphe, a circle of flags fluttered by the wind blowing over the prairie. The tall, sleepless man called the two Baltic poets, the extremely pale man and woman, so that they could help the blind Indians. Take them to live in the round house and then bring them to the Grand Theater so they can tell their dreams there, said the man with the bowler and walking stick, who had ears like Nosferatu, trembling as if he already knew that the two Indians from the plateau of the blind tribe dreamed everything they could not see:

"I hope you get your heart's desire, that you reach your goal, that your dreams become reality!" said the man in the bowler.

"Let's go to the round house," said the Baltic poet in Nahuatl to the Indian.

"Let's go," answered the Indian. "Let's go with my wife and my unborn son."

"Let's go," said the woman poet, taking the new arrivals by the hand in the Baja Oklahoma night, the mirages dissipated by now. "We're going to your house. My name is Astrid. My husband's is Ivar. But that's another story. Let's go."

And the Indian couple: We have nothing, we've come home, this land was always ours, we passed through here on our way south, one day a long time ago when we first walked on this land, do you remember, woman? We've brought our son to be born on our land, not strange land, not the frontier: our land, the North, the place of meetings.

13

It turns out that I, Christopher, am capable of finding relationships and analogies (I don't divine things: I relate things, make things similar!) others don't see because they have forgotten them. For example, all I have to do is establish the relationship between a couple on the run, two blind Indians from the mesa visited one day by my Uncle Fernando, she pregnant like my mother, he in search of something better like my father (see how I keep my faith in you, pro-gen-i-tor!), and the Indian fetus perhaps imagining my parents just as I imagine his. Accordingly, I establish the relationship between that couple in flight and the disunited couple constituted by my dad and mom: looking at the two Indians on the frontier between Mexamerica and Baja Oklahoma, I see my parents crossing other frontiers, and thus I conclude, in the first place, that we are always in frontier situations, either exiting or entering, as in stage directions—enter Hamlet and Ophelia—exeunt Quijote and Dulcinea, etc. But, the reader exclaims indignantly, your parents aren't even together, each one is in a different corner of the woods, one in Montesinos's cave, the other in El Toboso, we left your mother a hostage in the bosom of Hipi Toltec's Nahuatl-speaking family, with you (inevitably) in her belly, sharing with them (with Them) a dinner of cactus salad and orange slices (Plato's banquet in a somber thieves' den: by the way, what page are you on, Mom?), while your father climbed up into the truck of the albino driver, Bubble Gómez, which Colasa Sánchez had flagged down with tricks worthy of Claudette Colbert, of enchanting memory: your father in the company of the Discalced Carmelite dazzled by the jukebox lights and the pictures of Guadalupe, Virgin, Thatcher, Margaret, and of Doctor and Mother, so where's the comparison, Christopher (finally you wake up, Reader, and you ask me something!)? Only this one, I note, I newt:

We're all different, but it's good that we resemble one another as well. In this world, everything is different, but only if everything is related to everything else. Readers, I don't know another secret to be truer after my eight months of gestation: we've always got to be in the situation where difference is in tension with sameness. We are recognized because we are different, but also because we are similar: I, Christopher, am likely to be recognized because of the form in which I share and admit the sameness of my gestures and my words with those of others. We human beings are not the only animals who need and recognize the scattered members of our species: the lamb, ladies and gentlemen, can always recognize his mother (who happens to be a female) in an anonymous flock of one hundred animals.

In the same way, I recognize, from my solar center, which orders, establishes hierarchies, yet is most free, my distant father and my infinitely close mother and I join them in my vision as one with the pair of illegal Indians, and I'll stake my reputation on it:

My mother Angeles is sitting in the cave of tin water tubs and cardboard that belongs to Hipi & Family, bereft of hope, when suddenly an unusual disturbance resounds in the jailed night and the fires of the circular wall of garbage join together and run like the proverbial scalded cat. (Do proverbial cats have nine lives?) (Or should those who keep proverbial cats as pets be tickled with a cat-o'-nine-tales?) Don't forget, dear Readers, that the vast Cittá del Messico is totally surrounded by garbage dumps, its genetic chain is a circular mountain of trash dumps all linked together as if to announce to the city: Garbage is Your Destiny. And now it seems that the foreseeable is happening:

The fire burst into life at the very door of Hipi's family's house, and everyone ran to put it out, all of them (the old, the babies, the huehuetiliztli and the xocoyotzin grab what they can); the suffocating smoke billows, asphyxia is imminent, there is no water, so one man quickly makes some orange juice and throws it on the blaze, another man shouts, laughs, and urinates powerfully on the fire (my mother remembers the day she reached the city and peed on the flame in the monument to the Revolution, remembers her dream about urinating until she refills the Lake Texcoconut; she remembers and I dream about the lost city of lakes! the place where the air is clear!), but it isn't enough, they all scatter through the thief-ridden slum (dolorous city, lost city, city without a name), all except one old man as stubborn as a stone. He remains seated in the cave when our buddy Egg rushes nervously in and pulls my mother to her feet (and me along with her, horrified—it goes without saying!), telling her, Angeles, get a move on, if this fire really catches, it'll consume all the oxygen in the city, the city will suffocate, and then they see the old veteran sitting there, immobile, waiting for the catastrophe, immutable, his face fixed, the inexpressive screen of the play of lights and shadows, and the philanthropic Egg tries to pull him to his feet as well, he warns him about the danger, but the old man is wrapped in his serape, and with his immobile face he says something in Nahuatl and our buddy Egg abandons him and swiftly guides my mother (and me, Readers, and me!) out of the dark shack to an Army jeep, where the grandparents, Rigoberto and Susana, wait and hug my mother and the general does the driving, throws it into reverse, gets stuck for an instant in the garbage. Hipi Toltec fighting the fire, but when he sees us, he becomes disconsolate. He picks up a long stick, sets it on fire, raises it as if to threaten us, then acts as if he were going to toss it on the garbage pyre, but instead he smiles in an ugly way, blows out the burning point of his javelin, and throws it at us. It looks like he's let us get away, let us save ourselves, my mother and I, Egg, and the grandparents, in an Army jeep, vintage 1944, about which General Palomar says: "This relic has finally come in handy! You drive, Mr. Egg, all right? I'm getting too old, and get us out of here, head for Oaxaca! Aaaaah, the city is burning! Let's head for the pure air, Susy, don't be afraid of anything. I've been in worse situations! Don't be afraid, Miss Angeles! Or your unborn baby!"

General Rigoberto Palomar falls forward, his face smashing against the windshield, then back, into the arms of his wife Doña Susana Rentería. In his back is the spear thrown by Hipi Toltec. My mother screams. It's the same lance that killed Tomasito down in Acapulco. Exactly the same. Doña Susana smiles and caresses the shaved head of her dead husband.

Hipi sheds his skin before the incredulous eyes of Egg and Angeles, and it's our fat friend, accelerating in horror, who shouts out a description of him, they were real tight, they played in the same group, he was tying up his trousers with a belt made of snakes, and he was shedding, he always was, but now in the light of the fire all his skin was vanishing. Hipi is peeling, right down to the muscle, his skin is coming off in huge chunks, like a peeled banana, right down to the white but corrupt, worm-eaten bone: in the distance, Hipi's skull shines after a while, smiling, amid the red night, and they can no longer see, no longer know, no longer imagine that new skin grows on him instantaneously, only the skull smiles, and we flee, and Doña Susy Rentería caresses the shaven head of her old husband, and Egg drives the jeep like a soul who is carrying the very devil who brought us here.

At the same time, my father is traveling next to Colasa, who sits alongside the albino driver, and no one can talk because of this man's constant chatter, this man the radio calls Bubble Gómez. He gives instructions nonstop, avoid the curve at mile 8, there's been a land-slide, there's an unnoticed Smokey at the Atlixco exit, slow down with the Manila provisions at the intersection of Highway 2 and the Christopher Columbus Highway, Inclán knows about your load, use your radar detector so they don't pick you up on Huamantla, the Tijuana Taxis at Teziutlán look funny to me, this is Bubble Gómez, do you read me, Bubble Gómez here, I'm protected, I'm carrying a little girl dressed like a religious nut (watch those personal comments now, son), accompanied by a guy who looks like a fag (come on now, son, you're charging a lot for this ride!), and it seems to me they could be like camouflage to screw up the cops if I have close en-counters of the worst kind, okay? Okay, Bubble Gómez, you're the man of the hour, you know your mission, but stay out of the way of the gringo Marines headed toward the Chachalacas River, and our own soldier boys, too, because some haven't been notified by Inclán, remember the situation is confused, a huge fire has broken out in the slums, it's hard to breathe here, go south young man, stay out of trouble, good buddy, roger, Bubble Gómez effectivesuffrageno-reelesion, no more lesions, CB radio signing off, good night.

"I'm hungry!" exclaimed Colasa Sánchez when Bubble Gómez turned off his CB. "Don't you have anything to eat?" she asked, and he just laughed. "What are you carrying in back?" A big old refrig-erator, said the albino. "Is it empty?" asked the girl. No, no way, answered Gómez, my job is to bring food back and forth to D.F. "So can we take a little to eat?" If you like, baby, but why don't you tell your main man here to take a nap and to stop looking at me like that, I don't like people to look at me like that, tell him it's dangerous to look at me like that, *tell him* later we'll stop and have some salt pork for breakfast! The driver laughed, and my father has no desire whatsoever to think or act, he prefers to tell himself you're an idiot, Angelito, you don't hear or understand anything, take Colasa's hand, it's there so you don't feel so alone and so fucked up so suddenly, go ahead, better than nothing, go ahead, pimp, aren't you hungry, too?

14

I'm an honest guy: the reader should know that a third situation is interpolating itself between these two, involving the circumstances of my mother and father; it's as if the citizens band the truckers use had squeezed between the AM and FM bands on the radio, so that if on the first band Colasa says I'm hungry, on the second Egg translates they've been tricked, they take shadows for reality, but on the third, the intruder band, Minister Federico Robles Chacón laughs and, like a child kept after school, writes one hundred times: You can't beat the system, you can't beat the system. He suddenly forgot which number he was on and bucked like a bad-tempered horse when the flow of his inspiration was cut off by the buzz of the telephone.

Robles picked up the presidential hot line with a stratospheric storm of curses; he felt, suddenly, full of self-pity. In the simple act of picking up the receiver of that green apparatus, he proved once again that he was sacrificing his time and his talent to the common good, to the highest goals of the state. And what did the community, personified in the voice of President Jesús María y José Paredes's private secretary, say to him? What? Whatwhat? Whatwhatwhat?

The secretary had left his temporary office in the National Palace to return to his regular office on Avenida Insurgentes, the one decorated with Roche-Bobois furniture. It was a sign that the crisis had passed. And now—whatwhat?—were they saying that Mamadoc was refusing to give the Cry this year? What the fuck was all that about? Say that again, Mr. Private Secretary? She refuses . . . ? But what the hell . . . what the fuck does that old slut think she's here for, anyway? Does she think we brought her here to knit booties and watch soap operas? You get her over here now! Whatwhat? She's already in my waiting room? That that's what she wants, to see me, to speak to me, or she won't give the Cry? The President says to go easy with her, that this monster is more useful to us than ever, that, after all, she's your Frankenstein, you invented her, Mr. Secretary, you imposed her on us. Of course, of course . . .

He hung up in a rage and ordered his toady to be sure that the Mother and Doctor of Mexicans was in his waiting room.

Meanwhile, the secretary of the SEPAFU calmed down, carefully put his papers away in a schoolboy's botany portfolio, and neatly tied the ribbons with bows.

Smiling, he received the apparition, as serene, certainly, as she, who came to ask him for God knows what, one of those little caprices of women in power, send the presidential jet to carry my angora sweater from Mexico to Rome, fire those three functionaries for having taken me to a fifth-rate restaurant, and get rid of these other five for having made jokes about me over the telephone, build me a swimming pool in the center of the Zócalo, burn the writings of my predecessors, their hospitals, movies, schools, there can be nothing before or after LITTLE OLD ME!

But now it was nothing like that, and he would have expected anything but this: the Holy Lady, wearing a riding cape of orange suede and chaps decorated with silver, and underneath a Mexican riding outfit, in the Jesusita in Chihuahua mode, suede, silver, short jacket, Andalusian riding skirt, and a riding crop in her hand, with which she instantly slapped Robles Chacón's face. Now he was astonished; she then dropped to her knees before him, weeping, damn it, with almost the same words as Concha Toro begging for the body of the Ayatollah, oh, my love, my little love, turn around and look at me at least, my little lovey-dovey, be nice, it's your honey talking to you, don't make me suffer, do it to me pretty, sweetie pie, give your honey what she wants, don't make me stay here on my knees like this, don't you see I'm dying for love of you?

No one had ever said anything like this to the vibrant but austere Robles Chacón: My honey man, give me some honey. (Mamadoc hugging the knees of the minister, who felt he was living through the worst nightmare of his life, but for that very reason he kept hoping that this one, like all the others, would end: this was merely an unpublished chapter in the Ayatollah saga. He closed his eyes and said: I am living through something that man I had the obligation to have killed should have lived through, this must be my punishment, these things don't happen to me, this is a scene from the theater of the incomplete, the incomplete that accompanies each and every one of our acts, this is the shortened apocalypse, only I had to live it because I killed that witch doctor. We have not gathered the One Hundred and Forty-Four Thousand Just Men. Forgive me, oh Lord—jabbered Robles Chacón, with Mamadoc still hugging his knees—nor have we left the Babylon that dizzies nor has the seventh cup been filled—I'll drink the others in Guanajuato!—with the wine of God's vengeance, and I did not find the number 666 on Matamoros Moreno's hirsute body when I carefully examined it, and I don't know if there is a woman in the jungle, but the harlot in purple did appear. Here is this great whore, hugging me, squeezing her cheek against my fly, God help me! and it's getting hard against my will, and she, give me your rod give me your son give me your come don't deny to me what you have given to all Mexican women, the right to a son on October 12.)

"There's no time!" the minister stupidly exclaimed.

"We can extend the contest a year or even ten years, we have the power to change dates, and if we don't, what good does it do to be us? Ten years, why not? it doesn't matter as long as our little boy wins the contest and the dynasty is ours, honey man! yours and mine, my little lovey-dovey, you and I can play with time, set the clocks back, put them ahead, whatever we want, I've been thinking a lot while I've been all alone, why do we have power if we can't change time? What good is power if you can't stop time and even tell death to get lost, tell me, boss man?"

She opened her eyes wide and looked at him, her mascara running because of her tears, potholes in her plastered-over face where she'd been rubbing against his fly, her original dark skin showing through here and there.

"We can't do that," the cornered minister whimpered meekly,

convinced that the Lady had gone mad. "It's a law, we have to obey it, laws are meant to be obeyed . . ."

"But not carried out!" She gave vent to her emotion, spattering her viscous saliva over the functionary's trousers.

He looked at her as if she were some apparition fabricated by Maybelline: he realized that this woman had been born expressly to play this scene; her whole life had been a preparation for this moment she was now living out. For that reason, Robles Chacón concentrated his intelligence and said the best thing he could:

"Dear Lady: laws are terrible, but customs are even worse."

With that sentence, which he felt was worthy of him, Federico Robles Chacón began to reconstitute his shattered aplomb. He realized where he was, but the outrageous woman at his feet was whimpering, either you make me yours or I don't give the Cry, either you give me a son or I go on strike, either you extend the time for the contest or I kill myself, I swear I will! I was living very happily with my boyfriend Leoncito and my job as a stenographer, you came and transformed me, now pay up, I'll kill myself, I swear, and the chaps whipped against the ministerial carpeting like slaps.

Federico Robles Chacón painfully pulled himself back together again. He was in the SEPAFU Secretariat Building on Avenida Insurgentes, almost at the intersection with Viaducto, at the ill-named Insurgentes Bridge, fifteenth floor, private telephone number 515-1521, the place from which the Ayatollah Matamoros had observed the most terrible action in the life of FRCH (as the press called him), his having ordered the death of several thousand rioters (innocent? guilty? the system doesn't judge, it concludes: you can't fight the system, it is all of us, but it is more than all of us, not better, all of us with power, said Robles Chacón, trembling, he who considered himself a liberal man, on the left, humanitarian, enlightened, sensitive), and at his feet his creature, the Mother and Doctor of all Mexicans, who negated everything he thought about himself, kneeling, weeping, threatening to ruin all the symbolic ceremonies of the nation: FRCH thought of himself as a little Christopher (just like me!): in looking for the Orient, he fails and finds America; his success derives from his failure, his perception tells him the world is flat, but his intention tells him the world is round: someone else's perception negates his visionary intention, but it is intention that triumphs.

Could that be true once again, here, tonight, with this serpent woman, this Cihuacóatl hugging his knees?

He stretched out his arms, tried to stand her up, rejected the vision that succeeded the one about Columbus: now the Minister of State's perception told him that the country was flat and repetitive and that hell must be the same, everything repeats itself eternally in Mexico, the same cruelties and injustices, the same useless jokes that exorcise each other, the same stupidities, so it's ultimately in stupidity repeated eternally where injustice and jokes blend and dissipate and become eternal.

Now all of it (the fatal perception of the country) was getting mixed up, the effect of the cause, the cause of the effect, with national planning: economics = fatalism. And a woman at his feet asking him for something that wasn't economics and wasn't fatality either . . .

FRCH felt overcome by the kneeling embrace that Mamadoc was bestowing on him, screw me or there's no Cry: fornicate with me or there will be no contest, give me a son or give me death, come on, don't be a fag:

What was better, to succumb to economics or to succumb to fatality? And suddenly my direct line was disconnected, my vision of that scene faded, and I was left without knowing what Federico Robles Chacón decided or what the ex-stenographer from the SE-PAFU secretarial pool decided. But in this I shall from now on resemble you out there. Enjoy yourselves, your mercies, and remember that whatever you do, Minister Federico Robles Chacón and the Mother and Doctor of all Mexicans are going to be short of breath because the oxygen in the city is disappearing, consumed by the flames from the garbage . . .

You give them their destinies, svp! This novel belongs to you, dear Readers!

15

 "I'm *hungry!*" Colasa Sánchez shouted again at dawn; my father opened his eyes and woke up from a long dream in which my mother appeared to him, always close and always (reach for her!) untouchable! no matter how far my father stretched out his hands and repeated to himself: "I'm not worthy of her. Not yet. I have to deserve her."

He's a romantic, a knight errant. Colasa is hungry. Bubble Gómez pays no attention to Dad's reasons. On the other hand, he does share, with a trace of cruelty, her reasons. He knows that the reasons belong to all three of them, and that the dawn has overtaken them in a new landscape, as different from the uplands all consumed in fires and asphyxia as heaven is different from hell: here a rolling plain announced in the glare of the morning light its descent to the sea. The mists were lifting along the wide rivers, and the coconut palms, the lemon and orange trees, charmingly shook off the dew, indifferent to their fate at the hands of the Tropicana juice company; the warm breeze shakes the clothes left to dry on the red stone and the roof tiles shine as if varnished; the whitewashed façades of the houses, the smell of the early-morning coffee and papaya opened by machete, the pineapple and tamarind reach the most secret corners of the tongue and palate.

This is the albino driver's supreme cruelty. Like Lucifer in the desert, he shows the pilgrims this temptation of sweet, tropical Veracruz, with its hint of the nearby Gulf and the Caribbean, where all the sweetness of life in the New World given by Columbus to Castile and Aragon is concentrated, between Cartagena de Indias and New Orleans, Havana and Campeche, Barbados and Jamaica: the prodigious cornucopia of red snapper, lobster, oysters, and swordfish; dyes, baroque pearls, and huge turtles.

And once he's tempted them, Bubble Gómez says: "We'll eat raw meat."

He opens the rear doors of the trailer. A polar exhalation paralyzes their facial muscles. Bubble Gómez, used to it, does not flinch; he jumps into the icebox, similar to a bank vault, where the steers become visible, hallucinations dreamed, Uncle Fernando Benítez once said, by Soutine, red and skinned, their blood and fat congealed, decapitated, their hooves cut off, swinging on the black hooks: a red, white, and black world where the albino driver is totally at ease, choosing the steer he likes best, bored, whistling that old song about the old milch cow, and how, and how, until he raises an arm as white as the frost surrounding it, rose-colored like the dry blood of the beasts, and unhooks a peculiarly shaped steer, long and narrow, small in comparison to the others, but tasty, very tasty, says Bubble Gómez when the three of them kneel down around the skinned, decapitated animal, which has a metal band encrusted with frozen blood on its rear leg. That's how they hang up this animal: the leg bracelet is connected to the frozen hook.

Bubble Gómez cuts off slices of raw meat, and Colasa looks interested in the metal bracelet, and Angel tries to be friendly, saying that all they need are these slices and some chiles, and nosy Colasa lifts the beast's leg and reads the inscription on the bracelet

FF   ♥   FB

and she stops a second, closes her eyes, and eats quickly, while the driver comments as he devours the steer that it's like eating steak tartar or beef sushi, or deer stew, or beef broiled creole-style, he knows about these things, tricks of the trade, and then goes back to singing: she ambles through the meadow, killing flies with her tail, tail, tail.

16. Why Are We in Veracruz?

The belly of the jungle is like my mother's belly, mud and water, but why am I so happy where I am while this ghostly man runs flees wishes he could scream surrounded by the night and the luminous eyes shine as if they were imagining themselves seeing because they do not see in the dark seeing what they should imagine: running out of the jungle and occasionally looking back desperate running and always seeing how close the pyramid is in the jungle like a back projection gigantic in the distance.

Villa Cardel on the banks of the Chachalacas River has everything you could want for your vacation: Pepsi-Cola and Raleigh (ralley-rattle-railing) cigarette signs, mud streets and equally attractive mudholes, an astonishing variety of insects an entire zoo walking around the streets freely amusing groups of black, ravenous pigs with raspberry-colored markings among the tightly packed antennas of TV CANTINAS, from which only half the citizens who enter ever leave alive abundant discotheques with tin roofs where you can dance to the latest hits of the Four Fuckups the best bordellos on the Gulf an everlasting unparalleled offering of pretty girls who came down from the mountains to give pleasure to the motley crew of white and black gringos in perpetual rotation never more than 179 days in Cardel troops from the Central American Army made up of Salvadorans and Hondurans trained by the gringos and also dark-skinned gringos Chicanos Puerto Ricans who aren't noticed here in Veracruz and don't have to be rotated in accordance with the law since they are identical to the little boys who show their swollen bellies and tiny penises among the shacks and alleys of Villa Cardel but the little boys don't screw and the troops do with the sad whores down from the highlands in search of dollars whores up from Honduras when Operation Big Pine moved to Veracruz women from Panama Colombia Venezuela known as Contadora widows when the peace collapsed whores who came from the halls of Moctezuma and the shores of Tripoli suffering from IRS (Illnesses Related to Sex) who came here to give them to the gringos and their collaborators from Honduras and Salvador and saddest of all the Señoritas Butterfly from Veracruz the local ingenues seduced and abandoned with their children as green as the jungle blond like the golden eyes of the fallen Angel of Independence which my mother saw from close up the day of the earthquake always crying these hated, hateful children: at the entrance to Villa Cardel a hand-lettered, badly painted wooden sign that says in red letters: Now Entering Little Saigon, and beyond, a horizon made up of tents stained with oil and field-kitchen smoke, tortuous mud paths and mudholes abandoned jeeps helicopters that fell down for lack of fuel or screws dogs and on the promontory where the officers live the CAT HUTS with mosquito netting at the doors to let the rancid breeze in and to keep the insects, the bat shit, and the wild pig snouts out he never stops running while the back projection of the El Tajín pyramid grows and grows. The man shouts call me Will in order to get out of the jungle and enter a novel because he has forgotten that this jungle is in a novel in the same way that I, Christopher, am inside my mother's belly OUCH! an extremely tall man bald but with a long mass of yellow ash cascading down the shoulders of his black leather jacket he plays bowls in a jungle clearing he has in his hand a wooden ball he throws it down an improvised path and the ball is going to smash against the pins set up on a platform of rough boards the ball does smash against the pins, which don't fall but break into pieces under the impact of the wooden ball painted with white stars on a blue background call me Will. Will Gingerich running with no force left out of the jungle wanting to abandon forever the pyramid

surprised by the permanently navy-blue sky of this night which is
really day but he doesn't know it under the shadow of the pyramid
and the foliage woven like a wet overcoat over the jungle of Veracruz:
Will Gingerich feels trapped inside the pyramid he cannot distinguish
between open air and trapped air makes no distinction between stone
and foliage.

NOW ENTERING LITTLE SAIGON: at the door of a one-story house
painted indigo blue with a sign that says THE CELESTIAL EMPIRE
a diminutive Oriental man with shaven temples an aroma of opium
dressed in an anachronistic, suffocating Mao uniform is sitting in his
straw rocker and fanning himself (his feet never touch the ground)
while he shouts to and solicits the blond, dark, black soldiers from
Detroit Mongoloids from Vermont Chicanos from Chicago Neori-
cans from Amsterdam Avenue disturbed violent homeless people
recruited from the cities of the North Entel the most bootifull gills
of the two seas, the Pacific and the Atrantic, await you he says fanning
himself unhurriedly with no apparent sadness only his long yellow
fingers clutching the fan as if it were a life preserver his eyes more
veiled than ever as if once the light had disguised itself as fire because
that day the sun just imagine that day the sun came up in the west
. . . I Little Christopher in my mother's belly
You, Reader
My enormous superhuman effort (I swear it) to listen to the OTHER
in order to know myself to be UNIQUE
That day the sun rose in the west: like an angel made of yellow ash
and black leather, the tall man with watery eyes and square jaw,
which he shaved every six hours so it would shine with a chrome-
plated luster, his face is bluish and his cheeks metallic, a shiny gray:
he wears a black shirt with a clerical collar and a black leather jacket
and blue chinos combat boots two cartridge belts cross over his flat
stomach and are held up by his hook-like hips, which are obscenely
narrow, and from the cartridge belts hang hand grenades and from
the man's hand flies a ball decorated with the Stars and Bars and on
the back of his jacket he wears his title: THE PRIEST OF DEATH
The frightened eyes of a tiger in the jungle night two yellow me-
dallions set in the foliage that covers the pyramid CAT HUTS is an
acronym for Central American Tropical Habitat created for the War
of the Isthmus and the invasion of Nicaragua during the eighties:
their peculiarity is that they last only six months in the Central

American climate and then they disintegrate: a cute way of suggesting
that we get our job done in six months and get out no Vietnams a
limit of six months to the campaign before the Nervous Nellies of
Nebraska and the Anxious Aunties of Alabama go crazy seeing so
much blood spilled right out of their TV sets onto the floors of their
living rooms furnished by J. C. Penney's seeing so many boys come
home dead in black plastic body bags dead in the jungles of Veracruz
all of it planned as a lightning campaign no need even to take into
account troop movements governed by law number —— which man-
dates giving official notice of troop movements only when those troops
have remained more than 180 days in a single place and around here
no one stays a minute more than 179 days so no one knows anything
and nevertheless the number-one bestseller during the year 1992 in
the United States is called *Why Are We in Veracruz?* by Norman
Mailer the always *energetic* (sixty-nine years of age) Brooklyn-born
author: Why does Norman Mailer dare to write this book? Why is
he trying to dishearten the national effort to eradicate the Communist
threat on our frontiers? Doesn't Mailer believe in the domino theory?
Doesn't national security matter to Mailer? Or is he only interested
in fame? Doesn't he see the red tide rolling toward Harlingen, Texas,
bringing with it the destruction of American youth by the Managua-
controlled drug traffic? asked President Dumble Danger from his
hospital room, where he was surrounded by plastic flowers and
TelePrompTers. (The President was wearing a World War II para-
trooper's uniform, ready, as he said, for the final jump, and had a
quilt over his legs, on which pious hands had embroidered his motto:
GOD IS MY CO-PILOT.
The pins split apart under the impact of the ball with the stars on it
and a nine-year-old boy, as green as the forest, retrieves the wooden
ball and returns it to the man with the long, ash-yellow hair tumbling
down his back and wearing the black jacket: The boy goes back to
the platform and sweeps away the splinters with a broom
Will Gingerich running out of the jungle under a permanently navy-
blue sky
I in my mother's belly one month before my happy arrival in the
world a Mexican boy like me but he already born and I not yet he
picking up the broken pieces of clay the broken earth varnished blood-
red the boy picks up the pieces of idols vessels ceramics and patiently
replaces them with another twelve figurines and the man with the

title THE PRIEST OF DEATH written across the back of his black leather jacket again throws the ball and breaks only ten of the twelve figurines and then turns his fury against the promontory where the CAT HUTS are crowded together: he looks at the ruins-to-be of the prefabricated shacks set to self-destruct in September they've been here since April replacements have not arrived he turns and looks with a resigned ardor at the eternal ruins of the Totonacas how long is this going to go on I thought we were going to clean this up in six months and get out I thought we would never have to request more CAT HUTS because we weren't going to be here in this clearing between the pyramid and the temporary housing for the invading Army more than six months what frightens the tiger?

the officers' city on the hill is surrounded by concertina wire, the entrance is flanked by twin machine-gun towers and a sign legible at a distance of a quarter of a mile:

RESTRICTED AREA. USE OF DEADLY FORCE AUTHORIZED

I, Christopher, do not understand why the Priest of Death again tosses the ball, sending it spinning against the clay figurines, and this time he rolls a strike because within a month I will be BORN and now I must take more and more account of the presence of the OTHER, that OTHER to whom I speak even if he doesn't speak to me and I only have you, READER, to understand finally what I intuit outside my chamber of genetic echoes you must tell me for example that . . . Reverend Royall Payne looks one day with his eyes of burnished steel at his intelligence officer, Professor Will Gingerich, and he says in his most truculent tone stroke my chopper Prof go on just feel how smooth its sides are close your eyes and tell me please if it doesn't make you as hot as I am to wipe out these greasers in a single day, which I could do by firing my portable Minuteman 92 against Jalapa and make pickled jalapeños out of those spicy jalapeño chicks hahaha tell me the truth egghead why are we in Veracruz?

Will Gingerich's terror as he flees through the jungle has an echo: the jungle of red suns and blue nights tells him it isn't possible you can't come back to me there is no possible reconciliation none none The Priest of Death little Christopher is a veteran of the Contra wars in Central America, Grenada, and Vietnam his name is Royall Payne (Reverend Royall Payne) and he's a fundamentalist preacher who made a fortune by refusing merely to preach comfortably and only practicing his preaching under the protection of a pleasure dome built by the contributions of the faithful in a southern city, instead he decided to put his anti-communist, fundamentalist crusade into practice and be present on all the battle fronts where the red menace is being confronted: when Royall Payne returns from his sanguinary tourism in praise of the Lord, multitudes crowd the entrance to his pleasure dome in Savannah, Georgia (it was a beautiful Southern port with a muggy, sugary Caribbean atmosphere until Payne turned it into the seat of his fundamentalist crusade, surrounded it with gas stations built in the shape of tabernacles, turned the mansions into motels and filled the labyrinthine streets and plazas with shops that sold the Bible on cassette—read by Reverend Payne—Bible videos— acted out by Reverend Payne, his family, and his associates—rubber baby bottles stamped with the picture of Reverend Payne blessing the city and the world, and plastic bottles of holy water to put into the formula so that children would learn from the cradle on to recognize the preacher who would guide them toward their reunion with Jesus, outwardly Protestant but actually Catholic the Reverend, since he sells holy baby bottles and also sells holy enemas the extremes meet but, brothers and sisters, be very careful not to mix up the orifices), his only condition being that wherever he was there be television cameras the Reverend would never abandon the faithful but instead of appearing every Sunday on TV wearing shiny shantung or costly double-knits and Cardin shirts or lizard Lacoste shirts like the other TV preachers, now utterly displaced by the energy of the most Fundamental of Fundamentalists, he would always appear in battle dress wearing his black jacket with THE PRIEST OF DEATH emblazoned on the back like the prophets of the Old Testament, the OT in the Reverend's personal shorthand, his fax machine to the Almighty his direct line to Divine Grace: he marched out to battle just as Joshua had tumbled down walls and crossed rivers and made the sun stop in its path across the sky and now they don't let him carry out his mission, they force him to be content stroking the metallic body of his Apache attack helicopter, as smooth as the cheeks he shaves four times a day, petting the decals tenderly stuck onto the fuselage and being satisfied with climbing up to the cockpit of his chopper and sermonizing his intelligence officer, Professor Gingerich, the greenish boy who sets up the Totonaca figurines on the board, the inimitable ruins of El Tajín, the parrots, the tigers, the river:

GOD IS PLEASURE! shouts the Reverend to his intelligence officer in this wasteland of Veracruz as long as we carry on His work on earth He rewards us pleasure is only odious when we do not deserve it when we seek pleasure before we seek the Lord but if we first seek the Lord we shall always find Him He is only absent when we do not seek Him out all we have to do is seek Him to find Him and the nothing is a sin NOTHING NOTHING is impossible and everything is possible is permitted in the name of the Lord everything is permitted to him who has found the Lord and the voice of the Lord has said: Go forth and be my soldier exterminate my enemies and then I shall receive you and you will have the pleasure which I am! says the Reverend to Professor Gingerich of Dartmouth College and Will Gingerich realizes that the Reverend is surrounded by a luminous, orange-colored square and the feline purring of a TV camera (a tiger in the jungle): If you turn your back on Jesus, Jesus will turn his back on you, concludes Royall Payne, followed by organ music and a list of thanks to the program's patrons and an announcement that this program reaches your home via satellite thanks to a subsidy from the Union Carbide Corporation from somewhere in Veracruz: now you know why we're in Veracruz! Close-up of the Reverend's fists and slow fade:

Royall Payne jumps off his designer helicopter picks up a towel to wipe off his sweat lathers up his cheeks picks up his razor and reminds Will Gingerich you are here to tell Washington what it wants to hear nothing else don't work so hard don't even leave your CAT HUT just write your weekly report saying there are Communists in Veracruz Soviet agents Cuban bases even if it isn't true: modern intelligence consists in telling your superiors what they want to hear: the rest of the time, well, there's a case of beer over there and in Cardel there are very pretty girls if you don't mind dying of some venereal disease but what can stop sex, eh, Professor? Go on tell me what can stop it. I'll tell you: the fear of God, but you, an agnostic secular humanist, what do you do, Professor? Screw and die!

The helicopters that still work leave the jungle clearing near El Tajín in search of nonexistent targets / they see a nosegay of roof tiles and they drop a bouquet of napalm / they seek out the thickest places in the forest / the mangrove swamps the rotten vines / the wavy fronds of the palm trees and they open the valves of Agent Orange to exterminate all greenery /a chemical, dark-red cloud to defoliate the jungle / an orange-colored juice to defoliate its inhabitants: they come back late from their incursions when the tiger opens his golden eyes and begins his nocturnal prowling / they withdraw to their CAT HUTS and open their refrigerators and drink Iron City beer and tear open their cellophane bags and eat pretzels Doritos and individual-sized pizzas: then they drop a nickel into the beer bottle and try to see, while they laugh and make jokes about Thomas Jefferson's being a shithead, if what they say about Iron City beer is true, that it can dissolve a nickel, but they don't know that the orange pesticide is dissolving them and they that now are twenty, thirty years old and then go home with medals and beer bellies and hearts swollen with patriotism to Allentown, Pennsylvania, and Lansing, Michigan, years later will wonder why is my pancreas my liver my fucking brain my colon my rectum dissolving?

they don't wonder about this now now they go out on patrol carrying their Backpack Nukes: this is a green knapsack which contains a nuclear device equivalent to 250 tons of TNT and they go down to Villa Cardel spend a jolly Saturday in the cantinas where half of those who enter do not leave alive but they emerge safe and sound: who's going to mess with a Detroit black six feet tall and carrying 250 tons of nuclear explosives? or with a Puerto Rican from the island of Vieques armed with / who walk in shouting THIS IS RAMBOWAR! and later on they decide to visit one of the bordellos they've been in all of them except one: the one that belongs to the old Chinese / he's put them off / but they have bet each other that before leaving Veracruz they are going to screw every available woman and they're about to reach 175 days here so they know that in four more days they'll be transferred so that there will never be any official record of their ever having been in Veracruz they walk out singing happy tunes by Stephen Foster and Irving Berlin America America from sea to shining sea: the Oriental guardian of the Celestial Empire fans himself and rocks smiles at them and invites them Amelica? flum sea to shiny seamen? you go in now see mos' elotic woman flom sea to shiny seamen smiles the diminutive Deng Chopin inviting the gringo soldiers in with his long mandarin pianist's fingers and the boys from Detroit or PR look at each other, elbow each other with a joking air of complicity and they enter the Celestial Empire giggling Will Gingerich doesn't know it but he's delirious and in every one of the jungle's shapes he sees a frightened tiger he imagines he's a big sports hero a pitcher for the St. Louis Cardinals a fullback for the Los Angeles Rams the oldest winner at Wimbledon he's delirious but not even that can diminish his fear they're going to come back they're going to get him he walks in circles through the jungle they're everywhere and he nowhere; the navy-blue sky splits open: the moon parts the veil and sticks to the sky like a silver decal: Will Gingerich flees and the Reverend Payne argues: why are we in Veracruz? Caressing the metallic body of his Apache attack helicopter, as metallic as his cheeks shaved four times a day, caressing the tenderly applied decals on the Apache each decal a star with a skull in its center and surrounded by statements in which only the geography varies: I WAS IN VIETNAM. I WAS IN GRENADA. I WAS IN NICARAGUA. MEXICO NEXT: Reverend Payne begins to pound desperately on the fuselage of his helicopter scratching the decals saying with a hoarse voice: Why are we in Veracruz? and Gingerich trying to quiet him down telling him we're here to protect the oil installations in the Gulf of Mexico without which the free world would be strategifucked . . . and the Reverend interrupts him with an open, hard slap on the body of the helicopter that echoes like a gigantic can of Campbell's soup allowed to swell monstrously in the boiling humidity of the jungle: the truth! shouts the Reverend the truth! We've got to terminate this country that exports greasers who are invading us like the plague of locusts that destroyed Pharaoh's power! Michigan is not growing South Carolina is not growing Georgia isn't growing, not even your own home state Texas is growing, Professor, we aren't having kids but all these greasers grow and grow and cross over and cross over and they'll end up coupling with our own daughters and mothers and wives who have emerged like Venus from the Caucasian genetic pool Are you listening to me, Professor? haven't you heard how often they call each other motherfuckers? well I want to send them back to their mommas air-mail with my faithful Minuteman 92 kill them in their father's seed before they enter their mother's belly repulsive filthy greasers invaders of other people's clean white American property / camping out on our green lawns Are you going to allow it, Professor? But you're opposed to abortion, Reverend, how are you going to halt the demographic explosion of the Hispanics if you are an apostle of the anti-abortion movement in the good old U.S.A., but they are not U.S. of A. nor are they good nor are they old said the Reverend in a horrible explosion of rage, throwing himself on the unarmed figure of Professor Will Gingerich and killing an unborn child is not the same as killing a grownup Mexican with a mustache to keep him from procreating, it isn't the same, Prof, admit it! Will Gingerich, assaulted by Reverend Payne, lands face-down next to a slow river surrounded by burning tigers

there is only one room in Deng Chopin's bordello: it is divided by a vaporous but stained gauze curtain stained with what only God knows / semen from an onanistic Chicano, bat shit or beer or guacamole it's impossible to tell: the tiny Oriental lets the men in invites them to undress and then silently approach the canopied bed, which in turn is wrapped in complicated mosquito netting arranged like theater curtains, without waking up the sleeping woman: she is the sleeping beauty that's the secret of this celestial house, that there is *only one prostitute* here and she makes love *asleep*: asleep? The two gringos laugh and Deng Chopin closes his eyes significantly and invitingly: asleep and the two soldiers nudge each other and laugh finally Nat what we always wanted none of these pigs let us listen Macho Nacho making love at the same time you from the front and me from the rear then we trade places why not smiles Deng Chopin: only in Caldel can you carry out your illusions he invites them to undress and take off their backpacks ah no laugh Nat and Macho Nacho never, we can be naked but we never give up our BACKPACK NUKES even for a second they laugh but don't you worry now Chink man, the only rockets that be gonna go off here are when my buddy and I come inside your sleepin' beauty they cackle Deng Chopin fans himself doesn't laugh only raises his eyebrows and goes back to his rocker on the main street of Villa Cardel: Now Entering Little Saigon

they told me there wouldn't be any killing! exclaims Professor Gingerich they recruited me to help the cause of peace to avoid a war between the United States and Mexico I got out of the Acapulco catastrophe and they told me in the U.S. Embassy that the way to work for peace was to do some intelligence investigation in Veracruz the alternative? we send you to Texas to work on the border I'm a professor in Dartmouth College it doesn't matter it says here that you're a Texan it doesn't matter where you work but where you're from as far as repatriation is concerned Professor Gingerich the honorable way out of this fix is an intelligence mission in Veracruz our reward to you will be to send you back to Dartmouth College where Christmases are indeed white and the mountains are green and the

summers are as slow and hot as deep lakes and the pale dahlias and
yellow jasmines flower: don't worry Professor there won't be any
killing it's a reconnaissance-intelligence mission: we've got to find a
reason, Professor Gingerich: why are we in Veracruz? Reverend Royall Payne gets into his black helicopter, which is like a spider a
caterpillar a hidden diamond a diabolical crown the devil's cloven
hooves the anus of the vampire as black as the night of the day in
which the sun set in the east and the cats closed their eyes and the
dogs did not dare to bark / the Reverend gets into his Apache attack
helicopter, which he learned to fly on direct orders from President
Rambold Ranger who told him: "Royall, you are God's co-pilot. If
I weren't here, you would make the Big Decision in my place": the
President personally gave him this marvelous apparatus, which can
fly at 327 miles per hour for six consecutive hours at thirty thousand
feet detecting and calibrating the distance to every aircraft that comes
within three hundred miles: capable of locating more than 250 targets
and making thirty air interceptions: but the most beautiful aspect of
Royall Payne's chopper is its rotodome, the disk that holds the radar
and radio antennas of the craft with a range that duplicates that of
the most advanced systems currently known—it looks like a white
emblem mounted on top of the helicopter and thinking about the
decals stamped with the death's-head and the anxious difference
between stamping the skull on the name of Mexico and adding the
address of the newest decal: CANADA NEXT COLOMBIA NEXT
TRINIDAD NEXT said Royall Payne, who had decided in that instant
to speak to the world through the microphone of his trusty Apache
broadcasting his message of war and salvation with each steel pulse
of the blades of his helicopter blades that shine like the shining blades
that every six hours shave the shining cheeks of the man of steel the
Priest of Death striking fear into the air of the old Totonaca cemeteries
bending the trunks of the palm trees beating the zinc roofs against
the cardboard walls shortening the life of the CAT HUTS, which are
already on the point of disintegration: someday you'll thank me the
Reverend whines as if in a stellar sermon but the voice from the radio
says don't come back Roy go back to your base no roars Reverend
Royall someday you'll thank me he shouted in pain biting his hands
on which was tattooed

DEATH BEFORE DISHONOR

but the voice from the radio a distant faggy voice paid by the reds an anti-American insolent Massachusetts voice Roy don't forget that we are only here to protect the oil supply we do what we have to do we follow orders Roy we apply the instructions of the CIA pamphlet we try to neutralize all Mexicans within a radius of ten miles around Villa Cardel and the banks of the Chachalacas but we cannot go any farther there is an agreement with the Mexican government not to go any farther you can't launch your missiles against Mexico City not even against Jalapa Roy: pay attention to the Gulf of Campeche Resolution! Then we're involved in the same old thing we won't win this war either! shouted the preacher, his hands bleeding bitten by his own teeth don't be stupid Roy remember that this little war is only a media event an informative show covered by TV and the press to prove to the world but above all to ourselves that we really are macho and it's also being staged so that the Mexican government can prove to its people that they have to unite in order to defend this shitty country it's important for both of us don't forget that what are you going to do Roy where are you going Roy Roy! don't forget how the script goes don't do anything weird remember that at the end we're going to say we won the war then we get out we win and we get out Roy don't forget that everything's already set WE WIN AND WE GET OUT ROY!

A river appears in the middle of the night it flows luminous and slow like a caress a distant guitar is heard and Will Gingerich wonders why all this makes him afraid Christopher don't you ever feel terror amid the placental pleasures and protection of your mother Angeles's womb?

She doesn't move Nat told Macho Nacho the chink told you that she's asleep go on open the curtain Nat one mosquito net after another sure so she can sleep in peace but if my black dingaling doesn't wake her up I don't know how yours will better measure mine why do you black guys always think that God gave you bigger bananas than anybody else? okay set her up so we can have some fun with you in front and me in back then we switch listen look at her lift up her legs and look at her she's not very young see around here who cares if they're young or old the important thing is a piece of ass forget if it's young or old Macho it isn't that her legs weigh a lot heavy sleep Nat try to turn her over I'm telling you she weighs a ton

the equivalent of 250 tons of TNT

BACKPACK NUKE
FRONT-ROW DICK
NEVER LEAVE HOME WITHOUT THEM

and her arms are real stiff let's see these marble tits frozen spread her legs and what about her ass? frozen too frozen and locked tighter than a safety-deposit box at Chase Manhattan Bank stick your finger in it doesn't go in Nat this ass is a dry CAT BOX! no one's gone through there in a hundred years and what about behind? BACK DOOR! something's going on back here and the face what's it like Harry made of porcelain it looks like a doll's face made of Chinese porcelain it's pretty but it's old white real white with closed eyes powdered and with red hair touch her hair Nat do it for me I'm looking down here Nat it isn't hair it's a wig what the fuck it slipped off there's a liquid running out her ears what's she got in her nose cotton wads holy shit Harry what she's got running down her ass stinks like hell like disinfectant it smells like formaldehyde holy shit she just now opened her eyes Macho Nacho but she isn't moving them they're made of glass holy papaya this bitch is sick Nat this bitch's got something wrong with her this bitch is dead don't be a moron this fucking bitch is spoiled cold cuts don't shout like that Macho for the sake of Luis Rafael I beg you Sánchez don't make such a racket that's right be careful watch out what you're doing don't clench your teeth don't clench fists don't move your BACKPACK NUKE like that if you pull on that string shiiiiiiiiiiiiiiiit
someday you'll thank me
the greasers breed like rats so they can go for the good life
so they can end up the way everybody wants to end up
as in a stellar sermon
TV and refrigerators and football stadiums and
white asses and things that work and hospitals
and cereals that snap crackle and pop and bread without flies
and American cars Akutagawas and Togos and Meijis and Kabuki 2002s
each one of your little brothers who stays here means one red-blooded American home saved thanks to me!
Cardel Chachalacas Tajín Totonacas
Reverend Royall Payne looks at the vision of the Peak of Orizaba which is rapidly approaching his whitish-blue eyes reverberating looking at the frozen peak of the volcano an image of his own gaze as if

the humble toiler in the Lord's work could transform himself into
nature
tall white eternal rock and ice: permanent
NO MORE DEFEATS! MORE DEFEATS MEAN MORE REVENGE!
NO MORE VIETNAMS! LETHAL FORCE IS AUTHORIZED!
NO MORE DEFEATS!
in the river crossing the river under the water masked by the fiery
water imagining that his pantheistic anthropologist's dream is finally
going to resolve itself in the nightmare of dying and becoming hamburger repeats Will Gingerich under the slow and flaming river but
the flames only consume the town of Cardel the river is a border and
the professor of Dartmouth College crosses to the other side and falls
face-down on the fertile mud of the river
the United States lost its innocence in Veracruz muttered Professor
Gingerich when the hands of others (friendly? unfriendly?) grabbed
him under the armpits and pulled him out of his mud bed on the
banks of the slow river surrounded by tigers with golden eyes and
backs of fire the butterflies crowning the waters the ghost of the moon
in the eternal blue black night
in Veracruz
in Vietnam
in Korea
in Hiroshima
in Dresden
in Santo Domingo
in Bluefields
in Managua
in Port-au-Prince
in Santiago de Cuba
in Manila
in Andersonville
in the Little Bighorn
in Tripoli
in Chapultepec
in Chapultepec
in Chapultepec
and in El Tajín
the broken clay
bells of the moon

hummingbird magician
serpent skirts
stars of the south
the tiger said: fire in half of the night
the clay said: mirror of smoke
I said crisscrossed with voices:

17. *The Other Bank of the River*

 After he'd been rescued from the mud on the floodplain, Professor Gingerich said all these things as he was eating some hamburgers cooked up by the albino trucker. My father and the girl dressed as a Discalced Carmelite listened to him.

The Yankee spoke to her, raising his voice slightly above the din behind us, endless said my father: Gingerich only stared at the girl, recognizing her, as he spoke near the low, hospitable fire in this forest clearing.

He stopped occasionally to chew the hamburger. Then he revealed, staring at Colasa Sánchez, that he was speaking and imagining at the same time; such was the scope of his gaze. When I am born, I may perhaps have a better opportunity to understand how people look at things and persons and to read in looks the names of desire. Although from this moment on I do know (my father looks for me, you understand, Reader) that if desire is only the imitation of another desire it's because when we want something we want at the same time to be wanted. That's the way Gingerich and Colasa look at each other. Both know what the Professor heard from the lips of his deceased friend D. C. Buckley. Be careful with that woman. Use a wooden penis. Penis du bois.

Tonight my father divines in the trembling of Gingerich's features, a man just saved from death in the jungle, an availability in the face of another's desire. An aperture. She needs no introduction: Colasa Sánchez, Matamoros Moreno's bastard. He says simply, as she swallows a piece of hamburger, which she holds delicately between her fingers, the way one might pick up a host, that he came from the other bank. What did he want? Something huge, something very difficult, for him to have risked death by crossing over.

The other bank: my father was going to interrupt, by saying something banal: he swam. He stopped just in time. The night, the light of the fire, the clamor behind us (I am my father! you are the reader!) transformed her; Colasa Sánchez was a necessary being, she revealed herself as a daughter of necessity, more even than her father Matamoros Moreno and her mother Anónima Sánchez. She needed; that was her supplication that night.

The other bank: Will Gingerich stretched out his hand and touched Colasa Sánchez's fingers with his own. Cinnamon-colored skin, tea-colored, Carmelite-colored. Guess: where are the scapularies? Will closed his eyes and accepted the necessity of Colasa. Desire is necessary and it must run the risk of transformation. We desire what we desire not only in order to have it but also in order to change into the image of our desire: into our own image.

Would the object of desire resist?

Would it admit its own need, the need of the other, even at the cost of transformation?

When my father saw their fingers touch and when he imagined the cruel union of their sexes, he stood up trembling, masked his emotion in the frontier darkness, and said to himself what he would say to my mother and me, turbid and luminous in her bosom, when he found us once again:

"I saw this couple take that risk and I saw things clearly in the darkness of the jungle. I am not risking anything by returning to you, who are my love, Angeles, and to our about-to-be-born son. Accept my return. Let me explain why I love you and how much I desire you."

Colasa and Will, holding hands, staring at each other with passion, conscious of the danger, laughing at the myth, at Matamoros dead, at the bitten Manhattanite's wooden dildo, at the Mexican Ms., the mortal manuscript: Will Gingerich had no book, Matamoros's words would not be eaten: he was the owner of a body,

"My body is yours," said the girl Colasa, free at last.

The Discovery of America

. . . why do I have to find you if I
never lost you . . .

Gabriel García Márquez
The Autumn of the Patriarch

1. Your Truth of Blessed Bread

Pay attention now, Reader: wait for me because I'm going to need you more than ever, don't hide from me, don't go away: you have to be *there* when I need you to lend me a hand so that I can recover everything I shall lose, I'm certain of it, when I abandon my mother; not yet: my mother is alive and I am inside her during these last days of my gestation, my mother is alive, sitting in the Church of San Felipe Neri in Oaxaca, surrounded by fleurons and looking (since she still can't look at me!) at a Holy Child of Atocha dressed in brocade and rose-colored feathers and as she looks at the Holy Child our buddy Egg looks at her with a mixture of melancholy and unbounded passion but she and I know that something is going to happen, a tremulous premonition makes both of us see you, Dad, blazing along the highway on a broken-down Kurosawa motorcycle ripped away from the body of a Yankee sentinel, far from the temptations of sweet tropical Veracruz, far away and returned to the sacred highlands, rapidly along the road from Orizaba and Tierra Blanca and the Tuxtepec River, over hill over dale, through Cuicatlán toward Oaxaca. My father, who left Bubble Gómez and his refrigerated truck full of edible cadavers as well as

Colasa Sánchez with Professor Will Gingerich united for better or
for worse, while you, Dad, you have no reason to doubt it, it's for
better, for better it will be that you ride toward us, toward my mother
and toward me, certain of the place where we're all going to meet,
come on, where else could it be?

Oh, how I see you, Pop, tall and gypsy-colored and green-eyed
and myopic and tense, every muscle on your angular face more
sharply drawn than ever, the bad roads beating you and bouncing
you on your balls, which is where you feel the physical danger of
the highway, its violence, its potholes, and that I feel with you because
that's about where we relate, you and I, what the fuck, that's where
we begin: that's where America was invented, that's where it was
desired, that's where it was needed, and nowhere else: America is in
my father's balls!

He's biking along toward Oaxaca on the Christopher Columbus Highway, a rioting sea of potholes, and my father says son don't be born
without me don't be born halfway my son wait for your father I'm
on my way to you I'm almost there wait just a little longer Christopher
wait for me hope stop time I'm just about there Angeles don't get all
self-absorbed without me don't give birth without me don't close the
circle yet without me don't just be you two but we three always three
don't leave me out of your halo Angeles let me enter your light don't
finish your light without me don't take your air away without me
don't have our son without me look I'm coming back forgive me and
forgive me above all for not explaining to you that I left you for
reasons I will never understand completely, but that I began to understand, know when? when I saw the gringo professor and Colasa
Sánchez risk sharing everything even the fearsome myth even the
painful past to transcend, in the dangerous love of a couple, the social
stupidity of reputation appearances conventions. Because if two people really love each other Angeles that's the most revolutionary thing
in the world that changes the world just that there's nothing more
to do but live a love telling to go fuck themselves all those who will
tell who told what happened before will be or will not be will do or
will not do with those whom the middle class fills its days without
imagination without love withoutwithout the substitution of possible
quantities of love for equivalent quantities of things and I lost and
disoriented never reached this but between my conservative revolution
and your leftist revolution I inserted a passion called jealousy and a

justification called machismo and because of them I was unable to imagine the worst thing that could happen to me: not that I would cheat on you, Angeles, but that you would no longer think about me, that killed me with jealousy, that is what pulled me out of my sensual justification: a world in which you could go on living with our son without loving me anymore without even thinking about me: I was no longer jealous of anyone but of myself Angeles in the instant in which I imagined not only your absence I confess it or that of the child but *my absence* from your world and that of our son: your light without me your air without me your body without me is what I cannot stand from now on and that's why I'm returning so that you pardon me and admit me once again into your light your air your flesh: listen to me Angeles and Christopher: my words are a call for help! I put on the brakes, I skid, the dust covers me.

My father entered the church in Oaxaca: golden glory, intense perfume of flowers and the neighboring bakeries, incense and recently washed tile floors; he went to her, touched her shoulder. She did not look at him. She raised her veil and showed him the nape of her neck.

My mother dropped the volume of Plato published by the UNAM with green covers and the black shield THROUGH MY RACE THE SPIRIT WILL SPEAK.

She had to lift her long hair, which she promised not to cut until she finished reading the *Cratylus*.

Egg looked at them together and stood up from the pew.

Egg and the Baby Ba walked out, he with his flat feet and his bald head, she wearing her plaid schoolgirl's smock, with her tresses and little round face.

And my saddened heart: don't go away, little girl, don't leave me alone, Baby Ba! Suppose that now, as it seems, everything is forgiven and the couple reunite and I'm left alone: who but you can be with me, little girl, Baby Ba: remember I'm the only one who sees you as you are! Don't forget that! Don't forget me!

Ah, the egoism of love. No one does anything to get me closer to the girl, who goes off, following Egg along the nave of the Church of San Felipe Neri in Oaxaca an October morning in 1992. She turns back, holding the hand of our buddy, and looks at me:

She waves goodbye to me with her little hand raised to the height of her cheek.

Bye-bye. Ciao. See you soon, sweetie pie!

The church is empty at this hour.

My father holds up my mother's long hair. He brings his lips to my mother's perfumed nape. He bares only her back, her shoulders, her nape. My father kisses the incomparable softness of my mother Angeles's body. Angeles gives him the ecstasy of the acid fragrance of her armpit; she gives him her shoulders, good for a copious, liquid cry; she gives him the wingèd virtue of her soft bosom and the sleepy quintessence of her light back: breathing all of her in, forever in love with what is soft about my mother, how I want to fall asleep in your arms, to forget everything, Penny, Lucha, and Ulises and the Ayatollah and Colasa and Bubble Gómez's truck and the Veracruz war. I wanted to sleep in the crackling sheets and imagine her as I saw her, dressed in the radiant mourning of resonant starch, with her coppery eyes and her ruddy cheeks, and I wishing she would caress me as she caressed the beads on her rosary with her fine, agile fingers . . . the luxury of ivory and mother-of-pearl.

He told her again that he could not desire her and only desire her, that she had to give him whatever she had even if it were on the threshold of the cemetery. Her feet. He dreamed wide awake of her feet. He asked for her feet. But at that moment she said no. She then spoke for the first time to say no. Not this time. Everything will repeat itself except this.

"Why?" asked my father.

"I don't want you ever to see me insane, dried out, or sick. That's why."

My father understood then (I understood, says my father) that this time he was not going to take off her shoes (I did not take off her shoes), nor was she going to offer (her feet) so that I wouldn't get sick (because of absolutes) here in Oaxaca (where the best and worst of me began) (my mission, Angel my father now laughs): (your love, the best of me, says my father, and she repeats it with him).

She raised her thaumaturgical eyes and looked into my father's green eyes.

My mother gave my father the water she held in the hollow of her hands to drink.

When we left the church, nevertheless, the unexpected was waiting for us: a white Shogun limousine right in the Oaxaca plaza, a uniformed Oriental chauffeur wearing a black cap, obsequiously opening the car door, next to which, on foot, leaning against the half-open window, one little Gucci-poochie foot coquettishly posed on the carpet of the limousine, the other posed unceremoniously on the cobbles of the Oaxaca plaza, dressed, all of him, in white as if for an extemporaneous First Communion, in his hand an elegant malacca cane which he twirled in his idle fingers before our astonished eyes, his jowly face perfectly polished, shiny, pulled tight, well shaven except for the tiny black spot of a mustache on his permanently sweaty upper lip: our Uncle Don Homero Fagoaga Labastida Pacheco y Montes de Oca, of the best etc. . . .

"Ah, dearly beloved niece and nephew, don't gape at me in such an astonished fashion." Don Homero laughed musically. "Rather, you should repeat as the sublime poet Don Luis de Góngora said in disquieted contemplation of these Fabio, oh grief, you see before you, fields of solitude, faded hills were once famous Cempoala, or as his worthy successor, the poet Don Octavio Paz, in the same place but three centuries later: Only the fat academic is immortal! Here I am, and as your favorite poet might say (Homero said, wagging his censorious sausage finger), you seek Acapulco in Oaxaca, oh pilgrim! and Acapulco in Oaxaca you do not find because Acapulco turns out to be in Acapulco, and, oh Quevedo, grandfather of terrorist dynamiters, only the ephemeral remains and lasts! Which is to say, niece and nephew, October 12 is coming and with it the Quincentennial of our discovery, or as the Indians of Guanahaní said when they saw the caravels approach, Hurray, hurray, we've been discovered! But I, modest man that I am, only desire that the child of our blood, destined to win, if God wills it, the national contest of the little Christophers, come into this world with comforts and auguries worthy of his high destiny, for which I place at your and your comrades' disposal my humble carriage—and inside the limousine my parents saw with horror Egg seated between Homero's little sisters Capitolina and Farnesia, they full of smiles, kind, of course, wearing summery flowered dresses and wide-brimmed straw hats with ribbons, Scarlett O'Horror style, beckoning with maternal solicitude to my mother (with their hands) and to my father (with their eyes), and Egg with a gesture that said there's no way out! shrugging his shoulders and Baby Ba is not there, *she is no longer there*, SHE IS NO LONGER THERE! I shout from my solar center invisible but no one pays me any mind—in order to travel to Acapulco and await the blessed event in my house, whose rustic comforts you will have to excuse (as my singular friend Don Enrique Larreta said, sipping at the straw in his *hierba mate* in a smoky little ranch near Paysandú) but whose austere virtues you know only too well.

And since he detected that my parents were somewhat hesitant, he imperiously and impatiently tapped them with his walking stick, lightly, on the shoulders (the very shoulders my father had been kissing only a few minutes earlier), on the knuckles (the very hands in which my mother had held the water she had offered to my father only a few minutes earlier) (and this gentle rapping reminded my father of the sado-erotic spankings that his uncle had given him with a lady's shoe when he was a boy), and said come along now, my patience is limited as is my time, my little sisters here, Capitolina and Farnesia, certified virgins both, will gladly play the part of midwife: holy little hands! Acapulco is being reconstructed slowly but surely, under new and more propitious patronage than that of that deplorable petty political boss Ulises López, and it is important for our future (which is also that of your baby, beloved niece and nephew!) that the little Christopher come into the world there, that Acapulco be the site of the Grand Celebration of the Quincentennial, and that our face, which received the Illustrious Navigator, who was coming from his East which was our West, search another East that was still farther off. Let us now turn toward the true, classical Orient, the Pacific, which in reality is our nearest Occident, as we, by God, are their true Orient! But, in a word, I don't know what I'm saying, except this: that the child be born on October 12 in the port of Acapulco, which faces the new constellation of the Pacific. Let's declare our faith in the future at this opportune moment, upward and onward, Tomasito, as Our Candidate exclaimed as he raised on high our PRIstine banners in the Far-Off Campaign of 1970, because tonight we must sleep in Pichilinque, on the eve of October 12, and go, all of us, to ask a blessing and to give thanks in the Cathedral of Acapulco.

My parents took their place on the car's jump seats, staring at the smiling faces of Capitolina and Farnesia as well as the ovoid face of our astonished buddy while Don Homero assumed his place in front next to the chauffeur Tomasito.

"How easy it is to see that our brother is of the same blood as we"—Farnesia sighed—"just as we call all our maids Servilia, he calls all his drivers Tomasito . . ."

"Enough of these vagaries, Farnesita," Capitolina interrupted her. "Better make the Sign of the Cross quickly because this is indeed a cardinal sin, being out of our house two days in a row, and traipsing around these mountains, filled with who knows what dangers, and ending up as midwives in Acapulco, that capital of vice, the Babylon of the Pacific coast . . ."

"Oh, Capitita, they were right in the convent, no doubt about it, and in the first place . . ."

My father Angel brutally dropped the silver bracelet with the initials FF and FB separated by a heart he'd saved from the Veracruz jungle into Farnesia's lap.

Miss Farnesia Fagoaga's eyes almost jumped out of her head; she trembled and then wept with her head hung low. Capitolina bit her lip and hugged her, little sister, little sister . . . My mother raised her thaumaturgical eyes and looked at my father. I know what she thought:

Angel Palomar, you finally learned to use your violence to humanize your fellow man.

Girls were strolling around the plaza hand in hand, with a resignation overflowing with rage. Night fell suddenly on that city of greens and blacks and golds, which is eternally sculpting itself.

2. I Love You Not As a Myth

 (The three of us alone back in Acapulco: She, I, He.)

I searched for Agueda and I did not find her.

I searched for the Sweet Fatherland and I did not find it.

I found Angeles, your mother.

I found her in the same way I lost Agueda.

"Let's never hurt each other. We're all here together."

And when you met him, Mom, when you found out who he really was, when you followed him to Acapulco, to Oaxaca, to Mamadoc's contest in Mexico City, when you played the passive part in his adventure, the destruction of Aca, Uncle Homero's campaign, the encounter with Matamoros Moreno, the return to Maksicko City, the search for the city in the city, the Boulevard, the conch-shaped chariot, the contest offices, the . . . When you finished up living all of it, then what, Mom, what remained of your first impression or your first illusion, what did you say to yourself, Mom?

This is what I said to myself, Christopher. From the moment I met your father I never again doubted: I have a body, my son, look, touch me, I have two breasts bursting with milk, I have hard, heavy buttocks, touch them, son, caress my neck, son, feel how it pulses, my waist exists, it's flesh and movement and heat, touch my navel, son, caress my sex and hold your little hand over the hot lock of the uterus through which you will leave: go ahead, son, I'm your mother, it's your last chance to be inside your mother, look upward, from your position, now that you're about to be born, tell me what you see, tell me, please.

Who are we? Who are you, Mom? Angeles? Agueda?

Both of them, son, both. I learned to be both.

How many of us are there, Mom?

Just three, son, the three of us, reconciled, with fewer illusions but with infinitely more tenderness.

Where are we, Mom?

Back in Acapulco, son, giving thanks because you are going to be born.

When, Mom, when?

Right now, son, between Sunday, October 11 (we are on the beach), and Monday, October 12 (we are in Acapulco), 1992.

Who is with us, Mom?

Our friend Egg, the Orphan Huerta, and Tomasito, the second Tomasito, the chauffeur who drove us from Oaxaca and who turned Uncle Homero over to Uncle Fernando, who was waiting for us in the Chilpancingo airport, where that day they were holding the funerary ceremonies for a local favorite son, Don Ulises López, and his family, who etc. etc., loading Don Homero forcibly into the broken-down two-motor plane of the Institute for Indian Studies with Don Fernando and heading for new horizons while Tomasito took charge of the Shogun and headed for Acapulco.

And the little sisters?

An albino trucker picked them up at the Chilpancingo exit. He said he would bring them to Mexico City. He told them to sit in the rear, where they'd be much cooler.

And us?

Mom, I see a lamp, a burning light above my head, here inside your stomach, a light bathes me and says: Thanks to me you know everything, everything, everything, Chris,

> Christopher
> Christopher Critic
> Christicritic
> Christopher Crisis
> Christopher Crime
> Christopher Incriminated
> Chri Chri Christopher

Mother! that light has been there for how long, from when you conceived me, above my little head, and I never saw it until now, Mother, hurry up, don't let that light go out yet, give me a few minutes more of that wisdom, don't take it away from me yet, how it shines, how it shines, how right you were to teach me everything here inside, how right it was for me to learn everything here inside, a burning fire above my little head, that's the origin of the light, a fire that shines and that is consumed inside your plexus and that illuminates my little head, telling me also, Mother:

"Let's never hurt each other. We're all here together."

I HEAR WHAT IS GONE, WHAT I STILL DO NOT TOUCH

We are facing the sea, at Revolcadero beach, facing the Pacific Ocean. There are twelve dead dolphins on the beach: a perfect dozen dolphins murdered by the contamination in the bay and the insane swirling of El Niño sent from Peru.

Twelve white dolphins implacably turning purple as if they were losing their innocence, which was identical to their beauty: their tender eyes, marine brothers of paschal sweetness; their smooth bodies, changing color; and their open jaws: naïve sharks. At our feet.

The Oriental boy turns his back on the setting sun. He has taken off his chauffeur's cap, revealing a youthful head and straight hair, he wears a black uniform that gives him an air somewhat like that of an admiral in the Japanese Navy on the eve of Pearl Harbor and he tenderly takes the hand of Orphan Huerta, naked at his side, both of them looking at my father and mother (and me inside her belly!) and at Egg barefoot with his trousers rolled up and his shirt open, revealing his hairless, almost feminine breasts, Egg does not look at us nor does he look at the couple made up of the boy dressed in black and the naked Orphan: Egg looks toward the ocean, where one day the other Tomasito sailed, dead. He thinks perhaps about the symmetry of the speared destinies: the first Tomasito in the sea, Grandfather Rigoberto in the mountains, and Hipi Toltec incinerated in the upland, and the bombs of Reverend Payne in the Gulf: the end of the world that came to die there, the Mediterranean, the Atlantic, cradle and prison, mother and stepmother of the world for five centuries: now they do not look toward the Gulf, the Antilles, the Atlantic, and the Mediterranean: now they look toward the Pacific, and the Oriental boy takes the hand of his brother the Orphan Huerta, my brother, my brother he calls him again and again, I could not come for you until the right moment, I knew that my brother had to carry out his destiny and that his destiny was inseparable from that of all of you and your child: you had to reunite, you and your child, who were separated, so that all of us could be together on this beach and so that I could reveal myself to you:

"He's my lost brother," said Orphan Huerta with an astonished seriousness. "The lost boy I told you about . . . He's come back for me . . ."

And for you, said the Oriental boy, whom it was difficult to imagine, as my parents were trying to do, in a nameless slum, a lost city in the D.F. adipose, eddyfeet calcified running from the settlement of squatters burned down by Doña Lucha Plancarte de López: and it was he, vomited out by the subway on the corner of Calle Génova and Liverpool; nevertheless, it was from there he emerged and now it was this: and he gave his hand to his brother: and he extended his other hand to my parents (and to me), come with us, let's go to Pacífica, the New World is no longer here, it's always elsewhere, celebrate the Quincentennial by leaving behind your Old World of corruption, injustice, stupidity, egoism, arrogance, disdain, and hunger, we've come for you: here is our hand, the child will be born at midnight, as was written, quickly one day, very soon the ships will come for us and we will leave for Pacífica, Pacífica awaits you, there you are necessary, here you are superfluous, said Orphan Huerta's brother, don't hand your about-to-be-born son over to the unsalvageable horror of Mexico, save him, save yourselves: come to a better world of which a part of Mexico already belongs, the whole Pacific coast from Ixtapa north, the whole Pacific basin from California to Oregon, Canada and Alaska, all of China and Japan, the peninsulas, the archipelagos, the islands, Oceania: a basin of 108 million square miles, three billion inhabitants, half the world's population, working together, three-fourths of the world's commerce, almost all of the world's advanced technology, the maximum conjunction of labor, technical know-how, and political will in human history, said the Lost Boy, found boy, intoning all this as if it were a psalm, using his hands with their long fingers, come with us to the New World of Pacífica, turn your backs on the tyrannical Atlantic which fascinated and dominated us for five centuries: end your foolish fallacious fascistic fascination with the Atlantic world, turn your backs on that past look to the future because it's there we men and women are triumphing who simply said this to ourselves, only this: Behind the mask of glory is the face of death; let us renounce glory, force, domination, let us save the West from itself by teaching it once again to deny power to power, to stop admiring force, to open its arms to the enemy (yes, sweetie, look at him now), to choose life over death: We have enough to be moderately happy, in the name of what are we going to sacrifice the technical means we have now of achieving abundance, peace, intellectual creation, in the name of what? We asked ourselves that and we got no answer: we had it all in our hands, technology, resources, inventiveness, labor, we have what we need to invent a new world—the Orphan Huerta naked with his eyes closed turned away from the sea imitates with his hands the movements of his brother's hands—beyond the old frontiers separating nations, classes, families, races, sexes: why don't we use it? What's stopping us? We decided that all this was possible in a new community, not a utopia, because in Pacífica we never lose sight of the fact that we will never escape destiny, that was the West's madness, to think they had dominated destiny and that progress would eliminate tragedy (Nietzschevoice); that's how tragedy became a crime, by taking advantage of the dream of consciousness, sentencing tragedy to take refuge like a hunted animal in a concentration camp and to appear anonymous and bloody in historical massacres, without finding its place in the community and saying to history: there are too many exceptions to progress, happiness is capable of attacking itself (fe-de-rico!), we have to admit what it denies us in order to know we are complete, our face is that of the other, we don't know ourselves if we don't know what we aren't and we admit it: we are unique because

we are alike: in Pacífica we helped both the rapid advance of technology and the tragic awareness of life by taking seriously what a
novel, a poem, a film, a symphony, a sculpture says: we decided that
the works of culture were as real in the world as a mountain or a
transistor, that there is no real life without a still life to compensate
for it in art, no living present with a dead past, no acceptable future
that does not allow exceptions to progress, and no technological
progress that does not incorporate the warnings of art:

My father and my mother saw the two brothers—one dressed as a
Japanese chauffeur, the other nude, holding hands—begin to say all
these things in unison, in a chorus whose setting was the crepuscular
ocean: my parents saw what was behind the brothers: Angel, Angeles:
my father and mother looked at each other and their eyes shone,
they understood:
     Others give us their being.
     When I complete you, Angeles.
     I complete you, Angel.
     They exchanged the gift of their perfectible existence the way the
two brothers did and the four of them now sought (the five of them:
I inside my mother's womb; the six of them: Egg stops staring sadly
toward the distant horizon and turns toward us, doubtful as to whether
he should join with the brothers or with us: he waits, a big buddy,
he waits a bit, we're coming, we're understanding):
     Come with us to Pacífica, we can't force you, we merely suggest
it, although we can tell you that in all this, friend Angel, friend
Angeles, as yet unborn child Christopher, there is something definitive, something inexorable: friend Angel, in your house of bright
colors in Tlalpan there are many portraits of men named Rutherford
and Planck, Einstein and Pauli, Bohr and Broglie, Heisenberg, above
all Heisenberg, your favorite, Angel, isn't that right?
     To observe all phenomena simultaneously is impossible: we must
choose a time and place within the vast continuum which it is given
us to imagine because it exists in reality: our slice of the global
phenomenon is our limit but it is also our liberty: it is what we can
affect, for better or for worse: what we can see, touch, it is only one
face of reality: the position or the movement of something, one or
another, but never both at the same time: that's our limit, but it's
also our power:

We depend on the vision of others to complete our own vision: we are half eye, half mouth, half brain, half face; the other is I because it completes me:

The two brothers slowly touched each other's face, each one with his eyes closed, each one speaking now in the sudden tropical night with modulated alternations, a surprising hymn:

Knowing this was understanding at the same time our grandeur and our servitude, our freedom and our dependence, and by knowing them, it was possible for us to attain what our understanding of limits would seem to have forbidden us: precisely because one only knew his position perfectly while the other only knew his movement perfectly. When the two united, each knew what the other didn't know and they could, complete, be what neither was alone (the Pacific is a horizontal flame; the sky moves quickly to take possession of it, extinguish it: we do not see the light that is born elsewhere when here everything becomes darkness): in that way, we manage in Pacífica to conciliate destiny with technology, unite what we know spiritually with what we know technically and make a new life because we don't control freedom but we do dominate technology:

Come with us, said the two brothers, and my parents, turning to look at each other, marveled as, in the renewed Acapulco dusk, the memorious port of his childhood, the happy scale of his vacations, was reborn in my father's eyes: my parents saw themselves splendid as they saw the tongues of fire on the horizon like a literal message from the ocean: the distance of the voices of the other side came closer in the presence of the magician who came from the sea, the Orphan Huerta's brother: the Lost Boy now found them, he returned on the voyage opposite to that of the Europeans, not Columbus's caravel but the China galleon, not Cortés's brigantine but the Philippines galleon: the other half of our face, our blind eye, seeing once again: we have two horizons and a single face and the Lost Boy was saying: No one can catch up to us technologically, we've gone beyond the fifth generation of computers, what your parents wanted without knowing it, Angel, we've left behind the four serial, arithmetic generations of computers that simply added up one operation after another, in order to enter the generation of computers that process various currents of information simultaneously: Look—said the Orphan Huerta with a strange return to his habitually nasal voice—before, it was only possible to put one tortilla at a time on the fire, heat it, flip it, and toss it into the basket: now, see? we can heat up all the tortillas at the same time, all at once, flip them all over at once, and put them all in the basket at the same time

> the multitrack mind of Mamma Mia
> reading Plato getting my old man hot in Aca
> the inconsumable taco of my Grandparents Palomar
> the Curies of Tlalpan
> antimatter: life not death
> Federico Robles Chacón wants to dictate two letters at the same
> time

In Pacífica we've already won the technological race, and for that very reason we do not want power: we offer well-being: whoever dominates computers dominates the economy dominates the world: we don't want to dominate but to share: come with us, Angel, Angeles, Christopher yet-to-be-born, leave the corruption and death of Mexico behind, leave the interminable misery and the ageless vices of your fatherland in order to save it someday, pulling it little by little, piece by piece, out of its corrupt stupidity and its historical madness: the two reunited brothers spoke in chorus, now our buddy as well, and with them my father and mother: and I on the point of being born.

3. Fatherland, unto You I Give the Key of Your Good Fortune

As they were crossing from Guerrero into Michoacán, a group of armed peasants demanding the restitution of their lands—stolen by a lumber company—were cornered in the hills: hungry, weak, they were hunted down and summarily shot in the town of Huetámbaro, under the naked flanks of the deforested mountain. Colonel Inclán, under orders after the night of the Ayatollah to restore order wherever and however necessary in the Mexican Republic, pronounced these peremptory words:

"Bury them without coffins. They were fighting for land, right? So give them land until they choke on it."

The loudspeaker in the Huetámbaro plaza blared out "Jingle Bells," drowning out the shots.

Homero Fagoaga shook with fear watching the peasants fall one after another because instead of shots all he could hear was "Jingle Bells," as if Christmas had killed them.

"Look, you wretch, look straight in front of you," said Benítez to Uncle Homero, digging the muzzle of his rifle into the rolls of fat hanging off Homero's ribs. "Take a good look."

"Fernando, I was having a good time in my Acapulco house, protecting my niece and nephew . . . right, *our* niece and nephew . . ."

"You were taking advantage of them to set up a new scam, Homero you con man, you know that the child will be born exactly at midnight tonight, October 11, and you want to have him in your power so you can walk into Pacífica carrying him in your arms: that's what you want, you miserable tub . . ."

"So what's wrong with that?" Don Homero got upset, then calmed down instantly when he felt the Mauser digging into his lard. "What's wrong with that, I ask you?"—His voice now a whisper—"That's why I went about having myself kidnapped by another unfaithful Filipino. I can be useful to our niece and nephew and to the baby, I have contacts in the Philippines, I know the . . ."

Benítez paid him no attention. He watched the scene with Homero from a window protected by wrought-iron bars: the Santa Claus music, the scattered cadavers, and Colonel Inclán walking around with his riding crop in his hand, okay, spread their legs, laughing, let's see which ones shit themselves out of fear.

"Homero," said Don Fernando, "take a good look at what you've never wanted to see in your life."

A bulldozer or a match could end all this, murmured Don Fernando Benítez. The mountains of Mexico are bald, worn away by erosion. Topsoil has become as fleeting as life itself. For him, he said to Homero Fagoaga, trembling behind the bars over the little plaza of Huetámbaro, reality was animated by the past.

Does life become more resilient because of that? A woman wept in the same room from which Fernando and Homero watched the atrocious scene acted out by Colonel Nemesio Inclán and the executed peasants.

"Don't cry," Fernando said to the woman. "There's nothing you can do. Tomorrow . . ."

"Life's always been terrible here," the sobbing woman said. "And, besides, who's going to fight against helicopters?"

How well Benítez knew it. Today's weapons were no longer those of yesterday's revolution. Could Zapata have withstood a barrage of white phosphorus or napalm? But how did Ho Chi Minh survive it? How did the Sandinistas manage to topple Somoza? Because their societies were much simpler, much more black-and-white, less complicated, and with fewer complicities than the Mexico of 1992? With what weapons was it possible to fight today without exposing everyone to a useless death? With what weapons, without playing the game of the cynics who control power? With what weapons, so one could say to oneself: I haven't asked anyone to give more than what I am willing to give? I haven't ordered anyone to go to his death by asking him to do what I would not be willing to do? I haven't said to anyone: the only option is armed revolt, romantic suicide? To no one.

". . . but, Fernando," Homero Fagoaga was saying, since he had no reason to listen to the barely murmured thoughts of his relative, "what's wrong with the kids joining up with Pacífica? Things are hopeless here, you can see that for yourself, if you brought me here to prove it to me, you were certainly successful, Fernando, you've scared me to death, don't you think that as far as shocks are concerned, enough is enough? Listen, and even from the nationalistic point of view, Pacífica is our salvation, we refused to form a common market with the United States and Canada in the seventies, but now Japan and China dominate the United States and Canada. Pacífica is our ace in the hole; we'd be walking into commerce and technology through the front door, plus we wouldn't owe a thing to the gringos!"

"First we've got to finish up what we began here," Don Fernando Benítez said, through clenched teeth.

"Bah, here and everywhere else the main idea is to make money and get power, the rest is words, words, words," said Don Homero Fagoaga bluntly, but the words froze on his rose-colored lips: "Fernando, Fernando, what are you doing?" Benítez aimed his rifle through the window bars, shot, and Colonel Nemesio Inclán fell down next to the peasants' bodies: there was no surprise on his face because it already was a skull. Green slime poured out of his cheek instead of blood. His black glasses smashed against a bullet-riddled wall. The soldiers pointed at the small, three-story building. They surrounded it instantly. Benítez waited with his rifle at the ready.

Homero shook like Hegelatine. The imperturbable loudspeakers blared out the bolero "You Have to Know How to Lose." The music was drowned out by the roar of the helicopters.

4. *Land!*

Reader: all this is happening in my head, because now I think that the world outside has ceased to exist, and if something does live there, today only my memory or my imagination can bear witness to it. I could be wrong. Or worse: perhaps what I'm saying to myself can escape my own mind and be heard outside. What would happen then? would happen if the voice of an unborn child were heard outside before birth? What witchcraft would they accuse the mother of? Of what traffic with the Holy Spirit would they accuse the father? And me too, of what would (or won't) I be accused of before I'm born, what would they call me?

Reader, that's why I need such a web of complications, like the ones I've been weaving over the course of my nine months here enumerated. You know that I haven't narrated anything alone, because you've been helping me ever since the first page. Your mediation is my health; just imagine my terror without you: me blind, veiled, enclosed, I would have spent my time going around in circles (vicious, vicos: tight little vicolini), asking myself:

"Where are the people who brought me here? I don't see them!"

You know, Reader, that without you I would not have done what I want, which is to communicate to the living my nightmares and my dreams: by now they are *your* nightmares and *your* dreams. My ghosts accompany me; now I also share my nightmares with them: my genes (my gegels, my gegelatines?) that for each one of the six billion inhabitants of the planet, there are thirty ghosts who accompany him: thirty progenitors, physically disappeared, but alive and kicking, your mercies benz should know, in each one of the 100 billion individual genes that occupy each one of the cells of my imminent little body! and in each one of these cells is written ALL THE INFORMATION necessary to reconstruct every function and every structure in the body: READER, TRY TO UNDERSTAND WHY I CHRISTOPHER KNOW EVERYTHING AND AM AFRAID OF LOSING

IT ALL: Ah, Reader, my pact with you is not disinterested—it goes without saying: I'm going to need you more than ever *afterwards* (will there be an *afterwards* . . . ?), after I'm born, according to what people say and what they call what is going to happen, shit, it's as if I were dead already!

Afterwards: when I need you to stretch out your hand to me so that I can recover everything I'm going to lose, I'm certain of it, when I abandon my mother. Not yet. My mother is alive and I am inside her on the last day of my gestation, my mother is alive and is lighting the fire over my head and I on the point of being born: the dead dolphins on the Revolcadero beach and a desperate scream from my mother: and as if in response to her scream, the ships appear in the distance, shining on the crepuscular sea, and my mother falls on her knees in the hot sand, Egg and my father Angel run to help her, my God, what's wrong? What shaking is this? Since when does my house, my pool, my moist, humid, warm cave tremble like this, beyond the boomboomboom rhythm of the rockaztec outside and my mother's identical heart inside?

Soon, please, you must decide, says the Lost Boy blinded by the light of the ships (the galleon of China? the galleon of the Philippines? how they shine in the night of my death!), and my father looks toward the farthest point on the horizon: Pacífica, the New World of the New World, and in that instant in which I fumble in horror for a handhold in my communication with the world outside, everything that has taken place is passing through my head, and I think that at the same time the world outside has ceased to exist, and if something is going to remain alive of it one day, today only my memory or my imagination can attest to it. I may be wrong. Or worse: what I'm trying to say to myself may escape from my mind and be heard *outside*. What would happen then? I repeat this fear of mine: what would happen if my voice inside here were heard outside? Would they kill me and kill my mother in the process? Witch doctors, did I say? monsters? But my voice cannot be heard out there, simply because complicity with my father has been reestablished, and my father should think about unborn me, but I'm on the point of saying what we are both saying when the Lost Boy urges us to choose: are you going to stay here or are you coming to Pacífica? New World: eternal obligation to complete the world: New World!

America is in my father's balls, from which I emerged, New World

is what Columbus gave Castile and Aragon: the double hemispheres
in your egg sack, my dear progenitor, steady producer of millions of
sperm, constant from puberty to old age: ready to abandon your body
at a moment's notice, whenever someone shouts: Go!; because the
fly flies, and goes to meet my mother's rationed-out egg, her stingy
cervix, protected from the world by a hard mucous stopper, and only
once a month, one glorious day, is it unstopped, and then it becomes
a river of glass, a sliding board for the sperm; the egg found the snake,
the serpent found its fecund nest, and ME VOILÀ!

And to think that in those testicles of yours that created me, father
of mine, can be found all the sperm necessary to produce the current
population of the world: in the hemispherical duplicity of a single
man: you, my father, Angel Palomar y Fagoaga, twenty-two years of
age, of an uncertain and failed life, youthful errors behind you (or
so you think), new horizon, promising aurora before you (or so you
think): in your balls, Pop, is all the sperm necessary to invent six
billion Aztecs, Quechuas, Patagonians, Caribs, Chinese, Filipinos,
Japanese, and arrogant Aryans, polyracial Polynesians, hungry Hungarians, Finlandish finalists, and basking Basques fallen from the
moon: all your semen would fit in a shot glass; patriarch!

all the eggs necessary to re-create the populations of the planet
would fit as well, Mamma Mia, you who produce them, in a test
tube:

thank you, thank you, for creating only me!

me instead of the six billion other possibles (plus pixies, Gasparine
ghosts, Nahuatl poltergeists, children of the night, and other Fran-
kedenics who accompany us)

thanks for ejaculating me among 300 million other sperm all com-
peting in the same contest and whom I defeated

thanks for allowing me to travel the eight inches from my father's
penis to my mother's egg, which to me, dear Readers, seemed as
great a distance as that from Jupiter to Venus (but I will never be a
hungry little Saturn and eat my parents, I am no patriphage!)

thanks for giving victorious me lodging

thanks for my nine months and for what I've learned in them: I
have lived for nine months, I am a gerontonone at birth: I note that
I am a not-yet-neonate! and above all, are my little brothers from
the New World of the New World, the Utopia of the Pacific, inviting
us to leave this land for a better one? As if my father's sperm which

I say could not re-create and repopulate the earth which fell to us!
As if my father's Hegelatinegenes could invent a different past, different information, in the technological paradise being offered to us
by the second Tomasito, the heretofore Lost Boy, and his brother
O. Huerta both standing hand in hand! The new Columbuses arrived
from the Orient: New World of the New World!

We are all Columbuses, those of us who bet on the truth of our
imagination and win; we are all Quijotes who believe in what we
imagine; but, ultimately, we are all Don Juans who desire as soon
as we imagine and who quickly find out that there is no innocent
desire, the desire to complete oneself takes over the other, changes
him, makes him one's own: not only do I desire you, I desire besides
that you desire as I do, that you be like me, that you be I: Christopher,
Quijote, Juan, our fathers who art on earth, our everyday Utopia,
give it to us tomorrow and forgive us our debts ($1,992 billion,
according to this morning's *Gall Street Journal!*), although we (Aztecs! Incas! Sioux! Caribs! Araucanians! Patagonians!) will never forgive our debtors: yessir, make us fall into temptation, because pleasure
without sin is not pleasure, long live Thomistic Catholicism which
presents us with unattainable ends in exchange for inexcusable
means, long live Augustinian Catholicism, which protects us from
personal responsibility before God and obliges us to seek His grace
through the intermediary of the hierarchy, long live Ignatian Catholicism, which allows us all ways to conquer souls in the name of
God and death, Angeles, death above all to the worst enemy of our
Mediterranean, Catholic, Thomistic, Augustinian, Jesuit, Marianite
tradition: not this pacific Confucianism being offered to us with such
conviction and tenderness by the Lost Boy, but the false revolutionaries, the modernizers, be they Russians, gringos, or just local up-
starts, Angeles my wife, Christopher my son, the destroyers of our
faithful image and our modest destiny: says my father, in the first
place the gringos, the greatest revolutionaries in Mexico, those who
have upset everything, those who really set us on the trail of the
mirage of the future, those who mutilated our territory and turned
silver into plastic and filled bakeries with smoke and broke the mirrors,
the Yankee revolutionaries who made us dream about progress but
who invaded us, humiliated us, persecuted us, and slugged us every
time we made a move toward progress by being ourselves; death to
their puritanical and militant hypocrisy; to the gigantic agonic and

pentagonic corruption that allows itself to point at us with the finger of one hand and hold its nose with two fingers of the other because of our skimpy corruption of playful dwarfs; death to all their imitators, Mexican modernizers-at-all-costs, those drunk on paper, cement, and mercury juice wealth and the right to steal and to export earnings and total amnesia about what happens in the blind mountains and the mute slums; and death, too, to all the left-wing modernizers, who secularized the ecclesiastical tradition and offer it now disguised as progress: let them have their German, abstract ideology passed through a sieve of Slavic Cesareopapism for a people whose Counter-Reformation authoritarianism is enough and more than enough for it, thank you: let's toast all of them with a glass of filthy water from the bay of dead dolphins: Angeles, Christopher, I don't want a world of progress which captures us between North and East and takes away from us the best of the West, but at the same time I don't want a pacific world which we will not deserve as long as we don't resolve what's going on inside here, my father says to us, with all that which we are, good and bad, bad and good, but still unresolved; wife, son, we shall arrive at Pacífica one day if we first stop being North or East in order to be ourselves, West and all. That would be Kantinflas's categorical imperative: Mock de Summa! Mere Cortésy won't take Cuauhtémoc off his bed of roses! All the cold rains of the world come to us from the Escorial! Queen Juana the Mad-der of Fact! Isabel the Chaotic, the tour brulée (and the Abolished Prince) and the Inky Session: I've drunk enough juice of the Cal Vine and swallowed enough Jacobites that I could shit a Constipated Luther and a J.-J. Rousseau, long live my chains! Condor Ché, long live my past! Chief Er Sun, Jamil Tun, and Rubberspyre: Calmás and We Dawn, Le Nin Le Nain Le Non, Engels Angeles Engelschen: let your halo shine once more, my love: my mother's aureole shines intensely, the galleons from the Orient shine, as well as the Lost Boy's golden hands, the argentine voice of he who was the Orphan Huerta, begging us, come, asking us, are you coming with us or not?

But my parents don't seem to heed this supplication.
My father and mother kiss.
She is still on her knees.
It must be an ancestral posture.
On her knees in the sand that grows cooler minute by minute.

We share in a moment of pleasant solitude (placentic, I mean). How much time between each apocalyptic tremor in Mamma Mia's belly? Nothing moves and I take advantage of the free time to count time and tell myself: I still haven't been born yet I already feel as if my soul were ancient. I still haven't been born yet I already fear that I'm going to act again the way my ancestors acted. Glory and ambition. Love and liberty. Violence. A land of sad men and happy children: how many children are born and die and are reborn with me?

I know that this is the calm before the storm. I know it.

Ayayay, here comes the earthquake again, I knew it, I knew it, you loved me, you loved me, Dad! Mom! Reader! Tell me, all of you! What's happening to me? Am I going? How I grab on to my destiny now that the racket's starting up again, my mother's commotions, her belly as agitated as the deepest tide of the deepest part of the ocean over which the Lost Boy and the Orphan Huerta are urging us to flee: I repeat to myself like a prayer: my destiny is defined by the genes of my father and mother—I am unique—I am the product of a conjunction of genes that had never combined before in the same way—it's possible that the genetic combination that fell to me will make me happy—it's possible it will make me unhappy—but I'll never know it unless I'm born, and what I'm feeling as my mother's contractions grow more frequent is that I'm going to be thrown out of my home sweet home, once again to wander, but if the first exit of little Christopher took place during pleasure, this one—I can smell it—will take place amid pain; why, my God, why conceived in pleasure and born in strife? My fear is yellow like the faces from Pacífica: am I going to be born? or am I actually going to die? I have aged irremediably in my mother's belly, yes, what they call being born is a deception, I am going to die a little old man; nobody gets any more time than nine months, we all die at nine months of age; the rest is death because it is oblivion (how you tremble, holy little Mother, calm down, for heaven's sake: give your little Christopher some peace! Not so hard, Mom, I feel like a marble made of blood rolling down a tunnel of smoke! Are you casting me out into the world? And suppose the world also only lasts nine months, what then? Mommy, Mommy, holy God, Daddy, Dada, Dada . . .). I'm forgetting everything I knew, the light is going out, here inside I knew everything, genes and Hegels, Hegelatines, my ancestors lived nine months keeping me company, my telephone book's full of lawyers, and more lawyers, shysters, rhetoricians, yakkers, ambulance chasers, prosecutors and prostitutors, hearings and seeings, syndicates and cynicates, tried and retried, executors and executioners, houses of detention and houses of correction: well, correct me if you can, let's see you correct the world.

What's happening, from the lunar center of my mother I hear them, smell them, oh Granny: it's the coyotes of Acapulco, have they come back to be present at my entry into life? into death? I smell their wet fur, their reddish eyes penetrate my mother's transparent belly, they could sink their sharp fangs between my fed navel and her exhausted navel: the coyotes form a circle around us, my father, my mother, and me, separating us from the Lost Boy and Orphan Huerta, who urge us: Soon? There's no time left! Choose: Pacífica or Mexico?

Or Mexico: will I be born here? You know where? Will I leave this country? Owing a thousand dollars, dead or alive! Will I be led to the D.F.? To breathe from birth eleven thousand tons of sulphur, lead, and carbon monoxide every day? To join a half million annual births—anal birds, antic words? To join a quarter of a million kids who die of asphyxia and infection each year? To shit, to add my shit to that of millions of dogs, cats, mice, horses, bats, unicorns, eagles, serpents, plumed coyotes? To swallow thirty thousand tons of garbage per day? To join the vultures that devour the rot: blessed art thou, Our Lady Tlazoltéotl, first star of the eternal night and of the invisible day, you who cleanse by devouring and then dirty it all in order to have something to clean; lady, can you compete with seven million automobiles, five million bureaucrats, thirty million pissers, shitters, eaters, fuckers, sneezers? Am I going out into that country? So that they can tell me that thanks to oil we're in good shape? That from now on we have nothing to worry about, just to administer our wealth? That I'll have my refrigerator even though I may not have electricity, and my Walkman so that people can be jealous when I walk the streets that are buried in garbage and fires?

READERS, RESOLVE MY DILEMMA:
Is it worth it to be born in Mexico in 1992?

Please! I'm forgetting everything! With each maternal shake something else slips out of my memory, I'm talking to my ancestors to see if they remember, but now they, too, have slipped away and with them everything I knew, now I won't know anything, goo, be-a-ba, here comes the ahhhhh: the fire above my little head went out, and outside I can hear the ubiquitous loudspeakers that travel the streets and plazas of my Sweet Fatherland, announcing that the celebration has been postponed, presidential decree / speech by Mamadoc and her / Columbus was colonial / there is nothing to celebrate the little Christophers are finished / Mexican time is postponable time, postponable, postponable: everything's happening tomorrow, not today, what do you say? All this happened tomorrow! (My mother trembles even more, now she howls like the coyotes that surround us.) Will my birth be postponed? So, *after all that*, I won't be born? Am I being given the right not to be born? Can I choose? Can I perhaps stay here forever in my soft salon, swimming in my Olympic pool, living in ease on the blood, the pâté, and the mucus of Madonna Angelica? Aaaaay here comes the aaaaaah: she is screaming in pain, the killer quake of '85 is being reproduced in its entirety in my mother's city, on uterus avenue (labyrinth of solitude! Luther's Expressway!), and I curse my mommy,

> MOTHER
> NAME WHERE BIOLOGY ACQUIRES A SOUL!
> WHERE NATURE BECOMES TRANSCENDENT!
> AND WHERE SEX BECOMES HISTORY!

Can you hear me, Mom? Why don't you answer me? You, too, are forgetting—are you forgetting me? I kick I dive I bend like a reed, I hear, ever more faintly, your voice which during nine months accompanied me, soothed me, sang to me, celebrated me, what's happening to me, Mommy? History's happening to me, the past is happening to me, the nation is happening to me and the narration of the nation is happening to me, the earth is happening to pass me toward you who lead me, I hear you say it, weakly now, the gas is passing out of me, my memory and my desire are passing out of me, my imagination and my language, love and envy are passing out of me, resentment and celebration are passing out of me, narrowness and symbols, analogies and differences all passing out of me, tacos, eggplant parmigiana (Anna? Anna, like manna, banana, banana split? That's it!), I'm heading for the earth, Mother, on this beach you received me and on it you are going to toss me, just as Uncle Homero was tossed, flying, naked, and spraying the world with blood and shit to celebrate my arrival: do you know what you are doing when you expel me into the world, Mother? Have you taken account of your responsibility and my own? You expel me to earth knowing that I am going to violate it, just as you, and my father and Homero Fagoaga and a pair of blind Indians with wooden hoes and Don Ulises López armed with lawsuits and checkbooks and bonds without bonds: will the very earth that we violate receive us, will you tell me, you and my father? We kill the earth in order to be able to live, and then we expect the earth to forgive us, absolve us of death even though we kill it? I'm being thrown, Pop and Mom, into a world where there is no possible reconciliation: we cannot be at one with the exploited earth, she gives us fewer punishments (death) than we give to her (violence): now I take revenge on you, world, to take out my portion of violence on you, violence on nature, violence on men, violence on myself: I am going to that destiny, beyond the ephemeral idiocies of smog, debt, the PRI, our national symbols, that's what I'm coming into, taking revenge on myself: to exploit the world from the moment I walk on it and to spend my life trying to expiate the guilt of my first exploitation, which was to suck your milk, which was to spit in a stream, which was to eat a jar of pureed Paschal Lamb sacrificed for me: am I arriving just to share this guilt? Can I do something to redeem it? Can I love a woman, write a book, free a people? Not even that, not even that: I'll do it all, gentle Readers, except allow the good earth to speak for itself, to express itself directly, not through my song or my curse, that I will not permit because I think (that's his father talking, you say) that art or politics or science (that comes from his grandparents!) is a sufficient compensation for our crime; that's why I go resigned to debt, oh Readers, to the PRI, to the smog, and to Mamadoc, because an instant before leaving my mother's womb I know (and I will forget it!) that neither I nor any other child about to be born, here or anywhere, could stand being born in a perfect world, a just world: it would horrify us, deprive us of all our pretexts, we need, oh Lord, oh Reader, oh Pro-Gen-I-Tors, an unjust world in order to dream about changing it, by ourselves, into a better world: the earth smiles before paying us, mercifully, with death . . .

I ask myself: I ask you: I ask all of you:

Will I have the right, at least, to intimacy with the world?

I do not have (I don't have, we don't have) time to answer; the contractions are more and more frequent; my father embraces my mother; they kiss; the two of them are kneeling on the beach, on their knees in the sand that grows colder by the minute, and their fingers are buried in whatever is left of the heat. Now my father takes her hand. He guides her finger over the sand. Their fingers write:

It is burning ice, frozen fire,
a wound that pains yet is unfelt
a dreamed-of good, a present ill
a brief rest which is no rest.

A wave breaks and washes away the poem—by whom? just written on the wet sand: . . . *what* is the name of that poem?

The wave takes away something else: I tremble as I hear that poem my father recites aloud, where have I heard it before? where? by God, before I knew everything, I heard that poem before. Now the fire over my head is going out, I knew who wrote it before, what its title was, now even the verses are disappearing just as lifelines disappear when the dead grow old: am I growing old, am I dying, am I forever leaving behind my ancestors, my memory, and my future imagining here inside as well? What do I hold on to, my God? I invoke you, see? I shall not end my poor unborn novel without directing a prayer to you, without recognizing you (just in case), but I'll be brief: I'll leave you this spot, you will decide whether to occupy it or not!

I'll be brief because now events are starting to rush ahead, Readers, and I am the victim of the blessed simultaneity that frees us from fearful symmetry, but both, my last (or penultimate) memory tells me, are lies, nothing is simultaneous and nothing is symmetrical; at least, then, nothing is linear, thank God all of us are circular or spiral observers, it's our privilege, yours and mine, Reader, here on this beach at midnight at the edge of the sea of waves, one chained to the next where float the galleons of Manila and China, which have come to bring me to the next Utopia.

—Pacífica—

Remember with me that portrait in the house of bright colors, the young Werner Heisenberg, dressed as a mountain climber, blond and smiling, telling us by way of farewell that the observer introduces instability in the system because he cannot separate himself from one point of view and therefore the observer and his point of view are part of the system and therefore there are no ideal systems because there are as many points of view as there are observers and each one sees something different: truth is partial because consciousness is partial: there is no universality except relativity, the world is unfinished because the men and women who observe it still have not finished, and truth, unexhausted, fugitive, in perpetual motion, is only the truth that takes all arbitrary positions into account and all the relative movements of each individual on this earth to which I am vertically heading, far from any lamps above my noggin: by god, Readers! it's my grandparents, the ones that created the Inconsumable Taco, who are telling me all this, I don't know if through the chain of my genes or by means of a sonar device in the shape of a hanging gourd that shines black from the highest mast on the China galleon, and that this is the conjuncture: on one side, the Lost Boys urge us one last time, are you coming or not? On the other side, I try to hold on to whatever I can, I stretch out my arms in my mother's convulsed belly, under a downpour of coagulations, my holy little hands hit a cellophane wrapper, they tear it, and they seek, in the way cartilage follows after bone, in the way little feet seek water to splash around in, that's how my hands seek out the fraternal twin: the dizzygothic twin, born from the other egg fertilized at the same time as I was, I seek him with my blind little fingers, my sweet little fingers that find another present wrapped in cellophane, they tear it open, they sniff the other being in the way the coyotes know how to smell and distinguish the differing scents of the twins: I touch those neighboring little fingers even if they are those of another and I know whose they are: Baby Ba! She was here all the while! She was here and I didn't know it! Gestating with me! I am not alone! The girl was gestated with the same semen and the same egg that I was! The woman appeared at the same time as I did! Christine appeared with Christopher! I am not alone: I never was, Electra! I quickly think before I forget everything: I see a powerful city, a big-shouldered city, windy, early snow, the hut of a mute Indian woman, a grandmother who didn't learn English and who forgot Spanish, receiving into her hands another child who appears between the dark and bloody legs of a blind woman, the blind father holds the woman's head to make her comfortable, the blind boy is being born in Chicago, my fellow, my brother, he frozen and me hot! I who stretch out my fingers and tell Baby Ba my fraternal twin, I no longer have to choose, girl, of course I could see you, come on, come on, let's go out together, you are my supreme reason for leaving, repeat that with me, we need each other, I cannot see half of the world without you, Baby Ba, nor can you without me, let's go out to answer the world, to be responsible in the face of reality, stretch out your little hand and touch mine, please, repeat with me the last thing I say to you:

I tell you this: with the same facility that we leave behind the achievements and the ruins. Everything builds and feeds the future, success as well as failure. Everything, therefore, will be ruins. Except the present, girl. Except the present instant in which we were chosen to remember the past and desire the future. Memory and desire, girl. Desire and memory, goo, dada, ma, heeeeere comes the aaaaaaah, clown begins with *c*, Baby, we're together, play with me, let's be playmates on earth, don't be afraid anymore, Baby Ba, hold my little hand, I'm here with you, don't you see, Baby, play with me, play sea serpent, booboo, agoo, dada, mama, papa . . .

Angel Palomar refused with a shake of his head: "We're not going with you."

I think my father feels that in this moment he is a desperate apparition.

Alone again! What an absolute solitude. Only my mother's halo shines intensely. Egg left with the Lost Boy and the Orphan Huerta. We stayed behind. The caravels from the Orient went out to sea, foggy, radiant, their red sails unfurled on the masts, Chinese characters painted on them. Their three masts piercing the deck like stakes made of gold, heading out to sea, far from the dying beach, far from the turbid fever of El Niño and the mortal whiteness of the dolphins and the red and gray circle of coyotes, far from the poem erased by the white tongue of the sea, far away, the caravels shine far away on an ocean where the dolphins live again their pleasurable time, their perpetual leaping and diving in the sea, from the surface to the bottom and from the bottom to the surface, as regular as a clock, as pragmatic as an anchor, as serene as a plumb line, from the bottom to the surface and from the surface to the bottom, eternally, until they die. They have no other fun.

The distant sea, the entire sea, murmured my father, watching the ships from Pacífica sail away without them, the water revived with *a puff of air printed on smoke.*

A country of sad men and happy children.

A child is being born just as October 12, 1992, is born, on the beach at Acapulco. He comes into the world holding the hand of a little girl whose eyes are closed. The boy has his eyes wide open, as if his eyelids had never formed. He looks fixedly at the earth that awaits him. The boy swims toward the land, softly, carrying the girl with him. He emerges from the belly of his mother as if he were crossing the pacific sea, carrying the girl on his shoulders, saving her from death by water. The light went out; the fire over their heads went out. The boy comes out. From the sky a swift Angel descends, an Angel with a golden helmet and green spurs, a flaming sword in his hand, an Angel escaped from the Indo-Hispanic altars of opulent hunger, from need overcome by sleep, from the coupling of opposites: body and soul, wakefulness and death, living and sleeping, remembering and desiring, imagining: the happy boy who reaches the sad land carries all this on his lips, he bears the memory of death, white and extinguished, like the flame that went out in his mother's belly: for a swift, marvelous instant, the boy being born knows that this light of memory, wisdom, and death was an Angel and that this other Angel who flies from the navel of heaven with the sword in his hand is the fraternal enemy of the first: he is the Baroque Angel, with a sword in his hand and quetzal wings, and a serpent doublet, and a golden helmet, the Angel strikes, strikes the lips of the boy being born on the beach: the burning and painful sword strikes his lips and the boy forgets, he forgets everything forgets everything, f
o
r
g
e
t
s

ABOUT THE AUTHOR

In November 1987 Carlos Fuentes was awarded the
Cervantes Prize, the highest award offered a Spanish-
language author. Until recently Robert F. Kennedy
Professor in Latin American Studies at Harvard University,
he now lives in Mexico City with his family. Among his
books are *The Old Gringo*, *The Death of Artemio Cruz*, and
the newly published *Constancia*.